# LOVE AT FIRST SIGHT

## A FIRST IN A SERIES COLLECTION

### KRISTEN PROBY

AMPERSAND PUBLISHING, INC.

COME AWAY
with me
A With Me in Seattle Novel
New York Times and USA Today Bestselling Author
KRISTEN PROBY

Come Away With Me
A With Me In Seattle Novel

By
Kristen Proby

*This book is dedicated to my mom, Gail Holien. Thank you for giving me the love of reading a good love story and for being the best woman I know. I love you, Mom.*

# CHAPTER 1

The light this morning is perfect. I hold my Canon to my face and press the shutter. *Click.* The Puget Sound is covered in color. Pinks, yellows, blues. And for once the wind is almost still. Waves gently lap against the concrete barrier at my feet, and I'm lost in the beauty before me.

*Click.*

I turn to my left and see a young couple walking along the sidewalk. Seattle's Alki Beach is pretty much deserted, aside from a few die-hards, or early morning insomniacs, like me. The young couple are walking away from me, hand in hand, smiling at each other, and I point my lens at them and *click.* I zoom in on their sneaker-clad feet and locked hands and shoot some more, my photographer's eye appreciating their intimate moment on the beach.

I inhale the salty air and stare out at the sound once again as a red-sailed boat gently glides out on the water. The early morning sunshine is just barely beginning to sparkle around it, and I raise my camera again to capture the moment.

"What the fuck are you doing?"

I twirl at the sound of the angry voice and gaze into blue eyes that reflect the bright morning water. They are surrounded by a very, very pissed-off face.

Not merely angry. Livid.

"Excuse me?" I squeak, finding my voice.

"Why can't you all just leave me the fuck alone?" The handsome—really handsome—stranger in front of me is shaking in rage, and I instinctively step back, frowning and beginning to get pissed right back at him. *What the fuck are you doing?*

"I wasn't bothering you," I respond, happy that my voice is stronger with my anger, and retreat back another step. Clearly, Mr. Beautiful Blue Eyes and Sexy Greek God Face is a loony tune. Unfortunately, he follows my backward motion, and I feel the panic start to take hold in my gut.

"I have had it with you following me. Do you think I don't notice? Give me the camera." He extends a long-fingered hand, and my mouth drops open. I pull my camera into my chest and wrap my arms around it protectively.

"No." My voice is amazingly calm, and I want to look around for a means of escape, but I can't stop looking into his angry, sea-colored eyes.

He swallows and narrows his eyes, breathing hard.

"Give me the fucking camera, and I won't press charges for harassment. I just want the photos." He's lowered his voice, but it's no less menacing.

"You can't have my photos!" Who the hell is this guy? I turn to run, and he grabs my arm, whipping me around to face him once again, grabbing for my camera. I start to scream, not believing that I'm being mugged practically outside my front door. Then he lets go of me and braces his hands on his knees, bending at the waist, shaking his head, and I notice that his hands are shaking.

Holy hell.

I take another step back, ready to run, but with his head still down, he holds up his hand and says, "Wait."

I should run. Fast. Call the police and have this whack-job arrested for assault, but I don't move. My breathing starts to calm, and my panic recedes, and for some reason, I don't think he's going to harm me.

Yeah, I'm sure the Green River Killer's victims didn't think he'd harm them either.

"Uh, are you okay?" My voice is breathy, and I realize I'm still clutching my camera to my chest almost painfully. I relax my hands and start to lower them when his head snaps back up.

"Do not take my fucking picture." His voice is low and measured, controlled, but he's still shaking and breathing like he's just run a marathon.

"Okay, okay. I'm not going to. I'm putting the lens cap back on." I do as I say, not taking my eyes from his face, and he watches my hands carefully.

Geez.

He takes a deep breath and shakes his head, and I get a good look at the rest of him. Wow. Beautiful face, chiseled, stubbled jaw and those deep, clear blue eyes. He's got messy, golden-blond hair. He's tall, much taller than my five-foot-six, lean and broad-shouldered. He's wearing blue jeans and a black T-shirt, and both hug that lean body in all the right places.

Damn. He'd look fantastic naked. Ironically, I'd love to get him in front of my camera.

He looks me in the eye again, and he looks vaguely familiar. I feel like I should know him from somewhere, but the fleeting recognition is gone when he speaks.

"I'm going to need you to give me the camera, please."

Is he serious? He's still going to mug me?

I let out a short laugh and finally break eye contact, looking up to the now blue sky and shake my head. I close my eyes then look back over to him, and he's staring at me intently.

I find myself smiling as I say, "You are so not getting this camera."

He tilts his head to the side and narrows his eyes again. Muscles low in my belly clench at his sexy stare, and I silently castigate myself. No getting turned on by your sexy early morning mugger!

"You are not getting this camera. Who the hell do you think you are?" Now my voice is rising, and I pat myself on the back.

"You know who I am."

His response throws me, and I narrow my eyes, staring back at him again, and get the strange feeling once more that I should know him, but I shake my head in frustration.

"No, I don't."

He raises an eyebrow, puts his hands on his lean hips, and he smiles, showing off a perfect line of teeth. The smile doesn't reach his eyes.

"Come on, honey, let's not play this game. Either give me that camera, or delete the photos, and we can get on our way."

Why does he want my photos? Suddenly it occurs to me that he must think I've been taking pictures of him.

"I don't have any photos of you on here, *honey*," I reply.

His eyes narrow again, and his smile slips away. He doesn't believe me.

I take a step toward him. I stare deeply into his widening blue gaze and speak very clearly. "I. Don't. Have. Any. Photos. Of. You. On. My. Camera. I'm not a portrait photographer." I feel my cheeks flush, and I look down for a moment.

"What were you taking photos of?" His voice is level now, and he looks confused.

"The water, the boats." I gesture out toward the sound.

"I saw you point your camera toward me when I was sitting on that bench." He points to the bench behind me. It's near where I shot the photos of the couple holding hands. I pull my camera in front of me again. He tenses up, but I ignore him, turn on the camera and start flipping through my images until I find the ones he's afraid are of him. I walk over to him and stand next to him, my arm almost touching his, and I feel the heat from his sexy body. I make myself ignore it.

"Here, these are the photos I took." I point the screen toward him and start to page through them, showing him all of the images. "Would you like to see the others I took as well?"

"Yes," he whispers.

I continue to show him the images of the water, the sky, the boats, the mountains. I can't help but smell his clean scent as he intently looks at the photos, scrutinizing each one while pulling his lower lip through his thumb and forefinger. His brow is furrowed.

Sweet Jesus, he smells good.

I've taken over two hundred photos this morning, so it takes a few minutes to page through each one. When I'm finished, he looks up into my eyes, and I see his embarrassment, and I'm not sure, but he looks almost sad.

My heart gives a flip as he smiles, a true full-blown, no-holds-barred smile, wiping away the sadness, and shakes his head slowly. He could melt glaciers with that smile. End wars. Resolve the national debt crisis.

"I'm sorry."

"So you should be." I turn the camera off and start to walk away from him.

"Hey, I'm really sorry."

"You must be awfully full of yourself if you think that everyone with a camera is taking your picture." I continue walking, and of course he's caught up with me, matching my stride.

Why is he still here?

He clears his throat. "Can I ask your name?"

"No," I respond.

"Um, why?" He sounds confused.

Hell, I'm confused.

"I don't give my name out to my muggers."

"Muggers?" He stops midstride and pulls me to a stop beside him, his hand on my elbow. I look down at his hand and, raising my eyes back to his, pin him with a glare.

"Let go of me." He does immediately.

"I'm not a mugger."

"You tried to steal my camera. What do you call it?" I start walking again, realizing I'm heading in the opposite direction of my house. Shit.

"Look, I'm not a mugger. Stop for a minute, will you?" He stops again, rubs his face with his hands and looks at me. I face him, put my hands on my jean-clad hips, my camera hanging harmlessly around my neck, and glare at him.

"I don't know who you are," I say in my best no-nonsense voice.

"Clearly," he responds, and a smile tickles his lips, and I can't help but feel my stomach clench, hoping he gives me that big grin again. My not knowing him seems to make him happy, but it's pissing me off. Should I know him?

"Why are you smiling?" I find myself smiling back at him.

He looks me up and down, taking in my dark hair, currently tied up in a haphazard bun, casual red T-shirt that hugs my breasts, jeans, curvy hips and thighs, and returns his deep blue gaze to mine. His smile widens, and I lose my breath.

Wow.

"I'm Luke." He holds his hand out for me to shake, and I look at it, still not fully trusting him, then back up to him. He raises a brow, almost as a challenge, and I find myself putting my small hand in his big, strong one and clasping it firmly.

"Natalie."

"Natalie," he says my name slowly, looks down at my mouth, and I bite my lower lip. He inhales sharply and looks back into my eyes.

Fuck, he's beautiful. I pull my hand out of his grasp and look down, not knowing what else to say, and still confused as to why I'm still standing here with him.

"I...I have to go," I stammer, suddenly nervous. "It was...interesting meeting you, Luke." I start to walk around him toward my house, and he steps in front of me.

"Wait, don't go." He runs a hand through his already messy golden hair. "I'm really sorry about all this. Let me make it up to you. Breakfast?"

He frowns slightly, like he didn't mean to say that, and then looks at me hopefully.

Say no, Nat. Go home. Go back to bed. Mmm...bed with Luke... Sweaty bodies, tangled sheets, his head between my legs, my body writhing as I come...

Stop!

I shake my head, trying to push the fantasy aside, and find myself saying, "No, thanks. I should go."

"Husband waiting at home?" he asks, glancing at my ringless finger.

"Uh, no."

"Boyfriend?"

I give him a small smile. "No."

His face relaxes. "Girlfriend?"

I can't stop the laugh that comes. "No."

"Good." He's giving me that big smile again, and I want desperately to say yes to this beautiful stranger, but my common sense kicks in, and I remind myself that this is not safe, I don't know him, and as swoon-worthy as he is, he's still a stranger.

I, of all people, know about stranger danger.

So I ignore the clenching between my legs, give him another small smile, and I say as politely and as forcefully as I can, "Thanks anyway. Have a good day, Luke."

Of course, politely and forcefully sounds all whispery from me right now.

Crap.

I hear him murmur, "Have a good day, Natalie," as I walk briskly away.

~

I WALK HOME QUICKLY, feeling Luke's eyes on my Kardashian-esque backside until I turn the corner toward my house. Why didn't I wear a longer shirt? My heart is thumping, and I just want to be safe inside, safe from sexy-smiled muggers. My body hasn't responded to a man like this in a long time, and while I admit it feels nice, Luke is just entirely too… Wow.

I close and lock my front door then follow my nose to the kitchen. Jules is making breakfast!

"Hey, Nat, get any good photos this morning?" Much to my delight, my BFF is flipping pancakes, and I smell bacon crisping in the oven. My stomach growls as I place my camera on the breakfast bar and pull up a stool.

"Yeah, it was a good morning," I reply. I wonder if I should bring up Luke. Jules tends to be on the romantic side, and she'll most likely have us married off by the end of the conversation, but she is the one person I confide in about everything, so why not? "I got some good shots. Almost got mugged…pretty standard morning."

I smile to myself as Jules twirls around, dropping a pancake on my tile floor, gasping.

"What? Are you okay?"

"I'm fine." I let out a snort. "Some guy was pissed that I might have taken his picture." I describe my encounter to her, and she smiles sweetly when I'm finished.

"Sounds like he likes you, friend."

I snort. "Whatever. He's just some random guy."

Jules rolls her eyes and turns back to the pancakes. "He might just be some random guy, but if he's as hot as you say he is, you should have gone to breakfast with him."

I scowl at her. "Gone out to breakfast with the hot mugger?" I ask incredulously.

"Oh, don't be dramatic." Jules flips the bacon in the oven then ladles more pancake batter onto the griddle. "It sounds like he was really nice."

"Yes, when he wasn't trying to steal my obscenely expensive camera, he was a perfect gentleman."

Jules laughs, and I can't help but smile in return. "What do you have going on today?" she asks.

Pleased with the change in conversation, I walk around the breakfast bar and start loading a plate with delicious food. "I have a session at noon, and I need to make some deliveries this afternoon. I really need to try to get in a nap this morning."

"Couldn't sleep again?" Jules asks.

I shake my head. Sleep never comes easily for me.

I reclaim my stool and take a bite of bacon. Jules is next to me. "How about you?"

"Well, since it's Tuesday, I guess I'll go to work today." Jules is a very successful investment banker in downtown Seattle. I couldn't be more proud of my longtime best friend. She's beyond smart and beautiful. She's the whole package..

"We gotta make a living." I devour the delicious pancakes on my plate, then rinse both our plates and load the dishwasher.

"I can do that." Jules starts to come into the kitchen, but I wave her back.

"No, you cooked. I got this. Go to work."

"Thanks! Have a fun session." She wiggles her eyebrows at me and heads for the garage.

"Have a good day at the office, dear!" I call after her, and we both giggle.

I climb the stairs to my bedroom and strip naked. I really need some sleep. My clients pay me very well to give them a fun, beautiful photo session, and I need to be well rested.

My room is large, with floor-to-ceiling windows. This is the one room of the house that has any pink in it. I love my soft pink duvet and fluffy pink pillows. My bed frame is simple, but the headboard is an old barn door that I nailed to the wall to give the room a rustic feel.

I fall into my king-size bed, the soft sheets hugging my naked body, and gaze out the window to the ocean view. I love this house. I never want to move. Ever. This view alone is priceless. The sapphire-blue water outside calms me, and as my eyes get heavy, I think of deep blue eyes and a killer smile and slip into sleep.

# CHAPTER 2

*J*'m out and about, delivering framed photos of flowers and beach scenes to the restaurants and shops along Alki Beach.

"Hi, Mrs. Henderson!" I smile at the gray-haired, plump woman behind the counter in Gifts Galore, one of my favorite trinket shops. I happily note that my work is hanging behind the cash register. There are shelves and shelves of beachy knickknacks, jewelry, and other artwork. It's a fun place to wander around in.

"Hello, Natalie! I see you have a delivery for me!" She smiles and comes around the counter, pulling me into a big hug.

"I do. I hope you can use them."

"Oh yes, I'm just about out of the others you brought in last week. You've become quite the popular young artist." Mrs. Henderson starts looking through my work, oohing and aahing, and I feel the pride in my chest as she tells me that she'll take all I've brought her today.

We chat at the counter while she writes me a check for last week's sales, and I turn to leave, but stumble into a very firm chest.

"Oh, excuse me…" I take a step back and look up.

"Hello, Natalie." Luke's staring down at me, a smile tickling his lips. He looks a bit surprised, happy, and just… Oh my.

"Hello, Luke." My voice sounds breathy again, and I mentally wince.

Mrs. Henderson heads to the back of her store to check on a customer, leaving Luke and I alone. I stare down at my sandals, reminding myself I need a pedicure.

What am I supposed to say?

"So, you're an artist." Luke glances over at my framed photos still stacked on the counter.

"Yes." I follow his gaze. "I sell my work in the local shops."

He grins, and I feel that pull again in my gut.

"What are you doing in here?" I ask "This doesn't seem like your kind of store."

"I'm looking for a gift for my sister for her birthday." He starts shuffling through my frames. "These would be perfect. She just bought a new condo. Which ones would you suggest?" He glances back at me, and I have no choice but to join him at the counter and lean close to him as we look through the twenty-plus photos together.

"Does she prefer flowers or scenery?" I ask.

"Er." He swallows. Am I having some kind of effect on him? I lean a little closer to him, pretending to inspect the photos on the counter and hear him catch his breath. "Probably flowers."

"I'd go with these." I smile to myself, enjoying his nearness now that I don't feel threatened by him, and select four photos of flowers, all different kinds and colors, and arrange them in a square for him to see.

"Perfect." His smile lights up his face, and I can't help but smile back. "You're very talented."

His compliment takes me back for a second, and I feel my cheeks flush. "Thank you."

Luke pays Mrs. Henderson, and then follows me as I head out of the store to my car.

"Where are you headed?" he asks as he catches up to me.

"Well, that was my last delivery, so I'll be heading home."

"Or," he says nonchalantly, "I could take you out for coffee."

My stomach tightens excitedly. He's still interested! Am I? He could be an ax murderer. Or worse.

"Happy hour?" he continues.

I smile and look away from him, still striding toward my car.

"Dinner? Can I buy you an ice cream cone?" He runs his free hand through his messy hair, and I mentally hug myself.

Somewhere public should be safe, so before I can put too much more thought into it, I hear myself saying, "Let's go get a drink. There's a bar one block over that has a good happy hour."

"Lead the way!" Damn, I would do just about anything for that grin.

"Don't you want to take your sister's photos to your car?"

"I walked." He shrugs.

"Here, stow them in my car." I open the trunk of my Lexus SUV and pull the door up for him.

"Nice car," he says, surprised. His eyebrows are raised as he gazes at me.

"Thanks." I flip the lever for the door to close and lock the car again as we continue down the sidewalk.

Luke pulls his aviator sunglasses from the neck of his soft white T-shirt and puts them on, looking around him as though he's making sure no one is watching him, and I frown. Is he embarrassed to be seen with me? If so, why did he ask me out?

I'm still puzzling over this as he holds the door to my favorite Irish pub open for me, and we walk into the cool bar.

"Hi! Welcome to the Celtic Swell." A young server smiles at both of us, paying special attention to Luke, and I mentally roll my eyes. "It's a beautiful day out there," she continues. "Would y'all like to sit inside or outside?"

I glance up at Luke, and without pausing or asking me what I'd prefer, he says, "Inside."

"Sure thing. Follow me, handsome." She winks at Luke, ignoring me completely, and leads us to a booth near the back of the bar.

We are seated, and Miss Flirty points out the happy hour menu displayed on the table, smiles broadly at Luke again, and then leaves us alone.

"Are you embarrassed to be out with me?" I am determined to get to the bottom of this.

Luke gasps, takes off his sunglasses, revealing his wide blue eyes, and looks horrified. The knots in my stomach slowly release.

"No! No, Natalie, not at all. In fact, I'm thrilled to spend time with you." He looks so sincere. "Why do you ask?"

"Well…" I gratefully sip the water the waitress has set down before me. "You just seem…"

"What?"

"Quiet all of a sudden." It's the best I can come up with. Damn, why does he make me so nervous?

"I'm happy to be here, with you. I just…" He shakes his head, runs a hand through that beautiful hair. "I am a private man, Natalie." He exhales quickly and closes his eyes, like he's struggling through some difficult internal debate, before turning his bright blue gaze back to mine.

"It's okay." I hold my hands up in front of me as if in surrender. "I was just checking. No worries."

I smile reassuringly and grab the happy hour menu before he can say any more. His change in mood and the reasons behind it are none of my business. We're just out for a drink. Let's keep it light.

He smiles at me, and I'm rescued from having to start small talk by Flirty Waitress taking our orders.

Luke raises an eyebrow in my direction. "What would the lady like?"

"A margarita on the rocks, no salt, extra lime." My eyebrows climb when the waitress' cheeks redden and the only acknowledgment to my statement is her scribbling ferociously on her notepad. Luke is hot, I can't blame her for paying attention to him, yet something primal in me wants to scratch her pretty brown eyes out.

And he's not even *mine*.

Luke chuckles. "Make it two."

"You bet. Anything else?" she asks Luke, pointedly ignoring me, and I smile to myself as Luke hardly spares her a glance before muttering, "No, thanks."

"I deserve a margarita after the day I've had." I sip my water.

"And what kind of day was that?" Luke leans forward, and I love that he genuinely looks interested.

"Well." I sit back, look up at the ceiling like I'm deep in thought. "Let's see. I couldn't sleep much last night, so I decided to take an early morning walk to get some work done. At which point, I was almost mugged." I look back at him and give him a sarcastic look of horror. Luke laughs, a full-out belly laugh, and my own belly clenches down again. Holy Jesus, he's so beautiful!

"And then…?"

"And then, after I made my very daring escape"—I smile at him, and he is grinning from ear to ear, his chin resting in his palm—"I went home, had breakfast with my roommate, then took a short nap."

"I would have loved to see that." His eyes have narrowed, and I feel myself blush.

"Loved to see me have breakfast with my roommate?"

"No, smart-ass, loved to see you nap."

"I'm sure it's not that exciting." I thank the waitress for my drink and take a long sip. Oh, that's good.

"And when you woke up?"

"You really want to know about my whole day?"

"Yes, please." Luke sips his drink, and I watch his lips pucker over his straw..

"Um…" I clear my throat, and Luke grins again, enjoying my reaction to him. "I had a photo session at noon. It wrapped around two. Then I made some deliveries around the neighborhood and ran into this handsome mugger I know, whom I am now enjoying a drink with."

"I like that last part the best."

Oh.

"And what did you do today, sir?" I rest my elbows on the table, happy to have turned the attention back to him.

"Coincidentally, I couldn't sleep well last night either, so I got up early to take a walk and enjoy the water." He pauses to take a sip.

"Mmm hmm…"

"Then I made an ass of myself with this incredibly sexy and beautiful woman that I ran into."

I gasp and bite my lip. Sexy and beautiful? Wow.

Luke's eyes narrow on my lips.

"Did she forgive you for being an ass?" My voice sounds breathy.

"I'm not sure. I hope so."

"Then what did you do?"

"I walked home to do some reading."

"What kind of reading?" Mmm, this margarita is delicious.

Luke frowns a bit then shrugs. "Just some reading for work."

"Oh? What do you do?" I motion to Miss Flirty for a refill, raise my eyebrow at Luke and signal for his refill as well at his nod.

"Why do you want to know?" He whispers this and suddenly looks ashen.

What the fuck? Is he really a serial killer? A spy? Is he unemployed and looking for a sugar mama? I dismiss that last thought. He wouldn't be able to live in this neighborhood if he were unemployed.

"Well, now I'm intrigued." I lean forward. He looks so uncomfortable, I decide to put him out of his misery. "But it's really none of my business. So, you read, and then?"

Luke visibly relaxes, and I can't help but be more than a bit disappointed that he won't tell me what he does for a living.

"I also took a nap."

I grin and look him up and down. "To be a fly on the wall."

Oh, I almost forgot how much fun it is to flirt!

He laughs, and it tickles me, making me laugh, too.

"Then I went shopping for my sister's birthday gift and found the perfect thing."

"Oh? And what was that?" I tilt my head to the side, enjoying this flirty game, sipping my delicious drink.

"Well, there's this brilliant local artist that takes beautiful photos, and I was lucky enough to find some of her work." He almost looks proud, and it gives me a warm, happy glow.

"That's great." I don't know what else to say.

"So, you had a photo session today?"

Whoa…change of topic.

"Yes." I think I need another margarita if this conversation is about to take the turn I think it is. I signal to Miss Flirty and, without asking, order him one, too.

He raises an eyebrow. "I didn't think you did portrait photography."

"Why did you think that?" I ask with a frown.

"Because you said so this morning during our most unusual meeting."

"Oh, that's right. I don't do traditional portrait photography." I clear my throat and look around the bar, anywhere but at him, praying he doesn't ask his next question, and grimace when he asks anyway.

"What kind of portrait photography do you do?" He looks confused.

I take a deep breath. Crap.

"Well, it varies. Depends on the client." I'm nervous again. I don't tell many people about this side of my photography business. I find that most people are too judgmental, and it's honestly no one's business but mine and my clients'.

"Look at me." His voice is low and serious, and he's not playful anymore. Shit.

I look into his eyes and swallow.

"You can tell me, Natalie."

Oh, he's so…sexy. And nice. Is that possible?

"Perhaps one day I will. When you tell me what you do for a living." I smirk and kick him under the table, and his mood immediately lifts.

"So there's going to be a 'one day'?"

Oh, I hope so! "If you play your cards right."

"Sassy little thing, aren't you?"

"You have no idea, Luke."

"I'd like to learn, Natalie." And there is that serious face again, making me squirm.

"You're quite the charmer, aren't you?"

Luke grins his wide, gorgeous grin. I smirk again and finish my third drink. My head is getting fuzzy, and I know I'd better stop with the alcohol.

"Another drink." Luke starts to call for Miss Flirty, but I shake my head.

"I'd better go back to water."

"Of course. More water for my lady friend and I, please." The overly friendly waitress saunters away, deliberately swaying her hips, hoping to get Luke's attention, but he's staring at me, ignoring her.

"What kind of movies do you like?"

Huh? Is he asking me out to the movies?

"I don't watch a lot of movies."

He tilts that beautiful head to the side and looks at me like I just told him that pigs fly. "Really?"

"I don't have a lot of time for it."

"Who's your favorite actor?" He smiles, and I feel like this is some sort of test, but I haven't been given the study notes.

"I don't even know who's popular right now." I sit back into the booth seat and purse my lips, thinking about it. "When I was a teenager, I loved Robert Redford." I shrug.

Luke looks like he's been kicked in the stomach, and I'm suddenly embarrassed. Then that beautiful face transforms into his smile, and his eyes soften as they take me in. "Why? Isn't he a little old for you?"

I giggle. "Yes. But I saw *The Way We Were* with him and Barbra Streisand when I was fifteen and fell in love with Hubbell. He was dreamy. I don't pay a lot of attention to movies. There's too much drivel out there."

Luke laughs. "Drivel?"

"Yes! If I see a trailer for one more stupid vampire movie, I'm going to kill myself."

He frowns again, looks around the bar and back to me, his eyes narrowed and apprehensive.

"What? What did I say?"

"Nothing. You're just very unexpected. What are you, twenty-three?"

Why does he want to know my age?

"Twenty-five. You?"

"Twenty-eight."

"So, you're old then." I giggle.

"You have a great laugh." His eyes are shining with happiness, and I mentally hug myself again, forgetting to be nervous, and I realize I'm just really enjoying him. He's just so easy to talk to.

I check my watch and gasp at the time. We've been sitting here for three hours!

"I should go." I smile up at him. "We've been here a long time."

"Time flies when you're with someone beautiful." He leans over and grabs my hand, and I am so caught up in his spell right now. My eyes focus on his lips, and he licks them, making me squirm. Before I know it, he retracts his hand, and I'm left feeling frustrated and missing the warmth of his touch.

"Right back at you." I put my sassy smile back on my face and reach for the check.

"Oh no. That's mine." Luke pulls the check from my fingers and digs out his wallet.

"I'm happy to pay for my own drinks."

He glares at me, and I'm stunned that he looks genuinely mad. Whoa.

"No."

"Okay. Thank you."

His smile is back as he says, "You're most welcome."

Luke settles the bill, and we head back out onto the sidewalk. He hastily puts his sunglasses back on and is visibly aware of who's around us. My heart flips as he takes my hand, and we start to walk toward my car.

The sun is just starting to set, and I look out over the gorgeous sound, the blue water, the boats and the mountains, and long for my camera. I glance up at Luke, and his jaw is tense. He's looking down, and we're walking briskly.

"Hey, slow down." I tug on his hand a bit and deliberately slow my steps. "Are you in a hurry to be rid of me?"

"No, not at all." He looks around us again, then grins down at me, slowing his pace.

"It's going to be a great sunset. Wanna walk along the water? I promise, no camera." I hold my free hand up to show him it's empty.

Luke smirks, and then looks around once more, and I follow his gaze. There are a lot of people out and about enjoying the beautiful day on Alki Beach. Luke shakes his head and looks forlorn for a moment.

We stop by my car, and I think he's looking down at me, but it's hard to tell through his dark glasses.

"I don't like crowds, Natalie. It's kind of a phobia." He shakes his head again, runs his hand through that sexy hair and releases my hand, putting his hands on his hips.

"It's no problem." I feel sorry for him in that moment and want to comfort him. I've never wanted to comfort any man before, ever. I've never had soft feelings toward a man. They've always just been a pleasant diversion, or my worst nightmare. Confusingly, I find myself reaching up and cupping his face in my palm to soothe him.

"Hey," I say softly. "Don't sweat it, Luke."

He leans into my touch and exhales, puts his hand over mine, then clasps it and kisses my knuckles.

Oh my.

"Come on." I deliberately interrupt this lovely moment, needing just a little space. "I'll drive you home."

Luke's jaw drops open.

"I'm not going to make you walk home, carrying these brilliantly genius photos, through the crowds. Hop in."

He flashes me his sexy, face-splitting smile and hops into the passenger seat.

Oh, Natalie, what are you getting yourself into?

# CHAPTER 3

*L*uke's home is a very short drive along the coast, and it strikes me that his place is less than a quarter mile from mine. He directs me to pull into a gated driveway. I can see only a single-lane drive ahead of me. There is no house in view.

"The code is 112774," he directs me.

"Wow, you trust me with the code to your gate?" I am trying to keep the banter between us light to mask my nervousness of going to his house. Will he even invite me inside?

"You'd be amazed at what I'd trust you with, Natalie." I glance back at him and catch his frown. "In fact, so would I."

I ignore his comment and pull through the gate, winding to the left, and gasp at the beautiful modern home before me. It's not huge, it's simple, but the view of the sound is breathtaking, and the white home itself is newer, with clean lines, tons of large windows, beautiful purple and blue hydrangeas lining the front of the house, and pruned shrubs lining the driveway.

"Wow, Luke, this is beautiful."

"Thank you." The pride is back in his voice, and it's evident that he loves his home. I smile at him, completely understanding the feeling.

I park so the passenger side is facing the front door and don't make a move to take my seat belt off. Luke has already jumped out and, to my surprise, walks around the front of my car to my door and opens it.

"Please, come in." He holds a hand out to me, but I pause.

"I should go…"

"I'd really love for you to come inside." He gives me that charming grin, and I feel myself softening. "Let me show you the view. Maybe make you dinner. That's all, I swear." His eyes shine with mischief, and I just can't resist him.

I don't want to resist him.

"I'm not keeping you from anything?"

"Nope, I'm a free man, Natalie. Come on."

I shut off the car and take his hand. Wow. The electricity from his touch is still there, and my eyes widen as they find his. His smile is gone, and he's staring intently into my eyes. He pulls my hand up to his lips, then closes my door behind me and leads me up to his door without letting go of me, as if I could run away at any minute.

I can't help but appreciate the way his jeans hang on his hips, molding around his very fine ass. His white T-shirt is untucked and hugs the muscles of his shoulders and arms just perfectly. I want to hug him from behind and sink my nose into his back, inhale his scent, and kiss him there between his defined shoulder blades.

It should seriously be illegal to be that beautiful. He clearly takes very good care of himself. Suddenly, I feel out of my league. He is a ten, and I'm lucky if I hit a seven after I've been buffed and polished at my favorite salon. Not to mention, I have hips and an ass and a bit of a belly bulge that no matter how many sit-ups or yoga exercises I do, it just won't go away. I know I'm not fat, but I'm not supermodel thin like Jules, either.

And, until today, that never bothered me.

Luke unlocks the door and turns to me, and the look in his eyes tells me that he's not looking at my flaws. He seems to be just fine with what he sees, and hope starts to spread through me.

"Welcome, Natalie. Make yourself at home." I follow him inside and can't stop the face-splitting smile that comes at the sight of his magnificent home. The great room is large, with double-height ceilings and pale khaki-colored walls. The back wall is all glass, and the view is of the Puget Sound. The furniture is big, in blues and white and a touch of green. I could curl up in his love seat and stare outside all day.

I wander through the room, my sandals echoing on the dark hardwood floors, and gaze out the windows for a few moments. The sun is hanging low, just above the mountains, reflecting on the choppy blue water, and pretty white sailboats are coasting along gracefully. I turn to see Luke still on the other side of the room watching me, his arms crossed in front of him. I wish I could read his mind.

"What?" I ask and mirror his stance, crossing my arms in front of me, pushing my cleavage up a bit, exposing it through the V-neck of my red T-shirt.

"You are so beautiful, Natalie."

Oh.

I drop my arms and open my mouth to speak, but nothing comes out, so I just shake my head and look to my right at his very lovely kitchen.

"You have a great kitchen."

"Yes." It's a simple agreement, and Luke is on the move, slowly walking toward me. There's no humor in his eyes now. It's hunger. Hunger for me.

I couldn't move if I wanted to.

"Do you like to cook?" My voice is higher than normal, and the nervousness is back, but this nervousness is not fear. I'm definitely not afraid of him. I'm a bit intimidated by him.

"Yes," he says again, and as he approaches me, he raises his long-fingered hand to run the backs of his fingers down my cheek. I swallow hard and hold his blue gaze.

"You don't want to talk about your kitchen?" I whisper.

"No," he whispers back.

"Oh." I look down at his mouth and back up into his blue eyes. "What do you want to talk about?"

"I don't want to talk, Natalie." Since when has whispering been so sexy? My thighs tighten, and I'm suddenly wet and hot and panting.

Luke grasps my face between both of his hands, still gazing intently into my eyes, as if he's trying to convey some kind of deep message, or perhaps he's asking my permission? I slightly tilt my head back, and he oh so slowly lowers his lips to mine. He rests them there for what feels like minutes, chastely kissing me, loosely resting his soft lips on mine. I reach my hands up and grab his forearms, and he groans as he takes the kiss deeper, persuading my lips open and tickling my tongue with his.

Oh God, he smells so good, and his expert lips are a drug that I just can't resist. He nibbles at the sides of my mouth, nibbles my lower lip then invades my mouth again. He pulls the hair tie out of my hair, spilling my long, chestnut hair around my shoulders, and plunges his hands in it.

"You. Are. So. Beautiful." He murmurs against my mouth, each word between his sweet kisses, and I am completely intoxicated. I run my hands up over his shoulders and twist his hair in my fingers and hold on for dear life.

Oh, this man can kiss!

He slows the kiss down again, gently cupping my face in his hands, and leaves sweet kisses on my jaw, cheeks, my nose, then plants his lips on my forehead and takes a deep, deep breath. I run my hands back down his shoulders—holy shit, is he toned!—over his sexy arms and hold on to his forearms, and I am more than just a little dizzy.

And I don't want him to stop.

As my blurry sight clears, Luke leans back, still cupping my face, and smiles gently down at me. "I've wanted to do that all day."

Where is that music coming from? I realize my phone is ringing inside my purse, still slung across my body, and I break our intimate contact to rummage through and find it. Maroon 5 is whaling on about being at a payphone, and Luke's smile breaks into a big grin as I answer the call.

"Hi, Jules." I mouth *roommate* at him at his raised eyebrow.

"Nat! You haven't answered my texts. Are you okay?" She sounds annoyed, and I roll my eyes.

"I'm fine. Sorry, I didn't see your texts. My phone has been in my bag, I must not have heard it." I take another step back from Luke, trying to clear my head, and he rests his hands on those lean hips.

"Do you have dinner plans?"

"Dinner?"

Luke leans in and whispers in my free ear, "I'm making you dinner." He winks at me—winks!—and then walks around me toward the kitchen, leaving me to my call.

"Um, yeah, I have dinner plans." I wince, knowing that I'm about to get the Jules Third Degree.

"Oh?" I know her expertly plucked brows are raised. I so do not want to have this conversation with Luke in earshot. I hear Adele start to sing and turn to see Luke has paused by a sound system, fiddling with his iPhone.

"Yeah, something just came up. Why? What's going on?" Luke is now in the kitchen, rummaging around in his fridge, and I have a great view of his jean-clad ass. Holy crap.

"I was going to invite you to go to dinner with some of my coworkers, but if you have plans, I'll just see you tonight." There is a pause. "Is it the mugger?"

I gasp. Leave it to Jules! "Maybe."

"Awesome! Have fun, be safe, take pictures if you can. Toodles!" She's hung up, and I can't help but laugh at her. Oh, to have my friend's carefree attitude.

"So, that was your roommate?" Luke asks as he pours us both a glass of white wine. I take a sip and am pleasantly surprised by its fruity sweetness.

"Yeah, she was checking up on me." I sit at the lightly colored granite breakfast bar and page through my texts. I have three, all from Jules.

*Hey, Nat, wanna go to dinner tonight?*

*Nat? Turn your phone on!*

*Natalie, I'm making reservations...dinner?*

Oops. I lay my iPhone on the counter top and take another swallow of wine. Luke's watching me.

"Sorry, that was rude." I smile apologetically. "She was worried when I didn't respond to her texts."

Luke shakes his head. "You are definitely not rude, Natalie. So, how do you feel about Alfredo sauce?"

I grin at his flirty tone. "I have a long-standing love affair with Alfredo sauce."

"Really?" He chuckles and tucks a strand of my now messy hair behind my ear. "Lucky Alfredo sauce."

He turns again and starts pulling out pots and pans and ingredients from his pantry and fridge. He's so...competent in the kitchen.

When he whips back around to start making order of his chaos, he sees me watching him and gives me a half smile. "What are you thinking?"

"You're very competent in the kitchen."

"Why, thank you." He bows grandly and makes me laugh.

"Who taught you to cook?"

"My mom." He puts a pot of water on to boil and starts grating cheese.

"What can I do to help?"

"Sit there and be beautiful."

I blush. "Really, I want to help."

"Okay, you grate this cheese, and I'll get the chicken going."

I happily come around the island and take over the cheese grating, watching Luke move about his kitchen with ease. Soon, the room smells of grilling chicken, making my mouth water. Luke moves up behind me and puts his arms around me, checking the cheese status, without actually touching me.

My skin is on fire. Touch me! Hold me! But he doesn't. Before I know it, he's moved away, and my body is almost quivering with need.

I don't remember ever feeling this physical pull toward a man before. It's a little scary, but it's a lot of fun.

"Okay, I think we're almost ready to dish up. Can you strain this pasta?" I gladly assist him as he finishes the sauce, and my stomach growls.

Mmm...a sexy man who can cook!

Luke pulls down plates, silverware and napkins. "Let's eat outside, enjoy the view."

"Great idea." I smile as we dish up, grab our wine and head out to the deck off the great room. The outside eating space is spectacular. Warm tones of reds and browns, the table seats six, and there is a huge stainless steel grill with outdoor kitchen counters, fridge and sink.

We sit, and my nerves from our earlier delicious kiss are gone, and I'm just plain hungry.

"Hungry?" he asks, reading my mind.

"Starving!"

"Dig in."

I take a bite and close my eyes. "Mmm…s'really good."

I cover my mouth with my napkin and laugh.

Luke's eyes dance, and he smirks, taking a drink of his wine. "I'm glad you like it."

"So"—I scoop up another bite—"your mom taught you to cook?"

"Yeah, she always said that all of her children needed to be able to feed themselves after we left the nest."

I watch him stab some chicken with his fork. "How many siblings do you have?"

"I have one brother and one sister."

"Older, younger?" I ask. God, this man can cook.

"Older sister, younger brother."

"And what do they do?"

"Samantha, my sister, is an editor for *Seattle Magazine*." Luke's eyes are full of pride. "Mark is wasting his college education as a fisherman in Alaska."

"I take it you don't approve?" I raise my brow at him as I take a sip of wine.

"Well, he's young. I guess it's good he sows his wild oats now." Luke shrugs.

"Your parents?" I like hearing him talk about his family. He clearly loves them very much.

"They live in Redmond. Dad works for Microsoft, and Mom is a homemaker." He glances down at my empty plate.

"It was delicious, thank you." I lean back in my chair and stretch out my legs.

"You're very welcome." He looks so young with his shy smile. "Would you like some more?"

"Oh no, I'm full." I pat my belly and gaze out at the water. "This is a fantastic view."

"Yes, it is."

I look over at him, and he's gazing at me. My cheeks warm. "You're very complimentary."

"You're easy to compliment."

I smirk.

He tilts his head to the side and picks my hand up in his, bringing it to his mouth. This is the first time he's touched me since that thigh-clenching kiss, and I sigh at the heat of his touch.

"You are quite beautiful, Natalie. Why don't you believe that?"

I'm stupefied. No one has ever called me out on my insecurities because I've never shown them to anyone. I shrug. "I'm happy you think so."

He frowns at my answer but doesn't press me. "I do."

"I wish I had my camera." I don't realize I've said this out loud, and I feel him tense beside me.

"Why?" His voice is cold, and looking into his eyes, I see they're arctic.

"Because of this view." I gesture out to the water. "This would make a wonderful image."

He relaxes beside me. "Maybe one day you'll be able to capture it."

"There's that 'one day' again." I grin at him, and he grins back.

"One day." He says again, and I can't help but feel a little giddy inside. I shiver a bit as a breeze rolls through his patio. The sun has set, and the sky is all purple and orange, and it's cooling off.

"Are you cold?" he asks.

"No, I'm good."

"Really?"

"I'm a tiny bit cold, but I don't want to go inside."

"I'll be back." With that, he stands and gathers our dirty plates.

"Hey, I'll clean up. You cooked."

"Nonsense. You're my guest, Natalie. Besides, I have a housekeeper who will do most of it in the morning. Sit. Stay." He pins me with a serious gaze, then heads inside.

He's so bossy. I think I like it. No one has ever had the audacity to be bossy with me before. It's fun.

I hear the iPod change from Adele to something soft and bluesy, and a few moments later, he's back with a plush green blanket and my iPhone.

"The light was blinking on your phone. I thought you might want to check it." He hands it to me, but before I can look at it, he holds his hand out to me. "Come with me."

"Where are we going?"

"Just over there." He points to a soft love seat closer to the edge of the patio. I take his hand, and he leads me over and I sit, sinking into the cushions. He sits beside me and covers us both in the blanket. His arm is draped around me.

"This is quick." I look into his blue gaze, unsure if being in his arms like this, this quickly is altogether safe, yet I want to be here.

"We're just admiring a pretty view, Natalie." He pulls me closer to him, runs his hand down my side, and I lean on his shoulder. I remember my phone in my hand and pull it out from under the blanket to read it, not bothering to hide it from Luke.

*Hey, gorgeous, plans tonight?*

It's my friend Grant, and while we haven't had sex in a while, sometimes, if we're drunk or lonely, we indulge. I haven't heard from him in weeks, and of course it has to be now, as I'm curled up in this sexy man's arms, that he texts me.

Crap, crap, crap. Luke tenses beside me, and I cringe but hit Reply, still not pulling it out of his eyesight. I have nothing to hide.

*Yeah, I have plans. Sorry.*

Luke doesn't relax beside me, and I know he's mad. Shit.

Grant responds almost immediately.

*Tomorrow?*

*Sorry, Grant, not interested.*

*Okay, bye, Nat.*

I put my phone in my pocket and just lean my head back on Luke's shoulder, not saying anything. What can I say? He lets out a sigh and tightens his hold on me, not saying anything for a long time. Finally, I glance up at him.

"Are you okay?"

"Why wouldn't I be?"

"Um, I don't know. Just checking." The last two words are whispered. He seems mad at me, but I didn't do anything wrong. I told the guy to take a hike!

Suddenly, he shimmies and pulls his iPhone out of his pocket. "What's your phone number?"

My wide gaze finds his, and he raises a brow. I rattle it off to him, and he punches it into his phone. "What's your last name?"

"Conner." He finishes programming my name and number into his phone, and I close my eyes and inhale his clean scent while he continues to fiddle with his gadget.

My phone buzzes in my pocket.

# CHAPTER 4

I retrieve my phone from my pocket and pull it out of the blanket.

"Oh my, look at that, I have a text! Whoever could it be?" I bat my eyelashes at him and smile sweetly.

Luke laughs. "Maybe you should check it."

"Oh! Good idea." I chuckle and slide the arrow at the bottom of the screen, waking the phone up and open the text from a phone number I don't recognize. I want to squeal like a schoolgirl, but simply smile and open the message.

*Hey, Natalie, save this number. You're going to be seeing it a lot. —Luke Williams*

I grin at him and save the number and his name to my phone.

"So." The smile leaves his face, and he's serious again.

I pull back, out of his grasp, and turn my body toward him, my leg tucked under the opposite knee, mentally preparing myself for a serious conversation.

"So?"

"So." He gazes at me almost warily, and I feel a moment of alarm. "Who's Grant?"

"Just a friend." I shrug.

He raises an eyebrow. "That wasn't just a friendly text, Natalie. I am a man. I know the difference."

I cringe and look back out over the darkening water.

"Look at me." His voice is sharp, and I whip my eyes back to his.

"He is just a friend, Luke. Yes, there has been a physical relationship there in the past, but it's been awhile."

"How long is awhile?"

"Months."

"How many months?"

"Since last fall."

"Is there anyone else?"

"Why is this any of your business?"

"Because you're the first woman I've brought into my home, and all I can think about is getting your beautiful body naked and fucking you senseless. I need to know if there is any competition. I don't share, Natalie." His eyes are on fire, his beautiful lips parted as he breathes heavily, and his hands are in fists.

I open my mouth to speak and close it again. Holy Jesus, he wants to fuck me. Well, back at you, bossy man.

"Saying that you don't share implies that I'm already yours, Luke."

"Aren't you?" he whispers.

This is too much. I've known the man less than twenty-four hours, and he wants to stake a claim! Part of me is yelling, *Yes!* But that damn reasonable side rears her ugly head and shakes her head adamantly. *No!*

I stand abruptly, untangling myself from the blanket.

"Look, Luke…" He's suddenly at my side, his strong hand on my chin trapping my gaze in his.

"Answer my question, please." His touch is gentle, but his gaze is raw, and it pulls at me in a way I've never known.

"There is no one," I whisper.

"Thank Christ." And his lips are on mine, but instead of the passionate fervor I'm craving, his lips are gentle and tender, as though he's memorizing my mouth with his lips. He lets go of my chin and wraps my hair in his hand, while the other curls around my lower back, and he pulls me to him, my front against his, and I moan low in my throat. His chest and stomach are hard muscle. I wrap my arms around him and hold him to me, my hands clasping on to his back.

Bravely, I close my teeth over his lower lip and suck him gently into my mouth. His eyes fly open, meeting mine, and he plunges his tongue in my mouth, sliding it along mine in a beautiful rhythm. Our breathing is ragged, and my hands just can't stop moving up and down his back, feeling the hard muscles flex as he moves against me.

Both of his hands slide down to my backside, and he clenches it tightly while nibbling from the side of my mouth down my neck.

"Oh my." I lean my forehead against him, and I feel him smile against my neck.

"You have a great ass, Nat." He pulls me more tightly against him, and I feel his erection against my stomach. I run my own hands down to his derriere.

"Back at you, Luke." My voice is breathy, and he pulls back, his eyes a bit glassy with want and desire, and I know they mirror my own.

Fuck, I want this man.

Our arms are still wrapped around each other, clasping each other's bottoms. I give him another squeeze and run my fingers lightly up under his shirt to his bare skin and smile as he gasps. His beautiful blue eyes are watching mine, and I push my finger between the elastic of his boxers and his skin and run it along to the front of his jeans.

Suddenly, his hands are on mine, and he stills me, not taking his eyes from me. He brings both my hands up to his lips and kisses each finger, then steps back and lets go. The cold air around us is a slap to the face, and I frown in confusion and frustration and feel the sting of rejection.

What the hell?

"Why did you stop?" I hear the hurt in my voice, and I clear my throat.

"Nat, I definitely don't want to stop…"

I step toward him, but he backs up and raises his hands in surrender.

"Luke…"

"Natalie, let's slow down a bit."

Isn't this what men want?

"If you've changed your mind about me…" He's back in front of me before I finish the sentence. His hands are cupping my face, and he's making me look him in the eye, and the raw emotion is still there.

"Listen to me, Natalie. I have not changed my mind. I want you. You are beautiful and smart and sexy as fuck, but I don't want to take this too fast."

"I'm so confused." I close my eyes and shake my head.

"Hey." I look back into his eyes, and he smiles at me, running his fingertips down my cheek. "Slow."

"I don't know slow, Luke."

He frowns and whispers, "I don't either, so we'll learn together."

I'm so frustrated. My body is craving him, but his words intoxicate me.

"So, no sex? At all?" I sound like a child whose candy has been taken away.

"Not tonight," he says with a smile. He takes a deep breath, kisses my forehead, and takes my hand. I grab the blanket, and we go back inside. His music is still playing.

He takes the blanket from my hands and throws it on the long blue couch to my right. "Would you like a tour?"

I'm still frowning over the no-sex comment, but the idea of seeing the rest of his home perks up my mood, and I nod.

He laces his fingers through mine. "Thank you for joining our tour today, Miss Conner. We are delighted to have you with us."

I laugh at his tour-guide voice and relax a bit. He does have a way of making me laugh.

"You've seen the kitchen."

"I love the kitchen."

He smiles and pulls me down a hallway pointing out a powder room and a spare bedroom. At the end of the hall is another closed door, but he waves it off and says, "Just storage for now."

He leads me back to the great room and up a flight of stairs to a large loft area that he's using as a TV room, with more plush furniture. The flat-screen mounted to the wall is huge, and I can't help but laugh.

"What's so funny?" He looks at the TV, and I snicker.

"Boys and their big TVs."

He chuckles and leads me through to another spare bedroom and bathroom. On the opposite side of the loft, with more floor-to-ceiling windows showing off the view, is the master suite. It's huge, with large-scale white furniture and green, blue and khaki accents. It's incredibly peaceful.

His master bath is beautiful, with a large egg-shaped tub separate from the shower that could be a room all on its own.

I gasp in delight when he shows me the walk-in closet.

"Women and their closets." He's laughing at me, and I can't help but join him.

"This, my friend, is a fantastic closet."

"Yes, it is." He agrees and squeezes my hand, then leads me back through the bedroom and down the stairs to the great room.

I'm suddenly uncomfortable, and before I can change my mind, I pull gently on his hand and wrap my arms around his waist, linking my fingers together at the small of his back and drawing him into a big hug. His arms fold around my shoulders, and he kisses my hair, inhaling my scent.

"Thanks for dinner," I murmur into his chest.

"Anytime."

"Thanks for the tour."

I feel his smile against my head. "Anytime."

"Thanks for your phone number."

He chuckles and pulls back. "I recommend you use it."

"I will." I pull out of his arms and grab my purse. It's time to go home and think about this sweet, sexy man. I certainly can't think when I'm with him.

He walks behind me out to my car, pulls his photos out of the back and takes them inside, then returns to me to open my door.

"Let me know that you get home safely." The shadows from his house lights are playing across his face, the light reflecting in his gorgeous eyes.

"Okay, bossy man." I chuckle up at him.

"Bossy?" He purses his lips like he's giving it some thought, then smirks. "Maybe a little bossy."

He leans down and touches me, just with his lips, running them lightly over mine. "Good night, beautiful."

"Good night." Swoon! Geez, he's just so yummy. I'm thankful that I have enough wits about me to climb into my car and get my seat belt on. He walks back to his doorstep and waves me off as I pull down his driveway.

Holy shit.

∾

I SLING my purse on the hallway table by my front door, throw my keys in the key bowl and dig for my phone. I heard it ping when I was driving home, and I know exactly who it's from.

"Nat, is that you?" I hear Jules' stilettos click smartly on the hardwood between the living room and the foyer.

"Yeah, I'm home."

*Thank you for today. Please let me know when you get home. —Luke*

I smile and want to jump up and down in giddiness.

"Well, I guess it went well?" Jules has her hands on her hips, and her blond head tilted with a smile across that gorgeous face of hers. She's still in her cranberry-colored dress and heels from work, her long hair pulled back from her face.

"Oh yeah, it went well."

"So, not so much a mugger, huh?"

"No." I giggle. "He's really nice. And, oh my God, Jules, he's hot." I worry my lip between my teeth, but she reads my mind.

"He's not out of your league, Nat."

I frown at her. "I wasn't going to say that."

She rolls her eyes at me. "You were thinking it. You're hot, too, Nat. Enjoy him. He's lucky you're interested. We both know that doesn't happen often."

"Yes, that's what worries me, too."

I tell her about having happy hour, and how he seemed uncomfortable out and about with me, but when we were at his house, he was much more relaxed. I tell her about the best kiss on record, and the sunset.

Jules listens patiently, doesn't interrupt, or get all giggly or jumpy like she always does. She simply smiles at me, and before I know it, she's pulled me in for a big hug.

"You deserve a good guy, Natalie. Don't run from it. Enjoy it. Really."

I lean into her and suddenly feel like crying, which is mortifying. "I don't even know when I'll see him again."

She pulls back and grins. "Oh, I have a feeling it won't be long. Sounds like he's smitten." There's the Jules I know!

I smirk and kick my shoes off. "I'm going up to bed. It's been an eventful day."

"Okay, good night, sweetie." She briefly hugs me again and heads back to the living room and whatever she was doing before I came home.

I run upstairs and straight into my bathroom. I take my makeup off and brush my teeth and stare at myself in the mirror for a moment. I touch my lips. They're still sensitive from Luke's kisses. My cheeks have a glow, as do my green eyes. My dark hair, which he pulled out of my bun, is all disheveled and kinda sexy.

Remembering his comments about my ass, I turn and peer at it, giving it a good study. I've always considered my butt to be too big, too round and prominent. Yeah, I definitely have a round butt. I guess Luke likes round butts. I smile to myself, strip naked, turn out the lights and jump into bed to text him back.

*No, thank YOU for today. I had a good time, despite almost being mugged. I'm home and safely tucked in bed. —Nat.*

I smile, happy with my flirty response, and lie back on my pillows. A few seconds later, there is a ping.

*Glad to hear you are safe. What are your plans for tomorrow?*

Oh my! I quickly hit reply.

*No sessions tomorrow, thinking about going to take some photos at Snoqualmie Falls. What are your plans?*

I glare at my phone until I see his response.

*What time shall I pick you up? :)*

Pretty sure of himself, isn't he? I can't help but laugh and turn on my side while considering my response.

*Will it be safe? I will have my camera with me, and I know how that angers you.* I chuckle to myself, thinking I'm quite witty, when suddenly my phone starts to ring, and it's him.

"Hi."

"I thought you'd already forgiven me for this morning." He sounds frustrated. What the...?

"I was kind of being a smart-ass, Luke. I'm sorry, I guess texting is not a great way to flirt." I close my eyes.

He takes a deep breath. "No, I'm sorry. Would you mind if I join you tomorrow?" Gosh, he has a sexy voice, and he sounds hopeful. Who am I to say no?

"I would love the company. Shall we say ten a.m.?"

"That works for me." He sounds relieved, and I get the giddy feeling in my chest again. "I'll text you my address."

"Okay." He sighs. "So, you're in bed?"

Oh, now it's gonna get good! I smile and lie on my back. "Yes. You?"

"I am, too."

"We had a long day." I'm picturing him in that huge, gorgeous bed of his, naked and lying under the covers, and my mouth is suddenly dry.

"Yes, we did." I hear rustling as he moves in the bed.

"I hope you sleep better tonight."

"Me, too." I hear the smile in his voice.

"Why were you having a hard time sleeping last night?"

There is a long pause, and it's perfectly quiet, and I wonder if I've lost the call.

"Luke?"

"I'm here." He sighs again, then says, "I just don't require a lot of sleep. How about you? Why up so early today?"

I'm not entirely satisfied with his answer but let it go.

"I've suffered from insomnia for a couple years now. I usually only get a few hours of sleep here and there."

"That sucks," he breathes.

"Yeah, but I can take advantage of the early morning light."

"You're something of a workaholic, aren't you, Natalie?" I think he's laughing at me!

"No, I just enjoy what I do."

"And what are you wearing to bed tonight?" Geez! Change of subject!

"Good night, Luke." My smile is in my voice.

"Sweet dreams, Natalie. See you in the morning."

He hangs up, and less than ten seconds later there is a text.

*Can't wait to see you in the morning, and to one day see what you wear to bed.*

Oh, I definitely hit the nail on the head when I said he was a charmer.

*There's that mention of 'one day' again! I'm also looking forward to tomorrow. Sleep well tonight, Handsome, you're going to need it. :) xoxo*

For the first time in over two years, I actually fall to sleep quickly, have calm dreams, and wake with the sun.

# CHAPTER 5

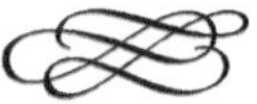

*F*uck! I'm late!

Luke's going to be here to get me any minute, and I'm still running around the house, grabbing my camera equipment, purse, and sandals. I'm pulling my hair up in a ponytail when the doorbell rings.

Shit!

"Hey!" I smile as I open the door, then my mouth drops at the delicious sight of him. His dark blond hair is still wet from his shower and all disheveled in that way he has. He's wearing a simple gray T-shirt, his sunglasses tucked in the collar, and khaki cargo shorts.

Yum.

His impossibly blue eyes shine as he smiles down at me. "Hi, beautiful. You look fantastic in red."

I feel my cheeks heat. I love this red sleeveless top and decided to wear the denim shorts that fit my rear just so. Just for him.

"Ready?"

"Almost." I step back to let him in and close the door behind him. "I'm running a bit late. Busy morning, but I'm almost ready."

"Couldn't sleep again?" He frowns down at me.

"The opposite, actually. Slept too well, was almost late for yoga, and had to run a couple errands." I pick up my camera bag and grab my purse off the table by the door. I hate feeling scattered!

Luke grabs my camera bag from me, slings it over his shoulder, and I grin up at him in thanks. "How about you? Sleep better?"

"Much, thank you."

"I'd show you around, but I'd love to get on the road. Rain check?"

"Absolutely, let's go."

I whistle when I see Luke's sporty little Lexus convertible parked in my driveway. He deposits my camera bag in the tiny back seat then opens my door for me with a huge, cat-ate-the-canary grin on his handsome face.

"Nice car."

"I figured it would be a good day for a drive with the top down."

"Sounds good to me." The leather seat is low and soft, and I can't help but be just a little impressed. He has good taste.

Before long we're zipping down the freeway through Seattle and heading out of town on Interstate 90. This car can move! The sun is warm, the wind feels great, and Luke cranks up some Maroon 5. There is no need for idle chitchat. We're just enjoying each other's company, and I find myself relaxing back into the seat and enjoying the lush, green scenery on our way to the falls.

It's obvious Luke knows where Snoqualmie Falls is, and as we get closer, he turns down the music, then rests his hand on my left thigh. Just that touch alone makes my libido sit up and take notice, and I take a deep breath to calm my erratic heart.

"You've clearly been here before."

Luke smiles at me. "Yeah, my parents used to bring us here when we were kids for picnics and stuff."

"Do you mind if I leave my camera bag in the car? I'll just take my camera."

"No problem, I'll close the top." Luke patiently waits for me to gather what I need out of my bag, then closes the top of the car, locks it, and we're off, hiking down the covered bridge that leads to the hotel and the falls access where tourists can ooh and aah over the beautiful water.

I sling the camera strap over my neck and check the settings as I walk.

"How long have you been a photographer?" Luke asks. He's intently watching me adjust the settings.

"All my life, actually. My dad bought me a digital camera when I was about ten, and I never wanted to do anything else." The memory brings a smile to my face, and I look up at him.

"He must be very proud of you," he murmurs.

The pain is swift and hard. "He's gone."

"Gone?"

"My mom and dad were killed almost three years ago." Shit, I didn't mean to say that!

"Damn, Nat, I'm sorry." Luke stops walking and pulls me into his arms, holding me tight, my camera squished between us, and I'm mortified to feel tears prick the backs of my eyes. I do not want this day to turn sad.

"I'm okay." I put my hands flat against his hard chest and look up into his face. "I'm okay. Let's not get sad today."

Luke's frowning down at me, his eyes full of compassion and, to my relief, void of pity. I don't want him to feel sorry for me.

"Hey, I'm okay. Really." I cup his cheek in my hand, and he turns and places a kiss in my palm.

"Okay." He releases me, and we resume our journey to the falls. It doesn't take long, as it's not far from the road.

I glance over at him, and he's still brooding, a small frown on his face. "Luke, cheer up. You didn't say anything wrong. I'm happy you're here."

He looks me in the eye again and gives me a half smile. I relax a little, happy that the mood is lifting, and pick up my camera as we turn the bend to see the falls.

"I'm so glad there isn't anyone else here today." I'm trying to change the subject.

"I'm surprised there aren't," he replies.

"Well, summer's almost over, and it's the middle of the week, so I figured we'd have the place mostly to ourselves." I start snapping photos.

Luke steps back and watches me work. I move up and down the path, getting different angles, stopping to adjust my settings, and take shots of flowers and spider webs and other things that catch my eye. The trees are just beginning to change color, so I aim my camera up and take photos of those, too.

"Ready to move on?" I glance back at him. "I hope I'm not boring you."

He shakes his head. His arms are crossed in front of him, and he's leaning on a fence. He looks relaxed, but his eyes are watching me intently.

"Nothing about watching you is boring, Natalie."

Oh.

He unfolds himself and takes my hand, kissing my knuckles, before leading me farther down the dirt path to get shots at the base of the falls. He again backs away and leaves me to my work. I feel his eyes on me as I move, and I smile to myself.

After about twenty minutes, I'm satisfied with the shots I've captured. "Okay, I think that's a wrap."

I turn to find his eyes have widened in surprise.

"What?"

He shakes his head. "You're done so soon?"

"Well"—I check my camera—"I've taken almost four hundred photos. I think I'll have some good shots out of these."

"I'm sure they'll be beautiful."

I grin and put the lens cap on my lens, careful not to point it at him, and let my camera fall down to my hip. I don't understand why he doesn't like to have his photo taken, but I can respect it. I wish I could talk him into posing for me. He'd be a treat to capture.

"What are you thinking?" he asks as we climb the trail back to the car. He's beside me, his hand on my lower back.

"Why don't you like to have your picture taken?" His eyes meet mine, then he quickly looks away. He shrugs nonchalantly, but I can see he's hiding something.

"Look at me," I say softly, smiling.

His wide blue eyes meet mine, and he's got that *where is she going with this?* expression. "You can tell me."

We've stopped on the trail, facing each other, and because of the uneven ground, I'm almost at eye level with him. I rest my hands on his shoulders. Luke's eyes widen further, and he swallows, and it looks like he's going to confess something. My stomach clenches. Talk to me!

Suddenly, he shakes his head and closes his eyes briefly.

"I just don't."

I frown up at him, but he shakes his head again and whispers, "It's just part of my phobia of being in crowds. Stupid, I know."

I want to probe him further, but he takes my hands off his shoulders, links his fingers with mine, and snakes our arms around my back, pulling me close. He rubs his nose back and forth over my own, his blue eyes intense.

"I've been thinking about kissing you all day."

"Less thinking and more doing." I'm surprised by my sassy response, or that I'm able to respond at all with my heart beating as fast as it is.

Luke smiles against my lips and sweeps me up in a hot, all-consuming kiss. He releases my hands and finds my ass like he did the night before, pulling me against him. I grasp his face in my hands, holding him close, and just like that I'm lost in him. He's so good with his mouth! He nibbles my lips, and his tongue makes gentle and patient love to mine. I groan and push my hands up into his hair, hanging on for dear life.

"Excuse us!"

I glance behind me to see a group of hikers trying to get around us on the trail. Oops! Luke laughs and pulls me out of the way so they can make their way down the path.

"I guess we got caught," Luke whispers in my ear, tucking a strand of hair behind it, and kisses my cheek.

"I guess so." I giggle breathlessly, and we resume our hike to his sexy car.

~

"YOU BROUGHT FOOD?" I can't hide the surprise in my voice as Luke pulls a small cooler and blanket out of the back of the car. I stow my camera and lean my hip against the car.

He gives me a shy smile. "Yeah, I packed a picnic lunch. I know a nice little spot up that trail there to relax for a bit. I hope that's okay? You said you didn't have any sessions today."

"Sounds good to me, I'm starving."

"Good. Come." He takes my hand and leads me into the woods on another dirt trail. The trees and ferns are lush and dense around us, not letting much sunlight in. After we walk for a few minutes, the path opens up to a clearing. There's a beautiful meadow with tall, green grass. A tall, lush oak tree stands in the middle, it's large, green branches providing plenty of shade.

"Oh, it's beautiful!" I let go of his hand and move quickly through the grass to the majestic tree and stare up into its branches. "This tree has to be two hundred years old."

I glance over to Luke, a huge smile on my face. He's standing near me, the cooler and blanket at his feet, his hands in his pockets.

"I'm glad you like it."

I look up again. "Luke, I love it."

I help him spread the big, green blanket we snuggled up in last night in the shade of the tree.

"Get comfy."

I kick my sandals off and sit on the soft blanket, my legs stretched out in front of me and lean back on my hands. Luke also kicks his shoes off—mmm, naked feet—and kneels on the blanket, opening the cooler.

He pulls out a fruit salad, sub sandwiches, and hummus and crackers. My stomach growls, and we both laugh.

"Did you make all this?"

He passes me a sandwich, and I dig in. Mmm...

"Yeah, I threw it together this morning." He passes me the fruit and pops a cracker full of hummus in his mouth. "I love a woman who likes to eat."

I stop chewing and look up at him, frowning, remembering my thighs and round butt. "What do you mean?"

"Just what I said. I like a woman who enjoys food." He shrugs and frowns at my expression. "What did you think I meant?"

Shit. "I don't know." I eat a strawberry.

His eyes narrow. "Don't tell me you have body issues."

"Don't be ridiculous."

"Natalie, you're beautiful. You have no reason to be self-conscious."

"Did you not just see how I devoured that sandwich? I'm not self-conscious." Stop talking about this.

He shakes his head.

"This is delicious." I smile sweetly.

He doesn't look like he's buying my change of subject, but he lets it go and starts packing the leftovers back into the cooler.

I lie on my back and take a deep, satisfied breath. Oh, this is nice. Warm late-summer day, good food, sexy man… Yes, it's a really good day. Suddenly, Luke is pulling my feet into his lap, and he starts to rub.

Make that a glorious day.

"Oh my. You cook and give foot rubs. I must be hallucinating." I hear him chuckle.

"Hey, what's this?" He runs his thumb just above the arch on the inside of my right foot.

Oh, that. "A tattoo."

He tickles my foot, and I squirm and giggle.

"Obviously, smart-ass. What does it say?"

"One Step at a Time," I reply, and sigh as he continues to work magic on the sole of my foot.

"In what language?"

"Italian."

His finger traces the letters, and I push up on my elbows and watch him. When his eyes meet mine, they're on fire, and the muscles low, low in my stomach clench.

"It's sexy." He grins.

"Thanks." I grin back.

"Do you have any more?" He cocks his head and reaches for my other foot.

"Yes."

His eyes shoot to mine again, and they narrow. "Where?"

"Various places."

"I don't see any others." His eyes skim up my bare legs, my arms, my chest.

"The one on my foot is the only one visible with my clothes on, and that's only when I'm barefoot," I whisper. Oh, this is fun!

He releases my foot.

"Hey! I was enjoying that foot rub."

He grabs my ankles and parts my legs, then crawls up my body on his hands and knees until his nose is almost touching mine.

"I want to know where your other tattoos are, Natalie."

I bite my lip and shake my head. Who can form words with his body so close?

"You're not going to tell me?" He leans in and lightly kisses the corner of my mouth.

Again, I shake my head no.

"Maybe I'll just have to find them."

# CHAPTER 6

e kisses the other side of my mouth, his eyes not leaving mine.

I nod, slowly.

Luke grins as he pushes me back down against the blanket and covers my body with his. Holy Moses, he feels so good! His long, muscular body seems to fit perfectly against my soft curves. He presses one leg between mine, and I can feel his impressive erection against my hip.

I push my hand under his shirt to caress his bare skin, up and down his ribs. His skin is so smooth and tight over sculpted muscles.

While he continues to make me crazy with that talented mouth of his, he runs his hand from my hip up over my shirt to my breast, and I can't help but bow up off the ground, pressing my breast into his hand. My nipple is hard, straining against my bra and shirt, and he runs his thumb over it.

"Open your eyes." I gaze up into his perfect blue eyes, gazing at me with passion and hunger. My breath catches, and I run my fingertips down his cheek.

"You are so sexy, Natalie. I just can't seem to stop touching you."

"I love you touching me."

"You do?" He caresses my face, pushing errant strands of hair off my cheek.

"Yes," I whisper.

"Your skin is so soft," he murmurs, his fingers still on my cheek. "I love your curvy body."

My eyes widen.

"Don't frown." He kisses me between my eyebrows, as if he's smoothing the frown from my face.

"I'm not so sure about my curvy body." It's a whispered admission that I've never made before, and frankly, I've never felt this vulnerable.

His blue gaze meets mine again, and each word is staccato: "You. Are. Beautiful."

I close my eyes, but he tips my chin, forcing me to look at him again.

"Thank you."

His lips find mine, gently now, lingering and caressing my mouth as if we have all the time in the world. I shift my hips and grind myself against his thigh, and he groans low in his throat.

My blood is on fire. I've never wanted a man like I want Luke. I want to consume him. I want him fast and hard, and I want him to take all day. I love how tender he is with me.

He sits up, pulling me with him and grabs the hem of my shirt. "I want to see you." He's breathless and needy, and in this moment I'd do anything he asked.

I lift my hands above my head, but before he can pull my shirt off, I feel drops of water on my face. I glance up and realize the sky has clouded over, and it's starting to rain, the water seeping through the branches of our oak tree.

"I'm getting wet," I whisper against his mouth.

He grins, his eyes laughing at me. "I hope so."

I can't help but laugh at him, and I wrap my arms around his neck. "That, too, but we're about to get rained on."

"Damn it," Luke murmurs, kissing me chastely. He runs a hand down my back, from my neck to my ass, and I think I purr.

"We should go." I raise an eyebrow at him.

"Don't think I'm not going to discover your tattoo secrets."

"Whatever happened to taking this slow?" My breathing is starting to calm, but my heart is still beating fast. Oh, what this man does to me!

"I think I've changed my mind." He's perfectly serious.

Thank God!

"And why is that?" I run my hands through his hair, completely happy on his lap, with his arms tight around me.

"Because I can't keep my hands off of you. I don't know what you're doing to me, but I'm under some kind of spell." He gives himself a shake and looks around us at the darkening sky.

"The rain is getting heavy. Let's head back." He lets me go, and we gather our things, jogging into the woods and to the car. By the time we get there, we're wet and laughing like kids.

"I don't want to get your leather seats wet!"

"Don't worry about it. Just get in!" He opens the door for me. "I don't want you sick, baby."

Baby? Baby! Am I okay with him calling me baby? He guides me into the seat, slams the door and runs to the driver side. He looks over at me, his hair and shirt soaked, breathing hard, his beautiful blue eyes full of humor.

Oh yes. I'm fine with it.

"Let's get you home and dry." He starts the car and pulls out of the parking lot, toward the freeway.

"So, tell me more about yourself." Luke merges onto the freeway and glances over at me.

"What do you want to know?" I ask.

"Favorite music?"

"Maroon 5," I respond easily.

"Favorite movie?" he asks with a grin.

"Hmm…we've had this conversation." I laugh. "I still like *The Way We Were*."

"Ah yes, you're a Robert Redford fan." He kisses my hand, and I sigh.

"I am."

"First boyfriend?" His eyes turn nervously to mine again, and I freeze. How do I answer this question?

"You know, I don't do this." I turn in the seat to face him.

He glances at me, then back at the road. "Do what?"

I shrug, trying to find the words and wondering why I feel the need to explain myself.

"Hey." He links his fingers with mine and kisses my hand before resting them both in his lap. "What is it?"

"I don't usually spend much time with men. I don't make out. I don't share meals. I don't spend time playing the twenty questions game. I just…don't." This is coming out so wrong!

He gazes at me again, surprised.

"Okay, what do you do with men?" He squirms in his seat, and I think he's mad.

"I fuck them." There. It's out there.

"What?" Oh yeah… I think he's really mad.

"Luke, I don't date." Oh, how do I explain this? I have never wanted to date anyone before. Before him.

"Are you brushing me off?" His voice is incredulous, and he lets go of my hand.

"No!" I close my eyes and shake my head. "Before I met you, I mean. I just don't want you to think that I'm promiscuous or that I go out with guys into the woods after knowing them for less than two days."

"But you fuck them," he snarls.

"Well, I used to." I turn back in the seat and stare out the windshield. "Before my parents died…"

He grabs my hand again, and I whip my head back to him, surprised.

"Go on."

"Before they died, when I was in college, I didn't think much of myself. And, therefore, neither did anyone else. I didn't date as a choice, Luke. But sex was something I understood. I've never wanted to feel anything else for a man." I swallow hard and close my eyes in shame.

"Did something happen to you to make you feel like that?" His voice is dead calm. Too calm.

"Umm…" I've never told anyone this. Except Jules.

"Look, Nat, I feel something here, too, and you can bet your sweet, beautiful ass that I'm going to make love to you tonight. I'm not going to fuck you. So I think it's pretty important that we're honest with each other now. No surprises." His handsome face is so sincere, and sweet.

"Last night you said you wanted to fuck me."

"I did. I do. And I will. But not tonight."

"Oh," I breathe.

"Yeah. So, what happened, baby?"

I pull my hand out of his and twist my fingers in my lap. Luke changes lanes, and I try to gather my thoughts. Oh, this hurts.

"When I was seventeen, I dated a guy for a few months who I thought was pretty nice. I was a virgin, which he would tease me about, but I didn't care. I was only seventeen, for Christ sake.

"Well, long story short, he took things too far one night. We were at my house. My parents were at some party, and we were alone, and he…" I stop talking and look out the window, not seeing the buildings and trees, swamped in shame.

"He raped me."

Luke inhales sharply, his face contorted in anger. "Motherfucker."

"That's not even the worst part." I laugh mirthlessly with the memory.

"This isn't fucking funny." He's glaring at me now, and my face sobers.

"Trust me, I know." I swallow. "You're very sweary."

"You haven't heard sweary yet. What happened next?"

"My parents came home." It's a whispered confession. Again, Luke inhales loudly.

"My dad almost killed him. The cops were called. He was punished. His dad was a senator, so along with the legal crap, my parents sued his parents and won. My dad was a very high-profile lawyer. I have quite a large trust fund from the lawsuit, which will never be touched by me. I don't need it. My parents made sure I was very well taken care of, and I don't want it anyway."

He doesn't say anything for a long time. He just drives and seems completely lost in thought.

"So," I interrupt the silence, "that's why I had so many issues with guys in college. It took a few years of counseling and my parents' deaths to wake me up and pull me out of some destructive behavior."

"Tattoos?" he asks.

"No, ironically, the tattoos had nothing to do with my past, and everything to do with healing."

He still won't look at me. Fuck, it was too soon!

"Hey." I grab his hand in mine. "I know that was a lot to dump on you, and we just met. If you'd rather just drop me off at home and cut our losses, I understand."

"No, Natalie, you're not getting rid of me that easily." He squeezes my fingers in his, and the relief I feel is incredible.

"You seem a little quiet."

"I don't honestly know what to say." He frowns and glances at me.

"I just…" I pause to collect my thoughts. "I feel this heading somewhere intimate, and I thought you should know." The last two words are a whisper.

"You've never dated anyone, ever?"

I shake my head.

"Honey, we have a lot of catching up to do." His voice is tender again, and I feel hope slowly spread through me.

"We do?"

"Oh yeah. I have one question, though."

"Okay."

"Where is that fucker?"

"I don't know. Why?"

"Because I'm going to kill him."

I can't believe he just said that! I chuckle softly. "No need. I'm sure he's a miserable man, Luke."

"He should be in hell."

"He will be." I grasp his hand tighter with mine. "Trust me, he's not an issue anymore. My dad saved me."

"Thank God." He kisses my knuckles, and I feel him start to relax beside me.

Wow, I told him the worst, and he still wants to see me? How did I get so lucky?

Luke pulls up in front of my house and turns off the car. He opens my door for me and lifts my camera bag out of the back, following me to the house. I unlock the door and motion for him to come inside.

"Jules!" I call out for my roommate, but the house feels empty.

"I don't think she's here." I smile at him and take my bag from him, setting it on the floor and my purse on the table. I take his keys from him and lay them on the table as well.

"Can I show you around?" I suddenly feel shy.

"Sure, after you."

I grasp his hand in mine. "Thank you for joining our tour today, Mr. Williams, we're delighted to have you with us."

Luke laughs, a full-on belly laugh, and I feel my shyness melt away. "Oh, I do love your sense of humor, Natalie."

I pick my camera bag back up off the floor, and he raises a brow. "I'll show you the studio and put this away too."

He nods, and I lead him through my house.

"I see you have a great view, too." He motions to the floor-to-ceiling windows off the great room, and I smile.

"I do. This is obviously the living, dining and kitchen." I glance at the reds and browns of our couches, dark wood dining furniture, and the simple elegance of the kitchen.

"Great kitchen." He winks down at me.

"Yes," I reply, and he chuckles. "But I don't cook much. Jules does a lot of the cooking."

"I'd love to cook for you here." His gaze is bright.

"I'd like that." I feel my cheeks heat. "Okay, let's go out to the studio, then I'll show you around upstairs."

"Out?"

"Yeah, I converted the guesthouse into a studio. It's my favorite part of the house. Come on."

I lead him out the sliding glass doors, across the backyard to the studio. I pause at the door and look up at him speculatively.

"What is it?" he asks, curiosity written across his face.

"Don't freak out on me, okay?"

"Why would I freak out?"

"Well, I told you I don't do traditional portraiture." I bite my lip.

"Baby, after our conversation earlier and the way I feel about you right now, I guarantee I will not freak out."

I watch his face and see that he means it and turn to unlock the door.

Here goes nothing.

I walk in ahead of him and put my bag on the floor. I switch on the lights, and Luke follows me inside. He stops just inside the threshold, his jaw dropped, his eyes wide, taking in my studio.

I turn and look with him. There is a king-size bed in one corner with white sheets draped over the canopy, ready for tomorrow's session. There are more floor-to-ceiling windows—perfect lighting!—across the room. I have racks of lingerie, corsets, boas, shoes, and other props. But what he seems to be focused on are the canvas photos hanging around the room.

He walks over to one and gazes at the couple in the throes of passion. It's in black and white, a side view of a couple lying on my king-size bed. The man is on top, braced over her, his mouth on her breast. Her head is thrown back, her mouth open, her leg wrapped around his hip, and her foot resting on the back of his thigh.

It's an erotic, intimate photo, and one of my favorites.

Luke turns in a circle, taking in all of the art on my walls, some of women or men in provocative poses, most of couples in different sexual positions. Finally, his eyes find mine.

"This is what I do," I whisper.

"Natalie"—he swallows and looks at my favorite photo again—"this is incredible."

"Really?"

He nods, his eyes wide. "Yeah, it's amazing. Sexy as hell. How did you get into this?"

I can't stop the smile on my face. "In college. Girls wanted me to take boudoir photos of them for their boyfriends, so I set up a makeshift studio in my apartment and started the business there."

"And the couples?"

"That sort of evolved. Most of them are return customers. The boyfriends or husbands loved the photos of their girls, and they wanted intimate photos of them as a couple."

"It's not porn." I just want that clarified and watch his face.

He frowns. "Baby, this is art. It's definitely not porn."

I smile, relieved. "There's a bedroom that I use to store props and furniture in for various shoots, and I use the kitchen to store refreshments for the clients. Sometimes, the girls like to have photos taken in there, too. It's fun."

He walks over to me, cups my cheek in his palm and kisses me softly. "You're amazingly talented."

Wow.

"Thank you. And for the record, I don't ever have sex in here. Ever."

His eyes dance with mischief. "Is that a challenge?"

"No, it's a fact."

"Why?"

"Because these aren't my memories. They're my clients'."

"So, you don't bring men in here?"

"Just you, handsome." I smile shyly.

"Good to know."

"Actually," I continue, looking him square in his bright blue eyes. "I've never invited a man to my home before."

His eyes widen, and he inhales deeply. "Your bed?"

"Just me."

"That's about to change." He grasps my hand and pulls me out of the studio, slamming the door behind us, leading me back into the house.

"Where is your bedroom?"

# CHAPTER 7

*H*oly hell, he's a man on a mission.

Luke is dragging me through the house, breathing hard, his eyes feral.

"Your bedroom?" he repeats, and I point up the stairs, unable to articulate words.

I don't remember my own name! And he hasn't even touched me.

Wow.

As he pulls me up the stairs, I get a great view of his tight ass, and my stomach clenches.

"To the right," I finally find my voice, and he pulls me into my bedroom, shuts and locks the door, and pulls me to him.

There's still plenty of light coming in the windows off the blue waters of the sound, and for just a moment I stand with his arms around my waist, my hands on his broad shoulders, and drink in the sight of his beautiful face.

"You're so handsome," I whisper.

He grins at me and leans down to nuzzle my neck, gently walking me backward to the bed. Thank God I made it this morning!

I'm expecting him to push me back onto the bed, but instead he steps back from me, not touching me at all, and his burning eyes run up and down my body, finally landing on my eyes.

"Are you sure about this?"

What? "Are you having doubts?"

"Hell, no, I just want to make sure this is what you want, baby. If you say no, that's fine, but please, God, don't say no."

Oh wow. He's giving me control, and I don't know if it's because of what I told him in the car, or if he's just being chivalrous, and frankly, I don't care. This is my choice.

*He* is my choice.

Staring him square in the eye, I say with a surprisingly sure voice, "Luke, please get us naked and make love to me."

He smiles, that huge, heart-stopping smile, and whips his T-shirt over his head.

Whoa!

He's all lean muscle and broad shoulders. His stomach is sculpted, with those incredibly sexy lines that run down the hips and to his cock. His arms are muscular…he's just so…*strong.*

I raise my hand to touch him, but he shakes his head, still smiling. "If you touch me, this will go much faster than either of us wants."

Oh. "We have all night."

"And we'll be taking advantage of it, baby, trust me. But this first time is going to be special."

I start to take my shirt off, and he stops me. "I'd like to do that."

"Well, then, hurry up!" I hear the whine in my voice but can't stop it, and I can't help but laugh with him.

"My pleasure." He shucks his shorts and underwear in one fast movement, and suddenly I'm getting a front-row view of Luke in all his glory.

He is simply a Greek god. His body is perfect in every way.

And he wants me!

He walks to me and grabs the hem of my shirt, pulling it over my head. He runs his fingers under my bra straps and leans in to nibble on my neck, just under my earlobe.

"Luke," I murmur.

"Easy, baby." He reaches behind me, deftly unclasps my bra and peels it down my arms. He makes quick work of my shorts and panties, pushing his hands between the fabric and my ass, cupping it, then slowly gliding them down my legs.

Oh, he's good with his hands!

He stands back up and lifts me, and suddenly I'm cradled in his arms. I wrap my arms around his neck, and he kisses my lips softly as he lowers me onto the bed.

"Sweet Jesus, you're beautiful, Nat." He whispers this against my throat, and I can do nothing but close my eyes and grip the blanket beneath me.

"Let's find those tattoos."

I smile as he kisses and licks his way down to my breasts, then gasp as he tugs one nipple firmly into his mouth and laves it with his expert tongue. Lightning shoots straight to my groin, and my hips start to shimmy of their own accord. I moan his name and twist his soft blond hair in my fingers.

"Hush, baby." He runs his hand down the opposite breast and tweaks it with his thumb.

"Oh God!"

My body's response to him is overwhelming.

I feel him smile against my skin, and he moves down, suddenly rolling me onto my right side. "What have we here?"

"Perhaps another tattoo?" My voice cracks as he runs his hand from my left hip to my shoulder.

"What does it say, baby?"

It's script, as are all of my tats, that runs up my ribs, but I'm too busy trying to remember to breathe to talk.

"Natalie, what does it say?" He kisses each letter gently, arms wrapped around my hips, braced on his elbows.

"It says, Be happy for this moment." I groan and continue. "This moment is your life."

"In what language?" His finger is rubbing it now. Oh wow.

"Sanskrit."

"Mmm…turn onto your stomach."

I oblige and groan as he kisses my shoulder, over to my spine and starts working his way down, down, down.

"God, your mouth feels good," I groan, and I feel him smile against my sensitive skin.

"And this?" He nibbles between my shoulder blades.

"It's Greek."

"What does it say, beautiful?" Oh God, his hands are just everywhere. My skin is on fire, and he wants me to talk?

"Love deeply."

"You're so fucking sexy, Nat."

"You're making me feel pretty fucking sexy, Luke."

He nibbles his way down to my lower back.

"No tramp stamp?" I hear his smile.

"Hell, no," I respond.

He plants open-mouth, wet kisses on my left buttock, then my right, and then I hear his breath catch.

"Christ, baby."

He nibbles my upper thigh, just under my right buttock, and I about come up off the bed.

"Easy. What's this one?"

I smile. "A tattoo."

"Oh, you are a smart-ass." He slaps me on the ass, hard, and I gasp.

"Ah!" I look back at him in shock, my eyes wide, and he grins.

"What does it say?" He raises an eyebrow, daring me to make a sassy retort, and I swallow.

Holy fuck, no one's ever spanked me before. It's…*hot.*

"Happiness Is A Journey," I whisper. "In French."

He groans and kisses it tenderly. I lie back down, flat on the bed and enjoy the nibbles and kisses Luke leaves up and down my legs. He stops and gives the arch of my right foot extra special attention again, making me grin and want to clench my legs closed at the same time.

Suddenly, he flips me onto my back, and he raises my left foot up, bending my knee, and kisses my ankle, slowly moving up my leg. He is a wonder to watch as he worships my skin.

His eyes narrow when he catches sight of my belly button piercing, but then they darken when he sees my freshly waxed pubis.

"Oh, honey, what's this?"

I start to respond with my witty tattoo retort, but it's caught in my throat when he bends that sexy blond head over and ever so gently rains tiny kisses over the one word scripted on my pubis.

"It says Forgive, in Italian."

He gives it one last wet kiss then climbs up my torso, kisses the silver heart in my belly, then up my sternum, until he's bracing himself on his elbows on either side of my head and smoothes my hair off my face. His blue eyes shine with need, his mouth open as he pants, and I've never felt so wanted, so needed, by anyone in my life.

"Do you have any idea how amazing you are?" He rubs his nose against mine and licks the seam of my lips lightly.

My ragged breath catches. "Not half as amazing as you make me feel."

"Oh my God, baby, I want you." I feel his amazing erection against me, and I tilt my hips up in invitation.

"Yes." I nibble his lower lip.

He reaches down between us and gently rests a finger against my clitoris. I arch up and gasp as I feel it all the way to my toes.

His mouth is hungrily on mine now, kissing me hard and deep, and suddenly I feel that fantastic finger slip lower to the lips of my opening, and he growls against my lips.

"Fuck, you're so wet."

"I so want you."

He slips his finger in and out of me, and then he adds another, and I think I'm going to die from the sensations zinging around my body.

I grip his ass in my hands and tilt my pelvis up in invitation. "Now."

"Hold on."

What the fuck? Hold on?!

Suddenly, he dives over the side of the bed to snag his shorts and pulls a foil packet out of his back pocket. I smile as he tears it open, his eyes locked on mine, and he rolls it down his cock.

He leans over me again, poised at my entrance. I run my fingers up his spine to his gorgeous hair and lift my legs up, tilting my pelvis again. He rubs his nose over mine and slowly, oh so damned slowly, eases into me.

"Oh my," I breathe, as he closes his eyes tightly and leans his forehead against mine.

"Natalie," he whispers raggedly.

He pushes into me, all the way, and stops. When I start to move my hips, he stops me, staring down at me again.

"Just wait."

I just want to move. I want him to pound in and out of me, to make me explode around him, and he looks so calm.

I squeeze my muscles around him, just once, and that's it.

"Fuck," he whispers, and he starts to move in and out, gaining momentum. I'm meeting him with my hips, and we establish a delicious rhythm. His lips are on mine again, sliding and tangling with mine, and his hands are cupping my head, tangled in my hair.

I run my nails down his back, and he pulls a hand down to my breast, then to my hip, and finally farther down to hook my knee around his arm, opening me wider, and I feel myself start to tighten, as all of the hair on my body stands up on end, and I bury my face in his neck.

"Yes, baby, let go."

And I do, convulsing around him.

"Oh, Luke!"

Suddenly, I feel him stiffen and push into me twice more, and he empties himself into me.

"Natalie!"

～

My breathing is starting to calm, and my vision clears, and I am cradling Luke against my chest. I run my fingers through his soft blond hair and gaze down at him as he catches his breath.

"I'm sorry, I'm heavy. I'll move in about an hour." Luke doesn't move but smiles.

I yank on his hair, then lean down and kiss his forehead.

"You're fine," I whisper and continue to pet his hair.

"Just fine?" He frowns playfully and pushes up off of me, breaking our precious connection. He discards the condom and lies down next to me, pulling me into his arms.

"Okay, you're better than fine."

"How are you?" he asks, serious now.

"I'm…" I search for the word. "Fantastic."

"Yes, you are." He kisses me lightly. "So, why the different languages?"

I shrug and look away, but he pulls my chin back toward him.

"I don't want anyone to know what they say unless I tell them."

"Who has been so lucky, Miss Conner?" He raises an eyebrow.

"You," I whisper.

"And?"

"You."

He gasps. "Really?"

"Yes."

He runs the backs of his fingers down my cheek, then his thumb across my bottom lip, and I bite it.

"Oh, you want to get rough, do you?"

"Maybe later."

"What do you want to do, baby?" Oh, he's so sweet.

"I think I need a shower." I grin up at him and sit up, shimmy off the bed and turn back to him.

"I do love your ass, Nat."

I laugh, turn and wiggle it for him, then saunter toward the bathroom.

"You'd better join me before I use all the hot water!"

# CHAPTER 8

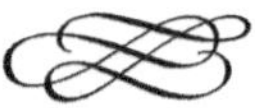

*Who* is this woman, and what has she done with me?

I can't believe how at ease I feel with Luke, especially naked. I've never, ever just walked around in the nude like it's no big thing. My clients do it all the time, and I admire their confidence, but that's just not me.

Until today.

Until him.

*I do love your ass, Nat.* The words he uttered before he clamored out of bed to join me in the shower still make me smile. He loves my full ass, my body art, my curves.

He seems to especially love my curves.

I glance up at him in the shower and smile. Oh, he's pretty. He's scrubbing his hair, and I can't help but pour some body wash in my hands and start washing his back.

"Mmm…" he growls, and leans his head back in the spray to rinse his hair.

"How often do you work out?" I ask.

"Just about every day." He turns, pouring the fragrant soap into his own hands. "Turn around."

"How about you?" he asks as he starts massaging my shoulders.

"What was the question?" I murmur.

He chuckles. "How often do you work out?"

"I do yoga three or four times a week when I can fit it in. My work is pretty physical, too. That's it." I shrug.

"It's working for you." His voice is sincere, and I glance back at him and smile.

"Back at you."

He rhythmically circles his hands over my back and down to my bottom, and then steps around me so my back is in the water and starts massaging my front.

"You have great hands," I whisper and brace myself on his hips.

"You have great skin," he responds. His hands run over my breasts and tight nipples, suds running down my torso. He eases one hand down my belly and finds my clitoris with a finger. He backs me up against the wall and pulls my earlobe between his teeth.

"Ah!"

"I would love to make love to you here, baby, but there's no condom dispenser in the shower." I feel him grin and look up into his bright blue eyes.

Before he can slip a finger inside me, I grab his hand and bring it up to my lips, pulling his finger into my mouth, sucking it hard. His pupils dilate, and he bites his lip.

"I have a better idea."

With that, I run my hands down his chest, over his abdomen and to his hips. I sink down to my knees and am at eye level with his impressive, very hard cock. I wrap my hand around it, moving up and down, looking up into his eyes.

"Shit, baby." He closes his eyes and leans both hands against the wall of the shower, and seeing the pleasure on his beautiful face empowers me.

I lean in and lick around the rim of the head, then take him in my mouth and suck hard.

"Fuck!"

Oh yes!

I push and pull him in and out of my mouth, my teeth sheathed behind my lips. I'm sucking and licking, swirling around the tip as I pull up. He starts to rock his hips against me, and I take him deeper and deeper, feeling the tip at the back of my mouth.

"Oh shit, Nat. Stop, baby, I'm gonna come."

But I don't want to stop, so I don't. I continue the torment, reveling in making him crazy. He grabs hold of the bun on top of my head and growls as he comes, and I swallow quickly.

He's panting, his forehead leaning against the tile. As he catches his breath, he looks down at me, his eyes molten blue, and pulls me to my feet, kissing me long and hard.

Oh my.

"Come on, let's get out of the water." He pulls away, turns off the water and hands me a fluffy towel.

"Are you hungry?" I ask.

"Starving." He grins wickedly, and I laugh at him, wrapping the towel around me as I walk around him and into my bedroom. I spy his gray T-shirt on the floor and scoop it up. I drop the towel and pull the shirt over my head. Mmm…it smells like him.

No panties. I giggle at my audacity and turn to find Luke standing in the doorway, a towel around his hips and his eyes on me.

"That's some show, Nat."

"Glad you liked it," I reply with a smile. "Come on, we'll find something to eat in the kitchen."

I wait for him to pull on his shorts—no underwear!—and we head downstairs.

Luke sits on a bar stool and watches me move about the kitchen.

"I have no idea what we have," I say shyly. "This is Jules' domain. Hmm…Caesar salad?"

I hold the bowl up out of the fridge, and he nods. I dish it out for both of us, and then walk around and sit next to him.

"So you don't cook at all?" he asks.

I grimace. "I can, I choose not to. Jules has always lived with me, and she loves to cook, so it works for us."

At the mention of her name, I hear the front door open. "Nat?" she calls.

"I'm in the kitchen," I call back.

"Do you have company?"

I frown. "Yeah."

"Okay, going to bed. See you tomorrow." I hear her shoes click up the stairs.

Luke raises a brow and looks at me. I shrug.

"Maybe she had a bad day," he says.

"Maybe." I frown but shrug it off. I'll ask her about it tomorrow. I figured she would have been curious to get a peek at Luke, but seeing as we're both half naked, I'm relieved. I don't really want anyone to see Luke without his shirt on.

I clear the few dishes we have and stack them in the dishwasher, then turn back and lean my elbows on the counter.

"Will you stay with me tonight?" I ask.

Luke's eyes widen, and he smiles. He doesn't say anything. He just stands and comes around the breakfast bar to me. Without touching me, he leans in and gently lays his lips on mine.

Geez, where did I find this guy?

"I'd love to stay tonight," he whispers against my lips. Oh, there's that sexy whispering thing he does so well.

"Okay, good," I whisper back.

Suddenly, he turns his back to me and says, "Jump on."

"What?"

"Jump on my back, we're going upstairs." He reaches his arms back like he's going to catch me, and I laugh as I jump up onto his back, wrap my arms around his neck and hitch my legs up around his hips.

I lean down and pull his earlobe between my teeth, and he takes off for the stairs, effortlessly climbing them, and we are both laughing like crazy when he stops next to the bed and pulls the covers back.

I squeal as he unceremoniously drops me on the bed.

"You know," he says, his face suddenly very serious, as he sprawls out beside me on his side.

"What?" I ask sarcastically.

He runs his fingertip along the neckline of his T-shirt. "You never did ask me if you could borrow my shirt."

"I didn't?" I widen my eyes and bite my lip.

He shakes his head. "No, you didn't. Very rude of you."

"I'm so sorry. How can I ever make it up to you?" I try to look contrite.

"I don't know. I'm very offended." He still looks so serious, and I want to break out into laughter, but I'm enjoying our game too much.

"Can I buy you a new one?" I ask.

"Well, I'm really very fond of that one."

"Oh," I bite my lip again and push him onto his back. "Can I take a picture of it and give it to you?"

I unfasten his shorts, and he raises his hips so I can pull them down his legs, his erection springing free. I pull a condom out of the pocket and discard them onto the floor.

"No," he whispers. "It's just not the same."

"Hmm..." I roll the condom onto his cock and straddle his hips. I look down at him, narrowing my eyes like I'm thinking very hard, trying to solve this problem.

"Well"—I cross my arms and grip the hem of his soft gray shirt, pulling it over my head—"I guess I'd better return it then."

I hand him the shirt, but he throws it on the floor and sits up so we're nose-to-nose. He grasps my ass in his hands and lifts me over his cock, and I slide down onto him.

"Fuck, baby, you're so wet."

"That little game turned me on."

He growls and kisses me, guiding me up and down with his hands on my rear. I plant my hands on his shoulders and push, and he lies back on the bed. I lean down and kiss him tenderly, my hips still moving, his hands still on my butt.

Then I sit up and start to really move, reveling in how deep he feels, clenching around him. He runs his hands up my stomach to cup my breasts and tease my nipples with his thumbs.

"Ah!" I throw my head back and grind down on him harder, faster, and feel myself tightening, and I'm going to come already.

"Come for me, baby." His hands are gripping my hips, pushing me down onto him harder and harder, and I explode around him.

Before I've had a chance to come down to earth, Luke has moved out from under me, pushing me onto my stomach. He's lying on my back, his chest hair tickling my shoulder blades. He kisses the back of my neck and then over my tattoo. He parts my legs with one of his and then he's inside me again.

"Oh God!"

"Oh, baby, you feel so good." He's braced himself on his fists on either side of me and is pushing into me over and over, hitting that sweet spot on the front side of my vagina, sending little glittery sparks of yumminess all through me. I feel myself being pushed to the edge again, and I cry out Luke's name as I come, my orgasm gripping my body and wringing me dry.

He cries out my name as he finds his own release and collapses on top of me.

"Wow," I mumble into the pillows, and I feel his smile against my back.

"What was that?"

"Wow," I say again, not moving my head.

He bites my shoulder, and I yelp, pushing him off me. He chuckles as he discards the condom and wraps us in the blanket, pulling me into his arms, his front to my back.

"I'm sorry, miss, I didn't hear you."

"I said, 'That was just so-so.' "

He lets out a full belly laugh and hugs me close.

"Is this the wrong time to tell you that I'm on birth control?" I turn in his arms as I say this to see his reaction.

"What?" His eyes narrow, and now he looks pissed. Shit!

"Well, yeah, I am. Why are you mad?" I back up a few inches to look in his face.

"I thought you said it's been almost a year since you were with anyone."

"It has been."

He raises an eyebrow.

"Women don't go on and off birth control just because they're in a physical relation-ship." I roll my eyes. "It would mess with our hormones too much."

"Oh." He frowns again and then looks at my tattoos.

"I've been tested each year at my physical. I'm perfectly healthy." I smile.

"So, I could have had you in the shower?"

I laugh and nod but then stop and eye him speculatively. "Well..."

"I also get physicals regularly, haven't had a partner in about the same amount of time as you, and am healthy as can be."

"Then, yes." Oh, I so do not want to think about him being with other women. No, no, no.

"Well, shit, I think we need another shower."

I laugh and snuggle back into his arms, resting my head on his chest. "Tomorrow. I'm sleepy."

"Maybe we'll solve each other's insomnia."

"It's worth a try." I yawn and kiss his chest.

"Go to sleep, baby."

~

I WAKE in the morning to bright sunlight and a heavy arm draped over me. I've never slept with anyone before, so this is new. And amazingly comfortable.

Luke is asleep on my pillow. He looks so young and relaxed. He needs to shave, and his hair is messy, as usual. I want to run my fingers through it, but nature calls, so I carefully slide out from under his arm and head into the bathroom.

When I tiptoe back into the bedroom, Luke is still fast asleep, but he's turned to his other side, wrapping his body around the covers so a naked arm, leg, buttock and back are all exposed.

Holy sweet baby Jesus, he is a sight to behold!

I just can't help myself. What self-respecting woman could have this in her bed and not touch?

Not me.

I climb back onto the bed and run the palm of my hand from the heel of his foot, up over his toned calf and hamstrings, over his tight derriere and up his back, then run my fingers through his hair. I nibble his neck and across his shoulders. I kiss his spine and make my way down to the base of his back where two very sexy little dimples live, right above his ass.

I hear him groan and grin.

I run my fingernails down his ass to his thighs and kiss my way up his side over his ribs.

He slowly shifts and turns onto his back, and I kiss up his body, nipping a nipple and resting my hand on the sexy V at his hips. I look up into sleepy, amused blue eyes.

"Good morning, handsome."

"Well, good morning, beautiful."

Suddenly, I'm flat on my back and Luke has laced his fingers in mine and pulls both my hands above my head. He kisses my neck and my chin and moves his hands down my arms to cup my head in his hands.

"How are you this morning?" he whispers against my mouth and rubs his nose back and forth on mine.

"I'm good."

"Just good?" He kisses my jaw, and I sigh.

"What were you going for?" I ask and tilt my head, giving him better access.

"Amazing," he whispers.

I smile and run my hands down his back. "That works, too."

He leans up to look down at me again, and I cup his cheek in my hand.

"How are you?" I ask.

"I've never been better."

My eyes widen at his serious reply. "Wow, I was just looking for good."

"Oh, honey, I surpassed good yesterday morning."

"You are quite charming."

He smiles down at me. "You are quite beautiful in the morning."

I snort at him and start to brush him off, but he holds my chin firm.

"You." Kiss. "Are." Kiss. "Beautiful." Kiss.

Holy shit.

"You aren't so bad yourself." I smile against his mouth.

"I want you, baby," he murmurs.

"I can tell." I grind my hips up against his erection, and he gasps.

"Jesus, you've got me horny like a teenager, Nat. What the fuck are you doing to me?" His blue eyes gaze into mine, and he moves his hips, the tip of his cock resting against me, and I tilt my pelvis, welcoming him inside me.

"Ah!" I grasp his shoulders as he pushes deeply inside me. He buries his face in my neck, gently sucking and kissing me. His thrusts become faster and harder, and our breathing is harsh.

"Oh, baby... I've never... Fuck, you feel good."

I cup his bottom in my hands and squeeze, pulling him in deeper.

"Come with me, baby." He's breathing raggedly, and I can feel him falling over the edge, and he takes me with him.

"Oh yes!" I cry and convulse around him.

Minutes later, after our breathing and bodies have calmed, he raises his head and kisses me gently. He eases out of me, and I find I'm a bit sore, but I don't mind.

"I'll be back." He gets up and goes into the restroom.

I sit up and stretch lazily. Oh, yes, I'm sore. Clearly, these muscles haven't been used in a while. I hug myself, then get up and throw on a T-shirt and yoga pants.

"You got dressed." I laugh at Luke's pouty face as he comes out of the bathroom. He wraps me in his arms and hugs me tight, and I sigh. Wow, is this just too good to be true?

"I'm going to go make some coffee. Meet me downstairs?" I stroke his cheek with my hand.

"Sure, I'll be right behind you."

# CHAPTER 9

"**W**ell, good morning, sunshine!" I greet Jules as I saunter into the kitchen. She's just back from a run, her blond hair pulled back in a ponytail, dressed like me in a white T-shirt and black yoga pants. She puts the coffee grounds back in the freezer and smiles over at me.

"Good morning, yourself. Did he leave?"

"No, he'll be down in a minute. We're having coffee."

"You invited him over." It's not a question.

"Yes."

"And let him stay."

"Yes."

Her blue eyes are sharp. "A little against your usual M.O."

"I know." I sigh and take three mugs out of the cabinet. "He's different, Jules. I don't know where this is going, but I want to find out."

She pats me on the shoulder and smiles. "I'm happy for you, sweetie."

I hear Luke walk in behind me, and Jules' eyes bulge. I know, he's hot!

I turn and smile at him.

"Luke, this is my best friend, Jules. Jules, this is…"

"Luke Williams!" Her voice is shrill, and now she's smiling, her hands in fists. She's practically jumping up and down.

"Ohmygod! Ohmygod! Ohmygod! Luke Williams is in our kitchen!" She shoves my shoulder and does a little circle happy dance.

What the fuck?

I look back at Luke, and he's gone perfectly still. He's completely pale. He swallows hard and looks at me but doesn't touch me.

Jules has stopped her happy dance. "You didn't tell me you were all gooey over Luke Freaking Williams!"

"I take it you know him?" I ask, my voice a whisper.

What am I missing?

Jules stops, her jaw drops, and her eyes widen.

"Of course I know *of* him. Nat, that's Luke Williams."

"I'm aware," I reply, but my face is flushed, and I'm starting to feel like everyone is in on some big joke and I'm the butt of it.

"No, Nat…"

Luke finds his voice. "Natalie, I can explain."

He reaches for me, but I move out of his grasp and round the breakfast bar to put space between us.

"Explain what?"

"Natalie." Jules swallows and looks at him, gets an irritatingly swoony smile on her face, then looks back at me. "This Luke Williams is famous."

"What?" I narrow my eyes and look at him again, and it suddenly all makes sense.

*Don't fucking take my picture.*

*Why won't you all just leave me alone?*

*I don't like crowds.*

"From the *Nightwalker* movies, Nat," Jules whispers.

Luke hasn't said anything, and he's no longer looking at me. His hands are on his hips, and he's hanging his head.

"You lied to me." I hate how broken my voice sounds.

His head whips up, and he pins me with those beautiful blue eyes. "No, I didn't."

"I asked you, more than once, what you do for a living, and you kept brushing me off." Oh, this hurts.

"I just…" He runs his hands through his hair. "Natalie, what I feel for you…"

"Stop." I hold my hand up. "You said yesterday in the car, no surprises."

He swallows.

"God, I feel so stupid." I close my eyes and want to lay my head on the bar and cry.

"No, baby…" He starts to move toward me, but I back away again, making him stop.

"No, you listen, *baby.*" The rage is kicking in, and I'm starting to shake with it. "I trusted you with things that I've never trusted with anyone else. And the whole time you were lying to me."

"It's not like that…"

"Natalie…" Jules steps forward, but I pin her in her place with a glare.

"So, I was a joke. 'Let's see how far I can get with this girl before she figures out who I am'? Well, you fucked her, Luke. Good for you."

"No!" He comes around the bar, ignoring my warnings of staying back and grasps my shoulders in his hands. His eyes are glacial, his face taut, as if he's in pain.

"No, Natalie. Nothing about us is a joke. And I did not fuck you, I made love to you."

I'm just so embarrassed. "Everyone in the country knows who you are, Luke."

"Not everyone," he replies.

"You're right. Apparently, I'm the only one who isn't bright enough to recognize you." I pull out of his grasp and back away. He drops his arms to his sides.

"Natalie," Jules tries again. "Why would you know who he is? You never saw his movies."

"His face is on millions of T-shirts, Jules! There are action figures in his likeness."

Luke grimaces and turns away.

"Girls of all ages squeal just the way you did five minutes ago and lose their fucking minds! It's my fucking job to know faces! God, I'm an idiot." I'm so embarrassed, I just want to run. I want him gone. I want him to hold me and tell me it's not true.

What the fuck would he ever want with me? He can have anyone in the world. Literally.

"Nat..." Luke reaches out for me, but I pull away, ignoring the pain in his voice.

"Just go."

"No, I don't want to leave." His beautiful face is in agony, mirroring mine.

I fold my arms around myself to keep from reaching out to him. "I don't want you here. I can't be with someone who lies to me." Oh, just go.

"I didn't lie! Natalie, that's not my life anymore. Let's talk about this."

I've heard enough, and I just need to get away from him. "I have a session in an hour, I need a shower, and I want you gone by the time I come out."

"You're overreacting!" His voice is manic, his eyes pleading with me.

"Get the fuck out of my house!" I scream at him, hot tears falling down my face.

"Natalie, don't do this..."

I turn and run up the stairs, through my room and into the bathroom, locking myself inside. I lean against the door and slide to the floor, my body convulsing as huge sobs rack my body.

"Natalie, open the door."

Fuck, he followed me.

"Just go away." There's no strength left in my voice. I just want him to go.

"I'm not going away, goddammit! Open the fucking door!"

"No!" I stand and lean my forehead on the door, my hands in fists and braced on the cool white wood.

"Natalie, so help me God, if you don't open this door, I'll break it down. Come out here and look at me." His voice sounds ragged and close to mine. And he's really pissed. But so am I! I don't respond, and suddenly Luke hits the wall to the left of the door.

"OPEN THE MOTHERFUCKING DOOR!"

I still don't respond. Hot tears are rolling down my face.

"Fine, Nat, if you want to act like a child, fine. I don't need this." I hear him stomp out of my room and down the stairs.

How did I get myself in this mess? How did I not recognize him? His hair is longer, and it's been a good five years since the last movie came out, so his body has filled out more, and he's older, but how could I not recognize that beautiful face?

Suddenly, I'm reminded of our talk when we had drinks at the pub. *If I see a trailer for one more stupid vampire movie, I'm going to kill myself.*

Oh God. Could this be any more humiliating?

Luke starred in three vampire movies that not only did well, but became such a huge sensation that you couldn't go anywhere without seeing news about the stars or merchandise of all kinds.

And I've just spent the past forty-eight hours falling in love with a man who is not only completely out of my league, but I don't even play the same sport.

Why didn't he tell me? Why did he let me tell him all of my secrets, while he didn't tell me any of his?

I sulk over to the tub and turn on the water. I have to pull myself together for my session. I cringe. Today's client is a couple, and I'm going to have to take intimate photos of them, encourage them to love each other, be romantic.

Shit.

I shower quickly, but let the water spray on my face for a few extra seconds. I'm going to look horrible with red, puffy eyes.

After I'm dry and dressed, I blow my hair dry and secure it back in a bun. I examine my face. Yep, red, puffy eyes. I don't bother with makeup and pray that my eyes calm down in the next thirty minutes. I just have to get through this session, then I can ball up in my bed and cry for days if I want to. Just two hours to get through and not think of Luke.

I poke my head out of the bathroom, but the bedroom is empty. Thank goodness. The wall next to the door where Luke hit it is unscarred. He didn't hit it that hard. I go into the spare bedroom and peek out the front-facing window. Luke's car is gone from the driveway.

He left.

Downstairs, Jules is still in the kitchen, a coffee mug in hand, tears in her eyes.

"Natalie, I'm so sorry."

I hold my hands up in surrender. "It's not your fault. I can't talk about this right now, Jules. I have a session in a few minutes."

"He's a wreck, Nat."

"Just stop."

"You have to talk to him."

"Stop! Jules, I can't talk about this." My voice catches, and I take a deep breath, willing the tears to stay at bay.

"Okay, we'll talk after the session then."

"Don't you have work?" I ask.

"I called out. I'm going to be here with you." She gives me a small smile.

"I love you, Jules." I turn to leave, but a thought occurs to me. "Do me a favor?"

"Of course. What is it, sweetie?"

"Strip my bed and wash all the bedding?" I couldn't stand to have to smell him later when I'm wallowing in self-pity.

"Sure."

~

It was the worst session of my life. I was scattered, sad, and edgy. The couple were great. They were very much in love, sexy, and I know that I got some great shots, but I feel badly that it wasn't the fun session I usually provide, so I'll refund the session fee. It's the least I can do.

I change into khaki shorts and a blue tank top, thanking the Lord above for my best friend when I see my bed has been stripped, washed and remade. My muscles have been reminding me all morning of last night's activities, and with every turn and stretch, my heart breaks just a little more.

Downstairs, I grab my iPhone to check messages and return calls, snag a tall glass of sweet tea from the fridge and join Jules on the back patio.

"How did it go?" she asks.

"It sucked." I shrug and sink into a red plushy chaise lounge.

"Sorry."

"I'll refund their money, but I think they'll still be happy with the photos." I turn my phone on and take a deep breath.

"Are you sure you want to check that?" Jules asks from the chaise beside me. Her eyes are closed, and she's drinking in the sunshine.

"I have to see if any clients called. I'll ignore him." I refuse to say his name out loud.

I have seven missed calls, five voice mails and three texts waiting for me.

There is absolutely nothing waiting for me from Luke, and I can't help but be disappointed. He said he didn't need this, so does that mean that we're over, just like that? Most likely, yes. Luke Williams can have anyone. Why would he want me?

I turn the phone off, slam it on the table beside my drink and pull my knees up to my chin, rest my forehead, and let the tears come full force.

"Oh, honey, don't cry." Jules climbs on my chaise with me and wraps her arms around me.

"I just feel so foolish," I mutter into her shoulder.

"You really didn't know who he is?"

"No. He looks a little different now," I reply defensively.

"Yeah, he does. He's aged well." Her smile is in her voice, and I can't help but agree.

"He has." I sigh. "Of course, now I see it. I should have known as soon as he mugged me at the beach."

"Maybe you were just too surprised."

"I guess, but what excuse do I have after that? I spent almost two solid days with the man, Jules."

"Hey, stop beating yourself up. You have been enjoying a sweet, sexy man for two days. There's no crime in that."

"I told him so much. I told him about Mom and Dad, the rape, everything. I even showed him my studio."

Jules looks down at me with wide eyes. "And you had sex in your own bed."

"Don't remind me."

"How did he react to all of it?"

I sit up and take a sip of tea. "He seemed sad for me that Mom and Dad are gone. The rape infuriated him, and he wants to kill that slimeball. He was really cool about the studio and said that it was sexy and I'm talented."

"Well, that all sounds encouraging."

"And last night was just…" How do I describe it? "Amazing and wonderful. He loves my curves, and when he touches me, just…wow." I can't stop the smile on my lips, and Jules smiles back.

"You made it with Luke Williams."

And my smile is gone.

"I'm sorry, but give me five minutes to gush. Is he as hot naked in real life as he is in the movies?"

"He was naked in the movie?" I squeak.

"From behind, yeah. It's my favorite part."

Oh, I definitely don't like it that all of America has seen Luke's ass. "I think his ass is better in person," I reply.

"Oh, you're killing me!" Jules sounds fifteen, and I giggle. "You know, he hasn't had a new movie since the last *Nightwalker* five years ago."

"Why?"

"I don't know." Jules shrugs and climbs back onto her chaise, taking a sip of my tea. "Rumor had it that some crazed fan broke into his house and hurt herself."

I gasp. "Was he hurt?"

"No, I don't think so. I don't think he was home. But who knows how much of the television tabloid stuff is true? I heard he just left LA and stopped acting. I had no idea he'd moved here."

"He's from here," I tell her. "His family lives around here."

"Oh, cool." Jules looks at me speculatively. "Are you sure you're done with him, Nat? You should have seen him after you ran out this morning."

"What did he do?"

"Well, he has quite a potty mouth, but then, so do you. He paced and swore, and I tried to stop him from running after you, because I knew that wasn't going to be the way to smooth things over."

"No, I didn't want to see him."

"He was a mess. He's mad about you. I think you should get to know him, the real him, better and give it a chance." I frown at her. "Besides, I've never seen you act this way about a man before. Don't give up on this yet."

"He lied to me, and you know how I feel about that!"

"Oh, Natalie, think. Have you stopped to think that maybe it was a nice change for him to be around someone who didn't want anything from him? Who didn't recognize him and squeal and ask him stupid questions? He was just a normal guy hanging out with a normal girl. I wouldn't want to ruin that, either."

I think hard about what Jules is saying, and yes, it makes sense.

"He still should have told me, at least yesterday." I am now sulking, and I don't care.

"You're right. Let him apologize. Maybe you'll get some good gifts out of the deal. Jewelry? Wine? Flowers?" She laughs when I stick my tongue out at her.

"Not today."

"Don't play games with him, Nat."

I scowl. "I'm not playing anything. He hurt my feelings. I just want to hang out with my best friend and do girl stuff today. Besides, when he stormed out of my room, he said he didn't need this, so I'm assuming he's no longer interested."

"Oh, he's interested." She waves the thought away with a flick of her wrist. "Wanna go shopping?" she asks hopefully.

"No. Ironically, I want to go to the movies. But nothing with Luke Williams in it."

"Okay, there's nothing with his name on it there anyway. I think we deserve extra butter on our popcorn."

"And no diet soda. And because you recognized him before I did, you're buying."

Jules pouts as we gather our things and get in the car, headed to the movies where I can lose myself in someone else's story for a few hours and spend time with the one person in this world whom I trust completely.

# CHAPTER 10

*I*t's late when Jules and I get home. The high-paced action/adventure film we caught—with Vin Diesel, no less—was exactly what I needed to escape reality for a few hours. And I ended up giving in to Jules to go shopping afterward. How can I, Natalie Conner, pass up new shoes? They are my vice.

"Those red Louboutins you found are to die for," Jules says as we're pulling bags out of the back of my Lexus.

"I know. I love them. I don't know when I'll get to wear them, but I couldn't resist them." I reach for the bag of shoes, and we head for the front door.

We stop abruptly when we see what's waiting on our doorstep. Dozens of bouquets of roses, in all different shapes, sizes and colors, are covering the porch, the front steps, every surface possible. The aroma is amazing. There must be fifty-dozen roses here, minimum.

"Oh, Natalie." Jules' eyes are wide, and her face gets all gooey, taking it all in.

I can't help but get just a little gooey with her.

"Wow." It's all I can say, and I'm just so relieved. Maybe it's not over? We walk up the steps, careful not to knock anything over, and I see an envelope taped to the door with my name written on it.

"Here!" Jules pulls it off and hands it to me. It's too dark to see well, so we step inside and drop our bags. Jules starts hauling bouquets in.

"Where should I put these?"

"Um…I don't know. Just put them throughout the house."

Her smile is huge. "He gets mad props for this, girl."

"Yeah, he does." I feel my own wide smile and stare down at the envelope and then carefully rip it open.

*Dear Natalie,*

*There is a rose here for every time I thought of you today. I wish you would talk to me and let me explain why I didn't tell you who I am, and I'm so deeply sorry that you had to find out from your friend. I have a lot of explaining to do, and I hope you give me a chance to make it up to you.*

*Please call me when you're ready to talk.*
*Yours,*
*Luke*

Oh, yes, he's charming. I tuck the note in my pocket and help Jules bring all of the flowers inside, scattering them all over the house. It looks like there's either going to be a funeral or a wedding in my living room in the morning, and it makes me giggle.

"See?" Jules smirks. "I told you he's crazy about you."

"Or just crazy," I reply, laughing.

"You'd better call him and thank him."

"Yes, Mom." I roll my eyes at her. We lock up after the final bouquet has been brought in and fussed over. "Here, take some of these up to your room."

"Don't have to tell me twice!" Jules tucks a bouquet under each arm and heads upstairs with her shopping conquests.

I grab my phone, which has stayed turned off all day, my new shoes, and a gorgeous arrangement of perfect long-stemmed red roses with pearls tucked into the petals, and go up to my room. I kick my sandals off, set the vase on my bedside table, and put the new shoes in their new home in the closet. Going back to the flowers, I can't help but fuss over them and bury my nose in a soft, fragrant bloom. I notice another note, tucked in the stems, and pull it out, sitting on the bed as I read.

*These reminded me of your gorgeous long legs and delicious red lips. And one day, I'd love to see you dressed in nothing but pearls.*

Oh my. Is this what it feels like to be romanced? I wouldn't know, but I think I like it. And it occurs to me that he's been romancing me all along. The delicious dinner at his house, cuddling on his deck watching the sunset, our amazing picnic lunch yesterday. He was right when he said that he made love to me last night. Sex has never been that intimate for me.

But he did lie, even if it was by omission, and that's a deal breaker for me.

I decide to give him a chance to explain. I'll go to his house tomorrow and hear him out. I already miss him. His touch, his smile, his belly laugh, the feel of that soft blond hair in my fingers. I desperately want something good to happen with this man, and maybe that's what scares me most of all, even more than his celebrity status and the fact that he could have any skinny little glamorous woman on the planet.

If things go too much further, he could hurt me.

But the thought of not seeing him again makes my chest ache.

I pull my phone and the letter from the front door out of my pocket. I fire up the phone and impatiently wait for it to wake up.

Three missed calls, two voice mails and two texts. Nothing from Luke.

Both voice mails are from clients, so I save those and remind myself to call them and the four from this morning back tomorrow.

I scroll down to Luke's number and hit Call.

He answers on the first ring.

"Hi," he says softly.

"Hi," I murmur, my eyes closing at the sound of his voice. "Thank you for the beautiful flowers."

"Do you like them?" I hear his smile.

"They are amazing. And bountiful." I can't help but chuckle.

"I thought of you a lot today."

"Apparently so."

"Natalie, I'm so sorry…"

"No, Luke," I interrupt him, the agony in his voice my undoing. "I'm sorry, too. I may have overreacted just a bit."

"No, I understand. I should have said something yesterday."

"Yeah, you should have." I sigh. "I don't want to talk about this over the phone. Are you busy tomorrow morning?"

"You want to see me tomorrow?"

I hear the excitement in his voice, and I melt even more. "Well, I was thinking I could come over to your place, and we could talk."

"Yes. Come now."

I laugh and turn on my side on the bed, feeling my stomach start to settle for the first time since this morning. "I'm tired and don't think I'm up for a long conversation tonight."

"What did you do today?" he asks.

"Jules and I did some shopping." Should I tell him about the movie?

"What did you buy?"

God, I love his sexy voice. "Shoes."

"You like shoes?"

"I'm a woman. I am desperately, irrevocably in love with shoes."

"What do the new shoes look like?"

"Red stiletto Louboutins." I grin as I think about my sexy new shoes.

He whistles. "Wow."

"Yes, they are wow." I laugh.

Suddenly, it's quiet, and I think I've lost the call. "Luke?"

"Yeah, sorry, I was just imagining you wearing nothing but those shoes and pearls."

"Wow," I murmur.

"Yes, it was wow." His voice is low, and I hear his grin, and I just want to touch him.

"What else did you do today?" he asks, interrupting my thoughts.

"Well, ironically enough, we went to the movies."

I hear him gasp. "I thought you didn't watch many movies."

"I don't, but I had a rough morning and wanted to forget for a little while, so we overdosed on popcorn and soda and a bare-chested Vin Diesel."

"Was it good?"

"A bare-chested Vin Diesel is always good," I reply haughtily.

"You wound me, Natalie."

"A bare-chested Luke is better," I whisper.

"That's better," he whispers back.

"I like it when you whisper."

"You do? Why?"

"It's hot."

"Really?"

"Very hot." Oh, I love this flirtiness that we have.

"I'll remember that."

I suddenly wish I'd taken him up on his offer to go to his house now, so before I can make an ass of myself and beg, I end the call.

"Nine o'clock tomorrow?" I ask.

"I'll have breakfast waiting," he murmurs.

"Good night."

"Good night, beautiful," he whispers.

～

I WAKE TO AN INCESSANT DOORBELL. I glance at the alarm clock. Who the hell is ringing my doorbell at seven-thirty in the damn morning? I fumble around for yoga pants and a shirt and grumpily trudge down the stairs.

Standing at my door is a young blond girl, maybe sixteen, holding a Starbucks to-go mug and a single red rose.

"Are you Natalie?" she asks with a smile.

"Yes."

"These are for you." She's excited as she pushes the coffee and flower toward me.

"Uh, thanks." I take them from her, pushing the rose against my nose.

"There's a note, too." She holds it out to me and claps her hands. "This is the most romantic thing I've ever seen in my life!"

I laugh at her excitement and open my door wider so she can see the dozens of bouquets of roses in the living room. Her eyes about pop out of her pretty little head.

"Holy shit! Wow. You're so lucky. Bye!" She waves and is off.

I take a sip of the coffee—oh God, that's good. How did he know white mochas are my favorite?—and open the note.

*Good morning, gorgeous. Just a little something to start your day off right. Can't wait to see you. Luke*

Holy Moses, he's just so sweet.

Jules comes down the stairs yawning. "Who was at the door?"

"Does Starbucks deliver?" I ask.

"Uh, I wish." She eyes my coffee and the rose.

"A girl just delivered these."

"Jesus, this is starting to get sickening." Jules heads for the kitchen, and I laugh, following her.

"I'm going to see him this morning."

"Good. I don't want the details." She starts making her own coffee. "Wait. You're the only one getting laid. Yes, I do want details. And pictures."

I grin and bury my nose in the rose again. "I'm not going to sleep with him. We're just going to talk."

"Right."

"We are."

"Okay. Let me know how that works out for you." She sets the coffee to drip, then smiles over at me. "I'm glad you're giving him a chance."

"Just because he's *the* Luke Williams?"

"No, because he's a good guy who finally treats you the way you deserve to be treated."

"What am I getting myself into?"

"Something fun." She shrugs. "Stop overthinking it and enjoy it."

"Okay. I'm going to shower and head over to his place for breakfast."

"Be safe." She calls after me.

"I always am," I call back.

～

I STAND at Luke's door and pause before ringing the bell. Am I overdressed? I glance down at my yellow sundress and strappy black sandals. Summer is hanging on with a vengeance, and it's going to be warm today. Maybe I should have worn shorts.

Maybe I should stop procrastinating and ring the damn doorbell.

A few seconds later, Luke opens the door, and before I can say a word, he wraps me in his arms and kisses me with a need I've never felt before. He runs one hand down to the small of my back, pulling me against him. His other hand cups the side of my head while his mouth moves deftly over mine, back and forth, his tongue pushing into my mouth to dance and move against my own.

Oh God, I missed him! It's only been twenty-four hours, but it feels like I haven't seen him in days. I run my hands up his back, under his shirt, feeling his smooth skin, and moan against his mouth.

He slows the kiss, gently touching my lips with his, and when I open my eyes, he rests his forehead on mine.

"Do you always answer the door like this?" I whisper.

"Oh God, Natalie, I was afraid I wouldn't see you again." His voice is raspy with anguish, and I grasp his face in my hands, imploring him to look me in the eye.

"I'm here."

"Thank God." He steps back, and I let my eyes slide over him. His body does amazing things to a white button-down shirt, sleeves rolled to the elbows, and jeans. He's barefoot. His hair is messy and sexy and is begging for my fingers.

"You look fantastic. Come in, make yourself at home." The smell coming from the kitchen is amazing, and my stomach growls.

"You're cooking?" I ask, glancing back at him.

"I promised you breakfast."

"You already sent me coffee, which was delicious and unexpected. Thank you." I lean up and kiss him chastely on the mouth.

"You're welcome." He smiles. "I hope you like French toast, bacon, fruit and coffee."

"Perfect."

"It's all set up outside."

I follow him out onto his magnificent deck, and he motions for me to go ahead of him. Was I really here just a few nights ago? It feels like a long time ago, so much has happened since then.

The table is covered with a white cloth. The food is on warming plates, under silver, domed lids. There is coffee and juice, but the red roses are what catch my eye. Three dozen, in three separate bouquets, are set in even distances down the table.

Tears come to my eyes as I feel Luke's hands on my shoulders from behind me. He's gone to so much trouble! Even after the way I spoke to him yesterday.

I turn in his arms and look up into his intense, beautiful blue eyes. "Thank you, so much."

"It's my pleasure, honey. I told you in the car, we have a lot of catching up to do. Get used to it."

I don't know what to say. He pulls me in for a hug and kisses my forehead.

"Come on, let's eat. I'm starving."

We sit in the same seats we sat in the other night. He uncovers our plates, and I breathe the delicious scents in appreciatively.

"Smells fantastic." I pour warm syrup over my French toast and take a bite of bacon. "Mmm...bacon."

He laughs and takes a bite of his own bacon. "I do love watching you eat, baby."

"Why?" I ask with my mouth full of the soft, delicious toast.

"Because you're so honest about it. Like everything you do, I guess. I love it that you enjoy food."

"Clearly. Have you seen the size of my ass?"

His eyes blaze as he glares at me over his coffee mug. "Don't ever put yourself down like that around me again, Natalie."

I frown and look down at my plate.

"I don't know how many times I have to tell you or show you how beautiful I think you are for you to get it through your head."

"Luke…"

He reaches out with his long fingers and grasps my chin, tilting my face back up to meet my eyes.

"Look at me. There is nothing for you to be uncomfortable about when it comes to your body. Eat whatever you want. I love watching you eat. I'd love to work out with you, just because I love watching you move. Your curves are beautiful, and I can't wait to get my hands on them again."

"Okay."

What else am I supposed to say to that?

"Are you trying to send the florists' kids to college?" I ask, trying to distract him.

# CHAPTER 11

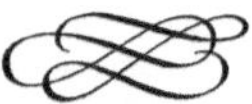

*L*uke laughs at my quip, and I relax a little. I really need to watch what I say around him about my body. I've never been so self-conscious with other men, but that's probably because I didn't really care what they thought of me. They could take me or leave me.

I want Luke to take me.

"Thank you for breakfast." I pick up my coffee and lean back in my chair, admiring the view of the water and the boats sailing across it.

"You're welcome." He stands and holds his hand out for me to take. "Come, let's get more comfortable and have that talk."

Wow, I'm not going to have to drag it out of him! This is good. I take his hand and abandon my coffee, but grab the orange juice, and follow him over to the plush love seat. I sit facing him and wait for him to start.

Luke sits on the edge of the sofa and runs his fingers through his hair. He's agitated, probably nervous. I don't really know what to say to put him at ease. And I desperately want him to start talking.

"Hey," I say and link my fingers with his. "It's okay. Tell me whatever you're comfortable telling me, and we'll go from there."

His eyes are worried, his brow furrowed, as he leans back and kisses my knuckles.

"First of all, I didn't mean to lie to you." He looks me square in the eye. "I should have been honest with you the night you were here, but frankly, I just got so caught up in you. You make me forget my own name sometimes."

So he has that problem, too, huh?

"Obviously, the morning we met I thought you were taking photos of me. That doesn't happen often anymore, but every once in a while it does, and I panic."

"I won't ever take your picture without your permission."

He squeezes my hand and gives me a sad smile.

"Thank you," he murmurs. He takes a deep breath and continues. "A few years ago things were pretty crazy. The paparazzi can be merciless, and sometimes the fans are worse. I've never been great in crowds, no idea why, but being literally chased down the street by hundreds of people on a regular basis pushed it into a full-blown phobia. Every moment of my life was documented for five years."

He turns toward me, his eyes wide and haunted. "I couldn't have had a girlfriend if I had wanted one. There was never a moment to myself."

"I thought I read something about you being with the co-star... Meredith Something or other."

He shakes his head with frustration. "That was all fabricated for the sake of the films. For the publicity. The studio owns you when you're in big-budget films, Nat. They dictate who you're with, what you do, where you go. I was too young to truly understand what that meant.

"Meredith is nice, but she was never my girlfriend, and that's just another example of how ruthless the paparazzi are. They can twist anything around until they get the story they want, rather than the boring truth." He swallows and frowns, and then his beautiful blue eyes find mine again.

"If you have questions about my past, you need to ask me. Don't go looking around online for answers."

Geez. "Okay."

"This is important. It could make us or break us, and I refuse to lose you over something that is no longer a part of my life."

"Is stuff still printed about you?" I ask.

"Sometimes. Not often anymore. Thank God."

"Have you really not made a movie in five years?"

"I haven't acted in one in five years," he replies.

"Why?"

He runs his hand through his hair again. "Because not all money is good money."

"What does that mean?"

"I made a lot of money from those films, Nat. I still do, thanks to merchandising, and my accountant and lawyers. And I could still be making a lot of money acting in films, but at what cost? So I can be hounded and have my life ruled?"

"What about actors like Matt Damon and Ben Affleck? They seem to lead fairly private lives," I remind him.

He nods. "Yes, they do, but they're also a bit older now and aren't starring in romantic comedies geared toward young women. They aren't great fodder for the rags anymore."

"So no movie business at all?" I ask, wanting to know more. He still hasn't told me what he does now.

"I didn't say that."

Oh. "Okay."

"I produce now, help movies get made. I'm not an actor anymore."

"So does that mean that you have to be gone for long periods of time?" I keep the panic out of my voice, but my blood runs cold. I don't want him gone most of the time!

"No, I do most of my work from home." He kisses my hand again. "I go to L.A. or New York for a few days here and there, but that's it. I also work with other producers who are able to do most of the hands-on work."

"Oh." Wow, he really does live in a completely different world from mine. "I have a question."

"Shoot."

"Jules said yesterday that she'd heard that someone hurt themselves in your house."

Luke goes pale, and his eyes suddenly look bleak.

"Yeah. I was in New York doing publicity for the last movie." He swallows. "A young girl, a fan, broke into my house. She lit it on fire."

I gasp. "Oh my God."

"That would have been bad enough, but she did a really bad job of it and got caught in the house and ended up dying in there."

"Holy shit, Luke."

"That's when I knew I was done. It's too crazy, and I'm just not made for it. Other actors manage okay in that world, but it's not worth people's lives to me."

"She was obviously a messed-up girl, honey."

His eyes dart to mine. "That's the first time you've called me anything other than my name."

I smile shyly and shrug.

"Yeah, she was messed up. It didn't make it right."

"Do you miss it?"

"I miss the work. Acting is fun, and I like to think I was good at it. Being on set was a lot of fun, and I learned a lot. But I don't miss the rest of it."

"Okay, so here's the million-dollar question. Why didn't you just tell me?"

"At first I didn't believe you when you said you didn't know who I am." He smiles sadly at me. "That rarely happens. And then when it became obvious that it was true, it was just such a breath of fresh air to be normal."

"You're not normal, Luke, and I mean that in a good way."

He smirks. "You know what I mean. You didn't become a fifteen-year-old like Jules did yesterday. You seemed to like me, not a character in a movie."

"I've never seen your movies," I state matter-of-factly.

"I love that." His voice is completely honest.

"But were you ever going to tell me? I was going to find out sooner or later. That's what I'm struggling with, Luke. That's why I freaked out on you yesterday. I confided things to you that I just don't share with anyone. Even Jules doesn't know about my tattoos."

His eyes smolder at the mention of my tattoos, but I press on.

"Clearly, after our conversation in the car, you should know that I have trust issues with men. All men. I don't keep men in my life."

"I'm hoping that's about to change," he whispers.

"This wasn't a great start to convince me to make any changes."

"Natalie, think about the rest of the time we've been together. I'm still the same man I was before we were in your kitchen yesterday morning. I still like to cook. I think your work is sexy. I can't keep my hands off you. I'm just a man."

"I know."

"You do?"

"Yes. I'm not an idiot. But you know me better than anyone, after less than a week, and I can't help but feel a little foolish. Yesterday was really embarrassing for me."

"It was embarrassing for me, too."

"Well, I'm glad that's over."

"What?"

"My first embarrassing moment in front of you."

He smiles, but it's fleeting. He gets serious again. "Can we start over?"

"No."

His face falls. "So it's over?"

"No, I don't want to start over because that would mean erasing everything we've had, and honestly, aside from yesterday, the past few days have been really good." I bite my lip and gaze over at him.

His impossibly beautiful face breaks into a heart-stopping smile. God, he just looks so…joyful. I can't help but match it.

"Natalie, these have been the best few days of my life, and I mean that."

"Wow."

Finally, he pulls me onto his lap and into his arms. I bury my face in his neck, wrap my arms around him and hold on, inhaling his sexy scent, planting soft kisses on his cheek.

I lean back and take his face in my hands, gazing deeply into his eyes. "Just don't ever act with me."

"Baby, you don't have to worry about that."

Suddenly he's kissing me, and we're on the move. He stands with me in his arms and heads inside the house. He's carrying me like I weigh nothing, and it's so…hot.

"Where are we going?" I ask against his lips.

"My bed."

Oh.

"We didn't clean up after breakfast."

"Later."

"We could get naked on the deck," I suggest and bite his earlobe.

He growls. "No, my bed." We're moving up the stairs. "I'm getting you naked and plan to spend about a week in bed with you."

I can't help but laugh. "I have clients on Monday."

"Okay, but today and tomorrow you're all mine."

"Yours?" I raise an eyebrow at him.

"Mine." He repeats and stands me gently at the side of his bed. He grabs the hem of my dress and pulls it over my head. "Sweet Jesus, you're not wearing any underwear."

I grin. "Nope."

"This whole time, you've been sitting six inches from me with no fucking underwear?"

"Yep." I laugh and start unbuttoning his shirt. His eyes watch mine intently, and I pop the buttons, one by one. I push the shirt over his shoulders, and he lets it fall to the floor.

Next, I push my finger between the elastic of his boxers and his skin, the way I did the other night when he stopped me. His eyes flash with need, and he makes no move to stop me this time. I smile and run my tongue along my lower lip. I glide my fingers along his stomach to his fly and open his jeans. I pull the soft denim and gray boxers slowly over his lean hips and down his legs. He steps out of them and kicks them aside.

"There, you've caught up to me," I murmur and gaze back up into his heated blue eyes.

He doesn't touch me, which is making me mad with longing. I want those skilled hands on me!

"I love it when you look at me like that," he murmurs and moves toward me.

I back up, the backs of my legs meeting the edge of the bed.

"How am I looking at you?"

"Your beautiful green eyes are looking at me like you just can't wait until I touch you."

"I can't."

"Lie back on the bed, baby."

I do as he asks and gaze up at him, enjoying the view that is Luke. All of the blood in my body has pooled between my legs, and I'm panting. All without him actually touching me.

"What are you doing to me?" I ask, surprised that I spoke the words aloud.

He grins and climbs onto the bed, straddles my legs, his hands planted on either side of my shoulders. He's still not actually touching me. He lowers his head and sweeps his lips across mine. Once, then twice.

"I'm seducing you."

"You're good at it." He smiles against my lips. I grasp his hips, but he pulls back, out of my reach. "Hey!"

"Grab on to the headboard."

"I want to touch you."

He lightly kisses me again. "Trust me, baby. Hold on to the headboard."

I reach above me and grab on to the white wooden headboard.

"Keep your hands there, okay?"

"Okay."

He smiles and kisses my lips once more, then my chin. I close my eyes and tilt my head back, giving him access to my neck. He takes advantage and licks all the way down to my collarbone.

He lowers his body down onto mine as he moves down my body. He clasps one breast in his hand, worrying my sensitive nipple between his fingers while he sucks the other one in his mouth, and it's a direct hit to my groin.

"Oh shit." I bow up off the bed, my body zinging in sensation. He blows softly on the nipple and moves to the other one to pay the same respects.

"So beautiful," he mutters against my breast. "I love your breasts. You fill my hands perfectly."

"Can I move my hands now?" I breathe.

"No way. Keep them where they are."

"I want to touch you."

"You will, but don't move yet."

I groan in frustration, and he starts kissing down my torso again. He laves my belly piercing with his tongue. "This is so hot."

"I was thinking about taking it out."

"Please don't, I love it."

"Okay," I say shyly.

He grins and moves farther down, his hands running down my sides to my hips. Suddenly, he grips the insides of my thighs and pushes them wide apart. He rubs his nose over the tattoo on my pubis and moans.

"Who did you have to forgive, baby?"

I gasp and stare down at him with wide eyes. His eyes meet mine, and I'm mortified to feel tears prick at the backs of my eyes.

"Myself," I whisper.

"Oh, baby." He kisses my tattoo sweetly, his fingers moving up my inner thighs to my center. He runs one finger down my cleft, from my clitoris to my anus, and I cry out.

"Argh!" Ohmygod!

"Honey, you are so wet." His tongue follows his finger, and my hips convulse. He holds my thighs firmly against the bed, spread wide open for him.

"So sweet." He runs that glorious tongue back up to my lips and then presses it inside me, kissing me intimately as if he were kissing my face, his nose pressed against my clitoris.

"Holy shit!" I cry and feel him smile against me. His hands move around to cup my ass and lift me, and he presses his face into me farther, and he's taking no prisoners. He rubs his nose back and forth over my clitoris as his tongue moves around and around inside me, and I am almost afraid of my orgasm. I come fast and hard, pulling myself with my hands still clenched on the headboard off the bed, calling out Luke's name, or I think that's what I'm saying anyway.

I may be speaking in tongues.

He continues the sweet torture until the last tremble moves through me, then he kisses his way up my body, stopping to pay special attention to each breast, and finally lying over me, resting his pelvis on mine, his elbows on each side of my shoulders. His hard shaft is lying against my very wet center, and when I roll my hips to wrap my legs around him, I feel it slide up and down.

Luke's eyes clench shut. "Oh God, Nat, you feel so good."

"So do you." I pull myself up and kiss his lips, tasting him and me.

He moves his hips now, sliding that deliciously large and hard cock up and down my folds, but not slipping inside me yet. The tip keeps bumping up against my clitoris, shooting sparks of sensation through me.

"Let me touch you," I beg.

"God, yes, touch me."

Hallelujah!

I grip his hair in my hands and pull his face to mine. He kisses me voraciously, and while what he's doing against my center feels so fantastic, I just want him in me.

"Luke," I breathe against his mouth.

"What do you need, baby?"

"You. In. Me. Now." Each word is staccato between kisses. He groans deep in his throat and finally slips inside me.

Hard.

Oh sweet Jesus!

"Ah!" He's pounding into me, over and over, each thrust harder than the last. His breath is ragged and broken. I reach down and grab his ass, pulling him harder.

"Oh, Natalie, come with me, baby." His words, his voice, are my undoing, and I explode around him. I am just sensation, as he pushes inside me to the hilt, grinding and grinding, moving back and forth, as he empties himself into me.

I run my fingers up his spine and push them gently through his damp hair as he shudders over me, whispering my name like a prayer.

# CHAPTER 12

*I* love his hair. It's just the right length for me to run my fingers through the softness, over and over. Luke sighs in contentment, his cheek resting against my sternum, and I cradle him in my arms. We stay this way for a long while, in companionable silence.

When his breathing slows, and I think he's gone to sleep, he raises his head, kisses my chest where his cheek has been, and our eyes meet.

"Stay with me this weekend."

"I thought we'd already established that," I reply.

"Damn right." He kisses me quickly then rolls off me and strolls into the bathroom. Yes, he has a fine derriere.

"I have a question," I call to him in the bathroom.

"Shoot," he calls back.

"Did you have a butt double in your movie?" I pull my dress over my head and begin finger-combing my hair, tying it back in a ponytail.

"Uh…" I hear water running in the sink, and he pokes his head out the door. "No."

"Oh." How do I feel about this?

"I thought you didn't see the movies." He flashes his half smile at me. Swoon!

"I didn't. That was a particularly favorite scene of Jules'," I explain.

"Ah." He disappears back into the bathroom for a few minutes then reappears in fresh red boxers—drool!—and pulls on his discarded jeans and white button-down shirt.

"I don't know how I feel about that," I murmur as I watch him dress.

"Why?"

"I don't think I like it that everyone in the free world has seen your ass."

He pulls me off the bed and against his solid chest, linking his hands at my lower back.

"Why, Natalie, are you jealous?"

"Of about a hundred million girls ogling you?" I raise an eyebrow. "What's to be jealous of?"

"Absolutely nothing." He gently sweeps his lips over mine in that way he has that makes my knees all weak. "Your hands and eyes are the only ones I want on my ass, baby."

"Okay," I whisper against his mouth. "If I'm going to stay here this weekend"—I step back out of his arms and grasp his hands in mine—"I need to run home and grab a few things. I hadn't planned on a weekend vacation."

"Let's go do that now, then come back here."

"You want to spend all weekend here at the house?"

"Most of it, yes." He brings my hands to his lips. "We can hang out here today, do whatever you want. Let me cook for you and take care of you."

My jaw drops. I'm unable to articulate words.

"And tomorrow, I want you to go to my parents' house with me for dinner."

"What?"

"They do a family thing every Sunday, and I think my brother's in town for the weekend."

"I can't meet your family!" I pull my hands out of his and wrap my arms around my stomach. Meet his family!

"Why not?"

"You've known me less than a week!"

"So?"

"So? So! Luke…"

He quickly grabs my hands again and smiles lazily down into my panicked eyes. "It's just some burgers on the grill, Nat. It's no biggie. I want you to meet my family."

"Aren't we moving kind of fast?"

He scowls and looks down at our hands then back into my eyes. "You're staying the weekend with me. Part of my weekend is spending an afternoon with my family. I want you to come."

He wants me to meet his family! I just can't quite wrap my head around this. But he looks so hopeful, and I must admit, part of me is very curious to meet his parents and see where he grew up.

"Okay, I'll come."

His eyes light up with boyish excitement. "You will?"

"Yes, I can't seem to resist your charms," I mutter sarcastically.

"Come on." He slaps my ass and ushers me toward the stairs. "Let's go get your stuff before I rip that dress off you again."

∼

I AM SITTING at Luke's dining room table editing photos. We spent an hour or so gathering my clothes, necessities and my computer, camera and memory cards from my house, then spent another half hour cleaning up our breakfast.

Things would have progressed faster had we not been too busy touching, kissing and stealing glances at each other the whole time.

Suddenly, Katy Perry's song *Teenage Dream* makes a whole lot of sense.

I gaze across the brightly lit living space to Luke's couch, where he's lounging casually, his bare feet crossed at the ankle, a stack of movie scripts on the ottoman. He's got one of the scripts open on his lap, and he's biting his thumbnail as he reads.

Visions of me straddling his lap and throwing the script over the back of the couch make me smile, but I turn back to the image on my computer screen.

I'm editing the photos I took while Luke and I were at the falls the other day. There are about twenty-five of them that are my favorites, and I'll print and frame them, offering them for sale around town.

As I close the file containing the falls photos, I sense Luke get up and head for the kitchen.

"Would you like something to drink?"

"Just some water, thanks." I smile at him and open the next file of photos to edit. These will be much more fun.

The couple I photographed yesterday fills my screen. Luke steps behind me and sets my water on the table.

"Wow."

I look up and grin. "They're good-looking, aren't they?"

"They are. They need to loosen up a bit."

I laugh. "The first twenty images get tossed out of every shoot. It takes at least that long for the client to relax."

I page through about twenty photos and stop.

"See? They don't even know I'm there anymore." The blond woman is in a black barely there teddy. The dark man is sitting on the bed, legs crossed, and she's straddling his lap, arms around his neck and fingers in his hair, kissing him.

"Yeah, much better." He starts to rub my shoulders as he watches me work. "When did you take these?" he asks.

"Yesterday." I lean into his hands and moan. He's amazing with his hands.

"After our fight." It isn't a question.

"Yeah. Oh God, don't stop doing that."

He kisses my head, and I feel him smile. "I prefer hearing those words come out of that sexy mouth of yours when you're naked."

I laugh and lean my head back, looking up at him upside down.

"Later. I have to finish these. The client's already getting a refund, and I want them to have their pictures as soon as possible."

"Why are they getting a refund? Nat, they're fantastic."

"Because it wasn't my usual fun session. I feel bad."

"I'm sorry." He kisses my head again.

"Don't be. They'll be happy with the shots and with getting their money back. Give me an hour."

"Okay, take your time, baby." He goes back to reading his script, running his hands through his unruly hair, and I can't help but grin, enjoying our easy camaraderie.

I put the finishing touches on the last sexy photo of my too-good-looking clients and grin in satisfaction. Despite my horrible mood yesterday, I rocked these pictures.

"Okay, come look."

Luke rises gracefully from the couch and stands behind me again. I page through each finished image, proud of how they turned out.

"They are amazing." He kisses my cheek gently, and I smile wide, glowing in his praise.

"Thank you. I hope they like them."

"They'd be idiots not to. Are you finished for today?"

"Yep, that's all of them. I'm all caught up until my session Monday." I close my computer down and stand up, stretching.

"How is the reading coming?" I ask, gesturing to his stack of scripts.

"Tedious. It's all been crap so far today."

"No blockbusters in that pile?" I run my hand down his cheek, unable to keep myself from touching him.

"Definitely not." He turns and places a kiss in my palm, and I feel my blood start to hum.

"I'm sorry I've been a boring companion this afternoon." I smooth both of my hands up over his shoulders and around his neck, pulling him in close, and kiss his chin.

"There is nothing boring about you, baby." He turns his head, giving me access to his throat, and I place chaste kisses down to his collarbone. "Although, now that we're both done with work…"

"Yes?" My fingers are in his hair now, pulling his lips down to mine.

"We could do something a little more energetic."

"What did you have in mind?" I love the way his hands feel against the small of my back as he pulls me closer to him.

"Are you still naked under this dress?"

"I don't know," I say innocently, and widen my eyes. "Maybe you should check."

"It's a tough job, baby." He gathers the skirt with his fingers, hiking it up around my hips, and cups my bare bottom in his hands.

"I love your ass." He's nibbling my lips and kneading my butt rhythmically. Mmm… feels so good. He slides one hand down between my legs and slips a finger inside me from behind, and I arch against him.

"Oh, Luke…"

"You're so ready for me, honey."

"I kept picturing myself attacking you on the couch while you were reading."

"You did?" His smile is delighted, and he continues to torture me with his finger.

"Yeah, it got me hot."

"Fuck, Natalie, looking at you gets me hot."

"Come here." I lead him back to the couch and motion for him to sit. He complies and gazes up at me with bright blue, lustful eyes.

Instead of straddling him, I kneel between his knees and reach for the clasp on his jeans.

"You're wearing too many clothes." My voice is breathy.

I open his jeans, and he lifts his hips so I can pull them down and discard them. His erection springs free, hard and ready for me.

I lick my lips.

Even his cock is pretty, which is a thought I never thought I'd have. It's large, and hard, nestled in a small patch of curly blond hair. No manscaping here, but he doesn't need to.

I run my hands up his thighs and grip him in both hands. He sucks breath in through his teeth, his jaw clenched, and his eyes are on fire.

My hands start to move up and down, and I lean down and brush the very tip with my tongue, tasting the bead of liquid at the end.

"Shit, baby."

He pulls my hair free from my ponytail and pushes his fingers through it, and I get bolder with my mouth, moving faster and pulling him in deeper, rubbing my tongue up and down the impressive length of him. My left hand moves lower and cups his balls, and he goes mad.

"Enough!" He grips me beneath my arms and pulls me on top of him so that I straddle his lap, and pushes into me swiftly, and I'm so thankful for my lack of panties beneath this dress.

"Ah!"

"I. Need. You." Our eyes meet, his hands on my hips, moving me up and down in a punishing, sweet rhythm, pushing so far inside me that it's just almost painful. I pull my dress over my head, and Luke's lips find a nipple, pulling it relentlessly into his mouth, and suckling.

I am gripping the back of the couch above his head, and I lean back, giving him unfettered access to my breasts, and surrender to the tightening of my womb, the flexing of my thighs, and I explode around him, my body singing in sensation.

Luke pulls me down on him, hard, and empties himself into me. "Oh yes, baby!"

~

WE ARE STRETCHED out on the couch, lying side by side. Luke is tracing the letters up my ribs with his fingertip.

"It's for my parents," I whisper.

"Why this phrase?" he whispers in response.

"Because it's important to remember to be in the moment. It can be over so fast."

"And why on your left side?"

"Because it's close to my heart."

He kisses my forehead and runs his fingers up and down my back, soothing me.

"Can I ask a question about them?" God, when he whispers like that, he can ask me anything he wants!

"Of course."

"What happened to them?"

I sigh and kiss his chin. "They were killed in a plane crash about three years ago. My dad used to fly, and he had a small plane that they would use for weekend trips."

"That's an expensive hobby."

"Yeah, he could afford it." I take a deep breath and look up into Luke's relaxed eyes. "I think I mentioned the other day that he was a high-profile lawyer."

"Yeah."

"Well, he was good at it. He did very well, and when they died together, I was the only beneficiary."

"Hey, I wasn't asking you about your financial situation." He grazes my cheek with the backs of his fingers.

"I know." I shrug. "Anyway, they were going down to Mexico for the weekend. I was supposed to go with them."

Luke's arms tighten around me, and I run my fingers through his chest hair.

"I decided at the last minute to stay home because I had finals at school the following week."

"I'm so sorry." He's resting his lips on my forehead now, and I'm curled into him, absorbing his strength, his heat. "They must have been amazing people."

"Why do you say that?" I lean back and search his blue eyes.

"Because you're amazing, baby."

Geez, charming doesn't even begin to describe this man.

"They were amazing," I whisper. "I know that my dad always wanted me to be something grander than a photographer, like a doctor, or a lawyer, or go into finance, something that would make a lot of money. But you know what?"

"What?"

"Neither of them even batted an eye when I said I was going to take pictures for a living. They just loved me. They just wanted me to be happy.

"My dad's job was ruthless and demanding, and he could be a complete asshole in the courtroom. I went and watched him once, and I didn't even recognize him. He almost scared me.

"But when he was home, he was so gentle. He was a big man, tall, with big hands. And he always smelled like fabric softener and coffee. And even when I was grown, he would let me curl up in his lap and hold me."

Luke swallows hard.

"What?" I ask.

"You don't have anyone to take care of you anymore."

"I've been taking care of myself for a long time, honey. Even when my parents were still here."

He briefly closes his eyes and clenches his jaw, as if he's angry, or frustrated. What did I say?

He leans in and sweeps his lips across mine, slipping me beneath him, and gently, tenderly, makes love to me.

# CHAPTER 13

*J* wake alone on the couch. A light blanket covers me, and I'm still naked from Luke's lovemaking. My skin feels sensitive and warm under the blanket. I could curl up and sleep here all night.

Wow. I've never had gentle, sweet, loving sex before, and I must admit, there's a lot to be said for it.

I sit up and stretch, looking around the great room. It's dark outside now, surprising me. How long was I asleep? Heavenly aromas are coming from the kitchen, but Luke's not in it. I stand and wrap the blanket around me and go to find him.

As I stroll toward the kitchen, I can hear Luke talking and look out on the deck. He's sitting on the love seat, talking on the phone. I turn to go upstairs and have a shower to give him privacy, but then I hear my name, and I can't help but stop to hear what he's saying.

"You'll like her."

Must be his family?

"No, Samantha, it's not like that. She's different. I wouldn't be bringing her to Mom and Dad's if that were the case. Look, I just wanted to give you a heads up that I'm bringing her with me tomorrow. I've already talked to Mom, and she's excited to meet her. Do not play the overprotective big sister tomorrow. Please."

I can't help but smile.

"I'm serious, Sam. Be nice. I love you, too. See you tomorrow."

He ends the call and runs his hands through his hair, standing to come inside and sees me inside the doorway. I give him a small smile, taking in his disheveled handsomeness in his faded jeans and white shirt.

"Overprotective sister, huh?"

"You have no idea."

"I can hold my own, Mr. Williams." He joins me inside, and I open the blanket so he can slide his arms around my waist, and I wrap the blanket around his back.

"I know, but she can be ruthless. Sam and I have always been particularly close because we're less than two years apart in age. She has a history of thinking she needs to protect me, so just don't be surprised if she's a little cool toward you tomorrow."

"She's never liked your girlfriends in the past?"

"She's never met anyone from my past."

"What do you mean?"

"I've never introduced anyone to my family before."

"Why me?"

He leans down and kisses me in that gentle way he has, and I sigh. "Because you didn't know who I am. And you have gotten under my skin. I don't think I'll ever have enough of you."

"I'd like to know you better," I whisper, intentionally missing his point.

"Ditto, baby."

"You know me better than anyone."

"There's still a lot to learn." He brushes my hair off my face, and I grasp his wrist so I can kiss his palm.

"How long was I asleep?"

"Just about an hour."

"It smells good in here." He grins down at me.

"Stir-fry okay for dinner?"

"Mmm...sounds great. Do I have time to take a quick shower first?"

"Sure, baby. You go shower, and I'll get dinner ready." He pulls out of the blanket and releases me.

"I could get used to being spoiled like this," I quip.

I turn from him and head for the stairway when I hear him mumble, "I'm counting on it."

~

THE DRIVE TO LUKE'S PARENTS' house is fairly short. It's a rainy Sunday afternoon, so we're in Luke's black Mercedes SUV. How many cars does he have? I look to my left and take a deep breath, trying to fight down the nerves. My stomach is in knots.

I'm flat-out terrified of meeting his parents.

This weekend has been wonderful. After dinner last night, we cuddled on the couch and watched old comedies from the eighties and laughed all night. Then he took me to bed and made sweet love to me like he had on the couch.

Wow, he can be so tender. I can't help but remember when he slapped my ass the first time we made love, and I wonder when he's going to do that again.

Variety is the spice of life, after all. Perhaps we'll play when we get back to his place later.

He looks so beautiful, sitting here in his black T-shirt and another pair of faded blue jeans. His strong hands are on the wheel, and I shiver as I think of how they feel on me.

"Are you cold?" He reaches for the climate controls on the dash, but I stop his hand.

"No, I'm not cold."

He glances at me, and then does a double take, raising an eyebrow.

"I love your hands," I say as I twine my fingers with his. He raises them to his lips and kisses my wrist.

"They're just hands." He gives me a wicked smile, and my stomach clenches.

"They do crazy things to me," I whisper.

"Behave, or I'll pull this car over and fuck you."

I gasp at his words. This is a completely different attitude from last night, and frankly, it's hot. Desire pools in my groin, and I smile as I decide to play with him a little.

"Don't make promises you can't keep."

"Oh, honey, trust me, that's a promise I can definitely keep."

I pick at an imaginary piece of lint on my red sundress. I'm wearing a soft blue denim jacket over it because of the weather and brown peep-toe sandals.

"Prove it."

He whips his head toward me and narrows his eyes. "Excuse me?"

"You heard me," I whisper and pull the hem of my dress up around the tops of my thighs, thrumming my fingers against my already sensitive flesh.

"You want to fuck in the car on the way to meet my parents?" His voice is incredulous, but his eyes are on fire, and his breathing is shallow.

"Yes, please."

He takes the next exit off the freeway and parks behind a strip mall. It's heavily lined with dense trees, and there is no traffic behind the long building. He parks at the far end and shuts the car off and pulls me over the console and into his lap. One hand dives into my hair and the other under my hemline and cups my ass.

"You are so fucking sexy. I want you all the time."

"I want you, too."

I'm panting and needy, and I want him in me now.

"Straddle me, baby." Luke shifts the seat back with the automatic button, and I lean back against the steering wheel as he unzips his pants, freeing his erection. He cups my ass in both hands, pulls my thong panties to the side and lowers me onto him.

"Fuck, yes, Luke."

"Argh!"

I move up and down violently in the small confines of the car. His hands stay on my ass, guiding me, our eyes locked and mouths open, gasping for air.

"Fuck, I'm gonna come."

"Yes, baby, come for me."

I grind against him once, twice and then explode, milking his cock with my muscles, and I feel him come apart beneath me, emptying into me.

I lean forward, resting my forehead against his as our breathing calms.

"Holy shit, Nat, that was just a little unexpected."

I pull up off of him and climb back over to my seat, straightening my dress.

"It turns me on to watch you drive."

"Well, hell, let's go on lots of road trips, baby."

I laugh and realize that it also helped to calm some of my nerves.

Luke zips himself up, rights his seat and starts the car.

～

We arrive at his parents' home a few moments later, just a few minutes late. I check my hair and makeup in the mirror, noting my bright eyes and rosy cheeks, compliments of a very satisfying bout of car sex.

"Nervous?" he asks me.

"Yes," I admit and offer him a smile.

He leans over the console and takes my chin between his thumb and forefinger and gives me a gentle kiss. "They're going to love you. You have nothing to be nervous about."

"I hope you're right."

"Come on."

He hops out of the car and comes around to open my door for me before leading me up to the entrance of the large, beautiful home.

The house is a white colonial-style home with manicured lawns and beautiful, colorful flower beds.

"Does your mom garden?" I ask.

"Yes, she's passionate about flowers," he responds, and I can't help but smirk. "What?"

"Like her son. My living room could rival her rose garden right now."

He laughs as we approach the door and kisses my hand. "Are you complaining?"

"Not in the least."

The red door opens, and a very small, petite blond woman greets us with a huge smile.

"Oh, darling, you're here!" Luke leans down so she can kiss his cheek and gives her a warm hug.

"Hi, Mom. I'd like you to meet Natalie Conner."

"Natalie, it is such a pleasure. Welcome to our home." She shakes my hand warmly, and I instantly like her.

"Thank you for having me, Mrs. Williams."

"Please, call me Lucy. Come in, you two."

We follow her through the vast foyer, toward the back of the house, which I assume is where the kitchen is. I briefly glimpse a formal living area with white furniture and a large formal dining room. Luke is still holding my hand and kisses my knuckles. I gaze up at him, and he smiles warmly down at me, clearly happy to have me here.

Damn, he's pretty.

"Luke and Natalie are here!" Lucy announces as we enter the eat-in kitchen. The kitchen is homey and large, in brown and bronze tones. The countertops are all dark brown granite, the appliances are stainless steel, and the oven is enormous. Any chef would covet this kitchen. There is a casual dining area, opening up to a family room with a large television and plush, inviting furniture in more shades of brown, copper and bronze.

It's incredible and comfortable.

"Welcome, Natalie." A very tall blond man is busy working in the kitchen. He wipes his hands on a towel and comes around the island toward me. "We're so happy to meet you."

"Nat, this is my dad, Neil."

"I'm delighted to meet you, sir." He shakes my hand firmly, and his kind blue eyes smile at me. Luke is a dead-ringer for his father.

Luke's younger brother, Mark, who also looks like his father and older brother, is helping Neil in the kitchen. "'Sup, Natalie?"

"You must be Mark." I smile at him, and he nods.

"Yep, I'm the best-looking one here, aside from you." He gives me a Cheshire cat smile, and I can't help but laugh. The Williams men are all handsome as sin and charming to boot!

"And this," Luke interrupts, glaring at his little brother, "is my sister, Samantha."

Samantha is sitting on one of the plush couches with an iPad in her lap and a wine glass in her hand. She is simply beautiful and petite like her mother, blond and blue-eyed, with delicate features. But her eyes are shrewd, and she is not smiling or welcoming me into the fold.

"Natalie." She nods at me once, and then goes back to her engrossing piece of technology.

I look up at Luke, but he's staring at Samantha. I can feel the tension in him, and remembering their phone call last night, I squeeze his hand so he looks down at me. Clearly, Samantha is going to be the hardest one to get to know in his family.

I shrug and smile at him, and he smiles back at me, some of the tension leaving his shoulders.

"Natalie, come sit with me at the table so we can chat while the boys cook. Luke, grab an apron, son. I think your dad needs help with the steaks."

"I do not need any help." Neil looks affronted, but I can tell this is a running joke in the family. "I can cook a steak just fine."

Lucy rolls her eyes at him and leads me to the dining table. "Would you like a glass of wine, dear?"

"Yes, please."

We settle at the table with our drinks, and I take a large sip, mentally preparing myself for the interrogation that is about to come.

"So tell me, what do you do, Natalie?"

"I'm a photographer." I glance over at Luke in the kitchen with his father, and my mouth goes just a little dry at the sight of three very handsome, virile men bustling around the kitchen. What is it about a man who can cook?

"Oh, how interesting. What kind of photography do you do?" Lucy leans her elbows on the table and takes a sip of her wine. She's genuinely interested in me, and it makes me relax.

"I mostly do nature photography. I live on Alki Beach, not far from Luke, so I have a lot of opportunities to take photos of the water, the boats and such. And I enjoy taking day trips around the area to take photos of flowers and just pretty things in general." I take another sip of my wine, and Luke catches my eye with a naughty grin. He smirks and goes back to chopping something.

"I'd love to see some of your work. Do you have a website?"

"No, I sell my work in shops around Alki and in downtown Seattle near Pike Place Market."

"I will have to look for it." Lucy smiles at me, and I can't help but lean forward so only she can hear me.

"I have to thank you for something," I whisper.

Her eyes widen in interest, and her grin widens. "What, dear?"

"Thank you for teaching your son how to cook. He's amazing in the kitchen."

She laughs, a full-on belly laugh, and clasps my hand in hers. "Oh, darling, you are welcome."

I glance in the kitchen, and Luke is staring at us open-mouthed. He frowns, and I smile to myself.

"What are you two whispering about?"

"Nothing," Lucy responds innocently. "How is my steak coming along?"

~

WE'RE all seated at the table off the kitchen. Neil is at one end, and Lucy is at the other. I'm seated to Neil's right with Luke next to me, and Samantha and Mark are across from us.

The guys prepared rib-eye steaks, roasted baby red potatoes and roasted asparagus with garlic and bacon. Luke refills my wine glass as serving plates are passed around the table.

"So, Natalie"—Neil hands me a basket full of rolls—"are you from around here?"

"Yes, I grew up in Bellevue."

"Oh? That's not far from here. Would I know your parents?"

Luke's fork stops midway between his plate and his mouth at his father's question. "Dad…"

"No, it's okay," I murmur softly and smile at Luke's father.

"My parents passed away a few years ago, but you may have known them. Jack and Leslie Conner."

Neil's eyebrows shoot up. "The lawyer Jack Conner?"

"Yes, sir." I take a bite of steak.

"He did work for us at Microsoft on occasion."

I look up and notice Samantha's brief scowl before she smoothes her face into a perfectly neutral expression and drinks about half the glass of wine in front of her in one gulp. She fills her glass again and drinks some more.

"I'm so sorry to hear about your parents, Natalie," Lucy says softly. "I'd heard of their passing on the news when it happened."

"Thank you." I desperately want to change the subject, but Mark comes to my rescue.

"How did you guys meet?"

I smile smugly at Luke and answer him myself. "Luke tried to mug me one morning."

All eyes go to Luke, and I can't help but laugh. Luke's cheeks flush as he looks over at me.

"You should know my brother doesn't need to mug anyone." Samantha's voice is cold and mocking, and she clearly doesn't find me funny. Mark elbows her.

"She's kidding, Sam." Luke grasps my hand under the table, and I resume eating with my left hand, content to keep my right one snuggled in his.

"I was taking photos down at the beach one morning, and he mistakenly thought I was taking photos of him, so he approached me. Quite angrily, really."

Lucy gives her son a knowing look and glances back at me. "How did you react, Natalie?"

"I was angry. I thought I was being mugged for my camera."

"You thought Luke Williams was trying to mug you?" Samantha's voice is incredulous.

"I didn't know who he was." I shrug and take a sip of wine.

"Right." She snorts.

"Samantha…" Luke's warning is unheeded by his now tipsy sister.

"Anyway," I continue, "we ended up running into each other later that same day when he was out buying a gift for your birthday."

"Which I'm now reconsidering based on your behavior," Luke adds.

"So you mean to tell me that you don't know what my brother does for a living?" Her face is openly hostile now.

"Samantha, what in the world is wrong with you?" Lucy's face is flushed, and she's clearly embarrassed by her daughter's performance.

"Of course, now I know what Luke does for a living, Samantha," I respond before Samantha can. "But I didn't recognize him at first, no."

"So you're not just fucking my brother because he's a rich movie star?"

Holy fuck.

# CHAPTER 14

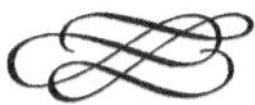

"Samantha!"

"What the hell!"

"Oh my God!"

The Williams family all start yelling at Luke's sister in unison, but she remains firm, her eyes blazing at me. Amazingly, I take a deep breath and find a Zen-like calm that is very *un-me*.

I grip Luke's thigh when he starts to come out of his chair in fury.

"Samantha, what the hell is wrong with you?"

"Luke, stop."

"No, Nat, I will not have you spoken to like that, least of all by my own family!"

"Hey." I grip his thigh again, and I feel all eyes on me as I look up him.

I turn my gaze back to his sister, and I know my eyes betray my outer calm. I'm just so pissed.

"First of all, and I mean no disrespect to your family, Luke, how dare you say such a thing about your brother?"

Samantha gasps, and I continue, "Not only are you intimating that I'm a whore, but you're also insinuating that your brother has the intelligence of a mud fence to be with a woman who would take advantage of him because of his celebrity or his money, and be perfectly okay with that.

"I don't need or want Luke's money. Not that it's any of your business, but I do just fine, thank you. I've never seen his movies, but I don't doubt that he's very talented. What I do know is that he's amazingly smart. He is honestly the kindest man I've ever met, and he is beautiful, inside and out. I will not tolerate anyone speaking about him like that, Ms. Williams."

I scoot my chair away from the table and stand.

"Natalie." Luke grabs for my hand, and I squeeze it reassuringly.

"Is there a restroom nearby where I can regroup?" I ask Lucy.

"Of course, dear, down the hall to the left."

I look down at Luke and then throw caution to the wind and lean down to kiss his lips. "I'll be back."

As I walk, more calmly than I feel, down the hall, I hear the table erupt in anger at Luke's sister. Good. She deserves everything she's about to get.

I find the bathroom and lock myself inside. Leaning my hands on the vanity, I hang my head, trying to keep the shaking at bay. I know it's from the adrenaline, but I can't make it stop.

Maybe I should have kept my big mouth shut, but she just made me so mad! I don't know what her problem is with me, but she's been openly hostile all night. And the last comment just pushed me over the edge.

I'm sure his parents now hate me for verbally castigating their daughter at the dinner table. Although, they seemed to be more shocked than anything when it was happening, and Mark had a wide grin on his face as I walked away from the table.

Oh, how am I going to go back out there and face them?

I take five deep breaths. The shaking starts to subside, and I don't know how long I've been locked in the bathroom. I open the door and start the journey back to the table.

Before I can turn the corner, I hear Lucy's soft voice. "Honey, she obviously loves you."

I stop in my tracks and listen.

"Mom…" Luke starts to speak, but Lucy interrupts him.

"I know, it's none of our business, but it's pretty clear how she feels about you, honey. Why else would she defend you like that?"

"She's a keeper." This is Mark's voice, I think.

I decide to stop eavesdropping and walk into the room, noticing that Samantha is no longer at the table.

Luke stands and quickly walks to me, wrapping me in his strong arms. "Are you okay?"

"I'm fine." I pull back and smile up at him, then turn to his family. "I'm so sorry for the way I spoke to your daughter…"

Neil holds up a hand to stop my speech. "No, Natalie, we are sorry for her behavior. Please, come finish your meal. Samantha won't be rejoining us."

I look up into Luke's eyes, and he looks nervous and unsure, his eyes searching mine. "Okay."

"You're sure you're okay?" he murmurs.

"Yes, let's finish dinner." We sit back in our places and continue eating.

"This is really delicious." I smile at Neil, and he grins back at me.

"I'm glad you like it."

"I love a man who can cook." I grin at Lucy, who beams back at me, and settle in to enjoy the rest of our evening.

~

LUKE IS quiet on the way back to his place after dinner. He's biting his thumbnail, which tells me that he's thinking. He's not touched me since we left, and I can't help but start to feel a little apprehensive.

"Are you okay?" I ask, breaking the silence.

He glances over at me and frowns. "Of course."

"Okay. Good." I clasp my hands in my lap and stare at the lights from the city in the distance out my window. As we pull up to his house, the silence is deafening. He opens my door for me and escorts me up his front steps to usher me inside. He turns on a light as I walk to the kitchen and lay my purse on the breakfast bar.

I turn to look at him and am surprised to find that he's not in the room. Where did he go?

I frown as unease starts to unfurl through my stomach. Oh my God, I really screwed up. He must be mad at me for the way I spoke to his sister at dinner. Where is he?

Maybe he wants me to leave, and he's giving me space to pack my things.

I climb the stairs and head for his bedroom, willing myself not to cry until I get home. I'll just pack my things and get the hell out of here. Then I can fall apart.

Just before I cross the threshold into his bedroom, my phone pings in my pocket. I pull it out, and I have a text.

From Luke.

*Natalie, would you please join me in my bathroom?*

Huh?

I walk through the bedroom and to the entrance to the bathroom and stop in my tracks.

He has drawn a bath in that huge egg-shaped tub of his, and the scent of lavender is hanging in the air. There are candles lit on the vanity and the side of the tub. Luke is standing next to the tub wearing only his jeans, the top button undone.

Finally, I find my voice, but all I can say is, "Hi."

"Hi."

"I thought you were mad at me."

"Why?" He walks over to me and grips my chin in his thumb and forefinger, tilting my head back so I can look him in the eye.

"Because you've been so quiet since we left your parents' house."

"I've just been thinking." His fingers caress my cheek, and he tenderly kisses my forehead.

"About?" I whisper.

"Let's get in the bath." Oh! I want him to keep talking.

"I'm overdressed for a bath."

"So you are, baby." He peels my jacket off my shoulders and down my arms and sets it on a nearby chair. He pulls my dress over my head and gently folds it and places it over the jacket.

"Step out of your shoes."

I comply, unable to take my eyes from his. He wraps his arms around me and leans down to kiss my shoulder, while unclasping my bra and pulling it down my arms. As he steps back, I hook my thong in my thumbs and push it off my hips, letting it drop to the floor. I stand before him and flush with pleasure at the way his eyes go glassy with desire as he runs them up and down my nakedness.

"You're overdressed, too," I whisper, and my stomach clenches as I see his pupils dilate.

"So I am." He unzips the jeans and pulls them and his boxers off in one smooth motion, leaving him gloriously naked before me.

"Come." He holds his hand out to me so he can help me step into the water. I sink down and sigh as the hot water envelops me.

"Aren't you going to join me?"

"Yes." He steps in and sits facing me, his legs on either side of mine, and leans against the opposite side.

"This is nice." It's the truth. The water is soothing after the difficult encounter with his sister, and he's naked, which makes everything nice.

"It is."

"You're very monosyllabic tonight, you know."

He grins at me almost shyly. "I'm sorry. I have a lot going through my head."

"Spill it."

He shakes his head.

"Oh, no, you don't. What's going on in that handsome head of yours, Williams?"

"I'm really sorry about the way my sister treated you tonight."

Oh.

"I'm just sorry for the way I reacted, Luke. I'm sorry that I made you uncomfortable and for speaking that way to your family."

"No, don't apologize. She was way out of line. I had a bad feeling that she'd act like that, that's why I called her last night."

"Luke." I pick up one of his feet and start to rub. His eyes widen and then he closes them and leans his head against the tub with a groan. "I don't have siblings, but I can understand wanting to protect someone I love. What I don't understand is, why the blatant hostility? I don't get it."

"Well, something you said tonight hit a little too close to home," he murmurs, then opens his eyes and sighs, looking everywhere but at me.

"What?"

"The part about me being stupid enough to be with someone I know is using me because I'm rich and famous."

I gasp and drop his foot. Oh my God, this is mortifying. "I don't understand."

He takes my right foot in his hands and rubs his thumb over my tattoo, frowning.

"My last relationship was with a woman who was with me for all those reasons."

"Oh." I do not want to hear this.

"Yeah."

"How long ago?"

"I broke it off over a year ago."

"I thought you said that you've never introduced anyone to your family." I lean my head back on the tub. I just can't look at him when I'm feeling jealous and nervous and unsure.

"I haven't. They never met her. They knew of her, more so after the fact."

I'm staring at the ceiling, listening to him, trying to find that Zen-like calm I found at his parents' dining room table.

"Why?" My voice is calmer than I feel.

"Because she went to the tabloids and said that she was pregnant when I decided to break our engagement."

"What the fuck?" My head snaps up, and I hold his gaze. "You're a father?"

"No!" He tightly closes his eyes and shakes his head in frustration. "She sold the lie to the tabloids to get back at me for breaking up with her."

"You were going to marry her?" I feel like I've been kicked in the stomach.

"Yes." He's watching me warily, no doubt gauging my reaction to all of this.

"And you never introduced her to your family?"

"She never had much interest in meeting them. Whenever I'd arrange it, something would come up." He shrugs.

"And you didn't find that odd?"

"I do now."

"Why did you break it off?"

"Because she wasn't right for me."

"That's a lame answer."

"It's the truth." He shrugs and then sighs. "I guess I finally realized that had I not been famous or wealthy, she wouldn't have given me the time of day. She didn't like it that I'd stopped acting and hoped that the producing thing was just a phase and I'd miss being the center of attention. She wanted to be a celebrity wife, and that wasn't something I was interested in."

"Do you still talk to her?"

"No."

I lean my head back again and look at my now wrinkled fingers. The water is starting to cool. Time flies when you're trying to hold a calm conversation about your lover's ex-fiancée.

"I guess that explains a lot."

"Nat…"

"Hold on." I hold my hand up to stop him. "Give me a minute."

"Okay." He frowns and continues to rub my foot.

Why do I feel so betrayed all over again? And then it hits me.

"I must have looked pretty stupid to your family when I didn't know about your ex-fiancée."

He abruptly leans forward and pulls me onto his lap, ignoring the water sloshing onto the floor, and wraps his arms around me.

"You were magnificent tonight. I didn't know if I should be proud or emasculated at the way you jumped to my defense like that."

"You should have warned me."

"I know."

I run my fingers through his hair and sigh. "We still have so much to learn about each other."

"We'll get there, baby."

"It made me crazy when your sister was talking about you like that."

He shakes his head and laughs ruefully. "Ironically, she was talking about you, baby."

"I know, but in doing so she made it about you, and I couldn't stand it."

"No one has ever jumped to my defense like that. You were so calm and sure of your-self, and so pissed off. Your green eyes were on fire, and you just looked so beautiful. I wanted to fuck you right there at the table."

"Luke Williams!" I pull back and stare at him, shocked.

"It's true. You turned me on, big time."

"I don't think that would have been appropriate with your parents sitting at that same table."

"I don't think I would have cared if the pope and Elvis were sitting at that table."

I laugh and snuggle up against him again.

"Oh, baby, what am I going to do with you?"

"Anything you want."

"Come on." He stands me up out of the water, and then climbs to his feet behind me. I can't get over how strong he is. He moves me around like I'm nothing at all.

He slings a towel around his hips and grabs another soft, white, fluffy towel off the towel warmer and wraps it around me. He pulls me against him and kisses me deeply, passionately, before letting go so he can dry my body.

Oh my.

He runs the towel up and down me, soaking up the extra moisture. I can't resist leaning forward and kissing his sternum, and I hear his quick inhale.

When I'm dry, I take the towel from around his waist and return the favor, enjoying the intoxicating sight of his muscular physique.

"There, all dry," I whisper.

"Thank Christ." He pulls me to him, his hands in my hair, and kisses me deeply. I wrap my arms around him and drag my nails down his back.

"God, baby, you'll unman here in the bathroom."

"Good." I scrape his back again, and he growls against my neck. He abruptly spins me and plants my hands on the vanity facing the wide mirror over the sinks. I look up and am taken aback by the sexy sight that is Luke standing behind me, about six inches taller than I am, all golden hair and bronze body, leaning down to kiss my bare shoulders. He cups the back of my neck in his hand and smoothes it down my spine, hovering for a moment over my tattoo, watching his own hand's progression, and his breathing increases. He pulls my hips back so I'm bent over, and I just can't stop watching his beautiful, expressive face as he touches me.

Finally, he runs a single finger down my bottom and slips it inside me.

"Oh, Luke."

"Baby, you're so ready." I feel him position the head of his cock on my lips and slowly, oh so slowly, push inside me. His eyes meet mine in the mirror as he pushes farther until he's buried completely in my folds.

"Spank me." Fuck! Did I just say that?

"What?" He stops, his hands on my hips, and he's gaping at me in the mirror.

"Spank me."

"You like it rough, baby?" He grins quizzically at me.

"Not until I met you." His face changes from curiosity to pure possession in a matter of seconds, and I can't help but clench around him.

"Fuck, Natalie." He raises his right hand and brings it down on my buttock.

"Yes!" I circle my hips, and he starts moving in and out of me, holding my hips. I'm backing up against him, and we find our rhythm. Finally, he raises his hand again and slaps my ass, and it's so fucking hot!

"Again?" he asks breathlessly.

"Yes."

He obliges, and I feel the tension beginning low in my belly. My legs clench, and I tighten around him, my orgasm ripping through me.

"Oh, baby, yes."

I watch in fascination as Luke tightly closes his eyes and grips my hips harder, his own orgasm pushing through him and explodes inside me.

He runs that beautiful hand down my back again, his breathing still choppy, and smiles at me in the mirror. "I had no idea you like it rough."

"It's a newly acquired taste."

He slips out of me and leans down to kiss the tattoo on my upper thigh, below my buttock, and I gasp.

"I think this is the sexiest tattoo you have."

"You do?"

"Mmm hmm." He's tracing it with his finger, and chills run up my back.

"Why?"

"Well, it looks fucking sexy."

"I'm glad you like it." I grin down at him, still through the mirror.

"I love them all," he says earnestly, and I can't help but fall just a little in love with his honest face.

"I want you happy, Nat."

"Oh." I turn at his words, and he stands up, wrapping his arms around my shoulders and pulling me into a big hug.

"I don't know what to do with these feelings I'm having for you," I whisper against his chest.

"We're just going to take this one day at a time, baby." He pulls back and gives me his tender kiss.

"Okay, I can do that."

"Good, let's get some sleep." He picks me up in his arms and heads for the bed.

"You know, I can walk." I laugh and press my face in his neck.

"No need, I have you."

"I love how strong you are."

"Do you now?"

"Yes. Speaking of, I have to get up early tomorrow for yoga, and then I have a session at eleven."

"Okay. Want me to pick you up for lunch?" He pulls the duvet back and lays me down on the bed, climbing in behind me, and pulls me into his arms.

"Aren't you sick of me?"

"Are you sick of me?" He pulls me around so he can see my face.

"Well, no."

"I want to see you for lunch tomorrow. Please."

"Okay," I mumble and curl up in his arms to sleep.

# CHAPTER 15

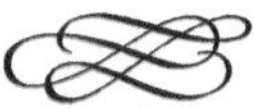

There are some days that the work just flows. This is, thankfully, one of those days.

It was tough leaving Luke's bed this morning, but I'm glad I went to yoga to get my blood pumping. I had a relaxed breakfast with Jules, where I filled her in on the weekend events, and I couldn't even be very mad when my eleven o'clock session was late.

Brad is a hot twenty-one-year-old with a lot of model potential. He's got the face and the body, and he's hired me to help him beef up his portfolio. I usually work with women or couples, but Brad is professional and sincerely wants to break into show biz, and I just couldn't turn him away.

Not to mention he's tall, dark and extremely handsome. Not a bad way to spend a few hours out of the day.

We've been having a lot of fun all morning. Brad is easily six-foot-three and completely toned. Not unlike Luke, but I push him to the side of my brain and focus on the job. Where Luke is bronzed and golden, Brad is tanned and dark, with dark hair and eyes and the hint of a five o'clock shadow on his sculpted jaw.

He's stripped down to an impossibly small pair of nude boxer briefs that barely cover the essentials, and he's wrapped from the waist down in a white satin sheet.

"You're good at this, Natalie. It doesn't even feel like work."

"Thank you." I raise the camera to my eye and start clicking. "These sessions should be fun."

"Are you single?" he asks as he gives the camera a sexy half smile.

"Uh, no." I frown at him. "No flirting, Brad."

"Sorry, couldn't resist. I'm in bed, mostly naked, and a beautiful woman is taking my photo."

I laugh and change memory cards. Man, it's hot in here! I take my blue hoodie off, leaving a fitted black tank over my sports bra. I have cropped yoga pants on, but go in the bathroom and change into yoga shorts. I refasten my hair up into a bun and kick off my shoes.

"Okay, Brad, back in bed."

"How can I resist that?" He is such a flirt! He climbs back on the bed and pulls the sheet low over his hips.

"Okay, on your back, one arm over your head. Good, don't move." I climb on the bed and straddle his hips with my feet, standing directly over him.

"This is a great shot." I'm snapping away, so pleased with the images I'm capturing.

"Should I look serious for some?"

"Sure, don't give me that sexy smile. Perfect!" Snap, snap, snap. I walk up his body, focusing down on his face. I almost lose my balance, but he reaches up and clasps his hands around the backs of my calves.

"Whew! Thanks." I giggle and continue to snap head shots while he throws one hand back up over his head, keeping one hand braced on my leg to keep me steady.

"What the fuck is going on?!"

Brad and I both jump, startled at the angry shout coming from my front door.

"Luke! You scared the hell out of me!"

Brad immediately releases my leg, accurately assessing that he may have his money-maker punched any moment.

"What the fuck, Natalie!"

"Stop yelling at me!" I jump off the bed and stow my camera. "Brad, you can go ahead and get dressed. We're finished here anyway."

Brad rises off the bed, letting the sheet fall, and I avert my eyes. He saunters into the bathroom to get dressed.

"What the hell is your problem?" I hiss at Luke.

"What do you think? You were on a bed with a naked man, and his hands were on you!"

I take a deep breath. "He wasn't naked, Luke. I am not naked."

"Close enough," he mutters.

"Hey, this is why I told you not to freak out on me when I showed you this studio."

"You didn't tell me that you work with young naked men." He's pissed all over again.

"I don't, usually. He's a friend of a friend who needs images for his portfolio. Don't be a jealous ass."

"You led me to believe that you work with women or couples, Natalie."

"Luke, I just told you, this is an exception."

"I don't like it."

"It doesn't matter if you like it."

Luke glares at me like I've grown a second head and runs both hands through his hair.

Brad saunters out of the bathroom, fully dressed in jeans, T-shirt and sneakers. "Thanks again, Natalie. I had a great time."

I smile warmly at him. "Me, too, and you're welcome. I should have them edited for you this week."

"Great. See ya." He leaves, shutting the door behind him.

I turn back to Luke to find his glacial blue eyes narrowed on me. He's royally pissed.

"What, exactly, are you mad about?" I ask as I turn back to the bed and begin stripping the sheets.

"Natalie, I just walked into this studio to find my girlfriend standing in what would only be appropriate as nightwear over a naked guy on a bed, and he's got his hands on her bare leg. What do you think I'm mad about?" His voice has risen several decibels, but I'm stuck like stupid on one word.

"Girlfriend?"

He stops his rant and stares at me. "Yes, girlfriend. I thought after this past weekend that that's where we are."

Oh.

Wow.

"Am I wrong?" His voice is worryingly calm.

"Well, no, I guess I just hadn't thought about it." I finish with the bed and turn to face him again. "Luke, this is my job."

"I don't like it."

"It isn't your place to tell me that I can't do this."

"I didn't say that."

"That's what you're implying. I've done this for years. No one has ever gotten out of hand. Remember, I told you I don't have sex in here, and I don't have sex with clients. Jesus, do you have so little faith in me?"

"No, it's just…" He runs his hands through his hair again and paces back and forth. "I wasn't expecting to feel the way I felt when I saw his hand on you."

"How did you feel?" I tilt my head at him, my curiosity piqued.

"Like I wanted to kill him," he growls.

"Oh."

"Nat, think of how you would feel if I had to do a love scene in a movie. It would be work to me, but I'd still have to hold another woman, kiss her…"

"Stop right there." I do not want to hear this.

"It's the same thing for me."

Geez.

I take a deep breath and sit on the side of the bed, suddenly weary. "I'm sorry, it didn't occur to me. Honey, I haven't had to explain my actions to another human being in years."

"I know."

"You were jealous."

"Jealous is too tame a word for what I was feeling."

Part of me wants to squeal and do a little happy dance, but I hold it in and gaze at him impassively. "You don't have any reason to be jealous. You're all I see, Luke, even when I'm not with you."

He closes his eyes tightly, as though some great weight has been lifted, and I take him all in. He's wearing another button-down shirt today, in black this time, and black jeans. He looks young and impossibly beautiful.

And I'm his girlfriend!

I stand and move to him, wrapping my arms around his waist. He puts his arms around me, linking his fingers at the small of my back, and we just gaze at each other for a minute.

"Please don't be mad at me," I whisper.

"I'm not."

"You were."

"Yeah, I was." He kisses my forehead. "Don't you have any real clothes in here?"

"Yeah, it got hot in here, so I took them off."

He narrows his eyes again, and they go cold. Shit.

"Don't freak out on me. It happens no matter who I'm photographing. I don't have AC in here."

"Why not?"

"Well, honestly, because a sweaty body is sexy on film."

"Oh." He furrows his brow.

"Hey, stop it. You have nothing to be jealous over, honey." I run my hands down his face, loving the roughness of his stubble against my palms.

"I love it when you call me that." He leans into my touch and closes his eyes.

"You do?"

"Yeah, you usually just call me by my name."

"You're a terms-of-endearment kind of guy, huh?" I stand on my toes and kiss his lips gently, and his eyes warm up.

"Obviously, *baby*."

"I love it when you call me baby."

Now his eyes light up like it's Christmas. "Why?"

"No one ever has before," I whisper.

He sighs and hugs me close. "I forget how inexperienced you are when it comes to relationships."

"Yeah, so cut me some slack. There has to be a learning curve." I pinch his tight butt, and he laughs.

"Okay, okay. Just do me a favor." His face is serious again.

"What?"

"No more single men. Please."

I frown and want to argue with him.

"Please, Natalie. For me."

"What if we have a chaperone?"

"Talk with me before you book another single man, and we'll discuss it. I don't like feeling like this. I'm asking you to respect how I feel."

Well, when he puts it like that.

"Okay, I'll talk with you first." It's a concession, but I can't help but think about what he said about love scenes, and I know I'd go out of my mind with jealousy if I were in that position.

"Did you do any love scenes in your movies?" I ask and search his face.

"Why do you think there was a butt shot?" He grins down at me.

"I don't ever want to see those movies, Luke."

"Fine by me, baby."

"So, I'm your girlfriend, huh?"

"Absolutely." He kisses me deeply, and I grip on to his shoulders, pulling him down to me.

When he pulls back, I can't resist running my fingers through his hair. "Okay, let's go get lunch. Fighting with you makes me hungry."

"You're putting on some decent clothes first."

~

I LEAVE Luke with Jules in the kitchen and run upstairs to get dressed. I smirk to myself, remembering the look of apprehension on Luke's face when confronted with Jules, but she was cool as could be, and I'm relieved that her adolescent behavior where he's concerned has subsided.

I throw on a pair of blue jeans that hug my ass, a green top and matching green heels.

It may just be lunch, but I never get to wear my heels, and Luke's tall enough that I could wear them all the time.

So I think I just might. He seems to like them.

I brush out my brown hair, leaving it loose so it frames my face, and apply some eyeliner and mascara.

I'm good to go.

I find Luke and Jules still in the kitchen, talking about all things cooking.

"I bake my bacon," Luke is saying. He's standing with his back to me so he doesn't see me enter the room. "That way there's less mess on the stove top."

"I don't care how it's cooked." I wrap my arms around his middle and press my nose between his shoulder blades, breathing him in. He smells of fabric softener and body wash, and his shirt is soft against my face. "As long as it ends up in my mouth," I mumble against him, and I hear him chuckle.

He turns to look at me and grins wide. "You are gorgeous in green. It matches your eyes." He runs his fingers down my face, and I sigh.

"Thank you. Is this better than what I had on earlier?"

"Much. Do you have any more sessions today?"

"I have one tonight around eight."

He frowns. "Why so late?"

"A lot of people work during the day, so I have to schedule evening sessions some-times. It doesn't happen often because I prefer using the natural daylight rather than my lighting equipment, but sometimes it's necessary."

"Who is it?" He eyes me speculatively, and I sigh.

"Just a girl who wants some pretty photos for her husband for their anniversary."

"Oh, okay."

I run my hand through his hair. "Don't worry, babe. There are no single men on my books right now."

"Can you let me know when there *are*?" Jules pipes in quickly. "All this mushy stuff is reminding me how long it's been since I got laid. Go to lunch. Or get a room."

We say our goodbyes, and he holds the door of the Mercedes SUV open for me so I can climb in. When he's behind the wheel, he leans over the console and kisses me lightly.

"Where are we going?" I ask as he starts the car.

"How does seafood sound?"

"We live in Seattle. I think it's a prerequisite to love seafood to live here."

"Seafood it is, then." He grips my hand in his and smiles over at me. "You look beautiful."

"Thank you." I feel my face flush, and I look down at our joined hands. "You always look beautiful."

He laughs and shakes his head. "It's just genetics."

"What did you do this morning?" I ask, changing the subject.

"I went to the gym and worked out with my trainer."

"You have a trainer?" Of course he does.

"Yeah, he kicks my ass." He grins at me, and I can't help but grin back. "How was yoga?"

"It was great. I love it. Have you ever tried it?"

"Um, no."

"Not manly enough for you?" I roll my eyes.

"It's not that. I just like a rigorous workout."

"Go with me Wednesday morning."

He frowns and eyes me speculatively. "I'll make you a deal."

Uh oh, where is this going?

"What kind of deal?"

"I'll go with you to yoga on Wednesday if you go to the gym with me tomorrow."

I bite my lip and look out my window. I'm afraid of looking like a fool. I don't have the tight, little body that most of the other women have in gyms. Yoga keeps me toned and flexible.

"You don't have to go with me," I whisper.

"Natalie, what did I say?"

"Nothing." I can't look him in the eye. I hate feeling self-conscious, and I'm just now to the point of not feeling that way naked in front of Luke.

"Baby, what's wrong?" He pulls into the parking lot of the restaurant and cuts the engine, turning toward me in his seat.

"Nothing, I..."

"Look at me." His voice is stern, and when my eyes meet his, they're ice blue. "Talk to me."

"No, you get mad at me when I talk about my body. Just leave it alone. We'll work out separately. It's okay."

"Why are you so hard on yourself?" He's bewildered.

"I'm not. Well, not until now," I whisper.

"Stop this. You have nothing to be ashamed of, baby."

"I'm not ashamed. I know you find me attractive, and I love that."

"Then what's the problem?"

"I don't want to make an ass of myself."

"But you want me to go to yoga and try to twist into a pretzel and make an ass of myself?"

Oh. Good point.

I giggle and put my fingers over my mouth.

"Are you laughing at me?" He's smiling again, and the tension in my stomach relaxes.

"I wouldn't dare."

"So, are you going with me to the gym or not?"

"I so wish you'd let me take your picture."

His eyes widen, and he goes very still, and I mentally kick myself. "Why?"

"Because I'd love to take your picture at yoga. This is going to be hilarious!"

He relaxes and laughs as he gets out of the car, coming around to open my door. "Come on, I want to watch you eat."

# CHAPTER 16

Salty's sits on a pier on Puget Sound. It offers great views and great food. The hostess seats us near the windows looking out on the water, and we are busy reading the menu. I glance up at Luke and can't help but sigh just a little. He's just so disarmingly handsome. He's biting that thumbnail as he peruses the menu.

"Can I have your hand, please?" I hold my hand out.

"You can hold my hand anytime, baby." He shoots me a sexy smile but gives me the wrong hand.

"No, the one you're biting, please."

He extends his hand to me with a frown, and I lean over the table and kiss the thumbnail. "You're going to make this bleed." I look up into his sea-blue eyes and am pleased to see that his breathing has changed and that my touch is turning him on.

"Don't start this here, please." His voice is low and sexy, and my stomach clenches.

"I don't know what you mean." I widen my eyes innocently. "I'm just making sure you'll have an appetite for your lunch."

"I'll tell you what I have an appetite for." He grins wolfishly, but before I can respond, the waitress is at the tableside.

"What can I get you two today? Would you like to start with an appetizer?" She glances up at both of us with a smile, but she freezes when she sees Luke, and all the blood drains from her face.

"Luke Williams! Oh wow! I'm such a big fan, Luke…er…sir. I've seen all of the *Nightwalker* movies, like, forty times. Oh my God, they are so good. I can't believe you're here! Can I get an autograph? Can I get a picture?" The words all come out in a rush, and I can't help but sit back and drop my jaw.

Luke glances at me but seems to find his balance quickly and pastes on a dazzling drop-your-panties smile, just for Miss Gushy, but it doesn't reach his eyes, and I know that this is the smile he uses for fans.

It's fascinating.

"I'm sorry, I don't give photographs, but I'm happy to sign something for you."

"Oh great! Here." She shoves her notepad and pen at him.

"What's your name, sugar?" Oh, he is really laying it on thick.

"Hilary. Oh my gosh, wait until my friends find out I met you! They will be so jealous." She's practically jumping up and down, and Luke's smile never falters.

"Well, I'm glad you enjoyed the movies. Here you go." He passes the pad back to her, and she clutches it to her chest, her face all gooey and swoony, and I have to look down to keep from laughing and rolling my eyes at her.

After a few lengthy seconds of her just standing there, staring at him, I decide to rescue him.

"So, um, we'd like to order now, if that's okay with you, Hilary."

She shakes herself out of her trance and blushes but doesn't meet my eyes. "Oh, of course. What can I get you?" She stares expectantly at Luke, and he smirks.

"What would you like, baby?" And my man is back.

"I'll just have the salmon Caesar salad, please, with extra lemon on the side. What kind of white wines do you have?" I am still staring into Luke's eyes and am relieved to see that his eyes are dancing with humor.

"Oh, um…" She rattles off the white wine list, and I order a sweet Riesling to go with my salad.

"And what can I get you, Mr. Williams…er…sir?" Her face is on fire.

"I'll actually have the same as my girlfriend. Sounds delicious."

Girlfriend!

"Okay, let me know if I can get you anything else. Thanks again for the autograph!" And off she goes.

"Are you okay?" I ask when we're alone.

"Yeah, that wasn't so bad. How are you?"

"Amused. I didn't know whether to laugh at her or feel sorry for her."

"Hey, are you saying that I'm not a heartthrob? I'm hurt." He sits back and clutches his chest, right over his heart.

"Oh no, you definitely make my heart throb, along with a few other areas, Mr. Williams…er…sir."

"You have a sassy mouth, Natalie."

"I'm glad you noticed."

We settle in to enjoy our lunch, but other waitresses and kitchen staff keep stopping by the table to get autographs or gush about how much they loved his movies and ask him why he's not acting anymore. Thankfully, the restaurant isn't terribly busy, so there aren't many customers bothering us.

Finally, when I've lost count of how many employees have come to interrupt our lunch, I excuse myself.

"You okay?" Luke asks me.

"I'm fine. I'll be right back." I give him a bright, reassuring smile, and leave the table.

I find Hilary near the bar. "I need to speak with the manager, please."

"Oh, sure. I'll grab her." She disappears into what I assume is the kitchen and reappears with a tall redhead, about my age, who hasn't managed to make it to our table yet.

"Can I help you, ma'am?" Geez, when did I become a ma'am?

"I hope so. Luke Williams and I are having lunch here, and your staff has been interrupting us to ask him for autographs and to speak with him. I'd really appreciate it if you'd ask them to stop."

She frowns as she listens to my complaint. "I'm sorry, they shouldn't have approached you at all. That's against policy. Can I comp your lunch?"

"It's not about the money. It's about the lack of privacy. I'm sure he's not the first celebrity to come to your restaurant."

"Of course not. I'll take care of it. I apologize on behalf of the staff."

I walk back to our table and overhear Hilary apologize to her boss.

There's a busboy standing next to our table when I return, and I tap him on the shoulder. "Your boss would like to see you."

"Oh! Okay. Thanks for the autograph!" He grins and leaves.

"That won't be happening again," I inform Luke.

"What did you do?"

"I went to management. Other customers are one thing, but it's not appropriate for the staff to interrupt us every five minutes."

"Nat, this is just how it is sometimes."

"Well"—I shrug—"they've had enough of you. This is my lunch date with my boyfriend, and I'm done sharing him."

His eyes light up, and the smile he gives me is even brighter than the drop-your-panties one he gave the waitress, and I melt just a little inside.

"Your boyfriend is enjoying this lunch date with you."

"I'm glad." I smile shyly and take a sip of wine.

The rest of the meal is delicious, and we aren't bothered at all, unless it's to ask if we want more wine or dessert. Hilary places the leather check holder on the table and walks away.

Luke opens it and frowns, then smiles and passes it to me. Instead of a check, there is a note.

*We appreciate your patience and generosity toward our staff. Today's lunch is on the house, and please accept this $250 gift card to join us again, uninterrupted, soon.*

*—The Management*

"Oh my. I guess my chat with the manager worked."

"Looks like a date night is in our future." Luke grins and slips the card in his wallet.

~

"NATALIE, I had such a good time tonight. I know my husband will love these photos." Darla gives me a smile and a hug before leaving the studio.

"He's going to swallow his tongue when he sees these, I guarantee it."

"Maybe we can come in sometime before the holidays and do a couples session. It sounds like a lot of fun." Darla slings her black Coach handbag on her shoulder.

"I would love that! Just let me know when you'd like to set it up. I'll walk you out."

I wave goodbye to Darla and start cleaning up from our boudoir session. Darla was a lot of fun, very pretty and flirty, and she had some great ideas, too. I gather some lingerie that will need to go to the cleaners and push furniture back in place. I'm turning off the bright photography lights when my phone pings.

My heart leaps, and I can't help but hope it's Luke. He dropped me off at home after our lunch date and said he had some work to take care of at home, which was fine, because I needed to do some laundry and work myself.

But I miss him, and the thought of not seeing him until tomorrow morning when I go to the gym with him—which still fills me with dread—is a depressing thought.

*Are you finished with your session, baby?*

I do love it when he calls me baby.

*Just finished, going inside now. What are you doing?*

I lock up the studio and head into the house. Fall is in the air now, and after the sun sets, it's really chilly, so I hug my hoodie around me as I cross the backyard.

Jules left the kitchen light on for me, and I stop at the fridge to grab myself a bottle of water and a handful of grapes before heading up to my bedroom. As I climb the stairs, I hear Adele crooning and wonder briefly if it's coming from Jules' bedroom.

I walk into my own room and stop.

Holy shit.

The music is coming from my room, and there's Luke, sitting on my bed, barefoot, in black basketball shorts and a black T-shirt. He's frowning at his laptop and biting his thumbnail.

"So this is what you're doing."

He smiles and looks up at the sound of my voice. "I hope you don't mind. Jules let me in. I thought I'd just wait for you here."

I walk over to the bed and crawl up next to him, offering him my last grape. "I don't mind. I was just thinking about you."

"Yeah?"

"Yeah."

He closes his computer and sets it on the floor, and when he sits back up, I climb on his lap.

"I was afraid you'd think I was being presumptuous."

I hear the smile in his voice as he kisses my head, and I settle in and nuzzle his chest. It's just so good to see him, to touch him. "You are being presumptuous, but I don't mind."

"I missed you today."

I pull back and run my fingers down his face. "You saw me at lunch."

"So I did. But that was hours ago. I can't seem to get enough of you, baby."

"Are you staying the night?" I ask breathlessly.

"If you'll let me, yes."

"Good."

I reach up and kiss the side of his mouth, his chin, his nose, while running my fingers through his soft hair. His beautiful eyes are watching mine, and he's patiently letting me touch and kiss him. His hands are softly rubbing up and down my back, and desire is lazily unfurling through me.

I grip the hem of his shirt in my hands and lean back so I can pull it up over his head.

"I love your body," I murmur as I run my hands over his shoulders, his chest and down his arms, and his hands tighten on my ass.

"Do you?"

"Hmm…" I kiss his neck and nibble up to his ear. "You're fucking hot."

"Jesus, baby, I want you."

I feel powerful and sexy, knowing that I'm making him crazy with my touch, and I just want us both naked. Now. "I'm yours, Luke."

His eyes smolder. "Damn right, you're mine."

He makes quick work of my hoodie, top and bra, and then pushes me back onto the bed so he can strip me out of my pants and underwear. His mouth is all over me now, on my breasts, my neck, my side. My hands are in his hair as he shimmies out of his shorts and boxers, discarding them on the floor.

"Oh, Luke." My blood is thrumming now, and I have to have him inside me.

"Yes, baby, what do you need?"

"You, in me. Now."

He smiles against my stomach and laves my piercing with his tongue. "Not yet."

I groan and move my hips under him.

"Not yet, baby." He stills my hips with his hands and climbs up my torso, leaning on his elbow at my side. He kisses me deeply, slowly, his tongue doing incredibly delicious things to my mouth. His strong hand is stroking up and down my side, and I grasp his face in my hands and return his kiss with equal ardor.

I gasp as his fingers find my nipple and pull relentlessly, sending little zings of pleasure down to my groin. I can't help but resume moving my hips, and I run my hand down his side and around to cup his ass, pulling him to me.

"Fuck, Nat, you're so beautiful." His wicked mouth is making its way down my throat. He runs his hand down my back, over my ass, and hitches my leg up around his hip. He pushes forward and slowly, barely, slips just the tip of his cock inside me.

"Oh God, yes."

"Is this what you want?"

"Yes!" I wrap my arms around him, pulling him to me. Suddenly, he rolls on top of me, and I hitch the other leg around him, and he thrusts into me, all the way. I roll my hips, and he groans, his lips on mine, his elbows at the sides of my head and hands buried in my hair.

I grip his ass in my hands, but he stops abruptly and gazes down at me. His eyes are molten blue, the look on his face absolutely serious and almost reverent.

"What's wrong?" I ask breathlessly.

He shakes his head and closes his eyes as if he's in pain, and a sliver of panic pierces my heart.

"What is it?" I smooth my hand down his cheek.

"I just…" He opens his eyes again, pinning me in his intense stare and starts to move his hips once again, pistoning in and out of me like there's more than just desire pushing him.

"You just feel so good, baby."

I groan and move my hips, meeting his, and then he sits back on his heels quickly, taking me with him, not breaking our precious contact. I wrap my arms around his neck and plant my feet beside his hips, and he guides me up and down his shaft, his hands planted firmly on my ass.

I feel the oh-so-familiar tightening of my body as my orgasm nears, and he must feel it, too, because he picks up the pace and pulls me down on him harder.

"Give it to me, baby… Come on, beautiful… Come for me."

And I shatter around him, completely exhausted.

He pulls me down one more time and erupts beneath me, calling out my name with his release.

~

LUKE IS WRAPPED around me in my bed, his front pressed against my back. It's warm and comfortable and just…safe.

"You've become quite insatiable since I met you, Natalie."

I can't help but laugh. "Yeah, I'm just using you for your body."

"I knew it!" He tickles my ribs, and I squirm in his arms, turning to face him.

"Are you going to kick my ass in the gym tomorrow?" I run my fingertip over his lower lip.

"No, I'd prefer to watch your ass." I giggle and kiss his chin.

"You can do that anytime. You don't need to take me to the gym to do it."

"It'll be fun to work out together."

"Okay."

"Trust me."

"I do, implicitly." The honesty in my voice is absolute. I do trust him, and it fills me with a warmth I've not felt since before my parents died.

Luke kisses my forehead and tucks me in against his chest. "Go to sleep, beautiful girl."

# CHAPTER 17

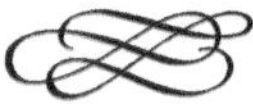

"Wake up, baby." Luke is brushing my hair off my face and gently kissing my forehead.

I want him to go away so I can bury myself in the covers and go back to sleep. It's too early!

"No."

"Come on, honey, open those pretty green eyes."

"I don't have to."

He chuckles and kisses my cheek. "Come on, morning girl, wake up. It's time to go get me all hot and bothered at the gym."

I roll onto my side and open one eye, peering at him uncertainly. "You hate me."

"No, baby, just the opposite. Come on, let's get up." He brushes his lips over my cheek and then my lips again, and I sigh.

"Let's stay here and get all hot and bothered, handsome."

"Oh, no, you don't. Come on, up." He slaps my ass and rolls away from me. He's already dressed!

"Oh Jesus, you're a morning person. This could change everything." I sit up and stretch and eye him warily.

"Gonna dump me already?" He smiles delightedly.

"I'm thinking about it." I rub my hands down my face and realize I smell coffee. "Do I smell coffee?"

Luke picks a mug up off the end table and takes a sip. "I brought this up for you, but since you're dumping me, I'll drink it myself."

I lunge up off the bed and dive for the mug in his hand. "Mine!"

"Ah, ah, ah!" He holds it out of my reach. "You hurt my feelings."

His grin betrays him, but I play along, enjoying this game. "I'm so sorry. Can I please have that coffee?"

I bite my lip and gaze up at him innocently through my eyelashes.

He purses his lips and moves his head from side to side as if considering my request.

"Well, maybe. If you kiss me."

I pucker up and lift my face to his, planting my lips on his cheek with a loud smack.

"Now?" I ask.

"Oh, I think you can do better than that. This is really good coffee." He takes another sip and moves quickly away from me as I lunge at him again.

Changing my tactics, I slide my hand in his shorts and grip his growing erection in my hand, rubbing up and down.

"Now?"

His eyes dilate, and he grins wickedly. "I do love the way you think, baby."

He hands me the mug, and I release him, walking toward the bathroom.

"Hey!"

"I'm gonna get you hot and bothered at the gym, not here," I toss over my shoulder and shut the door behind me while Luke laughs.

"Honey," he yells through the door. "You get me hot and bothered everywhere."

LUKE'S GYM is small and out of the way, which shouldn't surprise me. He's less likely to be recognized here, and I like that it seems to be a no-nonsense kind of place, with upbeat rock pumping through the sound system and no frills. No smoothie bar, no girls meandering about with hardly any clothes on. People come here to work out, not to be seen.

It's so him.

"Where do you want to start?" he asks me as he ushers me ahead of him through the door.

"We're not meeting with your trainer?" I'm relieved that it will just be us today. I don't feel confident enough to work with a trainer. I know that I'm strong and toned, despite my curves, but I don't like strangers touching me or looking at my body.

"Just us today, baby."

"Okay, I think I'll run for a bit."

"Sounds good." He leads me to a line of treadmills, and we choose two machines side by side at the end of the row.

"I brought music." I pull my iPhone and earbuds out of my bra and plug them in my ears.

"What else do you have in there?" He laughs, and I join him. I love his carefree mood today. He's having fun, and it makes me relax. "That's fine. I'm going to watch the news." He points to the flat-screen TV in front of us.

He shows me how to work the treadmill, gets me started, then jumps on his and breaks out into a steady jog.

My mouth goes dry. Sweet Mother of God, this man is amazing. He moves with no effort, and I have to consciously look away before I trip.

I crank up my music—Lady Gaga today—and set my pace with the beat of the music. I've always liked to run. I just never seem to find the time.

I watch the instrument panel in front of me and empty my mind, listening to Ms. Gaga sing about a bad romance. Within minutes, I'm in the zone, and I smile as Kelly Clarkson sings about being stronger.

Yes, I could get used to this.

Before I know it, thirty minutes and about three miles have passed, and I'm sweating like crazy. I slow the belt down to walk for five minutes, then hop off, reaching for my water. I look to my right where Luke was, but he's gone.

I frown and search across the gym, looking for him. I don't immediately see him, so I gather my towel, tuck my phone into my bra and wander out among the free weights.

"Can I help you find something?" I whirl around at the deep voice and then grin.

"Brad! Hey, how's it going?"

"Good."

He pats me on the shoulder, gripping me for just a few seconds longer than polite, and continues to smile widely. "I haven't seen you in here before. Thinking of joining?"

"Oh, I'm here with someone today."

"Cool. Can I get you some water or a fresh towel?"

"You must work here," I mutter drily.

"Oh, yeah, I do. Hey, I can show you how to use some of the weights if you want."

"That won't be necessary." Both Brad and I twirl at the sound of Luke's cold voice.

"Hey." Brad smiles at Luke and holds out his hand. "I didn't introduce myself yesterday. I'm Brad."

Luke shakes his hand and gives him a smile, but it doesn't reach his eyes. "Luke."

Brad's eyes widen, and he swallows. "Holy shit, you're Luke Williams."

Luke's smile doesn't falter. "Yes, I am."

"Well, um…" Brad gives me a quizzical glance then smiles back at Luke. "It's nice to meet you. Catch you later, Natalie." He nods at me and disappears among the weights.

"So it seems Brad is more than a friend of a friend." Luke turns to me, his eyes cold and distant.

Shit.

"No, that's exactly what he is."

"Didn't look that way."

"How did it look?" I back away from him and cross my arms across my chest.

"It looked like he was picking you up."

I shake my head adamantly. "He is just a flirty guy, Luke. He was being nice. I was looking around for you."

"I got a phone call. I have to leave, I'm sorry. I have to run home and do some work."

"Fine, let's go."

"Do you have to work today?" He opens my car door for me, and I slide in.

"No," I respond when he's behind the wheel. "I have today off."

"You're welcome to come home with me." How can he go from being pissed off and jealous to sweet and accommodating?

"That's okay, just take me home."

"Are you mad at me?" His voice is soft, and I can't look him in the face.

"Yes. Are you always going to overreact whenever a man speaks to me?"

"He's had his hands on you twice in two days, Natalie. He wasn't just speaking to you."

"But I didn't do anything wrong."

"He wants in your pants, and you didn't do anything to dissuade him."

"Luke, I'm more than capable of saying no. Trust me, that's all I've said all my adult life. Until you." My voice is raised in my frustration. Doesn't he see that I'm mad about him? That I don't want anyone else?

"I will never be okay with another man putting his hands on you. Get used to it." His voice is sharp, and his eyes are so cold.

He pulls up in front of my house, and I jump out without waiting for him to open the door. He leaps out of his side and follows me up to the front porch.

"Go home, Luke. Go work." I shove my key in the lock and turn it, but his large hand covers mine so I can't turn the knob.

"Natalie, don't be mad at me."

"Don't be mad at you? I may be your girlfriend, but I'm not your property."

"I didn't say you are." He backs up as if I've slapped him.

"Brad's just a flirty kid. Trust me, nothing is ever going to happen with him."

His eyes flare at Brad's name again, and I want to kiss him for caring enough to be jealous and smack the shit out of him for being so jealous he's almost blind with it.

I take a deep breath and decide to change tactics.

"Remember yesterday when you compared seeing Brad and me on that bed in the studio with seeing you onscreen in a love scene?"

"Yeah." He runs a hand through his hair and looks thoroughly frustrated.

"Am I supposed to get jealous every time a fan fawns all over you? They all want in your pants. All of them. They fantasize about fucking you and wooing you and about you being their boyfriend. Trust me, those girls have all spent more time thinking about you than I care to think about."

He starts to speak, but then closes his mouth and shakes his head.

"Don't you dare say that it isn't the same thing. A crush is a crush is a crush. Brad has as much a chance of getting in my pants as any one of those pathetic women has of getting into yours."

He exhales loudly. "Well, I guess I can see your point."

"Go work. I'm going to take a shower."

"Are you still mad at me?" He closes the gap between us and grips my hand in his tightly.

"A little. I'll get over it. Go work and call me later."

"Okay." He bends down and runs his lips lightly over mine, then pushes his fingers in my hair and pulls me to him, kissing me deeply, as if his apology is in his kiss, and I can't help but melt against him.

"You make me crazy," I murmur against his lips.

"Ditto, baby. I'll talk to you tonight."

He leaves me on the porch, and I watch him slip into his sleek black SUV. He smiles and waves and pulls out of my driveway.

I've fallen in love with a beautiful, sexy, sweet, jealous control freak.

Shit.

~

JULES IS in the kitchen when I go inside. I slam my purse on the breakfast bar and yank the fridge open, looking for a water.

"Well, hello, sunshine," Jules says sarcastically.

"What are you doing here? Aren't you supposed to be at work?"

"I'm working from home. Hey, you're really pissed. What happened?" She plants her hands on her hips and scowls at me, and I immediately feel better.

"He just irritated me at the gym. Luke has a jealous streak."

"Scary jealous or sexy jealous?" Jules asks, her eyebrows raised.

"Stupid jealous." I sigh and fall into the deep cushions of the red couch in the living room. Jules follows and sits in the armchair opposite me, her bare feet propped on the ottoman.

"He's obviously crazy about you." She takes a swig of her own water.

I shrug. "I guess. I'm new to all this, Jules. I don't like being questioned about things I do."

"He's not being a controlling asshole, is he?"

"No, but he does have a bossy streak. Not in a bad way. I know he cares about me. He's really sweet and gentle with me. But, boy, he does not like Brad." I roll my eyes and lean my head back against the cushion.

"Sexy model client Brad?"

"Yeah." I explain about Luke walking in on us in the studio yesterday and running into Brad at the gym today.

"Gee, I wonder why. That kid has it bad for you."

I scowl at her. "He does not! He's just flirty! Don't you start, too."

"You never could recognize when someone was interested in you, Nat."

"Luke has nothing to worry about."

"Oh, I know that." She brushes my words aside with a wave of her hand.

"Why doesn't he?"

"This is new to him, too."

"Whose side are you on?"

"Yours, sweetie. Always yours. Where is he?"

"He went home to work. Someone called while we were working out."

"Maybe you could use a day apart."

"Probably. Hey, what are you really doing here? You've been working from home a lot lately."

Jules frowns and shrugs. "Telecommuting is easy."

"Uh uh. I don't buy it." She's not telling me something. "I know you too well, Julianne Montgomery."

"My new boss is kind of a dick." She shrugs again, but she looks like she might be fighting tears.

Alarmed, I sit on the ottoman, making her lower her feet, and grasp her hands. "Has he hurt you?"

"No, he's just a condescending asshole." She shrugs again, but then breaks down in tears. Holy shit.

"Sweetie, what is it?"

She drops her head in her hands and cries, a hard, sobbing cry.

"I fucked him," she cries through her hands.

"What?" I sit back, my jaw dropped, shocked. Jules has a strict policy: no screwing coworkers.

"The night you first brought Luke home." I remember that night, when Jules went straight upstairs without coming to the kitchen to meet Luke.

"How? Jules, this isn't like you."

"I know." She wipes her eyes and her nose on the back of her hand. "We went out for dinner with some other people from the office, and I had too much to drink."

"Honey, is he trying to ruin things for you at work?"

"No! No, nothing like that." She takes a deep breath, and I hand her a tissue. "It's just so uncomfortable. And it doesn't help that he's freaking hot. Almost Luke Williams hot." She smiles at me, and my shoulders relax just a little.

"Wow, that's pretty hot."

"I know, right?" She shakes her head and looks sad again. I hate seeing Sad Jules. "And, Nat, you'd be shocked what he's hiding under those business suits he wears to work. Wow. It was the best sex of my damn life."

"Jules, are you hung up on this guy?"

"It doesn't matter even if I am. There is a no-fraternizing policy at our office. We could both be fired." Her eyes well again, and I just feel so helpless.

"What has his reaction been to all this?"

"Well, he was pretty pissed when he woke up the next morning and I was gone."

"Ah, so you did the whole sleep-with-'em-then-bail-when-they're-asleep move." I nod knowingly.

"Yeah. I didn't want to face the ugly morning after."

"Can't blame you there. But if he was pissed you were gone, maybe he really likes you."

"It doesn't matter. It's hopeless."

"But…"

"No, don't try to fix this, Nat. It's done. I'll go back to the office eventually. I just need a little time to regroup. I took a few vacation days, and now I'm working from home until I work up the nerve to see him again."

"Okay." I rub her arm soothingly, and then stand. "I'm going up to shower. Let me know if you need me."

"Thanks." She gives me a watery smile. "Oh, Nat?"

"Yeah?"

"Stupid jealous is kinda hot."

# CHAPTER 18

*I'm picking you up in an hour. Please dress formally.*

Oh my. I stare at the text and read it again.

I glance at the clock. It's five-thirty, and I'm definitely not anywhere close to being formal or sexy. I don't even know where to start.

This is a job for Jules.

"Jules!" I yell out my bedroom door, mentally thumbing through my closet.

"What?"

"I need to get sexy."

"What?"

I shove my phone in her hands, and she breaks into a huge smile. "Wow, he knows how to woo a girl."

"Jules!" I clasp on to her shoulders and shake her. "Help me. I'm not good at this."

"Come on." She grabs my wrist and drags me into my closet. "The new red Louboutins are a no-brainer." She pulls them off the shelf and hands them to me.

"What am I going to wear with them?" I'm in a panic.

"Don't you have a little black dress?"

"No." I frown. I don't have many dresses at all.

"Everyone has a little black dress, Natalie."

"Not me." I shrug.

"Get in the shower and scrub, shave and loofa. I'll be back."

"That sounds painful." My eyes widen in fear, and Jules smirks at me.

"We're just getting started. Go! Clock's ticking." She jogs back to her room, and I start the shower.

FIFTY MINUTES LATER, I am buffed and polished. Jules has curled my thick chestnut hair and managed to twist it up into some kind of sexy knot thing, with tendrils hanging around my face.

The face is a Julianne masterpiece. She's made my eyes look all smoky and sultry, accentuating the green in them. My cheekbones are defined, and my lips are pouty with a cranberry-red lip stain that is guaranteed to not smudge or come off for eighteen hours, which sounds too good to be true to me, but I'll take it.

My eyes run down the rest of my body in the full-length mirror hanging on the back of my closet door.

I'm hot.

Jules has lent me a to-die-for black dress. The neckline reminds me of something Elizabeth Taylor would have worn, just off the shoulder with a deep V-neck. The back swoops down low across the small of my back. It's sleeveless and gathered at the waist with a thick waistband. The skirt is floaty and soft and flirts just at my knees.

Under the dress is some impressive black underwear and a garter belt with nude stockings. I've never worn stockings before, but they're amazingly comfortable and feel silky and sexy.

My beautiful red stiletto Louboutins are killer with this dress.

Jules walks into the room and lets out a loud wolf whistle.

"Well, don't you clean up well, best friend of mine?"

I laugh and do a turn so she can see the whole effect. "Will I do?"

"Girl, he's going to die of heart failure the minute he sees you. You look amazing." She smiles and hugs me tight.

"Here, this wrap and purse will go with your outfit." She hands me a beautiful red wrap and a handbag that perfectly match the shoes, and I smile in gratitude.

The doorbell rings, and there are now about five million butterflies in my stomach.

"I'll answer. Take your time, make him sweat." She kisses my cheek and hurries down the stairs.

I stare at myself in the mirror for a few more minutes, and then put my things in Jules' red handbag.

Here goes nothing.

Do not fall down the stairs. Do not fall down the stairs.

This is my mantra as I walk down the stairs. I don't think I'm breathing, I'm too nervous. Where is he taking me?

I get to the bottom of the stairs and enter the foyer, and all of my wits completely scatter.

Luke is wearing a black double-breasted suit with a white shirt and a blue tie that perfectly matches his incredible eyes. His messy hair has been tamed somewhat, and it's begging for my fingers. He looks every bit the wealthy, sophisticated movie star, and he's all mine.

His eyes lock on mine, and a slow, delighted grin spreads across his face.

"Natalie, you take my breath away."

"You're not so bad yourself."

Luke closes the gap between us and hands me a bouquet of red roses. "These are for you."

"Thank you," I murmur as I bury my nose in them and breathe them in. "They're lovely."

"We should go. We have reservations." He takes my hand and kisses my knuckles, shooting shivers up my arm.

"Okay."

Jules magically appears from nowhere. "I'll put those in water for you. Have fun, you guys. You both look incredible."

"Thanks, Jules." I hand her the flowers, and Luke ushers me out of the house.

Instead of his Mercedes or the Lexus, there's a black stretch limo parked in my driveway with a sharply dressed driver standing at the open back door.

"Madam." He nods at me, and I smile in return.

Holy shit, Luke's gone all out! Is this how he says he's sorry? If so, we might have to argue more often.

I climb in the back of the spacious limo and slide over so Luke can follow. The inside must seat ten easily. It's all soft black leather seats and some sort of impressive sound system and other gadgets. The privacy glass is up.

Luke slides gracefully next to me and kisses my hand again.

"Luke, this is…amazing. Thank you."

"We haven't even gone anywhere yet." He looks so young and happy, and he's clearly excited for what he has planned for us tonight.

"It's already more than you should have done."

"No, it's exactly what you deserve, baby." He leans over and gives me his sweet, tender kiss, the one that makes my insides quiver. "You look gorgeous tonight."

I smile and flush at the compliment. "Thank you."

"Are those the new shoes?"

"Yes." I grin.

"They are wow."

"I know."

He laughs and pours me a glass of champagne as the driver pulls away from the house and heads toward Seattle.

"A toast." He holds his glass in the air, and I mirror him. "To a beautiful woman, who has become very special to me, and who is the most incredible person I've ever known. Thank you for being here with me." He clinks his glass to mine, and I blink back tears as I take a sip of the sweet pink drink.

"You are charming," I murmur and smile shyly at him.

"You are sexy as hell."

"Where are we going?" I take another sip of the champagne. Mmm…delicious.

"It's a surprise."

"Will it take awhile to get there?"

"A little while. Why do you ask?"

I take his drink out of his hand and place it next to mine on a small table near the minifridge.

"Because." I hike my skirt up a bit and straddle his lap. His eyes widen in surprise, and his strong hands glide up my stocking-clad legs. "I want to fuck you in this limousine."

"Holy shit, baby, you're wearing stockings."

I smile smugly and nod.

"I had a whole seduction scene planned for later." His breath hitches as I grind my center against his growing erection.

"Trust me, I don't want to ruin your plans." I lean forward and brush my lips over his. "But if you're not inside me in about twenty seconds, I'm not responsible for my actions."

"That's an offer I will never, ever refuse, baby." He slides me back on his knees so he can unfasten his pants, pulling his shirttails out of them and pushing them down around his thighs.

Instead of straddling him, I slip off his lap and onto my knees on the luxuriously carpeted floor. I smooth my hands up his strong thighs and stroke them up and down his cock.

"Holy shit, Nat, you are so fucking hot."

"You make me crazy." I smear the bead of moisture around the tip with my thumb and then put it in my mouth and suck, and his eyes go wide.

"Taste good?"

"Mmm…my favorite."

I take him in my mouth, just swirling my tongue around the tip and gliding my hands up and down his impressive length. I feel his fingertips just barely grazing my hairline around my ears, and I know he wants to sink his fingers in my hair but doesn't want to mess it up.

I grip his shaft with my lips firmly and sink down until I feel him against the back of my throat.

"Sweet Jesus, Natalie, stop."

I grin to myself and pull back but then sink down again, loving that I'm making him crazy.

"No, stop, I don't want to come in your mouth." He reaches down and lifts me onto his lap so I'm straddling him again. He reaches between us and pulls my panties to the side, and I rub my folds against him, feeling my wetness spreading over him.

"God, baby, you're so wet."

"You are so sexy, honey. I need you inside me."

He growls and kisses me hard while lifting my ass over him and sinks easily inside me. I grip the back of the seat behind his head and begin riding him, slowly at first, but his hands move me up and down faster and faster.

"Come for me, beautiful." He's kissing my neck and moves one hand between us to graze his thumb over my clitoris, and I'm lost. I shudder and clench down around him, crying out as he pushes up one last, hard time and empties himself into me.

"Fuck, Natalie." His breathing is ragged. I wrap my fingers in his hair and kiss him with all I have, pouring my heart and soul into the kiss, trying to convey the words that I just can't say: that I love him so much.

He tenderly cups my face in his hands and slows the kiss, pulling back so he can look into my eyes, and I see the love reflected back to me. It makes me glow inside, and it makes me want to run as fast as I can in the other direction.

"Thank you for tonight," I whisper.

"Oh, baby, it's just getting started." He gives me a slow, sweet smile and lifts me off of him. I rummage around and find a towel, and we clean up and straighten our clothes.

Settling back into our seats, Luke freshens our champagne and wraps his arm around me.

"I'm sorry about today," he murmurs.

"Me, too." I sigh and lean my head on his shoulder. "Did you get your work done?"

"For the most part. I'll have to make a few calls tomorrow."

"Oh good." He's running his fingertips up and down my bare arm, and I want to purr.

"What did you do today?"

"I hung out with Jules." I take his hand in mine and lace my fingers through his, reveling in how long and lean his hands are. "She's got some stuff going on, so I did the best friend thing."

"Is she okay?" He sounds sincerely concerned, and I can't help but grin. My sweet man.

"She will be. Man troubles."

"Ah. So, what does the best friend thing entail, exactly?" He kisses my forehead.

"Well, a lot of talking, eating ice cream and other things that I'm not allowed to divulge."

"Oh?" He chuckles and kisses my forehead again.

"Yeah, I could tell you, but then I'd have to kill you, and I've grown quite fond of you."

"Is that so?" He leans back so he can look me in the eye, and I nod gravely.

"Yes, very fond of you."

"And what are you most fond of, exactly?" He gives me his sweet smile, and I know that despite our teasing, he wants an honest answer.

"I'm fond of this." I lean up and kiss his lips softly. "You say such sweet things to me and make my body hum with it."

"Happy to hear that, beautiful girl."

I smile and kiss the palm of his hand. "And I enjoy your hands, and how expressive they are and how they feel when they're on me."

"Mmm…they love being on you, baby."

I lay my cheek on his chest, just over his heart. "Most of all, I love your heart. How kind you are and how gentle you are with me. Most of the time," I add and smile up at him.

His lips part as he exhales. "Natalie, I don't know what I did to deserve you, but I would do it again, over and over." He runs his knuckles down my cheek and kisses me tenderly as the limo comes to a stop.

"We're here."

Luke climbs out ahead of me and takes my hand to help me out of the impressive car. He pulls me to his side, and my eyes are glued to the enormous chateau before us.

"Oh my."

"This is Chateau Ste. Michelle. We're going to have dinner here tonight."

"I didn't know they had a restaurant." My wide eyes meet his.

"They don't. They do special events. Tonight, for a few hours at least, it's all ours."

I'm struck dumb. He rented out the entire chateau for me?

"Come." He leads me toward the front of the building where an older woman, in her midfifties, is waiting for us.

"Welcome, Mr. Williams and Ms. Conner. I'm Mrs. Davidson. We're delighted to have you. Would you please follow me?" She leads us on a cobblestone path around the side of the chateau. It's lined with old-fashioned streetlights illuminate the whole side of the building.

Luke tucks my hand in his arm and escorts me along behind Mrs. Davidson. As we round the bend behind the house, I gasp at the sight before me.

"Oh, Luke." I feel him grin down at me, watching my reaction to the most beautiful display I've ever seen. The stone path leads us beneath an arbor that is covered in grapevines. The vines are heavy with luscious, purple grapes. There are white twinkling Christmas lights draped over roughly ten two-person tables and wound through the arbor and vines lining the small space. There is soft, bluesy music crooning in the background.

The small table in the center of the stone patio is covered in a white tablecloth. The china is also white, but on one plate sits a single red rose. Luke walks forward and pulls the chair out for me, and I sit.

He picks up the rose, and I look up into his joy-filled eyes. He sniffs the delicate flower before extending it to me.

"For you, beautiful."

"Thank you." I put the bloom against my nose and sniff its sweetness.

Luke sits opposite me at the table.

"Honey, this is wonderful. Thank you." I reach over and grasp his hand in mine, so moved by this devastatingly romantic gesture.

"I'm glad you like it." He grins and gestures to the waiter.

"Sir, madam." The waiter is dressed in a white jacket and black pants and bow tie. He's an older gentleman with white hair and a British accent, and I can't help but fall just a little in love with him.

"Thank you for joining us this evening. We will be serving you three courses, in addition to an appetizer course and, of course, dessert. I hope you're hungry." He winks at me and motions to someone inside the building.

"Here is your appetizer. Chili garlic calamari, paired with our 2009 dry Riesling, and Hawaiian-style chicken skewers, paired with the 2008 Cabinet Riesling."

The plates are set in front of us with glasses of wine.

I meet Luke's eyes over the table. "It looks too pretty to eat."

"Enjoy, baby."

We dig in and enjoy the appetizers. The wines complement each dish perfectly, flooding my mouth with amazing flavors and textures.

Luke reaches over and holds my hand, rubbing his thumb over my knuckles as we finish our wine and wait for the next course.

"Are you having fun?"

"Much more than fun. This is…a fairy tale." I feel my cheeks heat, but it's the truth.

"This is a beautiful vineyard. We'll have to come again during the day so you can see the grounds."

"I'd love that."

"May I present your first course?" Our waiter is back and removes our empty plates and wine glasses. "This is our mojito-marinated halibut with mango, avocado and black bean salsa, served with the 2009 Midsummer's White. Enjoy." He backs away, leaving us with the delicious meal.

We're served two more courses of pork tenderloin and New York steak with Yukon gold potatoes and, of course, the perfect wines to accompany them.

I'm feeling very full and just a little lightheaded from all the wine when it's time for dessert to be served.

"Oh my God, Luke, I don't know if there is any room left in this dress for dessert." I sit back and rub my belly, and Luke laughs, his eyes alight with happiness. He's having a really good time and has been lighthearted and complimentary throughout our meal. He's so good at this.

He motions to the waiter, who immediately steps to the tableside. "Yes, sir."

"I think that Ms. Conner and I will share the dessert, please."

"Very good, sir."

"Good plan. Besides, we're going to work all these calories off at yoga tomorrow morning."

"Ah yes, yoga. You're going to make me go, huh?"

"No, I'm not making you."

"We could skip it and stay in bed all day." He winks at me over his wine glass.

"I can't skip it. I'm the instructor."

"I had no idea." He furrows his brow in confusion.

"I only teach three classes a week." I shrug. "Besides, I'm very flexible. You should enjoy the show." I smile smugly into my glass and watch his eyes glass over.

"I wouldn't miss it for the world."

The waiter reappears with our dessert of strawberry crème brûlée tart, on one plate, and two glasses of the Eroica Ice Wine.

He also sets a baby-blue Tiffany necklace-size box in the center of the table, bows to both of us, and walks away.

Oh. My. God.

# CHAPTER 19

*I* stare numbly at the perfect blue box tied with a white bow. What's this?

"It's for you," he murmurs and grips my hand. My eyes find his, and I just don't know what to say.

"You shouldn't have done this." My voice is a whisper.

"You haven't opened it yet," he responds drily, but his eyes are guarded.

I'm sure this is not the response he was expecting. I don't want to hurt his feelings.

He picks up the box and passes it to me. "Open it, baby."

I pull the ribbon off the box, and nestled beneath it on top of the box is a note.

*These remind me of you. Simply beautiful.*

*—Luke*

Oh my.

I smile up at him, and I see his shoulders relax a bit with his grin. He's sitting forward, leaning on the table, waiting in anticipation for me to open the box.

I pull the lid off the box and gasp.

Nestled in Tiffany blue satin is a string of exquisite pearls. They have a platinum clasp, and the pearls are milky white, with an almost iridescent glow that reflects the soft twinkling lights around us. I lift them out of the box, and they are smooth and cool to the touch.

"Luke, they're fabulous."

"Here." He gracefully unfolds his lean body from his chair and comes to stand behind me, taking the strand of beautiful pearls from my hands and unclasping them. He drapes them around my neck, and my fingers immediately touch them as he fastens them. They lay just at my collarbone. He leans down and kisses me gently on the cheek and offers his hand to me as Norah Jones begins crooning about coming away with her.

"Dance with me." His blue eyes are shining with happiness, and I'm so caught up in the romance, so caught up in him, I just can't resist him.

"It would be my pleasure."

He pulls me into his arms and begins whisking me around the patio.

"Thank you for the beautiful pearls," I whisper up to him.

"You are welcome, beautiful. They look perfect on you." As he sways me back and forth in time to the music, he leans down and places his lips gently on mine.

"You're good at this."

He smiles down at me. "The studio made me take lessons."

"I approve."

"I'm happy to hear it." As the song ends, he pulls me closer against his chest and wraps his arms around me, planting his lips gently on my forehead. "Come home with me tonight."

"You'd rather go to your place tonight?"

"Yes. I want you in my bed."

I smile and run my fingers through his soft blond hair, soaking in his beautiful face. His eyes are so blue, his freshly shaven jaw chiseled. I've never loved anyone so much.

"Okay. I'm going to need a few things from my house."

His fingers trace my skin just under the pearls, and a shiver dances down my spine. "Jules already took care of it."

I raise an eyebrow. "Pretty sure of yourself."

"Just hopeful, baby." He kisses my forehead again and cups my face in his hands. His lips find my nose, my cheeks and then settle softly on my lips. It's one of his special, gentle kisses, and I sigh as the muscles deep in my stomach begin to tighten.

"Take me home," I whisper against his lips, and his eyes blink open, burning with desire.

He leads me back to the table, and I see that our things have been gathered up and most likely taken to the car. The waiter appears with my wrap and handbag, and Luke tucks my hand in the crook of his elbow and escorts me back to the car, sliding across the leather seat behind me.

Inside, there is a fresh bottle of champagne and another fresh red rose.

"What is it with you and red roses?"

"You don't like them?" His voice is worried, and he furrows his brow.

"No, I love them. You're just spoiling me." I bury my nose in the blossom and peek up at him through my lashes.

"You look very beautiful right now, in those pearls and black dress and a red rose pressed to your face." He runs his finger down my cheek, and I sigh.

"Thank you."

"Come here." He lifts me effortlessly onto his lap, and I curl into him, burying my face in his neck.

"Tonight was the most magical night of my life, Luke."

I feel his smile as he kisses my forehead. "Mine, too."

〜

"WAKE UP, BABY, WE'RE HOME." Luke is kissing my forehead and brushing my cheek with his fingers.

"I'm sorry I fell asleep." I sit up and realize I'm still clutching the rose.

"I love holding you while you sleep, baby. Come on, let's go in."

The driver opens Luke's door, and Luke lifts me onto the seat next to him, ushering me out ahead of him. He thanks the driver and escorts me into the house.

My feet are starting to feel the effects of these fantastically beautiful shoes, but I don't want to take them off yet. Luke removes my wrap from my shoulders, skimming his fingers across my skin, and just like that my libido wakes up.

"Are your feet hurting?" He's always so aware of how I might be feeling, and it makes me smile.

"A little, but I'm okay."

He leans down and scoops me into his arms and begins the journey up to his bedroom.

"You do enjoy carrying me," I murmur and kiss his cheek.

"It's for purely selfish reasons."

"Oh? And what are those reasons?" I kiss his cheek again. I love the way his skin feels against my face.

"Well, one, I enjoy having you in my arms. And, two, I don't want you to take those shoes off yet."

He carries me into his bedroom and sets me down on my feet in the middle of the room. He flips a switch on the wall, and the light on the end table illuminates, throwing soft shadows across the room.

"Let me help you out of that dress."

I turn, and he kisses my shoulder as he lowers the zipper down the back and slips the straps down my arms. The dress falls and pools at my feet. He holds my hand, and I step out of it and turn back toward him.

He gasps and steps back from me, not touching me, and I've never felt more beautiful. His eyes are shining with adoration and desire, skimming over my hair and pearls, down to my breasts held firmly in place by a black lace strapless bra. He lowers his gaze over my belly piercing, black lace barely there panties that match the bra, garter belt, stockings and down to my killer red shoes.

Yes, I know I look amazing right now, and it's the most powerful, sexy feeling in the world.

I don't move toward him. I stand where I am, letting him drink me in with his eyes. I slowly reach up and unpin my hair, one thick curl at a time, and let it fall around my shoulders, dropping the pins to the floor.

"You are every fantasy I've ever had come true, Natalie." He swallows hard and flexes his hands in and out of fists, and I know he's dying to touch me.

I smile softly, not wanting to break this spell, and reach behind me to unclasp my bra and let it join the dress and pins on the floor, releasing my breasts. My nipples pucker under his hungry gaze.

"What would you like me to do now?" I whisper.

His eyes focus on mine, just a bit glassy like he's intoxicated, but I know it's not from the wine we've consumed all evening. He closes his eyes briefly, and then starts shedding his clothes, letting them fall unheeded to the floor around him.

Suddenly, he's standing before me, naked. "I'm almost afraid to touch you," he whispers.

"Why?" I cock my head, confused. Touch me! Please, for the love of all that's holy, touch me!

"I'm afraid you're not real."

And just like that I see the vulnerability in his eyes, and I walk to him, raising my hands up his chest, over his shoulders and into his hair. His blue gaze is on mine, and I smile tenderly.

"I'm real, and I'm yours." I push up on my toes and run my lips across his, and he shudders, exhaling deeply.

He reaches down and cups my bottom in his hands and lifts me, wrapping my legs around his waist, and walks us back to the bed. But he doesn't drop me. He wraps his impossibly strong arms around me and lowers me gently, without lifting his lips from mine.

He kisses me madly, voraciously, cupping my face in his hands while he lies over me, bracing himself on his elbows. My hands drift down his back to his butt and back up to his shoulders, over and over. His erection presses against my now wet panties, and he rocks his hips back and forth, sending zings of electricity through me.

"God, I've been fantasizing about this since the day I met you," he mutters as he moves his mouth from mine to my neck.

"About what?"

"You, in pearls and these shoes, wrapped around me."

"How's it working out for you?" I gasp as he rocks against me again, and I tighten my legs around his hips.

He smiles against my neck. "Better than I ever dreamed possible." He rubs his nose along my pearls. "You look so magnificent in these."

"I love them. Thank you."

He leans up on his elbows and pins me with those shining blue eyes, gazing intently into mine. He brushes his thumbs down my cheeks, and I run my fingers through his hair.

"What is it?" I ask, reveling in the intense way he's looking down at me.

"I love you."

The words are strong, firm, with no hesitation. His intense gaze never falters, and I know, undoubtedly, that he means it. My heart stops, tears fall from the corners of my eyes, and I clasp his precious face in my hands as I gaze up at my incredible man.

"I love you, too."

He brushes my tears away with his fingertips, and then leans down and kisses my eyelids.

"Don't cry, baby." His lips graze my cheek and settle back on my lips again, and I'm completely bewildered and lost to him.

"Make love to me, please." I want him more than anything. I want to feel him move through me. I want to see the passion on his face as he erupts inside me.

He smiles tenderly, sits back and hitches my panties in his thumbs. I raise my hips so he can slide them down my legs. He moves back on top of me and smoothes one hand up my leg, over the stockings, and lightly rubs his fingertips over the skin just above where the stockings end.

It's delicious.

That talented hand moves between my legs, and he slips two fingers inside me, his thumb wreaking havoc on my clitoris, and I bow up off the bed.

Oh God, it's just so good.

"Feel it, baby."

Oh, I do. My hips circle, and his fingers push in and out of me in a sensual rhythm. He leans down and kisses me, his tongue invading my mouth with the same rhythm of his fingers. Just as I feel my body quicken and the shudders start, he pulls them out of me.

"No!"

He grins down at me and swiftly fills me, burying himself inside me.

"Oh yes."

"Better?" His eyes burn down into mine, and he starts to move, and I'm overcome with sensation. My body is on fire. My heart is so full of love for this beautiful man. I can't find my voice, so I simply nod and hold on to him, gripping his tight rear, pulling him to me.

"Oh, baby, you're so tight." He clenches his jaw, and I grip him with my most intimate muscles, knowing that he's so close to his own violent explosion, and that I'm going with him.

"Come with me, my love." His eyes fly open and then shut again as he shudders inside me, and my body follows, clenching around him, pulsing with need.

"Oh, Natalie, yes!"

~

LUKE IS in his favorite spot, his head resting between my breasts, arms hugging my hips, and our breathing is starting to slow.

I can't believe that I had to wait twenty-five years for a man to truly make sweet, tender love to me.

Well, almost twenty-six years as of Saturday.

I also can't believe that we just let the L-word slip. I hope it wasn't just because it was in the heat of the moment, because of this impossibly romantic night. But as I think back on the look in his eyes as he said those three words, I know that he meant it. Even though we've only known each other for such a short time, and there's still so much to learn.

I also know that my heart has never been so full, and I have never met a man as kind, intelligent and as sweet as he is. I feel safe with him, and I feel beautiful and cherished.

Yes, he has a jealous streak, but don't we all?

"Don't overthink this, baby."

I look down and frown.

"Overthink what?"

"I hear the wheels turning in that gorgeous head of yours." He kisses my sternum, rolls off of me and lies next to me, facing me, bracing his head on his elbow.

"I'm not thinking."

"You're not a good liar." He leans over and kisses my nose and brushes a lock of hair off my cheek.

"I need to take my pearls off." I sit up and turn my back to him and feel him unhinge the clasp.

"Why?" He lays them on the nightstand, and I lie back down.

"I don't want them to snag on something and break in the night." I sigh and glide my hand down his side to his hip.

"I meant it, you know."

I smile and stretch lazily. "I know."

"What time are we getting up in the morning?"

I'm relieved that he's changing the subject. I have a lot to think about. "Class is at nine."

"Then we'd better get some sleep."

"I'm not sleeping in these shoes."

He laughs and sits up, sliding each shoe off my feet and placing them gently on the floor. He then unhooks the stockings from the garter and peels them down my legs.

"You have beautiful legs, baby." He kisses them and pulls the garter off me as well, tossing it on the floor.

He crawls up next to me and covers us in the duvet, scooping me into his arms. I rest my head on his chest and sigh, feeling his lips on my forehead.

"Go to sleep, beautiful."

"Good night," I mumble and drift into an exhausted sleep.

~

I WAKE SUDDENLY and reach for Luke, but he's not there. The bed is cold and empty.

Where did he go?

I pull on the white dress shirt he was wearing earlier tonight and leave the bedroom. He's not in the loft, so I go downstairs.

It's dark. I don't see him in the living room or kitchen, and I'm about to get really scared when I see movement on the deck.

I walk through the darkness to the open door, unnoticed. He's standing at the railing, bathed in moonlight. He's wearing a dark pair of pajama pants that hang on his sexy hips, and he's topless. He's leaning his elbows on the railing and is looking out on the midnight-blue water that is reflecting the moon.

I wish with all my might that I had my camera.

I walk up behind him and kiss his back, wrapping my arms around his middle. I love holding him like this.

"Did I wake you?" he whispers.

"No, I woke up because you were gone." I kiss him again. "Are you okay?"

"I'm fine, just couldn't sleep." He turns around to face me and leans his hips on the railing, wrapping me in his arms. His face is bathed in moonlight, his eyes gazing intently down at me. "How are you?"

"Lonely. Come back to bed."

"Okay," he whispers and kisses my forehead. "I see you've borrowed my shirt again."

"It's a nasty habit of mine."

"That's okay. You can return it to me upstairs." He scoops me into his arms, and I laugh as he carries me back to the bedroom.

<h1 style="text-align:center">CHAPTER 20</h1>

*J*'m surprised to wake before Luke. We have to be at yoga in an hour, but I can't resist lying here and watching him sleep.

The early morning light filters in through his floor-to-ceiling windows. I love his large bedroom with its large-scale furniture. The bed is enormous, the white sheets feel like Egyptian cotton, and they are soft against my skin.

Luke lies on his back, one hand flung over his head. His face is soft in sleep, his morning stubble so sexy along his jaw, and his usually messy hair even messier than usual.

And he loves me!

I saunter into the bathroom to answer nature's call, and when I walk back into the bedroom, I pick up the scattered clothes, shoes and hairpins from last night, a huge grin plastered on my face.

I notice one of my small suitcases is sitting on a chair near the windows, and I make a mental note to thank Jules.

I am happy to find my yoga gear, fresh underwear and other casual clothes and toiletries, including a toothbrush, all new, in the suitcase. I decide to unpack and settle in a bit. If he wants me to move back out, fine. If he wants to move some stuff into my place, that's fine, too.

I add my toothbrush and a stick of deodorant to his vanity and a bottle of body wash and shampoo to the shower. Jules must have gone shopping for all this last night, and I not only mentally thank her, I plan to surprise her with a special treat.

I leave the clothes in the suitcase, but pull on my yoga gear and look back over to the bed.

Luke's still asleep, and we still have plenty of time, so I leave him be and head downstairs to make coffee.

I poke around his kitchen, opening espresso-colored cabinets, and finally locate the coffee and maker, get it set to drip and find some mugs as well. As the coffee perks, I open the French door out to the deck and step out to enjoy the view of the beautiful Puget Sound and take a deep breath of fresh air.

It's a beautiful day. The sky is a brilliant blue, as the morning sun is up fully and shining on the deep blue water. The ferry is gliding gracefully toward Bainbridge Island. Seagulls fly over the water, and the breeze is blowing gently through my hair. It's a glorious day.

"I thought you weren't a morning person."

I spin at the sound of his rough, sexy voice. He enfolds me in his arms and hugs me close.

"Good morning, handsome."

"Good morning, baby."

Leaning my head back, I grin up at him. "I'm making coffee."

"So I smell. Thank you. Why didn't you wake me?" He kisses my forehead and takes a deep breath.

"You looked so peaceful, and we're in no hurry."

"You unpacked."

I lean my head against his chest, avoiding his gaze. "Yeah, I can repack if you'd rather I didn't leave my stuff here."

He grips my chin in his fingers and tips my head back, brushing my lips with his in a kiss that makes my toes curl.

"I like having your stuff here. Leave it."

"Okay." I smile shyly at him. "Let's get some coffee."

～

"ARE YOU READY?" I grin at Luke, who's now dressed in loose, black basketball shorts and a tank top. He looks fantastic.

"As I'll ever be." He looks nervous, and my heart melts.

"You'll be fine. Just remember what I said. Go at your own pace and stretch only as far as is comfortable. I don't want you to get hurt."

"I won't get hurt."

"Okay." I know he thinks this is going to be a piece of cake. I have no doubt that he's in excellent physical condition, but yoga is more physically demanding than most people realize.

I unlock the studio and usher him in. The glass windows are frosted so people walking by can't stop and stare. There are mirrors covering one whole wall with a barre mounted to it for the afternoon ballet class. Yoga mats are rolled up and stacked in a corner. I walk over to the sound system and choose some calming music.

"Okay, let's grab our mats. Clients will start trickling in soon."

"How many people usually attend this class?"

I can sense his unease about being recognized. "Only about eight or ten. It's a small class."

He nods, and we spread out our mats, me in the front of the class by the mirrors and him in front of me. Clients walk in and grab mats, spread all over the studio. No one even pays any attention to Luke, and I see him relax. I smile at him reassuringly, and he winks back at me.

"Okay, everyone, let's get started." For the next hour I lead the class through the series of poses, varying my poses to accommodate both novice and experienced clients. I typi-

124

cally lose myself to the music and the flow of the yoga itself, but I can't help but be distracted by Luke and his strong body. He's more flexible than I gave him credit for, and he's graceful. Watching his toned body move and flex is a delight.

He's watching me, too, with more interest than just to see which pose I'm moving into. When our eyes meet, the heat is unmistakable, and I know I'm turning him on as much as he's turning me on.

I can't wait to get him alone.

I'm in the downward dog pose, and I turn to look out over the class and see that Luke's gaze is on my ass.

I smirk.

Finally, class is over, and I'm so turned on I can hardly see straight. The clients all wave goodbye and shuffle out to get on with their day, and finally Luke and I are left alone. He walks over to the door and flips the lock, and my heart does a big ol' flip in my chest.

"Is there another class in here this morning?" he asks.

"No, not until this afternoon."

"Good."

"What did you think?" I ask.

"I think," he begins, as he walks slowly toward me, "that you are the sexiest woman I've ever seen in my life."

His eyes narrow, and his face is serious.

"Oh." I try to gather my wits. "So, I take it you liked it?"

"I had no idea you could move that gorgeous little body of yours like that."

"I've been doing this for a long time."

"Yeah, I see." He's finally standing less than a foot away from me, and I reach up to run my hand down his face.

"I'm glad you were here. It was a pleasure to watch you move."

He smiles, delighted with me, and cups my hand in his own, leaning in to my touch and closing his eyes for just a few moments. He opens those baby blues, and they are now on fire.

Holy hell, I love it when he looks at me like that.

He backs me up against the mirror and clasps my face in his hands, kissing me as if his life depends on it. I grip his hips and give myself over to his kiss, pouring all my frustration from the past hour into it.

"I want you," he murmurs against my lips.

"I've wanted you for the past hour. I'm surprised I was able to speak during class."

He smiles against my lips. "Let's take these off, shall we?"

He pulls my tank and sports bra over my head and throws them on the ground, then makes quick work of my pants and underwear. I repay the favor, divesting him of his black workout clothes, and he spins me around to face the mirror.

"Put your hands on the bar, baby."

I gladly comply. He kisses my shoulder and wraps his arms around my front, cupping my breasts and worrying the sensitive nipples with his fingers. Watching our reflection sends electricity straight to my groin. His large bronze hands span my chest, cupping my white breasts. His lips are on my shoulder, his eyes closed, and the look on his face is primal and needy and *oh my.*

"Ah!" I lean my head back against his chest, pushing my breasts into his hands.

"You made me crazy watching you in all those poses, baby. I don't know how I managed to control my hard-on."

I gasp and smile at him in the mirror.

He glides a hand down my side, tracing my tattoo, over my hip, across my buttock and finds my center.

"Fuck, baby, you're so ready for me." His lips are on my neck, nibbling, sending shivers down my spine.

Suddenly, he pulls back on my hips so I'm bent over, bracing my hands on the bar, and he smacks my ass hard before slamming his cock into me.

"Oh God!"

He grips my hair in one hand and my hip in the other and pushes into me, faster and faster, harder and harder, his stormy eyes on mine in the mirror.

Fuck, it feels so good! I push back on him and feel the orgasm rip through me, fast, hard, and I explode around him.

He thrusts twice more and shudders in his own release.

~

As we leave the yoga studio, I get a text from Jules.

*Birthday dinner at the folks' tomorrow night? Bring Luke.*

I frown. How do I bring this up?

"What's wrong?" He ushers me into his car and leans in to kiss me before getting behind the wheel.

"Nothing's wrong."

He raises an eyebrow at me, and I squirm.

"Talk to me, baby."

"Jules' parents have invited us over to their place for dinner tomorrow night."

"Oh? What's the occasion?" He starts the car and pulls out of the lot toward his house.

"My birthday," I whisper and bite my lip.

"What?" He glances over at me, his eyes wide, then back to the road ahead.

"Well, it's not really until Saturday, but they want to do a birthday dinner tomorrow night." I twist my fingers in my lap and gaze down. This is uncomfortable.

"Are you close to her family?"

"Yeah, they pretty much adopted me after my folks passed." This is much easier to talk about. "Her parents are great. She has four older brothers. The oldest, Isaac, and his wife just had a baby. I haven't met her yet."

"So it'll be a family thing."

Oh, what is he thinking? He doesn't look mad, but he doesn't look pleased.

"Yes. Will you go with me?"

"Of course. Sounds fun. But when were you going to tell me your birthday is this weekend?"

Oh.

I shrug and look out the window. "I hadn't really thought about it, honestly. I don't make a big deal out of it."

"Maybe I want to make a big deal out of it." His voice is deceptively soft.

"Don't be mad," I whisper. "It would make me feel stupid to say, 'So, let's go to yoga, and by the way, my birthday is Saturday.'"

"No, that would have been helpful." He pulls up to my house, dropping me off so I can work. He grabs Jules' dress and my shoes out of the back, and we go inside.

"So, I guess we're going to the dinner tomorrow night?"

"Yeah, we are." He hugs me tight.

"Thank you. Do you have much work today?" I ask, trying to distract him.

"Yeah, some. You?"

"I have two sessions, and I have to take Jules' dress to the cleaners."

He frowns deeply. "Jules' dress?"

Crap.

"Yeah, she lent it to me."

"Why?"

"Because I don't have any formal wear." I shrug. "It's no big deal."

"I don't want you to have to borrow clothes." He narrows his eyes and plants his hands on his hips.

"Luke, that's what girls do. We borrow each other's clothes. It's no big deal."

"I want to take you shopping for your birthday."

"No." I shake my head emphatically and walk toward the kitchen.

"Why ever not?"

"You do not need to buy me clothes. I can buy three-thousand-dollar shoes without batting an eye, Luke. I don't need you to clothe me."

"I didn't say you needed me to. I'm your boyfriend, for Christ sake. That's what we do. Let me spoil you."

"You do spoil me." I smile as I remember the flowers, the coffee, dinner last night. "You spoil me in all the ways that matter."

"Nat, I'm very wealthy. I can afford to spend money on you."

"Ditto." I cross my arms over my chest.

"You are so fucking stubborn!" He shakes his head and runs his hand through his hair, and I can't help but be amused.

"Are you smirking?" he asks.

"Kind of. You're funny when you're irritated with me."

He laughs and looks at the ceiling. "God, you're frustrating."

"I know. But I love you."

His eyes soften, and he pulls me into his arms. "I love you, too."

I lean up and kiss him sweetly on the lips, then the corner of his mouth.

"I'm serious, baby. Take my credit card, grab Jules and go shopping. Both of you, on me, for your birthday."

I open my mouth to argue, but Jules breezes into the kitchen. "Okay, don't have to tell me twice. Thanks." She winks at him and grins.

"Hey!" I say. "No way. I mean it."

"Jules, do you have plans tomorrow before dinner at your parents?" Luke is talking to her but looking at me, his jaw set.

I am so going to lose this argument.

"Nope. I happen to have a clear calendar." She smiles.

"Great. Will you please take my girlfriend shopping? And I think the spa is in order, too."

The spa, too? My jaw drops.

"It would be an honor and a pleasure, generous boyfriend-in-law." Jules laughs at her quip, and Luke joins her, and all I can do is look back and forth between them.

"I'm in the goddamn room, people!"

"I know, baby, I'm just planning a little something for your birthday." He flashes a wolfish smile and winks, and I don't know whether to smack him or really kiss him.

"I like your boyfriend, Nat." Jules smiles at me sweetly, and I know I'm sunk.

"Fine," I mutter.

"Your enthusiasm is inspiring." Luke's eyes are shining in humor.

"We'll go to the spa, but no shopping." I'm really hoping he'll accept the compromise, but I can see by the set of his jaw that there's no use in arguing.

"You will shop. Buy whatever you want. There's no limit on the card."

I shake my head at him. "Talk about stubborn."

He shrugs and kisses me hard, then pulls away abruptly, leaving me off balance.

"Will you come to my place when your sessions are over?"

"Yeah, I'll text you when I'm done." I sigh, resigned to my fate tomorrow. I know that Jules will make me follow Luke's instructions.

Traitor.

"Good. I'll see you later." He kisses me again and rests his forehead on mine. "I love you, beautiful."

And just like that my world is set right again, and in this moment I'd do just about anything he wanted.

"I love you, too, bossy man."

# CHAPTER 21

"Jules, I don't want to spend his money." I hear the whine in my voice, but I don't care.

"Sweetie, he wants to do something nice for you. It's your birthday."

We are wandering through Neiman Marcus in downtown Seattle. The crowds are light today given that it's the middle of the week. The perfectly coiffed saleswomen are very attentive and overeager to make a midweek commission.

"I feel like a gold digger."

Jules laughs as she pulls a blue blouse off a rack, then quickly dismisses it. "You are no gold digger. Here, try this." She hands me a black blouse, and we continue wandering.

We've already been to the spa this morning. We both had facials, massages, pedicures and manicures and had our bits and pieces freshly waxed. I have to say, it felt fantastic. "The spa was enough. It was generous and relaxing and perfect."

"Nat, stop fighting this. Luke is being incredibly generous and wants—*wants*—us to enjoy ourselves today. I agree that there's no need to go ape-shit crazy, but humor the man and get a few nice things. You'll probably need a few formal dresses if he continues to plan things like the other night, which, by the way, *holy shit*. Plus, you may have to go to a movie premiere or something sometime, and you have to look the part."

Holy shit is right.

I'd never considered that. Does he go to the premieres of the movies he works on now?

Hell.

Two hours, and a few thousand dollars later, we leave the store loaded down with bags and boxes. I can't believe she talked me into all of this. I'm happy that she also managed to snag a few things for herself. Luke would approve.

I have purchased three new evening dresses and the appropriate undergarments for them, a few blouses and jeans, two new pairs of shoes—Manolo Blahniks!—and a new Gucci handbag.

I might chicken out and return it all tomorrow.

Jules also scored a new pair of Louboutins and a handbag. She looks beautiful as we leave the store and head to the car. She's the happiest I've seen her since her tryst with her boss. Smiling, carefree and relaxed.

Three hours at the spa and two hours of spending someone else's money at Neiman's will do that to a girl.

We head back to our house to get ready for the party tonight. I'm really excited to see Jules' family and to meet her new niece, little Sophie.

Luke will be here in an hour.

"Are you going to wear that pretty new red top with the new jeans?" Jules pulls her new Louis Vuitton handbag out of its brown dustcover and makes quick work of moving all her things into it.

"Yeah, I think so. That's an awesome handbag." Aside from shoes, handbags are my weakness, and I can't help but ooh and aah over my pretty new Gucci bag.

"Have I mentioned that I like your boyfriend?" Jules smirks.

"He is an over-the-top guy, that's for sure."

"He really loves you, Nat. I can see it written all over him. He just wants you to be happy."

My heart goes a little gooey at her statement. She's right. And if spoiling me with some new things makes him happy, who am I to complain?

"Did you warn your family about him? I don't want them to go fan crazy on him today."

"Yeah, I did. They've had plenty of time to go fan crazy in private. You know they'll be cool. Besides, I have brothers. They don't care that he's sexy."

"Good point." We smile at each other and then head upstairs to primp for tonight.

～

"Hello, gorgeous." Luke pulls me in his arms and kisses me soundly.

"Hello, handsome." I smile up at him and usher him inside the house.

"Are you ladies ready?" He looks delicious in his black jeans and untucked white button-down shirt.

I run my fingers through his soft blond hair. "Yes."

"You look happy." He kisses my cheek and hugs me to him again. "And beautiful in this red blouse."

"It's new." I feel my cheeks flush.

"Yeah? I like it very much."

"Thank you, for everything." I kiss him, cupping his beautiful face in my hands.

"Did you have fun?"

"We had a great time. You spoiled us today. Thank you for including Jules."

"I'm fond of Jules."

"Oh?" I raise an eyebrow.

"She loves you, and she's your best friend."

Damn, he's just so sweet.

"Oh God, please don't be like this all night." Jules walks into the foyer and rolls her eyes.

"Hello to you, too." Luke laughs and kisses my forehead, then releases me.

"Thanks for today, Luke. We had a great time, and I am now the proud owner of this delightful handbag." Jules smiles sweetly.

"It suits you. You're welcome. Shall we go?"

I grab my camera bag and follow Luke out to the car. He raises an eyebrow, glancing at my bag. "Do you think I'm going to a family dinner with a brand new baby without my camera? I'm a girl, Luke."

He smirks and opens my door for me.

Luke and I follow Jules in a separate vehicle to her parents' house. They live in a new subdivision in North Seattle where most of the houses look alike. Well-kept lawns, small front porches with hanging baskets of colorful flowers and kids riding bicycles on the sidewalks. The house is average in size, with a large backyard.

No one, even the Montgomerys themselves, know that I'm the anonymous donor who paid their mortgage off earlier this year.

"This is a nice neighborhood," Luke comments, and I smile at him.

"It is. It suits Jules' parents. They're empty nesters, so the house is the perfect size for them. I'm glad it's a nice day today. We can all sit out in the backyard. Her dad has done a great job landscaping it. You'll love it."

We pull up to the house, and Jules' mom, Gail, comes running out to greet us.

"Oh, my girls are home! Hello, honey." She envelops me in her arms, and I feel tears prick my eyes. This woman is so special to me.

She pulls back and looks at me, her hands still gripping my shoulders. "You look lovely, dear. Happy birthday."

"Thank you, Gail. This is my boyfriend, Luke."

"Mrs. Montgomery." Luke offers his hand, but she also wraps him in a big hug.

"It's so nice to meet you, Luke. Please, call me Gail. Welcome."

His smile is wide and a little bit shy. "Thank you."

"Hi, Mom." Jules hugs her mom tightly.

"Everyone else is here. We're in the backyard. Your dad is grilling, and I'm praying he doesn't burn the house down."

Luke takes my hand, and we wander through the beautifully furnished home, past the state-of-the-art kitchen and out to the backyard. I smile at Luke's gasp.

"I told you," I murmur to him.

The back of the house faces a greenbelt, so there are no neighbors behind them. The yard is just under an acre. Beautiful shrubs and bushes border the tall privacy fence that encloses the yard. Stone paths lined with solar lights lead to different gardens. There is a riot of color from all the flowers, reds and yellows, purples, pinks. Some of the gardens have little benches next to them to sit and enjoy the day.

There are also large fruit trees for shade. Steven Montgomery spends endless hours on this garden, and it shows.

The patio is also large and covered. A huge stainless steel grill occupies the far left corner, smoke billowing out of it. Two round patio tables, with six chairs around each, sit in the middle of the patio, and to the far right is a seating area of two rocking love seats.

"I could spend all day out here," Luke murmurs, and I nod.

I glance at the tables and spot two familiar, but unexpected faces, and whirl around to Luke. "Your parents are here!"

He blushes a bit and shrugs. "Jules asked me if she could invite them, and I thought it would be a good idea. I want our families to get to know each other, Nat."

"Wow." I'm struck dumb. He never stops surprising me.

"Is it okay?"

Is it okay? I love him. His parents are lovely, and yes, I want them to know my family. Jules' family is the only family I have.

"It's great."

He smiles, relieved, and kisses my hand.

I lead Luke over to the tables and begin introducing him to Jules' large family, hugging Lucy and Neil.

"It's so good to see you, darling girl." Lucy holds me extra tight, and I return the embrace.

"Thank you for coming. I'm happy to see you both."

Jules' dad abandons the grill and jogs toward me. "Come here, birthday girl!" He sweeps me up in a big hug and twirls me around in a circle. "You're too thin. I'm going to fatten you up today."

I laugh and kiss his smooth cheek. He's a shorter man, but made of solid muscle like his sons, and balding on top, though he used to be blond like his daughter. He's one of the kindest men I've ever known. "I can't wait. I'm hungry."

"Good. Is this your man?" He turns to Luke and holds out a hand.

"Yes, this is Luke."

"Some kind of fancy movie star, aren't you?" Oh God. He's going to give Luke a hard time. A hush falls over the patio as everyone stops talking to listen to the exchange.

I blush scarlet and start to interrupt, but Luke puts his hand on my elbow and smiles down at me before shaking Steven's hand firmly.

"No, sir, I'm not fancy or a star. Thank you for including me and my family here today."

"Am I going to have to kill you for hurting her?" Steven keeps Luke's hand in his own, narrowing his eyes at him, and I just want to die. Now.

Holy fucking shit.

Luke laughs. "No, sir. Can I help you at the grill?"

"You know your way around a grill?" Steven smiles, and I exhale deeply.

"I do."

"Well, why didn't you say? We're cooking ribs and chicken." And just like that, Steven slaps Luke on the back and leads him over to the grill.

Jules' brothers wander over to introduce themselves to Luke and offer him a beer, and the chatter resumes.

Isaac's wife, Stacy, hugs me tight. "Happy birthday." She's a petite woman with red hair and laughing blue eyes.

"Thank you. You look fantastic! Where's the baby?" My eyes scan the patio until I find Sophie cradled in Jules' arms on one of the rocking love seats.

Stacy and I join her, and I hold my hands out. "Baby. Mine."

Jules laughs. "I just got her."

"I don't care. I've never held her. Hand her over, Montgomery."

Jules passes me little Sophie, and I just melt. She is tiny, less than two weeks old. Her dark hair is long and soft and a little wild in the way baby hair is, and Stacy has put a pretty pink headband on her. She's in a beautiful pink little dress with pink bloomers, and she's barefoot.

I run my hand down her cheek and press my lips to her forehead. She's sleeping, oblivious to the party going on around her.

"Oh, Stacy, I'm in love with her." I smile up at the new mother, and she preens.

"She's such a good baby."

"She's precious." I look down at her again and move her so she's resting on my chest, curled up under my chin. I rub her back and begin to rock and hum. There is just nothing like having a newborn on you.

"You're so sweet," I murmur down to her.

I look up to meet Luke's intense gaze. He's watching me, his look unreadable. What's he thinking?

I smile at him, and one corner of his mouth curls up, and his eyes soften.

I glance to my left and find Lucy's gaze also trained on me thoughtfully. A slow smile spreads across her face, and she winks at me.

Sophie makes a mewling sound, and I look down at her. I grab her pacifier and plug it into her mouth, and she sucks greedily as I run my fingertips down her soft hair.

"Natalie!"

"Huh?"

Jules is laughing. "I asked you if you brought your camera."

"Of course. I'm holding my newest model now. Maybe we can get some family shots after dinner?"

"Absolutely. Now give me back the baby."

"No."

"You're so selfish." Jules scowls at me, and Stacy laughs.

"Yes. Sophie and I are going for a walk." I stand with her and wander down one of the paths to a shady garden.

"Aren't the flowers pretty, Sophie?" I croon to the sleepy baby and rock her back and forth.

"You're good with her." Luke has joined us, and I smile lazily at him.

"I love babies. I never had siblings, so I'm living vicariously through Jules." I shrug and kiss Sophie's head.

He reaches out and runs the back of his finger down Sophie's cheek, and I feel my heart flip. His finger looks so big on her tiny little cheek.

"She's sweet," I murmur.

"You're sweet." He tucks a strand of my hair behind my ear and runs his thumb down my jaw before slipping his hand back in his pocket.

I gaze down at the sleeping baby, and for the first time in my life, I imagine that I might have this one day. A husband and a baby, and when I picture it in my head, it's this man before me by my side.

I've got it bad. Stop this. Get rid of the baby.

"Hey! Dinner's ready, and I want that baby back!" Jules is standing at the edge of the patio yelling toward us, and I smile at Luke.

"I'm gonna have to arm wrestle her later to get this baby back."

Luke laughs and escorts us to the patio for dinner.

~

THIS HAS BEEN the best birthday dinner of my life. The Montgomerys have seamlessly folded Luke's family into their own, engaging them in lively conversation and enjoying their company. Neil and Lucy seem relaxed and happy, laughing with Steven and Gail, sharing stories about when their children were young.

All of the brothers—Isaac, Will, Caleb and Matt—have teased Luke mercilessly about being a famous actor, asked questions about pretty actresses, and done a lot of talking about football since Will is currently playing with the Seahawks, and they're men.

What is it about boys and football?

Luke has laughed more than I've ever seen him, and I've fallen even more in love with him while watching him with my family. He's been attentive to me, refilling my drink, holding my hand and keeping tabs on where I am all evening. I suspect I would have felt smothered by anyone else, but he makes me feel loved.

Because he loves me.

Baby Sophie has been passed around all evening and is currently lying quietly in Lucy's arms. Lucy is cooing at her.

"Aren't grandkids the best?" Gail smiles softly at her beautiful granddaughter.

"We don't have any yet, but I can't wait." Lucy grins at Gail and then over at Luke, and he squirms in his seat.

I can't help but laugh out loud at him.

"Do you find me funny, baby?" Luke narrows his eyes at me, but I see the humor in them.

"Yes, that was funny."

"Okay, cake time!" Jules comes out of the house carrying a beautiful chocolate cake with twenty-six candles lit on it.

"You're going to burn the house down with that, Jules."

She smirks and sets it in front of me.

"Make a wish," Luke whispers in my ear.

I blow all the candles out in one breath.

Gail cuts the cake and passes it around. It smells heavenly. Gail makes the most delicious cakes.

"Thank you for making my favorite cake, Gail." I lean over and kiss her cheek.

"You're welcome, darling. I love you."

"I love you, too."

"Okay, now presents!" Jules hops up, and I frown.

"No presents. How many times do I have to tell you people? No presents!"

Everyone just laughs at me.

"We don't listen to you, brat." Isaac smirks at me, and I glare at him.

"I don't like you."

"You love me."

"You guys do too much for me already." I glance at Luke nervously. "It embarrasses me when you buy me stuff."

"It's not your birthday unless you have presents." Jules sets a red gift bag in front of me. "Open mine first." She's hopping in her seat in excitement, and my mood lifts.

She's bought me my favorite perfume and a beautiful silver bracelet. "Oh, thank you! I love it!"

"Can I borrow it?" Jules asks.

We all laugh, and I'm relaxed again, enjoying my family.

As usual, they've gone a bit overboard. The brothers all pitched in on a gift card.

"More shopping!" Jules and I exclaim in unison, and we break out into giggles.

Luke laughs next to me and kisses my temple, and I smile shyly at him.

Lucy and Neil give me a very generous gift card to use at the Microsoft Store in Bellevue. Wow.

"Thank you so much."

"Our pleasure, dear." Lucy smiles and kisses Sophie's sweet head.

"Ours next." Gail hands me a purple gift bag with purple paper.

"This party is more than enough!"

"You will not sass us." Steven shakes his finger at me and tries to look stern, but I've heard this before, and I giggle. "I will take you over my knee."

"Yes, sir." I open the bag to find a pair of earrings that I recognize, and I gasp, searching their faces.

They are both smiling tenderly at me.

"These are yours." I look back down at the beautiful diamond drop earrings and run my finger over them. They've been recently cleaned and sparkle in the soft evening light.

"We want you to have them." Gail has tears in her eyes, and I'm about to join her.

"They were your mother's. They should go to Jules." My voice is thick with tears.

"I have plenty of jewelry. They should be yours. Nana loved you." Jules is running her hand down my hair, and I just know that if I move I will cry. I'm so overwhelmed by the love this family has for me.

I shake my head but scoot my chair back and round the table to hug Gail and Steven tightly. Gail dabs at her eyes, and Steven cups my face in his hands and grins at me.

"We love you, baby girl."

"I love you, too. Thank you."

I take my seat and look up into Luke's beautiful face. He smiles and kisses my fingers.

"Last but not least." Luke sets a manila envelope before me.

"No, honey, you've done way too much already." I shake my head and scoot it back across the table toward him.

"Open it," he says, exasperated, and pushes it back toward me.

"Just open it already!" Will yells from across the table, and I glare at him. "I can't take the damn suspense!"

We all laugh, and I open the envelope. I pull out two passports and an itinerary. I read the itinerary and feel the blood leave my face and my jaw drop.

"We're going to Tahiti?!"

The table erupts with whoops and whistles and shouts of joy. The brothers applaud, giving Luke a standing ovation, and he laughs.

"Yes, tomorrow, for a week."

"But, we have work."

"My current project just wrapped, and I'm hoping you'll reschedule your appointments." He's gazing down at me with love shining from his blue eyes.

"Wow. Tahiti?"

He laughs and kisses me, square on the mouth, in front of my whole family.

"Get a room!" Matthew yells.

I clear my throat and look around the patio. "I just want to say," I begin and blink the tears from my eyes, "all the people I love the most in this world are here, and I can't tell you how thankful I am to have you. Thank you for all you've done for me, and not just these gifts, though they are wonderful. I am blessed. Even the boys have their good moments." I smile at them, and they salute me with their drinks and throw winks at me.

I take a deep breath. "Thank you for making me a part of your family. I love you very much."

I look up at Luke and around the patio into each face that is so dear to me.

"Now, give me that baby."

# CHAPTER 22

"*I* enjoyed them." Luke links his fingers with mine and kisses my knuckles as he drives us back toward Alki Beach.

"They enjoyed you, too. Thank you for coming, and inviting your parents. I had a great time." I can't hide my delighted smile.

"I'm glad. Are you excited about our trip?" His grin is wide.

"I have a lot to do tonight to get ready. Maybe I should stay home tonight so I can pack and make calls and stuff."

Luke frowns. "It won't take me long to pack. I can drop you off at home, go pack, and come back to your place." He swallows and glances at me.

"What's wrong?" Why does he suddenly look nervous?

"I don't want you to bail on me."

"Bail on you?"

"Yeah, decide you don't want to go."

Where is this vulnerability coming from? "I do want to go."

"Good." He smiles at me.

I find it doesn't take me long to pack either. A whole week in Tahiti entails a few bikinis, sarongs, pullovers and flip-flops. I also add one nice tank dress, in case we have dinner, and a pair of heels, some shorts and tank tops.

I'll throw my toiletries together in the morning before our nine a.m. flight.

I sit at the kitchen table and begin calling next week's clients to reschedule when I hear Luke come in through the front door.

"Baby?"

"In the kitchen!"

"Hey." He leans down and kisses me sweetly, and I sigh.

"Hi. Gonna make some calls. Make yourself at home."

"Okay." He saunters into the kitchen and grabs a bottle of water out of the fridge.

Half an hour later, all my calls are made, appointments rescheduled, and I'm officially on vacation.

Imagine that!

I have a huge, cat-ate-the-canary grin on my face as I crawl into Luke's lap where he sits on my couch. He's been reading a script.

"Well, hello, happy girl." He nuzzles my neck.

"Hi, obsessively generous boyfriend." He laughs and wraps his arms gently around me.

"I am looking forward to lying on a sandy beach with you, baby."

"Hmm…me, too. And snorkeling!"

"You snorkel?" He continues to nuzzle my neck and nips at my ear, and I squirm.

"Yeah, I have. It's been awhile."

"You smell so good. What else do you want to do?"

"Well, for one whole day…" I run my fingers through his hair and lean back so I can look at the pretty.

"Yes?"

"I want to stay naked and in bed with you."

"That's going to be my favorite day on this whole vacation." He runs his hand gently up and down my back, and I grin.

"Me, too. Are we staying in one of those huts that sits over the water?"

"Yes."

"Cool. We can skinny-dip."

He laughs delightedly. "Aren't you just the exhibitionist?"

"No, we'll do it at night." I lay my head on his shoulder and sigh deeply, suddenly tired but completely relaxed. "Can I bring my camera?"

"I assumed you would."

"I won't if it makes you uncomfortable." I made sure to be careful not to capture his photo tonight after dinner while I was taking photos of little Sophie and the rest of our families.

"I trust you completely. You can take my picture."

I sit upright in his lap, my jaw dropped and eyes wide. "I can?"

"Well, we're going to want pictures from our vacation, aren't we? Natalie, after everything that we've done, how can I not trust you to take my picture? We should have memories together."

I feel my smile grow, and I'm just so…happy. "I'm dying to take your picture, and before you freak out on me…"

"I'm not going to freak out on you," he says with a laugh.

"I want to take your photo because it's what I do, and you are so beautiful, Luke. There have been so many moments that I wish I could capture. I would never share any of our images with anyone unless I had your permission, but I want photos of you. I want photos of us together."

"I want photos of us, too."

I hug him tightly and then lay my head on his shoulder again.

"Are you sleepy?" he murmurs as he rhythmically runs his fingers through my hair.

"A little." I gaze up into his beautiful blue eyes. "Thank you."

"Baby, I told you, I enjoy spoiling you."

"No, not that." I shake my head and look down. "Although, yes, thank you for that, too. I just…"

"What?" He tilts my chin back up so he can see me.

"I love you."

His eyes flare, and he inhales deeply. "I love you, baby."

"Let's go to bed."

"My pleasure." He lifts me effortlessly in his arms and carries me upstairs.

~

"It's going to be a long flight." My voice is strong, but my stomach is in knots. Luke has hired a driver to take us to the airport, and we are in the back seat. I'm clutching on to his strong hand and worrying my lip with my teeth.

"We'll be fine." He pulls me over into his lap and nuzzles my neck. I recognize the distraction tactic, but it doesn't help.

"Do we have a layover in LA?" I ask.

"No."

"Oh." I frown and catch my breath when his lips graze the sensitive spot below my ear. "I didn't know there were direct flights from Seattle to Tahiti."

"I don't know if there are. A friend of mine is lending us his jet."

"Oh." Holy shit.

"Nat, have you flown since your parents passed?" He tilts my chin and looks into my eyes, and he looks nervous and worried about me.

I cup his cheek in my hand. "No."

"Baby, are you okay with this?" He kisses my palm.

"I'll be fine. It's like ripping off a Band-Aid. I just have to do it."

"If it makes you feel better, I plan to keep you fully occupied for most of the flight. You won't have time to be scared." He grins mischievously at me, and I giggle.

"Promises, promises…"

Before long, we arrive at SeaTac. The driver pulls onto the tarmac next to a large private jet. This is much bigger than anything my dad ever flew.

The driver opens our door and then begins transferring our luggage to the beautiful aircraft. Luke speaks with the pilot and co-pilot and the pretty flight attendant, but my ears are buzzing with too much nervousness to hear, or care, what they're saying.

The inside of the cabin is beautiful. It must seat twelve. The seats are large and plush black leather. Luke leads me to two that are side-by-side, and we sit.

"How are you?"

"How do I look?" I whisper.

"Pale and glassy-eyed."

"So, terrified then."

"Yes."

"That's accurate."

Luke buckles my seat belt for me—Geez!—and wraps an arm around me. "I've got you, baby."

"I know. I'll be fine in a little while."

His beautiful blue eyes are heavy with worry, and I pull his head down so I can kiss him. He sweeps his lips across mine in that way he has that makes me quiver inside and runs his fingers through my hair.

"You look beautiful today."

I'm just in blue jeans and a green tank top. I take in his black T-shirt and khaki shorts and grin. "Back at you, handsome."

The pilot's voice comes over the speakers announcing that we're ready for takeoff, what our altitude will be, and how long the flight will be. Thankfully, it should be a fairly smooth flight.

I hear the engines roar to life, and I pull out of Luke's arms so I can clutch his hand. Within seconds, we are racing down the runway and lifting off the ground.

I think I'm going to pass out.

"Breathe, baby."

I pull in a deep breath and let it out.

"Again. Stay with me, baby, just breathe."

God, I love him even more at this moment. His voice is calming me, and as we gain altitude and even out, I begin to calm.

"I'm okay," I whisper.

"Can I get you something?" The tall, leggy, blond flight attendant is at our side. I didn't notice how attractive she was before. "I can fix you some breakfast, if you like."

I shake my head adamantly. "Just water, please."

"Water for both of us, please."

We sip on the cool water, Luke's eyes still trained on my face, and I flush just a bit.

"So, whose plane is this?" I ask.

"Spielberg's." He grins at me.

Holy fuck.

"As in Steven?" I ask.

"The same. He directed the film that just wrapped that I helped produce. We've worked together a few times. I called in a favor." He shrugs.

"I am so out of my league with you." I shake my head.

"What the fuck does that mean?"

My head snaps around at his angry outburst, and my jaw drops at the glare he's sending me.

"I'm sorry..." I frown and gaze around the cabin of the plane. This is beyond rich. I know rich. This is *Forbes* 100 list, I-could-buy-a-Third-World-country rich.

"This isn't mine. I borrowed it. I thought you'd like it."

"I do. All of this is wonderful. You are wonderful. You just overwhelm me sometimes, Luke."

"Yeah, well, that seems to be contagious then, because you have completely beguiled me."

I'm feeling vulnerable and scared and excited and in love, and I just need to be in his arms. So I unbuckle my belt and fling one leg over his lap and straddle him. His eyebrows rise in surprise, and he grabs my curvy ass in his hands. I love that he's tall enough that even in this position we're practically at eye level. I grip his smooth face in my hands and lean in and kiss him like my life depends on it.

I feel his hands run up and down my back, and I grind my center against him.

"Fuck, baby, you make me crazy."

"Hmm..." I nibble at the corner of his mouth and open my eyes to find his blue gaze on me. "I want you. Make me forget where we are."

He takes control of the kiss, gripping my hair in his hands and holding my face to his, kissing me like he hasn't touched me in days.

As if we didn't make love just this morning.

He reaches between us and unbuckles his seat belt and lifts me easily, his hands planted firmly on my ass to hold me. I wrap my legs around his lean waist and tangle his hair in my hands, leaning my arms on his shoulders.

"Where are we going?" I murmur.

"Bedroom." Bedroom? On a plane?

"What's wrong with the chair we were in?" I lean down and bite his earlobe.

"I'm not giving the flight attendant a fucking show."

"Oh." I forgot. This is what he does to me. He makes me forget. And it's so hot!

He carries me to the rear of the plane and through a door into a small room with a double bed. It has beautiful, inviting linens and pillows in shades of browns and greens.

"Airplane sex!" I straighten in his arms and hold his face in my hands. "I've never had airplane sex."

He grins wide and kisses my chin. "Me neither."

I run my fingers lightly through his soft blond hair and gaze into his sky-blue eyes and can't help but wonder what I did to deserve this beautiful man.

"You are so beautiful." He frowns at my change of pace and just stands there in the middle of the room with me draped around him, not putting me down.

He shakes his head and plants a kiss on my collarbone. "I'm nothing special."

"Oh, honey." I wrap myself around him and hold on tight. "You are beautiful, inside and out," I whisper in his ear.

"Naked, now," he growls and sets me down.

I can't help but laugh, as suddenly we are just a tangle of clothes being flung off and flown about the room, both of us eager to get naked and touch each other.

When the last piece of clothing is shed, Luke grabs for me, pulling me to him in a passionate embrace, but instead of pushing us down onto the bed, he's cornered me against the wall, leaning his heavy torso and hips against me, his rigid erection pushing against my belly.

He slides his hands down my arms, links his fingers in mine and pulls our hands up above my head, pinning me in place. His gloriously soft mouth is on my neck, sweeping up and down. He captures both of my wrists in one hand and glides the other down my arm and to my breast to worry my nipple between his fingers.

"Fuck, Luke."

"God, you're so beautiful. I love how your breast feels in my hand."

I bow my body off the wall, my hands still pinned above me, in need.

"Hush, baby." His hand leisurely travels down to my hip and around to my ass where he rubs it softly, then slaps it. Hard.

"Ah!" I feel his grin in my neck, and I bite my lip. How does his slapping my ass turn me on so much? It's fucking sexy as hell.

"Again," I whisper.

"Oh, baby." He kisses my chin and the corners of my mouth, nibbling along my jaw. "You want it rough?"

"Only with you." And it's the truth. Only he can touch me the way he does and make my skin sing the way it does. It's intoxicating.

"Damn right." He slaps me again and hitches my leg up around his thigh, but he's too tall to rub his cock against my center.

"Lift me," I beg.

"Oh, I will. Patience, beautiful." That glorious hand of his slips behind me again, over my now warm ass, and down between my folds. He slips a finger inside me and moves it in a circular motion, sending me spiraling in sensation.

"Luke! Please!" I'm pulling my wrists against his hand to no avail. I want to touch him! I want him inside me!

"What do you want, baby?" He croons to me as he assaults my pussy in the most delicious way.

"You. Please." I whisper this against his neck.

"You'll have me. Be patient, my love. I'm making you forget, remember?"

"I don't remember my own fucking name right now."

He laughs and kisses me sweetly. "I'm going to let go of your hands now. Put them on your head."

"What?" He's not making any sense.

"Just put them on your head."

"I want to touch you." I pout, and he bites my lower lip.

"Not yet. Trust me."

He releases my hands, and I lower them to my head, weaving my fingers together and leaning my head back on the wall.

"Good. Don't move your hands, baby."

"Okay," I whisper.

He continues to kiss my face and neck, gently bites my earlobe and then heads south.

And I know exactly what he's going to do.

"Fuck." I look down at him as he kisses his way down to my breasts, pulling the nipples into his mouth. My breathing is ragged and blood is rushing though my body on hyperdrive.

I've never been so turned on in my life.

"Easy, baby. I've got you."

As he kneels on the floor, he hitches my right leg around his shoulder and wraps his arms around me, supporting me on his forearms and gripping my ass in his large hands.

"I'm going to fall."

"I won't let you fall." He kisses my belly piercing and then places three sweet kisses on my tattoo.

Without thinking, I lower a hand and run my fingers through his hair, but he jerks his head away and glares at me.

"On. Your. Head."

Oh.

"I want to touch you."

"Later. Come on, baby, play along."

"Okay." My hand goes back on my head, and without hesitation, his lips wrap around my clitoris, and he sucks.

Holy fucking shit!

"Fuck!" My hips push against his mouth, and he pulls back slightly to move down to my lips where he kisses me intimately, running his tongue up and down and around me, teasing me. He nibbles gently and then buries his tongue inside me while inhaling my scent.

I can't take my eyes off of him. Seeing his mouth on me is the most erotic thing I've ever witnessed.

His hands are kneading my ass. His right hand, still supporting my weight, slides closer to my center. He dips his littlest finger in my wet core and flexes it and pulls it out, and as his mouth resumes its delicious torture, he slips that little finger right...there.

His molten blue eyes are looking up at my face. I'm so overwhelmed with sensation it's weakening. That finger is moving slowly in and out, and the feeling is unimaginable. It makes me feel just a little dirty and wanton and oh so hot.

His presses his nose on my clitoris, and it's all over. He's pushing all my buttons—literally—and I fall apart, shuddering and pulsating, coming over and over. It just doesn't seem like it'll ever stop.

He pulls his pinkie out of me and kisses up my pubis, my belly, over my breasts and, finally, my lips. He's pinned me against the wall again with his body, because without him, I would collapse onto the floor.

"Please," I mewl, not recognizing my own voice.

"Anything, baby."

"Fuck me."

His gaze finds mine, and it darkens. "I just did," he murmurs against my mouth, brushing his lips back and forth. He grips my hands in his again and holds them over my head.

"Fuck me on that bed." I kiss him. "Please."

He holds me against his chest and twirls us across the short floor to the bed. He tears the duvet away from the sheets and guides me down onto it.

"On your stomach, baby."

I roll over flat on my stomach, and he's suddenly covering me, his hard cock pressing against my buttocks, his chest hair tickling my back. He kisses the very center of my neck and follows my spine down, paying extra attention to the tattoo in the center of my back.

"Why does it say Love Deeply?" he asks.

"What?"

"Why this tattoo?"

I have to blink and pull some brain cells back together to answer his question.

"Because that's what I always wanted, to love and be loved deeply."

He nuzzles the tattoo with his nose. "You are, Nat."

"I know."

I feel his smile as he resumes his journey down my back. He kisses my butt, one cheek at a time, and then sweeps his lips across the tattoo on my right thigh, under my buttock.

"And this one? Why does it say Happiness Is A Journey?"

"Because it was a long journey to travel for me to be happy again."

"Oh, baby." He parts my legs with his own and runs a finger from my anus down to my clitoris, making me angle my behind off the bed and into the air.

"Ah, Luke."

He grips my hips and slides into me, burying himself inside me as far as he can.

It's glorious. I feel full and happy and sexy and so loved.

He slaps the cheek that was ignored when he had me pinned against the wall and starts to move in and out of me, slamming into me hard, over and over.

I grip the sheets in my fists and cry out as I feel the familiar pull of the muscles around his cock and my legs clench. He grips my hips, almost painfully, as he slams into me once more and comes violently, erupting inside me.

# CHAPTER 23

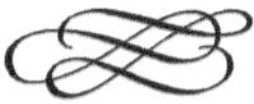

*I*'m standing on the deck of our gloriously beautiful hut, pointing my camera down at the water, snapping photos of the brightly colored fish. I take about a dozen photos, then look up and snap some shots of the island. It's almost sunset, and I can't wait to get some photos of the palm tree silhouettes in the sunset light.

"Hey, baby." Luke wraps his arms around me from behind and buries his nose in my neck. "How are you?"

"I think I'm going to be a little sore tomorrow, but I'm good. I forgot how exhausting snorkeling is." I smile and turn to face him.

He simply takes my breath away.

He's shirtless, wearing only black shorts that hang off his hips in that sexy way, showing off the muscles that form that V that runs down and disappears in the fabric. He's caught some sun while we've been here, turning his skin golden. My mouth goes dry every time I look at him.

And because I can, I raise my lens and snap his photo. He smiles shyly, and I take another.

"I love taking your picture."

"I've noticed. You've had that thing pointed at me more than anything else in the three days we've been here."

"That's not true." I laugh, and he takes the camera out of my hands, and suddenly I become the subject. "Hey! I'm on the wrong side of that lens."

"Turnabout is fair play, baby. Give me that sweet smile."

I lean back on the railing and pose for him playfully, cocking one hip to the side and planting my hand on my sarong-covered curve.

"We have to come here often," he murmurs as he continues to snap photos of me.

"Why?"

"Because I love watching you walk around all day in a bikini. I get to see your tattoos."

I smile and turn away from him. My left side is exposed to him, and I raise my left arm up next to my face, looking back at him through the crook of my elbow. "Take a photo of this tat, and you can look at it any time you want."

"God, you're good at this." He snaps away, his eyes shining with humor and lust, and I smile at him.

"Okay, hold on." I take off the sarong and let it fall to the floor of the deck and watch his eyes dilate. I love how he enjoys my body. My earlier insecurities have long vanished. I turn my back to him and pull my hair over my shoulder. My hands are out to my sides, resting on the railing. I know that from this view, he can see the tattoos on my back and my upper thigh. "There you go."

I hear my camera snapping to life, and Luke's breathing has changed.

"Finished with those?" I ask.

"Yes," he whispers.

I turn back to face him and jump up on the rail, sitting.

"Careful!"

"I'm fine. I won't fall in." I scoot so I'm sitting at an angle and pull my right foot up to rest on the railing. My tattoo is exposed. "Snap away."

He zooms in on my foot and presses the shutter about ten times.

"I hate to disappoint you," I mutter drily, "but the last tattoo will have to just remain our little secret."

His eyes darken as he steps back and takes more photos of me.

"So no one else has seen these tattoos?" he asks, the camera still up at his face.

"Most of them."

"What does that mean?" He lowers the camera and glares at me.

Crap.

"The one on my pubis is the newest one, and no one but you and the artist have seen it. The one on my back can sometimes be seen when I'm wearing a certain style of top or dress, but no one's ever asked me what it means. In fact, no one but you knows what any of them mean."

"And your side and leg?" he asks.

I shrug. "I wasn't a virgin when I met you."

He frowns and looks down, and I'm desperate to lift this mood.

"Hey." I hop off the rail and close the gap between us. "The past is over, Luke. For both of us."

"I know." He swallows and looks at me with those blue eyes. "It just makes me a little crazy that other men have touched you."

"Honey"—I smile and run my fingers down his face—"your touch is the only one that's ever mattered. You've introduced me to feelings I didn't know existed. Don't worry about before. You are all I see. Besides"—I take the camera back from him and put the lens cap back on—"you, my love, were certainly no virgin, either."

"How do you know? Maybe I was." He chuckles.

"There is no way that you can be as good as you are in bed and be a virgin."

"Oh? How good am I?" He winks at me and pulls me into his arms, running his hands down my mostly naked back.

"Hmm…you're fair."

He laughs as he bends down and places feather-soft kisses at the side of my mouth. "Fair, huh?"

"Yeah, I endure it. For your sake."

"You just endure it?" He continues to move those skilled, soft lips across my jaw and over to my ear.

"It's a real hardship, but somehow I find the willpower."

He chuckles and cups my face gently in his hands, sweeping his lips over mine, back and forth lightly, then sinks down into me and kisses me deeply but still softly. Lovingly. Like we have all day. I hold on to his hips, lacing my middle fingers through the belt loops, half of my hands on the fabric and half on his bare skin.

God, my man can kiss.

He pulls back and, still holding my face, gazes into my eyes.

"Wow," I murmur, and his face lights up with humor.

"Did you endure that okay?"

"You are really good at that."

"So are you. Did you bring a dress?"

I blink at the change of subject. "Yeah, why?"

"I have something planned for dinner."

"Oh. I was going to take sunset pictures."

"You still can. Bring the camera along."

"Okay. When are we leaving?"

"In a half hour."

"Where are we going?" I ask.

"It's a surprise, birthday girl." He smiles and runs his thumb across my lower lip.

"My birthday is over."

"This is your birthday vacation, so you're still the birthday girl." He kisses me chastely, then links my hand with his and leads me inside.

Our hut, although hut is really the wrong word for it, is absolutely breathtaking. It's really a bungalow over the water. No little hotel hut would be sufficient for my man.

Our space is large, sporting two bedrooms, a large common area and two bathrooms. The bigger of the two bathrooms has a two-person tub that sits right out in the open on a deck, with open views of the ocean. In fact, most of the rooms are open to the outside air with beautiful floaty curtains to pull for a little privacy. The floors are dark wood, but there are glass openings in most of the rooms so you can look down at the fish below.

The furnishings are plush, expensive and inviting. The master bed is large with soft white sheets, duvet and pillows. The common area has plenty of color: oranges, yellows and reds. It's truly beautiful.

"Have you been here before?" I ask as I pull out my dress and heels.

"No, first time. You won't need the heels."

"Oh, okay. Flip-flops?"

"Yeah."

"Are we going somewhere in the sand?"

He smiles and winks.

Okay, not gonna tell me. "Are you going to change?"

He pulls on a white short-sleeved button-down shirt and leaves it unbuttoned. "There, all changed."

I laugh and reach behind me to pull the strings on my bikini, letting it fall in my hands. Looking down, I do the same to the bottoms. I walk naked to the dresser and reach in for a thong.

"No underwear."

I turn and gape at him. His eyes are smoldering.

"But…"

"No. Underwear."

Geez. He's so bossy. And I like it. Weird.

"Okay." I pull the black tank dress over my head and smooth it in place and slip my feet in my black flip-flops. I run my brush through my hair vigorously, then tie it in a simple braid down the left side so it rests over my left breast. I brush on a light coat of mascara and turn to find Luke watching me, his expression unreadable.

"I'm ready."

He shakes his head as if pulling his thoughts together and smiles at me tenderly. "Let's go."

~

"So what has been your favorite part of our trip so far?" I ask Luke as I take a bite of my steak.

He's surprised me with dinner, in the water on a private tiny island. The resort boated us over, where the small table was already set with our meals and drinks, the table and chairs sitting in the shallow, perfectly clear water on pure white sand.

This almost rivals the vineyard on the romance scale.

"Snorkeling today was fun." He takes a sip of wine and shrugs. "My favorite part is being here with you."

I shake my head and smile. "Charming."

He laughs and continues with his meal. "How about you? Favorite part?"

"I also enjoyed the snorkeling today. The manta rays were incredible. But I really enjoyed exploring the town yesterday, too. Thank you again for the anklet."

"It's beautiful on you."

"What are we doing tomorrow?" I ask. I'm moving my feet around in the water, back and forth. It feels good between my toes.

"I seem to remember you saying something about spending a whole day in bed."

"Oh." My eyes go wide.

"Tomorrow is the halfway mark of the trip. Seems like a good time." He raises an eyebrow at me, and I grin.

"Skinny-dipping! We can scare the fish."

"And our neighbors." He smirks.

"Nah, the back of our room is secluded. I already checked."

He looks up at me, startled, and then breaks out into laughter. I smile smugly back at him and drink my wine.

"This is beautiful." I look out over the water and sigh. The sun is starting to set, and we've finished our meal. "Do you mind if I snap some pictures?"

"Go ahead, baby." He pours himself another glass of wine and sits back to watch me. I sling my camera strap around my neck—I wouldn't want to drop it in the water—and stand up, wading through the shallow water. It's warm around my ankles, the sand is soft, and the light is perfect.

I take about a hundred shots, of the water, the trees and of the tiny island itself. It's something out of a tropical island calendar. Then I turn the lens to my relaxed boyfriend and take a few shots without him seeing me. He's looking down at his wine, his expression thoughtful. He glances up at me and gives me that sexy half smile, and he's perfection. Open white shirt, black shorts, blond hair and golden skin, sitting casually at a romantic table set for two with a single red rose in a vase.

The sight is devastating.

Suddenly, he stands and walks toward me through the water and takes the camera from me. He wraps his arm around me and pulls me to his side, turning the lens toward us and snaps a picture of the two of us together.

For the past three days when we were out, if I had my camera with me, he would ask someone to take a photo of the two of us together.

Yes, we are capturing lots of memories, and it makes me smile.

He places the strap back around my neck and kisses my forehead.

"Thank you for dinner," I say. "It was delicious, and romantic."

"My pleasure."

"When are we being picked up?" I run my hands up and down his chest, under his open shirt.

"In about twenty minutes."

"Okay, let's go for a walk around the island. It's small. It should only take about ten minutes."

"Let's go." He links his fingers through mine, and we set off, wading through the ankle-deep water.

When we make it back to the table, our ride to the hut is pulling up. We board the small boat and set off across the darkening water.

~

I WAKE to the sun across my face and no covers over my naked body. Luke's face is between my legs.

"Holy shit!" I come up off the bed, bracing myself on my elbows, and gaze in pure shock at Luke tilting my hips up so he can bury his face in my pussy, licking and teasing my clit.

"Good morning, baby," he whispers against my core and blows on that most sensitive spot.

"Oh my God," is all I can say as I collapse back down on the bed. I feel his grin, and he slips two fingers inside me, making a *come here* motion and light erupts through me.

Holy fuck.

I bear down and come violently as he continues to suck on my clit and rock those fingers around inside me, my muscles shuddering around him. Finally, he kisses my tattoo gently and works his magic all the way up my torso until he's lying next to me, brushing my hair off my face.

"Good morning," I murmur. "Not a bad way to wake up."

"I'm glad you approve." He kisses me, and I taste myself on him, and it ignites my libido all over again. Surprising him, I grip his shoulders and push him back on the bed, lying on top of him and resting my pulsating sex on his hard cock. Playing his game, I link my fingers in his and push our hands up to the sides of his head and hold him down.

"What are you going to do with me?" He grins, his eyes shining with desire. I roll my hips on him, and he exhales sharply.

"Well"—I bend down and bite his neck softly, then lave it with my tongue—"after that fantastic wake-up call, I think I'll fuck you."

"Is that right?" He pushes against my hands, but I hold him down with all my might. We both know he could easily break my hold, but he plays along. "I'm not stopping you, baby."

I lean forward until I feel the tip of his cock against my lips and then I sink down on him until he's completely buried in me.

"Fuck," he whispers between clenched teeth.

"You feel so good."

I start to rock, slow and shallow, back and forth, taunting and teasing him. With each downward motion, I clench my muscles around him, then let go as I rock back up. I gently sweep my lips across his and tease the tip of his nose with mine.

Just when I think he's ready to come, I stop and loosen my muscles.

"Oh, you are such a tease. I should spank you."

"I have your hands," I reply and start to rock again.

"So you do." His eyes close, and he bites his lip as I increase the tempo, and the pleasure is just too much. I let go of his hands and sit up, riding him fast and hard.

"Grab on to the bed frame." I love being the boss, and his eyes dilate even more. He complies.

Suddenly, I roll off him and grip him in my hand, and take him deep into my mouth, sucking hard.

"Holy fuck!" He grasps my head, but I pull out of his grasp and glare at him.

"On. The. Bed. Frame."

He smiles and complies, and I resume the sweet torture, licking my sweetness off him, moving my hands up and down the hardness, and he erupts in my mouth.

As he calms, I kiss my way up his body, reveling in his sculpted stomach, teasing his belly button with my teeth. I run my fingertips up his sides, and he squirms and laughs. I kiss his neck, his chin and finally place a chaste kiss on his mouth.

"Turnabout is fair play," I whisper his words from yesterday back to him, and he groans.

"Jesus, Nat, you're going to kill me."

"Ah, but what a way to go."

He laughs and kisses me tenderly, then abruptly stands up and pulls me with him, throwing me over his naked shoulder.

"I have the best view of your ass right now, my love." I give it a little slap, and he returns the favor on my ass. "Where are we going?"

"Skinny-dipping!" He jogs—*jogs!*—with me over his shoulder out to the deck and down the steps that lead to the water, and just tosses me right in.

I hit the warm surface with a loud splash and come up sputtering. It's not too deep, only about six feet, and as I push the wet hair off my face, I see Luke dive in headfirst. He gracefully swims to me, and I can't help but admire the way his back muscles move.

"Hi." I smile shyly when he surfaces before me and wrap my arms and legs around him.

"Hi." He grins and plants his hands on my waist, then throws me through the air to land back in the water.

Oh, we're going to play! Naked!

I squeal when I surface and splash him, and he splashes me back with a laugh.

He swims for me again, and I try to quickly escape, but he catches me and tosses me again.

"Are you trying to drown me?"

"Maybe I want to do some mouth-to-mouth."

"You don't have to kill me to do that! I'm a sure bet." I giggle and splash him again, enjoying the way his naked body looks in the clear water, reflecting in his perfectly blue eyes.

"God, you look beautiful right now," he says.

"I was just thinking the same thing." I swim to him and wrap myself around him again.

"I enjoy playing with you," he says and kisses my nose.

"Me, too. In and out of bed." I smile sassily, and he bites his lip.

"I have to say, this morning was a first for me."

"A good first, or a bad first?" I run my fingers through his wet hair, loving the way our naked bodies feel twined together in the warm Pacific.

"Definitely good, although I have to admit I prefer being in control."

"Well, variety is the spice of life. I like to surprise you every once in a while." I kiss his chin, and he chuckles.

"No complaints here, baby."

"Hmm…good."

He lifts my hips and surprises me by slipping inside me.

I lean my forehead against his as he stills, filling me. "I love you," I say.

"Oh, baby, I love you, too. Let's frighten the fish."

<h1 style="text-align:center">CHAPTER 24</h1>

*I*t's our last morning in our tropical paradise, and I purposely wake extra early to make sure I'm up before Luke. He's done so much for me this week—hell, this month—and I just have to do something special for him before we go back home to reality. Not that reality is all that bad. It's just been bliss to have him all to myself this week.

After our Naked Day, as it will forever be known in my head, Luke surprised me with a shark-feeding trip, which before this vacation I would have assumed would include me as the menu but turned out to be one of the most exhilarating experiences of my life. I'll never forget standing in waist-deep warm water with dozens of docile sharks floating around us to take the food from our hands.

Yesterday was spent getting romantic spa treatments for two. I've been to the spa more in the past two weeks than I have in the past two years.

I'm not complaining.

But today is our last day. I poke my head back in the bedroom to make sure he's still sleeping and then go wait on the steps leading to the water below the bungalow for our breakfast to be delivered by canoe. I set the food and coffee on a tray and go into the bedroom.

After placing the delicious-smelling foods on the ottoman at the end of the bed, I climb up Luke's body and kiss his lips.

"Luke, honey, wake up." I nibble his lips and kiss over to his neck as he shifts beneath me.

"Mornin'," he mumbles.

"Good morning, love. Wake up. I have something for you."

He runs his hand down my back and frowns. "Hard to make love when you're dressed, baby."

I laugh as he opens those sexy blue eyes. "That's not what I have for you." I get up off him and walk to the end of the bed as he sits up, the sheet pooling in his lap, and runs his hands over his face and through his hair. His morning stubble is impossibly sexy.

"Breakfast!" I set the tray on the bed between us and pull the silver dome lid off the plate. There are large helpings of pancakes, bacon, eggs and fruit. On the side is a carafe of coffee and two mugs.

"Did you order this?" he asks.

"Yeah, I thought I'd feed you for once."

He smiles and cups my face in his hand. "Thank you, baby."

"You're welcome. I hope you're hungry." I hold a strawberry up to his mouth, and he takes a bite, then I pop the rest in my own mouth.

"Starving," he says, his lust-filled eyes on mine.

"Later," I whisper.

"You're no fun." He pouts as he pours himself some coffee, and I laugh.

"That's not what you said last night." Thoughts of making love in the bathtub that sits out on the patio flood my mind, and I bite my lip.

"No, no complaints last night."

"What time are we leaving?" I ask.

"Not until this evening. Why?"

"Do we have any special plans today?" I eat a bite of pancake and groan. "God, that's good."

"Damn, I love to watch you eat, baby. No, I thought we'd wing it today. Did you have something in mind?"

I shrug and take another bite of pancake.

"What is it?"

"Nothing. We can do whatever you want." I avoid his gaze, suddenly shy. I don't want to go anywhere today. I just want to be with him, and I don't know why I'm suddenly so shy about speaking up and telling him so. It's silly.

"Natalie." His voice is stern, and I catch his gaze. "What's wrong?"

"Nothing's wrong. I was just thinking…" I put my fork down and bite my lip. "I just want to stay here, until we have to go to the airport. I want to be alone, for as long as we can, here in our tropical bubble." The last few words are a whisper, and I glance up at him to see his reaction.

He's smiling sweetly. "Why does that make you shy?"

I shrug again and look down. "I don't know. I thought you might want to go have some grand adventure before we leave, but I just want you."

"Baby, look at me." I do as he asks without hesitating and am so relieved to see his beautiful smile. "Spending the day alone with you in this beautiful tropical paradise sounds perfect to me."

"Okay." I smile at him, relieved, and continue to dig into my pancakes.

We finish our breakfast, and while Luke is in the shower, room-service-in-a-canoe comes to take away the dirty dishes and linens. The man is quite large and is talkative while he gathers the things into a box to put on the canoe.

"Your husband is a very lucky man." He smiles at me, and I smile, but inside something doesn't feel right.

What an inappropriate thing to say. I don't correct his misunderstanding about my marital status and simply say, "Thank you."

"How long have you been married?"

"Um, not long." Why is this creeping me out? I learned long ago to trust my instincts, so I cross the room so I'm standing behind a large couch, near the bathroom door.

"Oh, that's nice." He wanders over to the couch and picks at some pretend lint on the arm of the orange fabric. My heart speeds up as fear takes hold. He's trying to move closer to me, and now his eyes are predatory. "I've noticed you this week. You're very beautiful."

"I think you'd better go now." I move around the other side of the couch away from him, but he's following me, and my heart is in my throat.

"Why?"

"Because I don't want you here. My husband will be out any minute, and I'm not interested. Get the fuck out or I'll have you fired."

"You can't do that. My uncle owns this resort." He laughs and starts to come at me faster.

"Luke!" I scream, but before the word is out of my mouth, the large man is thrown from behind and slammed into a wall. Luke, his breath heaving and his face contorted in rage, is gripping on to his throat. He punches him in the face, twice, and blood spurts out of the man's nose, and he screams like a girl.

I'm quite sure no one has dared lay a hand on him before.

"I'm going to make sure you don't ever try to touch another woman at this resort again, you fucker." Luke's voice is cold and calm, his eyes glacial, and this is a very angry side to him I've never seen before.

"Are you okay, baby?" He doesn't look at me as he speaks, doesn't take his eyes off of him.

"I'm fine." My voice is stronger than I feel, and I'm glad.

"Call the main desk and tell them to call the cops. Tell them what happened."

I do as he asks and within minutes a motorboat pulls up at our bungalow with management and police, and a man who must be the asshole's uncle.

The police take control of the situation and relieve Luke of his charge. Luke then races to me and enfolds me in his arms. I must be too shocked to do more than stare wide-eyed at what's happening around us.

"Are you okay?" His hands are running up and down my back, soothing me.

"Yes, I'm okay. He didn't touch me. He was just really creepy, and I know he would have if you weren't here. He felt off the minute he came in here, so I moved behind the couch close to the bathroom in case he tried anything, and he did." I shiver, and Luke pulls me tighter to him.

The uncle is yelling for the police to arrest him. It seems this isn't the first time this has happened. The Asshole is crying and blubbering, but no one cares.

As I watch what's happening around me, the fear is replaced with pure rage. I pull out of Luke's arms and walk over to The Asshole being handcuffed by the police. He's crying down at me, weak and afraid, and before I know what I'm doing, I jerk my knee up, right between his legs and bring him to his knees.

My chest is heaving, and there is sudden silence all around us.

"I am not a victim." My voice is hard and controlled and loud because I want him to hear every word. "And you are nothing but a piece of shit."

"Did you see what she did to me? I want to press charges!" The whiny Asshole is wailing, but his uncle raises his hand, silencing him.

"I didn't see anything that you didn't deserve. Get him out of this bungalow."

He's escorted out, and the owner apologizes profusely, offering comps and refunds and anything else I can possibly imagine. I'm sure he's praying we won't go to the press, which we won't anyway.

Luke wouldn't have it.

I turn and look at Luke, whose eyes are hooded, his face hard. He tells the manager that we will still be leaving today.

"We will press charges, but I don't want this to go to the press, either," Luke murmurs, and my heart stops.

Oh my God. This could make things really bad for him if it hits the tabloids. I suddenly feel so guilty. I leave Luke to handle the rest of the business alone and go into the master bedroom to start packing.

Luke comes in the room as I'm finishing with the underwear drawer. He walks straight to me and pulls me into his strong arms, rocking me back and forth, kissing my forehead. "Are you really okay?"

"I'm so sorry."

"For what?" He pulls back and frowns down at me. "You didn't do anything wrong."

"This could be really bad for you if the tabloids catch wind of it."

"Trust me, they won't. Neither the resort nor I want that. But that's not what's important. You are, baby. Did he hurt you?"

"No, I told you, he didn't touch me. But it felt good to knee him in the balls." I smile, and Luke pulls me back to him.

"I was so scared when I came out of the bathroom and heard you scream. I saw that bastard lunge for you, and I honestly don't remember much after that. I just had to make sure he didn't touch you." He's running his thumb down my cheek, and I kiss his palm.

"Thank you."

"I will always protect you, baby. That's what I'm here for. That's what I want to do."

"I know, and it's one of the reasons why I love you. I don't know why I'm not freaking out." I shrug and grin. "I guess I just felt strong, and I knew that you were here, and that he couldn't hurt me." I run my hands through his hair. "Are you okay?"

"As long as you're okay, yes, I'm okay. God, I love how strong you are, baby. It was quite a sight watching you take him to his knees."

"You might want to remember that, in case you ever get out of line." I press my body up against his and smile up at him.

"Oh yeah? You think you can take me?" He rubs his nose across mine, and I sigh.

"Probably not, but the wrestling around part would be fun."

He laughs and smiles tenderly at me. And now, for his other present.

"So, before we were so rudely interrupted, I was going to give you a present when you got out of the shower."

His eyebrows fly up. "You got me a present?"

"Sort of, yes." I'm wearing a bathing suit cover-up that is quite conservative, in black. It's a hoodie style that zips up the front and covers me from my knees to my neck.

I step back out of Luke's grasp and begin pulling the zipper slowly down, keeping the fabric closed. When the zipper is completely undone, I shrug the fabric off my shoulders so it pools at my feet.

Luke gasps, and his eyes widen, finding mine, and his face breaks out into a face-splitting grin. I plant my hands on my naked hips and cock my head. "Do you like my outfit?"

He walks to me and runs his fingers under my pearls and kisses me in that tender way he has, and I feel my knees go weak.

"Baby, you know I love this outfit. There is nothing like looking at you wearing nothing but these pearls."

"I love the way you look at me," I whisper.

Luke's eyes skim hungrily down my body, and when his gaze returns to mine he kisses me tenderly.

"I don't want to fuck you today, Natalie," he whispers against my lips.

Oh. "You don't?" I whisper back and roll my head back, as his lips wander down my neck.

"No."

"I love your whispery voice."

He grins. "I know."

"What do you want to do?"

"I want to make slow, sweet love to you." His fingertips are just barely touching me, brushing up and down my back, sending shivers through me, and his lips mirror them on my neck. It's sensation gone mad.

"That sounds lovely."

He lifts me in his arms, and I wrap my fingers in his hair as my lips find his in a soft kiss. He gently lowers me onto the bed and covers me with his body, his legs between mine. He glides his right hand up my left arm and links our fingers, but instead of holding them above my head, he simply rests them on the bed next to my head.

This isn't about restraining me, or playing with me. This is about him showing me how much he loves me, and it fills me with so much strength and reassurance and tenderness.

He runs the fingers of his left hand through the hair by my face as he continues to kiss me, softly, gently, patiently. I rest the bottoms of my feet on his calves, rubbing up and down, caressing him, as I thrum the fingertips of my free hand up and down his strong back.

I can feel his hardness against me, but he makes no move to sink inside me. Not yet.

"You are so beautiful," he murmurs against my lips.

"You make me feel beautiful," I whisper to him, and he groans.

He plants tiny kisses at the side of my mouth. I weave my fingers into his hair and gently caress him.

"I love your hair. It feels so good in my fingers."

"I figured that," he whispers, and I feel him smile against my neck. "You always have your hands in it."

"Don't ever cut it short, please." I love hearing his whispery voice.

"Okay." He kisses my earlobe and tickles it with his teeth. "You have amazing skin, so smooth and soft. And you always smell so good."

His words are seductive. His hand is still moving in my hair, and my body is humming.

My hips start to move beneath him, and I feel his grin at my throat. "You know what you do to me."

"You do the same to me, baby." He flexes his hips, pushing his cock against my wet center. The tip slides against my clitoris, and I gasp.

"I want you."

"I know. I want you, too."

I love the whispers, the soft sighs and gasps. This is the quietest our lovemaking has ever been, and it's no less intoxicating.

Oh so slowly he begins to fill me, one delightful inch at a time, until he's buried as far as he can go. He fills me up, physically, emotionally, and I feel tears roll from the sides of my eyes.

This sweet, protective, kind, sexy man loves me. And I love him, oh so much.

"Don't cry, baby." His whispered voice is rough with emotion, and he starts to slowly move, in and out of me. My legs hitch up higher around his hips, taking him in even deeper, and as he hits that most sensitive spot, I feel sparks begin to fly through me.

"Oh, I'm gonna come, my love."

"Yes," he whispers in my ear, and I am lost, my orgasm consuming me, but I barely make a sound, caught up in our quiet lovemaking.

Luke stills, pushes into me one last time and empties himself into me, whispering my name.

# CHAPTER 25

I've decided that being back in the real world does not suck.

We've been home from our romantic Tahitian getaway for a week, and we have fallen into a comfortable routine of work, flirty texts throughout the workday, hitting the gym or yoga together and alternating between his place and mine at night.

Tonight, we're staying at my place, and we're having dinner with Jules.

"That is not how you cook pasta!" Jules looks beautiful, as usual, as she glares at my boyfriend, and I smirk.

"How the hell do you do it?" Luke is thoroughly frustrated with her, and I'm sitting back with a glass of wine, enjoying the show.

"You have to put the salt in the water before it comes to a boil. Everyone knows that."

"You know what, you do it. I'm going to make out with my girlfriend." He leaves Jules to finish dinner and comes around the breakfast bar to kiss me.

"Is she being mean to you?" I ask and caress his face.

"No, she just doesn't know how to cook and won't listen."

"I can hear, you know." Jules glares at us, and we laugh.

I love spending evenings with these two. They both mean the world to me, and I love it that they get along so well.

"So, Luke, when does your new movie come out?" Jules is stirring the pasta.

"This Friday," he responds and takes a sip of wine.

"What?" I exclaim. I had no idea! Why doesn't he tell me these things?

"Um, I have a movie coming out on Friday."

I stare at him, dumbfounded.

Jules looks back and forth between us and then mutters, "Oops."

"Why didn't you say something?" My feelings are so hurt.

"It didn't occur to me." He frowns and shrugs.

"You have a major motion picture about to be released for millions of people to see, and it didn't occur to you to mention it to your girlfriend?" I turn and face him on my stool.

156

What the hell?

"I just did some of the production. I'm not starring in it or anything."

"I don't care, Luke. This is a big deal. Are you going to the premiere?"

"No, absolutely not." He shakes his head and runs his hand through his hair.

"Why? You should go. You're a part of it."

"No." He swallows hard. "I don't do that anymore."

"Either way, you should have told me. You never talk to me about your work, and you know all about mine." This is something that's been bothering me, and I'm glad Jules brought it up.

"What does a producer do, anyway?" Jules asks as she drains the pasta and starts layering lasagna in a glass dish.

"It depends on the producer. There are a lot of different roles. Some are on set during the entire production and run things there. Some work behind the scenes, securing money from a studio or wooing actors and directors. There are a lot of things to do, and there are usually a few producers doing different jobs."

"Okay, so what do you do, specifically?" I ask, sincerely interested.

"I've been doing the behind-the-scenes, preproduction stuff so I can work from here. Sometimes I have to make a trip to LA or New York for a brief meeting, but that's rare these days. Pretty much everything can be done on the phone or by e-mail. So, I talk to actors and directors, and sometimes sit in on conference calls to get money secured for a project." He's talking with his hands, so animated and enthusiastic, and it occurs to me that he really loves what he does. I smile at him and kiss his cheek.

"I'm proud of you."

"Why?"

"Because you're doing something you love, and you're good at it."

"How do you know?"

"I wouldn't be with someone who sucks." I respond sassily, and he laughs.

"So, how much money did you have to secure for the movie coming out on Friday? And who's in it anyway?" Jules slips the lasagna in the oven and leans across the counter, listening attentively.

"It's called *Rough Shot* with Channing Tatum. It's an action movie, lots of stunts and stuff blowing up, so it was high-budget. About a hundred million."

Jules and I look at each other and then back at Luke.

"I'm sorry, did you say a hundred million dollars?" My voice is very shrill. It's disturbing. Almost as disturbing as my boyfriend being responsible for raising a hundred million dollars.

"Yeah." He smiles shyly. "The action/adventure movies are always high-budget, because there's a lot of cinematography involved, CGI, and a lot of other stuff that I don't really understand but know it's expensive."

I swallow. Wow.

"So, this is a big-box-office movie then."

"Yeah, it's expected to bring in about a hundred and fifty million this weekend." He shrugs again, but I see the pride in his eyes.

"So, here's where I get personal, and you can tell me to mind my own fucking business, but I'm curious because money is what I do for a living." Jules' eyes are gleaming with curiosity, and I know exactly what she's going to ask.

"Okay, go ahead." Luke smirks. He knows, too.

"Well, I know how much actors usually get paid for big-budget films, but what about producers?"

"When all is said and done, after royalties and stuff, I'll probably bank about fifteen from this movie."

I narrow my eyes at him and bite my lip, not sure that I understand the words that just came out of his mouth. I look at Jules, and her mouth is opening and closing, also with no sound coming out.

Luke isn't looking at either of us. He's staring down at his wine.

Finally, Jules speaks first. "Please tell me you have a damn good entertainment lawyer and a team of entertainment accountants with excellent reputations. Because if you don't, I know some." She's completely serious.

Luke nods his head. "Yeah, that's all been covered for years."

"Good," she responds.

I just don't know what to say. I knew he was wealthy, but I had no idea.

Finally, Luke looks over at me. "Are you okay?"

"Fine," I whisper.

"You look a little pale." He looks worried.

"I'm okay." I shake myself out of my stare and look to Jules for guidance.

"Nat," she says, "you're no stranger to money."

"No, I'm not."

"Your parents left you, like, twenty million."

Luke blanches.

"I know."

"So, what's wrong?" she asks quietly.

I frown. "Well, I guess it's just a lot to take in." I look at Luke and finally, needing to touch him, grip his hand in mine. "I'm sorry, honey. The money isn't that big of a deal to me, you know that. I guess it's just surprising to hear that my man deals with actors and hundred-million-dollar movies and is friends with Steven Spielberg. It's easy to forget because we're so far removed from that life."

"Nat, I've removed myself on purpose."

"I know."

"Don't freak out on me," he whispers.

"I am not freaking out on you." I smile, finding my equilibrium.

"Um, can I ask one more question?" Jules raises her hand like we're in class, and we laugh. "Okay."

"Can I have Channing Tatum's number?"

We all bust out in a laughing fit, and I'm relieved to have the tension lifted.

"He's married, Jules."

"Damn it." She frowns. "All the good ones are taken."

"Luke"—I jump off my stool and stand between his thighs, rubbing my hands up and down his arms—"I want to see your movie this weekend."

"You do?" He looks completely shocked.

"Yes. This is what you do. I want to support you. Let's go opening night."

"I told you, I don't do premieres. I'm not going to LA for it." He's shaking his head adamantly.

"No, I mean here. Let's go to opening night here, in Seattle."

Jules jumps up and down in excitement. "I want to go, too! I'm sure I can find a date."

"Let's make a night of it. We'll double-date, go to the movie, maybe dinner. Let's celebrate!"

Luke smiles, a wide, melt-my-panties smile, and for the first time since I met him, he looks genuinely proud and excited about what he does. "You really want to?"

"Absolutely."

"Then I guess we're going. But let's try to go to an out-of-the-way theater. I don't want our night to be ruined because I get recognized and have to stand around signing shit for three hours."

"We'll go to a late show in a suburb after dinner. You can wear a trench coat with a hat and sunglasses." I smirk at him, and he narrows his eyes at me.

"You're such a smart-ass."

"But you love me." I smile sweetly.

"God, get a room." Jules pulls the lasagna out of the oven.

～

"I'M NERVOUS." I look over at Jules and cringe. "What if I don't like it?"

"Then you lie through your pretty straight teeth and tell him you love it. That's what girlfriends do, no matter what their boyfriends do for a living." She shuffles through my closet, looking for something to wear to the movie tonight.

"Who are you bringing tonight?" I ask as I pull my black dress over my head and step into my black Manolo Blahniks.

"Don't lecture me."

"Uh, okay."

"I'm bringing my boss."

"Holy shit! I didn't think you were seeing him anymore." What the hell?

"We're not really seeing each other."

"Are you sleeping together?"

"No. Definitely not. He's not as bad as I thought he was. Once the embarrassment faded…well, he's a pretty nice guy. I figured, why not bring him?" She bites her lip and slips on a pair of my silver earrings.

"I hope you know what you're doing, Jules."

"I'm not sure that I do, but it's just one night. Please, be cool, okay?"

"I am the epitome of cool. I'm offended you'd say otherwise. And here I was going to spring for dinner tonight, too."

She smiles at me as the doorbell rings.

"One of our guys is here." I head for the door, ready to go. "I'll get it."

I jog down the stairs and open the door to find a huge bouquet of red roses staring me in the face.

"Well, hello."

Luke pokes his head out from behind them and smiles at me. "Hey, gorgeous, these are for you."

"Thank you, my love." I bury my nose in them and sniff as he comes inside and closes the door behind him. He looks fantastic in a blue button-down shirt that matches his eyes and a pair of khaki pants.

"You look handsome," I murmur and kiss his lips softly.

"You are breathtaking." He runs his fingertips down my face, and I blush.

"Come on, I'll put these in water, and then I get to go see my boyfriend's movie tonight."

Luke laughs. "You do? That's cool."

"I know. He's very famous, but I can't tell you who he is because we are private people." I nod sagely at him, my eyes wide.

"Are you sure I can't get it out of you?" He wraps his arms around my middle as I arrange the flowers in a vase.

"Nope, my lips are sealed."

"Damn, and here I was hoping to get to take you out tonight." He nuzzles my neck, and I sigh.

"Well, I could probably go out with you later, after my other date."

Luke tickles my ribs, and I squeal. "Like hell. You're mine, baby. Get used to it."

I turn in his arms and run my hands through his hair, smiling up at him. "You are the only one I'll ever want, my love."

His eyes soften, and he gives me that kiss that makes me all gooey. "Ditto, baby."

"Oh my God, do you two ever stop?" Jules rolls her eyes as she comes in the room, and Luke smiles smugly and kisses my cheek.

"Nope."

"Gag. Nate just texted, he'll be here in a few—"

Just then the doorbell rings.

"He'll be here right now. I'll get it." She smiles and saunters to the front door.

"Who's the guy?" Luke asks.

"A guy she works with," I respond, and Luke's eyebrows shoot up.

"Really?"

"Yeah. Could be interesting."

"Come on in and meet them." Jules walks into the kitchen ahead of a very attractive man wearing dark jeans and a black long-sleeved button-down shirt. He's tall like Luke, with broad shoulders and slender hips. He has long dark, dark hair pulled back in a short ponytail at the nape of his neck, gray eyes and a nice, square jaw. Yes, he's swoon-worthy, like Jules said before. He also has kind eyes, and he can't take them off of Jules' face as she introduces him to us.

He's smitten.

"Nate, this is my roommate, Natalie, and her boyfriend, Luke Williams."

Nate shakes both our hands and smiles at Luke. "It's a pleasure. I can't say I was a fan of the movies you acted in years ago, but I do love the ones you produce now. I've been waiting for *Rough Shot* to come out for months." He smiles at us both and then steps back to drop his arm around Jules' shoulders.

"Here's hoping you like it." Luke seems relaxed, and I breathe an internal sigh of relief.

"Shall we go? I'm starving."

"Let's go." Luke takes my hand, and we all climb into his Mercedes SUV, me in the front with Luke, and Jules and Nate in the back.

"Where would you like to eat?" Luke asks us.

I turn my head to answer and see Nate kiss Jules' hand. Just friends, my ass. I'll drill her later.

"How about that little Mexican place you took me to last week?" I suggest. "It's quiet, and they have delicious margaritas."

Both Jules and Nate nod in agreement.

"Mexican it is." Luke picks up my hand and kisses my knuckles, and I smile shyly at him.

The restaurant is relatively slow for a Friday night. The owners know Luke, so they escort us to a private booth near the back where we won't be noticed.

After chips and salsa have been delivered and we've all ordered, we sit back to sip margaritas and get to know Nate.

"So, Nate, what is it that you do?" Luke asks.

"I work at the same investment firm as Julianne," he responds and smiles down at Jules.

My eyebrows climb into my hairline, and I meet Jules' gaze with my own.

Julianne? No one calls her that.

Jules narrows her eyes at me, telepathically telling me to shut up.

"How long have you been doing that?" Luke asks, oblivious to our silent conversation.

"About eight years."

We make small talk for the better part of our meal. Nate is polite, attentive, and clearly completely taken with Jules.

And it's completely mutual.

Luke lays his hand on my thigh and squeezes, and I link my fingers through his.

"Do you sail?" Nate asks out of the blue.

"I've been a few times, but I haven't in a while," Luke says. "You?"

"Yes, actually, I have a catamaran docked in Seattle. Would you two like to join us one afternoon for a tour around the sound?"

Luke looks down at me to get my take, and I nod and smile, catching Jules' slight nod.

"Sounds fun," Luke replies.

The check arrives, but I pluck it off the table before anyone else can.

"You're not paying for this." Luke digs for his wallet but I hold the check away from him.

"Yes, I am. We're celebrating your movie premiere, so I get to pay."

"Fuck no, give me that check."

"Mine." I hold it against my chest as I pull my card out of my wallet.

"Goddammit, Nat…"

I pull his face down to mine and kiss him, long and slow. When I pull back, we're both out of breath. "Let me do this. I'm proud of you, damn it."

"I can't argue with you when you do that," he mutters and looks disgusted, but I see the gleam of humor in his impossibly blue eyes, and I smile smugly as I pass the check and my card to the waitress.

Nate watches our exchange with curiosity and then breaks out in a wide grin.

"Dude, you've got it bad," he says to Luke.

"You have no idea," Luke grumbles.

# CHAPTER 26

"Four for *Rough Shot*, please." I pass my card through to the ticket girl at the movie theater and smile at her. We're quite early, but we want to get seats in the back so we can be inconspicuous and leave after everyone else when it's over.

"This is the last damn time you pay for me to go anywhere," Luke grumbles behind me.

Jules and Nate laugh at him, and I just smile serenely.

We buy two extra-large tubs of popcorn and buckets of soda to share and find our seats. Even though we're more than thirty minutes early, I'm surprised to see a handful of people already seated in the theater.

We climb up to the very top row of the stadium-style seats and sit in the middle, Jules and I between the boys.

Luke runs both his hands down his thighs and takes a deep breath.

"Are you nervous?" I whisper in his ear.

He smiles down at me and kisses my forehead. "A little."

"Do you watch your movies?" I ask.

"Yeah, but I usually wait until after opening weekend to see what audiences are saying. Opening weekend is nerve-racking, and usually busy."

"I'm glad we're here. It's exciting."

He laughs and takes a handful of popcorn out of the tub. "Me, too. I hope you like it."

"I'm gonna love it."

The theater fills up quickly, and finally the lights dim and the previews start.

I'm shocked to see that two of the five movies previewed are billed as being produced by Luke E. Williams. I look up at him, stunned, and he smiles shyly down at me. I shake my head and push some popcorn in his mouth, making him laugh.

I'm excited as *Rough Shot* begins and want to stand up and cheer when Luke's name flashes on the screen during the opening credits. Instead, I kiss him soundly and give him a ridiculously proud smile.

It's hard to tell, but I think he actually blushes.

The movie is fantastic. When a mostly naked Channing Tatum walks across the screen, Jules and I look at each other and start laughing. We can't resist. Luke throws popcorn at me in disgust.

It's a fast-paced two-hour film that keeps you on the edge of your seat until the end to find out "whodunit." There is indeed lots of action and stuff blowing up. There is also an intense love scene between Channing and his co-star, and I can't help but watch it in a very clinical way, knowing that Channing is married in real life, wondering how his wife deals with scenes like these.

I'm also incredibly happy that Luke has chosen to assume a different role in the movie business.

One particularly bloody scene makes both Jules and I squirm in our seats.

"Oh God, really?" I clasp my hand over my mouth as I realize I said that out loud, and both Nate and Luke laugh at us.

As the closing credits roll, I can't stop smiling. I do clap, inconspicuously, when Luke's name appears again, and he grins at me. We wait until all the other customers have left and the lights come up to leave the theater. As we stand, I wrap my arms around Luke and hold him tight, burying my face in his chest and inhaling his sexy Luke scent. I lean my head back and look up into his shining blue eyes.

"I loved it. I'm so proud of you. We are doing this for every movie. I want a schedule."

He runs his fingers down my face and smiles sweetly. "I'll get you one." He kisses me gently.

"Um, Nat? This is a double date. Stop making out with your super-cool, famous boyfriend, please."

I laugh and glance back at Jules. "I'm just appreciating his art," I say primly.

"Appreciate it in private. Come on, let's go." Jules and Nate walk ahead of us out of the theater. I move to follow, but Luke holds my elbow, keeping me back.

I turn back to him, and he kisses me again, passionately this time, lovingly. He pulls back and leans his forehead against mine.

"What is it?" I ask.

"Thank you for tonight. I love you, baby."

"I love you, too."

WE ALL DECIDE to continue the celebration and go out for drinks. We end up near our place at the Celtic Swell, and I have to smile as I remember the first time Luke and I had drinks together here. It feels like a lifetime ago.

The bar is pretty busy with locals, and no one is really paying attention to us as we snag a booth near the back.

"They make a pretty good margarita here," Luke comments and smiles down at me. He remembers, too!

I grin and nod, and we all decide to continue with margaritas.

Luke orders mine just the way I like it.

"So Nate"—I take a sip of my margarita. Delicious—"What did you think of the movie?"

"It was excellent, as I knew it would be. You?"

"Obviously, I'm biased, but I really liked it. Except that really bloody part."

"Yeah, what the hell is it with boys and blood?" Jules squishes up her nose prettily.

"I am man. I like blood." Nate beats his fist on his chest, and we break out into laughter.

"Mostly naked Channing Tatum is always pleasing on the eyes." I catch Jules' eye, and we wink at each other.

Luke nudges me with his elbow as Nate glares down at Jules, and I giggle.

"I do believe you have a hit on your hands, sir." I kiss Luke's smooth cheek, and he gives me his sexy half grin. Swoon!

"I'm glad you all liked it."

"What did you think of it?" Jules asks.

"I'm happy with how it turned out. I think the cast and crew did a good job, and the movie was entertaining. The audience seemed to like it."

I know I have a stupid grin on my face as he talks, but I can't help it.

"What?" he asks me.

"I just think you're cool." I shrug.

"You're pretty cool, too."

"Oh, I know." I take a sip of my drink and wink at Nate, who laughs at us.

"What are you working on now?" I ask.

"I've just started talking with a studio about another Marvel comic movie that will come out next summer. The movie I wrapped before Tahiti is a romantic comedy with Anne Hathaway that will release in the spring."

Hearing him talk about his work is just so...*sexy*. I run my fingertips up and down his thigh as he talks. He grips my hand and brings it to his mouth, kissing my knuckles, then lays our hands in his lap.

"Before I forget"—Luke takes a big sip of his drink—"My dad is throwing a big surprise anniversary party for my mom next Saturday night. Jules, you and your family are all welcome to come."

I smile at him, delighted that he wants my family at his parents' party.

"Oh, how fun! I'll let them know. Is it formal?" Jules asks.

"Yeah, Dad's going all-out. It's their thirty-fifth anniversary."

"Wow." I take a sip of my drink. Thirty-five years.

"What?" Luke gazes down at me, and I swallow.

"That's just a long time." I shrug.

"My parents have been married for forty years," Jules adds.

"Are your parents still together, Nate?" I ask.

"No, my dad raised me. He's always been a bachelor."

"Can I help out with the party?" I ask Luke.

He smiles down at me warmly and kisses my forehead. "No, I think Dad and Sam have it covered. Just come with me."

"So I'm just a piece of arm candy, is that it?" I frown as if I'm offended, and Luke laughs.

"Oh, you're much more than arm candy, baby." He kisses me gently, and Jules makes gagging sounds as Nate laughs.

"We'd better go while we can still pull them apart," Jules says and waves at the waitress for the check.

～

I WAKE Saturday morning to an empty bed. I sit up and stretch, the soft white sheet sliding down my naked torso and pooling in my lap. I listen to Luke's house, trying to decipher if I can tell where he might be, but all is quiet.

I run my hands over my face and then notice the Starbucks to-go mug and red rose on the night table, along with a note.

Oh, he does spoil me.

I take a sip of the coffee. It's still hot, so it hasn't been here long. I sniff the beautiful rose and open the note.

*Working this morning. In the office downstairs. I love you. —Luke*

Office? I don't remember seeing an office. There was one room downstairs that he said was storage on my initial tour. I wonder if that's it.

And, if so, why did he say it was storage?

I shrug and drink more coffee in his beautiful big bed. It's raining today, and his large windows are covered in drops, making the choppy water on the sound look blurry.

I pull on the blue button-down shirt Luke wore last night and go look for him.

Sure enough, when I get downstairs and head down the hall, the room Luke said was for storage is open, and I can hear him talking on the phone.

"Yes, I saw the numbers this morning. It's great news. I'm glad you're happy with it. No, we'll wait for Monday's numbers before we make that decision. Okay, we'll talk then." He hangs up as I walk in the room.

"So, not so much for storage." I look around his office and can't help but feel like I'm in a movie of my own.

This is where he keeps his movie memorabilia. The movie posters from his *Nightwalker* movies, with him on them, are framed and on the walls. There are awards and certificates, photos of him with celebrities and important people scattered throughout the room. He looks impossibly young in most of the photos.

I gaze back down at my man, sitting at his impressive desk. He's leaning back, wearing a white T-shirt and jeans, watching me apprehensively.

"What?" I ask and tilt my head to the side.

"Are you mad?"

"That you lied about this room?"

"Yes."

"No."

"Oh." His eyebrows rise, and he looks a bit thrown off-kilter.

"I know why you did. Any more surprises around here?" I ask as I come around his desk.

"No."

"Good."

Luke scoots back, and I sit on the desk in front of him, bracing my feet on the arms of his chair as he scoots in close and wraps his arms around my waist and buries his face in my belly.

I push my hands in his hair and lean down to kiss his head.

"You smell good," I murmur. "Did you shower without me?"

"Yeah, I got up early. The morning after a release is always busy. Plus, I had to get you coffee."

I smile against his head. "Thank you for the coffee."

"You're welcome."

His phone rings. He sits back and answers it, keeping one arm around my waist.

"Williams." His voice is short and business-like, and I smile down at him.

"Hey, Channing, thanks for calling me back, man. Just wanted to let you know that I saw the film last night. You did a fantastic job." He listens for a moment and then laughs. "I know. I'm glad you survived it. How is your beautiful wife? Good. Hey, I have another project I'm looking at for next year. Can I send you the script? It's pretty good." Luke nuzzles my belly again, and I can barely hear Channing—Channing freaking Tatum!—speaking on the other end.

"Okay, I'll shoot it over next week. Enjoy your weekend, you deserve it. Bye."

"He sounded happy," I murmur.

"He should, the numbers are good this morning."

"Did I mention last night how very proud of you I am?"

"You did. I especially liked hearing it when you were naked." He flashes me a wolfish grin, and I laugh.

"I liked that, too."

"In fact"—he cups my ass in his hands and pulls me more tightly against him—"you didn't get permission to wear this shirt."

"Gosh, I have to stop doing this."

"I know. You'd think by now you'd learn what happens when you wear my shirts."

"But I like your shirts." I pout down at him.

"I like doing this." He slowly unfastens each button, and I shrug out of the soft shirt, letting it fall onto the desk behind me.

He inhales sharply, his eyes level with my breasts, and he runs those beautiful blue eyes over all of me, like he's eating me alive with his gaze.

"Sweet mother of God, you're so beautiful." He leans in and rubs the tip of his nose against my right nipple, back and forth and around in a circle, and it puckers as he watches. "I love how your gorgeous body responds to me."

He pays the same attention to the left nipple, and I moan softly.

He's sitting in that chair, fully clothed, and I'm about to come unglued from just his nose.

Unbelievable.

He looks up at me as he takes a nipple in his mouth and suckles, then licks and kisses his way across my chest to the other side and does the same. His hands are caressing and kneading my ass as he kisses down my torso.

"Lean back on your hands, baby."

I do as he asks, and he kisses my belly piercing. "So fucking sexy. How long have you had this?"

"I got it on my eighteenth birthday."

"It's hot." He kisses it again and nibbles his way down to my tattoo.

He abruptly scoots me to the edge of the desk, making me lean back even farther on my elbows, exposing me to him. He places a chaste kiss on the dark letters. "Don't lie back. I want you to watch."

Fuck. That is maybe the sexiest thing he's ever said to me.

"Okay." My voice is heavy with need, and he grins up at me, his blue eyes molten.

He leans down and, with just the tip of his tongue, licks me from my clit down through my folds and back up again, and then settles his mouth right over my clit, rolling his tongue over and over it, and then suckling gently.

I throw my head back and moan his name loudly and then bring my head up to keep watching him.

It's so fucking hot when his mouth is on me.

He glides one hand around from my ass, over my thigh and slides a finger inside me.

I buck up off the desk, my feet still planted on the arms of his chair, but he holds me tightly against his mouth. His tongue slides back and forth over my clitoris, and that finger is working magic inside me. His deep blue eyes are on mine as I explode, loudly.

He runs kisses up and down my thighs and pulls his finger out of me.

"God, you taste good. I want you all the time, Nat. I never get enough of you."

"Inside me. Now." I'm panting, and I need him.

He stands and pulls his jeans down around his thighs. "Wrap your legs around me, baby."

He fills me as I wrap around him, leaning down to kiss me, cupping my right cheek in one hand and gripping on to the end of the desk with the other, as he pushes into me relentlessly.

"Oh God." My hands are on his ass, pulling him harder. I feel my orgasm already working its way through me.

"Come for me, beautiful." He whispers in my ear, and that sexy whispery voice sends me over the edge into another amazing climax that has me digging my heels into his buttocks.

"Christ, Nat." He shudders as he comes inside me, raining kisses on my face, pushing his hands into my hair.

"I recommend desk sex," I murmur and grin lazily up at him.

He laughs and pulls me up in a sitting position. "Yes, let's do this more often."

# CHAPTER 27

"*H*ey, Natalie! Thanks for meeting me here, rather than having me pick these up at your place."

I smile at Brad and give him a swift hug. We are meeting at Starbucks so I can give him his finished photos to add to his portfolio before he goes on some auditions this afternoon.

We sit at a table with our drinks as he pages through them.

"Wow, you're really good."

"I had a good subject." I wink at him and take a sip of my coffee. The days are getting cooler and rainier as fall approaches, and I'm thankful for the warm mocha.

Brad smiles shyly and continues to look through his photos. "You make me look good. When can I schedule another shoot?"

"Well, Brad, that could be an issue." I grimace and think of Luke. Hell, Luke wouldn't even like it if he knew I was having coffee with Brad.

"Oh?" He raises an eyebrow.

"My boyfriend doesn't like for me to shoot single men on my own. It's mainly a safety issue for him." I shrug and smile apologetically.

"I'd never hurt you, Nat." Brad frowns, and I feel like shit.

"I know that. Maybe I could arrange for Jules to be there, too, so we aren't alone. Luke would probably be okay with that."

"That's fine. You just do great work. I'm sorry if I was too forward before. You're beautiful, and I'd be stupid not to try, but I understand that you're not on the market. It's cool. I'll talk with him if you want." Brad looks so sincere, and I pat his shoulder.

"Thanks. We'll figure it out."

"Natalie?"

I glance up into familiar blue eyes, and my heart sinks into my stomach. "Hello, Samantha."

"I thought that was you." Her eyes shine shrewdly as she looks Brad over, then back at me and I want to shrink. Fuck! Of all the people to see me here with Brad!

"Will we be seeing you Saturday night at Mom and Dad's party?" she asks, a fake smile on her pretty face.

"Yes, Luke and I will be there."

"I'll see you then." She saunters out of the coffeehouse, and I groan, hanging my head in my hands.

"Who was she?"

"Luke's sister."

"She sure doesn't like you."

I look up at him and chuckle. "No, she doesn't."

"Why?"

"Long story. I'm glad you like your shots. I'll let you know when I've had a chance to talk to Jules and Luke about setting up another appointment."

"Okay, cool. Hey, I mean it, I'll talk to Luke if it will help and let him know that I'm not into you like that."

"I'll keep that in mind. Thanks for the coffee."

"My pleasure."

∾

SHIT.

How in the hell am I going to explain to Luke about meeting up with Brad today? I know Sam will say something to him, and I pray she hasn't called him before I get home to tell him myself. Luke's really possessive where Brad is concerned, and I know I should have run it by him ahead of time, but it just seemed silly to have to ask permission to meet with a client in a public place.

I think I'm going to be in trouble. Maybe I can distract him with sex.

"Honey, I'm home!" I let myself into the house, using the key he gave me when we returned home from Tahiti.

"In the office," he calls back.

I set my handbag on the couch and carry two large, heavy shopping bags back to his office.

He greets me with a warm smile and then he raises his eyebrows in surprise when he sees the bags. "What's in there?"

"I did a little something for your parents' anniversary." I smile at him, nervous.

"You did?" He grins, delighted with me. "What is it?"

"Well, I had some help from your dad this week." I begin pulling out frames. There are eight of them. "I asked him for photos of just him and your mom every five years they've been married, beginning with their wedding photo."

Pulling the last of the frames out, I arrange them on Luke's desk. His eyes skim over them and then settle on the last one.

"I made their wedding photo and this one I took at my birthday party the biggest two, and the others can be arranged around them."

He picks up the photo I took at the party, and he stares at it for a long time. They had been posing for me, all stiff smiles and bodies, and Luke had made a joke about something, sending us all into giggles. In this photo, Lucy is laughing into the camera, and Neil is smiling down at her, his face close to hers, and the love moving between them is touching.

It's my favorite photo of the day.

"You're so talented, baby. They're going to love these. My mom will hang them in the family room." He sets the frame on the desk and pulls me to him, kissing me in that soft way he does that makes me all weak in the knees.

"I hope they like them."

"You're so sweet. You didn't have to do this. I already put both our names on the gift I got them."

"I know." I hug him tight and bury my face in his chest. "But I wanted to do something nice for them. I've grown very fond of your parents. I put both our names on this, too."

I feel him smile against my head.

"What did you get them, anyway?"

"We"—he stresses the word, and I smile—"got them a second honeymoon in the south of France."

"Of course we did." I laugh and kiss his sternum.

"Is that funny?"

"No." I pull back and look up at his impossibly handsome face. He didn't shave this morning, and I rub my hand down his cheek, enjoying the roughness. "I love how generous you are."

He shrugs and looks uncomfortable. "They deserve it."

"Yes, they do."

"Have you decided what you're wearing Saturday?" he asks as I gather the frames back into their bags.

"Yeah, I picked something up the other day when Jules and I took Stacy shopping. Thank you again for including Jules' family. They're excited to go."

"My parents really enjoyed themselves with Jules' family. They'll be happy to have them there."

"Do you have lots of work today?" I ask, steeling myself to tell him about Brad.

"No, I'm done. You?"

"I just so happen to have a clear calendar for the rest of the day."

"Hmm…what can we do with a whole day off in the rain?" He raises a finger to his lips and pretends to be thinking really hard, and I laugh, but then remember that there is somewhere I need to be, and my mood shifts. Brad and meeting with Sam are the furthest thing from my mind.

"Actually, I'm sorry to burst your bubble, but I do have to run an errand." I look down at my hands and then back at him, biting my lip.

"Okay. Do you want company?"

"You don't have to go if you don't want to."

"I always want to be with you. Where are you going?" He looks concerned, leaning back on his desk, his arms crossed over his chest.

"The cemetery." I shrug nervously.

"Why?"

"I only go twice a year. On my birthday, which I missed this year because my incredibly sexy boyfriend whisked me away to a tropical paradise." I grin sassily at him, and he grins back. "And on their birthday."

"Their birthday?" he asks, confused.

I nod. "They shared a birthday, exactly three years apart. They always made a big deal of it, with a big party or a fun trip somewhere. They always made sure to include me, and so I want to always remember it for them." The last few words are a whisper.

He crosses to me and kisses my forehead. "Let's go."

~

MELANCHOLY SETTLES over me as we get closer to the cemetery. We took my car since I know where to go in the large graveyard, and I just needed something to occupy my mind.

Luke will most likely drive home.

"I'm sorry, honey, but this might turn into a sad day for me. I don't dwell on this often, but I'm usually not good company after I've been here."

He kisses my fingers gently and sighs heavily. "I wish you never had to go through this, Nat. It's something I can't fix for you, and I would do anything if I could."

"I know," I whisper.

I park on the single-lane-paved driveway a few rows back from my parents' large headstone. After getting out of the car, I reach in the back seat for two bouquets of flowers, lilies for my dad and sunflowers for my mom. They were her favorite.

I walk over to where they rest. Luke walks just a couple paces behind me, giving me space. He always knows what to do to comfort me. I'll have to thank him later.

This section of the cemetery sits up on a hill with a great view of downtown, the Space Needle, and the sound. I gaze around me, taking in their view, and then turn back to the large, black marble headstone.

I kneel before it, not caring about the wet ground, and brush leaves and grass off the base, cleaning it up, keeping myself busy and my eyes averted from their names and dates of birth and death. I place the flowers beneath their names and then sit back on my heels and look up.

CONNER is written in big, bold letters across the top, their names and dates are below. Written in script below that is: *I am my beloved's and my beloved is mine.*

I lean forward and place my palms flat on the smooth, cold marble over each of their precious names and close my eyes, letting the memories flood my mind.

Luke kneels next to me and places his hand on the center of my back.

"Talk about them, baby." His voice is rough, and he's rubbing my back gently.

I don't look at him. I just keep my eyes closed and my hands on the stone, but I find myself talking.

"My mom loved to bake. We would bake cookies every weekend, even when I was in college. She was pretty, and she hugged me all the time." The tears are flowing now, running unchecked and unheeded down my face, mixing with the rain falling around us.

"She had an MBA from Stanford, but rather than leave me in day care, she chose to stay home and raise me herself. And she always told me that it was the best thing she ever did and that she was so thankful for the opportunity to care for me and my dad.

"She was so smart and funny, and she was my best friend," I whisper and brush the tears off my cheeks before returning my hand to the marble.

"My dad was funny, too, but in more of a dry way. He was crazy about my mom. The sun rose and set with her as far as he was concerned. He spoiled her incessantly, which is one of the things that reminds me of him when I think of you." I smile to myself.

"No matter how hectic his job got, he always came home to us, every night. He was a ruthless businessman, but he was the gentlest man I'd ever known. And when it was time to defend his daughter, he was voracious and tenacious, and there was no stopping him.

"They were the center of my world." I hang my head in my hands now, rocking back and forth, letting the grief settle over me. Luke wraps his arms around me and settles me

171

against his chest, rocking me, murmuring words I don't understand against the top of my head. He kisses me and tells me he's sorry.

Finally, when there are no more tears left, I wipe my nose on my sleeve and look at the black stone, again reading their names and dates and the inscription below.

"They would have also been married thirty-five years this year."

He gasps and kisses my head again.

"They tried to conceive me for seven years. They tried everything, but it never worked, so they gave up and resigned themselves to the idea of not having kids at all, or maybe adopting later. My mom got a partnership at a firm, and their lives were taking a very non-child-conducive path.

"And then, suddenly, in the eighth year, she got pregnant. She almost lost me at five months and endured many months of bed rest, but here I am, safe and sound."

"Thank God," Luke whispers.

"I miss them." I begin to weep again.

"I know, baby."

We kneel there, on the wet ground with the rain falling on us, for a long time. It feels like hours, but it might only be minutes. Finally, Luke stands and lifts me into his arms, cradling me against his chest and takes me to the car. He buckles me into my seat and kisses my forehead. As he walks to the driver's side, I raise my knees and wrap my arms around them, pulling myself into a ball, and cry all the way home.

Luke carries me inside and up to his bedroom. I'm not crying anymore, but I'm exhausted, my eyes hurt, and I'm just sad.

He sets me gently on the side of the bed and takes my shoes off for me.

"Stand up, baby." I comply, and he takes my dirty jeans off. "Arms up," he says and pulls my shirt over my head.

He takes my bra off and grips my shoulders in his hands, guiding me back down to the bed. He walks to a dresser and pulls out a white T-shirt, moves back to me and slips it over my head. He strips out of his own dirty clothes and grabs a fresh T-shirt and pajama pants.

Luke pulls the covers on the bed back and lifts me into it.

"It's the middle of the day," I protest, but he kisses my forehead and runs his fingers down my cheek.

"Take a nap. You're wrung out, baby. I'm going to grab my laptop and sit with you, okay?"

"Thank you." I grip his hand and bring it to my face, nuzzling his palm. "Thank you for today. I love you so much. I don't know what I would do without you." I feel the tears start again, and I'm mortified.

"Hey, hush, baby." He's kissing my forehead and cheek, rubbing his free hand sooth-ingly up and down my back. "Nothing's going to happen to me. Go to sleep. I'll be right back."

He pulls out his phone and turns it off and does the same to mine, pulls the covers around my shoulders and walks out of the room.

A few minutes later, he's back with a large bottle of water and his laptop.

He crawls onto the bed next to me, and I turn so I'm facing him. Lifting his hand, he brushes my hair back with his fingers and smiles at me softly.

"I love you, beautiful girl. Get some sleep. I'll wake you in a few hours."

"Okay," I whisper, and close my eyes, enjoying the rhythmic caresses of Luke's fingers in my hair, and drift to sleep.

# CHAPTER 28

onight is Luke's parents' party, and I couldn't be more excited. I'm putting the finishing touches on my makeup—I'm getting pretty good at this!—while Luke is dressing in my bedroom. Jules keeps coming in and out of the room to borrow something, nag me about something, or just chatter because she is also nervous.

I love her.

I hear Luke laugh, and I walk out into the bedroom. He's on the phone, and at the sight of me, his eyes darken and get glassy, and I give a satisfied nod.

Mission accomplished.

I'm wearing a black dress that hangs off one shoulder. There are rhinestones along the high waist, and it falls to my red Louboutin-clad feet. I'm wearing my hair up, thanks to Jules' handiwork, and my pearls.

I feel sophisticated and sexy.

"Okay, Dad, I have to go. We'll see you at the club. Just tell her you're taking her out for dinner. Okay, bye." He hangs up and crosses to me.

He's so handsome in his black suit and white shirt with black tie. His blond hair is in some sort of order, but I'm sure I'll make a mess of it before long.

He rakes his gaze over my dress and hair and runs his fingertip under my pearls against my skin. "You are the most beautiful woman I've ever seen." He kisses me, in that way that makes me swoon, and I run my hands down his smooth cheeks.

"Thank you. You clean up pretty well yourself, handsome. Are you going to be okay tonight with all the people there?"

"Yeah, I'll be okay. I'm an actor, remember? I can play the part for one night."

"I don't want you to be uncomfortable." He doesn't fool me. I can see the nervousness in his eyes and the way he keeps fidgeting with his tie.

"I'll know most everyone there. My parents wouldn't invite a bunch of strangers, so it should be cool." He kisses my forehead, and his lips turn up on one side. "Are you worried about me?"

"Of course I am. I love you."

His eyes soften. "I love you, too."

"Hey, Nat, can I borrow… Oh God. We don't have time for this." Jules shakes her head in disgust and stomps into my closet, coming out wearing a pair of my earrings. "Can I borrow these earrings?"

"Yes." I laugh. "That dress is to die for."

"I know, right?" She flashes a Cheshire cat grin and turns in a slow circle, showing off her strapless red dress. She's stunning in red.

"Are you bringing Nate tonight?" I ask.

"No way, not introducing him to family." Jules shakes her head adamantly, and I let it go. She's still not talking much about Nate.

"Okay." I shrug and smile. "Want to ride with us?"

"No, Isaac and Stacy are picking me up. I'll see you there."

"Ready, baby?" Luke asks me.

"Let's go."

∽

THE ANNIVERSARY PARTY is being held at a country club in Bellevue that Luke's family belongs to. The ballroom has been decorated beautifully, with colorful flower center-pieces, twinkling lights and candles. There is a two-person wooden bench sitting near the entrance, along with black markers, for everyone to sign in lieu of a guestbook. Neil will place it by Lucy's favorite flower garden at home.

"Luke, this is gorgeous. Samantha and your father did a great job. Your mom is going to be beside herself."

Luke smiles widely. "She'll love it. Come on, let me introduce you to some people."

He snatches two glasses of champagne from a waiter and hands one to me as we begin mingling about the room. I am excited to see Gail and Steven have already arrived, and I hug them both.

"Oh my goodness, you both look so wonderful!" Gail is simply stunning with her short blond hair styled around her face, and she's wearing a beautiful royal-blue evening gown. Steven is dapper as can be in a black suit and tie. I couldn't be more proud of them.

"Darling, you are breathtaking." Gail hugs me close, her eyes shining with love and happiness.

"Thank you for coming, both of you. My parents will be delighted to see you." Luke shakes Steven's hand and kisses Gail on the cheek.

"Thank you for inviting us. You look so handsome, dear."

"Happy to be here," Steven responds and winks at Luke.

Huh? I look up at Luke, wondering what that wink was about, but Luke's face gives nothing away.

The room is filling quickly with people, and Luke sticks close to my side, his hand on my back, introducing me to his family and friends.

Finally, in a moment alone, he hands me a fresh glass of champagne and whispers in my ear, "You are unbelievably gorgeous tonight. And you are charming everyone in this room."

His smile is possessive and loving, and I warm at his words.

"You're the charming one. Are you having fun?"

"Yeah, I'm excited to see my mom's reaction. In fact"—he looks at his watch—"time to get everyone seated."

He has a word with the band leader who then announces, "Ladies and gentlemen, please find your seats. The guests of honor will be arriving shortly."

Luke and I are seated at the head table with his parents, Samantha and her date and Luke's brother, Mark.

"Luke, Natalie, this is my date, Paul," Samantha says.

Luke shakes his hand while giving him a speculative stare, and I smile to myself.

Overprotective brother.

"Hey, beautiful." Mark flashes me that signature Williams grin and pulls me into a hug. "Good to see you're still putting up with my brother's shit. When you've had enough of him, give me a call." He winks down at me, and I can't help but laugh.

"Stop fondling my girlfriend. Find your own." Luke pulls me out of Mark's grasp as Mark grins at him.

Yes, these Williams men are charmers.

Luke takes my hand and kisses my fingers as he guides me to my seat between him and Mark.

Suddenly, the ballroom doors swing open, and the room erupts into applause. Neil is smiling lovingly down at his bride as Lucy's mouth drops, and she looks around the large room, realizing that she recognizes everyone here.

She turns to Neil with a shocked smile, and he dips her way down low and kisses her tenderly. I can't hear what he says to her, but I'm quite sure he says, "Happy anniversary, my love."

I can't stop smiling.

Lucy is wearing a beautiful black evening dress, and Neil is in a black suit and red tie. They look young and happy and still very much in love.

As they make their way through the crowd to our table, they stop to shake hands and give hugs to other guests.

I turn to Luke and grin up at him. "They look so happy. I'm so happy for them."

"Me, too." He kisses my forehead, and I decide to be the bigger person here, to try to make things right with his sister.

"Samantha." I lean around Luke toward his sister to get her attention. "This is a great party. You did a fantastic job."

She looks stunned for a moment, then plasters the fake smile on her face, and my heart sinks. No smoothing things over tonight. "Thanks, Natalie."

I look up at Luke and shrug. He shakes his head ruefully, and we turn our attention back to his parents.

Lucy hugs me tightly on her way to her seat. "Oh, Natalie, this is amazing!"

"I'm so happy that you're surprised and happy, Lucy. Happy anniversary."

"Thank you." She kisses my cheek and then enfolds Luke into a hug.

"Hello, dear." Neil sweeps me up in a hug, all smiles. "Were you able to finish the project you were working on?"

"Yes, and I'll have it with me tomorrow at brunch." We are hosting brunch at Luke's house tomorrow morning to give his parents their gifts and have a private family celebration.

"Perfect. Thank you." He smiles at me kindly and moves on around the table.

"My parents love you," Luke murmurs in my ear.

"It's mutual."

We take our seats, and Neil stands, tapping his water glass with his spoon, and the room hushes. Someone hands him a microphone.

"I want to thank you all for coming tonight and extend a special thank you to my lovely daughter, Samantha, for being my partner in crime these past few months. It's been daunting keeping this little secret from my beautiful bride." He smiles down at her, and she blushes prettily. "I am a very lucky man. As of tomorrow, I have had the honor of spending every day with the best person I've ever known for thirty-five years. Luce, you are my best friend, the love of my life, and I would do it again every single day. Thank you for putting up with my shenanigans, for our three gorgeous children, and for teaching me how to cook a steak."

As we all laugh, Lucy wipes a tear from the corner of her eye and grins at her husband.

"Happy anniversary, my love. Here's to thirty-five more." Lucy stands amongst the applause, and Neil kisses her soundly.

The band starts to play a bluesy tune, and a delicious dinner is served.

"So, Natalie, how was Tahiti?" Lucy smiles warmly across the table at me.

"Warm, romantic, and completely perfect," I respond with a wink. "I didn't want to come home."

Luke kisses my fingers. "We'll go back."

The band begins to play *At Last* by Etta James, and Neil stands. "I believe this is our song, beautiful."

He takes her hand, and we all watch as he moves her effortlessly across the dance floor. They are gazing at each other as though they're the only two in the room.

"Your parents are so in love," I murmur to Luke.

"Yeah, it gets a bit gross for a kid to watch." He shakes his head, but his eyes are full of humor. "Shall we join them?"

"Sure."

As he leads me out to the dance floor, I see other couples, including Jules' parents, get up to dance to the sweet song. Luke pulls me into his arms, and we glide around the floor.

"I love dancing with you." I run my fingers down his cheek, and his blue eyes light up.

"We should do it more often then."

"Yes, we should." I smile up at him, and his eyes are suddenly so serious. What's wrong? Is he still nervous about the crowd?

"Nat, I..."

Jules sweeps by on the arm of one of Luke's cousins. "Definitely glad I came stag," she mumbles to me as she passes, smiles and shrugs, then gives us a finger wave, clearly enjoying her night.

"You were saying?" I ask Luke.

He exhales and pulls me tightly against him, nuzzles my ear with his nose, and whispers, "I love you."

The evening moves quickly, and magically. Luke keeps me tucked close to his side all night, glaring at anyone who dares ask me to dance, and I can't help but laugh at my possessive man.

No one asks for an autograph, and Luke poses politely for the photographer Samantha hired for the occasion, knowing the photos will be the property of the family.

"There you are!" I turn at Stacy's excited voice and hug her tightly.

"Well, hello, pretty girl! I told you when we bought it that that dress is a knockout." I stand back and admire her beautiful white off-the-shoulder dress. It fits her body perfectly, and she glows with happiness.

"Thank you. Yours is stunning, too."

Isaac pulls me into a hug. "Hey, brat. Thanks for helping Stacy find that dress. It's torture. I have two more weeks before I can touch her, and I think I'm going to die."

We all laugh at his pained expression, and I pat his cheek. "Poor boy. I think Sophie's worth it."

"Yeah." His face transforms into a sweet smile. "She is. Hey, dance with me?"

I look up at Luke, and he shrugs and turns to Stacy. "Do me the honor, beautiful?"

Stacy blushes bright red and takes his hand as he leads her onto the floor. I know how she feels. He's a heartthrob.

Isaac isn't too bad himself. He's tall and toned and tan, with dark blond hair and killer brown eyes. I had a crush on him for years.

"Are you having fun?" I ask him.

"Yeah, Stacy is especially, so I can't complain. Luke's a good guy. I wasn't so sure about him at first, but I like him."

"What brought that on?"

"Dad and I had a conversation with him the other day."

"What?" Why didn't I know about this?

"Yeah, you were working, and he invited all of us guys out for lunch." He shrugs and smiles like he's hiding something. I know Isaac. The man is like Fort Knox. If there's a secret, he won't spill it.

"Oh. He didn't mention it."

"Didn't he?" He shrugs again, like it's no big deal. "Well, my point is, I like him."

"Wow, am I getting the big-brother stamp of approval?" I widen my eyes and drop my jaw sarcastically.

"As long as he minds his manners, yes."

"I like it when he doesn't mind his manners." I wink at him and laugh as he cringes.

"TMI. Jesus, I don't want to know that. Are you happy?" He peers down at me, serious now, and I can't help but feel loved.

"I am. He's a good man, Isaac. He loves me. It's not about what he does for a living, or what I've done in my past, or how much money either of us has. It's about who I am when I'm with him." I shrug, a bit embarrassed. "He makes me feel special."

"Ah, Nat. You are special, honey. I'm just glad you finally figured it out. It's a pleasure watching you fall in love." He winks down at me. "Now, before I get too mushy, can you babysit one of these nights? I need some serious alone time with my wife."

I laugh. "Sure, shall we say in two weeks?"

"Oh God, yes. Thank you."

∾

As the evening draws to a close, Luke pulls me out on the dance floor for one final dance. My feet are killing me, but I can't refuse him. I love swaying in his arms.

I realize that the band is playing Norah Jones' *Come Away With Me*, and I turn my startled gaze up to his. He's smiling down at me tenderly.

"I do believe this is our song. You look as beautiful tonight as you did that night, in the vineyard, in these pearls. You take my breath away, Natalie Grace Conner."

Oh.

I feel the tears in my eyes as I gaze up at him. I run my fingers through his soft blond hair. "You sure know how to sweep a girl off her feet, Luke Edward Williams."

His eyes skim over my face as he moves me about the room. I swear, we're the only two here, and I don't care who's watching us.

He leans down and gently presses his cheek to mine. "Thank you," he whispers.

"For what?" I whisper back.

"For being mine."

~

WHEN WE REACH Luke's house, he leads me inside and shuts the front door. He tugs my hand gently, pulling me into his arms.

"You were wonderful tonight. You charmed everyone," he murmurs in my hair.

"I had a great time. Your family is wonderful." I nuzzle his chest and inhale his sexy Luke scent.

"Are you sure you're okay with us having the family here in the morning for brunch?"

"Of course. I'll even help you cook."

He chuckles. "Thank you for your service."

"It's a good cause. Let's go to bed." I pull away, but he stops me, his eyes suddenly serious.

"Not yet."

"Are you okay?"

"I'm more than okay. I have something to show you."

"Oh, okay."

He takes my hand in his and leads me through the room. He stops by the sound system and fires up his iPod, and something bluesy and slow starts to pour out of the speakers. He leads us to the deck, opens the French door, and flips a switch, and I gasp.

The deck has been transformed into soft and romantic. Bouquets of red roses with tiny white pearls tucked in the petals cover every surface. There are twinkling white lights strung back and forth, high along the ceiling of the space, and a small table is sitting by the love seat with a bucket of ice and champagne and two glasses.

I twirl and gaze up at him, my eyes wide. "When did you do this?"

"I had it done earlier while we were getting ready for the party at your house."

"Luke, it's magical." I turn to take in the beautiful space, breathless. He's so romantic.

He wraps his arms around me from behind and buries his face in my neck. "Do you like it?"

"I love it. Thank you."

"Come, sit." He leads me to the love seat, and we sit. My dress floats around my legs as I sit, and it feels soft against my skin. I smile to myself, remembering that I'm not wearing any underwear. Luke will enjoy that when he finds out.

He pours us each a glass of champagne, clinks his glass to mine, and I take a sip.

"It's nice tonight. It's not even very cold." I lean my head back against the cushion and close my eyes, listening to the water that we can't see in the darkness. Luke lifts my feet into his lap, and I turn my head so I can watch him.

He removes my shoes and starts to rub.

"Oh, sweet mother of God, I love you."

He laughs. "Feet hurt?"

"A little. Those shoes are worth it."

"Yes, they are. Did I mention that you look beautiful tonight?"

"Once or twice." I wink at him and sigh as his thumb pushes down on the arch of my foot. "You're good with your hands."

"I'm glad you approve."

"I could get used to this, you know. All these flowers and foot rubs and champagne and you, my handsome boyfriend."

He frowns, and my heart stills for just a moment. What did I say wrong?

"Hey." I pull my feet out of his lap and move toward him, lying across his lap. He wraps his arms around me, holding me to his chest, and I cup his face in my hand. "What is it?"

His eyes are on mine, intensely blue and serious, and I know that something important is on his mind.

"Talk to me, baby." I continue to caress his face, and he turns his head to press a kiss in my palm.

"I don't think I want to be your boyfriend anymore."

What?

I still and narrow my eyes at him. "Okay, I'll get my things." I move to get up, but he tightens his hold on me, clenching his jaw and his eyes closed tightly.

"No, that's not what I mean. I'm not breaking up with you."

"What are you doing?" I whisper.

"I'm fucking this up." He opens his eyes, and I see fear, and longing, and love.

What's this?

"I've wanted to do this all night, but I couldn't find the right time, and I'm glad I didn't because it should be here, while we're alone." He swallows and takes a deep breath. "Natalie, since I've known you, my world has changed. I found something with you that I didn't know I was missing, but that I wanted very much. You are such a beautiful woman, inside and out. You beguile me. I can't keep my hands off of you. You are so sexy and fun and smart. Your sassy mouth makes me crazy." He smiles down at me and runs his fingertip along my lower lip.

I'm speechless, which is good because he doesn't seem to be finished.

"I can't ever imagine my life without you. You are the center of my world, Nat. I want to love you, protect you, fight with you, make babies with you and spoil the shit out of you for the rest of my life."

He takes a deep breath and pulls a small Tiffany-blue box out of his pants pocket. I feel my eyes go wide, my heart rate spike and my breath catch.

My eyes search his as he holds the tiny box in his beautiful hand.

"Natalie, be my wife. Marry me."

# CHAPTER 29

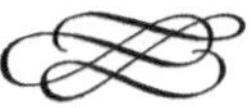

$\mathcal{O}$h. My. God.

My eyes are locked on his face, and all the breath leaves my body.

Marry him! *Marry him?*

It's so soon. We've only known each other, what, less than two months? Two incredible months.

His worried eyes are gazing deeply into mine, blue to green, and I know in my heart that the answer is yes. After everything we've been through these past two months, everything we've shared, I can't imagine life without him either.

And I don't have to.

He wants to marry me!

"Baby, you're killing me here." Luke moves to open the little blue box, but I put my hand over his, stopping him. He turns startled eyes back to mine, but I smile reassuringly.

"I just have a couple things to say." I am now giddy and jumping up and down on the inside, my heart in my throat, but I'm amazingly calm on the outside.

"Go ahead," he murmurs and still looks a bit scared and uncertain.

"When I see my future, Luke, I see you. I see *you*, not your money or what you do for a living, or who you know. I love and respect you for the kind, giving, loving man you are. I want what my parents had, what your parents share. I would be honored to be your wife, give you children, and make a life with you."

As I speak, tears run unchecked down my face. Luke's eyes soften, and his arms tighten around me.

"Is that a yes?" he whispers, and I giggle tearfully.

"Yes."

"Thank God." He brushes his lips across mine softly, and I cup his cheek in my hand.

"You had me worried there for a minute," he whispers against my lips.

Oh, I love whispery Luke.

I just love Luke.

"You surprised the hell out of me. I think I forgot to breathe."

"Can I show you this now?" He holds the ring box up and grins down at me.

"By all means."

He sits me up on the small couch and kneels in front of me. Oh my. Seeing my sexy man, disheveled blond hair, bright blue eyes, in a black suit with the tie loosened, kneeling before me, holding a little blue ring box, is an image I'll hold in my head forever.

"When I saw this, I knew it was yours. I've had it since the day I bought your pearls."

I gasp, my eyes widening. He's wanted to marry me since the night at the vineyard!

"I didn't think you were ready then." He chuckles as I shake my head.

He opens the box, and cradled in the velvet is diamond perfection. The center stone is princess cut and large, but not crazy big. It's nestled in platinum, with two lines of smaller diamonds on either side that twist around each other to meet at the center stone.

Tears prick my eyes again as he takes it out of the box, places it on my left hand and kisses it there.

"Thank you. It's perfect."

"Like you." He leans up and kisses me, passionately, and I wrap my arms around him, pulling him to me.

He gathers my long skirt in his hands and pushes it up around my thighs, skimming his hands along my thighs and up under the skirt to grip my hips.

"Jesus, I love this new habit you have of not wearing any underwear." I smile against his lips. "We're writing that into the vows. No underwear for you."

I let out a belly laugh, and then gasp as he pulls my hips forward and pushes me back against the soft cushions of the love seat.

He pulls in a shaky breath as he gazes down at me, exposed to him from the waist down, my black skirt hiked up, in my pearls.

"Do you have any idea how beautiful you look right now?"

"You make me feel beautiful."

He sits back on his heels and pushes one finger inside me, his eyes locked on my center, watching his hand. "You are the most beautiful woman I've ever met in my life, baby."

I moan as he continues to torture me with that finger. My breath hitches, and I start to pant. Jesus, what he does to me with just one finger.

"Luke, I want you."

"Oh, trust me, you'll have me." He pulls his now wet finger out of me and sucks on it. "You taste good."

He bends down and pushes my thighs wide with his palms, spreading my labia in the process. I grip the cushions of the couch, preparing for the incredible invasion of his mouth, and buck my hips when his mouth covers me, his tongue pushing between my lips.

"Oh my God!" My hands dive into his hair, my hips circling. He grips my ass, tilting my pelvis higher, and he continues to make me wild with that talented mouth. He rubs the tip of his nose against my clit, and I give in to my orgasm, convulsing and shuddering, calling out his name.

He nibbles my inner thighs as my body calms.

"Holy shit, you're good at that," I pant and run my fingers through his shaggy blond hair.

"Mmm, I'm glad you approve, baby. Stand up for me." He rises gracefully and takes his suit jacket, tie and shirt off, discarding them on the floor of the deck.

"After what you just did to me, my legs are jelly. I don't think I can stand."

He takes my hands and pulls me into a standing position and wraps my arms around his bare shoulders. "Just hang on to me."

"Happily," I murmur in his neck as his hands glide to my back, unzipping my dress. I lower my right arm so he can pull my dress off, and he lets it billow to my feet.

"God, no bra either? It's a good thing I didn't know this earlier. I would have locked us in a bathroom at the club and kept you naked all night." His hands smooth down my back to my bottom.

"You're not naked."

"Oh, did you want me to be naked, too?" he asks innocently, and I bite his collarbone.

"Get. Naked."

"Demanding little thing, aren't you?"

"Why aren't you naked?"

His hands roam from my bottom, up my back and begin taking the pins out of my hair, letting it fall around me.

"I love your hair," he murmurs and watches it fall, one strand at a time.

"I love your hair, too." I push my fingers through it, and he smiles.

"I know."

When my hair is loose, he takes my hands in his and kisses them, one knuckle at a time, his eyes on mine. He steps away from me, and the cool night air swirls around me, sending a shiver through me, making my nipples pucker.

"I love your body. I love that you're curvy, yet strong and fit." His eyes glide greedily up and down my curves.

"I'm glad." I smile shyly. "You're still not naked."

He raises an eyebrow. "Impatient?"

"I want my fiancé to make love to me," I whisper, and his eyes dilate.

"Say it again," he whispers.

"Make love to me," I whisper back.

"No, the other part."

A small smile spreads across my lips. "My fiancé."

"God, you said yes." He swallows, his eyes round, and then he smiles, a heartbreaking, wide, joyous smile, and I fall in love with him all over again.

I nod and glance down at my beautiful ring. I can't wait to get a ring on his finger, too.

"Did you think I'd say no?"

"No, I just…" He runs a hand through his hair. "I was just really nervous."

I close the distance between us and kiss his lips softly. "You have no reason to be nervous with me. You've had my heart for quite some time. Now, my gorgeous fiancé, please take me to bed and make love to me."

He sweeps me up in his arms and carries me to his bedroom, kissing me softly the whole way.

~

"HEY, BEAUTIFUL, WAKE UP." Luke nibbles my earlobe, and I turn sleepily to face him.

"You kept me up really late," I murmur, not opening my eyes. I hear him chuckle.

"I'm sorry. But we have to get up and start getting brunch ready." He kisses my cheek and then my nose.

My eyes flutter open, and I palm his cheek in my left hand, and my ring catches the morning light. I smile brightly at him, and he grins and kisses me softly.

"Let's stay in bed all day and make love."

"As good as that sounds"—he pulls back and rolls away—"everyone will be here in about two hours, and we have stuff to do. Coffee's on the night table for you. Go ahead and grab a shower, and I'll meet you in the kitchen."

"I love you."

He flashes a cocky grin at me. "I love you, too. Get up. I'll see you downstairs."

He leaves the room, and I sit in the bed for a minute and grin stupidly, gazing at my ring. I finally shake myself and grab my coffee, making a beeline for the shower.

~

"Okay, what can I do?" I ask as I stroll into the kitchen.

Luke is at the stove, a white kitchen towel slung over his left shoulder. He's wearing a white linen button-down shirt with faded blue jeans and bare feet.

Yum.

"Here, cut up some fruit." He pulls melons, strawberries, grapes and peaches out of the fridge, and I grab a cutting board and sharp knife and get started with my task.

"So, Isaac mentioned last night that you took the guys out for lunch the other day." I grab a cantaloupe and cut it in half, pull the seeds out and begin cutting it into wedges.

"He did?" Luke frowns slightly and mixes some pancake batter.

"Yeah, that's all he would say, other than he likes you, as long as you mind your manners. I told him I prefer it when you don't." I smirk and begin pulling stems off the strawberries.

"I wanted to ask them all if it was okay if I asked you to marry me."

I twirl at his words, my mouth gaping open. He shrugs and pours the batter on a griddle on the stove top.

"Why?"

"Because they're your family. They love you and protect you, and it's tradition." He takes a sip of coffee and eyes me speculatively.

Wow.

"What did they say?"

"I proposed, didn't I?"

"What if they'd said no?"

He laughs and shakes his head. "I would have asked anyway."

He flips the pancakes, and I wander over to him with a strawberry, holding it up to this lips.

"Here." He takes a bite, and I slip the rest of it in my mouth. "Mmm, that's good."

I lick my thumb, and he takes my wrist in his hand and licks my forefinger. "I love watching you eat."

Desire flashes, fast and hot, through me.

"Yeah?"

"Yeah."

I wander back to the fruit and pluck a grape from the stem. When I turn, Luke has taken the pancakes off the griddle and turned it off.

I do like the way he thinks.

I rub the grape across my lips, then pop it in my mouth and chew slowly.

"Want some?" I hold a grape out for him. He slowly closes the space between us and takes the grape out of my fingers with his lips.

"I like this game," he whispers, and I grin. He lifts me up onto the counter so my feet are dangling, steps between my legs, and puts another strawberry against my lips. I grip it in my teeth and then lean down so he can take a bite from my lips and kiss him at the same time.

He tastes of strawberries and Luke, and I moan against his mouth.

"God, you're so sexy."

I pull my green shirt over my head and throw it on the floor, then my bra follows it. Grabbing another strawberry, I look in his eyes, bite my lip, and swirl the red fruit around my nipples, making them pucker. Luke's quick intake of breath and tightening of his fingers on my ass tell me he likes the sight before him.

I pull the strawberry up my chest, against my skin, over my chin and push it into my mouth, enjoying the sweet juiciness of the fruit.

He doesn't move. He just watches me, his hands gripping my jean-clad bottom, me naked from the waist up, and I set about seducing my sexy fiancé.

I push a chunk of cantaloupe in Luke's mouth and lean down and kiss him, sucking the juice into my own mouth.

"You're making me crazy," he whispers against my mouth.

"That's the point," I whisper back.

He suddenly lifts me, and I wrap my legs around him as he twirls and rushes over to the dining table. He sets me down on it and pulls my jeans over my hips as I raise them and down my legs, taking my underwear with them.

He pulls his shirt over his head, not bothering with the buttons and pushes his soft blue jeans down around his thighs.

"I can't get enough of you." He covers me with his torso, his hands in my hair and face buried in my neck, kissing and suckling my sensitive skin.

"I don't want you to get enough of me." I wrap my legs around his hips, and he slides inside me, all the way to root of his cock, and I clench around him.

He grips my right hand in his left one and pulls it above my head and begins to move, in and out of me, at a steady pace.

"It makes me so hard to watch you eat. Your sweet mouth is the sexiest aphrodisiac I've ever seen." His lips find mine, and I'm lost in his words, in his body moving so gracefully and surely above mine.

I run my hand down his back to his tight ass and hold on tight as he increases the pace.

"Oh God," I moan.

"Look at me," he growls, and my eyes meet his. "I want to watch you come."

Fuck.

And that's all it takes to send me over the edge. He slams into me twice, then stills and bites his lip as he erupts inside me.

"God, Nat, you're going to kill me." He kisses me gently, then pulls out of me, helping me up off the hard table.

"I can't help it that you have a food fetish." I slap his naked ass and collect my clothes on the way to the bathroom to clean up and get dressed.

When I join him in the kitchen, he's fully dressed and has more pancakes cooking on the griddle.

I kiss his cheek and resume cutting up the fruit.

"I have to go to LA next week." Luke flips his pancakes and turns to me.

"Why?" I finish stemming the strawberries and move on to the peaches.

"I have a meeting that I need to be there for in person. I should only be gone one night."

"Oh, okay." I frown. This will be the first night we've spent apart since our magical night at the vineyard.

"Come with me," he suggests.

"I can't. I'm still catching up with clients from our vacation. I'm booked solid next week." I toss a pit in the garbage and grab another peach.

"It's just one night," he murmurs, and I realize he's standing behind me.

I'm suddenly feeling vulnerable, and I don't know why. It's just one night! Surely I can get through one night without him.

I turn and smile brightly, not wanting him to see my insecurity. "It'll be fine. What day are you leaving?"

"Early morning Wednesday. I'll be home Thursday around noon."

"That's a long meeting." I raise my eyebrows.

"I'm going to pack a few meetings in there, since I'll be there anyway. Are you sure you'll be okay?"

"Of course. I love you, but I think I can survive without you for one night. Jules and I'll have a girls' night."

"Okay." He kisses my nose and returns to his pancakes and slips some bacon into the oven.

"What are we going to do about all the flowers outside?" I ask, changing the subject.

"What do you mean?"

"Don't you want to eat out on the deck?"

"No, we'll eat in here. We can bring them in if you like."

I walk over to the glass door and gaze out at my beautiful flowers, trying to shake my melancholy mood now that I know Luke will be leaving overnight next week.

"They're beautiful. I don't know where we'll put them all."

"Leave them for now, and we'll figure it out later."

"Okay." I set the large dining room table for six, pour orange juice and coffee into carafes and set them on the table as the doorbell rings.

"I'll get it." Luke flashes me a smile, and I relax a bit, excited to see his parents and give them their gifts.

"Hello, darling." Lucy kisses Luke's cheek and comes into the great room. Neil and Mark follow with Samantha bringing up the rear.

They've obviously spent a lot of time in Luke's home. They're comfortable moving around the space, and I stand back for a moment, enjoying the view of Luke with his family.

My family now.

"Everyone, I'd like to introduce you to my beautiful fiancée, Natalie."

I laugh as Luke joins me and kisses my hand.

"Yes," I say drily, "we've met."

"Oh, Natalie, I'm so excited that you're going to be a part of our family." Lucy hugs me tight, and I blink back the sudden tears that threaten.

"Thank you."

"And here I thought you'd choose the right brother." Mark shakes his head ruefully and pretends to pout.

"I did." I laugh at his stricken face and give him a quick hug. "Don't pout. We'll find you a good girl."

Mark laughs and heads for the kitchen to steal a piece of bacon. "No need. I'm good."

"Stay away from that bacon!" Luke bellows.

Neil hugs me and cups my face in his hands, his kind eyes happy. "Are you happy, sweet girl?"

"Yes, thank you."

"Good."

Luke's parents are both so generous and welcoming. Samantha, however, rolls her eyes and pours herself a cup of coffee.

"So." Her eyes gleam with malice, and she glances at Luke, then back at me, and I brace myself for what's about to come out of her snarky mouth.

"Who was that delicious-looking man you were with the other day in the coffee shop?"

# CHAPTER 30

*I* frown, then the blood leaves my face, and I turn to Luke. His eyebrows are raised almost to his hairline. The room stills.

"I met with a client to give him some work he purchased." My eyes don't leave Luke's, but his face changes, and gone is my carefree, happy man. He knows exactly who I'm talking about, and he's pissed.

Fuck.

I forgot to tell him about meeting with Brad because it was the same day that we went to the cemetery.

"What's his name?" Sam asks and takes a sip of coffee.

"Brad," I murmur, watching Luke as he exhales and hangs his head. "I forgot to tell you because we went to the cemetery that day." My voice is low and thin.

Samantha frowns for a moment and swallows, and she almost looks guilty.

Luke stares at me, his eyes ice cold, and I feel tears threaten. "Don't be mad. I just gave him his photos, and he asked if he could make another appointment, but I told him you wouldn't like it. He offered to call you himself and talk to you to let you know that he's not interested in me like that. It was nothing."

"Why didn't you say something when you got home?"

"I really forgot. It was nothing."

"It didn't seem like nothing when you smiled at him and rubbed your hand all over his shoulder." Samantha shrugs smugly, and I gasp.

"Sam." Lucy's voice is sharp and loud.

Luke's eyes don't leave my face, and I shake my head.

I pin Sam with a glare and ball my hands into fists. How dare she?

"What the fuck is wrong with you?" My voice is shaking in rage.

"What did I do?" She widens her eyes innocently.

"I met with a client. I patted his shoulder when he expressed nervousness about talking with my protective boyfriend about the possibility of having a chaperoned photo shoot with me. We were in a fucking public place having a conversation.

"Is this how it's always going to be, Samantha? You questioning my motives with your brother for the next sixty years? Do you have any idea how much money I'm worth without Luke? I don't need his money or his contacts. When my parents died, I inherited over twenty million dollars."

Sam blanches, and I hear Lucy gasp, but I keep going.

"Your brother is famous. Get over it. I wouldn't love him any less if he flipped burgers for a living, if that's where his passion was. You seem to be the only one hung up on who he is.

"I am marrying him, Sam. I'm in it for the long haul. I'd prefer to have a friendly relationship with you. I think that if you gave me half a chance, you'd like me.

"But I will not continue to be disrespected by you. I don't deserve it."

"I don't trust you," she spits out through clenched teeth.

"I don't trust you either, so I guess we're even." I look at Luke to see what he's thinking. His hands are in his pockets, and he's gazing at me thoughtfully. "Do you want me to go?"

"No, don't go!" Lucy comes toward me, glaring at her daughter. "Samantha, you're being ridiculous."

I continue to look at Luke. He hasn't answered me. Neil and Mark are both also glaring at Samantha.

"Well?" I raise my eyebrow at him.

"No, this is your home," he says quietly, and his eyes warm. Oh, thank God.

"Sam," he says quietly and walks around the table to her. She's still glaring at me, but he turns her chin so she's looking in his eyes. Lucy grips my hand in hers, and I smile thinly at her. I'm shaking like crazy.

"Stop this. I am marrying Natalie. I'm in love with her, Sam. She's nothing like anyone from my past. You have got to knock the chip off your shoulder and move on. I have."

He runs his hands through his hair and looks over at me, then turns his attention back to her. "If you don't trust her, trust me. Give her a fighting chance. She hasn't done anything to you."

Sam shakes her head and closes her eyes, and she suddenly looks tired. "I can't bear to see you hurt again."

"*You* are hurting me, Sam."

She gasps as though he's hit her. "What?"

"When you hurt her, you hurt me. Stop. This is our home, and if you can't respect her in it, you're not welcome here."

Holy shit. He's defending me to his sister, and I just want to wrap myself around him and kiss him, but I stay where I am, riveted.

I look around the room, at Lucy, Neil and Mark, and decide this has gone on long enough.

"I'm hungry." My voice is calm and light. "Let's have brunch. I think Mark's about to eat all the bacon by himself."

Lucy smiles at me and squeezes my hand as we head to the kitchen to place the food on the table. Mark and Neil help us get everything settled, and I watch out of the corner of my eye as Luke murmurs something to Sam. He hugs her gently and joins me in the kitchen.

"I'm sorry." I hug him around his middle and breathe in his scent.

"Don't be. You didn't do anything wrong. I'm sorry for Sam."

I shake my head. "Let's eat."

"Okay."

We enjoy our delicious meal, and the mood lifts considerably. I'm relieved that the conversation isn't forced or uncomfortable after my altercation with Sam. She continues to eye me speculatively from across the table, but she's no longer glaring at me, so I figure we've leaped one hurdle.

"Natalie, let me see that ring." Lucy leans toward me, and I show off my beautiful ring, a silly grin plastered on my face.

Lucy smiles at her son. "I did such a good job raising you."

Luke laughs, and I nod. "That you did. He has good taste."

Luke kisses my hand and smiles at me, his eyes soft and loving.

After breakfast, we clear the table. Lucy, Sam and I clean up the mess and join the men in the living room with fresh coffee.

"Presents!" I jump up and down and clap my hands, excited to give Luke's parents their gifts. Everyone laughs at me, and I grin. "I love giving presents."

"You didn't have to get us anything at all," Neil informs me.

"You only celebrate your thirty-fifth anniversary once." I decide to give this olive branch thing another try and turn to Sam. "Will you please help me bring their gift in from the other room?"

Her eyes widen in surprise, but then she shrugs good-naturedly. "Okay."

I smile and lead her down to Luke's office, where the large box sits on his desk.

"Holy shit, that's a big box."

I laugh. "I know. I had a hell of a time wrapping this sucker. Here, you take that side and I'll take this one."

We lift it together—it's really not that heavy, just awkward—and carry it out to the living room.

"What did you do, buy them furniture?" Mark asks drily.

I stick my tongue out at him, and Sam and I set the box on the floor in front of Neil and Lucy.

"Open it." I sit next to Luke on the couch, and he drapes an arm around my shoulders.

They attack the box from opposite sides, tearing the paper and pulling the lid off.

"Oh my." Lucy's hand covers her mouth as she gazes at the contents. She begins pulling the black, framed photos out of the box, one by one, and Neil takes them from her, arranging them on the floor. At the bottom of the box are the two larger frames of their wedding day and at my birthday party.

"These are wonderful," Lucy says as they hold the image from the party in front of them and gaze at it. "Natalie, you're very talented."

I blush, delighted that they like their present. "Thank you."

Luke kisses my hand. "There's more."

"What?" Neil frowns, not privy to this part of the present, and I giggle.

"We're sending you on a second honeymoon to the south of France. It's all paid for, you can go whenever you like."

Their mouths drop, and Lucy looks back at their photos and starts to cry.

"Geez, Mom, what's wrong?" Mark awkwardly pats her back, clearly uncomfortable with a woman in tears.

"I'm a bit overwhelmed, I guess. First, last night's party, then my son is giving me a beautiful daughter-in-law, and now we're going to France. It's a lot to take in in such a short time."

Neil kisses her forehead and hands her a handkerchief. I didn't know men still carried those.

I freshen everyone's coffee, and we sit and chat about weddings for the better part of an hour.

"Have you set a date?" Lucy asks.

"No." I chuckle and look at Luke. "He asked me twelve hours ago."

"Winter weddings are lovely."

"I'm going to need help. Also…" I frown and peer at Luke, and he runs his hand over my back.

"What's wrong?"

"I don't want the paparazzi to get wind of it."

"Do you want a big wedding?" Neil asks.

"No, just family and close friends." I shrug. "I've never really thought about it."

"Every girl thinks about her wedding. It scares us men to death." Mark smirks.

I shake my head. "I'd never planned to get married. This wasn't even on my radar."

"I have an idea," Sam says softly. "What about a destination wedding? You can fly everyone somewhere and have a small wedding somewhere lovely, like Tahiti or something."

The idea takes hold in my brain, and I smile. I look over at Luke, and he's smiling at me.

"What do you think?" I ask him.

"I'm the man. You just tell me when and where to show up and what I'm supposed to wear, and I'll be there."

I grin at Sam. "I like that idea. Let's talk about it some more later."

Sam smiles at me—*smiles at me!*—and I have visions of Luke and I getting married on a white sandy beach with crystal-clear blue water surrounding us.

~

"So what are your plans for tomorrow night with Jules?"

Luke and I are snuggled up on the couch. It's Tuesday night, and he leaves for his trip tomorrow, which I've been trying very hard to not dwell on. I don't want him to go.

"I think we're going to be in the studio."

Luke raises his eyebrows and looks down at me. "Why?"

"She wants me to do some photos for her." I shrug. "I'm not sure why. She already has quite a collection."

"What do you mean?"

"You must not read *Playboy*."

"Not since I was a randy teenager. Why?" He looks perplexed as I turn on the couch to face him, then realization dawns, and his eyes go wide.

"You're kidding."

"Nope. She posed for them in college." I laugh as I think back on that time. "She's the person I practiced on the most to get good at what I do. She did some work for *Playboy* for about a year, and then abruptly stopped. She said she was over it, and it was time to move on."

"Wow."

"Do not go on the Internet and try to find naked pictures of Jules." I narrow my eyes at him and cross my arms over my chest.

Luke laughs. "No, thanks. She's beautiful, but I've grown to feel very brotherly toward her. I do not want to see her naked."

"I'm glad to hear it."

"No, there's only one woman I want to see naked."

"Oh?" I ask innocently. "Who could that lucky woman be?"

"Just this gorgeous brunette I know. She's all curves and has the sexiest tattoos I've ever seen in my life." He pulls me onto his lap, so my knees are straddling his hips. I'm dressed in one of his T-shirts and my panties because we've been watching TV before bed.

"Do I know her?" I ask.

"I don't know. She always steals my shirts, and she's wearing a very fetching ring on her left hand." He pulls the shirt over my head and nuzzles a nipple with his nose.

"I think I know who you're talking about," I whisper and close my eyes as he sends chills down my back with that nose.

"You do?"

"Hmm… she's hopelessly in love with you." I grind my center over his erection, reveling in the feel of his jeans against me.

"Fuck, baby, I can feel how hot and wet you are through my damn jeans." His hands are on my hips, and he's pushing up against me.

"I want you." I kiss his lips. "Now."

He slides me back to his knees, opens his jeans and shimmies them down around his hips. His large hands cup my ass and lift me over him, shifts my panties to the side, then lowers me down onto him.

"Oh God! Luke, you feel so good." I begin to circle my hips, riding him, looking down into his molten blue eyes. His mouth is open, his breathing coming hard and fast.

He sucks a nipple hard in his mouth, and I cry out. My nipples have been extra sensitive lately.

"Gentle," I pant, and he releases the nipple from his lips and lightly runs his tongue over it.

"Okay?" he asks.

"Oh yes, more than okay."

He stands in one fluid motion, me still wrapped around him and without breaking our precious contact. He lays me down across the length of the couch and covers my body with his. He lifts my left leg, pressing it against my chest and over his shoulder, spreading me wide and begins to hammer into me.

"Luke," I cry out as sensation rolls through me. My hips are moving against his, and he's gazing down at me with such possession, such feral need, I come fiercely.

"Yes." He lets go of my leg and pulls out of me abruptly, flipping me onto my stomach. He pulls my ass in the air and slams his cock back inside me, slapping my ass in the process.

"Holy shit!" I squeal and grip the cushions in my fists.

He reaches down and grips my hair in a strong hand and pulls back, just enough to tug, and grips my hip with his other hand, pulling me back hard and fast on his hard cock.

I love it when he fucks me.

His breath is coming hard and fast. "Come again."

"I can't." If I come again now, I'll pass the hell out.

"Come. Again." He pulls harder on my hair and slaps my ass again, and I can't stop it. My muscles tense and shudder in the most intense orgasm I think I've ever had. I scream incoherently, pounding my fist on the couch as my body bucks back against Luke, and he roars my name as he explodes.

"Fuck me." He pulls out of me and pulls me to him, kissing my face, my cheeks, nose, eyes, cupping my face in his hands. "Are you okay?"

"Of course." I frown, not understanding. "Why wouldn't I be?"

"I've never been that rough with you. Jesus, Nat, you devastate me. I forget myself with you." His hands run down my back, soothing me.

"Honey, I like rough sex with you. You know that. I trust you completely. I'm fine." I smile at him. "You can slap my ass anytime. It's fucking hot."

Luke laughs, still catching his breath, and crushes me to him. "God, I love you."

# CHAPTER 31

*I* haven't slept all night. My stomach has been churning, and I feel slightly queasy. I know it's because Luke is leaving this morning, and it makes me nervous. I'll worry about him until he's home safely. I hate that he's flying.

It's not like he can drive to LA for the day.

The green glow from the alarm clock says it's five a.m. Luke will want to get up and get ready for his eight a.m. flight, so I start waking him up.

I love waking him up.

I kiss his cheek and run my fingers through his hair. "Wake up, my love."

"Humph."

"Come on," I reply, laughing at him. "Wake up. You have to get ready to go."

He turns to me and wraps me in his arms, burying his face in my neck.

"Go back to sleep," he murmurs.

Oh, I love being in his strong arms.

"If we go back to sleep, you'll miss your flight." I kiss his lips and continue running my fingers through his hair.

"I wish you were coming with me."

"You'll be home tomorrow."

"I don't like leaving you."

I smile, and my heart gives a little lurch. "I'll be okay."

"Will you drive me to the airport?"

"Of course."

He sighs, his eyes serious as they take in my face.

"Are you okay?" I rub his rough cheek with my hand.

"I miss you already."

"Oh, you have it bad, Mr. Williams."

Luke laughs and rolls me onto my back. He runs his knuckles down my cheek and kisses me in that gentle way he has that makes me all gooey. "Yes, I'm afraid I do."

"I do, too," I whisper.

"I'm glad to hear it."

He sweeps his nose down mine as I raise my legs up and around his waist. We're still naked from last night's lovemaking. He shifts so his hard cock is lying against my folds and rocks gently back and forth.

I know this will be much different from the way he fucked me on the couch last night. This will be slow and sweet.

He's kissing me tenderly, his eyes open and on mine. He pulls his hips back, and then slides inside me oh so slowly.

"Luke," I sigh against his mouth.

"I love you," he whispers.

He doesn't increase the tempo, he just continues a steady, slow rhythm, in and out, cupping my face in his hands, and it's so beautiful I can't stop the tears from falling out of the corners of my eyes.

"Don't cry, baby." He brushes the tears away with his fingertips and rubs my nose with his again.

"I love you so much," I whisper back to him. "Please, be safe."

His eyes widen, and I know he can see the vulnerability in my eyes, and he finally understands my fear about this trip.

"Oh, baby." He closes his eyes tightly and buries his head in my neck. I wrap my arms around him, holding him to me, as he gradually increases the tempo and pressure inside me, and I come, pulsating around him, as he empties himself into me.

~

"THEY'RE GOING to be calling your flight. You'd better get through security." Luke's wearing a baseball cap and glasses in hopes that he won't get recognized in the airport. He looks hot.

He always looks hot.

"Have fun with Jules tonight." He pulls me to him and kisses me long and slow.

"Be good." I raise an eyebrow at him, and he laughs.

"I'll see you tomorrow. I'll call you when I get to the hotel." He kisses me again, then rests his lips on my forehead and takes a deep breath, like he really doesn't want to let me go.

"Okay. Safe travels, my love." I run my hands down his chest and step back and watch him walk toward security and his terminal.

~

"NATALIE?" Jules calls as I open the front door to my house. I have hardly been here all week.

"Yeah, it's me." I really don't feel well, and I don't think it has anything to do with Luke's trip.

"Did Luke leave this morning?"

I walk into the kitchen. Jules is buttering a bagel, and as the aroma hits my nose, it turns my stomach.

"Oh shit." I run for the hall bathroom and throw up, barely making it in time.

"Hey, are you okay?" She's standing in the doorway, watching me. Jules is one of the only people in the world I would let stand there and watch me hurl.

"I think I must have the flu. I've been feeling queasy all morning. I thought it was nerves, but apparently not."

My stomach convulses again, and I grip on to the toilet as I violently retch.

Jules disappears and comes back with a glass of water for rinsing my mouth and cool washcloth. She sets the glass on the sink and presses the cloth to my neck, and I moan.

"Thank you."

"Let's get you upstairs and in bed. Lie down for a while and see if your stomach settles."

"Okay."

Jules follows me upstairs. I don't feel too bad, just intensely nauseated. I hate throwing up.

My phone pings in my pocket as I climb on the bed. It's a text from Luke.

*About to take off. No one recognized me. I miss you already, beautiful.*

I smile and hit reply.

*I miss you, too. Be safe. I want you home in one piece, please.*

And, I have to barf again. I run for my bathroom and stay there for the next thirty minutes. Jules is hovering with wet rags and water and makes me shove a towel under my knees.

"I think we should go to the ER."

"No, I'm fine." I retch some more.

"Yes, I can see that you're in top form," Jules replies drily.

"Don't be a bitch."

"Nat, I'm worried. You can't stop throwing up."

"I don't have anything left to throw up."

"Yet you're still dry heaving. This isn't normal, even for the flu. You don't have a fever."

My abs are starting to ache as I continue to heave over the toilet.

"Nat, don't make me call my mother."

"She'll side with me," I reply.

"Fine, I'll call Luke."

"No, he can't do anything from LA anyway."

More heaving. God, there's nothing left in me! What is wrong with me?

"Okay, Nat…get in the goddamn car. Here's a bucket." Jules shoves a big plastic bowl under my face and helps me to my feet. "An hour of uncontrollable barfing is too much. You're probably dehydrated."

She helps me into the car and takes me to a nearby hospital emergency room. Surprisingly, it's fairly quiet, and I'm processed through triage and into a room quickly. I'm thankful that Jules is with me to give them my personal information. I can't stop heaving long enough to form a sentence.

I manage to give a urine sample and change into a hospital gown.

"Natalie, I'm Mo. I'll be your nurse today. Put this pill under your tongue. It's called Zofran, and it'll help the nausea." I gratefully accept the medicine from the kind, petite nurse and take a deep breath.

"Let's get another set of vitals." Mo smiles and takes my temperature, blood pressure and heart rate.

"Everything is normal. That's a good sign. Dr. Anderson will be here in a few moments."

"Thank you." Jules pulls a chair up next to me, and my phone starts to ring. It's Luke.

"Hello?"

"Hey, baby, I'm at the hotel. Everything okay?"

"Yes, everything's fine. I'm just hanging out with Jules."

Jules' eyes go round, and she mouths, *What the fuck are you doing?* I brush her off.

"Okay, good. I'm heading back out to my first meeting. I'll text you when I can."

"All right, have a good meeting. I love you."

"I love you, too." I hear the smile in his voice as he hangs up.

"Natalie…"

"Stop. He can't do anything from LA. There's no need to worry him. He'll be home tomorrow anyway."

"He should know that you're in the emergency room."

God, she's stubborn.

"That pill they gave me is helping with the puking. They'll probably just send me home."

"Knock, knock." A small blond woman pokes her head through the door. "I'm Dr. Anderson. I hear you're not feeling well, Natalie."

"I've been throwing up for about the last hour and a half."

"Has it been steady, or does it come and go?"

"Steady. Couldn't breathe until the nurse gave me that anti-nausea pill."

"Any other symptoms like diarrhea, fever, abdominal pain?" She is jotting down notes in my chart as we talk.

"No, just the vomiting. I was a little nauseous early this morning, but I thought it was just nerves. Then the vomiting started."

"Okay, well, it sounds like we've got that stabilized." She pushes on the skin on my hands and looks in my mouth and nose. "You're pretty well dehydrated, so I want to start an IV and get some fluids going. We'll take some blood and run your urine and see what we see, okay?" She smiles down at me kindly.

"Okay. Will I be able to go home today?"

"Most likely. Let's get some test results, and I'll be back in a little while."

"See?" I say to Jules after the doctor leaves. "I've probably just got the flu."

Nurse Mo bustles back into the room and starts my IV.

"Oh, no, I'm outta here!" Jules jumps up and runs out of the room.

I smirk at Mo. "She hates needles the way most of us hate spiders."

Mo laughs, draws some blood and bustles back out again, leaving me with Jules.

"How are you feeling?" she asks.

"Better. Still a tiny bit queasy, but I don't feel like I'm going to throw up anymore."

"Good. You were starting to scare me."

We sit in companionable silence for a while, both of us checking our phones and watching a bit of TV. We wait a really long time, about two hours, before we see the doctor again.

"I'm sorry for the wait. I had a few blood tests that I wanted to run, and they can take a little time." She pulls a chair up next to me, and it looks like she's settling in for a long chat.

Shit, what's wrong with me?

"I have some good news and some news that could go either way, depending on how you choose to look at it."

"Okay. I'll take the good news first, please."

"You're very healthy. All of your vitals are normal, and your labs all came back completely fine."

"Good."

"Except, and here's the other news, you're pregnant."

I hear Jules gasp beside me, but I don't understand.

"What did you say?"

"You're pregnant."

"No, that's impossible." I shake my head adamantly. There must be some mistake.

"Oh?" The doctor raises an eyebrow. "Why is that?"

"I'm on the Pill. I never, ever miss a pill. Never. I'm The Pill Nazi."

"The Pill can be very effective at preventing pregnancy, but just like all birth control, it can fail."

"No, if I take it the right way, which I do, I won't get pregnant."

I see Jules pick up her phone and start tapping the screen voraciously while the doctor smiles patiently at me and pats my leg.

"Natalie, the Pill is ninety-nine percent effective when taken correctly. There is a one percent chance that it can fail, and it seems that you are that one percent."

"What?!" The world starts to fall away from beneath me.

"She's right, Nat." Jules shoves her phone in my face. "Never mind that you have an educated MD right here telling you this, but WebMD concurs. Ninety-nine percent effective."

"I take it this is bad news?" Dr. Anderson asks.

I look at Jules, and she looks as shocked as I feel. "I don't know."

The doctor looks at my ring and smiles broadly. "Maybe it's just a shock. We ran both your urine and blood to confirm. I'd like to do an ultrasound to determine how far along you are."

Nurse Mo steps out of the room and returns with a little ultrasound machine on wheels. Instead of putting a probe on my flat belly, the doctor has me put my feet in the stirrups so she can use a vaginal probe.

"The baby is too small to see with the external probe," she explains.

Baby? *Oh. God.*

The nurse turns out the light, and we all look at the screen of the machine. Suddenly, there is a little black circle, about the size of a quarter, and inside is a flutter.

"There we are!" Dr. Anderson smiles. "I'd say you're at about six weeks along."

Jules grabs my hand, and we stare at the screen in awe.

"Is that the heart?" I ask, pointing to the fluttering on the screen.

"Yep. It's hard to make out much more on this machine, but the black area is the amniotic fluid, and that flutter is the heart. You're nausea and vomiting is something we call hyperemesis gravidarum. It's morning sickness times a hundred. You'll probably be pretty nauseated during this pregnancy, so I'll prescribe you some anti-nausea meds to use at home. They won't affect the baby. Also, stop the Pill immediately, start taking some prenatal vitamins with folic acid and make an appointment with your OB doctor in the next four weeks."

She hits a button on the machine, and a photo of the ultrasound prints out.

"Here, something for you to show off." She winks at me. "We're going to keep you for a while, push another bag of fluids and make sure your vomiting is under control, and then you can go home."

"Okay."

She leaves, and Jules and I just stare at each other.

"Are you okay?" she asks.

"No." I feel numb.

"I love your ring. The picture you texted me Saturday night didn't do it justice."

"Thanks."

"Okay, let's talk about this rationally." Jules takes my hand in hers and looks me in the eye. "He loves you."

"He'll think I'm trying to trap him."

She laughs—*laughs*—and squeezes my hand. "Natalie, that won't even cross his mind."

"His family will think that."

"Who gives a fuck?"

"He just barely proposed."

"Now you're just babbling. Natalie, look at me."

"It's too soon." My eyes fill as they find hers. Thank God she's here with me. "We just met. We're still learning each other, Jules. We've been engaged for less than a week. It's too soon."

The tears come in earnest as my phone rings again. I send it straight to voice mail.

"Nat, you have to talk to him."

"I'm not telling him this over the phone."

"No, he'll worry if you don't answer the phone, silly." My phone rings again, but I'm crying too hard now to answer it.

"You answer. Tell him I'm in the bathroom or something."

"Natalie's phone," Jules answers. "No, sorry, Luke, she's in the bathroom. Want me to have her call you back? Uh huh. Oh, okay, I'll tell her. Bye."

"Well?" I ask when she hangs up.

"He's going into another meeting, but he'll call you later."

"Good." I let my head fall against the bed. "Oh God, what am I going to do?"

"What are you talking about? You and Luke are going to be parents." Jules takes my hand again. "Nat, you'll be awesome parents."

"It's too soon," I whisper and put both hands over my face and weep.

# CHAPTER 32

My crying jag subsides, and I take a deep breath as Nurse Mo returns to change my IV bag.

How am I going to tell Luke that I'm pregnant? I know he wants kids, and so do I, but not yet. We're not even married yet. I couldn't bear it if he thought I was trying to trap him into something he doesn't want.

Jules turns on the TV and flips through channels, pausing when she finds a nightly entertainment gossip show.

"We spotted Luke Williams out today."

Holy shit!

"He was having a romantic lunch with Vanessa Horn, one of his former co-stars from the *Nightwalker* movies. Has Luke finally come out of hiding to rekindle his romance with the lovely Vanessa? They were engaged to be married for over a year before their split early last year. We smell love in the air! We will be sure to keep you updated on Luke and Vanessa as we get more details."

There is a series of photos rolling across the screen, taken today. I recognize the black T-shirt and jeans he wore on the plane. He and the beautiful blond Vanessa are indeed leaving a restaurant, his arm is around her shoulders, and he's smiling down at her, his nose pressed against her ear. Then there's a photo of him wrapping his arms around her shoulders and pulling her in for a kiss. The camera is angled badly, so I can't actually see the lip-lock, but it's obvious that's what they're doing. In the next photo, she's getting into a car, and he's holding the door for her. In the last photo, he's getting into the driver's side of that same car.

"Holy fuck, he's cheating on me."

"We don't know that."

"I just saw it with my own eyes!"

"Nat, it's the fucking paparazzi. They make everything up."

"Pictures don't lie. I know that better than anyone. You saw the way he was touching her and looking at her. He kissed her."

The jealousy running through me is primal. My heart is hammering. I'm breathing hard, and I feel my face heat. If I didn't have anti-nausea meds on board, I'd be hurling again.

"Natalie," Jules murmurs and takes my hand. "I'm sure it's not what you think."

I shake my head and give in to the tears. "It's over."

"No, Natalie. No. Talk to him about it tomorrow."

"There's nothing to talk about." I shake my head again, unable to believe what I just saw. "I can't trust him. I can't live this celebrity life with him."

"You're being silly."

"Shut up! You're supposed to be on my side! You're *my* goddamn friend, not his. He's fucking around on me! I just saw proof, so show some fucking loyalty, Jules."

"I'm sorry." She starts to cry, too, and I feel like a shit.

"Come here." I scoot over, and she crawls up onto the bed with me, holding me to her as we weep. "What am I going to do?"

"Take some time. You've just found out you're pregnant after being violently ill. You're not thinking straight. Take some time." She's stroking my hair, and I am so thankful for her.

"Okay."

My phone pings, and it's a text from Luke.

*Almost done with today's meetings, baby. Will call you tonight. Love you.*

"Fucker." I throw the phone down and don't bother to answer, but the floodgates open to more tears. About five minutes later, there's another text.

*I haven't heard from you all day. I miss you. You okay?*

"Nat, you have to talk to him."

"No." I turn the phone off and throw it in my handbag.

A few minutes later, Dr. Anderson returns with my prescriptions and discharge instructions. "You're free to go, Natalie. Good luck."

I'm going to need it.

Jules drives us to the pharmacy and then home. I'm loaded down with medication and vitamins.

When we get home, I go up to my room and crawl onto the bed, curl into a ball and weep like I haven't since my parents died. I feel like my world is literally falling apart, and essentially, it is. I can't be with Luke. He'll make up excuses for what I saw today, but he can't change it. He had his hands on that woman, in an intimate way. He used to be engaged to her, and he lied to me when he told me he never spoke to his former fiancée.

I press my hand to my belly. Oh God, and what am I supposed to do about the baby? Be a single parent? I guess I can do that. I don't see a choice. But the thought of it tears my heart out.

I fall asleep in the middle of my bed, sobbing and mourning the best relationship I've ever had, the loss of the one person I saw myself spending the rest of my life with.

~

"WAKE UP, NAT." I startle awake at Luke's voice.

"What are you doing here?"

His eyes are worried, and he's leaning over me, his face pale. "I couldn't reach you all day, and I was worried so I came home. Why didn't you tell me you were sick?"

"Who told you I'm sick?" I sit up and scoot back out of his grasp, and he frowns, confused.

"Jules said you'd been sick today, and she took you to the ER. Baby, you don't look very good."

"Yeah, I'm probably contagious. You should go home." I wrap my arms around myself, and I just can't look him in the face.

"Natalie, what's wrong?"

"I just don't feel good."

"Bullshit, look at me. Where's your ring?" His eyes are on my left hand.

"In my jewelry box."

"Why isn't it on your finger?" His voice is rising, and he's starting to look desperate, and I'm still sad and pissed and hormonal, and I know this is not going to go well.

"Luke, I think you should go home."

"No. Tell me what's wrong."

I can't stop the tears as they fall down my face. Luke reaches for me, but I pull back.

"Let me touch you."

"No." I shake my head. "I just want you to go home."

Luke pushes his hands through his hair in frustration. "Nat, let me help. Talk to me."

"You've done enough."

"What does that mean?"

"Just go home!" I shout.

"No!" he shouts back.

I hang my head in my hands and hate myself for crying in front of him. "Just go," I whisper.

"You're scaring the shit out of me. What is wrong?"

"I saw you." I raise my face and look him square in the eye. "I saw you with Vanessa outside of a restaurant in LA. I saw you with your arm around her and your nose against her fucking ear, your mouth was on hers, and you got into a car with her."

He frowns and swallows.

"Now get the fuck out."

"Natalie, that was a lunch meeting for a movie I'm asking her to do. There were three other people there. Did you see them in the photos, too?"

"I don't care."

"I'm not lying to you."

"I know what I saw."

"You saw exactly what the motherfucking paparazzi wanted you to see! I told you from the beginning, you need to talk to *me*, Natalie."

I'm shaking my head adamantly. "You lied to me when you told me that you don't speak to your ex-fiancée. You wig out on me about Brad, ask me to respect your feelings when it comes to working with men, but you don't give me a heads-up that you're going to be meeting with a woman you not only used to fuck but were supposed to marry? According to those photos, you more than talk to her. Did you fuck her in that car?"

"Jesus Christ, no! Is that what you think?"

"Just go. I can't trust you, and I don't want you here."

"You're making this more than what it is. I'm telling you, it was a business meeting."

"Okay. I still don't want you here."

"Fuck, Nat." He stands up and paces around my room, looking everywhere, running his hands through his hair. "Why won't you believe me?"

"You lied to me, and that's a line I can't deal with you crossing."

"I didn't lie!" he shouts. "I haven't spoken to her until this week when I asked her to do the fucking movie!"

Oh, why won't he just go? My tears are coming again.

"Baby, don't cry. I promise, I'm not lying to you about this." He steps toward me, but I hold my hand up, stopping him.

"You need to know what seeing that did to me. You didn't look like colleagues, Luke. You had your hands on her, and the look on your face was the one you give me when you smile at me." He swallows, and I continue. "You effectively ripped my heart out and stomped it to dust with just one look. Now, I'm upset and hurt and hormonal, and I can't deal with you tonight. I need you to give me some space, and I need it now because I just can't look at you anymore."

"Natalie, we've both done things we regret. Fuck, your whole body is a road map to your mistakes."

I blink at him. Did he seriously just say that to me?

"I guess this will just be an experience that I'll add to my road map. Now get out of my house before I call the police."

"I love you." He's looking me square in the eyes, his blue eyes bright with fear. "This is not over. I'll give you some time, but goddamn it, Nat, this is not over."

He leaves my room and slams the door behind him. A few seconds later, I hear the front door slam, too, and then I hear his car—the Lexus?—peel out of the driveway.

I lie back on the bed, too exhausted to cry or, ironically, sleep.

"I didn't tell him about the baby," I say as Jules walks into my room.

"I figured. Did he deny it?"

"He says it was a business lunch about a movie he's asking her to do." My voice is monotone.

"He could be telling the truth."

I glare at her, and she continues. "Natalie, if you hadn't just gotten the news about the baby five seconds before we saw the show, would you be reacting the same way?"

"Yes."

"I don't think so." Jules climbs on the bed with me but doesn't touch me. "Honey, I think today has just been an emotional roller coaster for you."

"That's the truth." I sigh and throw an arm over my face. "We hurt each other really bad tonight."

"I heard."

I glare over at her again, and she shrugs. "My room is fifteen feet away, and you were yelling."

"What do you think?" I ask, because I love her, and she loves me, and she'll tell me the truth.

"Do you want me to tell you the truth or do the best-friend-loyalty thing?"

"Um, both."

"Okay." She takes a deep breath and looks down at me. "Luke is the best thing that ever happened to you. I don't believe he was cheating on you today. I think that he needs to remember to be more careful of how he behaves, especially in public, because the fucking paparazzi will twist just about anything into a good story. But he's been away from all of that for years now, and I can understand why he let his guard down."

She pauses and gazes at me intently. "Natalie, he loves you. He had tears in his eyes when he stormed out of here. He knows he fucked up. Not only that"—she raises her hand to stop me from speaking—"you have to think about the baby, too. I'm not saying to stay with him for the sake of the baby, but I am saying that he needs to know, and you need to remember that you're incredibly hormonal."

I'm trying to process everything she's saying. She's right. I am probably blowing this way out of proportion.

"I don't want him to think I'm trying to trap him into being with me because of the baby," I whisper.

"Honey, why would he think that? You didn't do it on purpose."

"I'm scared."

"It's going to be okay." She wraps me in her arms and hugs me tight.

BY THE NEXT morning I'm starting to feel a little foolish. It's amazing what a night of sleep, some anti-nausea meds and a good cry will do.

Now, how do I make it right?

I take a long shower and frown at my puffy eyes in the mirror as I get ready for the day. I look horrible. I dress in some jeans and a sweater and pull my ring out of my jewelry box and put it back on my hand.

We have a lot of talking to do, but we'll get through this.

Jules is in the kitchen when I go downstairs. "You look horrible."

"Thanks. I feel a little better."

"Good. Going over there?"

"Yeah."

"Good."

"Okay, I guess I'll go."

"Everything is going to be fine."

"Thank you. For everything, Jules."

"I love you. Now go get your man." We grin at each other, and I leave the house, on foot. I'm going to walk to his place, get a little exercise and fresh air. He doesn't live too far away from me.

As I walk I think about all the ways he's shown me over the last two months that he loves me. The coffees, the massages, how he's always so concerned about how I'm feeling or what I'm thinking. Even his possessiveness is loving. And the flowers! All the hundreds of flowers.

Not to mention my birthday and taking me to Tahiti. Holding me on the plane. The way he held me at the cemetery.

My God, he loves me so much. And I threw it all back at him last night.

I have to apologize. I have to make it right.

I walk faster and make it to his house in less than fifteen minutes. I decide to knock on the door rather than use my key, because I'm not sure how I'll be received, but he doesn't answer. I ring the bell over and over, but still no answer.

Weird.

I let myself in with my key and wander through the house, calling his name. He's nowhere to be found. I go upstairs, and he's not there either. His bed looks like it hasn't been slept in since he and I left yesterday morning to take him to the airport.

Shit. Where is he?

I pull my phone out of my pocket and call him. It rings and rings and then goes to voice mail.

"Hey, it's me. I'm at your place, but you're not here. Please call me. I'm worried." I can't help but feel a little hypocritical after he came to me last night because he was worried and I threw him out.

I send him a text as well, in case he doesn't check his messages, and wander downstairs.

I go out onto the deck and sniff my flowers. They've stayed remarkably fresh-looking thanks to the cool, early fall weather. I sit on our love seat and can't help but remember Saturday night after Luke's parents' anniversary party when he proposed.

I look down at my ring and grin.

Where is he?

I try calling him again, but it goes to voice mail.

Suddenly, the doorbell rings, and I go to answer it. It's Samantha.

"Thank God you're here." She hugs me, and I automatically hug her back in shock.

"What's wrong?"

"I've been trying to find you. I don't know your phone number. I was just at your house, and Jules said you'd come here."

"What's wrong?" I repeat.

"It's Luke. Nat, he's been in an accident. We have to go to the hospital."

Oh, dear God, no!

# CHAPTER 33

"*W*hat happened?" I'm sitting in the passenger seat of Samantha's SUV, and she's driving like a bat out of hell. I brace myself against the dashboard as she makes a sharp right turn.

"I don't know the details. Dad called me about a half hour ago and said that he got a call from Harbor View Hospital to let him know that Luke is there. They had to wait for him to wake up to ask him who to call."

Her voice catches on a sob, and I instinctively grab her hand. Who cares if she hates me? I'm all she has right now.

"So he is awake?" The tears are rolling down my face unheeded. I just need to get to him, to hold him and make sure he's alive.

"He was. I guess he keeps coming in and out. Mom, Dad and Mark are already there. I don't know why none of us has your number. Well, I know why I don't, but no one else does either, but Luke told me where you live once, so I went to your place, and that's when Jules told me you'd gone to Luke's."

"Thank you for looking for me. I had no idea." God, drive faster!

"Natalie, I'm so sorry for everything." We're both sobbing now. "I didn't realize until Saturday morning how much you mean to each other, and I was just looking out for him. That bitch Vanessa did a number on him, and I just couldn't bear it if anyone hurt him like that again. But I can see the way you look at each other, you really love each other."

"I know. Don't worry about it, Sam. Just get us to him, please." Oh God, what will I do if I lose him? After all the horrible things I said to him?

What if he never sees his baby?

No, I mustn't think like that. He's fine.

Please let him be fine!

Samantha finds parking and scrolls through her text messages as we run into the huge Seattle medical plaza to find the text from her father instructing us where to go.

We hold hands in the longest elevator ride of my life. Finally, we find his room. Neil and Lucy are standing outside the door, talking with a doctor. Lucy comes to us immediately when she sees us hurrying down the corridor.

"He's going to be okay."

Oh, thank Christ.

"What happened? Can I see him?" I can't control the tears streaming down my face, and I just want to push her aside and run to my love.

"Yes, you can see him. They have him sedated." Lucy holds one of our hands in each of hers. "We could have lost him."

I look down at her and see the circles under her blue eyes, her pale skin. I hug her close.

"What happened?" I ask again.

"He was in a car accident very early this morning, around two a.m. A drunk driver sideswiped him and sent him into the median on Interstate 5." Lucy wipes the tears under her eyes, and I feel like retching.

It was after I sent him away. Oh, this is all my fault!

"Why was he out at that time?" Samantha asks.

"We got in a fight," I whisper. "This is my fault. Oh God, I'm so sorry."

"No, sweetie, no." Lucy folds me in her arms and rocks me. "It's not your fault."

"Nat, you go see him. I'll stay here with Mom." Sam pats my shoulder reassuringly, and I walk into Luke's room.

My world stops moving.

He's lying so still in the hospital bed. There's a bandage above his left eye and a large bruise on his cheek. He's in a hospital gown very much like the one I wore yesterday. There is a clamp on his index finger, a blood pressure cuff on his arm and an IV in the crook of his elbow. His left wrist is bandaged tightly.

I walk over to the side of his bed and grip his right hand in mine, then sink down in the chair and begin to weep.

"Please, baby, wake up. I need to hear your voice." I'm stroking his hand and staring him in the face, willing him to wake up.

Neil walks in the room and pats my shoulder. "They gave him some medicine to help him sleep."

"Are there internal injuries?" I ask.

"No, he has some bruised ribs and a sprained wrist, and he got knocked around a bit, but he's very lucky. If the car had spun in the other direction, he would have gone over the bridge."

I gasp and rest my cheek against Luke's shoulder. "I'm so sorry."

"Natalie, it's not your fault, honey. Couples fight."

I look up at Neil in surprise.

"Lucy told me that you'd fought and that that's probably why Luke was out so late." He smiles kindly and pats my shoulder again.

"I could have lost him," I whisper.

"He's going to be fine. He'll just need some TLC for a few weeks. I'm going to take Lucy and the kids down to the cafeteria for some breakfast. Take your time."

"I'm not leaving him."

"I'm not asking you to."

A pretty blond nurse bustles in and checks Luke's vital signs and smiles at me. "He's doing really well. Are you Natalie?"

"Yes," I respond, surprised.

"He was asking for you this morning when he regained consciousness. He'll be glad to see you when he wakes up." She winks at me and leaves the room, and Luke and I are alone.

"Oh, honey." I lean up and run my fingers through his soft blond hair. I hate seeing Luke like this, broken and vulnerable in this sterile bed. He's so strong and steady. This is not him. It's not right.

And I know that everyone says it's not, but I can't help but feel that it's my fault that he's here.

My phone rings, and it's Jules.

"Hello," I whisper, so I don't wake Luke.

"What the hell is going on?"

I can tell she's in a panic, and I start talking, low and fast. "Luke was in an accident after he left our place last night. We're at Harbor View. He's okay, just beat up, but they have him sedated."

"I'm on my way."

"Thanks, Jules."

I sit at Luke's side all morning as people come and go. His parents and siblings come in to hug me, and they take turns sitting vigil with me. Jules comes, bringing me a coffee and to also sit with me for a while.

The nurse and doctor both bustle in and out, reading machines and taking notes.

"How long will he sleep?" I ask the doctor.

"We gave him the medicine about six hours ago now, so he should wake up soon."

"Can I snuggle next to him?" I look at the doctor, pleading with my eyes.

"His left wrist is sprained, and a couple ribs also on the left side are bruised. Stick to his right side, and you'll be fine, but be gentle."

"Thank you."

I gingerly wriggle up next to his right side and kiss his stubbly cheek. I rest my head on his shoulder and run my fingers through his hair and down his face.

Oh, I love him so.

"I love you so much," I whisper to him. "I'm so sorry for the way I acted. I'm so sorry."

I continue to croon to him, laying my head on his shoulder and resting my hand over his heart. I stay very still so as not to move him and jostle him.

I wake to Luke's lips on my forehead. I lift my head and find his beautiful blue eyes gazing down at me.

"Oh God, Luke." The tears start again, but they're tears of relief. He's awake!

"Hush, baby, I'm okay."

I adjust myself so he can wrap his right arm around my shoulders, and I run my fingers through his hair. "I'm so sorry. For everything."

He kisses my forehead again. "I'm sorry too." He brushes his fingers through my hair, and I kiss his jaw.

"How do you feel?"

"Sore. Relieved that you're here."

"Sam found me this morning."

"She did?"

"Yeah, your parents called her, and she found me at your place."

His eyebrows shoot up. "My place?"

"I went there this morning to apologize, but you weren't home, so I was waiting for you there. Jules told her I was there." As I remember those horrible moments of not knowing if he was dead or alive, I shudder.

"Are you cold?" he asks.

"No, I'm worried about you. Why were you out so late?"

"I couldn't go home. You weren't there. You wouldn't let me stay with you, so I just decided to drive."

I close my eyes and shake my head, ashamed of how I spoke to him last night.

"Yesterday was rough," I whisper.

"Yes, it was. Will you tell me about it?"

I sit up, and he frowns. "First, let me get the doctor so he can examine you, and once we get you taken care of, if you still want to talk, we will."

"Don't leave me." He holds on to me tightly, clenching his eyes shut.

"Never again," I tell him, and his eyes open quickly, finding mine. "Never," I repeat.

I reach over and push the red nurse-call button.

"How can I help you?" a disembodied voice asks.

"Luke is awake," I respond, still stroking Luke's hair.

"Someone will be right in."

"Hello, Mr. Williams." The doctor smiles at Luke and, seeing me curled up at his side, winks at me. "I have good news for you. We're going to kick you out of here tomorrow. You're banged up pretty good, but nothing is broken, and according to the CT scan, you don't have any internal injuries. You are a very lucky man."

"Thank you. Can I eat?"

"Are you hungry?" I ask him.

"Starving."

"Sure, you can eat. Start with something light. No steaks today."

I get up off the bed so the doctor can examine Luke. Taking advantage of the time, I call Jules and ask her to bring Luke a light sandwich and cup of soup from our favorite deli, and then I call Luke's mom, using the number she gave me earlier, to let them know that Luke is awake and being released tomorrow.

They promise to visit later this evening.

The doctor finishes up as I hang up the phone.

"Jules is bringing you some dinner." I take his right hand in mine and bring it up to my cheek.

"You should go home and eat, get some rest."

"I'm not leaving until you do."

I expect a bit of an argument, but he smiles shyly and caresses my cheek. "Okay. Will you tell me about yesterday?"

"Persistent, aren't you?"

"I want to know what happened."

"Maybe we should talk about this tomorrow, after we're home."

"Talk to me, baby." His face is somber and a little sad, and I close my eyes. Should I tell him about the baby while he's here in the hospital, or should I wait?

I open my eyes, and he's still patiently watching me, and I know that he deserves to know the truth.

I take a deep breath. "I wasn't feeling well yesterday morning before you left, but I thought it was just nerves because you were flying, and I was scared."

I grip his hand in mine, and he squeezes gently. "I wish you'd told me."

"I didn't want to worry you. When I got back to my place, I got violently sick. I spent a good hour throwing up, even when there wasn't anything left to throw up." I squish up my nose in disgust. "Sexy, huh?"

"Keep talking," he responds.

"Jules made me go to the ER when the vomiting showed no signs of stopping."

"Why didn't one of you call me?"

"You were in meetings all day, and there was nothing you could do from LA."

"I could have caught the next flight out."

"I just wanted to see what the doctor said. I thought for sure I had the flu, and they would tell me to drink juice and sleep it off." I shrug.

"What did they tell you?"

I bite my lip and shut my eyes for just a moment. "Well, I'm healthy."

"But?"

Here goes nothing.

"I'm six weeks pregnant," I whisper.

I'm looking down at our hands. The room is silent.

Finally, after what feels like hours, he whispers, "Look at me."

I shake my head no.

"Look at me, baby."

"I didn't do it on purpose."

"Look at my face, Natalie."

I slowly look up at him, and he is gazing at me with love and wonder and a little confusion. But he's not mad.

"You're not angry?" I ask.

"Why would I be angry?"

"Because it's too soon." I shake my head and close my eyes. "It's just too soon."

"I'm not angry. But, Nat, didn't you say that you were on birth control?"

"I was. I'm OCD when it comes to taking my pill, but the doctor said that, just like all birth control methods, it can fail, and clearly, it did."

I look up into his gorgeous face and take a deep breath, steadying myself to finish the story.

"So, the doctor told me I was pregnant and did an ultrasound to see how far along I am. I have a picture. I'll show you in a minute."

"Okay," he whispers.

"After the doctor left, Jules was flipping through channels on the TV in the room and stopped on an evening gossip show, and that's when I saw you." I try to release his hand so I can stand and pace, but he holds on tight.

"Don't go. Finish the story."

"My world fell apart. I hated seeing those pictures, more than I've hated anything in my life. I hated the way you were looking at her..." My voice cracks, and I clear my throat.

"Nat, it was nothing."

"I know, but it didn't look like nothing, and then I learned that you'd been engaged to her, and I was hormonal and scared and sick, and I just wanted to be in your arms."

"Come up here."

I lie back down next to him, and he cradles me close to him.

"When I couldn't reach you yesterday, it made me crazy. I couldn't concentrate in any of my meetings. It's not like you to not respond or answer your phone."

"At first I didn't know what to say, and then I was mad at you."

"I caught a late flight back to Seattle and went straight to your place, and you know the rest."

"I'm sorry for the things I said."

"Me, too."

"Luke, I don't want you anywhere near that woman. I don't want you to work with her."

"I called her after I left your place last night and told her that I was going with someone else for the movie. I won't talk to her again. I'm sorry I hurt you. I wasn't holding her when we left the restaurant. I certainly didn't kiss her. I probably hugged her goodbye, but it didn't mean anything. I don't even remember what I was doing, but the rags always twist things to look the way they want them to. I was probably thinking about calling you."

"So," Luke says, and I tilt my head back so I can see his eyes, "we're having a baby."

He smiles, widely, and just looks so...*proud of himself.*

"Looks that way."

"I guess we'd better get married sooner rather than later."

"Luke, I don't want you to feel like you have to marry me just because I'm pregnant..."

"Stop right there. I asked you to marry me before we knew you were pregnant."

"I know, but..."

"No buts. Natalie, I love you so much. I want children with you. This is a wonderful thing. It is soon, sooner than I would have preferred, but a baby is never a bad thing. You're going to be a fantastic mom."

I didn't know I could cry so much in one day. More tears flow. I'm relieved and happy and so in love with this beautiful man.

He leans down and rubs his nose across mine and kisses me in that gentle way that makes me swoon. "I love you, baby."

"I love you, too."

"Oh God, Natalie, the poor man has almost been killed. Must you maul him?" Jules breezes in with a bag full of food. She shakes her head in exasperation.

"Don't be a brat, Jules." I sit up and start unloading Luke's food for him. My stomach grumbles, and I'm pleased to see that she brought some for me, too.

"We're having a baby." Luke gives Jules a wide smile.

"I know. I'm so happy for you guys." Jules walks to him and plants a kiss on his cheek, smiling at both of us.

"Lips off my man, Montgomery."

"Jesus, you're so selfish."

∼

WE'VE BEEN HOME for a week, and Luke has mostly recovered from his injuries. There will be no visits to the gym for a few more weeks, but the bruises have faded.

"The moving van is here."

"You are not lifting anything. Don't even think about it. Your wrist is still healing." He hasn't even lifted me lately, and I'm missing it.

"Well, that makes two of us."

"I didn't hurt my wrist." I raise an eyebrow at him as he crosses the great room to me.

"I do love your sassy mouth." He slaps my bottom, and I squeal, before he moves his hand around to settle on my belly. "There is no lifting for the beautiful woman I knocked up."

I laugh and caress his handsome face. "Are you sure about me moving in here?"

"Of course. We're getting married in two months anyway. It makes sense." He stiffens and frowns down at me. "Don't you want to?"

"I want to be wherever you are. It doesn't make sense for us to move in with Jules." I smirk. "Jules can live in the house as long as she pleases, and I'll still use the studio for work."

"But?" He raises an eyebrow.

"But I think that as our family grows, we might need more bedrooms."

His face softens, and he kisses me gently on the forehead. "I'll buy you any house you want."

"I want to stay here for now. We'll keep our options open."

"Okay." He kisses me again before the moving guys ring the doorbell and start unloading boxes and a few pieces of furniture. I left the majority of everything at the other house for Jules. All of the boxes go up into a spare bedroom, so I can sort through them at my own pace. The unloading doesn't take long.

"Do you need to work this afternoon?" I ask Luke after the men leave.

"No, you?"

"Nope." I walk toward the stairway and start ascending the stairs toward our bedroom.

"What in the world should we do to occupy our time on a rainy Thursday afternoon?" Luke murmurs in my ear at the top of the stairs.

"Hmm…we could read," I suggest.

"Nah, I've been doing a lot of that lately." He nibbles my neck and wraps his hands around my waist, spreading his palm over my belly.

"We could watch a movie."

"I'm not in the mood."

We finally make it to the bedroom, and I turn in his arms, kissing him softly while I run my fingers down his cheek.

"I'm all out of ideas," I whisper.

"That's okay," he whispers back. "I have a few ideas of my own."

# EPILOGUE

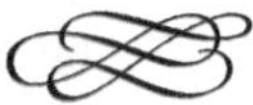

"*H*oly shit."

I'm standing in a beautiful bungalow in Tahiti, in front of a full-length mirror, and I don't even recognize the woman staring back at me.

I love my wedding dress. It's long and billowy. It's white chiffon with a beaded bodice and spaghetti straps, and the skirt falls from the empire waist all the way to the ground. I won't be wearing shoes today. My makeup is classic and simple, perfect for a beach wedding, and my hair is curled into an intricate bun behind my left ear with a red rose pinned to it.

I'm wearing my pearls.

"You are stunning." Jules kisses my cheek, and I smile at her nervously. She is also stunning in her simple pink chiffon gown.

I look around the bungalow and smile in happiness and warmth and love. I am surrounded by beautiful women. Luke's mom, Lucy, and Jules' mom, Gail, have their heads together in a corner. They both look lovely in their pretty pink dresses.

Samantha and Stacy are cooing over little Sophie, who is simply adorable in a soft pink dress with a pink headband.

Jules is, of course, my maid of honor, and Stacy and Sam are my bridesmaids. Sam and I buried the hatchet after Luke's accident, and we have become good friends. She did most of the legwork on planning this fantastic wedding.

"Are you nervous?" Stacy asks.

"I wasn't until I put this dress on. Now I'm a little nervous." I smile and look back in the mirror. Holy shit, I'm getting married!

Neil walks through the door and smiles widely when he sees all of us. "I've been sent in here to give you this." He hands me a wrapped box with a card attached and kisses my cheek. "It's almost time."

"Are the boys ready?" I ask.

"Yes, and your soon-to-be husband is a nervous wreck. He is ready to make you his wife."

I laugh and kiss Neil's cheek. "Here, take this back to him." I hand him a wrapped box, also with a note. "And tell him I'll meet him in a few. I'll be the one in white."

I walk into the bedroom to open the gift in private. My man does enjoy spoiling me. As if renting out this entire beautiful resort for our family and friends to enjoy for a whole week and our beautiful wedding weren't enough, he's given me little gifts every day.

I'm crazy about him.

Luke has written on the envelope of the card, *Open the box first, then read this.*

He's so bossy.

I unwrap the beautiful white paper, and there is a small Tiffany-blue box. Inside, nestled in the satin, is a pair of amazing diamond earrings. They are soft pink princess-cut diamonds with teardrop diamonds dangling from them. They take my breath away.

I open the card and sit on the side of the bed.

*My Love,*

*When you read this, you will be minutes away from becoming my wife. I can't express to you how honored I am that you are mine. I am ready to love you for the rest of my life, as your husband.*

*I love you, with all that I am.*

*—Luke*

Well, isn't he a charmer?

∼

NATALIE DECIDED that returning to Tahiti with our family and friends was where she wanted to get married, so I've flown everyone here and booked the resort for the week, just for our affair. I hope it's everything she ever dreamed it would be.

I button my white shirt and check my reflection in the mirror of the master bedroom of my parents' bungalow. Nat wanted the guys to wear khaki pants with white shirts for the ceremony, so that's what we're wearing.

She's the boss.

My hair is a mess, as usual, and it doesn't make sense to fix it, because Nat's fingers will be in it as soon as she sees me.

I smile as I think of my bride. I am one lucky son of a bitch. Natalie is, without a doubt, the sexiest woman I've ever seen, all long dark hair, beautiful green eyes, and smoking-hot curvy body. But her heart is what caught me. Her gracious, loving nature, and sassy mouth are what I can't ever imagine living without.

And I don't have to.

"Hey, Williams, stop mooning over yourself and get in here for a celebratory shot!" Jules' brother Isaac calls from the main room of the bungalow.

All the guys are here: My brother, Mark; Jules'—and Nat's—brothers, Isaac, Caleb, Matt and Will; and their father, Steven. My dad raises his glass as he hands me mine in a toast.

"To my son and Natalie. Thank God she said yes."

"Here, here!"

Everyone slams down the shot, and the room erupts once again in chaos, men yelling lewd jokes and throwing insults.

It does not calm my nerves.

I'm not at all nervous about marrying my girl. I'm just ready for it to be over already.

"Dad, I need you to take something over to Natalie." I hand my dad a small blue Tiffany box.

"No problem, I need to check in with your mother anyway. Are you about ready?" He smiles and pats my back.

"Yes, I've been ready. Let's get this show on the road." My dad laughs as he heads over to the bridal suite, and Isaac approaches me with another shot.

"No, man, I need a clear head for this." I wave off the shot and look out the door toward Nat's bungalow.

"This isn't for you, moron, it's for me." He grins and slugs back the tequila and winces. "Fuck, that's good. Are you ready for this?"

"Everyone keeps asking me that. Yes, I'm ready. I'm past ready."

"You're good for her, you know."

I look over into Isaac's face, shocked. All of Natalie's family have always been welcoming and friendly with me, but I know the brothers have had reservations, and as a brother myself, I can't blame them.

"How so?"

Isaac shrugs and looks back over at the other guys, then back to me. "She's opened up more, laughs more. Hell, I don't know, man. She's just happy. I've known her for a long time, and I don't remember ever seeing her smile this much."

"I'm glad." I nod and smile to myself.

"But if you hurt her, or that baby," Isaac continues, and I know what he's going to say, "I'll fucking kill you."

"No need. I'm not going to hurt her." I hold my hand out to shake his, and he takes it, then pulls me into a guy hug.

"Welcome to the family, bro."

"The girls are ready." My dad stalks back into the room with a wrapped gift in his hand. I told her not to get me anything. She and the baby are everything I need. "This is for you."

I walk into the bedroom to open the gift, and the note, alone, wondering if she likes the pink diamond earrings I sent over. Everything in this wedding is pink, and she should have pink diamonds, too.

*Luke,*

*I know you said that Baby and I are all you need today, but I couldn't help but get you a gift. I chose this particular gift because it symbolizes how precious time is. I am grateful for the time you give me, and for the many years we are about to spend together, as a family, and as lovers. You are what I was waiting for, Luke, and I can't believe that in a few short hours you will be truly mine, as I am yours.*

*Thank you for picking me to share this life with.*

*Love,*

*Nat*

*P.S. I can't wait to kiss you.*

And she calls me charming. God, I love that woman.

Inside the white box is a platinum Omega watch with a black face. On the inside is an inscription, which makes me grin. Nat is big on inscriptions. That sexy body of hers is full of them.

*You are my now, always, forever. —Nat*

Well, hell.

I fasten the watch on my left wrist and stomp back into the main room. "Let's go. No more waiting around."

Without waiting for an answer from anyone, I walk down the wooden boardwalk to the sandy beach where the ceremony will be held. The resort did a great job getting set up with white chairs, a small arbor with red roses, and candles lit and scattered over the sand, giving the beach a soft glow. It's almost sunset, and I know Nat would think the lighting is perfect.

I shake hands and wave at some of our fifty or so guests who have flown here for the week-long celebration and make my way up to the arbor with Isaac and Mark right behind me. The front row is reserved for our parents, and I made sure to have the resort place lilies and sunflowers on two of the chairs in honor of Natalie's parents.

Where is she? I see the girls, all in pink dresses. I'm relieved that my sister, Sam, and Nat have become friends and gotten to know each other better since I proposed. Sam happily helped plan this wedding.

Our mothers are escorted to their seats, and my heart starts to beat a little faster. Jesus, I can't stand the suspense. I need to see her.

Where the fuck is she?

Finally Jules, Sam and Stacy make their way toward us and take their places, and the music changes. Natalie and Jules' father come into view, and the rest of the world just falls away. Her beautiful dark hair has been curled and pulled into a loose bun behind her left ear with a rose tucked in it. Her dress is long and billowy, with a beaded top and spaghetti straps, and she's holding a large bouquet of red roses with the pearls inside. Her new diamonds sparkle at her ears, and, thank God, she's wearing our pearls.

I feel the grin spread across my face as I stare into her gorgeous green eyes, and my heart calms. This is it.

"Who gives this woman to this man?" the pastor asks.

"On behalf of her parents, I do," Steven responds, and places Nat's hand in mine.

Every time I touch her, I feel the hit to my gut. Every single time. I'm drawn to her in ways I never knew possible, and I will never grow tired of the feeling I get when she's near me.

"You are stunning," I whisper to her and grin as she smiles shyly and looks up at me through her long dark lashes.

"You're pretty beautiful yourself," she whispers back.

She can call me beautiful any damn time.

"Welcome, friends and family," the pastor begins. He says a quick prayer and moves right into the ring ceremony.

"With this ring, I thee wed," Natalie says, her eyes on mine, in her soft, sweet voice, and places my ring on my finger.

"With this ring, I thee wed," I respond and push the wedding band onto her small finger, next to her engagement ring.

The rest of the ceremony is relatively short. We decided against the unity candle ceremony and live music, wanting to focus solely on our vows to one another. We wrote our vows together, last week before we left for Tahiti.

We laughed, argued, and Nat cried, but we eventually came up with what we both want to say. Instead of each of us saying the vows in their entirety, we will say them together, alternating the lines.

"And now, Luke and Natalie will recite their vows together." The pastor steps back, and I take both of Natalie's small hands in mine, rubbing my thumbs over her knuckles.

"Are you ready?" I whisper and take a deep breath.

"Yes," she whispers back, her sassy smile in place. God, that smile does things to me.

I clear my throat, and as I look deeply into her eyes, we begin.

"I vow to love you."

"I vow to love you," she responds, her voice strong.

"To respect you."

"To be your best friend."

"To read aloud to you." I run my knuckle down her smooth cheek and see her eyes start to well up.

"To lead a charmed life."

"To write you love letters."

"To laugh at your jokes." She winks at me, and I grin.

"To always make the coffee, or have it delivered."

"To help you cook."

"To always believe that your newest haircut is the best you've ever had." I tuck a strand of her soft hair behind her ear.

"To be patient."

"To always support your hopes and dreams."

"To not overshadow you with my fame," she says, and I can't help but laugh with everyone else.

"To be your biggest fan," I respond. God, I love her.

"To wake you every morning."

"To wake *you* every morning. You are not a morning person."

"To kiss you every night."

"To hold your hand."

"To always remember where I left my keys and phone."

"To cherish you." I take another deep breath.

"To believe in you."

"To believe in us."

"To never give up." She clenches my hands in hers more tightly.

"To never, *ever* give up."

"To forsake all others and be true to you."

"To work every day toward being the man you deserve."

"To work every day toward being the woman you deserve." We both have tears in our eyes now.

"Do you vow to be my wife?"

"I do. Do you vow to be my husband?"

"I do." Fuck, yes, I do.

"It is my pleasure to present Mr. and Mrs. Luke Williams. You may kiss your bride."

I cup her beautiful face in my hands, and she runs her fingers through my hair, gazing up at me with such love, such trust, it takes my breath away. I slowly lean down and brush my nose down hers and sweep my lips over hers in the way I know she loves. She sighs against me as I slide my arms around her, pulling her more tightly against me, and cup the small baby bump between us in my hands.

Our guests are applauding, our mothers dabbing at their tears. I rest my forehead against hers as she runs her fingers down my cheek.

"I love you," I whisper.

"I love you, too. Let's go dance."

IF YOU ENJOYED THIS STORY, you can see a full list of all of the books in the With Me In Seattle series here: https://www.kristenprobyauthor.com/with-me-in-seattle

*Easy Love*

*New York Times* and *USA Today* Bestselling Author

# KRISTEN PROBY

A BOUDREAUX NOVEL

Easy Love
Book One In The Boudreaux Series
By
Kristen Proby

EASY LOVE

Book One in The Boudreaux Series

Kristen Proby



Cover Art:

Photography by: Kristen Proby

Cover Design: Okay Creations

Published by Ampersand Publishing, Inc.

# PROLOGUE

## ẼLI~

"You work too hard." The voice comes from behind me. I'm standing behind my desk, gazing out over the French Quarter and the Mississippi River from my fifty-fourth floor office windows in New Orleans. The sun is blazing already. It's only eight in the morning, but it's a stifling eighty-six humid-filled degrees out there, much hotter than the cool comfort of my office.

It seems all I do is watch the world from this office window.

And where the fuck did that thought come from?

"Earth to Eli," Savannah says dryly from behind me.

"I heard you." I shove my hands in my pockets, fingering the silver half-dollar that my father gave me when I took this position, and turn to find my sister standing before my desk in her usual crisp suit, blue today, her thick dark hair pinned up and worry in her hazel gaze. "And, hello, pot, I'm kettle."

"You're tired."

"I'm fine." She narrows her eyes at me and takes a deep breath, making my lips twitch into a half smile. I love getting her riled up.

It's ridiculously easy.

"Did you even go home last night?"

"I don't have time for this, Van." I lower into my chair and motion for her to do the same, which she does after shoving a banana under my nose.

"But you have time to stare out the window?"

"Are you trying to pick a fight today? Because I'll oblige you, but first tell me what the fuck we're fighting about." I peel the banana and take a bite, realizing that I'm starving.

Savannah blows out a deep breath and shakes her head, while mumbling something about pigheaded men.

I smile brightly now.

"Lance giving you problems?" My hands flex in and out of fists at the idea of finally laying that fucker flat. Savannah's husband is not one of my favorite people.

"No." Her cheeks redden, but she won't look me in the eye.

"Van."

"Oh, good, you're both here," Beau says, as he marches into my office, shuts the door behind him, takes the seat next to Savannah, steals my half-eaten banana out of my hand, and proceeds to eat the rest of it in two bites.

"That was mine." My stomach gives a low growl, not satisfied in the least, and I give a brief thought to asking my assistant to run out for beignets.

"God, you're a baby," Beau replies, and tosses the peel in the garbage. My older brother is taller than my six-foot-four by one inch and as lean as he was in high school. But I can still take him.

"Why the fuck are you two in my office?" I sit back and run my hand over my mouth. "I'm quite sure you both have plenty to do."

"Maybe we missed you," Savannah says with a fake grin and bats her eyelashes at me.

"You're a smart ass."

She just nods knowingly, but then she and Beau exchange a look that has the hairs on the back of my neck standing up.

"What's going on?"

"Someone is stealing from us." Beau tosses a file full of spreadsheets in my direction. His jaw ticks as I open it and see columns of numbers.

"Where?"

"That's what we don't know," Savannah adds quietly, but her voice is full of steel. "Whoever's doing it is hiding it well."

"How did you find it?"

"By accident, actually," she replies crisply, all business now. "We know it has to be happening in accounting, but it's buried so deep that the who and how is a mystery."

"Fire the whole department and start over." I shut the file and lean back, just as Beau laughs.

"We can't fire more than forty people, most of whom are innocent, Eli. It doesn't work like that."

"There has to be a paper trail," I begin, but Savannah cuts me off with a shake of her head.

"We're paperless, remember?"

"Oh, yeah, saving the fucking trees. Are you telling me that no one knows what the fuck is going on?"

"It's not a huge amount of money, but it's big enough to piss me off," Beau says quietly.

"How much?"

"Just over one hundred G's. That we've found so far."

"Yeah, that's enough to piss me off too. They're not just stealing post-its out of the supply closet."

"And it's not predictable. If it was a regular amount, on a routine, we could find it no problem. But I don't want to cause mass hysteria in the company. I don't want everyone to think that we're looking over all of their shoulders every damn minute."

"Someone is stealing, and you're worried about the employees' feelings?" I ask with a raised brow. "Who the fuck are you?"

"He's right," Savannah adds. "Having the co-CEOs of the company on everyone's asses isn't good for morale."

"What about having the CFO do it?" I ask, referring to Savannah, who shakes her head and laughs.

"No, I don't think so."

"So, we just sit back and let whoever the fucker is use us as his own private ATM?"

"Nope." Savannah smiles brightly, her pretty face lighting up. "I want to bring Kate O'Shaughnessy in."

"Your college friend?" I glance at Beau, who has no expression on his face whatsoever. Typical.

"This is what she does for a living."

"She looks over people's shoulders for a living? She must be everyone's favorite person."

"You're on a roll today," Beau says quietly.

"Kate works with companies who are dealing with embezzlement. She comes in as a regular employee and blends in, investigating on the down-low."

"Can she actually do the job? It won't work if she doesn't know what she's doing."

"She has an MBA, Eli. But I want to put her in as an administrative assistant. They see and know everything, and they talk to each other. She's likable."

"Okay, works for me." I glance at Beau. "You?"

"I think it's the way to go," he agrees. "None of us have time to do it ourselves, and I don't trust handing this off to anyone else. Like Van said, people talk. I'd like to keep this quiet. Kate will sign all the necessary non-disclosure agreements, and from what I've heard, she's excellent at her job."

"One thing," Van says, and leans forward to stare at me, the way she does when I'm about to be in deep trouble. "You're not allowed to mess around with her."

"I'm not an asshole, Van…"

"No, you're not allowed to get your man-whore hands on her."

"Hey! I am not—"

"Yeah, you are," Beau says with a grin.

I sigh and roll my shoulders. "Not having the same date twice doesn't make me a whore."

Van simply raises a brow. "Leave her be."

"I'm a professional, Van. I don't sleep with the employees."

"Is that what you said to that assistant that sued us a few years back?"

"Anymore."

"God." Van shakes her head as Beau laughs. "She's a nice woman, Eli."

Instead of replying, I simply narrow my eyes at my sister and swivel in my chair. Kate's a grown woman; one I'm most likely not attracted to anyway.

It's been a few years since much of anything has held my interest for long. That would require feeling something.

"Call her."

# CHAPTER 1

## ~KATE~

"$\mathcal{H}$ello?" I ask breathlessly, as the cab I'm in whizzes down the interstate, heading directly for the heart of New Orleans.

"Where are you?" Savannah asks with a smile in her voice.

"In the cab on the way from the airport. Are you sure I shouldn't check into a hotel room?"

"No way, Bayou Industries owns a beautiful loft that we'll pretend you're renting while you're here. Come directly to the office. I have a meeting, so I won't be able to greet you, I'm sorry."

"It's okay," I reply and bite my lip as the cabbie cuts off another motorist and my stomach rolls. "I'm hoping to make it alive. I might not survive the cab ride."

Savannah chuckles in my ear, and then I hear her murmuring to someone else in her office. "I have to go. Eli will meet you."

"Eli? I thought I'd meet with Beau—"

"Eli's not as scary as we've all led you to believe. I promise." And then she's gone. The cab swerves again, and I send up a prayer of thanks that I didn't eat breakfast this morning as I use my hand to fan my face.

It's darn hot in the Big Easy.

During all the years I went to college with Savannah and her twin brother, Declan, I never did make it down here to visit them, and I can't wait to explore the French Quarter, eat beignets, have my tarot cards read, and soak it all in.

Of course, I'd rather soak it all in while not wearing so many clothes. Who knew it would be so hot in May? I shimmy out of my suit jacket, fold the sleeves over so they don't wrinkle, and watch as above ground cemeteries, old buildings, and lots of people zoom by.

Eli is the one Boudreaux sibling I've never met. I've seen photos of the handsome brother, and heard many stories about his stoic, tough, playboy ways. Van says the stories are exaggerated. I guess I'll find out for myself.

Well, not the playboy part. That's just none of my business.

Finally, we come to an abrupt stop. There's a red cable-car on one side and mountains of concrete on the other. I stumble out into the hot Monday afternoon, and sweat immediately beads on my forehead.

It's not just hot. It's sticky.

But I smile despite the discomfort, tip the reckless cabbie, and roll my suitcase behind me into the blessedly cool building, where a woman sits behind a long, ornate desk, typing furiously on a computer while speaking on the phone.

"Mr. Boudreaux is unavailable at this time, but I'll put you through to his assistant, one moment." She quickly pushes a series of keys, then smiles up at me.

She's very smiley.

"I'm Kate O'Shaughnessy."

"Welcome, Ms. O'Shaughnessy," she says, holding that smile in place. "Mr. Boudreaux is expecting you." She types furiously and begins speaking into her phone again. "Hello, Miss Carter, Ms. O'Shaughnessy is here for Mr. Boudreaux. Yes, ma'am." She clicks off efficiently. "Please have a seat. Can I get you some water?"

"No, thank you."

Miss Efficient simply nods and returns to her ringing phones. Before I have a chance to sit, a tall woman in black slacks and a red sleeveless blouse walks out of the elevator and straight to me.

"Ms. O'Shaughnessy?"

"Kate, please."

"Hello, Kate. Mr. Boudreaux is in his office. Follow me." She smiles and offers to take my suitcase, but I shake my head and follow her into the elevator. She doesn't ask me any questions, and I'm thankful. I've learned to lie well in this business, but I don't know what she's already been told. I'm led past an office area and into the largest office I've ever seen. The massive black desk sits before a wall of floor-to-ceiling windows. The furniture is big and expensive. Comfortable. There are two doors, each on opposite sides of the room, and I can't help but wonder what they lead to.

"Ms. O'Shaughnessy is here, sir."

"Kate," I add without thinking, and then any hope of being able to think at all is tossed right out of those spectacular windows, when the tall man standing before them turns to look at me. The photos didn't do him justice.

*Yum.*

The door closes behind me and I take a deep breath and walk toward him, hiding the fact that my knees have officially turned to mush.

"Kate," I repeat, and hold my hand out to shake his over his desk. His lips twitch as he watches me, his whiskey-colored eyes sharp and assessing as they take a slow stroll down my body, then back up to my face. Jeez, he's taller than I expected. And broader. And he wears a suit like he was born to it.

Which, I suppose he was. Bayou Enterprises has been around for five generations, and Eli Boudreaux is the sharpest CEO it's seen in years.

He moves around his desk and takes my hand in his, but rather than shake it, he raises it to his lips and places a soft kiss on my knuckles.

"Pleasure," he says in a slow New Orleans drawl. Dear God, I might explode right here. "I'm Eli."

"I know." He raises a brow in question. "I've seen photos over the years."

He nods once, but doesn't let go. His thumb is circling softly over the back of my hand, sending my body into a tailspin. My nipples have tightened, pressing against my white blouse, and now I wish with all my might that I hadn't taken off my jacket.

"Please, have a seat," he says, and motions to the black chair behind me. Rather than sit behind his desk, he sits in the chair next to mine and watches me with those amazing eyes of his.

A lock of dark hair has fallen over his forehead and my fingers itch to brush it back for him.

*Calm the eff down, Mary Katherine.* You'd think I'd never seen a hot man before.

Because I have.

Declan, the youngest of the Boudreaux brothers, is no slouch in the looks department, and he's one of my best friends. But being near him never made my knees weak or made me yearn for a tall glass of ice water. Or a bed. Or to rip his clothes off his body.

*Whoa.*

"Did Savannah fill you in on what's happening?" Eli asks calmly, his face revealing nothing. He crosses an ankle over the opposite knee and steeples his fingers, watching me.

"Yes, she and I have talked extensively, and she's emailed me all of the new-hire paperwork, as well as the NDA's, which I've printed and signed." I pull the papers out of my briefcase and pass them to Eli. Our fingers brush, making my thighs clench, but he seems unaffected.

Typical. I don't usually inspire hot lust from the opposite sex. Especially not men who look like Eli. Which is fine, because he's my boss and my best friends' brother and I'm here to work.

I clear my throat and push my auburn hair behind my ear. With all of this humidity, it's going to be a curly mess in no time.

"That's a beautiful ring," he says unexpectedly, nodding toward my right hand, still raised near my ear.

"Thank you."

"Gift?"

He's a man of few words.

"Yes, from my grandmother," I reply, and tuck my hands in my lap. He simply nods once and glances down at the papers in his hand. He frowns and glances up at me, but before he can say anything, his office door swings open and Declan walks in with a wide smile on his handsome face.

"There's my superstar." I squeal and leap up and into his arms, and Dec squeezes me tight and turns a circle in the middle of the wide office. He finally sets me on my feet, cups my face in his hands, and kisses me square on the mouth, then hugs me again, more gently this time. "You okay?" he whispers in my ear.

"I'm great." I gaze up into Dec's sweet face and years of memories and emotion fall around me. Laughter and tears, love, sadness, affection. "It's so good to see you."

"Have you done anything fun since you got to town?"

"I almost lost my life in a cab," I reply with a laugh. "I came straight here."

"I'll take you out tonight. Show you the French Quarter. I know this great restaurant—"

"That won't be necessary," Eli interrupts. His voice is calm. He's standing now, his hands shoved in his pockets, his wide shoulders making the large office feel small. "You have a gig tonight," he reminds Declan.

"I can take you out before."

"Don't worry about Kate this evening," Eli replies, still perfectly calm, but his jaw ticks.

I feel like I'm watching a tennis match as my head swivels back and forth, watching them both with curiosity.

"You know what Savannah told you," Declan says softly to Eli.

No response.

Declan glances back down to me. "I really don't mind calling the gig off tonight and settling you in."

"I'll be fine, Dec." I grin and pat his chest. "Where will you be playing?"

"The Voodoo Lounge."

"I might just show up." I push up onto my tiptoes and kiss his cheek.

"I don't want you wandering around the French Quarter after dark."

"I'll take her," Eli offers, earning a speculative look from Declan, who then gazes down at me and kisses my forehead softly.

"I'll save a seat for both of you then," he replies with a happy smile. "Have a good afternoon. Don't let the boss man run you ragged." He winks at me and grins at Eli, then slips back out the door.

"You and Declan are close," Eli says when I turn back around. His hands are still in his pockets as he rocks back on his heels.

"Yes. He, Savannah, and I were sort of the three amigos in college."

"Are you planning on fucking him?"

"Excuse me?" I feel my jaw drop as I stare at the formidable man before me. I prop my hands on my hips and glare at him. "That's none of your darn business."

He purses his lips as though he's trying not to laugh. "It's none of my *darn* business?"

"That's what I said."

He tilts his head and looks like he's about to say more, but then he saunters to my suitcase and pulls it behind him, as he gestures for me to follow him.

*He's kicking me out?*

"Miss Carter, I'll be out the rest of the day. Reschedule my appointments."

His assistant gapes at him and then sputters, "But, Mr. Freemont has been waiting…"

"I don't care. Reschedule. I'll see you tomorrow." Eli calls the elevator, his eyes never leaving me as we wait for the car to arrive. "Do you have a change of casual clothes in here?"

"Yes. The rest of my things are being shipped down and should arrive tomorrow afternoon."

He nods and motions for me to lead him into the elevator.

"Eli?"

The air literally crackles around us as he glances down at me and raises a brow. He's barely touched me and my body is on high alert and my mind is empty.

"Where are we going?"

"To your place."

"You know where my place is?"

"I own it, *cher*." He sighs and finally reaches over and tucks my hair behind my ear, making me shiver. "Are you cold?"

"No." I clear my throat and step away from him. "If you'll just give me the address, I'll take a cab to my place."

"I wouldn't dream of endangering your life again," he replies with a half-smile, and every hair on my body stands on end. Good Lord, what this man can do with a smile.

I need to get my hormones under control. It's simply been too long since I got laid, that's all. And I'm not going to scratch this particular itch with this particular man. He's my boss. My best friends' brother.

*No way, nohow.*

"You coming?" he asks.

*Yes, please.*

I realize the elevator has opened and he's standing next to me, waiting for me to go first.

"Of course."

"Of course," he chuckles. "We can walk it…it's not far, but it's hot out, so we'll drive."

I nod and follow him to his sleek, black Mercedes, which he expertly drives down the narrow streets of the French Quarter. I can't help but practically press my face to the window, trying to take in everything I see at once.

"It's so beautiful," I murmur.

"Have you been here before?"

"No. I can't wait to walk around and soak it all in."

He parks less than three minutes after we set off, and kills the engine. "We're here."

"Already?"

"I told you, it's not far."

"I could have walked that, even with the heat."

"It's not necessary to make you uncomfortable," he replies simply and climbs out of the car, gathers my bag, and with his hand on the small of my back, leads me up to a loft that sits above an herb shop called Bayou Botanicals. I can smell sage and lavender as Eli unlocks the front door and ushers me inside, where I stop on a dime and take in the beautiful.

The outside of the building is well kept and beautiful with worn red bricks and green iron railings, but the inside is brand new and simply opulent.

"I'm staying *here*?"

"That you are," he confirms, his accent sliding along my skin like honey. "You'll consider this your home while you're with us. Here are your keys." He passes the keys to me, then turns his back and leads me to the kitchen, which boasts brand new appliances, dark oak cabinets, and matching granite countertops. "The bedroom is through there," he continues, and leads me into a beautiful room with a four-poster bed. "The linens are clean and fresh. The bathroom is there." He points to the left, but my eyes are stuck on the doors that lead out to the balcony, which offers a beautiful view of the street below and Jackson Square just a block away.

"There are times that it gets noisy with music and people, but there's never a dull moment in the French Quarter."

I nod and turn back to him. "Thank you. Shall we go back to the office?"

"It's mid-afternoon, Kate. Take the rest of the day to settle in."

"Oh, but, I'm here to work. Surely, I could—"

"It would look odd to bring on a new hire in the middle of the day, don't you think?"

*Of course it would.*

I smile sheepishly and nod. "You're right. I'll work from here." I toss my jacket onto the bed, pull my laptop out of my briefcase, and walk briskly into the kitchen. "It's going to be a process."

"Kate, I don't want—"

"I'm not going to be able to just dig in and start investigating. Van's right to give me an assistant position, but that's going to be even tougher." I tie my hair back off my face and lower into a kitchen chair as I talk briskly. If I talk about work, I won't be ogling him, and thus losing more brain cells.

"Kate."

"I'm going to have to play by the rules for a while, a couple weeks at least. I need people to trust me, so they'll open up to me."

"Kate."

"I—"

"Enough," he says sharply.

# CHAPTER 2

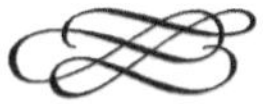

## ~KATE~

My head whips up to stare at Eli. He shoves his hands in his pockets and swears under his breath as he hangs his head then glances back up at me, looking at me like he doesn't really want to be here, and he's not quite sure if he likes me.

"You don't have to stay," I inform him stiffly.

"I don't expect you to work today at all, from here or the office."

"Why ever not?" I lean back in the chair and frown up at him. "You're paying me to work."

"You've travelled all morning, Kate. Settle in. Eat something. In fact, let me take you out to eat something."

"I don't think that's necessary."

"I do." He removes his suit jacket after taking his sunglasses out of the inside pocket and drapes it over the back of the sofa. He rolls the sleeves of the white shirt that molds over his muscled torso all the way up to his elbows, unbuttons the top two buttons, and removes his soft blue tie. "That's better. Go change into something more comfortable, and I'll feed you the best jambalaya you've ever had."

"I've never had jambalaya before," I reply with a raspy voice. I can't tear my eyes off his broad shoulders.

"This will ruin you for all other jambalaya; I promise you."

I frown and meet his gaze, trying to figure him out. "Are you sure?"

He nods and waits expectantly. I have a feeling not many people say no to Eli Boudreaux.

"I'm not going to sleep with you." The words are out of my mouth before I can reel them back in. I feel my face flame, but I tilt my chin up and square my shoulders firmly.

"I didn't invite you to," he replies calmly, but his eyes are full of humor.

I nod and walk back to the bedroom to change into a light summer dress, slather on sunblock with SPF 4000 to protect my white, freckled skin, and then rejoin Eli, who is now looking out my windows.

"You're always looking out windows," I remark with a smile. He turns to me and his eyes heat as he looks me up and down, and I suddenly feel very exposed.

"You'll burn, *cher.*"

"I'm wearing sunblock."

"Do you always argue?" he asks.

"I don't argue."

He holds my gaze for a moment and then tosses his head back and laughs, shakes his head, and leads me out into the hot afternoon.

"Let's go this way first." He turns to the left and rests his hand on the small of my back again, ever the gentleman, walking me down Royal Street. If you'd asked me yesterday if I thought I'd be walking in the French Quarter with the sexiest man I'd ever seen by my side, I would have told you to consult a doctor.

And Eli Boudreaux *is* sexy. But he's not mine, and he never will be. He's my boss, and he's being kind.

I take a deep breath, determined to pull my head out of the gutter and enjoy New Orleans, when Eli pulls me into a trendy shoe and accessory shop called *Head Over Heels.*

"Shoes!" I exclaim, already salivating. Okay, so the man is showing me shoes. I might sleep with him after all.

"Hats," he corrects me.

"Holy crap, what are you doing here?" A woman with short, dark hair and full lips smiles from behind the counter.

"Kate needs a hat," Eli replies and grins as his sister launches herself into his arms and holds on tight.

"Been a minute," she whispers in his ear in the same New Orleans drawl. Eli grins.

"You saw me at Mama's last Sunday."

"Been a minute," she replies and steps back, smiling at me. "Hi, Kate. It's good to see you again."

"You too, Charly." I'm pulled into another hug—the Boudreaux family is an affectionate bunch, and the middle sister, Charlotte, is no different from the rest.

"What can I do for you two?"

"Kate needs a hat," Eli repeats.

"I do?"

"Oh, yes, sugar, you do," Charly replies with a nod. "We need to keep the sun off your face and shoulders. Let's see..." She leads us to the back of the shop and pulls three hats off the wall, all wide-brimmed and pretty. "I think green is your color, with that beautiful auburn hair and your pretty green eyes."

"Thank you, but this hair is about to be a curly tangled mess with all this humidity."

"I know the feeling. I'll make a list of hair products to use while you try these on." She jogs back to her counter as I plop the first hat on my head. It's pink, not quite as widely brimmed as the green, and makes me look like a mushroom.

"Try the green one," Eli suggests, but instead I pull on one with a rainbow of colors. It looks like a box of Crayolas exploded all over it. Eli just watches me in the mirror with humor-filled eyes and crosses his arms over his impressive chest. "You do have beautiful hair."

"Thank you." His jaw ticks. If he doesn't like giving out compliments, why does he say anything at all?

"Oh no, dawlin', the green one," Charly says as she rejoins us. I smirk as I put the green hat on and sigh as I realize that she and Eli were right.

"Looks like this is the winner," I say with a grin. "I'll take it." I pull my wallet out of my handbag, but Eli lays his hand over mine and shakes his head.

"Bill me," he tells Charly, who smiles and nods happily, while handing me a list of hair products to try, waving at us as Eli leads me back out into the heat. "Feel better?"

"Hmm," I murmur, but, oh, God, yes, it feels so much better. "Thanks for the hat."

"You are welcome," he replies, his accent making me squirm again. I met this man just a few hours ago, and so far, everything he does makes me squirm.

Not good. Not good at all.

"Tell me about yourself," I say, surprising myself. All I know is, I need to get my brain on something other than the mass of testosterone walking next to me. We cross the street, me on the outside, and Eli immediately trades places with me, tucking me next to him away from the street. "Chivalry isn't dead," I whisper.

"No, dawlin', it's not." He flashes me a quick smile before leading me to a café with beautiful courtyard seating.

"It's surprisingly cool in here," I murmur after we're seated.

"The trees keep it cool," the waitress says with a smile. "Need a minute with the menu?"

"Do you eat seafood?" Eli asks me.

"Yes," I reply.

"Good. We'll both have the seafood jambalaya, please."

The waitress nods and walks away, leaving us alone.

"Now, tell me more about your plans to catch the person stealing from my company."

"You didn't answer my question first," I reply, and butter a piece of the bread the waitress just set down for us.

"What question?"

"Tell me about you."

"I don't matter." His voice is calm, but sure. Final. He leans back, folds his arms, and shutters immediately close over his eyes.

*Interesting.*

"It's your company, so yes, I do believe you matter."

"All you need to know about me is that I'm your boss, you'll be paid timely, and I expect nothing but your best on this job."

I set my bread on a small white plate and lean back, mirroring his pose with my arms crossed. "Actually, I believe it was Savannah who hired me, and I don't ever give less than my best. Ever."

He raises a brow and cocks his head to the side. "Beau, Savannah, and I hold equal shares and equal interest in the company. All three of us are your bosses, Kate."

"Understood." He watches me for several minutes. I can't figure him out. He has moments of being so kind, *nice*, and I think he may be attracted to me, and then the walls come slamming down and he's distant, impersonal, and borderline rude.

Which is it?

Not that it really matters, because starting tomorrow I'll answer to Savannah, and I'll hardly ever see the mysterious and sexy Eli.

I hope.

I tilt my head back, close my eyes, and take a deep breath of the thick New Orleans air. There's a light breeze now, cooling my heated skin. The trees above are green and lush, and I can see sprinkles of sunshine as it fights its way through the leaves.

Our meal is served and I stare down at the bowl of rice, shrimp, mussels and a bunch of stuff I can't make out dubiously, then glance up to Eli, who has already dug into his bowl heartily.

"You won't regret it," he says simply, and shovels another spoonful into his mouth. I watch his square jaw as he chews, and then glance back down at my own bowl.

Why not? I take a bite and my gaze finds his in surprise. "It's good."

"I wouldn't feed you something bad, Kate." He chuckles and reaches for the bread. The jambalaya is delicious, and I'm hungrier than I thought, devouring the bowl in just a few minutes. Finally, I sit back and pat my flat belly.

"That was great."

When the bill is paid and we're back on the sidewalk, walking back toward my loft, Eli glances down at me, and then sighs and pushes his hand through his hair.

"How did you get into your profession?" he asks softly.

"Oh, we're talking about ourselves now?" I raise a brow. "Look, you don't have to be nice to me. It's okay if you don't like me. I'll do my job, very well I might add, and be out of New Orleans in four to six weeks."

"Four to six weeks?" he asks incredulously.

"Yes. I told you earlier, it takes time to settle in, gain my coworkers' trust and confidence. I can't just sit down at a desk and start pilfering through files. I'm supposed to be a new hire, on the down low, remember?"

He shakes his head thoughtfully. "I didn't think it would be that involved."

"It's harder than it looks; otherwise, you wouldn't need me."

"Who said I don't like you?" he asks abruptly.

"What?"

"You just said 'it's okay if you don't like me.' What makes you think I don't like you?"

I stop on the sidewalk, stare up at him for a long minute, and then chuckle at the bewildered expression on his wickedly handsome face. "It doesn't matter, Eli."

I begin to walk again, and he hangs back, walking just a few paces behind me. I can hear the wheels turning in his head from here.

Finally, we reach my door. I glance back at him as he catches up to me. "Thanks for the hat, and for the meal."

"You're welcome."

I turn to let myself inside and move to shut the door, but Eli nudges his way inside and pushes the door shut behind him.

"Um, come on in?"

"I do like you."

I roll my eyes and toss my handbag on the couch, my hat on top of it, and see his jacket and his tie where he left them earlier.

"Oh, you almost forgot—"

Eli's very firm chest presses to my back as he reaches around me and takes the coat out of my hands and sets it aside, then swivels me around to face him.

"I do like you," he repeats. When I would look down, he catches my chin with his finger and tilts my head up. "But this is a bad idea."

"What is?" I whisper, hating the shakiness in my voice.

"This." He lowers his face to mine and sweeps his nose across my own, gently. His lips haven't touched mine yet, but they're tingling, already yearning for him. His hands glide up my bare arms to my neck, his thumbs gently draw circles along my jawline as he places a light, barely-there kiss on the corner of my lips. I hear a soft moan, and would be mortified to know that it came from me, if I could find my brain cells.

This man is dangerous. Everything about him screams *RUN!* but instead, I grip onto his lean hips and tug him closer. He needs no further invitation. He slips those amazing lips of his over mine, licks my bottom lip, and when I gasp at the fission of pure lust that moves through me, he moves in for the kill.

His tastes like the after-meal peppermint we both ate, and the light one or two day scruff on his chin rasps against my skin in the most tantalizing way. I can't help but wonder how it would feel on other parts of my body…behind my knees, between my breasts, between my legs.

Holy shit, I bet he would feel amazing between my legs.

I grip onto his biceps and realize that the one arm he's slung around the small of my back is the only thing keeping me upright. My knees no longer exist. We're both breathing hard as he drags his fingers down my cheek and pulls back, nibbling the edge of my lips once more, and then he's gone, staring down at me with shining whiskey eyes.

"That. That's a bad idea."

# CHAPTER 3

## ẼLI~

"So how was your date?" Beau asks, just before he attacks me from behind, his arm wrapped around my neck. I slip out of his grip, flip him onto his back, and glare down at him, sweaty and panting.

"What date?"

"Heard you left out of here for the day with Van's friend Kate," Ben Preston, a life-long friend of ours, and the Krav Maga expert that comes to train us four times a week, says with a smug grin. He's already shirtless and sweaty, but barely panting. Ben's not as tall as Beau and me, but he's much stronger, and he's fucking badass. "After Van told you to keep your hands off. She's pissed, by the way."

"It wasn't a fucking date," I mutter, and wipe the sweat off my forehead with a towel before switching my attention to Ben and throwing a punch, which he deflects, and we spar for a few long, hard minutes before I can continue. "Beau and Van were in a meeting. Someone had to meet her and show her the loft."

"And buy her a hat and take her lunch?" Beau asks with a wide grin. "Van's gonna cut your balls off."

"What are you, a bunch of gossiping women?" I whip my soaking wet T-shirt over my head, then prop my hands on my hips.

"Charly called me after you left her shop. She said you looked love sick."

"Fuck that," I mutter with disgust. "I don't do love sick, and you know it. So, Charly called you, and you used the family phone tree to spread the news that I was being nice to Kate?"

Beau and Ben both laugh, then Ben catches me off guard and takes me down to the mat. Motherfucker. "So, you're not taking her to Dec's gig tonight?"

"Do you want Mama's recipe for her pecan pie too?" I snarl.

"Wow, you're very defensive for someone who's not interested in the pretty Kate."

"She's not pretty," I mutter. *She's fucking beautiful.*

"Yeah, I'm not really into redheads with freckles myself. But the last time I saw her, she had a sexy little body," Beau continues, speaking to Ben, who nods thoughtfully.

I'm going to kill them both.

With my bare hands.

"When did you see her?"

"During one of my trips to visit Dec and Van at college." Beau strips out of his own shirt and tosses it away. "That was a while ago, though. Maybe she got fat."

"She's not fat," I reply, walking right into his trap. "Look, I'm just being nice to her."

"Right," Ben nods, just before he takes Beau down to the mat, but Beau pulls out, rolls Ben beneath him, and pulls up to throw a punch, which Ben rolls out of, and for the next few minutes they try to best each other.

I am *not* lovesick over Kate. Sure, she's sexy with her thick auburn hair and big green eyes, and the freckles on her face and shoulders simply beg to be kissed and traced, but for the love of fuck, she's an employee. It's just been longer than I care to admit since I last got laid.

That's a detail easily taken care of.

But the thought of any of the usual women I call to scratch that particular itch holds no interest.

*Fuck.*

"Not paying attention gets your ass kicked, man," Beau warns, just before he pulls my torso down and knees me in the stomach, then throws an elbow up, but I throw him off balance and he misses. Barely.

"Stop daydreaming about hot redheads and pay attention," Ben snarls.

"I'm done," I mutter, and suck down a bottle of water.

"We have ten minutes left," Beau says.

"You go ahead."

"Dude." Beau, panting and sweaty himself, props his hands on his hips and levels me with a somber look. "Be careful."

"I haven't done a fucking thing," I reply, but the memory of that hot kiss in her loft is right there, front and center. Her sweet body pressed to mine, her hair tangled in my fingers, and those bright green eyes, full of lust and mistrust, pinned to mine as I backed away and ran like a bat out of hell.

"Okay." Beau shrugs and shakes his head. "But if you decide to do the fucking thing, be honest with her."

"What the hell is that supposed to mean?"

"You have a habit of making women fall for you, and then you squish them like bugs," Ben adds.

"I do not."

"Yeah, you do. Dad never meant for you to—"

"This isn't therapy," I interrupt, and turn my back on both of them, headed to the shower. "I'm fine. Kate's safe from me. I'll make sure she gets to Dec's gig safely, and then I'll probably rarely see her after that."

"Eli."

I turn at Ben's voice.

"I do want that recipe. Your mom's pecan pie is the best."

I smirk, shake my head, and leave to the loud grunts of Beau getting his ass kicked.

～

KATE ANSWERS her door and I just about swallow my tongue at the sight of her. Her hair has been swept up onto her head, with soft wavy strands hanging around her face. She's in a silk black tank top that flows from the tops of her breasts to her waist, and white Capri pants.

And the sexiest strappy black heels I've ever fucking seen.

*She's safe from me.* No messing with her.

"Eli."

"Right the first time," I reply, and offer her a smile. I seem to smile at this woman a lot.

"What are you doing here?"

"I told you I'd take you to Declan's gig tonight." I raise a brow as she bites her lip and winces. "Problem?"

"I kind of figured that offer was off the table. Especially after—"

"After what?" She glances down at my chest and her eyes dilate. Oh, she's interested, all right. The chemistry is off the charts.

"After you kissed me." Her eyes return to mine, and she tilts her chin up defiantly. She's not going to back down and get shy, or play coy.

Good girl.

"I don't play games, *cher*." She frowns slightly at the nickname.

"What does that mean?"

"It means that I won't kiss you and then ignore you."

"No, *cher*. What does it mean?"

I grin and skim the tip of my finger down her nose. I can't seem to keep my hands off this woman. So much for not playing games.

*Jesus, get it together, Boudreaux.*

"It's a Creole term that means dear or darling. Are we going to stand in your doorway all night?"

She shakes her head and steps back, allowing me to pass. The place already smells like her, like honey.

"You really don't have to take me. Declan texted me with the address. According to my Google Maps app, it's not far."

"You shouldn't be walking around the Quarter after dark by yourself. You don't know your way around, and anything could happen. Besides, his club is on Bourbon. You're not walking down Bourbon looking like that."

"Looking like what?" she demands, and props her hands on her hips, making her shirt lift just an inch, giving me a glimpse of creamy white skin.

"Like a walking wet dream," I mutter and shove my hand through my hair.

"I live here. How can I never walk around after dark?" She raises a brow and is doing her best to look unaffected by me, but her cheeks have reddened and she keeps licking those plump lips of hers in agitation.

Those lips that taste like heaven and move effortlessly beneath my own.

I narrow my eyes and watch as she tosses her phone, cash, and other mysterious things that women carry with them into a small handbag and turns back to me.

"I'd feel better if I walked you."

"Suit yourself." She shrugs and glances around, as if she thinks she might be forgetting something. "How far is the walk?"

"About ten minutes."

I almost tell her that those heels are going to be a pain in the ass on the cobblestones and uneven sidewalks, but then decide against it. If the thought of keeping her held against me to make sure she's safe makes me an asshole, so be it.

I *am* an asshole.

Kate follows me down her stairs to the sidewalk below, and we set off toward Bourbon Street and Declan's gig.

"Are you sure you're up for this? You've had a long day." I catch her elbow as she cautiously makes her way around a wide hole in the sidewalk, then settle my hand on the small of her back. It just seems to fit there.

"I haven't heard Dec play in years," she replies with a smile. "I miss it. He's so talented. He could be doing so much more with his music than he is."

"New Orleans is his home," I reply softly, but with complete agreement. "He was in Memphis last month working on an album."

"I know. I was in town on a job, so we met for dinner, but I didn't get to hear him play."

"So, how close are you really?" I do my best to ignore the stab of fucking jealously that spears my gut.

"Very close." She nods and reaches for my arm as we cross a cobblestoned street, when she almost loses her balance on those sexy shoes. "He and Savannah and I were room-mates. Declan is one of my dearest friends."

*Naked friends?*

I want to ask, but hold my tongue. She was right this afternoon; it's none of my fucking business if she and Declan have a physical relationship.

Ah, fuck it.

"Have you two ever—"

"I believe we already had this conversation," she says with a laugh.

"I don't think it's funny."

"The thought of me having sex with Declan is hilarious," she replies and smiles up at me, her gorgeous green eyes glowing under the streetlights. "He's like a brother to me, Eli."

I nod and lead her to the left, down Bourbon Street, the hubbub of the French Quarter. At night, at least.

"Holy moly," she breathes, and takes in all the lights, the loud music, and the people leaning on the railings above the street. "It's like Vegas on steroids."

I laugh and tuck her hand in mine, linking our fingers. "That it is. It's still early, so this is pretty tame."

The streets have been blocked off for foot traffic only.

"There are a lot of sex shops on this street." Her frank observation startles a laugh from me, and I glance down to find her smiling up at me.

"It's Bourbon," I reply with a shrug. "The club that Declan is playing at is actually pretty classy. I think you'll like it."

"I think I like it all," she replies softly. "It's hard to believe this is the same city from one block over."

I nod and lead her through an iron gate into a wide courtyard with lights twinkling in the trees overhead. I introduce myself to the hostess, and she immediately guides us to the front of the crowd to two seats right in front of the stage, where Declan is playing a jazz song on the piano.

Dec's voice is deep and croony, reminiscent of Dean Martin and Frank Sinatra. He has a decent voice, but it's what he can do with a musical instrument—any instrument—that makes him stand out.

He's a freaking genius.

"Did it bother you that he chose music over the family company?" Kate asks from beside me, swaying back and forth to the song.

"No. That would be stupid. Listen to him."

She nods and then smiles up at me, a full-on smile that lights up her face, and I find that I have to swallow hard and fist my hands to keep from reaching out and cupping that amazing face in the palm of my hand and leaning in for a kiss.

No more kissing.

I make myself look back up at Dec, who's watching us. He shakes his head and finishes his song to delighted applause.

"Ah, that's awfully kind of you," he drawls, and winks at a woman in the front row who winks back. And they call me the man-whore. "I have some special guests here tonight, ladies and gentlemen."

He stands from the piano and reaches for a guitar, then pulls two chairs to the edge of the stage and grabs an extra mic as well.

Kate is already shaking her head no.

Interesting.

"My brother, Eli, is here tonight." He smiles down at me, and I just grin and raise a brow. "And a very old friend from college is here too. In fact, Kate and I used to sing together all the time, and I'm going to talk her into coming up here and joining me right now."

The room erupts into applause, but Kate is vehemently shaking her head and saying "No. Heck no."

*Heck no.*

Her aversion to cursing turns me on. I wonder what it would take to get her to talk dirty.

*I'm going to hell.*

"Come on, Kate. New Orleans wants to hear you sing."

I nudge her with my elbow and grin at the look of terror on her face. Finally, she swallows hard and stands, climbs the steps to the stage, sits next to Declan, and raises the mic to her mouth.

"Was this necessary?"

"Well, it's not as fun if you sing from down there," Declan replies and kisses her cheek. "Isn't she pretty?"

Why does everyone call her *pretty*? Can't they see that she's unbelievable?

I applaud with the rest of the crowd, and then Declan begins to strum the guitar. "Remember this one?" he asks her.

"I remember belting this one out after having a few too many drinks in Memphis at that dive bar you played in during college."

"That's the one," he confirms with a grin. And suddenly, Kate begins to sing *Crazy* by Patsy Cline, as if she was made to. It's effortless for her. Declan joins her on the chorus, adding harmony, and when the song is over, they're given a standing ovation. Kate stands and bows, kisses Declan's cheek, and returns to her seat at my side.

"Wow." It's all I can manage.

"He'll pay for that later." She takes a deep breath and clenches her shaking hands together.

"You have a beautiful voice."

She jerks one shoulder in a shrug and then settles back to listen to the rest of Declan's set. She gradually relaxes, moving in her seat, singing along with the songs she knows. And when it's all over, she stands and whoops and hollers, making Declan laugh from the stage.

"Thanks for coming, superstar," Declan says, as he pulls Kate in for a hug. "And you too," he says to me. "It's been a minute since you came to a show."

"Too long. I enjoyed it."

This seems to surprise him, and I feel like an ass. It has been too long.

"I'd walk you home, but—" Declan looks over at the girl in the front row he winked at earlier and shoots her a smile.

"I see things haven't changed," Kate mutters and shakes her head. "I'm fine. Eli walked me over."

"Do you mind walking her home?"

"If it's out of your way—" Kate begins, but I shake my head.

"Of course. Have a good night."

"He's so formal," Declan says with a grin.

"Not always," Kate replies, and then kisses Declan's cheek again, and before he can ask what she means by that, she says, "call me soon. We'll have lunch or something."

And with that, we leave, winding our way through the crowd.

"Would you like a drink for the walk home? There's no open container law here."

"Sure. I'd love some white wine, please."

I order two glasses, and we set off toward home, walking slower so she can absorb everything happening around us.

"We can walk up a block and get out of the crazy."

"No, I don't mind." Her eyes are pinned on a couple practically having sex against the wall of a building as we pass.

I take her hand in mine and keep her close, glowering at the drunker than fuck men that leer at her as we pass.

I'd rather not have her in the middle of this, and steer her down a block to walk up Royal, which is much more tame.

"I really didn't mind," she insists and sips her wine.

"I did." I glance down at her and lead her around the gaping hole in the sidewalk. "Promise me you won't go back there alone."

"Oh, I'm fine."

"Promise me, Kate."

"It's no big deal."

I sigh and stop us, right there on the sidewalk, steps from her front door, and turn her to face me. "Please, as a favor to me, don't go back to Bourbon Street at night alone. People get shot, raped, beat up down there all the time, *cher*. If you want to go, take someone with you."

Her eyes are wide as she watches me, her hand flat on my chest. I pulled her against me without even realizing it, and now the zing of awareness is a pulsing need. I can feel her, from knee to chest, and it immediately makes my dick stand up and beg.

This woman is going to be the death of me.

And she's off-limits.

"Kate."

"I won't," she whispers, and watches my lips as she licks her own. An involuntary growl slips from my throat as I tip my head down and lean my forehead against hers, breathing her in. "This is a bad idea," she whispers.

"Very bad," I agree, and reluctantly pull away and walk her down the block to her loft.

"This house is pretty," she says, gesturing to the four-story single family home right next to the building that holds her loft.

"Thank you," I reply.

"You own that one too?"

"I do. That's my house."

"You live there?"

I nod and watch her carefully.

"So, we're neighbors."

"We are."

"Well, thanks for taking me," she says, and doesn't meet my eyes as she climbs the stairs. "You don't have to walk me to the door."

"It's not a problem," I reply, but she stops me with a hand to my chest.

"I don't want you to walk me to the door, Eli. Have a good night."

And with that, she climbs the last of the stairs and lets herself inside without a backwards glance.

I stand on the sidewalk and watch her turn the lights on in her loft, then walk to my place and pour myself another glass of wine before I change into basketball shorts. It's hot enough outside to forgo a shirt. I sit on the balcony, listening to the music coming from Jackson Square, and settle in for a long sleepless night.

An hour later, Kate's lights go out, putting an end to a very long day. I picture her with her hair loose, climbing into bed, slipping between the sheets wearing nothing at all, and swear under my breath as I walk inside and close the doors.

Tomorrow will be business as usual. Forget her. I have no room in my life for a woman, least of all a woman who has forever and white picket fences written all over her.

I gave all of that up long ago.

# CHAPTER 4

## ~KATE~

"Good mornin'," Savannah says with a smile and hugs me after leading me into her office. "Thanks for coming in so early."

"I figured we could go over the details before I head down to HR and meet my new boss." I set my purse on the floor next to the chair and take in Van's office. "Nice place you have here."

"Thanks." Van grins. "Quite a step up from that apartment we all shared at college."

"It wasn't so bad," I reply. "But, yes, this is great. I'm proud of you."

"Okay, so tell me what happens now."

"Well, not much for the next few weeks. I need my coworkers to believe that I'm just another assistant. Then, as things settle and I'm not being watched as much, I'll start investigating. You know I'm good with the computer, I can hack and sneak around and no one will ever know I've been there."

"Do we lie and say we don't know each other?" Van asks with a frown.

"No." I shake my head and smile ruefully. "This is new for me, in that I've never worked in a place where I know the owners, but I think that if anyone asks, I'll just say that I went to college with you. Leave it at that."

"Why do I think we won't be having lunches together?"

"Because we won't. I need people to feel comfortable talking to me, and they won't if they think that I'm best friends with the boss."

"You are best friends with the boss."

I shrug. "They don't have to know that."

"This whole thing pisses me off," Van says with a sigh. "I love having you here, but I hate that someone is stealing from us."

"We'll find them. It's just going to take a little time." I reach across the desk and grip Van's arm reassuringly. "I promise."

She nods and then frowns. "Okay, change of subject. I'm sorry I wasn't available to meet you yesterday."

I sit back in my seat and school my features. "I told you, it was fine."

"Was Eli okay?"

"What do you mean?" I ask with a raised brow.

"I'm sure he was perfectly nice, but was he…*too nice?*"

"What are you asking me, Van?"

"Look, I told him to leave you alone, and then I practically dumped you at his feet yesterday."

"Wait." I hold my hand up and glare at my friend. "You told him to *leave me alone?*"

"Of course I did."

I blink at her and then stand and pace across the room. So, was he just hanging out with me, kissing me, yesterday as a rebellious act against his bossy sister?

"Why?" I turn and face her, hands propped on my hips. She looks down at her desk, suddenly looking flummoxed.

"Well, because, you know Eli—"

"Actually, I don't." I cross my arms. "I'd never met him before yesterday. But I'll tell you this," I lean on her desk, towering over her, suddenly so angry on both my and Eli's behalf that I'd be baffled if I stopped and gave it too much thought. "Eli was nothing but polite yesterday. He escorted me to my loft and to Declan's show last night."

"Look, Kate, I didn't mean—"

"I don't know why you think you had to warn your brother off me. I'm a grown woman, a professional woman, who certainly doesn't flop down on her back for any man who smiles at her and crooks his finger, which your brother *did not.* So, I think you've misjudged both of us."

"Wow, you're pissed."

"I am *so* bloody mad at you right now."

"When you get mad, your Irish shows through." Her lips twitch, but I'm not done being mad at her yet.

"I'm here to do a job, not start an affair. I won't be here that long."

"You like him," Van murmurs with narrowed eyes.

"I don't *know* him!" I repeat in exasperation. *Yes, I like him! He kisses like a dream, and I want to climb his hot body and have my wicked way with him!*

Not that I'm going to tell her that.

"I just didn't want him to set his sights on you and have you eventually hurt. I know you're still—"

"I'm fine." I shake my head, not wanting to go down this road with Van, not today. I have a long day ahead of a new job, and bringing my own baggage into it won't be productive. "I promise, I'm fine. Now, I need to get down to HR. I don't want to be late on my first day."

"I'll walk you down." She stands, but I shake my head.

"No thanks. No favoritism, remember?" I shoot her a grin and walk toward her door.

"Kate, if you want to talk about—"

"Do you want to talk about Lance?" I ask without turning around, and the room is suddenly filled with a heavy silence as I shake my head and open her door. "I didn't think so. Love you."

"Love you, too."

~

"THIS IS HILARY," Linda Beals, the head of HR informs me as she leads me to my new office. "She's been promoted to another position here in the company, but is going to stay with you today to show you the ropes."

Hilary, a woman who looks to be a few years older than me smiles and stands, offering her hand to shake. "Pleasure," she says.

"Hello," I reply and smile at Linda, as she assures me that I'm in good hands, and leaves me with Hilary.

"So, you're taking over as Mr. Rudolph's assistant," Hilary says, stating the obvious.

"It seems so," I reply and sit in the desk chair next to hers behind my new desk. "How long have you been with him?"

"Oh, gosh, about twelve years now, I guess." Hilary leans in as if she's about to tell me a big secret. "He's really very easy to work with, as long as you make his coffee just so."

"You make his coffee?" I ask with a raised brow. "That's a little old school."

She shrugs and starts pulling files out of her drawer. "I don't mind. Now, let's get started. You only have me for today, but I'll just be one floor up, so if you ever have questions, don't hesitate to call me."

"Thanks."

"Did Linda show you around?"

"No, she just brought me down here after she went over my paperwork." I glance around my small, simple office, and see exactly why Van put me here. It's a corner space, and I'm able to see down two corridors of offices, and into the windows of said offices.

"Sounds about right," Hilary replies with a roll of the eyes. "After we go over these things, we'll take a break, and I'll give you a grand tour."

"Sounds good."

"Are you new to town?"

"Yes, very new."

"Well, I think you and I will be good friends." She smiles and then stands when a man walks in, looking harried and busy. "Mr. Rudolph, this is your new assistant, Kate."

"Hello," he says with a distracted smile and shakes my hand, his grip firm. He's probably in his early forties, with thinning hair over a handsome face, with a nose just a couple sizes too big, and he wears thick-rimmed glasses on his face. He's not terribly tall, but he's wiry thin. "Hilary will show you the ropes, but let me know if you have any questions." And with that, he disappears into his office just off of mine and shuts the door firmly behind him.

"He's a man of few words," I remark with a smile.

"Yeah, he's not terribly chatty," Hilary confirms.

"Miss O'Shaughnessy?" A man asks as he walks into my office, carrying a large bouquet of happy sunflowers.

"Yes," I reply with surprise.

"These are for you."

I gape in surprise as he sets the flowers on my desk, waits for my signature, and then leaves.

"Wow, sugar, those are impressive."

I nod and pull the small envelope out of the plastic holder in the center of the bouquet and open it, facing away from Hilary, so she can't read over my shoulder.

*Kate-*
*Welcome. Have a good first day.*
*Best Wishes,*

*Eli*

"Who are they from?" Hilary asks.

*The sexiest man I've ever seen in my life, but I have no idea why he sent them because nothing good can come of it.*

"My parents," I lie easily, and shove the card in my pocket. Eli said he doesn't play games, yet he kisses me like he'd like to devour me, says it's a bad idea, and then sends me flowers?

"Oh, how lovely." Hilary begins to chat about her own family while she sets me up with new passwords on the several software programs we use and shows me her routine, and all the while my mind wanders exactly where it shouldn't: to Eli.

Does he think he can sweet talk me with a few pretty blooms?

Okay, maybe the flowers are sweet, but I don't get it. I was up long after I turned off the lights and climbed into bed last night. I could still feel him against me, hear his low, rumbly voice. My body was on fire, and the man had really barely touched me. Sure, that kiss was combustible, and just the casual way he laid his hand on my back, or linked our fingers, sent my body into a tailspin unlike any I've ever felt.

Even with my ex-husband, and I don't know for sure what that says about me.

By lunch time, I've been shown Hilary's complete routine from start to finish, I've been given a tour of the building and introduced to everyone in the department, and Hilary was kind enough to show me exactly how Mr. Rudolph likes to have his coffee made.

Oh, and it must be on his desk by 8:05 every morning. Sharp.

Because, apparently, this is 1956, and it's important to bring the boss man his coffee.

Hilary and two other assistants from our department, Suzanne and Taylor, invite me to join them for lunch, and I eagerly accept, hoping against hope that one of them lets something slip and I can wrap this case up early.

Of course, I'm not that lucky.

"So, where are you from, Kate?" Taylor asks, as she munches on her sandwich, careful not to get her perfectly manicured hands dirty. She's short and lusciously curvy with dark hair that is styled in a short bob and has big brown eyes.

"Yes, tell us about you," Suzanne, Taylor's exact opposite with blonde hair, tall, statuesque figure, and bright blue eyes agrees, while Hilary nods expectantly and pops a chip in her mouth.

"Well, I grew up in the Denver area," I reply, easily keeping the details vague. "Are you all from here?"

"Hilary and I are," Suzanne replies, "but Taylor just moved here from Florida last year."

"What part of Florida?" I ask.

"Orlando," she replies with a wrinkle of the nose. "I left one hot, humid city for another."

"What were you thinkin'?" Suzanne asks with a laugh. "I think we're going to try to take the kids to Disney World next year."

And just like that, the subject is redirected from me, and I sit in silence and listen while I nibble my sandwich and chips and sip my diet soda.

~

My phone is vibrating in my handbag as I push my way into my loft after a long day in the office. I drop my keys and briefcase on the kitchen table and dig out the phone, grinning when I see Van's name on the caller ID.

"Hey, boss lady."

"How was your first day, dear?" I can hear the smile in her voice.

"Pretty much the usual. Choose forty-five different passwords, each with a different number, symbol, and the blood of a virgin, then gossip about the boss, not *my* boss, mind you, and the two assistants having an affair three offices over, learn how to make the boss his coffee, and walk home in the sweltering heat in a suit jacket."

"So, it wasn't boring then," she replies dryly, as I eye the boxes that were delivered this afternoon and are now stacked in my living room.

"Nope, not boring." *Tedious, long, and I wanted to poke my own eye out with something hot and sharp, but not boring.* "I just got home."

"Do you like the loft?" I can hear Lance's voice in the background, asking Van something about where his golf glove is, to which she says no.

"It's really beautiful. I love the balcony off the bedroom. I think I'll have some wine out there before bed tonight. My stuff arrived today."

"Good. Settle in and make yourself at home. Do you want to have breakfast in my office in the morning? You could come the same time as today and I'll have everything ready."

"Sneaky breakfast, I like it." I grin and sigh happily. I missed her. "You don't mind going in that early?"

"Pshaw, no. I usually show up that early every day. This will be a much better start to my day."

I bite my lip to keep from asking her why she shows up to work before seven in the morning every day, because I already know.

Lance.

I wish she'd talk about it, but I know she won't. Maybe one night I'll ply her with a bottle of wine and get her to unload on me.

"Okay, I'll see you tomorrow morning then."

"It's a date. 'Night."

"'Night," I reply and end the call, then order in pizza and put the bottle of wine I bought on my way home from work into the fridge on my way to the bathroom for a long, cool shower.

It's bloody hot outside.

I need to start dressing in layers for work, with something light under my jackets, so I'm not so damn hot by the time I get home.

The shower is cool and rejuvenates me. Just when I'm pulling on my shorts and a tank top, the doorbell rings.

Thank God, I'm starving.

I carry the pizza to the kitchen, grabbing my iPad on the way, pour myself a glass of wine, then decide screw it and tuck the whole bottle under my arm and walk through my bedroom to the balcony. There is a small wrought iron table with two comfortable, plush chairs out here, and I settle in to watch the sun set and the people wander through the Quarter on their way home from work or walking their dogs, tourists wandering.

It's like a moving painting, never the same, but familiar. The person who owns the herb shop below me must have got some fresh lavender in today, because the smell is brighter and lovelier than yesterday.

I prop my feet up on the unused chair and nibble on a slice of pizza and sip my wine, perfectly content to stay right here until bedtime.

"Did you get my flowers?"

I turn my head to the left, and there is my neighbor, Eli, sitting in a similar chair, only about ten feet away. And, instantly, I'm pulled toward him in the most elemental way possible.

Which is ridiculous. He's only a man.

"I didn't hear you come outside," I reply.

"You were too busy munching on that pizza and looked about a million miles away." He props his feet up, laces his fingers behind his head, and flashes me a smile that I feel all the way to my core.

Does he have to be this handsome? Seriously?

I take a sip of my wine, finishing the glass, and refill it.

"Have you had dinner?" I ask.

"No, ma'am."

"Here." I pass the pizza box over the ornate railing that separates our balconies. "I have lots of food." Then I fill my glass and pass him the bottle of wine as well. "But only one glass."

He stands and disappears into his house, then quickly returns with his own glass and flashes me that heart-stopping smile as he reclaims his seat and takes a big bite of pizza.

"This is good."

"Hilary said they were the best in the neighborhood," I inform him.

"Who's Hilary?" He frowns in confusion, making me grin.

"The woman whose position I took. She trained me today."

"So, it went well then?" His gaze is sober, and if I'm not mistaken, concerned, making me soften toward him even more.

"It did. No problems."

"Good." He chews on his crust and tilts his head at me. "Did you get my flowers?"

I nod slowly. "Why did you send them?"

He opens his mouth to answer, and then chuckles and shakes his head. "I'm not sure. It just felt like the right thing to do."

"Because you kissed me?"

His smile fades as he watches me over the railing, and I know that the replay of yesterday is running through his head just like it is mine. "No."

"Did you kiss me because Van told you not to?"

He narrows his eyes in temper, his jaw ticking, and then simply says, "No."

"Why?"

"The kiss or the flowers?"

"The flowers." I can figure out the kiss on my own. It's called chemistry, and we've got it in spades.

He frowns and looks into his wine glass. "I don't know."

"That's…not helpful." I chuckle and offer him another slice of pizza, which he declines with a shake of the head.

"Honestly?"

"Well, I don't want you to lie to me."

"I've been asking myself why all day. And the only thing I can come up with is, I like you, and I wanted you to have a good day."

I sit and stare at him and realize that he's telling me the honest truth, and that he might be as confused by it as I am.

Huh.

"Well, they're beautiful. Thank you."

"You're welcome." He grins, as if he's thinking of an inside joke, and I can't help but smile back.

"What are you thinking?"

"The sunflowers reminded me of you."

"Big and yellow?"

"Happy. You have a great smile."

I exhale loudly and watch him carefully. "You confuse me."

"We're on the same page there."

"You said this is a bad idea, and you're right. Bad idea is tattooed all over it with huge neon letters."

He nods. "I know. So, for tonight, I'm going to stay over here and you're going to stay over there, and we're just going to enjoy the evening and this wine."

I watch as he raises a brow and waits for my response.

"When was the last time you sat out on the balcony to watch the sunset?" I ask.

"I haven't been home before the sunset in years," he replies honestly.

"Why tonight?"

He shakes his head again and watches a man jog by with a huge black lab on a leash. "I couldn't say."

I want to ask him if he *can't* or *won't*, but instead, I just nod and leave it be for tonight. "It's a good evening for sitting outside," I say instead.

"That it is."

# CHAPTER 5

## ~KATE~

*I*t's been a hell of a week.

By Friday night, I'm exhausted. Administrative assistants work their asses off. Not that I didn't already know this; I've just never personally worked as one, regardless of what my resume on file in Linda's office says. I'm ready to take a cool shower and curl up with a good book and a glass of wine.

I make it through the shower and change into sweat shorts and a tank, just as my doorbell rings.

I frown, tempted to ignore it, but when the bell rings for the third time, and then a fist pounds on the wood with a loud, "We know you're in there!" I walk over and swing open the door.

"Did I forget that we were having dinner?" I ask and watch with a wry grin as Savannah and Declan both push their way inside, stopping to kiss my cheek as they pass, their hands and arms loaded down with bags of food.

"We decided to surprise you." Declan sets down his bags and pulls me in for a big hug. "We're gonna sit around and eat fattening food and drink wine. Well, I have to leave after dinner for tonight's gig, but I'm still having a little wine."

"Just like the old days," Savannah adds with a grin. My cheek is pressed to Dec's chest, listening to his heartbeat, as he rubs his hands up and down my back. I didn't realize how badly I needed a hug until this very minute.

"You okay?" he asks and plants his lips on my head.

"Yeah." I don't pull away, and instead watch Savannah as she pulls white Styrofoam containers out of plastic bags, laying the food out buffet style on my table. She has dark circles under her tired hazel eyes, and she looks way too thin in her jeans and plain black T-shirt.

"You survived your first week," Van says, as she opens a bottle of wine and pours it into three glasses.

"Did you think I wouldn't?" I ask with a laugh, as I pull away from Dec and accept a glass.

"No, I just figured we'd use that as an excuse to celebrate," she replies with a wink. "I brought your favorite: Italian. With fattening Alfredo sauce and lots of extra bread."

"You do love me." I offer Van a wide smile and snatch the bread first. "God, I love carbs. Why do I love carbs so much?"

"Because they're bad for you," Van replies. "They're every woman's kryptonite."

"I thought that was shoes," Declan says, as he piles his own plate high with pasta, sauce, and bread.

"No, shoes are a necessity," I inform him soberly. "Like water."

"Women are weird," Dec says with a laugh, and makes himself at home on the floor, his back leaning against my sofa. His long, lean body is relaxed as he eats his dinner, and he reminds me of his older brother. Dec's just as tall and broad in the shoulders as Eli.

The Boudreaux men are prime examples of the male species.

"I don't think we're supposed to fully understand each other," I reply, and lick sauce off my finger.

"How are you?" Van asks, as she nibbles on a piece of bread. She barely took any food. I eye her plate and then stare her in the eye, but she shakes her head and narrows her eyes at me.

"I'm fine," I reply.

"No, really," Dec says, his usually smiling face sober now.

"No, really," I insist. "I'm fine."

"When was the divorce final?" Van asks.

"Sixty-four days ago," I reply before I can catch myself, then wince when they both turn surprised gazes on me, and share a glance with each other.

"You're counting the days and you're *fine*?" Dec asks.

"Heck, yes, I'm counting the days. That divorce was hard won." I stuff more chicken and pasta in my mouth and point at both of them with my fork. "You know that."

"You should have let me deck him," Declan insists. He lowers his fork to his plate, his eyes hot with temper as he glances at me. "Only a lowlife son of a bitch does what he did to you."

"It might have been satisfying to watch you hit him." I lick my fork clean as I think of my strong friend kicking my ex-husband's ass. "Do you still do that Krave Magnus stuff?"

"Krav Maga," he corrects me with a laugh. "And you should do it too. It's great self defense."

"I'll just add that to my list of things to do." I tilt my head as I watch Van push her pasta around her plate, lost in thought. "I'm thinking about becoming a lesbian and joining a nudist colony."

"Now, that, I'd like to see," Declan declares with a roguish grin, but then follows my gaze and swears under his breath. "She's not listening."

"Not even a little bit," I agree. "Earth to Van."

"Huh?" She jerks her gaze up and takes another long sip of her wine, then refills her glass.

"Now it's your turn to talk."

"We haven't finished with you," she says, but I just grin at her.

"Yes, we have. Dec and I just discussed me turning lesbo and joining a nudist colony."

"I'm all for it," Declan agrees, earning a glare from his twin sister.

"How bad are things, Van? And don't deny it. You look like poop, and you deflect when asked. I'm the master of those tactics."

She glances nervously at her brother and then back at me. "You don't need to worry—"

"Spill it, Van." Dec's voice is calm, his posture relaxed, but every muscle in his body is on high alert.

He's ready to kick butt.

And so am I, for that matter.

"Things just aren't going very well," Savannah murmurs softly.

"Is he hurting you?" Declan asks.

"He's…ignoring me." She sets her plate aside and pulls her knees up into her chest, hugging her legs tight. "Unless he can't find something, he just pretty much does his own thing."

"Who else is he doing?" I ask, and set my own finished dinner aside, then just raise a brow when Van stares at me and chews her bottom lip.

"I don't know."

"I'm going to grab Eli and Beau, and we're going to—"

"Nothing," Van insists, laying her hand on Dec's shoulder. "You're going to do *nothing*."

"Fuck that, Vanny," he says and stares at her as if she's lost her mind. "He's fucking around on you and you want us to ignore it?"

"I don't have proof." She shrugs and smiles sadly. "It's just a hunch."

"Promise me," Dec says and pulls her close to hug her, "that you'll call me, day or night, if you need me."

"I will."

"If you find proof—" I begin.

"I'll kick his ass myself," she finishes. She pulls out of Declan's embrace and begins cleaning up.

"See, this is exactly why I'm not ever getting married," Dec says. "I'd kill myself before I'd hurt a woman, and that seems to be all marriage is good for. Pain."

"Mom and Dad were married for more than thirty-five years," Van reminds him.

"Mine have been married for thirty-five," I add. "They're not all bad."

"Still, I'll stick to the way things have always been."

"Why are all my brothers man-whores?" Van asks me, as if Dec's not sitting right next to her.

"Because they're all hot and sexy and have women falling at their feet?"

"You think I'm hot and sexy?" Dec asks with a charming smile. "Aww, dawlin'. That's the sweetest thing you've ever said."

"Are you falling at Eli's feet?" Van asks, surprising me. Declan sobers and they both stare at me with matching hazel eyes.

"Heck no," I insist. "I don't fall at any man's feet."

"Atta girl." Van salutes me with her wine and drains the glass.

"Oh, by the way, Mama has given us instructions to bring you to dinner on Sunday." Declan grins. "I'll pick you up on my way over."

"I don't want to intrude on your family dinner."

"She might kill us if we don't bring you," Van assures me.

"Or not feed us, which would be worse," Declan adds. "You're coming."

"Thank you," I reply and grin at my friends. "It's good to see you guys."

"It's you we're happy to see, dawlin'," Declan replies with a wink. "Did you bring dessert, Vanny?"

"Of course."

"Stop holdin' out on me."

~

I SLEEP LATE the next morning. My biggest vice is sleeping late on the weekends. I despise the alarm clock. I open my eyes slowly and stretch in the soft king sized bed, then lie on my back and stare out the French doors at the bright blue sky.

As I begin to ponder what might be on today's agenda, my doorbell rings.

I glance at the clock and scowl. It's nine in the freaking morning on a Saturday. Who in the world could be ringing my bell?

I climb out of bed and don't even bother to throw a robe over my tank and pink frilly panties. Whoever is stupid enough to show up at my place at this hour is just going to have to take me the way they get me.

It's most likely Savannah anyway. She always was a morning person.

I hate that.

I yank the door open and scrub my free hand over my face. "Seriously, Van, you just left here like six hours ago. Did you forget something?"

"Savannah was here until three this morning?"

I drop my hand and stare up in shock at a grinning Eli. His whiskey eyes are shining as he takes in my sleepy appearance, from the top of my ratted head, down my braless front, making my nipples pucker, thank you very much, to my pink tipped toes. On his way back up, his jaw drops when he sees my panties.

"Yes," I squeak and cross my arms over my chest. "She and Declan came over for dinner and ended up staying. We always could talk for hours."

"Did I wake you?" he asks, his voice low and intimate as he steps toward me. I move back, letting him inside, and close the door.

"No, I was just waking up." I bite my lip. "Um, what are you doing here?"

"I need a favor."

I feel my eyebrows climb into my hairline as I watch his eyes smile, but he purses his lips to keep the smile at bay. It's…endearing.

"A favor?"

"Yes, dawlin', a very important one."

I tilt my head and feel my lips quirk into a half smile. "I'm listening."

"I need an escort around the Quarter this mornin'."

I prop my hands on my hips, and Eli's eyes slowly sober, heat, and move from my eyes to my mouth and down to my breasts. He swears under his breath as I remember that I'm showing him way more than I should and recross my arms.

"You need an escort?"

He nods and catches my gaze in his again. "Yes, please."

"I don't know my way around," I reply softly.

"I do."

"So, why—"

"I'd like to show you around our neighborhood, *cher*," he says softly. "What do you say?"

I chew my lip for a few seconds, and finally smile gratefully. I've been dying to walk around and explore the famous French Quarter. "I'd be happy to escort you."

"You might want to choose a different outfit," he says, as he gestures to my clothes. "I would hate to have to beat every man we walk past into the sidewalk for looking at you."

I wave him off and turn to walk into my bedroom, but hear him mutter, "Although, you look amazing in anything you wear."

This is not helping my nipples calm down. I close the door to the bedroom, lean back on it, and take a deep breath. This man is pure walking temptation. But he didn't touch me. He smiled and invited me on a tour of the neighborhood. Sure, he checked out my chest, but I am braless, and my damn body reacts to him on a purely visceral level.

I can control myself for the day. No problem.

I nod and mentally pat myself on the back, then quickly tame my hair, brush my teeth, and pull on some denim capris and a blue sleeveless blouse. On my way out of the bedroom, I grab the green hat Eli bought me the other day, and slip my feet into a comfortable pair of Toms.

"Okay, I'm ready."

Eli is standing at my window, his hands in the front pockets of jeans that mold to his bottom and thighs just perfectly. His black T-shirt is stretched over his broad shoulders, and his dark hair is still wet around the collar from his shower.

He turns and smiles when he sees me holding the hat.

"Good plan. It's going to get hot today."

"It's hot every day," I reply with a wry grin. He hands me my handbag and escorts me down to the sidewalk.

"This way." He leads me to the right, his hand in its spot on the small of my back, and within two blocks, we're at Jackson Square, in front of the St. Louis Cathedral where jazz musicians play enthusiastically on a variety of instruments, palm readers are just setting up their tables, and artists have set up their canvases on the iron fence surrounding the beautiful park that holds the large statue of President Jackson on his horse, giving the square it's name.

"It's beautiful down here," I murmur, and smile at a man as he plays his saxophone.

"That it is," Eli agrees, and leads me around the park toward a green building with a green and white awning and dozens of round tables with chairs under it. "We'll start with breakfast."

"There's a long line," I reply, and eye the line of people waiting patiently for a table.

"It moves fast," he assures me, and leads me to the end of the line. "And it's worth it."

"Okay, tell me about Café du Monde," I request, reading the sign on the awning.

"Best beignets in New Orleans," he assures me. "This place has been here forever and hasn't changed much."

Before I know it, we move up the line and find a table near the sidewalk.

"The menu is on the napkin dispenser," Eli informs me, and tilts it toward me. "But do you mind if I order for you?"

"I don't mind." I sit back and listen as Eli informs our server that we'll each have an order of beignets and a frozen café au lait. I watch in fascination as horse-drawn carriages glide down the street before us, the drivers giving their passengers all kinds of information about Jackson Square, which is directly across the street from us. "Thank you for bringing me out today."

Eli quirks a brow. "It's *you* escorting *me*, remember?"

I grin and nod. "Right. Except you're showing me around."

"You're new to town." He shrugs as if it's no big thing, but somehow I think it is a big deal. "And I haven't wandered around in a long while."

"Does it change much?"

"Not much," he says with a smile, as the beignets and coffees are delivered. "My father used to bring all six of us here every Saturday morning for as long as I can remember. We came until he passed away."

He stops talking and frowns, his eyes trained with determination on his beignets.

"I'm sorry for your loss," I say softly. I know his dad passed away two years ago, and I remember the heartbreak of the entire family with the loss of the larger than life patriarch of the family. "Oh, my gosh," I whisper, eyeing the square doughnuts covered in a heaping pile of powdered sugar. "This is just..."

"The best," Eli finishes on a groan and eats one of the treats in two bites. He licks his lips, and my ninety-dollar black lace panties are soaking wet.

This man should come with a warning label.

"Are you going to eat them or continue to stare at me?" he asks with a laugh.

I shake my head, pulling myself out of the trance of watching Eli, and take a bite. "Oh, wow."

"Right?"

"I need these every day."

"I can arrange that." His eyes are perfectly sober as he watches me.

"I'm kidding. I'd weigh four hundred pounds within a month."

"No, you wouldn't, and I'm not kidding. Say the word, and I'll get them for you."

I sit back in my seat and watch him as I chew the doughy goodness. What can I say to that? Instead of responding, I finish my beignets, then drink the delicious frozen coffee and wipe my mouth and brush the fallen powdered sugar off my shirt and pants.

"Ready for what comes next?" he asks and stands, holding his hand out for mine.

"Sure." He leads me to the sidewalk, settles my hat on my head, and leads me up and down the streets, wandering through gift shops and antique stores, jewelry stores, and even novelty voodoo shops. I soak it all in, looking in every nook and cranny of every store, and Eli patiently waits for me, not saying much, letting me lead him where I want to go.

He's protective while we're walking from store to store, sure to keep his hand on the small of my back, but when I'm poking around, he gives me space to explore.

In an antique jewelry store, I find a silver and ivory cameo locket that I must have for my mother for Mother's Day. When I pull my wallet out to pay, Eli beats me to it, handing the clerk his card.

"Eli, I'm buying this for my mom."

"She'll love it."

"Yes, but *you* just bought it."

He raises a brow and watches me with an amused tilt to his lips, as the clerk bags it up and hands it to me. "You're not paying for anything when you're with me, *cher*."

Before I can respond, he turns and leads me out of the store, and we're back to the palm readers and musicians before Jackson Square. A woman with deep mocha skin and a bight white smile waves at me, and I immediately sit at her table and pay her before Eli can blink, making him glare at me.

I stick my tongue out at him.

"Well, hello there, I'm Madame Sophia." She grins and begins to rub hand sanitizer on her hands.

At least she's a clean palm reader.

"Will I be reading both of your palms, then?"

"No," Eli replies and shoves both his hands in his pockets. He always does that when he's uncomfortable.

It's kind of adorable.

"Scared?" I ask with a grin.

"Skeptical," he replies, matching my grin and sending me off my axis.

"That's okay, baby girl, he can just listen. Please give me the hand you're most comfortable writing with." I lay my right hand in hers, palm up, and settle in to be entertained.

"Ah," she whispers and traces her finger around the outside of my palm. "You're an emotional one, aren't you, baby girl? You wear your heart on your sleeve."

I bite my lip and glance up at Eli, who rolls his eyes. I know what he's thinking: half the population does that.

"A smart one, you are. Oh, look at that! You're a good liar." She glances up at me, narrows her eyes, and then looks back down.

*I lie for a living.*

"Oh, baby girl." She's not looking at my palm anymore. Now she's looking me in the eye, her chocolate brown eyes full of sympathy. "He didn't deserve you, and you're better off without him."

I frown and glance at Eli, then back at Sophia. "I don't think—"

"But you gonna be just fine," she continues without a beat. "Sometimes, love be right under your nose, y'know?"

"I don't think I really need love advice," I reply nervously. She winks at me, and then returns to my palm.

"Ah, you're stubborn, but that's good. You don't let people take advantage, but you are a sucker for the puppy dog eyes." She chuckles when I simply blink at her. "Your parents miss you, way over there in Ireland."

I gasp and move to pull my hand away. "How did you know—?"

"It's just here," she replies. "You'll get a call soon that will change things for you."

"Change them how?"

"That's enough," Eli says, and lays his hand on my shoulder, sending electricity down my chest, making my nipples pucker and Sophia's eyes widen as she looks between the two of us, her hand still hanging on to mine.

"This is a powerful connection."

"I said that's enough. Thank you for your time," he says and helps me to my feet.

"I don't think she was done," I say with a frown, and glance back to see Madam Sophia watching us walk away with a thoughtful frown on her worn face.

"She was done."

His jaw is clenched and his eyes are narrowed as he leads me down the cobblestone street.

"Eli."

He doesn't stop, so I dig in my heels and pull him to a stop next to me.

"I'm fine."

He tucks my hair behind my ear. "You should be wearing your hat."

I settle it on my head, tipped a bit too far forward, so he has to bend at the knees to see my face. Finally, he smiles and tips the brim back.

"Why did that freak you out?"

He shrugs. "She was upsetting you."

*She was freaking me out.*

"I'm fine," I repeat stubbornly. He simply smirks and kisses my forehead.

"Are you ready for lunch?"

"More food?"

"You're in New Orleans, dawlin'. There's always more food."

~

"I'M EXHAUSTED," I sigh, as Eli walks me up to my door several hours, many shops, and two meals later.

"In a good way, I hope."

"Definitely a good way. I had so much fun today."

He smiles softly and takes my hat off my head, then tucks my hair behind my ear and drags his fingertip down my jawline. "I had fun too."

"I'm glad you rang my bell at the crack of dawn."

"I believe it was nine, not the crack of dawn."

I shrug. "Same difference."

He chuckles as I fish my keys out of my handbag and unlock my door.

"Do you want to come in?" I ask.

"I have a bit of work to do this evening," he replies. His eyes look almost...determined.

"Okay, well thanks again."

He nods as I close the door and toss my hat on the sofa. Holy crap, today was fun. The chemistry is still off the charts, but he was a perfect gentleman the whole day. He barely touched me, but we laughed a lot and he was...*friendly*.

Huh. Eli Boudreaux and I are friends.

I grin as I walk through my loft, and my iPhone lights up with a FaceTime call from my cousin Rhys. I grin as I press accept and sit out on my balcony to take the call.

"Well, hello, gorgeous. You are a sight for sore eyes."

"Hey, handsome. Back at you."

# CHAPTER 6

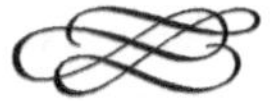

## ẼLI~

"*D*o you want to come in?" she asks, her green eyes smiling up at me.

*Fuck, yes, I want to come in.* Which means, I'd better not go in there because I've kept my hands off of her all day and my resistance is dying a slow, painful death.

"I have a bit of work to do this evening," I lie easily. She immediately looks down, disappointment shadowing her eyes, and I feel like the first-class asshole I'm known to be. But I'd be an even bigger asshole if I followed her in and seduced those expensive panties off her.

"Okay, well thanks again." She offers me another of her sweet smiles, then closes the door behind her and flips the deadbolt lock with a loud click.

I lean my forehead on her door and quietly take a long, deep breath.

I can still smell her.

I walk down her stairs and stroll to my own empty house, thoughts of Kate still running through my head. I don't remember the last time I took a whole day away from the office, and I certainly don't remember the last time I enjoyed myself so much.

Kate's enthusiasm for everything new is contagious. Her love of the music, the food, hell...even that crazy palm reader. She jumps in with both feet and relishes the experience, making being in her company simply effortless.

And maybe that's what has me scared shitless.

I've taken my home for granted my whole life. My father always pointed out to us that we live in a special place, but until I spent the past week sharing it with Kate, it never occurred to me to truly appreciate it.

Her delight in red beans and rice and a shrimp po' boy this afternoon brings a smile to my lips. The woman can eat unlike anyone else I've ever been with. Most women pick at lettuce and turn their nose up at walking *anywhere*, not to mention walking for blocks and blocks, wandering through shops full of overpriced gaudy knick-knacks.

Not that I typically pay attention to those sorts of things, as long as they're fun in bed and don't get too attached.

But Kate's different. Yes, I want to tumble her into bed and mess her up more than I want my next breath, but I enjoy her company just as much. Making her smile makes my stomach clench. Listening to her laugh makes my chest ache.

And when she slid her hand in mine and linked our fingers when we crossed the street, it was the easiest touch I've ever had.

I walk up the stairs to the master bedroom, toe off my shoes, and stare at my balcony, wondering if she'll go out to enjoy the rest of her evening.

And if so, would she mind if I join her?

God, I've become a pussy.

I just saw her five minutes ago, and I'm already craving her company. And that's exactly what it is: I crave her. Her body, her thoughts, her smile.

All of her.

She's made parts of me come alive that have been long dead, and I'm not sure if I can trust this yearning in my gut, yet I can't stop it.

I cross to the doors and open them, but before I can step out onto the balcony, I can hear her voice. And a man's.

I shove my hands in my pockets and finger the half-dollar in my right hand.

"Well, hello, gorgeous. You're a sight for sore eyes."

"Hey, handsome. Back at you."

"How are you down there in the Big Easy?"

I inch outside and see that her back is to me, and she's talking via FaceTime on her iPhone.

"Things are great down here. How are you? Are you taking care of yourself? I know you work so hard, and I worry, you know."

"Stop worrying about me, love. I'm strong as an ox." I raise a brow at the term of endearment, and feel my breath catch in my throat.

"Stubborn as one, too," she replies. I can hear the smile in her voice.

"You miss me and you know it."

"I do," she replies with a sigh. "I miss you very much. When do I get to see you?"

I turn and quietly let myself back into my house, gently closing the doors behind me. So, she does have someone. I shake my head and laugh ruefully. I'm such a fucking fool. Sharing beignets and palm readings means nothing.

*She* means nothing.

I can hear her laugh trickle in from my door, and every hair stands up on the back of my neck.

She's not nothing. She's the least nothing I've ever met in my life. And I can't have her.

～

"Uncle Eli, I want to go outside and play catch." My youngest sister's son, Sam, is staring at me with hopeful hazel eyes, his Chicago Cubs hat planted firmly on his head, baseball mitt and ball in his grubby little boy hands.

"I know you don't have a hat on in my kitchen," Mom gives Sam a stern look, and he takes the hat off and lowers his chin to his chest.

"No, ma'am."

"After dinner," I inform him, and pull him in for a hug and to ruffle his shaggy dark hair. "You can take both me and Beau on."

"I throw better than both of you," Sam says, and grins at Beau, who is chopping vegetables for Mom on the other side of the counter, across from where Sam, Gabby, and I are sitting.

"You don't throw better than me," Beau insists with a frown.

"Do too," Sam says, and eyes the pecan pie sitting on the counter cooling. "Nannan, can I have some pie?"

"Don't even think about touching that pie until after dinner." Mom shakes her spatula at Sam, making him grin. "You're just like your uncles. Always diving into dessert first."

"I'm a growing boy. Right, Mama?"

Gabby smiles down at her son and kisses his head before he can pull away with a cringe. "You are a growing boy. Growing on my nerves."

Sam smiles and walks toward the back door. "I'm gonna go toss the ball in the air until dinner."

"Good plan. Stay close!" Gabby calls, as the screen door slams.

"He's adorable," Charly, at the stove next to Mom, says with a grin. "And knows it."

"He's seven going on thirty-five," Beau says with a laugh. "He tried to talk me out of twenty bucks the other day when he dragged the garbage cans down to the road."

"He what?" Gabby asks with a gasp. "I'll kill him."

"Oh, please," Mom says with a scoff. "Y'all tried to pull off more 'n that with your daddy 'n me when you were young."

"Never got away with it, either," Charly says happily, and tosses some corn on the cob into a boiling pot. We've been wealthy for generations, but we've never hired household staff. Mama and Dad always said that there was no reason to live in a house too big for the eight of us to take care of. Mama loves to cook, loved raising us kids, and we had our own share of chores growing up. "Where are Savannah and Dec?"

"Here we are," Van answers, as she comes into the kitchen, passing hugs and kisses out to everyone.

"You did not!"

I freeze at the sound of her voice, then feel my hands clench into fists and my eyes narrow when Kate and Declan walk into the kitchen, his arm around her shoulders and hers around his waist, leaning into each other and laughing their fucking asses off. It's the leaning that pisses me off the most. They're way too cozy for my comfort level.

*What is she doing here?*

"Kate!" Mama exclaims, and hurries around the kitchen counter to pull Kate in for a hug. "Ah, dawlin', it's been too long since I laid eyes on you."

"You look wonderful, as always," Kate returns and hugs my mom tightly. "Thank you for inviting me."

"You're family, babe. You don't need an invitation. You'll come for Sunday dinner while you're still in town."

I take a deep breath, but feel my blood boil. She was invited, but she didn't call me to give her a ride? Instead, she chose to ride with Declan?

What the fuck?

Suddenly, Sam comes running in from outside, letting the screen slam loudly behind him. "Mama! I threw the ball way up high and it hit the oak tree and bounced off the trunk and hit the roof!" He comes to an abrupt stop when he sees Kate, pulls his hat off his head, and shuffles the toe of his worn sneaker on the hardwood floor. "Ma'am."

"Sam, this is Kate," Declan says, smiling at our nephew. "She's a very good friend of the family."

"It's a pleasure, ma'am." He holds out his hand to shake Kate's, making us all grin. Gabby's raising Sam very well.

"The pleasure is all mine, Sam. It's nice to meet you."

"Yes, ma'am."

"What were you saying about your baseball?"

Sam smiles widely, the excitement filling his dark brown eyes again. "It hit the roof and then rolled off and I caught it!"

"Good job," Kate says with a smile. God, her smile kills me every time, even when it's aimed at someone else.

"Don't you hit any of my windows, now," Mom warns and kisses Sam's head as she passes back into the kitchen.

"No, Nannan," Sam agrees. "I'm still working off the last window." He cringes and glances at his mom.

"He broke another window?" Charly asks with a laugh.

"Hey, don't laugh, that's the third one in six months," Gabby replies, but can't help the smile that forms on her pretty, young face.

"I do chores to pay for them," Sam informs us all. "When can we have pie?"

"Come on, shorty." Declan snags Sam's ball from his mitt. "Let's go out and toss some."

"You don't have a mitt!"

"I'll make do." Dec winks at Kate, setting my teeth on edge, and follows Sam outside.

"Lance isn't coming?" Beau asks Van. She just shakes her head no, and Beau's gaze meets mine.

Yeah, he and I are going to have to have a conversation with Lance soon. Something's going on there, and it isn't good. Seeing Van hurting is killing all of us.

"I got some new shoes in, ladies," Charly says with a sly smile. "Some really gorgeous, knock you on your behind, beautiful shoes."

"I'll be there tomorrow," Van says and links her arm through Kate's. "I'll bring Kate too. We'll clean you out."

"Not fair," Gabby says with a scowl. "This is what sucks about living so far out of town. I don't get to just walk down the street and shop."

"I brought you some in your size," Charly replies and winks at our baby sister. "I can't have you living in the Bayou with ugly shoes."

"You're my favorite sibling. You know that, right?"

"Hey!" Beau scowls at Gabby and wags his sharp knife at her. "I'm the one that lives out there with you, so you're not alone, and commute in to work every day."

"I've been telling you for months to move into town," Gabby replies and leans her elbows on the counter.

"I don't want you out there by yourself either," I reply. "You and Sam alone in the Bayou makes us all nervous."

"I'm not alone. I run a very successful bed and breakfast, thank you very much. There are always people around."

"People we don't know," Charly replies, and Mama nods in agreement.

"We love you, babe," Mama adds and cups Gabby's face in her hand. "Beau's keeping you safe."

"Beau needs to get himself a woman and leave me alone," Gabby replies, glaring at Beau, who just shakes his head and laughs.

"Tell me about the bed and breakfast," Kate says and fishes a carrot out of the salad bowl. God, I love her appetite. She looks amazing today in a soft, flowy black skirt and a green button-down top with a black belt cinched around her slim waist. She left her hair down and applied minimal makeup, leaving her gorgeous freckles uncovered, and has clear gloss on her lips.

Fuck, I want to kiss those lips.

"I turned the family plantation house into an inn," Gabby replies proudly. We're all fucking proud of her. Inn Boudreaux is thriving and booked solid for months.

"Oh, that's awesome," Kate says. "I bet it's amazing. Is it right on the river?"

"Yes. You can't see the river because of the levy, but yes. Guests love the old oak trees, and we've restored some of the slave quarters and stuff so they can also wander around and learn about the plantation."

"I'd love to see it," Kate says, and I immediately decide to take her out there next weekend. She'll love it. "Maybe I can get my parents to come visit and stay out there. It would be right up their alley."

"Are they still in Ireland?" Savannah asks.

"Yes, and they love it there. But I miss them."

"What about Rhys?" Charly asks, as Gabby and I set the table and Mama sets bowls and platters full of way too much food on the table as well. I still at Charly's question and watch Kate.

"He's great. Busy. I haven't seen him in a couple months."

"He's adorable," Charly says with a grin. "In a sexy, delicious kind of way. Is he available?"

"This is Rhys we're talking about," Kate says with a laugh. "Who knows? But I was able to FaceTime with him last night, and he looks as great as ever, and still stubborn as heck."

So, she was FaceTiming with this Rhys guy.

*None of my business.*

"Boys!" Mama calls out the back door. "Dinner's ready! Come eat these groceries!"

Kate sits next to me at the table and smiles up at me sweetly, and I find myself returning it, despite this perpetual frustration I can't shake.

"You okay?" she asks softly.

"Why wouldn't I be?"

"You haven't said two words to me since I got here."

"Hello, Kate." She narrows her eyes and tilts her head, but before she can ask any further questions, Sam and Declan join us and we all dig in. I glance up to find Charly watching Kate and me with a raised brow, but I shake my head, giving her the silent message to leave it be, and eat silently.

Kate laughs, asking more questions about Gabby's inn, Charly's shop, and how Sam likes the second grade, charming my whole family. How has she been friends with Dec and Van for so long and I'd never met her before?

*Because you've been too busy keeping the business the way Dad wanted you to.*

"Eli, you're more quiet than normal," Mama says softly, watching me with shrewd eyes. "What's going on with you?"

I shake my head and wipe my mouth with a napkin. "Just the same old thing, Mama."

"Hmph," she replies and glances around the table. "Why do I feel like I'm out of the loop here?"

"You're not," I reply with a smile. "Work as usual."

"You work too much."

"Not you too," I reply, and rub my forehead with the tips of my fingers. "I get this lecture from Savannah at least once a week."

"Well, you'll be gettin' it from me too. You're *my* baby boy."

*Oh, God.*

Kate smirks next to me and hides her smile behind a tall glass of lemonade.

"I'm fine, I promise."

"He even took the day off yesterday," Kate adds nonchalantly. Mama's eyes widen as she looks between Kate and me.

"He did?"

"Yes, ma'am."

"How do you know?"

*Don't say it.* I lay my hand on Kate's thigh, but she ignores me and says it anyway.

"Because he was with me. He showed me around the French Quarter all day. It's his fault that I'm now addicted to beignets from Café du Monde."

The table is silent for a few beats, then Mama clears her throat.

"You went to Café du Monde on Saturday mornin'?"

I meet her bright eyes with my own and nod. "Yes, ma'am."

"I've always wanted to see the French Quarter. It was amazing," Kate continues, oblivious to the tension between us siblings. They're all staring at me like I've grown a second head.

Finally, in the innocent way that only a seven-year-old can, Sam speaks up.

"Pawpaw used to take us there on Saturdays," he says, and takes a bite of the corn on the cob, missing some pieces, thanks to the gap in his front teeth. "It was fun."

"That's right," Gabby says and runs her hand over her son's hair.

Suddenly, Kate lays *her* hand on *my* thigh and I glance down into understanding eyes, and it's all I can take.

"I'm sorry, Mama, but I just remembered that I have some work to catch up on." I stand quickly and take care of my own dishes, then kiss her cheek. "Thank you for dinner. I'll call you tomorrow."

"Eli—"

But I don't stop to hear what she has to say. I walk quickly to my car and peel out of the driveway. My heart is beating quickly, and for the first time in more than two years, I'm consumed with *emotion*.

What in the hell is wrong with me?

And who the fuck is Rhys?

This is all Kate's fault. Before she showed up with her gorgeous green eyes and touchable red hair, I was fine, consumed by work. I had a routine that worked well for me, with no interruptions.

Certainly no Saturdays spent in the Quarter and evenings listening to Dec's gigs.

I just need to get laid. That's all there is to it. It's been more than a minute since I last enjoyed the company of a warm, willing woman.

Yes, that's it.

Before long, I'm back at my house, pacing through the silent, empty rooms, my phone in my hand, paging through my contacts list. I'm going to scratch this itch and get over it. Erase Kate from my mind completely.

I pour myself three fingers of brandy, sit behind my desk, and thumb through my electronic black book.

Ah, yes, I could call Amanda. She's always fun. Tall, leggy. But she has strawberry blonde hair, and that'll just remind me too much of Kate.

I skip to the next name.

Collette! I met Collette three years ago at a charity function. She's smart as a whip and likes to be blindfolded. I grin, but then I remember that Collette has freckles on her shoulders, and that won't do.

*Fuck.*

Fredericka. I haven't seen her in a while. She's curvy in all the right places with the best tits I've ever seen.

Scratch that. Kate has the best tits I've ever seen.

And I've never actually *seen* them.

I sigh loudly and swallow the rest of the brandy, then smile when I see Stephanie's name.

Steph and I have had a mutually satisfying arrangement for the better part of five years. She's long and lean with a runner's body and an enthusiasm in bed that can't be matched. She has jet-black hair and chocolate brown eyes with the whitest, smoothest skin I've ever seen. She's not afraid to make noise, and she can suck a cock like no one else.

Yes, I do believe I'll call Steph.

My thumb hovers over her name, but suddenly I see laughing green eyes smiling up at me as she gets her palm read, her face set in rapture when she first tasted the beignets. God, my dick throbs at the thought of what those eyes will look like when I'm buried so deep inside her I can't tell where she ends and I begin.

*Motherfucker.*

I throw my phone across the room, aiming for the couch, so it doesn't break, then pick up my glass and consider throwing that too, needing to hear the shatter of glass, when Charly's voice comes from the doorway.

"Sam would be impressed with that arm."

I whirl and glare at my sister. "What the fuck are you doing here?"

"Well, I'm not here for your sparkling personality," she replies, and plants her hands on her hips.

"Look, I'm not really fit for company tonight, Char."

"Clearly." She smiles, her hazel eyes softening, and I feel my chest loosen too. "You're handsome when you're pissed."

"Don't try to charm me."

She tosses her head back and laughs, then plops down on my couch and rescues my phone from the cushions. "What did your phone do to you?"

"Nothing."

"Wanna talk about Kate?"

"Fuck no."

"Wanna talk about anything?"

I glare at her and cross my arms over my chest.

"That may work in the boardroom, but it doesn't work with me."

"You're a pain in my ass." I sigh and stare at Charly. She's the second to the youngest, and I've been wrapped around her little finger since the day Mama and Dad brought her home from the hospital.

"You love me."

I simply grunt and then cave under her hard stare and scrub my hands over my face.

"You took her for beignets."

"Shut up, Char."

"I'm just saying, you haven't had beignets since Daddy—"

"I've had beignets since Dad died."

"Yeah, the ones you make your assistant go get for you. But you never go there."

I raise a brow and smirk at her. "I'm a bit too busy to just run out for beignets when the mood strikes."

"You know, I may not be the genius of the family, leading the family business into the new millennium, but I'm not slow, Eli."

"I'm sorry." I close my eyes and pinch the bridge of my nose. "I don't know what you want me to say."

"Say that you like Kate."

"It's not a matter of liking her."

"Well, why are you here, alone, while she's right next door, also alone? That's ridiculous."

"Because she's an employee, a friend of the family, and it sounds like she already has someone in her life."

"Yeah, an asshole of an ex-husband."

My jaw drops as I stare at Charly. "Rhys?"

"What?" She frowns and shakes her head. "No, Rhys is her cousin. Her very hot, base-ball star cousin. Daniel is her asshole of an ex."

I stand, circle my desk, lean my hips against it, and push my hands into my pockets. "What did he do to her?"

"Oh, no, that's her story to tell." Charly shakes her head as she stands and crosses to me, wraps her arms around my waist, and hugs me tight. "Daddy wouldn't want you to live like this, Eli."

I cringe, but don't reply. No one was in that room with Dad and me right before he died. No one else knows what he said.

What, exactly, he expected of me after his death.

"I'm fine, *bebe*," I reply, and smile reassuringly as she pulls away.

"But you want me to leave now."

"No, you know you can stay here for as long as you want." There are four women in my life that I'd do anything in the world for. My three sisters and my mother.

Scratch that. Five. It seems Kate has wormed her way onto the short list.

"I love you, big brother."

"I love you too, brat." I grin as she laughs and walks back out of the room.

"Get some sleep! You look like shit!"

"Thank you!" I call just before the front door closes. She really is a pain in my ass. I pour three more fingers and let myself out onto the balcony, my eyes immediately turning to the left, and sure enough, Kate is sitting out with a glass of wine in her small, perfect hand.

She turns her head, leveling me with a cool glare.

"Problem?" I ask and sink into my chair. She's sitting only a few feet away, with a simple wrought iron railing separating us. I could reach out and touch her.

But I don't.

"Yeah, I think there is a problem," she replies, as calmly as if we're talking about the weather.

"Would you care to share it?"

She's quiet for a moment, then sets her wine on the table beside her and turns to face me, and her green eyes, full of anger and frustration, take my breath away.

"I promised myself that I would never again let a man determine the way I feel about myself. I wouldn't play games. I'm worth more than that."

I raise a brow. "Agreed."

She laughs humorlessly and stands to pace around her small balcony.

"You confuse the heck out of me! You were so fun and easy to be with yesterday. I actually thought we were…*friends.*"

*Friends.* That particular word leaves a bad taste in my mouth.

"And then I see you today and you barely speak to me, then run out on your own family dinner!"

I stand and lean my hands on the railing, looking her in the eye. "I'm trying to keep my hands off of you, Kate."

"Oh, please." She rolls her eyes and crosses her arms over her chest. "I'm not irresistible, Eli. Trust me, I know."

"You're wrong. You're practically family—"

"I'm *not* part of your family."

"And I didn't know if you were already taken."

"I wouldn't have spent all day with you yesterday, not to mention let you *kiss me* the way you do, if I were taken."

"Is your divorce final?"

This makes her pause. "Of course it is."

"And Rhys is your cousin?"

She scowls. "Are you kidding me right now? You can't be jealous of my *cousin.*"

"Oh, dawlin', it seems I'm jealous of my own fucking brother when it comes to you. I wanted to rip Dec's arm off his body when y'all came in Mama's kitchen today."

"Declan and I are *friends!*" She stomps away again, really worked up now, and I have to work to keep the smile off my face.

My God, she's magnificent.

"*Friends* the way you and I are friends, Kate? Does he kiss you like I do?"

"It's none of your bloody business!" She points her finger at me and keeps railing. "You don't want me anyway! I'm bloody divorced, and I have bloody male friends, and I'm not going to apologize about any of that to you!"

"Come here," I reply softly. She stops in her tracks and stares at me, chest heaving with temper.

"No."

"I won't tell you again, *cher.*"

She narrows her eyes and steps closer. "You don't get to talk to me like—"

Before she can finish, I cup her face in my hand and brush my thumb across her soft cheek. Her skin is smooth and simply irresistible. I lean across the railing and stop my lips from covering hers by just a breath.

"Say *fuck*, Kate, it's okay."

"I don't swear," she whispers. "I have enough Catholic guilt as it is."

"Just this once. I won't tell." My lips are tickling hers as I talk, and I feel the shiver run through her. She licks her lips and swallows thickly, and I've never been so hard in my damn life. "Say it."

"Fuck," she whispers, and I crush my mouth to hers, kissing her with all the pent up frustration and need that I have inside me. I push both hands to the nape of her neck, holding her still as my tongue tangles with hers, then lick to the corner of her mouth to tease.

She moans, gripping onto my forearms, but not pushing me away. I want to be in her arms. I want to wrap my arms around her and pull her into me and lose myself in her.

I want to strip her bare and feast on her.

But I pull away, gently caressing her face, tucking her auburn hair behind her ears, keeping her gaze caught in my own.

"Say goodnight, Kate."

"Bad idea," she whispers, still gripping my arms with all she's worth.

"Maybe not such a bad idea," I reply hoarsely. *But not tonight.*

"Eli—"

"Say goodnight, Kate," I repeat and back away when I'm sure she has her feet under her.

"Goodnight, Kate." She presses her fingertips to her mouth and watches me with wide green eyes for a long moment, then turns and walks into her loft, locking the door behind her.

# CHAPTER 7

## ~KATE~

*I*t's too hot in here. I jerk my right leg out from under the covers and roll to my left side, staring into the darkness. I swear I can still taste Eli, but it's been hours since that crazy kiss on the balcony.

He confuses me unlike anyone I've ever met, including Daniel. It's clear that he's attracted to me, and let's face it, it's reciprocated. But he's fighting it as if he's almost *afraid* of it.

How could he possibly be afraid of me?

And, honestly, it's probably for the best that he fight it, and I should be fighting it too. I'm only here for six weeks, tops. I love his siblings as if they were my own, and sleeping with Eli could make things awkward.

Although, things seem to be awkward already, so that's probably not a great argument. Now I'm too bloody cold.

I pull the covers back over me and roll onto my back, staring at the ceiling. A car drives by outside, sending light and shadows over the walls, and then my phone pings next to me.

I frown and reach for it. Who the heck is texting me in the middle of the night?

*I'm thinking of you.*

Eli.

I bite my lip and reply. *Why are you awake?*

A moment later, he responds with: *Because I'm thinking of you.*

And now I'm too hot. I whip my covers off me, but before I can reply to him, he sends another message. *Did I wake you?*

*No.*

*Why are you awake?*

I shrug, even though he can't see me.

*Dunno.*

His next message makes me smile. *Do you need anything?*

I shake my head and answer. *No.*

270

*Are you only going to give one word answers?*

I laugh. *I have lots of words for you, but for now? Yes.*

It takes a minute for his response. Long enough for me to get too cold and then too hot and too cold again.

*Okay, then just listen. I enjoy making you smile. Your smile slays me. You taste sweeter than any beignet, and I want to spend more time with you tomorrow after work.*

I sigh, suddenly way too warm, and it has nothing to do with the temperature in the room, and everything to do with this confusing man.

*Are you trying to charm me?*

I bite my lip as I wait for his response.

*Maybe.*

I giggle and turn on my side. Now he's giving me the one-word answers.

*It might be working. What do you have in mind for after work?*

I grin and bite my lip as I wait for his answer. *I have many things in mind.*

Oh, flirty Eli is so fun!

*I look forward to hearing about those things.*

*Meet me on the balcony?*

I want to say yes, jump up, and run out there to see him, just for a few minutes, but instead, I take a deep breath and reply with: *No, thank you. Say goodnight, Eli.*

My eyes are getting heavy as I wait for his response. Finally, long minutes later, he replies.

*Goodnight, Eli.*

~

WHEN I WOKE up this morning, there were no more text messages from Eli. I almost thought I'd dreamed them, but when I looked, there they were.

He likes making me smile.

And now that I stop to think about it, he does make me smile. Quite often, actually. He has the best smile, and when he laughs, his whole face lights up, showing off a small dimple in his right cheek. His whiskey eyes are intoxicating, and when he pins me in his sexy I-want-you stare, well, he makes my panties melt right off me.

Yeah, I enjoy making him smile too.

"Earth to Kate." I blink rapidly and glance up to find Hilary laughing at me.

"I'm sorry."

"Hon, you were a million miles away."

I cringe and glance at my computer, which has been idle so long it went to sleep.

"Yeah, daydreaming. Sorry." I smile and gesture for her to sit in the chair across from me. "What can I do for you?"

"Oh, nothing. I decided to take my lunch break a few minutes early and come see how you're gettin' on here."

"Is it lunch time already?" I check my watch, and sure enough, the day is half gone. "Wow, time flies. I'm doing well. How are you?"

"Oh, I'm just fine." Hilary pats her pretty blonde hair and grins. "I had a date on Friday."

"Really? How did that go?"

"Well, it ended on Sunday afternoon, so I'd say it went well."

We both giggle, and suddenly there's a delivery boy at my doorway. "Miss O'Shaughnessy?"

"Yes."

"I have your lunch order here."

I frown, but quickly recover, playing along. I don't want Hilary to suspect anything.

"How much do I owe you?"

"Nothin', ma'am. Have a nice day."

There's a note stapled to the plain brown paper bag.

*Kate,*

*This should hold you over until tonight.*

*E.*

I tuck the note in my pocket, my heart suddenly beating fast and doing the happy dance in my head, as Hilary watches with blatant curiosity. I open the bag and practically groan.

"Shrimp po' boy and red beans and rice," I announce. "I can't eat all of this. Please, tell me you'll stay and help me."

"I've never passed up a po' boy," Hilary says with a grin, as I split everything in half and we settle in to eat at my desk.

"So, tell me more about this two-day date." I take a bite of my sandwich and sigh with happiness. The man does feed me the best food.

"Well, his name is Louis, which made me think that he'd be a bit of a geek at first. I mean, his name is *Louis.*"

I nod as I chew, and chuckle as Hilary gets the dopey I-got-laid look on her face.

"Where did you meet him?"

"Online." She blushes and then shrugs. "Once you reach a certain age, it's hard to meet people."

"You can't be more than thirty," I reply, and take a heaping bite of the red beans and rice.

"I'm thirty-two. No, not old, but I work all the time, and it's not like I go to school or meet new people all the time. So, I'm doing the online thing. So far, it doesn't suck."

"What does Louis do?"

"Well, he does this thing with his tongue—"

"Ew! No, what does he do for a living?" I laugh and throw a plastic-wrapped spork at her, making her giggle.

"I don't know. I think he said he works at a Starbucks."

I raise an eyebrow. "Not that I'm judging, but *you think?*"

"Honey, once he took his shirt off, and I got a look at his chest and abs, he could have told me he hunts whales for a living, and I still would have gotten naked for him."

I smirk, but I know exactly what she means. I wonder what Eli looks like under all of his perfectly tailored suits, worn blue jeans and hot T-shirts. He's muscular, I know that much just based on the little I've touched him. I wonder if he has tattoos?

"Also, Louis has these tattoos," she continues, as though she can read my mind, "all down his left arm. I spent a good few hours tracing them with my tongue."

"*Hours?*" I ask with a snort.

"Trust me; it was totally worth it," she replies with a wink. "He used his tongue in other ways that made me a very happy woman."

"Oh, my gosh, stop it with the tongue talk!" I cover my ears with my hands and shake my head. "I beg you!"

"He was begging all right."

I dissolve in a fit of giggles. "I like you."

"I like you too." She sighs and sips half my Coke. "So, who put that look I saw on your face when I walked in here?"

I shake my head adamantly. "No one."

"Bullshit."

"Seriously. I'm not currently having sex."

"No, you're currently having lunch with me. But you were thinking about having sex. I know that look." Hilary narrows her eyes. "Spill it."

"Honestly, I'm not seeing anyone, naked or clothed. I am, however, going to go buy some new shoes after work."

"New shoes are almost as good as really good sex," she concedes, and I silently blow out a long breath. "Not quite, but almost."

"New shoes are great, but I'm even more addicted to handbags."

"Me too!" she exclaims and shimmies in her seat. "Have you seen what's coming this fall from MK?"

"No, is it delicious?" I ask, and suck Coke through my straw.

"To die for," she confirms with a nod. "And I just picked up a cute little number at the Coach outlet last week."

"The outlets are my weakness." I grin at Hilary. I really do like her. She's someone I could be friends with. I'm glad she's decided to befriend me here at work.

"Now, tell me you like to read, and we'll be soulmates."

"My iPad is full of trashy romance novels."

A slow smile spreads across her pretty face. "I'm keeping you."

~

"You keep feeding me," I say to Eli as he escorts me, hand in hand, down Royal Street to the pretty little restaurant that he's taking me to for dinner.

"You like to eat. I like that in a woman." I laugh up at him, and then sigh as he leads me across the street, protectively laying his hand on the small of my back.

"How was your day?" He links his fingers with mine again as we stroll down the street.

"Long. I found out that I have to leave tomorrow morning for a business trip to New York. I also kept thinking about getting you alone. Do you know what a pain in the ass it is having you in the same building as me all day long and not being able to walk into your office and kiss you whenever I want to?"

"No, why don't you tell me."

His lips quirk as he glances down at me. "You're sassy. One of these days I'll just have my assistant send down for you and you can come to my office."

"Just so you can kiss me?"

"We can start with that, yes." His voice is suddenly rough, and my knees turn to jelly at the thought of being in Eli's office with him, and all the things we could do in that office.

"I don't think that's a good idea. People will talk, and we can't have that."

"So professional," he murmurs, then stops us on the sidewalk and leans in to whisper in my ear. "I can't wait to see you all flummoxed and writhing and *unprofessional* beneath me, *cher*. Trust me, we're about to get as unprofessional as possible."

My breath catches in my throat as he leans back and pins me in his hot stare. He drags his fingertip over the pulse in my throat. "I see that thought turns you on."

*Heck yes that turns me on!* I can only swallow hard and watch as he pulls away and leads me to the restaurant.

"Café Amelie," I read aloud. "That's a pretty name."

"And good food." He turns to the hostess. "Reservation for Boudreaux."

"Of course." She grins and grabs two menus. "Would you prefer courtyard seating?"

Eli raises an eyebrow at me. It's cooler this evening, and the courtyard is pretty with lights in the trees above. "The courtyard is beautiful."

"The lady wishes to sit in the courtyard," Eli replies with a soft smile, his eyes never leaving mine.

This man is potent.

We're seated in the corner of the courtyard, giving the table an intimate atmosphere. Soon, a very tall, handsome waiter arrives to take our drink order and to tell us about the specials.

"I'd enjoy a lemon drop martini, please." I smile at Eli as he orders his own drink and tells Joe the waiter that we need a few minutes with the menu.

"You're not ordering for me?" I ask when Joe leaves.

"Do you want me to?" Eli asks. "I certainly can."

I shrug a shoulder. "It's not necessary. You just usually enjoy ordering for me."

Joe delivers our drinks and takes our order. Eli orders an appetizer of Brussels sprouts sautéed in butter and bacon with dates, and assures me they are to die for.

"They're Brussels sprouts."

"You'll like them," he insists, and takes my hand in his as I drink my lemon drop.

"This is delicious." I take another sip. "So, you're leaving tomorrow?" I try to keep my voice nonchalant, but my stomach is suddenly tight. I don't want him to leave.

"Just until Friday afternoon." He kisses my palm. "I'll miss you."

"You'll be too busy to miss me."

"I'll miss you," he insists. "How was *your* day?" he asks and leans in, giving me all of his attention.

"It was good, despite not getting a lot of sleep last night. A handsome man sent me lunch."

"He did," he replies with a satisfied grin. "Did you enjoy it?"

"Yes, I loved it. I also shared it with a co-worker, because it was way too much food for just me."

"And this handsome man? Do you like him?"

"Well, he can be frustrating, but he's also fun and charming. Yes, I like him."

His eyes heat as he watches me talk. His thumb is tracing circles over the back of my hand.

"Another lemon drop, miss?" Joe asks as he walks by.

"Yes, please." Joe nods and leaves. "Thank you for lunch."

"You're welcome. I would have delivered it myself, but—"

"But people will talk." I chuckle and shake my head. "It's okay. It was a nice surprise."

"I have to tell you, I'm a bit confused as to why I didn't know you were recently divorced." His face sobers with the change of conversation, and I cringe, the subject of my ex being the very last thing I want to talk about.

"It really isn't a secret." He raises a brow. "It's been several months since the divorce was final, but I haven't lived with him in more than two years, Eli. It's not something I talk about freely, certainly not with someone I don't know well."

"Why did the divorce take so long?" he asks and leans back, but doesn't let go of my hand. I eagerly sip the fresh drink that Joe just set at my elbow.

"Because Daniel is a selfish, proud, arrogant man who didn't like having the word *divorcee* after his name. Well, until he was ready to marry again, anyway."

"He's remarried already?"

"One week after the divorce was final, yes." I sigh and then just shrug. "Honestly, I didn't care. I wasn't in a position emotionally to be dating anyone, and the important thing was to simply not be living with him anymore. The rest was just gravy."

"Did he hurt you?"

"Oh, he hurt me more than any one person should be allowed to hurt another," I reply easily, but sip my drink to hide my face behind the glass for just a moment to gather my wits around me.

"Look at me."

I raise my gaze to find Eli's eyes hot with anger and his jaw ticking, but the hand holding mine is still amazingly tender. This man has amazing control.

"Did he hit you?"

"Yes."

"*Fuck*," he whispers.

"But that wasn't the worst part."

He cocks his head and raises a brow when I don't want to answer. My lips are starting to feel numb.

"These drinks are strong. They make my lips talk."

His sexy lips quirk up in a smile. "They make your lips talk?"

"Yep."

"Okay, so keep talking. What was the worst part?"

I shake my head and finish the second drink, then signal to Joe for another. I can't tell him the very worst part. Not yet. "He would yell at me. He was a bully. Sometimes it's better if they just hit you once and then get on with their day."

"Bullshit," he says calmly. "I could teach you some self-defense, you know."

"Oh, I took self defense classes." I wave him off and drink the new lemon drop. "He used to call me a whore." I giggle, barely noticing that Eli has pulled his hand away and curled it into a fist. "Which is actually pretty funny."

"Why in the fucking hell is that funny?"

"Because, counting him, I've only been with..." I count in my fuzzy head. "Two and a half men. Hey, isn't that a TV show?"

"How is it possible that you were with half of a man?" he asks with a surprised laugh.

"Because he never got it in. It didn't count." I slap my hand over my mouth and giggle. "These drinks are really delicious. You should have one."

"That's okay, one of us will have to get you up to your front door."

"I can walk." I compose my face and sit up straight. "See? I'm perfectly sober."

"Right. So, back to what you were talking about. Why couldn't he get it in?"

"Who couldn't get what in?" I ask with a frown, and then prop my chin in my hand as I watch Eli smile across from me. "Gosh, you're pretty."

"Excuse me?" He laughs and tucks my hair behind my ear. His fingers feel good on my skin.

"I bet they'd feel good everywhere."

"I think I just missed half of that conversation," he replies. "You're hilarious when you've had too much to drink. I think you've had enough." He takes my drink away, earning a scowl from me.

"I have not."

"What would feel good everywhere?" he asks, distracting me.

"Your fingers."

This makes him pause. He blinks rapidly, and if I'm not mistaken, all three of him blush.

"You're blushing after what you said to me on the sidewalk?"

"I'm certainly not blushing," he replies. "And, yes, I do believe my fingers would feel good everywhere."

"I have no doubt," I reply, and reach up to push his dark hair off his forehead. "You are pretty."

"You already said that."

"It's true."

"I think our sprouts are here," he replies and kisses my hand before leaning away.

"Well, hello, Joe." I smile up at the sexy waiter as he sets my food before me.

"Hello there," he replies with a grin.

"You're handsome," I inform him. "May I please have another lemon drop?"

"You're flirting with the waiter?" Eli asks with a laugh.

"He brings me delicious drinks," I reply seriously and turn to Joe. "I would flirt with my date, but he took my drink away. That means no flirts for him."

"I would be happy to bring you a water," Joe replies and sets his hand on my shoulder. "And then another lemon drop after you get some food in you."

"You have strong hands, Joe." Eli growls next to me, but I ignore him. "Are you sure I can't have just one little teeny tiny drink now?"

I bat my eyelashes, but Joe just laughs. *Laughs!* Maybe my flirter is broken.

"I'll be right back with that water."

"My flirter is broken."

"No, it's doing just fine," Eli replies and holds a Brussels sprout up on the end of his fork for me to eat. "Try this."

"It's a bloody Brussels sprout."

His eyes flare at the word *bloody*, and suddenly I'm thinking about his lips against mine telling me to say fuck.

"Fuck," I whisper, watching his lips. He swears under his breath, then leans in to whisper in my ear.

"Eat, Kate. Please. You're killing me here."

"I am?" I smile widely, ridiculously proud of myself.

"Yes." He takes my hand in his and guides it under the table to his lap. "See?"

"Wow," I whisper, letting my hand roam over the bulge in his pants. "This is impressive."

"Thank you." He laughs and takes a drink of water, and when I squeeze my hand, just a little, he chokes on it. "Kate."

"I mean, you won't have any problem getting this in."

"Stop." He tugs my hand away, kisses my palm, and lays my hand back on the table. "The bartender gave you some strong drinks."

He offers me the Brussels sprout again, and I open my mouth, obliging him.

"It's good," I say, surprised.

"Told you."

"You're good at food."

"I'm glad you think so."

I eat two more of the delicious vegetables. "I do."

"Here's your water, miss." Joe smiles down at me with those super blue eyes, and I sigh, just a little.

"It's too bad you didn't give in to my flirting, Joe. You're almost as delicious as these Brussels sprouts."

"Kate." I glance at Eli, who is pinching the bridge of his nose with his thumb and forefinger.

"What?"

"So, liquor makes you come on to men, then? Is it true that tequila makes your clothes fall off?"

"No, tequila makes me throw up. Vodka makes my clothes fall off." I grin and sip my water. "You might want to take notes."

"No need. I don't think I'll ever forget anything about you."

"Oh." I sigh and lick my lips. "You say really great things."

"Only the truth."

I want to say more, but I clench my lips together, determined to not give too much away in my drunken stupor. Thankfully, Joe returns with our entrees, and Eli and I both dig in, enjoying the sounds of the diners around us, the night birds, and crickets. My cheeks feel warm from the alcohol, but the fuzzy haze is clearing from my head a bit with the food. Eli finally places the rest of the lemon drop he confiscated in front of me to finish with a grin.

"I've learned something about you tonight, *cher.*"

"Yeah? What's that?"

"You have a three drink limit," he replies with a laugh. "And, from now on, I'm asking for the oldest, ugliest waiter on staff."

"I probably wouldn't have dumped you for Joe," I inform him with a grin. "Although, the man is pretty hot. And has strong hands. And brings me drinks."

"Are those your requirements?" Eli asks.

"Some of them."

"What are the rest?"

"What are your requirements?" I ask, rather than answer him.

"As of about a week ago, I only have one requirement. That she be *you.*"

I blink at him, unsure that those words actually came out of his mouth.

"You're charming."

He shrugs one shoulder, watching me closely. "Call it what you want."

Eli settles the check and then holds his hand out for mine, pulling me to my feet. He leans in and kisses the corner of my mouth sweetly, then whispers in my ear, "You're all I want, Kate."

My nipples tighten, and the expensive lacy panties I'm wearing under my black maxi skirt are soaked as he leads me back to the sidewalk and toward our homes. I slip my hand in his and link our fingers, loving the way his big hand feels in mine. I lean back just a bit and take a quick look at his tight butt in his khaki slacks. He's wearing a white button-down with the sleeves rolls up on his forearms, showing off the sinewy muscles that flex and move under his skin.

"You okay?"

"Yep, I was just checking out your butt."

He shakes his head and laughs. "And?"

"It's there."

"Is that all?"

"And it's impressive."

He moves my hand to his other hand and cups my ass in the palm of his hand, gives it a pat, then takes my hand back in his. "Likewise, dawlin'."

"My loft feels really far away right now."

"It's right there," he says, and points to the building just a half of a block away.

"Really far."

But, before I know it, we're climbing the stairs to my door, and when we reach the top, Eli spins me, pins me to the door, and kisses me like a man starving. I grip his hair in my hands, loving the way the soft strands feel between my fingers, and press my belly against his pelvis. He's hard and thick, and I need to get him naked.

He pushes his hand under the hem of my top and glides his magical hand up to cup my breast over the lace of my bra.

"God, I fucking love your lingerie choices," he mutters, and drags his lips down my jawline to my neck, nibbling as he goes, sending shivers all over my body.

"I have a thing for pretty underwear."

"Thank Christ." His other hand cups my ass and he boosts me up high on his thigh. I shamelessly rub myself on his thigh, needing to get closer. God, he's just hard, *everywhere*.

"Come inside," I murmur and kiss his cheek when he rests his temple on my forehead, then turns his face and kisses me lightly on the lips. His thumb brushes my nipple again, making me gasp and press harder on his thigh, but he pulls away, breathing hard, and swallows thickly.

"I can't."

"What?" My eyes snap up to his. He's panting, and just as turned on as I am.

"Kate—"

"No, it's okay." I look down, disappointment singing through my veins, but he tilts my head up and kisses me sweetly.

"I'm not turning you down, and trust me when I say, I'm going to have you in every way there is to have you, but you've had too much to drink, and I'm not convinced that you trust me all the way yet. We're getting there, *cher*."

"I trust you. I trust you to give me a few of the best orgasms of my life."

"Killing me," he whispers, before planting his lips on my forehead and taking a deep breath.

"It's this door." I pull the hem of my shirt down and try to gain my balance. "I think you have an aversion to this door. Should I buy a new one? Is it the color you don't like?"

He laughs and cages me between his hands. "I don't want to fuck this up before we really get started, Kate."

"And then you say things like that that make me swoon and my panties all wet."

"Are your panties wet, Kate?"

"My panties have been wet for a week, Eli."

"Good." He kisses me softly, ending it on a growl. "Please tell me you can get yourself to bed."

"I can't get myself to bed." I grin and bat my eyelashes. "You might have to help me."

"Why do I think you're not as impaired as I originally thought?"

"I'm fine." I clear my throat and rest my hand on his rock-hard chest. "I'll get myself to bed."

He nods and steps away. "I'll see you Friday."

"Friday."

# CHAPTER 8

## ~KATE~

*I*t's early and I'm dragging, getting ready for work, when there's a loud knock on my door. I check the clock and frown, wondering who in the world would be here at six in the morning.

Did Eli come home early?

My heart starts to beat frantically as I dash to the door.

"Oh, Declan."

He flashes a smile, and then laughs. "Gee, don't look so excited to see me, superstar."

"Of course I'm happy to see you." I step back and invite him in. "But *why* am I seeing you at this time of day? You're typically going to bed right about now."

"Yeah, well, I haven't been to bed yet." He smiles again, making me roll my eyes.

"You're a man-whore."

"The ladies like a man who knows his way around a musical instrument." He shrugs as though it's no big deal and yawns widely. "I've come to take you to breakfast."

"I have to be at work in two hours," I remind him.

"Plenty of time for breakfast," he insists.

"Let me finish my hair." I wave for him to follow me to the bathroom, where he leans his broad shoulder against the doorjamb and watches me with humor-filled hazel eyes.

Eyes just like his older brother's. I haven't heard one word from Eli in four days. No flirty texts or phone calls. I know he's away for work, and he's probably busy, but I can't help but be a little disappointed.

I miss the sexy charmer.

"Did you have a gig last night?" I ask and pull my flat iron through my hair.

"Yeah, at a new place. The owner is trying to get me to commit full time, but I like bouncing around."

"*Bouncing* being the operative word," I reply, and smile brightly at him in the mirror.

"There wasn't a lot of bouncing happening last night, actually."

"I don't want to know." I put the finishing touches on my hair, smooth gloss over my lips, and turn to Declan. "I'm ready."

"Good, I'm starving." He takes my hand in his and leads me out of the loft and down the street.

"So, who was the lucky lady this time?" I ask, as we stroll hand in hand into the heart of the Quarter.

"Clarice," he replies, and a slow grin spreads over his lips. "She's a dancer."

"Oh, God. Clarice? *Seriously?*" I giggle and lean my forehead on his strong bicep, then glance up into his handsome, frowning face. "Does she hear the lambs screaming?"

"Stop it right now. You know that movie scared the hell out of me."

I laugh loudly and shake my head. This is too good to pass up.

"Did you drink chianti?"

"Kate—"

"You're right. I'm sorry." I try to school my features, but it's no use. I dissolve into laughter again.

"I'm never going to be able to see her again after this," he complains. "Do you know how flexible dancers are?"

"Does she also have a moth collection?"

He glares at me as he holds the door to the restaurant open for me, making me laugh all the louder. We're seated quickly, not many people are out at this time of day, and I chuckle all the way to the table.

"Damn it. She was fun."

"Oh, come on. You had to know it was doomed from the beginning with a name like Clarice. You had nightmares about that movie for months. The only thing that would have made it worse is if you swung for the other team and went for someone named Hannibal."

"You got mean," he replies, glaring at me over his menu.

"You know I love you," I reply, and blow him a kiss. "I forgot how much fun it is to rile you up."

The waitress arrives and takes our order. When she leaves, I lean back in my chair and study my friend. "You look tired."

"I am tired."

"So, why are we out to breakfast?"

"Because I miss you."

I narrow my eyes and feel my heart catch. I love this man with my whole heart. He and Savannah are like siblings to me. But I can also tell when he's not telling me the whole truth.

"You just saw me on Tuesday when you and Van took me out for drinks after work."

He shrugs a shoulder and sips his coffee. "Eli's due home tomorrow."

Ah, there it is.

"Yes, that's what I heard." I sip my orange juice and study the little placard on the table, announcing the daily lunch specials.

"Okay, I'm not Van." He leans forward, getting right to the point, which is his usual M.O. "You're a grown woman, and my brother is a good man, so if y'all want to bounce on each other, who am I to say you shouldn't?"

I roll my eyes at the *bounce* word, but he keeps going.

"But I want you to be careful, and if he hurts you, I'll kill him. Brother or not."

"That's so sweet," I reply sarcastically, and fake a tear rolling down my cheek.

"I'm fucking serious, Kate."

"I love you, too," I reply, serious now. "Eli and me, well, it's been confusing and exhilarating at the same time. But I haven't even spoken to him since Sunday night."

I shrug, but I can't help the stab of pain in my chest. I miss his voice.

"He's working. He rarely calls home when he's working."

I nod and sip my juice, just as Dec's phone rings.

"Hello, Clarice," I whisper in a creepy voice. Dec flips me off as he answers his phone.

"Hello, big brother."

I still as my eyes whip up to find his. He simply nods.

It's Eli.

"Yes, I spoke with her. Beau is taking care of it today." He pauses. "I'm having breakfast right now with Kate."

I raise a brow and inwardly cringe as Eli's words from the other night fill my head. *It seems I'm jealous of my own fucking brother when it comes to you.*

"I'll tell her. Safe travels." He clicks off and sends me an apologetic smile. "He's heading into a meeting."

The waitress arrives with our food and I simply nod.

"If it helps, he didn't sound pleased that I'm here with you."

I laugh and wave him off. "I'm sure he doesn't care."

"Oh, I'm sure he does. He's been glaring at me since you came to town. I'm just too easygoing to call him out on it."

"I don't want to cause any issues in your family, Dec."

"Now, that's funny." He laughs and covers my hand with his. "Trust me, you haven't caused any issues. You're helping us fix some issues, and well, Eli just has *issues*. Mostly asshole issues." He smiles fondly, then looks at me and sobers. "I mean that in the best brotherly way possible. He's not really an asshole."

"I know." I chuckle and decide that we've talked about this long enough. "So, tell me more about the lovely and flexible *Clarice*."

"Damn it. I liked her."

I AM sick of my own company. I check my phone for the hundredth time since I got home from work three hours ago and blow out a disgusted breath.

Nothing from Eli.

What in the world is wrong with me? I'm not this needy woman. So what if I haven't heard from him in three days? He gets home tomorrow.

It's not like we're sleeping together. We've only been out together a few times and shared some kisses.

Some amazing, mind-blowing, ruin me for all other kisses kisses, but just kisses all the same.

But I've missed seeing him on his balcony in the evenings.

Maybe he hasn't missed me.

I glare at my phone, then bring Eli's number up in my text box and send him a quick message: *How is your trip going?*

I bite my lip and hit send. It's a friendly message, but doesn't sound too needy.

Good Lord, I'm such a girl.

I flop onto the couch and turn the TV on, flipping through the channels and stopping on a show that I've heard good things about, but have never watched before, and try to get lost in the handsome actors and suspenseful story line.

Two hours later, after no response from Eli, and staring at the TV without following any of the shows that have played, I snap it off and scrub my hands over my face.

I want something sweet. That'll make me feel better. Now, ice cream or beignets? Café du Monde is open 24/7, thank goodness, because when I glance at the clock, I realize it's almost midnight.

Eli warned me not to wander around at night by myself, but the café is only a few blocks away. It'll take me less than five minutes each way to walk it. I can almost taste them now, and my mouth waters at the thought of the sugary goodness.

I'll stock my freezer with ice cream later for future emergencies such as this.

With a decisive nod, I slip my feet into my sneakers, grab my keys and some cash, and dash out the front door, walking briskly. There aren't many people out at this time of night. Some homeless people with their dogs curl up in doorways, sleeping. Someone is playing a saxophone on a balcony nearby, filling the night air with beautiful notes, making me think of Declan.

When I come upon Jackson Square, I decide to walk around the park rather than walk through it. That would just be asking for trouble.

Before long, I'm at the café and standing at the take out counter where I order a bag of the doughnuts and wait for just a few minutes while my order is filled. I glance around at the mostly empty café. There are a few people out, but it's mostly deserted, making me regret the walk out by myself.

I just have an uneasy feeling.

I check my phone, frowning when there still isn't a response from Eli. I understand that he's working, but he could have at least returned the message. Now, it's after one in the morning in New York, and he's most likely asleep.

Or with someone.

I shake my head in disgust, pay for my pastries, and set off back to my place. My stomach is in knots; this time, it's not because I miss Eli, but because it's actually kind of spooky in the Quarter at night.

"Really shouldn't have done this, Mary Katherine," I murmur to myself, as I clutch my warm bag of beignets to my chest and walk quickly, head up, constantly watching my surroundings. I pass Jackson Square and turn the corner near my loft when I see a taxi pass me and slow down, and then I'm suddenly jerked from behind.

"Scream and I'll kill you," a mean, hoarse voice snarls in my ear, as I feel something sharp pressed to my ribs. "Give me your money."

"I don't—" I begin, but lean forward, stomp on his foot, and smash the back of my head into the man's face, making him wail.

"Kate!"

I turn and jab my elbow into the man's stomach, but suddenly, I'm pulled away and Eli is there, landing a hard blow to the man's nose, knocking him cold.

"I almost had him," I say, panting and beginning to shiver as Eli dials 911 and reports the attempted mugging.

"What in the hell are you doing out here?" Eli spins, plants his hands on my shoulders and glares down at me.

# CHAPTER 9

## ĒLI~

"**W**hat were you doing?" I ask again when she only stares at me, her green eyes dilated in shock as she begins to shake. I pull her against me, wrap my arms around her shoulders and hold on tight, as sirens can be heard in the distance.

"Sir, the cab fare?" The cabbie approaches us, and I swear under my breath, wrap one arm around Kate and fish my wallet out of my pocket. I pay the cabbie and keep an eye on the man beginning to moan on the sidewalk.

"The luggage?"

"Leave it on the fucking sidewalk."

I want to fucking kill him.

"I'm sorry," Kate whispers in my arms. She's clinging to me now, her eyes pinned on the asshole waking up and dabbing at his nose.

"If you fucking move, I'll knock you back out."

"I just—"

"Shut the fuck up!" I reply, my voice hard and cold. Kate flinches, burying her face in my chest, then takes a deep breath and pulls away, meeting my eyes with hers.

"I'm okay."

"Kate—"

"I'm okay," she repeats stubbornly and glares at her mugger for roughly ten seconds until the police show up. For the next thirty minutes, Kate and I are questioned by the police, and the mugger is cuffed and taken away. We are finally given the okay to go home.

"I'm sorry about this," Kate says, as we reach my luggage on the sidewalk in front of my house. "Do you need help in with your bags?"

"No," I reply shortly. I'm so fucking pissed. Adrenaline is still coursing through me. I wanted to keep punching that fucker for just *thinking* of putting his hands on her.

"Well, I'll see you tomorrow."

"You're not going home," I reply, and take her hand in mine and lead her into my house.

"Eli, I'm fine."

"I'm not," I reply and unlock the front door, wait for her to walk in ahead of me, then leave my suitcase and briefcase just inside the door, lock it, and tug my tie off as I lead her up the stairs to the living area, shocked to discover that my own hands are shaking.

Kate stands in the middle of the room as I pour two glasses of brandy, pass her one, and take a long swallow, watching her as she also takes a drink and cringes as it burns on the way down.

"Why were you out there so late?"

"I wanted beignets," she whispers, her eyes trained on her drink.

"You wanted *beignets*?" I ask incredulously. "What the fuck, Kate?"

"Don't swear at me!" she shouts back, pointing her pink-tipped finger at me. "I was craving sugar, and it was either ice cream or beignets. The beignets were closer, darn it. I missed you, and you didn't answer my text, and I'm such a girl!"

She says this like I'm supposed to understand the logic, which I completely don't.

"What does your gender have to do with it?"

She glares at me like I'm being obstinate on purpose, then sets her glass on my desk and moves to walk out, but I catch her arm in my hand and pull her against me.

"You just scared ten years off my life, *cher*." I bury my face in her hair and take a deep breath. "I missed you too. I couldn't answer your text because I was on a flight home when it came in."

"Why are you home early?"

"Because I needed to see you." God, she smells amazing and feels incredible against me. "And then, when we drove past in the cab and I saw that fucker come up behind you, my heart stopped in my chest. God, Kate, he could have—"

"He didn't." I feel her smile against my chest. "I was kicking his ass."

"Yes, you were, tiger." I grin and plant my lips on her forehead. "You weren't lying when you said you took self defense classes."

"I'm no victim," she says fiercely, and another part of me softens.

"You're amazing," I reply and then sigh. "Scared me."

"Me too." She hugs me tightly before stepping away. "It's late, and I have to be at work in the morning."

"You're not going to work in the morning."

"Of course I am."

"No, you're not. I'm the boss, Kate. You were mugged tonight." Before she can shake her head and fight me further, I pick her up in my arms and carry her up another flight of stairs to my bedroom. "I want to spend tomorrow with you."

"Apparently, you're spending tonight with me too?" She pushes her fingers into my hair and smiles softly.

"I can't let you out of my sight tonight," I reply honestly, before sitting on the edge of the bed with her in my lap. "I need to keep you safe."

"Is that all?"

I bury my face in her neck, skim my nose up to her ear, and kiss her softly. She shivers, making me smile. "No, that's not all, *cher*."

"Have I mentioned that I'm glad you're home?" She cups my face in her hands and kisses my lips lightly.

"Are you?"

She nods, her fingers moving gently over my face. God, just having her against me has me hard, but her magical fingers, the way she's looking at me, has me tied in knots.

I need her.

And I don't need *anyone*.

"Kate, tell me now if you're not okay with me making love to you, because in about two point four seconds, I won't be able to control myself anymore."

Her lips curve in a purely feminine, seductive smile as she pulls herself out of my arms, stands, and in one fluid motion, whips her T-shirt over her head and tosses it on the floor by her feet. I'm struck dumb as she hooks her thumbs in the waist of her black leggings and works them down her legs, and suddenly she's standing before me in a matching lacy light pink bra and panty set.

Jesus Christ, she's breathtaking.

She moves to unhook her bra, but I shake my head and stand, just inches from her.

"You are stunning." My voice is nothing but a hoarse whisper as I take her in. She's slender, but has curves in all the right places. Her breasts...Fuck, I can't wait to get my hands on her breasts.

She lifts her hands and unbuttons my white shirt, then tosses it down with her things, and her intoxicating green eyes take a journey down my torso.

"Wow," she whispers, and traces the muscles of my chest and stomach with her fingertips, sending heat through me. "You're even better than I imagined."

Her hands land on the waist of my slacks and she pops the clasp open, and just as she slides her hands inside to nudge them down my hips, she leans in and plants her lips right over my heart.

*Fuck me.*

When my pants hit the floor, I lift Kate back into my arms and lay her in the center of the bed, then brace myself on my elbow next to her and run my fingers over the lace of her sexy as fuck underwear.

"I didn't hear from you this week," she murmurs, and watches my face as my hands roam over her body. "I thought maybe you'd changed your mind."

"Hell no," I reply and nudge her nose with mine. "I knew if I heard your voice I'd get on the next plane out and come straight here." My finger pushes under the cup of her bra and brushes over her nipple, making her gasp. "I've thought of nothing but you." I glide my finger to the other breast and repeat the movement, making her squirm next to me.

God, she's responsive.

Her hand cups my cock over my boxer-briefs, making my eyes cross. I take her hand, kiss her palm, then hold it over her head as I cover her body with mine and lay kisses on her lips, her neck, her collarbone, and begin working my way down her warm, writhing body.

"Oh, gosh," she breathes, shoving her hands in my hair.

"I want to learn every inch of you," I murmur, my lips against her belly. "I want to know what makes you gasp." I cup her sex in my hand and grin against her hip when she arches into my hand with a low groan. "God, you're soaked."

I glance up in time to see her bite her lip and her cheeks flush as I push one finger under the elastic of her panties and rub her wet pussy with just the fingertip, not sinking inside, just gliding over her lips and clit.

"Oh, that feels good," she whispers. I kiss my way across her lower belly to her other hip, then down to her thigh and hook my fingers into the material at her hips to pull them off, throw them over my shoulder, and spread her wide.

"Fucking hell, you're gorgeous, *cher*." And she is. God, her freckles are *everywhere,* sprinkled all over her body, even her pussy, which is waxed clean. I spread her wider and drag my fingertips up and down her thighs, making them quiver.

"Eli," she moans.

"Yes, babe, moan my name." And with that, I lean in and take one long swipe with my tongue from her wet opening, all the way up to her hard clit.

"Holy crap!" She jackknifes, but I press one splayed hand on her belly, holding her down, and nuzzle that hard nub with my nose as I pull her lips in my mouth and tug gently. "Eli, oh my."

I grin against her, still charmed that even in the throes of sex she refuses to swear.

I drag my fingertips down one thigh, around her ass to her crack and slide one finger over her anus and into her slick opening, making her moan all the more.

I love how fucking vocal she is.

I begin to slowly fuck her with my finger and kiss my way up her body. I tug on her nipples through the lace of her bra, kiss up her neck, and finally her lips. She wraps her arms tightly around my neck, holding me to her, still riding my hand and kissing me for all she's worth.

I'm going to fucking explode.

"Kate." Her feet are pushing my boxer briefs down my hips, just as anxious as I am for me to be inside her. "Kate."

"I'm sorry," she replies and arches against me. "Kate's not available right now."

I chuckle and bite her shoulder and her pussy clenches like a vise on my finger. "God, babe, you're so tight."

"Eli, I need you inside me."

Just the sound of her sweet voice against my neck while she's squeezing the fuck out of my finger makes me want to come. She's not going to get any more ready.

I reach into the bedside table and retrieve an unopened box of condoms to protect us both. I take myself in my hand and guide the tip through her slick folds, making us both moan.

"Are you trying to kill me?" she asks. Her eyes are bright green and wide as she pants and stares up at me in wonder and longing, matching every emotion running through me.

"No, *cher*, making sure you're ready."

"Never been more ready for anything in my life," she confirms and reaches between us, wraps her small hand around me and guides me to her opening. "Now."

I slide in, in one long, fluid motion and pause when I'm buried balls-deep. She's closed her eyes and is biting her lip, her fingernails digging into my shoulders.

"Open your eyes, dawlin'." She obliges and surprises me when she smiles up at me and circles her hips, inviting me to move. "You feel—" I shake my head, not having any words for the way it feels to be buried inside her.

And I know, in this moment, I'll never grow tired of her. I'll never want anyone else.

She rotates her hips again and I pull back, almost all the way, then push back and she closes her eyes.

"Keep them open," I instruct her. "I want you to see what you do to me."

Her eyes soften as she cups my face in her hands and kisses me deeply, and that's it. I can't stop my hips from setting a rhythm, moving in long strokes in and out of her, claiming her.

*She's mine.*

Her legs begin to shake and her whole body tenses. Her eyes widen in alarm.

"Oh, God."

"I'm right here," I whisper and nibble the corner of her lips. "It's okay."

I reach between us and press my thumb on her nub, and that's all it takes. She cries out, arching off the bed and coming spectacularly. I've never seen anything like it. Her pussy spasms around my cock, her arms tighten around my neck, and I have no choice but to follow her over into the most amazing orgasm of my life.

Our breathing is ragged and loud in the quiet room as I roll us and tuck her under my chin, cradling her on my chest. Her fingers are trailing up and down my ribs, in the same rhythm of my fingers on her back as we regain our senses.

"Eli?"

I plant my lips in her hair. "Yes."

"Kate's available now."

I chuckle and tilt her head back so I can look in her eyes, needing to see that she's okay. Her eyes are glassy with happiness, her cheeks flushed, and her hair a mess. She looks quite satisfied.

"She's about to be unavailable again."

"She might be tired."

I grin.

"I'll do all the work."

# CHAPTER 10

## ~KATE~

"*G*ood morning, beautiful."

I feel my lips lift in a soft smile. Most of my face is buried in a pillow that smells of Eli, clean with a touch of his body wash. I'm lying on my stomach. We aren't touching, but I can feel the warmth from his body next to me.

He suddenly brushes a fingertip down my temple and hooks my hair behind my ear. I pry one eye open and gaze over at a rumpled, sleepy, deliciously sexy Eli.

"'Morning," I whisper. My arms are folded under the pillow, bracing my head. He drags his fingertips down my arm to my ribs, and traces the words tattooed from just under my armpit to just above my hip.

"*I am enough the way I am,*" he recites softly and smiles at me, his eyes bright with curiosity, but he doesn't ask why these words. He simply waits, that happy expression on his handsome face, and continues to lightly drag his fingertips over my skin, which is on hyper-alert after the night we just spent together.

I lost count how many times we made love, how many times he woke me up with his lips, his hands, his cock. My body is deliciously exhausted.

"You're not terribly chatty in the morning," he finally says quietly, and leans over to kiss the ball of my shoulder. I chuckle and bury my face in the pillow, then gaze over at him again.

"Good morning."

"There she is," he says. The house is quiet around us. It must be very early morning because of the gray light coming in through the windows. "How do you feel?"

"Hmm…" I take stock of my body and my heart, and smile. "I feel surprisingly limber and sated. You?"

"I don't think I've been better," he replies, and traces my tattoo again. "I was also surprised to find this during the night."

"Surprised good or bad?"

"It's sexy as hell, *cher.*"

"Are you going to ask me about it?"

"No." He exhales deeply and finally pulls me into his arms, kisses my forehead, and tucks me against his chest. "You'll tell me about it when you're ready."

I grip onto his naked side and sigh in happiness. He's warm; his skin is smooth over toned muscles. He kisses my forehead, and his scruffy chin rasps against my skin.

It's sexy.

"We should be asleep," I murmur against his chest. "We couldn't have gotten more than a couple hours of rest."

"Go to sleep," he whispers against my hair. His hands are drawing patterns on my back, his lips are planted on my head, and with his heart beating in my ear, I could easily drift off and sleep happily for hours.

But it seems a shame to waste an opportunity to have Eli naked.

Again.

My hand drifts down beneath the sheet to cover his ass, which flexes under my touch. His body is just crazy. All of those hours I spent daydreaming about what he would look like beneath those suits of his were a waste of time, because the reality is just stellar.

"That's not going to sleep," he murmurs. I can feel him grin against my head as I turn my face and plant a kiss to his chest.

"Not particularly sleepy right now," I whisper, as I press my belly against his growing cock.

"No?"

"Nope."

He growls as I press him back onto the bed and pepper his torso with wet kisses, my hands roaming all over him in lazy caresses. His hands drift up my back to push my hair off of my face. When I glance up at him, he's grinning wickedly.

"You're so fucking beautiful, Kate."

I feel my face blush as I hide it against his hard abs. "Thank you."

Eli grips my shoulders and flips us, so I'm suddenly beneath him, his pelvis cradled between my legs, and his arms braced under my shoulders. He brushes my hair off my cheeks and stares down at me intently.

"You. Are. Beautiful," he repeats, kissing me deeply between each word, and my body flares to life beneath him, my nipples puckered against his chest and my hips circling against his hardness. "Jesus, just when I think I've had my fill, it's as though I've never touched you before."

"Love the way you touch me," I murmur against his lips. I freaking *love* the way he touches me.

"Do you like it when I do this?" He drags his nose down my jawline to my neck and lightly scrapes his teeth over my skin.

"Oh, gosh yes."

"Gosh yes," he repeats with a grin. "Oh, I think we can do better than that."

I whimper, knowing where this is going, but I have no energy to try to talk him out of it.

I'll say extra Hail Mary's the next time I go visit my parents.

"I want to hear that sweet mouth of yours get a little dirty, *cher.*"

I bite my lip as he kisses down to my breasts and circles my nipple with his nose before taking it in his mouth and sucking firmly.

"We'll start with something easy. What's this?"

"My breast."

He tweaks my nipple, sending a zing up my spine. "Ow!"

"Dirty."

"Um, tit?"

"Very good." He laves the abused nub with his tongue, and then kisses his way down my stomach, nuzzles my navel and the piercing there, then scoots down the bed further and spreads my legs wide. "Look how wet you are."

I bury my hands in his hair and try to guide his mouth down to me, but he pulls away and grins. "Use your words."

"Eli..."

"Yes, that's a start. Keep going."

"Please, kiss me."

He presses his lips to the inside of my thigh and then grins up at me.

"Please kiss my..."

"Your what, Kate?"

"My." I swallow hard and clench my eyes closed. "Pussy."

He growls and licks me from my opening up to my clit, and then proceeds to drive me out of my ever loving mind with his lips and tongue, making my head thrash back and forth on the pillow.

"Do you want my fingers inside you?"

"Yes!"

"Ask me."

"Please put your fingers inside me."

"Inside your what?"

I lift my head and stare down at him in confusion. "My pussy."

"Say cunt, Kate."

I blink. *You're nothing but a fucking cunt. I can't stand the sight of you.*

"Never." I try to close my legs and move away from him, but he immediately covers me again with his body and holds me tenderly. Tears have sprung in my eyes, pissing me off. "I won't ever say that."

"Okay. I'm sorry."

"That word isn't okay. Ever."

He holds me to him, braced over me, and combs his fingers through my hair. "I'm sorry, *cher*. I didn't know that was a trigger for you."

"It's just that one word. I can't deal with it."

"Understood." He kisses my cheek and the corner of my mouth before pulling back and gazing down at me. His eyes look a bit angry, and I'm sure he has a million questions, but he simply offers me a soft smile and palms my breast once more. "No more c word. Any other words we should avoid?"

"I'm not particularly fond of being called a bitch either."

All humor leaves his face as his hand stills on my breast. His eyes narrow.

"Let's get something straight right now, *cher*. I would never call you that, or cunt, or any other despicable word that could hurt you. You are beautiful and sweet, and there will never come a day, regardless of what happens with us after today, that you or anyone else will ever deserve that. Are we clear?"

"Yes." I hate the relief in my voice, but my whole body relaxes beneath Eli as he watches me for another long moment, and then lays his lips over mine and kisses me sweetly. His hand resumes with its ministrations on my breast, making me tingle.

"I love your skin," he whispers against my neck. "You're so soft. And your freckles make me crazy."

"My freckles!" I giggle and slap his arm playfully. "They're out of control."

"They're amazing." He grins down at me. "You even have freckles on your pussy."

"I know." I wrinkle my nose, making him chuckle.

"Sexy."

"Silly."

He slowly shakes his head no and reaches over for a condom, slips it on, and settles between my legs.

"Are you sore?"

"In a good way."

"I'll do my best to take it easy."

I drag my fingertips down his cheek as he positions himself against my lips.

"What do you want, Kate?"

"You," I reply with a confused frown.

"What part of me?"

*Ah, so we're back to the game.*

"That large, impressive part of you."

He laughs and kisses my forehead. "Words, Kate."

"Eli."

He raises a brow.

"I'd very much enjoy feeling your *cock* inside me now, please."

His eyes darken as he slowly pushes inside me, all the way, and holds himself still.

"Say it again."

"Please."

His lips tickle mine as he grins.

"Just a few more words."

I rotate my hips and clench around him, making his body tighten around me.

"Eli."

"Yes."

"Fuck me already."

"Damn." He begins to move, in long steady strokes, panting and groaning, but holding my gaze in his. "I fucking love it when you talk dirty."

"I kind of like it too," I admit, and moan when he slips his hand between us and presses on my already screaming clit. "God, Eli, I'm gonna come."

"That's right." He kisses my neck and hooks one of my legs over his shoulder, opening me wider, pushing deeper as he grabs my ass and pulls me harder onto him. "I'm right here with you."

His strength never ceases to amaze me, and the way his body is working me over is just too much. I can't help but cry out as I'm consumed by the orgasm, pulsing around him and rocking against him, as I continue to ride the aftershocks.

Eli rests his forehead on mine and swears under his breath, as every muscle in his body tightens and he follows me over into his own release.

We're both gasping for breath and sweaty when Eli slips out of me and collapses on the bed beside me, his arm draped over my stomach.

"Well, good morning."

He chuckles and kisses my shoulder. I gaze over at him, and can't resist pushing his hair back off of his forehead.

"You're so handsome."

"Thank you." He kisses me again, then rolls away. "We have to get up."

"Why? I thought we decided we aren't going in to work today."

"We're not." He shoots me a naughty grin. "I have a surprise for you."

"What kind of surprise?"

"A surprise surprise." He rolls his eyes as he saunters into the bathroom. "But you'll need to stop over at your place and pack a bag for the weekend!" He yells out at me.

"Okay, I'll just go over there now, take a shower, and get ready."

"No."

My head whips up at the tone of his voice as he comes back into the room.

"No?"

He shakes his head and takes my hand in his. "We'll be showering together."

"Eli, I'm as adventurous as the next girl, but I don't think I can go another round right now."

He chuckles as he kisses my knuckles. "I can't either, *cher*. But I'm not letting you out of my sight that long. Besides, it's my mess. I should clean it up."

"Well, when you put it like that…"

～

AN HOUR LATER, we're settled in Eli's car and headed out into the Bayou.

"It's amazing how, just a few minutes outside the city, we're in the middle of nowhere." I stare at the forests, the swamps, and wonder if there are alligators in the water.

"Not so different from most cities," he reminds me. He links his fingers with mine and kisses my hand before resting them on his thigh.

"Where are we going?"

"I thought we'd spend the weekend at the Inn."

"Oh, fun!" I grin and shimmy in my seat. "I've been dying to see it."

"We'll have my nosy sister and brother hanging around, but I think you'll enjoy it."

"You have such a great family." I gaze over at him as he drives effortlessly down the interstate. "They may be nosy, but they love you."

"Nosy," he insists with a grin.

"If you hated it, you would have left long ago."

His jaw clenches and his hand tightens on the wheel, but he takes a deep breath and finally nods. "True."

I tilt my head and watch him closely. There's something here he's not telling me, but rather than pry, I leave it be for now and decide instead to start telling him a bit about my past.

"I got it after I left my ex-husband," I say, and turn to look out the passenger window. "Because after being told every day that you're not good enough, it's easy to buy into it. But I'm not that person. I am enough."

"You're more than enough, *cher*." He kisses my hand again. "Look at me."

I turn to face him and am surprised to see him smiling.

"You're a strong woman, Kate. Which is a good thing, because it takes a strong woman to put up with my family."

He didn't make it awkward. Or turn it into a long soul-searching conversation.

He simply accepts me.

"I love your family."

He nods and changes lanes. "Tell me about your family."

"I love them too." I grin as I think of my ma and da. "My parents live in County Claire, Ireland."

"Did you grow up in Ireland?"

"No. I grew up outside of Denver. My da got a job there before I was born, so he and Ma moved there. Had me. Then about three years later, my da's brother and sister-in-law were killed in a car accident, leaving their son, Rhys, behind. So he came to live with us. He's really more like my big brother than a cousin."

"Rhys O'Shaughnessy? The baseball player?"

"Yes, that's him. You watch baseball?"

"When I can. Sam loves baseball, thanks to Beau."

"Where is Sam's dad?" I ask, as Eli takes an exit off the freeway and we merge onto a two-lane highway, headed deeper into the bayou.

"He's never met Sam." Eli shrugs, then shakes his head. "Gabby got pregnant right out of high school. When the boyfriend found out, he cut out right quick."

"That's horrible."

"It's probably for the best. Sam is loved by a great family."

"I agree with that, but it has to be hard for Gabby."

"We help her," he insists.

"Of course you do, but Eli, it's not just about being a single mom. She's *single*. I'm not saying that men make everything better, but I imagine she gets lonely. She has a young boy to care for, a business, and a large, successful family. She has a lot of responsibility."

He rubs his hand over his lips, thinking. "True. I don't think she's dated since Sam was born."

"Maybe she's not interested, and it's certainly none of my business, but I doubt it's as easy as she wants all of you to believe it is."

His eyes slide to mine. "You're an intelligent woman, Kate."

"Well, that we knew." I laugh and lean over to press my lips to his shoulder. "I'm excited to see her inn."

# CHAPTER 11

## ẼLI~

"Oh, my God, Eli," Kate gasps and grips my thigh with her strong hand. It's the same tone she uses when she's about to come, and it makes my cock twitch reflexively, but I just grin over at her in the passenger seat.

"Pretty, isn't it?"

She turns her wide green eyes to me, her mouth dropped open, and then back to the plantation as we drive up to it. "Those oak trees are incredible! And the house! No wonder Gabby loves running this place. I'd never leave."

I smirk and look at the green, lush land, trying to see it for the first time. The white, three story home with it's pillars, black shutters and wrap around porch, and second floor balcony sits back from the road about one hundred yards. Leading to it is a row of oak trees, creating a tunnel to the majestic home and the land it sits on. Sunlight filters through the leaves and limbs, sprinkling the green grass in light.

"How old are those trees?" Kate asks.

"About six hundred years," I reply, and pull around the side of the house. "They've been here far longer than the house."

"They're amazing." She bites her lip and continues to stare at the trees, and I can't resist reaching over and tugging the delicate skin from her teeth, then smoothing the pad of my thumb over it. "I want to see everything," she says, as she nuzzles my palm with her cheek.

"And I'll show you." I kiss her lips quickly before we climb out of the car and walk around to the front of the house.

"Uncle Eli!" Sam exclaims and tosses his ball in the air, catches it, and runs over to hug me. "Are you really stayin' here tonight?"

"We are," I confirm. "You remember Miss Kate?"

"Hello, ma'am," Sam says, and holds his hand out for Kate's, making my lips twitch.

"You can call me Kate," she offers with a smile, but Sam shakes his head no.

"I'm not supposed to call adults their real names," he says seriously.

"Can you call me Miss Kate?" she asks, and squats down so she can look him in the eye. Sam looks up to me for confirmation.

"You may."

"Okay, Miss Kate." He offers her his toothless grin just as her phone rings.

"Oh, this is Rhys FaceTiming me. Sam, do you know who Rhys O'Shaughnessy is?"

"Only the best baseball player on the whole Chicago Cubs team," he replies in awe. I step back, shove my hands in my pockets, and watch Kate with my young nephew. She grins and accepts the call.

"Hey, handsome."

"Hey. Whatcha doin'?"

"Actually, I have a young man here who is your biggest fan. Would you mind saying hi?"

"I get to say hi?" Sam asks with a big smile.

"Sure, here." Kate turns the phone for Sam, and instead of getting embarrassed or shy, he launches into a million questions.

"Oh, my gosh! You're the best batter in the league! What kind of bat do you have? How do you hit the ball so hard? Do you have to practice every day?" He takes the phone and sits on the porch, chattering at Rhys, who is chuckling and trying to get a word in edgewise.

"That'll keep them both busy for a few minutes," Kate says, and loops her arms around my waist, her face tilted up to mine. "Rhys loves kids."

"You might have just made my nephew's year."

"Well, I have ulterior motives." She grins as her hands travel up my back and down again, over my ass.

"Do tell," I reply and kiss her forehead.

"I was thinking about doing this." She stands on her tip-toes, but she's still too short to kiss me, so I happily oblige her, leaning down to take her lips with mine. It starts as a soft, simple nibble, and quickly escalates to tongues and panting and me gripping onto her lower lip with my teeth.

"There's a child ten yards away," she whispers against my mouth.

"I know." I cup her face in my hands, kiss her forehead one more time, and breathe in her fresh, Kate scent, then lead her down the brick walkway between the enormous, ancient oak trees. "They were planted hundreds of years before the house," I begin.

"It's so cool out here," she says.

"Yes, thanks to the river just on the other side of that levy, and with the way the trees were planted, it creates a wind tunnel effect. No one ever imagined that air conditioning would be a thing. This was the first form of AC."

"Amazing. Look at how some of the branches rest on the ground!"

Jesus, I can't take my eyes off of her. She's pulled her thick, auburn hair into a knot at the back of her head. She's wearing a strapless sundress and flip flops.

I wonder if she's wearing panties under there.

I intend to find out very soon.

"This is seriously the most beautiful thing I've ever seen."

"You'll get no argument from me," I reply, my eyes trained on her gorgeous face, just as she turns to me and smiles shyly.

"Way to lay on the Southern charm," she says.

"I am Southern, and it may have sounded charming, but it doesn't make it less true."

"Miss Kate! Miss Kate!" Sam comes running down the walk at full speed, the way only a young boy can, with Kate's phone waving in the air. "He wants to talk to you!"

"I'm dizzy," Rhys says dryly, as Kate takes her phone and smiles at her cousin.

"He looks happy," she says.

"He talks more than anyone I've ever met in my life, and that includes you. Cute kid."

"I have to go tell Mom!" Sam takes off back to the house, and I begin to follow him.

"I'll be up at the house, *cher*. Take your time." She shakes her head, as if to keep me here, but I simply kiss her hand and smile. "I have to say hi to Gabby."

Her soft laugh follows me as I saunter behind the excited boy to the house. I glance around at the freshly mowed grounds of the plantation and the flowers around the house. Birds are singing in the trees, and the breeze Kate mentioned brushes through my hair.

Why haven't I ever noticed before how lovely it is out here?

Because I haven't noticed much for years. I haven't given two fucks about anything for years.

Except for my family and the business, and not necessarily in that order.

I climb the steps of the porch, then turn and look out at the trees and the amazing woman chattering away at her phone, smiling and laughing.

She's the reason I've come alive.

~

"GABBY MAKES INCREDIBLE COOKIES," Kate says, as she pops the last bite of an oatmeal raisin in her mouth and tilts her head back to the let the sun warm her cheeks. "I could get used to this."

"What, cookies?"

"Cookies and sunshine and just…" she shrugs.

"Just what?"

We're wandering through the gardens behind the house, toward the slave quarters and caretaker's home, which is where Beau currently lives. I take her hand in mine and bring us to a stop, turn her to me, and cup her neck in my hand. "Just what?"

"Just being happy." The last word is said in a whisper, tugging at something unfamiliar in my gut. Before I can pull her into my arms, she smiles and continues walking. "What's over there?"

"Slave quarters," I reply. "Gabby had them refurbished, just enough to make them safe, so guests can learn and check them out."

"You owned slaves?" she asks with a gasp.

"Not me personally, no." I chuckle and tuck her hair behind her ear. I can't fucking stop touching her. "Many generations ago, slaves lived here, yes."

She frowns and bites her lip.

"It was two hundred years ago, Kate. That wasn't uncommon in the South."

"I know."

"This way." I lead her away from the slave quarters, through a rose garden in a riot of color.

"I want to check them out," she says, pointing to the small slave buildings.

"Later. Let's walk through the gardens."

"What's over there?" She squints her eyes, looking in the nearby field. "With the fence?"

"That's the cemetery."

"Is it old?" she asks with glee.

"Yes." I raise a brow. "Do you have a thing for cemeteries?"

"I know it sounds weird, but yes. Especially old ones. They're so interesting. Can we go look?"

"Let's go."

She walks quickly through the gardens, barely paying attention to the flowers. The gate to the graveyard is rusty, and a bit stuck, and I make a note to have it repaired, as I wrench it open and Kate hurries inside.

"I bet this is creepy at night," she says reverently, looking about like she doesn't know where to start, then makes a beeline for the very back and studies each headstone as she walks by. "There are dates here that go back to the 1700's."

"And there are graves on the property older than that, but the Boudreaux family started this graveyard around that time."

"Why aren't these graves above ground like the ones in the city?"

"Because the water table is different here. We're close to the river, but we sit higher. Even during Katrina, we didn't flood. We simply had wind damage."

"Amazing." She folds her arms and continues to walk through. The headstones have moss grown over them. Some are so faded that you have to really get close to read them. Several oak trees are planted throughout the space, giving shade and shelter from the elements, but their roots have made some of the stones go a bit cockeyed.

It is exactly what it looks like: an old cemetery.

"Oh, there are babies," she murmurs sadly, trailing her fingertips over a lamb carved in the stone.

I simply nod, my hands shoved in my pockets, my fingers rubbing the half dollar I keep there. The closer we get to a certain grave, the more nervous I become.

And that's ridiculous. He's been dead for two fucking years.

"The dates are getting more recent. Here's 1977." She sighs. "And these are sisters. Look," she points at the dates on the stone. "They were only two years apart. Died in the same week."

"They were spinster aunts," I inform her, remembering the stories I'd been told of the old maids. "They lived together, here, their whole lives. They were odd."

"Odd?"

I grin. "This is the Bayou, dawlin'. Let's just say they enjoyed the eccentricities that living here brought them. And if you ever made one of them mad, well...Bad things usually happened."

"They were witches?"

"Of course not." I chuckle and kiss her cheek. "They were simply Bayou women."

"Oh, this one looks new."

*It is new.*

She reads the stone and her eyes grow wide. "Your daddy."

I nod and read the stone for myself.

*Beauregard Francois Boudreaux*

*1947 ~ 2012*

*Beloved Husband & Father*

*I've adjusted my sails.*

"I've adjusted my sails," Kate reads aloud, and looks at me with a raised brow.

"Daddy always said, you can't control the wind, but you can adjust your sails. It was his way of reminding us that you can't control most of what happens in life. You can only control your reaction to it. I imagine he did the same in death." I smirk. "I'm quite sure he's running Heaven by now."

"I met him once," she says. "You get your height from him."

"Yes, and if you ask Maman, I got my stubbornness from him too."

"Naturally." She tilts her head as she watches me. The coin in my pocket is hot in my fingers, from me rubbing it hard, but I can't stop. "You're tense."

"As I always am when I'm around my father."

"You didn't get along?"

I shrug a shoulder, every instinct in me screaming at me to shut it down, walk away from the conversation and take Kate back to our room where I can sink inside her for about two days.

"I loved him fiercely," I say instead, surprising me. "And there were days that I hated him just as much."

"Those are extreme emotions."

"I spent my entire life trying to live up to what he wanted me to be," I say quietly, and remember the man now six feet under the ground. His loud laugh. His cold hazel eyes. His disapproving shake of the head.

"I'm sure he was very proud of you."

"No," I reply, and let Kate fold herself into my arms for a long hug. "He wasn't."

"How do you know?"

"He told me."

"What?" She pulls back with a frown. "He *told* you that he wasn't proud of you?"

"Let's sit." I guide her to the bench beneath a nearby magnolia tree. She sits facing me, waiting to hear more.

*Am I seriously going to tell her something that I've never spoken aloud before?*

"He told me to pull my head out of my ass and do what I was born to do, which was take care of my family's business."

She blinks for several seconds. "That seems harsh."

"He was right." I sigh and rub my hand down my face. "He'd already groomed Beau to take over as CEO of Bayou Enterprises, which makes sense because he's the oldest. I have a master's degree in business, but I spent ten years partying, taking advantage of the perks that money brings. Fucking random women."

I sigh and shake my head. "I was irresponsible and old enough to know better. I would have been disappointed in me too."

"You're not those things now," she says.

"No," I agree. "Sitting beside my father as he took his last breath, his last words being, 'You can be so much better than this,' will turn a man around." She takes my hand in hers and places a sweet kiss to my knuckles. "So, I focused all of my energy on the business, on the family. I work stupid hours."

"That's a good description."

"It's accurate. Working twenty-hour days is stupid, but I can't stop. I work, I look in on my family, and I go back to work. Occasionally, I call up one of the several women I know to hook up with and scratch that particular itch, and then I go back to work."

Kate flinches. "You seem to respect women more than that."

"Of course I respect women," I reply. "My mother would kill me herself if I treated any woman with anything other than respect. But sex is sex, Kate."

She nods. "I'm following."

"Women don't usually understand that."

"I do." She shrugs. "I haven't been divorced long, and the relationship I just came out of was…*combative.* I'm not looking to replace it."

"Combative," I repeat, and just like every time she begins to talk about the hell—a hell I don't even fully understand yet—that her ex-husband put her though, my hands want to clench and I want to simply kill him.

With my own bare hands.

"Mmm," she confirms with a nod.

"He hit you."

"I told you he did."

I nod. "What else?"

"What do you mean?"

"Don't play stupid, Kate. You're a smart woman. Did he ever put you in the hospital?"

"Pshaw," she tips her head back, staring up into the branches above, but doesn't directly answer. I grip her chin in my fingers and thumb and pull her gaze back to mine.

"You don't have to tell me everything, just don't ever lie to me, Kate. Did he put you in the hospital?"

"Once," she whispers. I close my eyes and take a deep breath. "So, you see," she clears her throat, "I'm in no hurry to jump into anything serious."

"I wasn't trying to warn you off, *cher.*"

"I know. But even if I did want something serious, this," she points back and forth between us, "has an expiration date."

"Really."

"I'll be gone in a few weeks. But I need to make something very clear, Eli."

"Keep going."

"While you're doing…*stuff* with me, you're not doing that same stuff with anyone else."

Is it any wonder that I can't get enough of her? She's fucking adorable.

"What kind of stuff?" I grin as she blushes.

"You know perfectly well what kind."

I lean in and tuck her hair behind her ear, then drag my nose over the apple of her cheek to her ear and plant a kiss there, making her shiver.

"Walks around the Quarter?"

"No." She sighs as I nibble down her neck, then back up again and kiss the tip of her nose.

"Pizza on the balcony?"

"Now who's playing dumb?"

"I want to hear the words."

"You always want to hear the words." Her hands grip onto my T-shirt. I love that I can turn her on so easily. She's so fucking responsive.

I grin wickedly and kiss her forehead, and then it occurs to me: My life has been in black and white for the past two years, and the minute she walked through my office door, everything was in blazing color.

I don't know what the fuck to do with that.

Except enjoy her, for every moment she's here.

"What is the stuff that we do?" I ask again.

"The sex stuff."

"You can do better than that."

"Do you have any idea how many Hail Marys I'm going to have to say because of you?" she demands.

"A lot," I reply with a laugh. "I haven't seen you go to church while you've been here."

"I only go when I'm visiting my parents." She shrugs one slender shoulder. "Okay, I'll make it clear. While you're fucking me, you don't fuck anyone else."

*Fuck.*

I have to swallow hard as I stare down at her determined green eyes. Fuck someone else? I can't think of anyone else.

"And you can't fall in love with me," she adds primly.

"I can't?"

"No. No love. Just friends, and laughs, and…stuff."

I narrow my eyes.

"And sex. I'm not saying the other word again today."

I watch her for a long moment, then tug her into my lap, cup her face in my hands, and kiss the fuck out of her. "You're all I see, Kate. I don't give a shit about other women. So you don't have to worry about me fucking anyone but you for as long as you're here."

"And no love."

*Why does that statement make my heart hurt?*

"I don't do love, *cher.*"

"Me neither."

*Liar.*

"But one other thing," I say, my lips against hers.

"What?"

"You're going to say fuck again today. You're going to say it a lot."

"Why does that turn you on?" She giggles and sinks her fingers into the hair on the back of my head.

"Because hearing those dirty words come out of your pretty mouth makes me hard." I kiss her, long and deep, then pull away when we're both gasping for breath. "Jesus, everything you do makes me hard."

"Maybe it's just been a while since you got laid."

*That's what I thought too.*

"No, it's you. It's just you."

# CHAPTER 12

## ~KATE~

"*A*re you sure you don't want to go to Mama's for dinner?" Gabby asks us as she gathers her handbag and car keys and settles Sam's baseball cap on his head.

"We'll be fine here," Eli replies with a grin, sips his sweet tea, and keeps his sexy, naughty eyes on me. "I'll show Kate around."

"I thought you showed her around yesterday," Gabby replies dryly. Eli simply shrugs one shoulder and takes another sip of his tea, watching me. God, he's potent. He showed me around yesterday, all right. Around his body, and mine, and I'm pretty sure he discovered erogenous zones that I didn't even know I had.

And muscles. I'm sore today. *Sore.* My inner thigh muscles are singing. How does that happen?

"How is it that you don't have any guests tonight?" I ask.

"I always have an empty inn on Sunday nights. That gives me time to catch up on laundry and cooking for the upcoming week, and I can get away to Mama's for dinner."

"Convenient for me," Eli says, and laughs when Gabby glares at him.

"You're my brother."

"That's the rumor," he says with a smile.

"No, you are," Sam adds solemnly. "Nannan says so. Plus, you look alike. I don't have any brothers."

"No, you don't," Gabby says with a laugh.

"I want some, though," Sam adds.

"Let's go." Gabby sighs and shakes her head. "Clean up your own messes, big brother."

"Yes, ma'am," he replies in that slow, sexy accent that never fails to make me weak in the knees, and the grin spreads over his face when Gabby's engine starts and drives down the driveway. "Alone at last."

"We're alone quite often," I remind him.

"Mm," he replies, leaning his hands on the kitchen island, just staring at me with that smirk on his face as I lean on the breakfast bar opposite him.

"Are you going to just…do me here on the counter?"

"*Do* you?" He tilts his head back and forth, as if he's considering it. "Probably. But first, I'm going to cook for you."

"Cook for me." It isn't a question. "You cook."

"I cook just fine, thank you very much." He cocks a brow.

*I bet he does. He does everything very well.*

"And what are you going to cook?"

"You'll see." He turns to the fridge and begins gathering supplies, moving about the kitchen as if he's perfectly comfortable here. Which kind of throws me, because let's face it, watching the uber successful billionaire businessman, who admits to being a workaholic, work in the kitchen like it's second nature is...*hot.*

"Where did you learn to cook?"

He chooses a knife from the butcher block and begins chopping up an onion.

"Mama taught us all to cook."

"What do you want me to do?"

"Just look gorgeous and keep me company."

"Charming," I reply with a sigh. He's in another black T-shirt and blue jeans, which I think is unusual for him, but look amazing on him. His forearms flex and bunch as he chops. Just like they bunch when he's over me, gripping onto the mattress as he thrusts in and out of me. His whole body gets tight. And this man isn't short on muscles.

I want to lick him.

"Kate?"

"Huh?" I blink rapidly and try to focus. "What did you say?"

He sets the knife on the cutting board and smiles. "What were you just thinking about?"

My first reaction is to say *nothing*, but instead I walk very slowly around the island toward him. "I was thinking about licking you."

He leans his hips against the island and crosses his arms, making his biceps flex, and just like that, I want to tear his clothes off.

"Is that right?"

I nod.

"Where would you like to lick me?"

I grin and drag a fingertip down his neck. "Right here."

He swallows hard, making me even wetter. I love turning him on.

"You're distracting me," he says evenly, and it would bruise my ego if his eyes hadn't just dilated and the pulse in his neck sped up.

"I think that's the point."

He shakes his head and returns to chopping. "I'm cooking dinner."

"I don't particularly give a crap about dinner."

He smiles, like he always does when I don't use the usual curse words, but doesn't look me in the eye.

"You'll give a shit later, *cher.* You'll need the energy for what I have planned."

"That sounds fun." I cup his very firm, stellar ass in my hand and kiss his bicep. "Let's skip to that part."

He laughs, turns and lifts me into his arms, my legs wrapped around his waist, and kisses me mindless, until I can't think; I can't even feel my fingertips.

But I can sure as heck feel the pulsing between my legs.

The next thing I know, he sets me on the counter top, plants a smacking kiss on my lips and backs away, returning to the cutting board just a few feet away.

"Stay."

I stick my lower lip out in a pout and bat my eyes at him, but he just reaches over and smooths the pad of his thumb over my lip, drags his knuckles down my cheek, and whispers, "Trust me. Let me feed you. Let me pamper you a bit. I like it."

*Well, how in the heck am I supposed to say no to that?*

"Can I snack while you cook?" I ask, as he chops through celery surprisingly quickly.

"Sure." He passes me a celery stalk. "Wine?"

"Always."

He pours us each a glass of white, we clink our glasses together, and take a sip before he resumes chopping and I munch my celery.

"You feed me a lot."

"You're a good eater."

I pause with the celery halfway to my mouth and frown at him.

"What are you implying?"

"That you eat well?" He asks with a shrug.

I glance down at my small-ish chest and flat-ish stomach and then back at him. "Am I fat?"

He busts out laughing, not breaking his stride in his chopping.

"No, Kate. You're not fat. You enjoy food. And in doing so, I enjoy watching you eat. I'd feed you every meal every day if I could."

*Oh.*

"Can I have more celery?"

He grins, passes me the celery, and kisses me soundly before pulling away to get back to work.

Sitting here, watching him cook, is not a hardship in the least.

DINNER WAS DELICIOUS. Eli is just one big surprise after another. It's amazing to me how *normal* he is. The whole family, really, and it shouldn't, because I've been so close to Van and Dec for so many years, but this family is rich beyond my wildest dreams, yet they're as grounded and down to earth as anyone else. There aren't servants bustling about. Their cars are new and expensive, but no Aston Martin.

And on a Sunday afternoon, I'm lying on the couch with this powerful man, who has the ear of governors and high-powered people, who runs a multi-billion dollar enterprise with ease and efficiency.

He's snuggling me, on his back, with me lying on his chest, watching some stupid movie on cable, while his fingertips glide up and down my bare arm, my shoulder, my neck and into my hair and back down again.

If I could purr, I so would right now.

"We have the whole house to ourselves, and you want to watch a movie?" I ask lazily. He plants his lips on my head, takes a deep breath, and hugs me tight before his fingers resume their trek over my skin.

"Is there something else you'd rather do?"

"Well…" I grin and kiss his heart, over his T-shirt, breathing him in. He smells good. Clean. A little citrusy. I shift my pelvis over his and feel him start to harden, and his fingers still on my shoulder. "Yes."

His fingers sink into my hair as I kiss down his torso, lifting his shirt as I go, and plant wet kisses over his flat, chiseled abdomen. His breathing speeds up, but he's quiet; the only sounds are the TV and my lips smacking on his smooth, warm skin.

I could kiss his stomach all day long.

His T-shirt slips back down, and I frown up at him. "Can we dispose of this, please?"

He sits up and pulls his shirt over his head, tosses it on the floor, and shuts the TV off before lying back down. "Better?"

"Hmm." I push up to kiss his lips, tug on the lower lip with my teeth, then work my way down his throat, chest, and back to his stomach, enjoying the ridges of the muscles there. "I thought the six-pack was a myth. Or the work of Photoshop."

"Not if you work your ass off for it," he replies. His breath hitches when my tongue finds the groove of that V in his hips and trace it down to where it disappears into his jeans. I make quick work of the button and zipper, and smile when I see he's not wearing underwear.

Convenient.

His erection springs free into my hand, and I immediately grip it and pump it twice. Eli tosses his head back and groans, then turns his hot eyes back on me as I slowly lick from his scrotum to the tip in one long, fluid motion and rub the underside of the head on the flat of my tongue before taking him in my mouth and sucking, not too hard, but enough to get his attention.

And by the way his hand tightens in my hair, right at the scalp, where it feels so darn good when he pulls, I've got his attention.

"Fuck, that feels good."

I take him deeper, until the head is at the back of my throat, and I swallow, massaging him, loving the way it seems to grow even bigger in my mouth, firm my lips and pull up, lick the head, and repeat the motion.

"Look at me."

My eyes find his. They're hot, narrowed just a bit. His mouth is open as he pants. The hand not gripping my hair is behind his head, and his whole body is heaving.

It's sexy as hell that I can turn him on like this after just a few moments.

I lick down his shaft and over his tight balls, lightly suck them, then work my way back up to take him into my mouth once again. He begins to gently guide me into a pace that he likes, barely thrusting up to meet me. Not forcing me, but rather guiding me, and I love it.

"Grip your lips just a little tighter."

I comply and he hisses out a breath.

"Fuck, baby." His hips are moving faster, and suddenly, he's pulling my hair, but I stay where I am. "Kate, I don't want to come in your mouth."

I hum and stubbornly stay put, but after only two more pushes and pulls with my mouth, he grips onto my shoulders and pulls me up his body, claims my mouth with his, and effortlessly reverses our position, pinning me beneath him on the cushions of the couch.

"I was having fun," I pout.

"That's not how this works, *cher*." He nibbles my lips, brushes his nose over mine, and then plants soft kisses on my cheek.

"How what works?" I ask breathlessly. Good God, this man can kiss. Is this legal in the state of Louisiana?

Probably not.

"This." He repeats softly as he continues to pepper my skin with kisses. "You're not going to just suck me off and make me come and call it a day."

"Well, that wasn't really my plan. I was just having fun."

"Hmm." He kisses my collarbone. "I'll be back. I don't have a condom on me."

"Wait." I grip his arms, keeping him still. "I have the birth control covered."

He raises a brow. "Are you sure? I don't mind using them." He kisses my collarbone again. "I've never *not* used them."

"I don't mind," I whisper. "Unless there's something you need to tell me."

He offers me a wicked smile and kisses me deeply.

I glide my hands down his naked back to his ass, under his loose jeans, and hold on tight as he presses his pelvis to mine, grinding against me and making me even wetter, if that's even possible. Is there anything sexier than a man's ass when it's barely covered by undone jeans?

No. No, there's not.

"Eli," I whisper.

"Yes, baby."

"My clothes are still on."

He grins against my lips and settles over me, his elbows planted on either side of my head. "Yes, they are."

"Take them off," I demand softly and wiggle beneath him, still gripping his ass, and the arch of my foot rubbing over his denim-covered calf.

"No."

He grips onto my hair and tilts my head to the side as he drags his lips down my jawline to my neck and proceeds to drive me out of my ever-loving mind with his talented mouth and tongue. My nipples have puckered, my hands grip him tighter, one still on his ass, the other now buried in his soft hair.

My hips tilt up, pressing against his hard on, and I want him inside me.

*Now.*

"Eli, please. Need you inside me."

"I'll get there," he replies lazily, and works his way around to the other side of my neck.

"Can we go a bit faster here?" I ask breathlessly, and then groan when his tongue skims over my sweet spot. "God, I love it when you hit that spot."

"I know," he whispers and does it again, making my toes curl.

"Eli." I'm whining, and I hate myself for it, but for the love of all that's holy, why isn't he naked and inside me?

"Kate," he says and bites the tender skin at the top of my shoulder. "It's Sunday."

I frown, but then sigh when he finally pulls my shirt up my body and guides it over my head. "What does the day of the week have to do with anything?"

He pulls the cups of my bra down and slowly circles one puckered nipple with his tongue, then blows on it and repeats the motion on the other side.

Moving as slowly as humanly possible.

He's trying to kill me.

"You're in the South. Don't you know that we don't do *anything* quickly on Sunday?" He's kissing down my stomach now, and I'm a bit self-conscious because hello, I don't have a six pack. Or any kind of pack.

But he doesn't seem to mind as he moves down my body, and I'm expecting him to pull my denim shorts off, but instead, he bypasses the center of my universe and begins kissing my legs.

*My legs.*

"Really?" I demand with a laugh, earning a sharp bite on the inside of my right thigh.

"Patience, Kate."

"Not patient."

He chuckles and drags his fingernails down my outer thighs, calves, to my bare feet and back up again while his mouth does something completely crazy to the back of my knee.

Apparently, he didn't find all of my erogenous zones yesterday.

"Oh, my God," I murmur, and can't keep my hips from shifting and moving. He's going to make me come without even *touching* me.

How is that possible?

"Open your eyes, sugar." My gaze meets his, and I'm surprised to find his eyes on fire, watching me as he unzips my shorts, guides them down my legs, and tosses them over his shoulder. "No underwear for you either?"

I shrug and smile at him, but he doesn't return it. He's still watching me intently, braced on the back of the couch, as his fingers glide up my inner thigh and brush, ever so gently, over my lips, my clit, and then…my stomach.

Really? He's not going to hang out in the one place that's screaming for him?

I must frown because a wicked smile breaks out over that impossibly handsome face of his and he cocks a brow. "You don't like that?"

"You're teasing me."

"Yes." He watches my face as his fingers find my core again, but it's just his fingertips tickling over my lips, the crease where my leg meets my center. I reach for his wrist to guide him inside, but he quickly grips my hand in his, kisses it, and places it above my head. "You're not controlling this." His lips are barely touching my own. "You're going to be patient, and enjoy. It's Sunday."

"You've never been lazy on a Sunday in your life," I whisper against his lips. Jesus, I can't catch my breath.

I'm going to die of asphyxiation before I get to come. That's not fair.

"There's a first for everything," he replies softly, bites my lower lip, then resumes the torture happening between my legs. He glances down. "Fuck me, you're wet."

"That happens when you do stuff to me," I reply and circle my hips.

"*Stuff*?" he repeats. "What kind of stuff?"

I'm not strong enough to fight him on my language. I don't care if I swear. All I can focus on is having him over me, in me. Now.

"When you kiss me and touch me and tease me with fucking me," I reply, and feel very satisfied when his eyes widen.

"I do love hearing those filthy words come out of your pretty mouth," he murmurs in that slow Cajun accent that makes me crazy. His fingers are rubbing my lips harder now, gliding effortlessly through my wet folds. Finally, he scoots down, kisses my navel piercing, slides one finger inside me, and plants his mouth on my clit, not sucking, just *being* and I cry out, gripping the cushions at my hips, pushing my hips up to grind on his lips.

He pulls the finger back out, and gently licks over my lips, clit and folds, plants the flat of his tongue over my clit, and pushes two fingers inside me; I push up onto my elbows, watching as he turns me inside out.

"Oh, my God, Eli, you're gonna make me…"

He pulls away, kisses me between my navel and pubis, and grins when I growl at him.

"Your pussy is so soft," he says, as though he's just making casual conversation. His fingers are moving in and out, slowly, methodically. If he'd just press his thumb on my sweet spot, I'd come spectacularly.

But I have a feeling that's not going to happen yet.

"You have this spot…" he shoves his fingers all the way in, and makes a *come here* motion that makes me see stars. "Right behind your pubic bone. Don't close your eyes," he orders. I look up at him as his fingers pick up speed. He's watching me as he pushes on that spot again.

"How didn't I know about this spot before?" I ask breathlessly, and then cry out when he settles the tips of his fingers there and rubs gently.

His eyes flare in male satisfaction. "You're good for my ego, *cher*."

"You're good for my," I swallow, "pussy."

"Fuck yes, I am." He rubs a little harder and I arch up off the couch. "Come, baby."

And that's all it takes, his voice, his breath on my skin, his fingers doing crazy amazing things inside me, and I come apart. I go blind, my core tightens, and I ride the wave of the orgasm as it shoots through me.

When I open my eyes, Eli is smiling down at me. He pulls his fingers out and covers me, guides himself inside me until he's balls-deep, and stays there, not moving.

I grip onto his cock with my muscles and grin when he swears under his breath. His jeans are still on, which for some reason, I find very sexy.

Everything about him is fucking sexy.

I grip his ass and pulse against him. "Move, Eli."

He shakes his head and tips his forehead against mine. "Not yet."

His whiskey eyes are trained on mine. He watches me as he pulls his hips back, then pushes back in slowly. "Your face is so expressive," he whispers. "And this feels so fucking amazing."

"The ridge of your cock rubs against that spot you've discovered," I whisper.

"Like that?" His smile is more than a little naughty.

"So good."

I bite my lip and tighten on him as he drags in and out of me. His eyes are on me, hands buried in my hair, gripping onto my scalp as he moves, and it occurs to me: this is what the fuss is all about. This is how a woman is supposed to be touched, looked at.

Respected.

Protected.

It's so unfamiliar to me, and sad at the same time, because I was *married* damn it, and I had no idea. How is it that sex with the man I was supposed to love was just…*empty*? And sex with Eli is…*everything*?

But Eli and I agreed. No love. Just fun.

This has an expiration date.

"Stop," he demands and begins to move faster, a bit harder.

"Stop what?"

"Thinking." He does something with his hips that has me gasping for breath, and in this moment, I can't remember my own name. "Grip my cock, Kate."

He pulls one of my legs up onto his shoulder to open me wider, and he sinks deeper inside, bumping my pubis with his, and holy shit, I see stars.

"Eli."

"That's right, baby." He smiles down at me. "You're amazing. I can see it building. Come for me."

I bite my lip and close my eyes, bear down on him, and fall apart all over again, shocked that it's so soon.

"Fuck," he whispers as he cups my ass and clutches me close to him, grinding inside me as he finds his own release. "Fuck, Kate."

"Yes," I sigh. "You just fucked Kate."

"As soon as I can move, you're getting spanked for that."

"You like it when I say fuck."

"I like spanking you too."

I feel him grin against my chest where he's resting and smile in return. I rather like the spanking myself.

I like Eli. And that could be dangerous.

# CHAPTER 13

## ~KATE~

*'m gonna spank your ass for that.*
And, boy, did he.

I grin and bite the end of my pen as I sit at my desk. I had a productive morning, but now all I can do is daydream about being at the inn…Making love until the wee hours of the morning…Breakfast with Gabby and a very chatty Sam…Walking in the gardens.

Eli finding my G-spot.

I also thought that was a myth. Apparently, I was wrong.

So very wrong.

I giggle and touch my suddenly very warm cheeks. Is it hot in here?

"Hilary!" Mr. Rudolph calls from his office, and I roll my eyes. That's the third time today that he's called me Hilary.

Seriously, I've been here for three weeks. Shouldn't he have figured out by now that I'm not Hilary? Kate isn't a hard name to learn.

I walk briskly into his office. "My name is Kate, Mr. Rudolph."

He glances up and flicks his hand, as if it doesn't matter. "Whatever. I need you to run the month end tax reports for payroll." He goes on about the other tasks he wants me to handle—tasks that are normally *his*—and keeps checking his watch. He seems twitchy. Nervous. Even his brow is sweaty.

He's kind of creepy.

But then, he looks up at me, and his brown eyes are kind.

"Thanks for doing all of this. Kate, right?"

I nod and turn to leave his office, my to-do list out of control.

"I'm leaving for the rest of the afternoon," he informs me, as he follows me out of his office and closes and locks the door. "I'll see you in the morning."

He wipes his fingers over his mouth and hurries out, and I'm just…*pissed.* It must be nice to not have to work much. The man is out of the office more than he's in it. He leaves every day at 1:30, like clockwork. Which really annoys me. Why would Eli have someone with such a poor work ethic working for him?

I set the list Mr. Rudolph just handed me aside, and decide to get some of my own work done. I examine the spreadsheet of all of the transfers of large sums of money that are unaccounted for so far, and try to find a common link. The amounts are all different. They range in size of a few hundred dollars to several thousand. It seems that lately, they've gotten bigger. One was almost ten thousand dollars. But they're not sent on the same day, or even on a regular schedule.

The only consistent thing is that they're transfers to Western Union. No name on these reports.

Don't you have to have an I.D. to pick up money from Western Union? I call a local branch, and sure enough.

Okay, who were they sent to?

Just as I'm about to start digging to find a name, something else occurs to me. The time of day the transfers were made were all around 1:00 in the afternoon, give or take a minute or two. I flip through them all, and sure enough, every single one is around the same time.

Interesting.

I glance at the time on the computer and frown. Mr. Rudolph leaves at 1:30 almost every day. I find each transaction in the computer, and I search for the name of the recipient at Western Union.

H. Peters.

*Who in the hell is H. Peters?*

I frown and pull up the roster of employees, not finding an H. Peters in the bunch.

Well, shit.

I dial Savannah's office number, but get her voice mail, so I dial her cell.

"Hello?" I can hear road noise and raise a brow.

"You've left early."

"Lance asked me to meet him at home," she replies with a sigh.

"Why?"

"No idea. What's up?"

"I have a small lead, and I'm going to need some help. Is there a person that you prefer I use internally to do some snooping, or can I call in my own private investigator?"

"We usually use someone internally, but let's bring in someone from the outside for this."

I nod in agreement. "Will do, thanks."

I place a call to Adam, a local investigator that a colleague recommended, and leave him a voice mail, outlining what I need, then hang up and study the transactions again. I've looked through them a hundred times, but didn't see the time stamp similarities until today.

What else am I missing?

"You look serious."

I gasp and throw the papers on the desk, startled, then cover my heart with my hand and sigh. "You scared me, Hilary."

"Sorry." She grins. "I have to go run some errands, but do you want to meet up for happy hour this afternoon? Say, around four?"

I frown and shake my head. "No, thanks. I had a long weekend. I really just want to go home and relax."

"A long weekend, huh?" She leans on the doorjamb and crosses her arms. "Who is he?"

I laugh and shake my head at my new friend. "You're incorrigible. It's not always about sex, you know."

"Of course it's always about sex." She laughs and tucks her hair behind her ear. "And you're having some. I can tell. I want to hear all about it. And you look like you could use a drink."

I sigh and start to shake my head again, but she rolls her eyes. "You're not saying no. Meet me at Huck's at four."

"Fine. Have a lemon drop waiting for me."

"Can do."

~

"So, talk. Who is it?" Hilary asks, as I sit and take a sip of a delicious lemon drop.

"Not telling." *No way, nohow.*

"You're not fun. I need details."

"I'm not telling you who it is, but I'll spill some details about the sex itself."

"Right on." She shifts in her seat and signals to the waitress for another drink.

"How long have you been here?" I ask.

"A little while. I'm a drink ahead of you. You have to catch up."

I take another drink and lick the sugar on the rim of the glass. I love this damn sugar. It's probably why my hips are so wide. Damn hips.

"So, was the sex good?" Hilary asks.

"The best sex that was ever invented," I confirm, and click my glass to hers.

"Impressive." She sighs and rests her chin in her hand. "Does he do fun oral stuff?"

"Indeed."

"Good. If a man won't go down on you, it's a red flag. Life's too short for that."

I giggle and nod. "For sure. My ex-husband refused to do that. It should have been a clue to his ass-hattery."

"My ex-husband only wanted to have missionary sex," she says with a wrinkle of her nose. "What's the fun in that?"

"Missionary is good," I reply.

"Yes, but every time? Let's switch it up a bit."

"True."

"Was he a pushover, or did he wear the pants? Pun intended." She sips her Bloody Mary through a straw and leans in.

"Oh, he's bossy for sure."

"I love the bossy ones."

I nod in agreement, then watch in wonder as she drains her Bloody Mary and signals to the waitress for another.

"Slow down there, Speedy Gonzales."

She giggles and shakes her head. "I'm celebrating."

"Oh! What are we celebrating?"

"My new car." She smiles proudly. "I just bought a new Mercedes."

I blink at her, stunned. "Seriously? How can you afford that on our salary?"

"Oh, honey, where there's a will, there's a way." She winks and sips her new drink, and all the hairs on the back of my neck stand up. But before I can say anything, my phone rings.

"Hello?"

"We need you. Now."

"Dec?" I frown and immediately reach for my purse; I mouth *got to go* to Hilary, who just nods and waves me off, already paying attention to her own phone. I reach the sidewalk and pause. "Where am I going? What's happening?"

"Come to Savannah's, now."

"Is she okay?"

"No."

My stomach drops and a cold sweat breaks out on my skin that has nothing at all to do with the heat of summer.

"Is she alive?" I whisper.

"Yes. Get here."

"Wait! Where does she live?"

Declan swears under his breath. "Fuck, you don't have a car. Get to Charly's shop and she'll drive you both here."

"On it." I end the call and run to Charly's just two blocks over. She's locking up the front door, her phone pressed to her ear, tears running down her pretty face. "Charly!"

"She's here. We're coming now."

"What is going on?"

"I'm not sure; Declan didn't want to waste time giving info, he just said Van's been hurt, and we need to get there. Get in."

We climb into Charly's car and she speeds off.

"How far away is her house?"

"Three minutes."

"How far is it normally?" I ask, and brace my hand on the dashboard as Charly weaves in and out of traffic.

"Ten."

I hold my breath and pray as Charly gives the cab driver from my first day a run for his money in the crazy driving department, and finally she comes to a screaming stop in a driveway, cuts the engine, and we both go running for the front door.

"Van?!" Charly screams as she pushes inside. "Where is everybody?"

"Upstairs!" Beau calls, and we run through the beautiful home, up the stairs, and come to a halt when we find all three Boudreaux brothers and a man I don't know just outside of Van's bedroom. Beau is talking into the door.

"Who are you?" I ask the handsome, tall man with sandy-blonde hair and deep blue eyes. Eyes that look tortured and worried.

"This is Ben," Eli replies. "He's been a good friend for many years."

"Vanny, you have to open the door, baby. Let us in."

"What is going on?" Charly demands.

"Van called me," Declan says. "She was sobbing; I couldn't understand much, but she said she was home and needed help. I called everyone. But she won't come out of her bedroom."

I'm staring into Eli's scared, angry whiskey eyes. He pulls me hard against him and hugs me close, takes a deep breath, as if he needs this to anchor him, then lets me go and moves to the door.

"Savannah, Charly and Kate are here. Will you open the door for them?"

"Only they can come in," comes a small voice from the other side.

"Jesus, what the fuck?" Beau asks, pushing his hand through his hair. Ben is silent, but clearly agitated, as he paces back and forth.

The door opens a crack and I lead Charly inside and immediately feel the blood leave my face.

"Christ," Charly says, as we both rush to her side. Savannah is sitting on the edge of the mattress of her bed. It's been stripped bare, the sheets and blankets thrown about the room, along with lamps, the alarm clock, anything that could be thrown has been. There is glass shattered. Savannah is wearing her white dress shirt, but no pants. I immediately cover her with a white bed sheet. "What happened, baby?"

Van's hollow eyes are on mine, and I know. I know exactly what happened. I want to fall apart, but I pull myself together and know that I have to get through this for Van.

"Where did he hit you?"

Tears fill her eyes. "He kicked my ribs."

I lift her shirt and bite my lips to keep from crying out at the blazing bruises across her ribcage.

"Where else?"

She shakes her head, but she's cradling her right arm against her.

"Is your arm hurt, honey?"

She nods. She's begun to shake. "Yeah, he pulled it behind my back really hard."

I look up at Charly, who has tears streaming down her face. "Tell the boys to call an ambulance."

"No." Van shakes her head and starts to stand, but I keep her next to me.

"Yes. Savannah, you're hurt."

"Can we come in?" Dec asks from the doorway.

"I don't want them to see this," Van whispers.

"They need to," Charly says, and nods at Dec. The four big men fill the room, and all four look like they're about to kill someone.

"What happened, baby?" Beau asks softly, his voice in direct contrast to his tense body.

"Let's finish figuring out where she's hurt," I interrupt. "He wrenched your arm behind your back?"

Savannah nods, and won't look any of the men in the eyes.

"Are you afraid of us, *bebe*?" Eli asks quietly as he squats in front of her.

"No, of course not. I'm embarrassed," she replies quietly, and watches Eli's face as her tears spill over. "How could I let this happen?"

"What *did* happen, Vanny?" Declan asks.

She swallows and looks at me. "My shoulder is dislocated. I'm pretty sure. I think a rib is broken."

The men all still and watch very carefully as I smooth her tears from her cheeks. "Okay. What else?"

She shows me her wrist, which has bruises in the shape of fingers around it. "Check my other shoulder," she says.

I pull her shirt away and we all gasp at the sight of more finger-shaped bruises on her opposite shoulder.

"He pulled my arm around my back and held onto my shoulder with the other hand."

"And kicked you in the ribs," I confirm, and Van nods.

"Why are you wet, honey?" Charly asks, and I frown as I realize that Van's hair and clothes are all sopping wet.

She starts to shake her head, but Eli takes her face gently in his hands and says, "Why are you wet, my sweet girl?"

Ben stomps into the bathroom and swears ripely. Beau follows, then both men come back into the room.

"He tried to drown her in the tub," Beau says, as Declan calls for an ambulance. "He's a dead man."

"Why?" Savannah asks, still staring into Eli's face. "I don't understand. He called me and said he wanted to tell me something, at home, in private. So, I came home. And he was in here, pacing back and forth. He looked...*frustrated.* Said that he'd been fucking some young thing that decided that she couldn't fuck him anymore because he's married and it's wrong. So, it's my fault.

"I told him that was easily fixed. He can fuck whomever he wants, for the rest of his life, and I'll happily sign papers. But that only made it worse, because Daddy made him sign a prenup, and he won't leave me just to lose out on all the money after all these years."

"A fucking dead man," Beau repeats, and Ben simply leaves, the door downstairs slamming behind him.

"Did he say he was going to kill you?" I ask her.

She nods stiffly, shaking in earnest now, shock setting in. "He kept holding my face in the water, until I thought for sure I was going to die, and then he'd pull me back out. Oh, my God," she breaks down crying. "And then he dragged me back in here by the hair and..."

"And what?" Declan asks.

"I don't want you to hear it," she says to her brothers.

"Vanny, we love you," Beau says softly. "It's okay."

She looks around the room, then settles her gaze on mine and whispers, "He raped me."

I swallow hard. I want to throw up. I want to run away. I don't want to hear this, hear how brutalized my best friend was by the man who was supposed to love her more than anything. But, instead, I lean in and kiss Van's cheek.

"You're safe. The ambulance is coming. We need to take pictures, Van."

"What?" she gasps.

"To press charges, we need photos," I repeat.

"Am I pressing charges?"

"If he lives long enough, yes," Eli confirms. He and his brothers are scary. Lance should be very afraid.

"Of course you are, honey," Charly says, and caresses Van's hair soothingly.

"You're leaving him," I say firmly. "This is it. No more."

"What do you mean, *no more?*" Declan asks.

Charly sighs and winces in pain. "Not the first time."

"What?" Beau demands, and Eli stands to pace, unable to keep still any more.

"But, it's the last," I repeat, before her brothers can ask more questions. "Eli, can you please have the locks on the house changed today?"

"Done."

Sirens call in the distance as the ambulance gets closer. My fingers shake as I push Van's hair behind her ear. I want to fall apart. For me. For Van. For this whole family that has been shaken to the core by an evil that none of us quite understand.

But I can't. Not yet.

"Come with me," Van whispers.

"Every step of the way, friend."

"Love you so much," she says, and begins to cry again.

"Love you more."

# CHAPTER 14

## ẼLI~

"**W**here the fuck is he?" Beau asks the room at large for the fourth time in twenty minutes, and continues to pace my office.

"We've been all over the city," Declan answers, clearly as frustrated as the rest of us. And, out of all of us, Dec is the calmest one. Seeing him agitated is always unnerving. "Maybe he skipped town."

"We'll find him," I reply and sip my brandy. "He can't go far. We've frozen his bank accounts."

"Maybe we shouldn't have done that," Beau replies. "If he uses the bank accounts, we know where he's been."

"He's not getting one more dime from this family," I reply coldly, my gut churning as I remember the look in sweet Van's eyes as they held mine and asked *why?*

Why?

Because he's a piece of shit. Because he wouldn't know what it is to be a man if it fucked him up the ass without lube.

Because he didn't know a good thing when he had it.

But none of that would have made her feel better. *Nothing* can make her feel better, except time and love.

"We should have known," Declan says as he rubs his face, his elbows planted on his knees. "*I* should have known."

"We all should have known," Beau replies in resignation.

"We did," I say, and sip the brandy. "We knew he wasn't a good man. Even if Savannah never would confirm it; we knew *something* wasn't right."

"It was her choice to be with him," Beau says, and holds a hand up when Declan starts to argue. "Think about it. She was young and convinced and proud, Dec. There was no talking her out of it."

"But it's our mother fucking job to protect her," I reply softly. "And we didn't."

We all blink at each other for a long minute. Our fists clenched. Our jaws tight.

"Dad would have killed that fucker himself."

"He would," I agree with a nod. "No one ever fucked with his family and lived to tell the tale."

"Dad never killed anyone," Beau replies with a half smile, as though the thought is entertaining.

"No one dared fuck with us before to test him," Declan says.

"He's going to pay," Beau says, and swallows his glass of brandy.

"He already has," Ben says, as he stalks into my office. We all still when we see him. He's sweaty, dirty, and has blood on his shirt.

"What the fuck?" Declan demands.

"What happened?" I ask, much more calmly than I feel.

"You don't need specifics," he replies, and takes my drink from my hand, gulping the brandy, and holds the glass out for more. "I found him."

"Is he alive?" Beau asks.

"He's wishing he wasn't, but yes."

"Do you need an attorney?" I ask my friend since childhood. He shakes his head and swigs more brandy.

"Not necessary. He's already turned himself in."

"He's turned himself in to the police?" Beau asks incredulously.

Ben nods and leans his hips on my desk.

"How did you pull that off?" Dec asks.

Ben simply smiles, a cold, hard smile that would make most grown men piss in their pants. "I made it very clear that it was either turn himself in, or I'd kill him."

"You would have," I say, with a bit of surprise, although it shouldn't surprise me. Ben has been in love with Savannah since puberty.

"Without hesitation," he replies coldly, and takes another sip of brandy. When his glass is drained, he slaps it on the desk and walks toward my door.

"Ben," Declan says, stopping our friend when he grips the doorknob. "What exactly is Savannah to you?"

Ben glances over his shoulder at Dec, shakes his head, his eyes suddenly sad, and leaves without a word.

"Fuck," Beau whispers. "This could turn into a shitstorm."

"It won't," I reply. "Our people will take care of it. He'll pay. Dearly."

"What an idiot," Declan says with disgust. "He did this over a piece of ass?"

"He did this because he's an evil son of a bitch," Beau replies. "It really has nothing at all to do with Savannah. It was never about her."

"I'm going to go grab a shower and then head up to the hospital," Declan says.

"I'll go with you," Beau replies, just as my phone rings.

*Kate.*

"Hello, *cher.*"

"Hi." Her voice sounds tired. "Gabby is here at the hospital with Van. She's going to stay with her tonight."

"They're keeping Van overnight?" I ask and check my watch. Damn, it's almost midnight.

"Yeah, it's late, and she's pretty hurt. They want to watch her. Can you please come get me? I wouldn't ask, but Charly already went home and—"

"Of course I'll come get you." I grab my keys and head for the door. "I'll be there in fifteen minutes."

~

I HATE HOSPITALS. The smell, the sounds. I fucking hate that Savannah is lying in a bed here.

I walk into her room and curl my hands into fists. Her face isn't marked at all. The fucker was sure to not bruise up her pretty face. But her arm is in a sling, and she's cradling it against her like it aches.

My own chest aches.

Gabby sees me first and runs to me, launching herself into my arms. Our girls are always so strong. So fierce. But they aren't afraid to lean on their brothers when they need us.

And, as far as I'm concerned, that just makes them all the stronger.

"It's okay, *bebe*," I murmur and kiss the top her of head. Gabby is not just the baby, she's also the smallest. The rest of us are tall, but she's petite. And if you didn't know her, you'd mistakenly think she's fragile.

"I just need a hug," she murmurs before pulling away and smiling reassuringly at Van.

"You're a sweet girl, *bebe*," I whisper in her ear. "Who has Sam?"

"He's with Mama. She took him home with her. I called Cindy and asked her to watch the inn for tonight."

I inwardly cringe, but nod. Cindy has been Gabby's friend since grade school.

And she spent an out-of-control, mistake of a night in my bed.

"How are you feeling?" I ask, as I lean in and plant my lips on Van's forehead. She's cool to the touch.

No fever from shock or infection.

"Sore," she says, and smiles as I pull away. *Strong women.* "I'll be okay."

I kiss Kate and drag my knuckles down her smooth cheek before sitting on the bed at Van's hip.

The looks that Van and Gabby exchange aren't lost on me. They'll grill me later.

"I have news." I take Van's hand in mine and look her dead in the eye.

"Tell me."

I exhale, wondering how much information I should give her. "He's in custody."

She closes her eyes in relief and her body seems to sag. "Thank God."

"He won't hurt you ever again." She frowns and looks back into my eyes.

"Is he in custody, or in the morgue?"

I grin ruefully. "He's not dead. Unfortunately."

"But he's hurt."

*Strong and smart.*

I nod, but don't elaborate.

"You've never lied to me, E. Not once."

"No, ma'am."

"So, why are you now?"

"I'm not lying."

Gabby snorts and I send her a hard stare, shutting her up.

"You're not telling me everything. How did you find him? Was he arrested?"

"I didn't find him."

She tilts her head to the side, and there she is. My Van. She narrows her eyes, and I know I'm in for it.

Thank Christ.

"What. The. Fuck."

"Ben found him." Her eyes widen, but I continue. "I haven't seen him yet. But I saw Ben. Swollen knuckles, sweaty. A little blood."

"Blood!"

"Don't you dare defend that fucker," Gabby says angrily.

"No, I want to know if it was *Ben's* blood!"

I smirk. "Honey, nobody makes Ben bleed."

She sighs in relief, but then frowns again. "So, Ben called the cops?"

"I honestly don't know how it went down. I'm assuming we'll find out tomorrow. Ben found him, and made him see that turning himself in was best for Lance's well-being."

Van's lower lip quivers, making my gut tighten. "He did that for me."

"We would do *anything* for you, *bebe*." She grips onto my hand with her uninjured one and squeezes, holding my gaze in hers, and an entire silent conversation passes between us.

*I love you. Thank you. I don't know what I would do without you.*

*I love you. Always. You're welcome. You don't ever have to know what it is to live without us.*

"Go home," she whispers instead. "Take Kate home. She's tired, but she won't admit it."

"I'm not tired," Kate lies easily.

"She's lying," Van says.

"I know," I reply with a grin and glance over at Gabby, who still has tears in her eyes. "You got this?"

"Of course." She grins, the dimples in her cheeks showing. "Vanny's stuck with me all night. It'll be like when we were kids and I'd sneak into her room and sleep with her because my room was haunted."

"Your room wasn't haunted," Van replies with a roll of the eyes. "You just liked my bigger bed."

"My room was haunted," she insists, talking to Kate now. "My things would be mysteriously moved. I heard voices."

"Those voices are in that hard head of yours," I reply and grin when she sticks her tongue out at me, just like she did when she was small. "But I am going to take Kate home now."

"Kate appreciates it," Kate says sarcastically. "She also loves it when you talk about her like she's not here."

"She's testy," Van says. "She's been bossing the nurses around all day."

"I'm right here," Kate says.

"I know how to reel that bossy side in," I assure Van, and laugh when Kate mutters *right here, people*. "We will check in on you in the morning."

"Good night."

I take Kate's hand in mine and kiss it as I lead her out of Van's room and into the hallway. As soon as we're out of view, she pulls her hand from mine and walks ahead of me to the elevator, keeping her distance as we wait.

"Are you okay?" I ask.

She simply nods, her eyes trained on the door of the elevator.

*Another lie.*

I move to brush her hair behind her ear, but she flinches away from my reach. My first reaction is frustration. Does she think that I would hurt her? But then she turns her sad green eyes to me and just shakes her head, and I relax.

It's not me. She's hanging on by a fucking thread.

I nod once and keep my distance to the car. Halfway home, I try to take her hand in mine, but she pulls away and clasps her hands tightly in her lap. Her whole body is tense. Her eyes trained on her lap.

For the first time in my life, I want to make it better for a woman. I want to hold her and protect her, and *she's not mine.*

She's never going to be mine. And the thought of her leaving makes me feel...

I don't know what, it just makes me *feel.*

I park and she jumps out of the car, walking quickly to her loft.

"Kate. You're coming up to my place."

"No. I'm not." She doesn't stop walking.

"Yes, *cher,* you are."

She stops and turns to glare at me. "No, I'm not. I don't want you tonight, Eli."

"You're getting me."

"You know what?" she rails, her eyes fierce, her gorgeous hair a riot of curls around her face. She advances toward me, anger vibrating in every muscle of her body. "I don't need this. I don't need another *man* telling me what I will and will not do."

"You shouldn't be alone."

"Shouldn't. Won't. Can't." She gets up in my face, and I've never seen anything like her. She's on fire, standing out here on the sidewalk in the French Quarter, yelling at me. "You're an asshole!"

*Shot to the gut.*

"I've never claimed otherwise, *cher.*" My voice is perfectly calm. My hands are in my pockets, so I don't reach for her and pull her in.

Not yet.

"You just play with people and their emotions! You're just selfish and heartless!"

My eyes narrow on her face. Her eyes are tearing up, her cheeks rosy, and her bottom lip quivers as she shoves her fists into my chest, knocking me back a step.

She's surprisingly strong for such a little thing.

"You just hurt people!" she yells.

"Who are you talking to right now, Kate?" I ask softly. Her eyes focus on me, and her face crumples as she begins to cry. "Ah, *bebe.*" I hug her tight to me, and she fights me, trying to wrench her way out of my arms, but I hold firm. "Shhh. You're safe, Kate. Let go. Cry. Scream. Do whatever you need to, sweetheart. I have you. I'm not letting go."

"I don't want you to see this."

"God save me from proud women," I mumble into her hair, as I press kisses to the top of her head, breathing her in. She begins to cry in earnest now, gripping onto my shirt rather than trying to get away. I scoop her up into my arms and carry her inside as she buries her face in my neck and cries; loud, body-shaking sobs making their way through her as though the storm has finally washed over her and all she can do is ride it out and survey the damage later.

And it's killing me. I don't take her upstairs to the bedroom. Instead, I carry her into the living room, sit on the couch, and simply hold her in my lap, my arms tight around her, and let her cry.

I brush her hair off her face, wishing I had a cool washcloth. Her back is slender under my hands as I caress her slowly, trying to comfort her.

Finally, after long minutes, the sobbing slows, and she is reduced to hiccoughs, then sniffles. Her small body still shaking. Her hands still clinging to me, as if I could let her go.

Not happening.

"Made a mess of you," she whispers roughly.

"Doesn't matter," I reply in the same whisper. The house is quiet around us as we sit here, holding onto each other.

"I know what she felt," she whispers, but then doesn't elaborate, and I don't ask her to. Finally, she says, "I know how it felt every time he kicked her. Pulled her hair. Wrenched her arm. Held her down while he—" The last word comes on a sob, and I tighten my arms around her as I wish for the chance to have Kate's ex-husband alone in a room for just five minutes. "At least I was never almost drowned."

I have to swallow the bile that rises up in my throat.

"Do all men hurt women?" she asks softly.

"No."

She simply nods.

"I hate that this happened to her. She'll question herself for a long time. *What did I do to make him hurt me? Why wasn't I good enough, smart enough, for him? If I had just done this or that, he wouldn't have gotten mad.*" My hands reflexively fist in her shirt. "Long after the bruises fade, and her shoulder heals, she'll still be broken."

"Do you think you're still broken, Kate?" I ask softly. She stills, then loops her arms around my neck and hugs me close, burying her fingers in my hair, and I return the hug, enjoying the way she feels in my lap, pressed against me.

"Sometimes I think I'll always be broken," she whispers into my ear, tears in her voice.

I cup her cheek in my hand and tip her face up so I can look her in the eye. Her tears make me feel so fucking helpless. I don't do helpless.

Shit, I don't do *feelings*. Or I didn't, until I met her.

"Do you want to know what I think?"

"Maybe," she replies with a sniffle.

I grin and tuck her hair behind her ear, then let my fingertips trail down her wet cheek. "I think that you are smart, funny, and sexy as fuck."

She grins and her green eyes darken, making my cock stir.

"I also think you're stubborn." She sniffles and raises an eyebrow. "I know you're beautiful." She tries to look down, but I tip her chin back up with my finger. "You are beautiful. Every freckle on your gorgeous little body drives me crazy. But, more than that, Kate? You're strong. Determined. You have a backbone."

Tears fill her eyes again, and I can't stand it. I tip my forehead against hers. "You're not broken, *cher*. He hurt you. But no one broke you."

"Thank you for that," she whispers, and kisses my lips softly before tucking her face back into my neck and beginning to cry again. Softly now. A cleansing cry. The kind of cry that sweeps out the demons and makes room for the good.

Kate deserves so much good.

~

There's a buzzing in my pocket.

And a woman lying on top of me.

I open one eye and squint at the light in the room. We're still in the living room, stretched out on the couch, cuddled up much like we were at the inn when we watched the movie.

Well, pretended to watch the beginning of the movie.

Kate's face is snuggled against my heart, her arms wrapped around my sides, legs entangled with mine. The only way we'd be able to get much closer is if we were naked. And it feels fucking amazing.

Imagine that.

The buzzing begins again in my pocket.

"Are you going to answer that?" Kate asks without moving, making me grin. I fish my phone out of my pocket, with Kate's dead weight on me, and frown when I see Declan's name on the caller ID.

"Hey," I answer. "What's wrong?"

"Nothing, as far as I know," he replies. I can hear street noises. "You sound funny. Were you still asleep?"

"No," I lie, and Kate pokes me in the ribs and hisses, "No lying."

"It's after nine, Eli."

"Are you the morning police?"

"Don't you have to be at work?"

"That's the thing about being the boss. I can go into work when and if the desire strikes." I kiss Kate's head and grin again as she shimmies against me, getting more comfortable, and succeeding in making sure my morning semi-hard-on is now just a hard-on.

But then she looks up at me, and everything in me just goes...*tender.* Her eyes are swollen and red. Her hair tangled around her face. Lips swollen from licking and biting them as she cried.

If I have anything to say about it, she'll never have another reason to be devastated like this in her life.

And that's ridiculous because *she isn't mine.*

Except, she's mine for right now, and that's all that matters.

"Eli?"

"Sorry, what?"

"If you tell me that you're having sex while on the phone with me, I will deck the fuck out of you when I see you."

"You don't scare me."

"He's not having sex," Kate says into the phone, and giggles as she snuggles into me again.

I've never loved to snuggle. I mean, it's a necessity to snuggle right after sex. Otherwise, you're just a prick who wanted to fuck her. And I am, but even I know the importance of the obligatory snuggle.

That isn't what this is.

"I might have sex after we hang up," I clarify, earning another giggle from Kate.

"No, he won't. At least not with me."

I slap Kate's ass and laugh when she pinches my side. "What's up, Dec?"

"Just wanted to give you an update on Van. She's doing better this morning. Stiff and sore, but her ribs aren't broken, and there's no bleeding. They'll let her go to Mama's this afternoon."

"She'll love that," I say dryly.

"Gabby wanted her to go to the inn, but I put the nix on that. Van will try to help. If we have her go to Mama's, she'll be pampered and taken care of."

"She'll die of boredom in a week."

"Maybe in a week she can go to Gabby's," he reasons, and I agree. "Anyway, I wanted to let you know so you can look in on her at Mama's tonight. I'll be by too."

"Thanks."

"And just so you know, Eli, she doesn't look good."

"I know. I saw her last night. But she's going to be fine, Dec."

"Yeah. Yeah, she will."

We ring off and I toss my phone on the floor and hug Kate close. "Now, what's this about me not having sex this morning?"

"I don't have time."

"Do you have somewhere you need to be?"

"Yes," she laughs. "I need to go in to work. As it is, I'm very late."

"You're with the boss, Kate."

"No one else knows that." She moves to climb off of me, but I tug her back into my arms and turn us on our sides, her between me and the back of the couch, and kiss her softly.

"Are you okay?"

"Yes."

I lean back so I can look at her clearly, and aside from the puffiness and redness, I can see that she's telling the truth.

"Strong girl," I whisper and kiss her forehead.

"I'm also late."

"Are we back to this?"

"I'm serious, Eli. I have a mountain of work, and I have some leads that I'm following."

"What leads?" I ask.

"Let me see if they go anywhere. All I have are hunches right now. I'll fill you in as soon as I have anything solid." She smiles and kisses my chin. "So, I really do have to go to work. And so do you."

"I do." I sigh and don't move. "I'm going to go check on Savannah this afternoon."

"I'll go this evening."

"Just ride with me this afternoon."

"I can't." She rolls her eyes and I grin because she's adorable. "You and I aren't doing…*stuff*."

"If by stuff you mean kissing," I kiss her lips, "and touching," drag my hand down her side to her hip, "and fucking," pull her against me so she can feel my hard cock against her abdomen, "yes, we are."

"No one else knows that. I can't arrive late and leave early, Eli. But I will let you do stuff to me later."

"We're going to keep working on your vocabulary, *cher*."

She grins up at me as she slides her leg up mine and presses her center against me, making my eyes cross.

"I'm looking forward to it."

# CHAPTER 15

## ẼLI~

"*H*ow are you adjusting?" I ask Van as I lean back in my chair and prop the phone between my ear and shoulder, returning an email.

"You know I love the inn," she replies. It's good to hear the smile in her voice. "And I love Mama too, but after the eighth day, I was ready to make an escape."

"Mama enjoyed babying you for a while," I reply.

"I really could go home, you know. I'm feeling pretty much normal again. I need to work."

"You need to relax."

"I have work, Eli."

"We may fall apart around here without you," the sarcasm in my voice is thick, "but we'll muddle our way through. Just enjoy the inn. Get well."

"I forgot how much I love being out here," she concedes. "And Sam is so adorable. He brought me breakfast in bed this morning. Gogurt and Goldfish crackers."

"Breakfast of champions."

"Oh, I have to go take a call for Gabby. I'll call you later."

"Bye."

I hang up and sigh. I'm restless. It's been more than a week since Van was hurt. She's doing well. The past week has been a blur of police statements, long days at work, and short nights with Kate.

*Kate.*

She's been working her own ass off. She works late into the evening, and is up early again the next morning. I see her long enough to sink inside her sweet body, then curl up around her and sleep.

I rub my hand over my mouth as it occurs to me that *I miss her.*

What the fuck is wrong with me?

I turn my attention back to work, but it's no use. I can't focus. I can't think of anything but Kate, and quickly decide to rectify the situation.

"Put me through to Kate O'Shaughnessy's office," I instruct my assistant and grin when I hear Kate answer with an irritated, "This is Kate."

"This is Eli," I reply. "I need you to gather all of your notes and files on your project and come to my office, please."

"Is there a problem?" she asks.

"Ten minutes," I reply, rather than answer, and hang up the phone. I answer several emails and calls before Kate is announced and shown into my office. I gesture for her to have a seat, then stand, cross to the door, lock it, and return to my own seat behind the desk.

"Good morning." My voice is formal, professional, and makes Kate frown.

"Hello," she replies. "Eli, is something wrong?"

"No." I shake my head and steeple my fingers. "I just want an update."

She narrows her eyes on me for a moment. I cock an eyebrow and simply wait, and finally, she opens a file and begins to talk.

And I don't even know what the fuck she's talking about. Her words mean nothing to me. All I can think about his how that skirt fits tight on her hips and ass and her white blouse fits tight across her tits. She loves expensive underwear, which makes my cock hard and my heart pound, and I want to know what she's wearing under that outfit.

She crosses her legs, drawing attention to the sexy emerald green fuck-me heels on her slender feet, and I swallow hard as I picture her naked, sprawled on my desk, her legs over my shoulders with just those heels on.

*Jesus Christ, I want her.*

"Eli?"

"Yes."

"Did you hear a word I just said?"

"No."

She shakes her head and watches me like I'm crazy. And I am. I'm completely fucking crazy about her.

"Do you want me to go through it again?"

"No, I don't really give a shit right now."

"You don't care that someone is stealing from your company? That's the whole reason you hired me, Eli."

"Right now, in this moment, no. I don't give a fuck."

"What do you want, then?"

"You."

Her green eyes flare, and her pouty mouth opens in surprise. The pulse in her neck speeds up.

I'm going to bite her there.

"You called me up here to—"

"To fuck you." I finish her sentence for her, because I didn't call her up here to do *stuff*, as she calls it.

"We are not going to do that here," she hisses, looking scandalized, but I simply grin and lean over the desk toward her, keeping her gaze steadily in mine.

"Let me make it clear; we can have sweat dripping, sheet ripping, furniture breaking, screaming, trembling, hair pulling, ass smacking fucking for hours, or soft, sweet, quiet, intense lovemaking for days. You can have either or both, but we're not leaving here without me being inside you, sugar."

Her legs shift as she clenches her thighs together and she swallows hard, processing my words.

"Right, because we can just stay here for days."

"Don't tempt me. I can make that happen."

She tilts her head and watches me for a moment. "You're intense today."

"I'm intense every day." I stand and slowly walk around my desk to her, pull her to her feet, and smirk at how short she still is, even with those amazing shoes on her feet. I turn her in my arms, glide my hands around her sides to her belly and up to her tits, bury my nose in her hair and whisper in her ear. "You're going to have to be quiet while I fuck you. My assistant is just on the other side of that door."

"I can't believe you want to do this."

*I don't want to. I need to.*

"Do you think you can do that, Kate? Be quiet?"

"I'm not good at quiet," she replies breathlessly, and pushes her ass back against my already hard cock. I grip her tight skirt in my hands, gathering the fabric, pulling it above her sweet, round ass.

"Did you wear this skirt just to make me crazy?"

"No, but if it does, that's a great bonus."

I bite her earlobe, thankful that she wore her hair up today, giving me access to her neck. "It does. And so does this fucking amazing underwear."

She's wearing black lace today.

"Lean on the desk." She bends over, pushes her ass out, and gasps when I squat behind her, rip her underwear, and toss them onto the desk.

"Those were expensive."

"And I don't give even one fuck," I murmur, as I drag my fingertip from the top of the crack of her ass, over her anus, and through her already sopping wet folds. "You're already turned on."

"Mm," she moans softly.

"No noise," I remind her, right before I pull her pussy lips into my mouth and suck, push my tongue into her, then over her folds, making sure she's good and wet. Her hips are moving desperately, searching for release, but before she can come, I stand and sink two fingers inside her while I unfasten my pants, desperate to be inside her. Jesus, it feels like I'm about to come out of my skin. I'm hot, swollen, and breathless.

I push into her from behind as I tilt her face back and kiss her hard, masking her moans. She can't stay quiet.

And that's another fuck that I just don't give.

I get only two pumps in, then pull out, spin her around, lift her onto the desk, pushing anything in our way aside so she can lie back, and coffee spills all over my iPad, right before my monitor tips over and cracks the screen.

"Oh, no!" Kate gasps, but I laugh as I prop her legs on my shoulders, kiss her ankle, and push back inside her.

"Thank God for the cloud," I murmur, and begin fucking her hard and fast. Her eyes are on mine, she's panting, and her cheeks are flushed. She licks her finger and reaches down to rub her clit. "Yes, baby, rub yourself. Fuck, that's hot."

She clenches around me, and I can't hold back. I come hard, and feel her come with me, milking my cock with her muscles. She covers her mouth with her free hand, trying to keep quiet, and failing miserably.

I pull out and help her off the desk.

"Just needed to take the edge off?" she asks, and begins to shimmy her skirt down her legs, but I stop her and lead her to the couch.

"I didn't say we were done." I strip us both out of the rest of our clothes and cover her body with mine on the couch.

"We already had furniture breaking sex," she says with a grin. "Or, electronic breaking anyway."

"And now we'll have the slow and sweet," I whisper against her lips. "You're beautiful, *cher.*"

"You're charming," she whispers back. I love how shy she gets when I give her compliments, and turns it around on me, calling me charming.

I'm just being honest.

"Your eyes are so green," I murmur and slide my already recovering cock through her folds, up to her clit, and down again. She gasps and closes her eyes. "Open."

"You're so bossy," she moans and bites her lip.

"You like it."

"I like it *so much*," she groans and circles her hips, inviting me back inside. I pin her hands over her head with one of my hands, cup her face with the other, and kiss us both mindless as I sink inside and stop, balls deep, and enjoy how tight, wet, and hot she is.

"No one has ever turned me inside out the way you do," I say against her mouth, then tug her lower lip with my teeth. "You make me forget myself. You make me fucking crazy."

"You do the same for me," she says, and whimpers as she circles her hips again. "Please move."

"You need me to move, baby?"

"Yes." She pushes against my hands, using my strength as leverage to lift her hips, creating just a tiny bit of eye-crossing friction.

"Ask me," I reply.

"Please."

I pull out slowly and push back in and stop again, making her frown.

"Ask me better than that."

She narrows her eyes on me, earning a cocked brow from me. "Eli?"

"Yes, Kate?"

"Will you please—" she clenches her muscles on my cock, making me swear under my breath. "Please fuck me?"

"Now you're just using the dirty words to get what you want," I say, but comply, moving slow and steady, in and out, and she smiles up at me. A gorgeous, full-on, happy smile, and my heart catches.

"I love the way you feel inside me."

*Heart fucking catches.*

I can't respond. I'll say something ridiculous. Instead, I pick up the pace and grind my pubis on hers, hitting her sweet spot, and watch her come apart beneath me, pulling me with her.

I release her hands and lie on her chest, in her arms. I can hear her heart, thundering in her chest. I can't see it, but I brush my hand down her side, over the sexier than fuck tattoo there. *I am enough the way I am.*

She's so much more than enough.

She sinks her fingers into my hair and holds me tight.

"You're a sweet man, Eli Boudreaux."

She kisses my head, and suddenly, everything in me simply calms. This feels…*right.*

It feels like home.

And that's ridiculous.

*Isn't it?*

"I hate to have to be the party pooper, but I really do have to go back to work," she says softly, but continues to hug me to her, gliding her fingers through my hair. I could sleep like a baby, right here.

"I have work too. But this feels good."

"Hmm," she agrees. "I like your hair."

"My hair?" I ask with a laugh.

"It's soft. And it feels good in my fingers." She rubs my forehead with her fingertips and I sigh. This woman can touch me as much as she wants, whenever she wants. "I like it."

"I'm glad."

"And I like your ass."

"Are you making a list?" I ask with a grin.

"Shh." She continues to make me sleepy and calm with her fingers. "I like your ass. It's firm, and you have the sexiest dimples right above it."

"I'm happy you like them."

"You have lots of likeable parts."

"What about the most important part?" I ask and glance up at her to wiggle my eyebrows.

"God, you're such a man."

～

"Hey, Van, it's Eli."

"Two calls in one day? I'm fine, Eli. Seriously."

"I'm happy to hear that, but that's not why I'm calling this time."

"What's wrong? Do I need to come to the office?"

I laugh and shake my head. "No. You're not coming in to work. I need your advice. You're Kate's best friend. I want to do something nice for her. Surprise her. She's been working hard, but I don't know what to do. Give me ideas."

There's a long, pregnant pause.

"Is this Eli *Boudreaux*? My brother?"

"Funny."

"So, what exactly is happening between you and Kate, Eli? And don't tell me it's none of my business."

"It's none of your business," I reply, just to rile her up.

"Really?"

"Kidding. Honestly, I like her. A lot. We spend time together."

"You're fucking her."

That pisses me off for reasons I can't explain. Yes, I am fucking her, but it's more than that, and to hear it put like that makes it sound…*cheap.*

"We are engaging in a physical relationship, yes."

"Is that it?"

"Are you going to help me or not?"

"I will if you answer my question."

I sigh and drag my hand down my face. I washed up after she left my office, but I swear I can still smell her on me, and it makes me want her all over again.

This is getting ridiculous.

"She's not like the others, Vanny," I say quietly…voice aloud for the first time what's been brewing in my head for weeks. "I like her. I respect her. And I want to do something special for her."

"Are you going to ask her to stay when the job is done?"

"No," I reply without hesitation. Van sighs.

"Okay, stubborn ass, I know exactly what you should do."

~

HER HEAD IS bent over her desk as she reads through what look like financial reports. She doesn't even see me as I lean against the doorjamb, watching her work. It's early evening, at least two hours past the time that the last person left for the day.

I do believe I've met my match in the workaholic department.

"I see you," she murmurs without looking up. Is it any wonder that I'm crazy about her?

"It's time to go, *cher*."

"I have a few more things before the weekend."

"Kate, it's almost eight on a Friday evening. It's the weekend."

"I'm almost done."

I cross to her desk and tip her head back with my finger under her chin. "Shut it down. I have a surprise for you."

Her eyes flare in happiness. "You do?"

"Yes."

She begins plunging her hands in my pockets, patting me down. "Where is it?"

"This is a new side to you."

"I love surprises."

*So noted.*

"What is this?" She pulls the half-dollar out of my pocket and gazes at it. "Does this say 1860?"

"It does. Dad gave it to me when I was just out of college. He used to carry two of them. He gave the other to Beau."

"What does it mean?"

*Smart girl.* "They were handed down from my great-grandfather as the first measurable profit from the company. And Dad said that it was to remind us that every penny we make is important, whether it be fifty cents, or fifty million dollars."

"I like that." She replaces the coin in my pocket and keeps searching. "I can't find my surprise."

"Well, we have to go to it. I don't have it on me."

"Oh." She pouts, but then stands and launches herself into my arms. "Thank you."

"You don't even know what it is."

"It doesn't matter. Thank you."

"You're welcome. Let's go."

She locks her desk and gathers her things, and then frowns as I escort her down the hall.

"You know, you shouldn't come down to my office."

"Everyone is gone, Kate. We're the only ones here."

"Still." She sniffs as she steps into the elevator, then does a little happy dance. "What's the surprise?"

"I'm not telling," I reply with a laugh and tug on a piece of her hair.

"Can I guess? Is it…?" She bites her lip as she thinks. "Is it a show?"

"No."

"Is it…Dinner?"

"No." I pull her in for a hug and kiss her head. "Stop trying. You'll never guess."

"Give me a hint."

"You must be impossible to live with at Christmas."

She simply grins and climbs into the car, a bundle of nerves the entire drive through town.

"We're leaving town?"

"We're not going far."

"You're a good surprise giver."

I laugh and glance over at her where she's watching me with happy eyes. "Is that such a thing?"

"Yes."

I pull into the parking garage at the airport, and Kate watches me with shocked curiosity. "Where are we going?"

"You'll see."

"But, I didn't pack a bag! I don't even have a toothbrush, since I took my spare out of my purse—"

I yank her to me and kiss the fuck out of her, just to shut her up, then lead her into the baggage claim area. I watch as her eyes skim over the people waiting for their bags, and when they land on a familiar face, she smiles and runs to her friend.

"Oh, my God! What are you doing here?"

The tall, dark man who was speaking with Kate's friend steps away, gathers his own bag, and waves at Lila as he walks away.

"Eli! This is Lila," Kate announces, as she and the dark-haired, beautiful woman turn to me.

"I know," I reply with a grin and shake Lila's hand. "Pleasure to meet you in person."

"Likewise."

"Wait. Why didn't I know that you were coming?" Kate asks Lila, as they lead me back into the parking garage. I'm happy to bring up the rear with Lila's small suitcase in tow.

"Well, I was going to come down in a few weeks for a job interview anyway, and then Eli called and asked if I'd like to come see you, and *hello*! Of course I did! So, I called and had my interview moved to Monday, and here I am."

Suddenly, Kate launches herself into my arms and hugs me tight. "Thank you," she whispers into my ear.

"My pleasure, *cher*."

"First things first," Kate says, after we all get settled in the car. She and Lila are sharing the back, so they can talk without one of them craning their neck to see the other. "Who was that tall drink of water you were chatting with at the baggage claim?"

"Noticed that, did you?" Lila asks with a laugh.

"Um, hello, he was *hot*."

I growl as I catch Kate's eye in the rear-view.

"Did he just growl?" Lila asks with a laugh.

"He does that," Kate says. "Spill it."

"All I know is, his name is Asher, and he's in town for some work thing." She shrugs. "That's it."

"You didn't get his number?"

"No."

"Did he get yours?"

"No."

"What is wrong with you?"

Lila laughs and kisses Kate's cheek. "Let's talk about you. How are you?"

"I'm good."

There's a moment of quiet. "I believe you," Lila finally replies.

"You really didn't get his number?" The girls bust up laughing, and it makes me smile to hear Kate so happy. So carefree.

I plan to keep her that way.

"I think this calls for girls' night out tomorrow night," Kate says suddenly. "I'll call Van, Gabby, and Charly, and we'll hit the town."

"Excellent idea! I haven't seen them in forever."

"Do you know my sisters?" I ask.

"Yep, I met them a few times when we were all visiting Kate at college. This is gonna be epic."

"So fun," Kate agrees. "We'll start at Café Amalie and flirt with Joe."

"Who's Joe?" Lila asks as I growl again.

"My favorite waiter."

"Is he hot?" Lila asks.

"So hot," Kate answers, and I grip the steering wheel tighter.

"I'm so in," Lila replies.

# CHAPTER 16

## ~KATE~

"Can I borrow these earrings?" Lila asks, holding my silver chandelier earrings up to her lobes and looking in the mirror to my right. "They go with my shoes."

"Your shoes?" I chuckle and look down, and sure enough, she's right. "You're going to have a hard time walking in the Quarter in those heels. Trust me."

"It's GNO," she says with a shrug. "I'll be fine. I'll kick them off and dance barefoot at the bar."

"Ew. You won't want to do that on Bourbon."

"Are you saying the French Quarter is unsanitary?"

"At night it is," I confirm, and smooth lip gloss on my lips. I step back and take stock. My hair is down, and thanks to the products Charly recommended, it hangs in pretty waves past my shoulders. Makeup is done, bolder than usual, because hello, girls' night. "Is this dress okay?"

Lila examines me thoughtfully, then nods. "The color matches your eyes, which I kind of hate you for, because I can't wear green, and it shows off your boobs. Excellent choice."

"Right on." Lila is gorgeous, as usual, in a one-shoulder little black dress and strappy silver heels. Her black hair is also down, straight and sleek. Makeup put together.

She's always put together.

"You look awesome," I say, and offer her a fist to bump.

"We're hot bitches," she agrees, just as the front door opens and Charly yells, "We're here!"

"It was a good idea to meet here," Gabby says, and holds a bottle of liquor up. "We'll have shots before we leave."

"Why do I feel like I'm back in college?" Van asks and hugs Lila tight, still careful of her shoulder. "Hi, sugar."

"Hello, friend."

"You all look amazing," I announce and find shot glasses. Charly pours us each a shot of Patron.

"Should Van be drinking with pain meds?" Gabby asks.

"I haven't taken a pain med in a week," she says with a roll of the eyes. "But maybe I should try it. It could be fun."

"Hey, Karen used to swirl her meds in her martini for a reason on *Will & Grace*," Lila reminds us.

"Bingo," Van agrees with a laugh, and we all take a shot, then another.

"Are we ready to go?" I ask. "We have a reservation at Café Amalie in fifteen minutes."

"Let's go wreak havoc on the streets of New Orleans, ladies," Charly says, and leads us out the door and to the sidewalk. "Lila, honey, those shoes are gonna be a bitch when you're drunk and walking through the Quarter."

"Told you," I say and smirk.

"They're pretty," Lila says.

"Oh, they are that," Charly agrees. "Trust me, I know good shoes. But you'll need to be careful."

"I'll hold onto you," I tell Lila, and loop my arm through hers.

"Oh, good, we'll both be on our asses," she laughs.

"Are you saying I'm clumsy?"

"Yes," they all say at once, making me laugh. The walk to Café Amalie is short, and we're seated quickly.

"Ladies," hot waiter Joe says, as he approaches the table. "Welcome."

"Hi, Joe," I say with a smile. "Ladies, this is Joe."

"Well, hello, Joe," Charly says, blatantly looking Joe up and down. "You're delicious."

"As is the food," Joe says without missing a beat, and I mentally high-five him.

"You're going to get along with us just fine," Gabby says with a laugh.

"What can I bring you to drink?" he asks, and lays his hand on my shoulder.

His very big, very firm hand.

"Lemon drop?" he asks with a wink.

"I really love you, Joe." He laughs and takes all of our drink orders, and when he's gone, Charly lets out a low whistle.

"Dear, sweet God, the things I could teach that man."

"I don't know, I think Joe looks like he already knows his way around a woman," Lila says, and watches Joe unabashedly at the bar.

"He's good with his hands," I agree.

"He touched your *shoulder*," Van reminds me with a grin.

"Exactly. And that woke my girl parts up, so there you have it."

Joe delivers our drinks, and Gabby keeps craning her neck to see the iron entrance.

"Who are you looking for?" I ask.

"Cindy is going to join us, but she didn't know if she'd be able to make it here, or if she'd meet up with us later for dancing."

"So, who is this Cindy?" I ask and glance toward the bar, just in time to see a woman walking away toward the rest room. I'd swear it was Hilary from work, but she's gone before I can tell for sure. "I remember you mentioned her before."

"She's been a friend of mine for a long time," Gabby says, and smiles at Joe as he sets her mojito in front of her. "You'll like her. She's fun."

"Are you having dinner tonight, ladies?" Joe asks.

"Maybe just appetizers?" Charly asks.

"I don't know, we're going to be drinking. A lot," I remind her. I glance back toward the bar, hoping to see the woman again, but she's not there. I must have been mistaken.

"May I suggest then that you put something on your stomachs?" Joe asks seriously.

"I'm starving, so yes," Lila says, and orders her entrée. The rest of us follow suit, then clink glasses when Joe leaves. "These drinks are strong!"

"I know. I'm only allowed to have one," I reply. Dinner is full of laughs, awesome food, and lots of flirting with Joe, who takes it all in stride. When it's time to leave, night has fallen over New Orleans. The air has cooled comfortably, and the walk over to Bourbon Street is lovely. We find a fun club with a DJ, claim a large table, and settle in for a night of dancing and laughter.

And lots of drinks.

"To good friends and shenanigans!" Charly announces, as we all hold our drinks in the air and take a sip. "Let's dance!"

Gabby and Lila join her, just as a beautiful young woman approaches the table. Gabby hugs her, tosses her purse on the chair next to mine, and pulls her with them to the floor.

"That must be Cindy," I say to Van, as we watch the girls dance on the mostly empty dance floor.

"Yep," Van says with a nod. "She's a nice girl. Kind of slutty, but nice."

That makes me smirk, just as I've taken a drink of my lemon drop, and I clamp my hand over my mouth so I don't spew it everywhere. "Van!"

"It's true," she says with a laugh. "I'm so glad you're here."

"Me too. How are you feeling? Really?"

"Much better." She smiles, and when I would question her further, she shakes her head. "Let's not talk about it tonight, okay? Let's just have fun."

"Okay," I agree. She deserves this fun night. "Although, now that I have you alone, can we talk business for a minute?"

"Sure."

"I have the PI looking into some things, but he still hasn't gotten back to me. I'm a bit concerned about Mr. Rudolph."

"Why? Has something happened?"

"It's all circumstantial," I reply with frustration and sip my drink. "I discovered that all of the transfers were made at about the same time of day. Less than an hour before he typically leaves for the day. And Van? He leaves super early, like around 1:30, almost every day. I do the majority of the work he should be doing. What's up with that?"

"I should have told you, and it didn't occur to me," Savannah says. "His daughter is very sick. She's been in the Children's Hospital for a while, and that's where he goes every afternoon."

"Oh, that's horrible."

"He's a nice man. He's been with our company for longer than a decade."

"But, if his daughter is so sick, he has medical bills to pay. This doesn't make him look any more innocent."

But Savannah shakes her head adamantly. "No, we have excellent insurance, and anything they don't cover, Eli is picking up. We take care of our own, Kate. Mr. Rudolph's daughter is getting excellent care, and he has no out of pocket expenses for it. It wouldn't make sense for him to skim money. He's still making the same salary, despite needing to be gone so much."

"Geez, remind me to work for you guys from now on," I say with some surprise. "That's very generous."

"If you're loyal to your employees, they'll be loyal to you. That's what Daddy always used to say."

"Makes sense," I reply, and chew my lip as I think over this new information. It still doesn't add up.

"Oh, hello, Kate."

I glance up in surprise to find Hilary standing by our table, a wide grin on her face. She's looking between me and Van, and I cringe inwardly.

*Crap. How am I going to play this off?*

"Hi, Hilary. Do you know Savannah?"

"Of course. Hello, Ms. Boudreaux."

"When we're not in the office, I'm Savannah," she replies, and smiles at Hilary.

"Van and I went to college together," I say, hoping that Hilary won't ask any questions, and wondering just how long she was standing nearby, listening to our conversation.

"I see. It's not what you know, it's who you know, right?"

I tilt my head, but before I can say anything further, the others return from the dance floor.

"Hi, I'm Lila." Lila holds her hand out to Hilary, who shakes it and continues to smile. "Hilary."

Introductions are made, and Hilary is invited to join us, and rather than decline, like I was hoping she'd do, she takes a seat and settles in across from me.

*Darn it.*

Another round of drinks is delivered, and suddenly a tall, handsome man is standing next to Charly, inviting her to dance.

"Darling, I'm a nightmare dressed like a daydream. Trust me, you don't want a piece of this." She pats him on the cheek and the man walks away, a look of pure confusion on his face.

"I wonder if he's confused because he got shot down, or if he's never listened to Taylor Swift before?" I ask.

"To Taylor Swift," Gabby says, holding her glass high. "For giving us fantastic one-liners for years."

"The girl writes some great ones," Lila agrees. "Oh! Fun drinking game. Every time someone uses a Taylor line in conversation, we take a drink."

"You're on!" Gabby says.

"This is so fun!" Cindy agrees, and we all drink in honor of the daydream line.

"Let's dance some more," Gabby says.

"Everything will be alright if we just keep dancing like we're twenty-two," Cindy says, we all drink, and then hit the dance floor while Pitbull and Ke$ha sing about Timber.

Charly and Van stay behind and are approached several times by cute men, and when the men leave after being shot down, they drink.

I wonder what lyrics they just used.

When we're all back at the table, our minds a little fuzzier, Hilary sits back in her seat and nudges her head to the side, indicating that I should look. "Three o'clock," she says.

"Which one? The bald one?" I ask.

"Fuck no, the one with the tattoo sleeve," she replies.

"Ah, I see him. Is that Mr. Starbucks?" I ask. "Louis?"

"Yes." She grins when Louis cocks his brow at her and shrugs a shoulder like, *you wanna?* "Looks like I'm getting lucky tonight, ladies."

"Lucky bitch," Gabby says with a frown, just as a waitress sets a basket of peanuts right in front of me, which Van quickly picks up and places at the other end of the table.

"You don't like peanuts?" Gabby asks.

"I'm allergic," I reply and shrug.

"Remember that time in college when you accidentally ate some and your face got all swollen? It was horrific," Van says with a dramatic shiver.

"Okay, back to me," Gabby says impatiently. "Do you know how long it's been since I got laid? *Years.*"

"Good Lord," Lila says in sympathy. "Honey, we can fix that. Like, right now."

"Oops! I'm out! Thanks for the drinks, guys." Hilary jumps up and scrambles over to Louis, who has just stood and paid his own tab, then they leave together with his tongue down her throat.

"She seems kind of fun," Charly says thoughtfully and sips her drink.

"I don't like her," Lila says with a shake of the head.

"Why?" I ask.

"I don't know. Just something about her."

"Anyway, back to me," Gabby says primly. "I haven't gotten laid in forever."

Just as the words leave her mouth, a shorter man, in his mid-thirties approaches her, leans in and says, "Why don't you let me help you out with that, sugar?"

Gabby blinks at him for a moment, then says, "I knew you were trouble when you walked in."

"Huh?" he asks in confusion as we all laugh, raise our glasses in salute, and drink.

"That means no," Van says helpfully, and the guy saunters away, shaking his head.

"Come on, Gabby," Lila says, "Why you gotta be so mean?"

More drinks.

"That was creepy," Gabby says.

"It's okay, I'm not getting laid either," Charly says. "It's been longer than a minute."

"You could always call Ryan," Van says with a smug smile. "He'd do you in a hot second."

"We are never, ever getting back together. Like, ever," Charly says, and we all laugh and drink.

Damn, these drinks are good. And strong. Am I still drinking lemon drops? I don't even know.

Maybe.

"But he was good in the sack," Charly clarifies. "And he did this thing with his tongue—"

"Stop," Eli says as he walks up to the table. "I don't need to know what any man does to you with his tongue."

"Why are you here?" Van demands. "It's *girls'* night out. Only girls."

"Ah, shake it off, Vanny," Gabby says, prompting us all to drink. "Declan's right behind him."

"Hi, Eli," Cindy says from next to me. She's been very quiet all evening, listening, laughing, and now that Eli's here, she's chatty?

I look between her and Eli, and frown.

"Have you fucked her?" I ask, probably way too loudly, but once I'm this drunk, I can't stop the words.

Damn words.

Cindy blinks rapidly, but Eli doesn't react at all. No frown. No denial.

*Nada.*

"Did you just say fuck?" Savannah asks in surprise.

"Yeah. I know, it's new. Eli's been teaching me."

"He's teaching you to say fuck?" Lila asks. "That's cool. Way to go, Eli."

He's watching me with hot eyes, but he's not giving anything away. He won't answer me.

Which, of course, means yes.

I turn my blurry gaze back to young, perky, skinny, perfect-skinned Cindy. "Was loving him like red?" I ask, and we all drink.

"It was fire-engine red," she confirms, and I kind of want to smack the hell out of her.

"Uh," Lila says, but Declan interrupts.

"Why are you all using Taylor Swift lyrics?"

"New drinking game," I say. "If we use the lyrics in conversation, we drink."

"We've been using a lot of them," Gabby says sloppily. "It's fun."

"Do you guys want a drink?" I ask them and signal for the waitress. "You should play."

"No, we're your drivers," Eli says. His jaw ticks, just a bit, and I think maybe he's mad at me, but I don't care.

I didn't fuck Cindy.

"No drinks for them," Van says to the waitress. "But another round for us."

"So, does that mean you're not ready to go home?" Declan asks with a laugh.

"Are you guys going all the way back to the inn tonight?" I ask Van and Gabby.

"No, we're staying at Mama's. She's at the inn with Sam and the guests."

"Cool."

"Eli, will you please give me a ride home?" Cindy asks, and bats her eyes at the man who's been spending every night in *my* bed, but before I can curl my hand into a claw and tear her fake-eyelashed eyes out, Declan speaks up.

"I get that honor, *cher*."

Eli is watching me.

*Eli is watching me.*

I grin and stand, make sure I'm steady on my feet, and say, "Excuse me."

"Where are you going?" Eli asks.

"Over there. Alone."

I nod decisively, walk to the bar, and get there just in time. My feet are slow. I'm glad I didn't wear heels.

"Hi there," the tall man next to me says. He's hot. Both of him.

"Hi."

"Having a good time?" he asks.

"Yes." I blink, and then exclaim, "I know you!"

"You do?"

"Yes! You were on the plane with Lila yesterday. Asher?"

"That's right." He shakes my hand and grins. "Is Lila with you this evening?"

"Yep. She's my BFF. We drink together. One time, in college, we made out, but it was no biggie."

"Okay," he laughs.

"You didn't ask her for her number," I accuse him, and poke my finger in his chest. He looks down at it.

"You just assaulted an officer."

"I did?" *Oh, crap.*

"Yes. I might have to arrest you."

"With handcuffs?"

"Would you like me to arrest you with handcuffs?"

"Hell to the yes!"

"Kate?" Eli's voice is cold and hard, and I'm sure he looks all scary and stuff.

"I'm talking to the hot Asher," I inform him. "I assaulted him, and he's a cop, and he's going to put me in handcuffs."

"No, I don't believe he will."

Asher laughs. "There's nothing going on here, man."

"Come see Lila!" I take his hand and lead him past Eli, who I glare at, because…*Cindy*, and am surprised to find that Gabby, Van, Charly, and slutty Cindy are all gone. "Where did everyone go?"

"Declan took them home," Lila says, and then her eyes go wide when she sees Asher. "Hi."

"We meet again," Asher says with a smile. He's super handsome, with dark hair and blue eyes and a great smile that's just a little crooked. Total hottie. I give her a thumbs up behind his back and sit down.

Eli joins me, lays his arm across the back of my chair and leans in to say in my ear, "We will talk later."

"About you fucking that young harlot?"

His eyes narrow. Yep, totally pissed.

"Among other things."

"Whatever," I say, and wave him off as if it doesn't matter. "You're not mine, Eli. Fuck whomever you please. There, there's a girl giving you the googly eyes right over there."

"Enough." His voice is cold and firm, and now he is glaring at me. I turn away and smile when I see that Asher and Lila have their heads together, chatting.

"So, I'm Kate," I say and hold my hand out to Asher, who shakes it with a smile. "But, I'm not telling you my last name, in case you really do want to arrest me."

"Her name is Mary Katherine O'Shaughnessy," Lila says. "Do you want her social security number?"

"How do you know my social security number?"

"I'm your person. If something happens to you, I have to know all your shit. Just like you know mine."

"Oh, right. She's my person," I inform Eli, before I remember that I'm mad at him.

Even though being mad at him is stupid.

"Kate tells me that you and she had a thing going in college," Asher says with a wink to me.

"We totally did," Lila agrees. "You know how crazy college kids are."

"The threesome only happened one time," I add, and the *look* passes between Lila and me. You know, the one that BFF's understand that says, *play along.*

"And we decided that we much preferred lesbian sex when it didn't involve a man," Lila says.

"Makes sense," Asher says thoughtfully, and I hear a noise beside me. It's Eli.

Laughing his ass off.

"Do you find threesomes funny?" I ask him.

"They can be," he says, and wipes his eyes. "But I'm still laughing at your name. Mary Katherine? Really?"

"What's wrong with my name?"

"It is kind of funny," Lila says.

"Is that why Dec calls you Superstar?" Eli asks. "Because of Mary Katherine Gallagher on SNL?"

"Yes." He's totally killing my buzz.

"Fuck, that's funny," Eli says.

"That part is super funny," Lila agrees.

"Okay, it's kind of funny," I say. My buzz is dying, it's getting late, and now all I can think about is going to bed. "Will you please take me home?"

"Of course, *cher*." Eli kisses my cheek and stands.

"Coming?" I ask Lila, who laughs at something Asher said that I couldn't hear.

"I'm gonna have Asher take me home," she says and smiles.

"Atta girl," I say and high five her. I fish the key to my loft out of my small purse and hand it to her. "I brought the extra key for you. See you tomorrow."

Then I point at Asher and make my serious face. "And, listen up, buddy. If you hurt her, I don't care if you really are a cop, I'll make your life hell. Okay?"

"Okay." He nods sincerely, and I back away.

"Okay then."

Eli leads me outside into the fresh, not-so-fresh, Bourbon Street air.

"Did you bring your car?" I ask. "'Cause it's not far. We can walk."

"We will drive, *cher*."

He leads me to the car, gets me settled the way he always does, which always makes me feel special, then climbs in the other side.

"I'm not special," I sigh, surprised when the words actually come out instead of stay in my head where they belong.

"What are you talking about?"

"Nothing." I shake my head, sober enough to know that I do *not* want to repeat that. "Are you really not interested in the threesome story?"

"Oh, I'm interested. I'm a man, Kate."

"Yes, you are."

"Okay, tell me."

"It was fun," I begin and smile at him. How long should I let this story go? "I mean, it's hard to say no to any of you Boudreaux brothers, and in college, Declan was *hot*. Look at him now, he's still hot, but back then, holy crap."

"Stop." He brakes in front of our building and turns to face me in the seat. "Are you telling me that you and Lila fucked my brother?"

"Well—"

"Because, if you are, you're also telling me that you lied to me when you told me that you'd never been with Declan."

I frown. "Eli, it was a joke. We never did a threesome. We never even had lesbian sex. We kissed once, when we were drunk. I think Declan saw that, I'm not sure."

He shakes his head and pushes out of the car, and I follow.

"Seriously, Eli. I won't curse because of the Catholic guilt. Do you honestly think I'd have a *threesome*?"

He laughs and meets me on the sidewalk.

"That's not the part that made you mad," I realize. "It was the *who*."

He shrugs.

"Why does the thought of me being intimate with Declan make you so mad?" I ask softly and cup his face.

"It's not rational," he says and kisses my forehead. "But it's probably because he's my brother, and I've laid a claim on you, and the thought of him seeing your body, being inside you, loving you, is completely out of the question."

"Well, it was a joke."

He takes my hand and leads me inside. I'm still a bit wobbly on my feet, so he wraps his arm around my waist.

"Now." He helps me out of my shoes. "Let's talk about Cindy."

"Oh." I make the *I just ate something disgusting* face and sag my shoulders. "I don't want to."

"I do."

"Can't we just have sex?" I ask and tug his white T-shirt out of his jeans, then glide my hands over his hard abdomen. "I love your stomach."

"It was one night, Kate."

"I don't care."

"It was a mistake. She's much younger than me, and Gabby's friend, but we were drunk, and it just happened."

"I don't care, Eli." But I do. I so do. I walk away from him and take a deep breath. "Okay, I don't lie. Yes, I care. I *hate* it."

I turn back to him, and he's standing there, his hands in his pockets, watching me.

"Why?" he asks.

"I don't know. We've both been with other people, and we'll be with others again when this is done." His jaw ticks at that. "It's not rational to hate it, but I do. I don't want to think about you touching her, or anyone else. I don't want to think about some other bimbo seeing you naked, or touching you, or being intimate with you. Does that make me a crazy jealous fuck buddy? Probably. But that's the way it is."

"One," he says in a low voice as he advances toward me. "You are not now, nor have you ever been, my *fuck buddy.* That's disrespectful to both of us, and I won't have that."

I frown, but he holds his hand up, stopping any words that might have come out.

"Two, I agree. I know you were no virgin when I met you, but I don't want to think about your partners. Nor do I want to think about you with anyone after me. Because this is just between you and me, Kate.

"And three," he whispers as he stops just inches in front of me. I can feel the heat from his body; I can smell his shampoo.

*I want him to touch me.*

"Three, all I can see, all I can think about, is *you.* I want you. You don't just cross my mind once in a while, you live in it."

My eyes widen as I watch him carefully, completely sober now. He's still not touching me.

"We said this would only last for as long as you're here. Only us. No one else, and damn it, Kate, that hasn't changed for me."

"Me too," I whisper. "Eli?"

"Yes."

"I really need you to touch me now."

He takes a deep breath, his hands flexing in and out of fists at his sides, his eyes traveling from my eyes to my lips and back again.

"I want you," I whisper.

He backs me up to the wall, and finally presses his body to mine, takes my face in his hands, and plants his lips on mine, kissing, nibbling, devouring me in the most delicious way. This man can kiss like no one I've ever met.

He kisses like it's his damn *job.*

His hands skim down my sides as he slides my dress down until it's magically pooled at my feet, and I'm standing before him in a black strapless bra and black thong.

"Fuck, Kate."

"Yes, fuck Kate," I agree with a grin, but when his eyes find mine, they aren't laughing. "What is it?"

He shakes his head and kisses me again, and his hand dives under the scrap of lace to cup my pussy in his hand.

"This?" He pushes two fingers inside me, and I'm so wet they glide in effortlessly. "This is mine, Kate. Do you understand?"

I nod and bite his lip, and cry out when he presses the flat of his palm against my clit and makes me come, right here, this fast, against the wall. His whiskey eyes are watching as I cry out.

"That's right, *cher*. Mine." He pulls his hand out, lifts me, and carries me up the stairs to the bedroom. Before I know what's happening, he's discarded my underwear, stripped out of his own clothes, and joins me on the bed.

Just when I think he's going to spread my legs and slide inside, he flips me over, presses my legs together, straddles them and slides his cock inside me, with my thighs pressed together and my ass just barely in the air.

And, holy hell if it's not the best thing *ever*.

Like, *ever*.

"Oh, my God," I groan. I can't move much with him pressing me into the mattress, holding me down with his body, and in this position, his cock feels even bigger, and hits that amazing spot every single damn time he pushes inside me.

"What are you feeling?" he asks, out of breath.

"You," I reply.

"More."

"I can feel the head of your cock pushing on my spot. I can feel your hands on my hips, holding me down. Your legs on my thighs. Oh, yeah, right there."

"Good girl," he murmurs, and slides his hand up my spine and into my hair, then grips my hair at the scalp, so there's no slack, and pulls.

Hard.

"Shit, yes," I moan.

"You like to have your hair pulled, Kate?"

"I guess so."

"You guess?"

"This is new."

"No one's ever pulled your hair?"

"Not like this."

He chuckles and pulls just a touch harder and begins to seriously fuck me. Hard. His hips slap against my ass, and I feel the most amazing orgasm working its way through me.

"Eli!"

"Say it again."

"Eli. I'm gonna come."

"Come, baby." He releases my hair, leans over and bites my neck, near my shoulder, and that's it. It's over. I come hard and long, clenching him tightly and crying out.

"Fuck," he growls and follows me, grinding into me as he comes, then collapses next to me. "Mine."

# CHAPTER 17

## ~KATE~

"**G**ood morning," he whispers in my ear. I'm on my stomach, my arms under my pillow. I can feel him against my side, rubbing my bare back with the flat of his hand, kissing my cheek, and I want to just stay, right here, forever.

"Mm," I reply.

"Open your eyes," he says. I can hear the smile in his voice.

"Mm mm," I reply and frown, making him chuckle.

"For me?" He kisses my cheek again and cups my ass in his hand, then drags that amazing hand back up my spine and brushes my hair off my back, so he can kiss my neck and shoulder.

I'm awake.

"Your skin is so soft," he murmurs, dragging his lips across my shoulder. "I love your freckles."

"My mother calls them angel kisses. Every time an angel kissed me in heaven before I came to her, I got a freckle." I smile and suddenly miss my ma. I manage to get one eye open and smile at a rumpled Eli lying next to me, his head braced in his hand as his fingers travel over my skin. He's smiling softly at me.

"Good morning," he says.

"Good morning," I reply. "What time is it?"

"Don't worry about it." He kisses my cheek again, and I close my eye. I feel him move around, and then hear the shutter on his phone.

"Did you seriously just take a picture of me?" I ask, and open my eye again to glare at him.

"I did," he replies. "You look beautiful in the morning."

*He's such a damn charmer.*

I quickly pull his phone from his fingers and turn over, scoot up against him, and hold the phone out to take a selfie of the two of us.

"Morning selfie," I announce, and we both smile at the phone. I snap the picture, but before I lower it, he kisses my cheek, so I snap that too.

"Keep the phone up," he whispers, and turns my face to his, kissing my lips.

I snap that one as well.

"Kissing selfies," I whisper and he kisses my nose. "You're sweet in the morning." I set his phone aside and turn to snuggle in his arms, press my face against his solid, muscular chest, and take a long, deep breath when he closes his arms around me and holds me close.

"I'm not sweet, *cher.*"

"Mmm hmm," I reply and rub my nose against him. "Sure you're not. You smell good."

He chuckles and kisses my head.

"Your hair smells good."

"It's the new shampoo I bought downstairs," I reply.

"I like it."

I sigh and could definitely fall back to sleep right here, in Eli's arms, but I have a feeling we need to get up and out the door to work.

"Seriously, what time is it?"

"After seven," he replies.

"What?" I pull back and try to get out of bed, but he tugs me effortlessly back into his arms. "Eli, we have to get up."

"Five more minutes."

"I don't have five minutes to give you."

"Yes, you do." He hugs me again, rubs his hands down my back and kisses my forehead. "Let me just enjoy having you in my arms for five more minutes."

"Well, it does feel good," I concede, and snuggle against him.

"Nothing feels this good," he whispers, making me grin. I don't care what he says, in these quiet moments, he's very sweet.

If I'm not careful, I could tumble right over into love with him.

It's a good thing I'm the very definition of careful.

"Eli?"

"Hmm."

"I don't want to, but I have to get up."

"I know." He sighs and loosens his grip on me. "Thanks for the extra five minutes."

I grin and roll away, then gasp when I see the time. "It's almost eight!"

"Yes."

"You said it was after seven."

"It is."

I glare at him, but he just stares at me with humor-filled eyes.

"Oversleeping on a Monday means the rest of the week is going to be crappy," I announce, as I stomp into the bathroom, pull a brush through my hair, then tie it back and stare in despair at my makeup-free face in the mirror. "I don't have time for makeup."

"You're beautiful without it," Eli says calmly, as he hands me a steaming mug of coffee and kisses my cheek. "Stop freaking out."

"I don't want to be late," I reply, before gratefully sipping the coffee. "Where did this coffee come from?"

"Timer on the pot," he replies. "You're fine, *cher.*" He wraps his arms around my waist and finds my gaze in the mirror as he kisses my cheek. "You didn't sleep that late."

I lean back against him and enjoy the feel of his chest pressed against my back for just a moment before slipping out of his arms and reaching for my makeup.

And then my phone rings.

Of course.

"Rhys is FaceTiming me at 8:00 on a Monday morning?" I ask with a frown. Eli just shrugs and saunters into his closet to dress. "Rhys, I can't talk now."

"Just give me ten," he replies, and I can tell just by looking at him that something is very wrong.

"What is it?"

"You didn't watch last night's game?"

"No," I reply guiltily. "Sorry."

"I'm hurt." The sarcasm is thick. "I thought you watched every game."

"Right. Of course I do. What's wrong?"

"I got hurt." He swallows and winces as he shifts in his seat. "Tore my rotator cuff."

"WHAT? Oh, my God, Rhys—"

"I'm fine."

I look into his green eyes, and I know he's lying. "No, you're not."

He sighs and pinches the bridge of his nose. "I'll need surgery. I'm out for the season."

"Rhys." I wish I could hug him. Baseball has been his life since he was five years old. It's been the one constant in his life, even after his parents died.

It's his life.

"I'm going home to Denver," he continues. "I'll see the doctors there, do some therapy. I'll be fine."

"Rhys."

He sighs again, and finally he says, "Careers end because of this, Kate. I can't lose baseball. I'm only twenty-eight, for Godsake."

"I'll be home in a couple weeks, tops, and I'll take care of you."

He smirks. "I don't need a mommy."

"Maybe I just need to be there to be helpful."

He clears his throat and talks to someone else in the room. "I have to go. I wanted to fill you in."

"Have you called Ma and Da?" I ask.

"They're next. Love you. See you soon."

"Love you too."

"He'll be okay," Eli says from the doorway, fastening the cuff-links on his shirt. I nod and set the phone aside, quickly brush on some mascara and lip gloss, resigned that this is as good as it gets today, and walk out of the bathroom.

"I know. Let me get some clothes on, and let's go."

"Hi Kate, this is Adam, the private investigator you spoke with last week?"

"Yes! Please tell me you've found something." I shift in my chair, gathering papers and a pen to make notes with.

"I have; I just hope it's something you can use. You mentioned that there is no employee named H. Peters at Bayou Industries, in any department."

"That's right."

"I had to do some digging into each of the employees and their families, and let me tell you, there are a lot of people who work there."

"Tell me about it."

"You have an employee there named Gerald Rudolph. Didn't get to him until I hit the 'R's." All of the hair on my body stands on end.

"We do."

"His wife's maiden name is Hannah Peters."

*Bingo.* I shimmy in my seat, doing the happy dance.

"Thanks, Adam. Can you email that information to me?"

"Sure thing. There is other info in the reports too, including a description of the woman who picks up the checks."

"Great job, Adam. Thanks again." I immediately call Eli's office and sigh in relief when he answers. "I need a meeting with you, Beau, and Van ASAP."

"What's wrong?"

"Nothing. We're about to wrap this case up."

There's a long pause, and then, "Be in my office in thirty minutes."

"But Van is at the inn."

"She's at the doctor for a check up. She'll be here."

He hangs up, and I sit for a second and frown at the phone. Why did he sound so...*cold*? Solving this case is what I was hired to do. He should be happy that it's almost over.

I use the next twenty minutes to print out all of the information I've gathered, along with the email from Adam when it comes through.

The elevator seems to take forever. This is the part of my job that I love so much. The part when I get to sit before those who hired me and tell them who and how. The satisfaction of knowing that the job was done well. My whole body is humming with excitement when I walk into Eli's office and see that Beau and Van are already there.

"Thanks for meeting with me."

The door closes behind me, and I sit in a seat between Beau and Van, facing Eli.

"Who is it?" Beau asks immediately.

"Gerald Rudolph."

"Impossible," Eli says calmly.

"No, it's not impossible." I explain the suspicions I brought to Van's attention over the weekend, and then show them the evidence that Adam sent over. "His wife's maiden name is Peters. Hannah Peters. Every transfer went to Western Union to an H. Peters."

Savannah is shaking her head. "This doesn't make sense. He has no reason to steal, Kate. He makes a very good salary. He's been with us for a very long time."

"That's how it usually is," I reply gently. "The person responsible is typically someone that is trusted. Loyal, even."

"I guess that people make poor decisions when they have a lot of stress in their lives," Savannah says slowly.

"Thank you, Kate," Eli says and stands, showing me the door. He's suddenly a stranger, and I don't like it. "We will go over this evidence, and discuss, and let you know if we need anything further."

"Are you okay?" I ask, frowning at him.

"Of course."

I stop in the middle of the office and stare at him. Finally, he simply leans in and whispers in my ear. "We will talk later. Have a good afternoon."

And with that, I'm shown through the door.

I return to my office and decide to make additional copies of all of the reports I just gave to Eli.

Why was he so cold just now? Not four hours ago he was holding me tight, being so sweet, so tender. Treating me like I'm special and sexy and someone he enjoys being with.

And, in his office, he was distant, as if he's never seen me naked or been inside me.

How can men do that? Go from hot to cold in a matter of hours?

Is he mad that I solved the case and the person responsible is someone he likes?

*Or maybe...*

I sit back and stare at the wall as it occurs to me that me solving this case means that I'm leaving. My time here is almost over.

And that just makes me sad.

I've loved spending time with Savannah and Declan again. I didn't realize how much I missed them until I had them available to me all the time.

But, most of all, I've enjoyed Eli. He's amazing sexually, and has given me a new confidence physically that I'll always be indebted to him for. He showed me how a woman is supposed to feel when she's with a man, in and out of bed. He makes me laugh. He turns my body inside out and makes it sing.

And I suspect that I wasn't as careful as I thought I was, and I've already done the irresponsible thing and fallen in love with him.

*I don't do love.*

He has been honest with me from the beginning. He's attracted to me, enjoys me, but he doesn't love me.

And I *am* leaving. I have a life in Denver. A job that sends me all over the country. I need to make sure that Rhys is going to be okay.

I have responsibilities.

"Are you okay?" Hilary asks, as she walks into my office, pulling me out of my daydream.

"Hi," I reply with a grin. "I'm okay. Just a lot on my mind."

"Wanna talk about it?"

I shake my head no with a sigh.

"I'm your friend, you know. You can always talk to me about stuff."

"I appreciate that. How was your weekend with Louis?"

"Even better than the last time," she says with a wink, and sits in the chair in front of my desk. She sets a to-go container on my desk. "I brought you lunch."

"You didn't have to do that. Is it lunch time already?"

"It is," she confirms. "I tried a new soup recipe and had a ton left over. This is why I rarely cook for myself. Cooking for one is just a waste of food."

"I hear you. Thanks." I take the lid off and sniff it. She even warmed it up for me. "Smells great. So, what else did you do this weekend?"

"I took Louis shopping. I needed some new shoes." She lifts her leg and shows me a gorgeous pair of sling-back Choos. "And I might have needed a new bag too," she says with a laugh, and shows off a gorgeous black Gucci handbag.

*Wow.*

"Those are gorgeous," I agree.

"Your friends are fun," she says with a smile, changing the subject.

"I know." I swallow, but keep my face impassive. This is the job. Lying. I'm excellent at it when I need to be.

"I didn't realize you were so close to the Boudreaux family."

"I wouldn't say we're super close," I reply easily. "I did go to college with Savannah, and when I decided to move down here, she offered me a job."

"Convenient."

*So, Hilary has a bitchy side.*

"I'm going to work through lunch," I say, ready for Hilary and her crappy attitude to leave. "Thanks again for the soup."

"Anytime." She stands and heads for the door. "I'm out for the day."

"Oh?" I check the clock. "At noon?"

"I have to go to the doctor. Yearly fun stuff." She wrinkles her nose, then waves and saunters off.

And I can't help but feel like I'm missing something.

I open the soup and take a bite and think back on the past few weeks with Hilary. She has more experience than me in this position, but I know she doesn't make enough money to buy close to five thousand dollars worth of shoes and handbags.

Unless she has a ton of credit card debt.

Which, she might. I mean, not everyone manages money well.

But...

One thing's for sure, she makes a heck of a soup. I continue slurping it up, eating it quickly. I was hungrier than I thought.

*Where there's a will, there's a way.* Hilary's statement the day we met for happy hour when I asked how she could afford her new car passes through my mind.

New shoes and bags.

Leaving early from work.

*And she was at the club when I was talking to Savannah about my suspicions regarding Mr. Rudolph!*

I wonder how much she really heard?

Having eaten all of the soup, I close the lid and come to a complete and utter stop. Written on the top in marker is **H. Peters**on, with the 'on' almost completely worn off.

H. Peters.

It can't be!

I scratch my neck, which has just begun to itch, and log into the employee time clock program to bring up Hilary's logs, print them out, and compare her comings and goings to the dates of the transfers.

Sure enough, every day there was a transfer, Hilary clocked out right around 2:00. Not long after Mr. Rudolph would have left for the hospital.

I page down Adam's email, looking for the description of the woman who picks up the checks.

*A woman in her mid-thirties. Blonde hair, average height, average build.*

Hilary.

I swallow, but realize my tongue suddenly feels thick. My throat itches. Cheeks are tingly.

"Shit!" I stare down at the empty bowl and my heartbeat triples. It's getting harder to breathe. My lips feel funny.

"Kate?" Mr. Rudolph is standing in the doorway, frowning. "Are you okay? Your face looks swollen."

I shake my head and pull my purse out of my drawer, looking for my EPI pen, but I don't have it. "Peanuts."

But my mouth is so swollen, it sounds like *veanuth.*

"What?"

"Ate peanuts," I repeat and point to the bowl. "Ambulance."

I'm struggling for breath now. My eyes are swelling shut.

*I'm going to die. The bitch killed me!*

"I need an ambulance," I hear Mr. Rudolph say. "She has an allergy and can't breathe."

And suddenly, everything goes black.

~

"KATE?"

Someone is yelling at me. I try to open my eyes, but can't. Everything is dark. My throat hurts.

"Kate, did you eat peanuts?" The same voice keeps shouting at me. I can only nod.

"It's a nut allergy," I hear another person say, as I'm being wheeled in a bed. "Gave her an EPI shot, and got her airway open."

"What's her name?"

"Kate O'Shaughnessy," someone says. I don't recognize any of the voices. Where is Eli? I want Eli. I can't see. I touch my face, and it feels totally foreign. "Here's her ID and insurance card."

*Someone has been going through my purse.*

"Okay, guys, wheel her back to room nine."

I'm shuffled about, lifted onto a new bed, changed from my clothes to a gown. All blind. My tongue is too big for my mouth. I itch *everywhere*.

"You can't talk to me, can you, Kate?"

I shake my head.

"I'm Dr. Coggin," the kind man says. "Just nod yes or no, okay?"

I nod yes.

"I hear you have an allergy to peanuts, and ate some?"

I nod.

"Do you know how much?"

I shake my head no.

"Are you itchy? Warm?"

I nod vigorously.

"Still having problems breathing?"

I hold my hand up and tilt it, as if to say *so-so*.

"Okay, we are going to give you some Benadryl and steroids in an IV, and it's going to make you sleepy, but it should calm all of this down. If you have visitors, can they come back to see you?"

I nod and lie back, frustrated that I can't talk or swallow. I'm quite sure I'm a drooling mess.

I want to cry, but my eyes are so swollen, my tear ducts don't work.

There's a prick in the back of my hand. "I'm putting in your IV, Kate. I'm your nurse, Mona."

I nod.

"Because this Benadryl is going directly into your bloodstream, you'll get sleepy pretty fast."

*Good.* Maybe I'll wake up half-way normal.

"Kate?"

My head turns at the sound of Savannah's voice. She takes my free hand in hers.

"Oh, my God, Katie, are you awake?"

I nod and squeeze her fingers, but the medicine is already making me tired. I need to tell her that it's all because of Hilary, but I still can't talk around my tongue, and now my body is feeling heavy from the drugs.

"Sleep, Kate," Van says. "You'll feel better when you wake up."

"Where's Eli?" I hear Beau ask Van as he also comes into my room.

"I don't know," Van responds. "We can't find him."

What does she mean they can't *find him*?

I moan, frustrated, but can't fight sleep as it slips over me.

# CHAPTER 18

## ĒLI~

"*L*ook, it's just government bureaucracy," Sal, the shipyard foreman, says in frustration. "It's their job to find these kinds of things."

"It's OSHA, Sal," I reply coldly. "I don't give a fuck if what you say is true, the bottom line is, you either fix that hydraulic system to their specifications, or they will shut down that whole line."

He shakes his head and paces his office in frustration.

"There's nothing wrong with it," he insists. "It's perfectly safe."

I raise an eyebrow. "Sal, you've been with us since I was a kid. I respect your opinion, and I'm not saying that it's *unsafe*. I am saying that it didn't pass the OSHA inspection, and it has to be fixed. I don't want to be called back down here for another ass-chewing by that inspector. You know the regulations. We operate within them, one hundred percent of the time. If you don't want to work that way, I'll find someone else who does."

"Are you threatening me?" He scowls and props his hands on his hips.

"No. I'm explaining what I expect to happen. Get it done. You have twenty-four hours."

I walk out without another word, frustrated that I was brought in on this in the first place. I've just spent three hours away from the office, where I have to fire a man who I've known almost half of my life.

*Fuck.* And have charges brought against him.

But not before I sit down with him, man-to-man, to ask him just exactly what in the ever loving fuck he was thinking.

Not to mention, now that the case is closed, Kate will be leaving.

And why does the thought of that make me want to punch a wall? I've known since the day I met her this was temporary. We've had fun. I've enjoyed her.

I'll enjoy women after her.

I stop next to my car and shake my head before opening the door and lowering myself inside.

The thought of other women does nothing for me except turn my stomach.

I pull my phone out of my pocket and frown when I realize the sound had been off. Four missed calls from Beau, all over two hours ago.

He can be damn annoying.

I punch the button for voice mail and pull out of the shipyard.

"Eli, Savannah and I are on the way to the hospital. Something's happened to Kate." My heart stills, then trips over. "I'm not sure what's happening. Where are you?"

The next message fifteen minutes later: "I'm almost to the hospital. Answer your fucking phone."

I floor the accelerator and try to call Beau, but it goes straight to voice mail, as does Savannah's phone.

What the fuck has happened to Kate? Panic sweeps through me, picturing her broken and hurt in a hospital bed. Sweet, loving Kate is the last person on this Earth that deserves to be hurt. She's so damn *good*.

Living in a world without her is incomprehensible, even if she's not mine.

And she can't ever be mine.

But she'd sure as fuck better be okay.

I find parking, run into the hospital and ask for Kate's room number, rushing away as soon as the numbers are out of the receptionist's mouth.

It seems to take forever to find Kate's room, and just as I walk through the door, I see Kate reach up to Beau standing next to her, place her hand on the back of his neck, and pull his ear down to her lips.

"Hey, wrong brother—"

Beau puts a finger up, stopping me. Savannah and Lila are listening closely.

"Go ahead, Kate. What is it?" he says softly.

"Hilary," we all hear her rasp. "Not Mr. Rudolph. She stole the money, gave me peanuts. I have proof."

We all gather around her. I grip her leg, thankful that she's alive, but fucking pissed at how swollen her beautiful face is. She looks like she went ten rounds with the devil himself.

"Enough for me to go have her arrested now?" Beau asks anxiously. Kate nods, and Beau kisses her forehead and leaves immediately, pulling his phone out of his pocket as he hurries out.

"What's happened?" I ask Savannah and Lila, as I take Beau's place next to Kate. Her hand is small and warm in mine. "Are you okay, *cher?*"

"Wanted you," she says.

"Don't talk," Lila says soothingly. "Someone, *Hilary*, slipped her peanuts. She's very allergic."

"We told Hilary that at girls' night out," Savannah adds with mutiny in her eyes. "That little bitch knew exactly what she was doing."

"Lunch," Kate adds.

"She brought you lunch?" Lila asks and Kate nods. I brush her hair off her forehead and cheeks, kissing her lightly. I can't stop touching her, reassuring myself that she's okay.

"Thank God for Mr. Rudolph," Savannah adds. "He walked in just as the reaction happened. Her airway closed up. He called the EMT's and they brought her here. She's been sleeping since I arrived, and her tongue is just now small enough for her to talk."

"I knew I didn't like that woman," Lila adds.

"Sleepy," Kate says.

"Sleep, baby," I whisper in her ear. She tightens her grip on my hand. "I'm right here. I'm not leaving. I'll be here when you wake up."

She nods and slips into sleep.

"I'm going to make that woman's life a living hell," I announce calmly.

"Good," Lila says. "I'm going to go call Rhys and her parents. I'll be back."

Lila leaves and Savannah leans back in her chair and watches me quietly for a long minute.

"You're in love with her."

"I love her so much I can't breathe," I admit, surprised. "I think I just figured that out."

"But you're still going to let her leave." It's not a question. I glance up and hold my sister's gaze for a moment, then look back at the sweet woman lying in this bed.

"I am," I reply quietly.

"Eli—"

"It's the way it should be. She deserves so much more than me, Van. I am a toxic, broken asshole."

"Well, the asshole part is true enough, but the rest? No, you're not, Eli. You're one of the best people I know."

I shake my head and kiss Kate's hand. "No, I'm not. I'm your brother. You're supposed to think that."

"No, you're wrong there," she replies. "But I'm not going to fight you on this today. It'll keep."

We sit in silence, watching Kate sleep. She's so still. Lila returns, and not long after, Declan. He looks as distraught as I feel when he lays his lips on her forehead and kisses her softly, whispering how sorry he is, how we all love her, that she's going to be okay.

Words *I* should have said.

"Love you too," she whispers to Dec and opens her eyes.

"You're awake?" Dec asks.

"Hard to sleep with you hanging on me," she says, making Dec laugh.

"May I please come in?" Mr. Rudolph is at the door, looking shy and uncomfortable. I stand and shake his hand.

"Thank you. For everything."

He nods and approaches the bed, smiling kindly at Kate. "I see that you're feeling better."

*Jesus, how bad did she look when they brought her in?*

"Getting there," she says. "Tongue is smaller." Her eyes fill with tears. "Owe you 'pology."

"No," he says, and covers her hand with his. "Beau filled me in. It never occurred to me to tell you about Serena. She's been sick a long time, and everyone in the office knows. I would have suspected me too."

"Thanks," Kate says, and closes her eyes, tired again.

"Get well quickly, sweet girl," he says, and stands to leave. "I need to get over to see Serena. Take care of Kate."

"How long are they keeping her?" I ask after Mr. Rudolph leaves.

"Just until tomorrow. They'd let her go today, but she had so many breathing problems, they want to continue the IV steroids to make sure she's in the clear." Lila's gaze never leaves Kate as she relays the information to me. "She scared the shit out of me."

"All of us," Declan says. "Is it true that she wasn't breathing when the paramedics got there?" he asks Van.

She simply nods.

*Hilary is going to wish she never stepped foot in Bayou Enterprises.*

~

IT'S LATE. The hospital is surprisingly quiet, with just the occasional sound of footsteps walking past Kate's door. She's been in and out of sleep all day, and I haven't moved.

I know she's going to be okay, but I can't make myself leave her side. I sent Savannah, Declan, and Lila home hours ago, promising them that I'd stay, and call if there was any change.

Now I just want her to wake up, which is utterly selfish because she needs to sleep and get well.

The swelling in her face has gone down. Now, just her lips are a little puffy, and her eyes look a little bruised. Every once in a while during sleep, she'll scratch her arm or her neck.

She's still itchy.

She has one hell of an allergy.

I lean in and whisper, so as not to wake her, but I have to say this out loud, while I still can.

"You are so special, Kate. So beautiful. I'm going to miss you every day. You made the man who's incapable of love fall in love with you." My throat tightens, and I stop talking. I simply bury my face in her neck and breathe her in, already missing what she brings to my life. The light. The laughter.

Already missing who I am because of her.

~

"WHAT ARE WE DOING TODAY?" Kate asks two days later. And what a difference two days make. The swelling is completely gone, and it seems that she's back to her old, energetic self.

"Sleep," I reply, and close my eyes beside her, goading her.

"No. No sleep."

"You need to rest."

"Eli, I'm fine. All recovered. You can even have sex with me and I won't die."

"That's not funny," I reply calmly and turn to face her. "You could have died."

"I didn't," she says, and cups my cheek in her hand. "I'm fine. And you've kept me in bed—*not* for the fun stuff, I might add—for two days."

"Fun stuff?" I ask and kiss her forehead. "You want fun stuff?"

"Yes."

"Not yet."

"Eli, my face swelled, not my...*other places.*"

I laugh. I can't help it. She's so fucking funny when it comes to the swearing.

"These places?" I ask and brush the backs of my knuckles over her nipple, making it stand at attention.

"Yes," she whispers and closes her eyes. "That's a good place."

"What about this place?" I ask and drag the same knuckles down her stomach to her navel, circling it softly, loving that fucking piercing.

"That doesn't suck."

I grin and kiss her collarbone. God, she's soft. And expressive.

She's addictive.

*How am I going to live without her?*

Because I will live without her.

But not today.

"And this?" I ask as my fingers drift down between her legs, lightly touching her warm skin. "What about this place, *cher?*"

"Best. Place. Ever." Her hips move, wanting me to press harder, deeper, but I hold back, barely tickling over her tiny pink pussy lips, watching in satisfaction as she squirms next to me. Her neck and cheeks pinken; her breath quickens. She grips the sheets at her hip opposite me and bites her lip. "That feels nice."

"Just nice, huh?"

*Oh, we can do a whole lot better than fucking* nice.

I kiss down her torso, lick the underside of her breasts, enjoying every gasp and moan that comes out of her delicious mouth. Her fingers find my hair and hold on tight as I nibble down her ribs, kiss a circle around her navel, then travel down between her legs. I spread her wide and growl when I see how wet she already is.

"You're so pink." I press a kiss to her pubis. "So wet." Her clit, making her gasp. "So sweet." I sweep my tongue through her folds, then pull back and look up into her shining green eyes. "I could do this all day."

"You'd kill me," she replies, and lets her head fall back as I grin and press a kiss to the delicate skin of her inner thigh, the crease where leg meets torso, then pay the same attention to the other side. "You *are* killing me."

"Just taking my time, *cher.*" It seems we always take it so damn fast, because I can't wait to be inside her, can't wait to feel her come apart at the seams. But this time, I want to enjoy every movement, every sigh, every moment. "You're quite fun, you know."

"I am?" She smiles down at me, decidedly happy with that compliment.

"You are." I lap at her now, from her pussy all the way to her clit and back down again. Her fingers tighten in my hair, pulling in the best way. She's sweet. Just a bit tangy.

Perfect.

"Eli, I want you inside me."

"I'll get there."

"No, really." I glance up at her tone. "This is *so good*, but I really want to feel you inside me. Please."

I kiss my way back up her delectable body, rest my hard cock against her folds, and prop myself on my elbows beside her head, careful to keep my weight off of her.

She takes my face in her hands and pulls me down to kiss her thoroughly, lapping at my lips, licking every drop of her own juices off of me, and if that isn't the sexiest fucking thing ever, I don't know what is.

I pull my hips back, and Kate reaches between us to wrap her little fingers around me, making my eyes fucking cross, then guides me inside her in one long, slow stroke.

"Oh, God," she whispers, her green eyes never leaving mine. "You always feel so good."

"It's all you, *cher,*" I reply.

She shakes her head and bites my lip. "It's *us.*"

I close my eyes and lean my forehead against hers, unable to keep from moving any longer. She squeezes around me with each thrust in the most amazing way, making my balls lift and tighten, my spine tingle.

I'm not going to last like this.

"Look at me," she says softly.

"Bossy thing, aren't you?" I say as my eyes find hers. She doesn't reply. She simply lifts her legs higher on my hips and clamps down, hard, her pussy rippling as she comes in waves.

She doesn't cry out. She just grips onto my arms and lifts her head off the bed, resting her forehead on my chest as she comes harder than I've ever felt her. I'm helpless to stop the orgasm that tears through me, also so damn strong, but quiet.

She lies back and smiles up at me, trying to catch her breath.

"That's the best medicine ever."

I grin. "You'll never hear me complain."

I brush loose tendrils of hair off her sweaty cheeks and kiss her forehead, her nose, and her lips. When I move to pull out, she holds me close. "Not yet."

I'd move the earth for her right now if I could.

Her fingertips glide up and down my back, to my ass, then up again lazily. "I have to go to the office today," she murmurs.

I frown. "I thought you were done."

"I need to put together the last of my reports, then I need to pack."

Her eyes are sad as she looks up at me, almost as though she's silently begging me to ask her to stay. "When are you leaving?" I ask instead.

"Day after tomorrow."

"I want to spend every minute with you."

She smiles, then shakes her head.

"You don't have to. We know this is finished, Eli. We can just cut it off."

"No, I don't want that." I kiss her lips softly. "I want to spend every minute with you that you're here. I'll take you to the airport myself."

"Why?"

I swallow hard and call myself a selfish fucking bastard, and a coward, when I say, "Because I'm not quite ready to say goodbye."

"And if I am?" she asks. I pull up so I can clearly look her in the eye.

"Are you?"

She bites her lip, thinking about her response, and then finally shakes her head quickly. "No."

"Okay then. When are we going to the office?"

"After you fuck me again."

She grins naughtily and squeezes my ass, and just like that, I'm hard again.

"You know what those filthy words to do me."

"No, what do they do?" she asks with wide, innocent eyes.

"This," I whisper against her lips as I begin moving inside her again. "I'll just keep reminding you until you figure it out."

"Maybe I'll stop using the dirty words."

"Oh, I think we'll make sure that doesn't happen."

～

"Here." I walk into Kate's bedroom and hand her a glass of lemonade. She's been working most of the afternoon, packing her things. Why I'm here watching, I have no idea. The only explanation I have is I've suddenly become a masochist.

Because this fucking hurts.

"Thanks." She grins, kisses me quickly, then returns to neatly folding her sexier than fuck underwear and placing them in a suitcase.

"I haven't seen these before." I retrieve a pair of leopard print boy shorts from the bag and hold them up. "I like these. Put them on."

"No." She laughs and snatches them out of my hand, refolds, and returns them to the case, right after I pull a purple, lacy thong out.

"Wow. I haven't seen this either." It's dangling from my index finger when she grabs it and glares at me as she folds and replaces it.

"Stop undoing everything I'm doing."

"I just want to know why you've been withholding sexy underwear from me. You know how much I love it."

"I haven't been withholding it," she laughs with a shake of the head, making her hair move about her shoulders.

My fingers itch to dive into that thick, soft hair.

So they do.

I comb my fingers through her hair and watch it fall back to her shoulders, then repeat the motion.

"I have a system," she informs me primly. "And you're messing it up."

"I am?"

"Yes."

She sighs and closes her eyes as my fingertips rub her scalp.

"That feels good."

With her eyes closed, I retrieve a sexy red nightie from the suitcase.

"And who, exactly, were you planning to wear this for?"

She gasps and steals the scrap of lace from my hand.

"Seriously. Stop touching all of my underwear."

"You don't mind when I take it off of you, *cher*."

"That's different." She sniffs, her nose in the air. "And I wasn't *planning* on wearing it for anyone."

"Wear it for me, before you go." The request is quiet. Sincere. She watches my eyes solemnly as she sets it aside.

"I can do that."

"You're good at taking orders," I comment with a grin. She narrows her eyes at me.

"I'm no one's submissive."

"Indeed," I agree, and run a finger down her cheek. "But I like that if I make a request, you're eager to comply."

"Why do I do that?" she asks with a frown. "Is that what got me into trouble with my ex-husband? I was too *easy*?"

"You didn't get into trouble with your ex-husband," I say, and take her face in my hands, making her look at me. "He was an asshole who didn't know a good thing when he had it. He doesn't know how to treat a woman, Kate. And wanting to please people you love isn't a bad thing, when it's done sincerely."

"Thanks," she whispers.

"So, you'll wear the sexier than fuck nightie?" I ask with a grin, lightening the mood again.

"We'll see," she says with a wink. "I don't want you to think I'm a sure thing."

"Oh, sugar, that ship has sailed." I laugh and pull her in for a hug, delighted with her. "You make me laugh."

"Do I make you want to pack things?" she asks, making my heart still at the reminder of her leaving. "Because I need to finish this and you're distracting me."

"You make me want to undress you," I reply, but she backs out of my reach.

"Oh, no." She points a finger at me and glares.

"You don't scare me."

"No hanky-panky. This has to get done."

"*Hanky-panky?*" I ask with a laugh. "What, exactly, is *hanky-panky?*"

She giggles and backs further away. "You know what it is. I have to get this done, Eli. I don't have time for shenanigans."

"Oh, there will be shenanigans, *cher.*" I slowly saunter toward her. She's run toward the balcony, caging herself in. "Admit it. You like the shenanigans."

"No. I don't." She giggles.

God, I love her giggle.

"You also like it when I get you naked."

"Stop it." Now she stands firm, her hands on her hips, as though she's a teacher and I'm an unruly student. "I'm serious, Eli. I have work to do."

I grin. "So do I."

# CHAPTER 19

## ~KATE~

"I never did ask you what happened with Asher." I'm chatting on the phone with Lila. "I was too busy looking like a blow fish."

"A lot happened with Asher," she says.

"Was there sex?" I ask, and throw the last of my things in my carry-on bag.

"Oh, indeed, friend. There was lots of sex."

"Was it good sex?" I grin and flop on the couch, wishing Lila was still here, rather than back in Denver.

"Maybe the best sex that has ever been had on this planet. Every time."

"*Every* time?"

"Every. Time."

"So, was there the exchange of phone numbers?"

There's a pause, and I sit up straight, stare at my phone, then, "Seriously? Lila!"

"I don't have time for a relationship."

"Who said anything about a relationship? Just call him up now and again have the best sex on the planet."

"Impossible," Eli says as he walks through the door. "We have the best sex on the planet."

I laugh and hold up my hand, signaling that I just need one more minute.

"He lives in Seattle, Kate," Lila says with a sigh. "I never go to Seattle."

"Maybe he goes to Denver," I suggest.

"I'm not going to be in Denver much longer either."

"You're not? Why?"

"Because, while I was in New Orleans, I had that interview with Tulane University, and I have a new job beginning this fall."

"Shut the front door!" I exclaim, and jump to my feet, dancing around the living room. "I'm so excited for you!"

"Thank you. So, I have enough to keep me occupied for now."

"It's not like being occupied by the best sex on the planet is a hardship," I remind her dryly.

"Seattle, Kate."

"Fine." I sigh. "I guess it doesn't matter anyway, since you didn't get his number."

"When do you come home?"

"Tomorrow." I bite my lip and glance back at Eli, who's sipping a bottle of water and leaning against the countertop, watching me. "I get in around noon."

"Want me to pick you up?"

"Sure."

"Okay, send me your itinerary. I'll see you tomorrow. Go enjoy your sexy business man. Have the second best sex on the planet."

"You're sick," I reply with a laugh. "Bye."

"How is Lila?" Eli asks and joins me in the living room.

"Good. She got the job at Tulane." I grin and stand on my tip-toes, so I can kiss him. He still has to bend down to meet my lips.

"Good for her." He cups my neck in his hands and takes the kiss deeper, in that way he does that makes my toes curl and my fingertips tingle.

The man can seriously kiss.

"What would you like to do this afternoon?" he asks.

"I want to take one more walk through the Quarter. It's so pretty this afternoon."

"Grab your hat," he instructs me, making me grin.

"Yes, sir."

"Don't sass me."

"No, sir."

He swats my butt. "Smart ass."

"Yes, sir." I tug my hat onto my head, grab my purse, and Eli leads me down the steps to the sidewalk.

"Which way?"

"I get to choose?"

"Of course." I stop on the sidewalk and take him in, standing so tall, his dark hair moving in the summer breeze, his sunglasses hiding his whiskey eyes. He has a little dark scruff on his face, and his lips are tipped in a half-smile, as if he finds me amusing. His body is perfectly comfortable in a white button-down and jeans, and despite having had him mere hours ago, I want to climb him.

"*Cher?*"

"Oh, what?" I shake my head and look up into his face.

"Where would you like to go?"

"Oh. Let's start in here." I lead the way into the amazing botanical shop beneath my flat. "I love the way it smells in here."

"After you." He holds the door for me, then follows me in, hanging back as I wander through the racks and tables of lotions, soaps, oils, and extracts. I saunter through, smelling the potions.

"Hi there," a woman with long, thick dark hair and bright, happy blue eyes says from the checkout counter. "Can I help you find anything?"

"No," I reply with a grin. "I've been staying upstairs, and I've wanted to stop in to look around. The smells that drift upstairs are delicious. I stopped in briefly one day to buy shampoo, which I love, but I didn't have time to browse."

"Well, I'm Mallory, the owner, and just let me know if I can answer any questions."

I nod and smile, and before I'm done, I've gathered more shampoo and conditioner, cucumber lotion for my eyes, lip balm, and an eye-pillow full of lavender.

Mallory rings me up and Eli pays before I can pull my wallet out of my purse, earning a glare from me.

"You're not paying for anything when you're with me, Kate."

"Thank you. That was fun," I say with a smile, as we step out onto the sidewalk. "I should have gone in there before. I love girlie stuff."

"Well, you are a girl, so I guess that fits," Eli says with a laugh, and takes the bag of goodies out of my hand.

"You're quite chivalrous, you know."

"Mama raised me right," he replies. Damn that accent gets me every time. Especially when he was in my hospital room, whispering in my ear.

*You made a man who's incapable of love fall in love with you.*

He thought I was asleep, but I heard him.

Not that it changes anything. I'm still leaving tomorrow, and I refuse to be the one to tell him that I love him when I'm not full of medication.

Because, what if I was wrong? What if I was hallucinating?

How embarrassing would that be?

He takes my hand, kisses the back of it, and leads me down the sidewalk, toward Jackson Square, toward the sound of music and people and the smell of beignets.

I'm going to miss this.

I'm going to miss *him*.

I glance up, and for just a moment, the words are on the tip of my tongue.

"What is it, *cher*?"

"I just—" I take a deep breath and chicken out. "I'm going to miss this place."

He smiles softly and kisses my cheek, but doesn't say anything in return, and I swallow my disappointment and decide to simply enjoy our last day together.

∼

"Another lemon drop?" Joe the waiter asks, as he delivers our Brussels sprouts.

"No," Eli answers for me, giving me a stern look. "I'd like to actually have a coherent conversation with you this evening."

"Come on," I reply with a laugh. "I'm fun when I'm drunk."

"You are fun," he agrees and spears a sprout with his fork, then holds it up to my lips. "But since this is my last night with you, let's keep it semi-sober."

"Deal." I chew the delicious vegetable and sit back in my seat, enjoying the courtyard of Café Amalie. "This place is so beautiful. I love the pretty lights in the trees. Isn't it pretty?"

"Yes," he replies, but when I look over at him, he's not looking at the trees. He's looking at me.

"Charmer," I whisper, and take the last sip of my drink.

"You look beautiful in this dress." He takes my hand in his and kisses my knuckles, sending electricity up my arm.

"Thank you."

"Your dinners," Joe announces, as he places our entrées before us. Dinner is delicious and filling, and when Eli suggests that we take a longer walking route back to his place, I readily agree.

I need to work off some of this food.

"Oh, look at this gallery," I breathe, and stop at a window with canvasses full of black trees and colorful leaves and backgrounds. They look almost...weepy. "I love this one with the yellows, golds, and oranges." I point to the one that has caught my eye. "It reminds me of Denver in the fall."

"Hmm," Eli murmurs and kisses my cheek before leading me further up the block. We stop several more times to admire window displays, walking slowly, hand-in-hand, laughing and talking.

*Enjoying.*

Did I ever honestly think this man was intimidating? Cold? Distant? It's amazing to me the difference in him from when I first walked into his office to that same man walking next to me tonight.

"What are you thinking so hard about?" he asks quietly, his accent thicker, perfect for this lazy, easy moment.

"Nothing."

"Now, that's a lie," he replies with a soft smile. "I can hear your wheels turning."

"I was thinking about you." I squeeze his hand a little tighter, and then bring it up to nuzzle it with my cheek. "And that I'll miss you when I leave."

He grows quiet for a moment, not responding at all, and then he surprises me.

"I've enjoyed every moment with you, Mary Katherine O'Shaughnessy," he says, making me smile at the way he says my last name with his accent. "You are a special woman."

We're standing in front of his townhouse now. Based on his last statements, I'm wondering if he's not saying goodbye.

"Thank you for a lovely evening."

"No, *cher*, I'm not cutting our night short." He leads me inside, up to the bedroom. "I just wanted to make sure I told you how much I've enjoyed you, in case I don't have enough blood supply to my brain later and I forget."

"Definitely charming," I laugh. Eli's phone rings, making him frown. He checks the display, dismisses the call, and sets his phone aside.

"I do believe I'd like to pamper you a bit this evening," he says, as he slowly saunters toward me.

"How so?" I ask, feeling a bit breathless at the look in his eyes, the way his body moves so effortlessly, his muscles bunching and moving beneath his smooth skin.

He's simply delicious.

"Well, I'll begin by slowly taking this dress off of you," he whispers. He's pressed against me now, his arms around me as he lowers the zipper on my back, pushes the black fabric off my shoulders, and watches it fall to my ankles. "You pulled the leopard print back out," he says with a cocked brow.

"You seemed to like it." I swallow at the hot look in his eyes as they lazily roam up and down my body.

"I didn't realize there was a matching bra."

"Of course there's a matching bra," I reply dryly. "There's always a matching bra."

"I do love your taste in underwear," he says, just before he hooks his fingers in the straps on my shoulders and tugs them aside, then lays his lips on my skin, kissing me gently all the way to the ball of my shoulder. He pays the same attention to the other side, just as his phone rings again.

"You should answer it," I whisper in his ear, then kiss him, just below his earlobe, on that soft skin that feels so good on my lips.

"No."

"It could be important."

He shakes his head and unhooks my bra in the back; his fingertips drag over my skin as he pulls it down my arms, then lets it fall. I tug his shirt out of his pants, then slide my hands up his stomach, over his smooth, warm skin.

God, I love touching him.

"This is supposed to be about you," he whispers against my collarbone.

"It is," I reply softly. "Touching you makes me happy."

He pauses, and then kisses me, right over my heart.

*Tell him!* My mind screams. *Tell him you love him and you don't want to leave!*

"Eli."

His phone rings again, and we both moan in frustration, but he ignores it.

"Eli, you really should answer it."

"Fuck no," he replies stubbornly. "Whoever it is can fuck off."

I slide my hands down the back of his pants and grip onto his very firm, very fine butt.

"I like your butt," I whisper, making him laugh.

"I'm glad you do," he says.

"I think you're wearing too many clothes," I say, just as my own phone rings. Our eyes meet and wait, and sure enough, as soon as mine stops, his starts. "Seriously. Answer. Something is wrong."

He swears and stalks over to his phone. "What." He frowns as he listens. "Are you sure?" He sighs and pinches the bridge of his nose, then scrubs his hand over his mouth in agitation. "Fine. I said fine, Beau. I'll be there in twenty."

He clicks off and turns to me with regret and anger written all over his face.

"You have to go."

"I'll be back in an hour."

I laugh and shake my head, then cross to him and simply wrap my arms around him and hug him tight. "It's okay, Eli."

"I swear, I'll be back in an hour. Two tops." He braces his hands on my shoulders and sets me away from him. "Take a hot bath, drink a glass of wine, relax. I'll come back and we'll pick this back up."

"Okay." I grin and kiss his chin, then his lips. "I'll go back over to my place and finish up a few things, so I don't have to do them in the morning. It'll buy me ten more minutes of sleep."

"I'll come get you when I get back," he promises, kisses me once more, hard and long, then tucks his shirt back in, grabs his keys and wallet, and rushes out. I take my time pulling my dress back on, not bothering with the bra, and walk over to my own flat.

Once I've finished gathering the last few things for tomorrow morning, sure that I'm ready for my flight, I take a hot shower, shave my legs, *again*, because really, you can never have legs that are too smooth, and decide to wear the pretty red nightie that Eli admired the other day.

He did ask nicely, after all.

I check the time on my phone, frowning when I realize he's been gone for over an hour. Should I go to bed and let him wake me up when he gets back?

It's getting late, and I have an early flight. I try his phone, to let him know that I'll be asleep, but I just get his voice mail.

"Hey, just wanted to let you know that I'm going to sleep for a while. Come on in and wake me up when you get home. See you soon."

I lie down, and the next thing I know, my phone is ringing.

"'Lo?"

"It's Eli. I'm sorry, Kate."

"What time is it?"

"It's after two. I'm not going to make it back tonight. I got hung up here. I'll have to send someone to take you to the airport in the morning."

*Um. Wait. What?*

"Okay."

"I'm so sorry, Kate. I have to go. Please take care of yourself. Thanks for everything. Take care and safe travels."

And with that, he's gone.

"Thanks?" I ask the empty room. "Take care and safe travels?"

I sit and blink into the blackness. Did that really just happen, or did I dream it? I check my phone, and sure enough. It was real.

He's not coming back.

I stare at my phone as it goes black and feel my eyes well. He's just my *friend.* This shouldn't upset me at all. So I don't get to have sex with him one more time. So I don't get to feel the weight of him on top of me, or his lips on my skin. So I don't get to hear that sexy accent of his as he whispers in my ear because he's so darn turned on he can't help himself.

So I don't get to feel his hands on my back as he holds me, or see the special way he smiles at me when he thinks I'm being particularly adorable or ridiculous.

So what?

It's a clean break. Like ripping off the Band-Aid quickly. It's probably for the best.

*And hurts worse than any slap in the face.*

I thought I'd at least get to say goodbye in person.

I lie back and can't stop the tears that flood my eyes, and that only pisses me off more. I refuse to waste one more tear on a man. *Any man.* Especially a man who doesn't love me and says goodbye with *safe travels.*

No more tears.

Not one.

I roll onto my belly and bury my face in the pillow, crying angrily. Why did I let myself fall in love with him? Haven't I learned anything?

～

"Hey, superstar," Declan says, when I open the door for him and turn to gather my luggage.

"Good morning. Thanks for picking me up."

"No problem. Eli said he—"

"I don't care what Eli said," I interrupt, and then scowl. "That sounded really bitchy."

"Kind of." He helps me gather my bags.

"The moving people will come get the rest later today or tomorrow."

Declan nods and follows me down the steps. I glance to my left, and also coming down Eli's steps is Gabby's friend, Cindy.

She glances over at us, smiles and waves, and then walks to her car, climbs in, and leaves.

*Are you fucking kidding me?*

"She's a little slut," Declan mutters, as he loads my bags into the back of his car.

"So is your brother," I reply. *"That* is what he got hung up with last night?"

"Hey," Dec holds his hands up in surrender. "I honestly don't know. I was simply asked to come take you to the airport." He winces and offers me a sympathetic smile. "I'm sorry."

"Whatever," I reply and get in the passenger side. "It was over anyway."

"Was it?"

"It sure as heck is now."

# CHAPTER 20

## ẼLI~

*J* drop into the chair behind my desk, lean my elbows on the smooth wood and prop my head in my hands, gripping my hair in my fists. It's after eight in the morning, and I just got here.

I never went home.

All I want to do is sleep, so I'll take a cold shower, get dressed, and get back to work.

Back to my life.

But first, I dial Kate's number, needing to hear her soothing, sweet voice after the fucked up night I just had, and frown when I'm immediately sent to the automated voice of her mailbox.

Her plane has taken off.

And it's probably for the best.

"You okay?" Beau asks, as he walks into my office and flops into the chair across from me, looking every bit as exhausted as I feel.

"I feel the way you look," I reply. "I told Sal to replace that hydraulic. *I told him*. I made it very clear what would happen if he didn't."

"We just never planned on a guy being killed in the night shift because he didn't do it fast enough," Beau replies, and rubs his eyes with the pads of his fingers.

"It was pride," I spit out. "I bruised his fucking ego, so he drug his feet."

"Well, he can drag his feet all the way to the unemployment office."

I nod grimly. "That doesn't help that young man's widow and two small kids."

"We'll make sure they're very well taken care of."

"Something tells me she'd rather have her husband," I whisper sadly.

"Eli," Beau begins and scratches his scruffy cheek. "I wanted to tell you, I was really fucking proud of you last night."

I raise a brow and watch my older brother. He's my best friend, and we respect each other, but we're men.

We don't get mushy.

I shift in my chair, uncomfortable, but he keeps going.

"You handled the situation perfectly."

"I didn't do it alone," I remind him. "You were right there with me, taking on your fair share of the work."

"Yes, and I'll continue to, but you did great. Dad would have been impressed."

I smirk. "Right."

Beau cocks his head, narrows his eyes. "Dad loved you."

"I know."

And I do. But, he didn't respect me, and wasn't *impressed* by anything I did once in my life.

"You're a good man, Eli. A fair one. A good leader. *I'm* proud of you."

"Thank you."

"Is she gone?" he asks suddenly, changing the subject.

"Yes."

He sighs. "And you let her go."

"She doesn't live here, Beau. She has a life and a job."

He shakes his head at me. "I'm sorry you missed last night with her. She was good for you."

*So am I. So fucking sorry.*

"Did you at least call and say goodbye?"

"I'm not a dick, Beau. Of course. I called and wished her safe travels."

His jaw drops. "That's it?"

"What else was there to say? Discuss the weather? Exchange recipes? Pledge my undying love?"

"You're wrong," Beau says quietly, as he stands and shoves his hands in his pockets, the same way I do, looking very much like our father. "You are a dick."

"Never claimed otherwise," I mutter as he walks away. I check my phone, for what I'm not sure. She may have landed by now. I tried to call Declan earlier to ask him how she was this morning, but he's not answering my calls.

He's probably either asleep or bouncing on one of his groupies.

I'd give just about anything to hear her voice right now, to smooth the rough edges left from holding that young widow through the night while she cried long, heartbroken sobs against my chest for a man who's never coming home. From being awake for too fucking long.

From already missing her.

But she's gone, and I have a business to run. So I schedule a mid-morning mandatory meeting with the men at the shipyard and hurry to shower and dress to make it there on time.

This is my life. This is what's important. Kate was just a pleasant distraction. It's time to get back to business.

~

"I don't give a fuck. I want it done. *Today.* Understood?"

"Yes, sir."

"Good." I hang up and bring up an email, just as Savannah and Declan saunter into my office.

"I see you're just your usual puppies and rainbows self," Declan says dryly, as he lowers himself into a chair, a smirk on his face.

"What do you want?"

"We want to talk to you," Savannah says. She folds her hands in her lap, sitting straight in the chair, head high, the way she always does. But her eyes are sad, and that kills me.

"How are you, *bebe*?" I ask her softly.

"Worried about you," she replies.

"Alright." I sit back in my chair and rub my fingers over my mouth. "What's up?"

"We've come to point out that you're back to your old asshole ways," Declan says.

"How would you know?" I ask with a raised brow. "You haven't spoken to me in two weeks."

"And I'd rather not speak to you now either, but Van talked me into it."

"Since you're talking to me, would you like to explain *why* you'd rather not?"

"Because you're a fucking dick, and you made Kate cry."

"What?" I scowl at them both. "I haven't spoken to Kate since she left two weeks ago."

"Oh, we know," Savannah replies. "And you're back to your BK attitude."

"*BK*?"

"Before Kate."

"Is this an intervention?" I ask with a laugh, and immediately wish for a glass of bourbon.

"Yes, if you'd like to call it that," Van replies. "It's an asshole intervention."

"Noted. You can see yourselves out."

"You don't even want to know if she's okay?" Declan asks incredulously. "No, *so, how's Kate?*"

"So, how's Kate?"

His jaw and fists clench, but before he can say anything else, Savannah jumps in. "She's...*fine.*"

*What the fuck does that mean?*

"Why did you let her leave?" Savannah asks.

"I have a better question," Dec interrupts. "Why did you fuck Cindy while Kate was twenty feet away, worried about you, wondering when you were coming back?"

I blink at my siblings, not exactly computing what the fuck they're saying.

"Excuse me?"

"Cindy? Gabby's slutty friend? The woman that Kate and I saw leaving your townhouse as we took her luggage to the car. The leggy blonde with the big tits."

"So charming," Van murmurs, while she glares daggers at me.

"I didn't fuck Cindy." Just the thought has bile rising in the back of my throat.

"Bullshit. We *saw* her, Eli."

"I don't know what the fuck you think you saw, but I didn't fuck her. I wasn't home, Dec. I was at the shipyard. Jesus, I haven't been home since I left Kate that night."

"Wait." Van thinks it over and then nods. "That's right. He was at the shipyard. And what do you mean, you haven't been home?"

*What's the point? Kate's not there. She won't be on her balcony with wine and pizza. Or next door listening to her music too loud. Or in my bed.*

"I have work."

"So, you're living *here*? How?"

"I have clothes here. Showers. A couch. And I'm pushing thirty-one, so I can pretty much do whatever the fuck I want, little sister."

"Are you eating?" Savannah asks, and I simply sigh.

"Hello, pot, I'm kettle. Have you seen you lately? Your clothes are hanging off of you."

"We're not talking about me," she says defensively.

"You never answered why you let her leave," Declan says quietly. "You didn't ask her to stay."

"Her job was finished."

"You love her," Savannah reminds me softly. "You told me you love her so much you can't breathe."

*And I haven't taken a deep breath in two weeks.*

"You hurt her!" Declan exclaims.

"I don't deserve her!" I shout back. "What am I going to offer her? You've said it yourself, I'm an asshole. I'm consumed with my job. This," I gesture to my office, "is what I eat, sleep, breathe, fuck. I made a promise to Dad that I'd get my shit together and focus on this family and this company, and that's what I'm doing! No woman wants to take second place to a job!"

"Eli, Dad wouldn't want you to give up love for this company," Savannah says. "You don't have to put the company above anyone you love on your priority list."

"Daddy never made us feel like we were second place. He sure as fuck never made Mama feel that way. They were a team, E," Dec says quietly. "You have so much more to give than that."

I stare at Dec for a moment. "What did you say?"

"You have so much more to give."

*"You need to take responsibility for your actions, son. Beau is going to need your help with the company. The family needs you. You have so much more to give this life than what you've been giving it. Riding along, screwing every pretty thing in a skirt, is not the way to live your life.*

*"The love of one good woman is worth more than all of those tarts combined. What your mama and I have had for the past thirty-five years? You can't buy it. You can't drink enough to fake it. It's soul-deep. I love her so much I can't breathe, Eli. Even when she makes me want to strangle her tiny little neck. She makes me feel so much. She gave me six amazing children. She makes me laugh.*

*"I want that for you. You are capable of so much in this life, Eli. I want you to love what you do. I know you're going to make our company better than I ever did. But more than that, I want you to fall in love. Have babies. Love her so much you can't breathe."*

"But, you know what?" Declan continues as I blink hard, coming out of that moment with my dad that I'd forgotten. "It doesn't matter. Kate's not hard to please, Eli. All she's ever wanted was someone to be kind to her. To love her. To be someone she can trust to protect her. Someone to *fight for her*."

"And you just let her go," Savannah agrees.

*I just let her go.*

"Look, man, if you don't love her, fine. It's not a requirement to love Kate, although how anyone could *not* love her, I don't know. But calling her at 2:00 with *safe travels*, after everything you'd done and been through was a dick move."

*Such a fucking dick move.*

"I love you so much," Savannah says with tears in her eyes. "I saw how different you were with her. You smiled so easily. You were tender with her. It was the Eli that hasn't been around in a long time. And now that she's gone, so is he. And I miss him."

"I'll let her know that we misunderstood about Cindy," Declan says, as he and Van stand to leave.

"No." I shake my head as they both spin around to stare at me.

"What? Why?" Savannah says.

"I'll tell her." I swallow hard and stand, push my hands in my pockets, fingering the half-dollar.

"If you're planning to call her, she won't answer," Savannah warns me.

"I'm going to see her."

"She won't want to see you," Declan says with a smile. "I kind of wish I was gonna be there to witness this."

"You also have a dick side," I comment calmly. "Must run in the family."

"Rhys is there," Dec says. "He might try to beat the shit out of you."

"He lives with her?"

"Yeah, they share a place, since neither of them are there often. But, come to think of it, he has a bum shoulder. You can take him."

"Duly noted."

"Good luck." Van grins, and comes around the desk to kiss my cheek. "You *do* deserve her. No one else does."

I hug her tight and pray she's right. Because living without her is pure agony.

I need her.

KATE AND RHYS'S house is in a newer development in Denver. The homes are modest, but nice, with trim yards and enough space between houses to be comfortable.

I pay the cabbie and walk to the door, not sure what in the hell I'm going to say.

*Sorry* just sounds…lame.

I ring the bell and am not surprised when a tall, broad blond man answers the door.

"Yes?"

"Is Kate available, please?"

"Who wants her?"

"Eli Boudreaux."

His nostrils flair, eyes narrow, and just when I think he's going to slam the door in my face, he steps back, and gestures for me to come in.

"I'm Rhys," he says and holds his hand out for mine, which I shake firmly.

"I figured," I reply, as he leads me into a living area littered with chocolate wrappers, popcorn, and used wine glasses. "Did you have a party?"

"Something like that," he replies. "Kate has stepped out for a few minutes, which is convenient, because I'd like to have a word with you privately."

"Okay." I look him in the eye, ready for him to rip me a new asshole, but instead, he blows out a gusty breath and sits in the chair opposite me.

"If you're here to fuck with her head some more, you can just get the hell out of here now. I won't have her hurt anymore. Not by anyone. Ever again."

"I'm not here to fuck with her head."

He licks his lips and leans back in the chair, crossing his ankle over his knee.

"Look, Rhys, I understand that you're protecting her, which I respect. I have three sisters, and if anyone even looks at them sideways, I want to rip into them. I don't want to hurt Kate. I'm *nothing* like her ex-husband."

"There are few people out there like her ex-husband. He's a murdering sonofabitch motherfucker," Rhys says matter-of-factly.

I nod, in complete agreement, when one word brings me up short.

"Murdering?" I ask, much more calmly than I feel.

"I know a lot of people don't consider the loss of unborn life to be murder, but in this case, it was brutal murder, man."

I frown, lost, and then the conversation from the graveyard comes to mind.

*"Did he ever put you in the hospital?"*

*"Once."*

"Are you saying he—"

"She didn't tell you," he mutters and curses, pushing his hand through his hair. "Yes, he did."

"I know that he hurt her."

Rhys lets out a humorless laugh.

"Yes, he hurt her. He used her for a punching bag. For sport." He clears his throat and has to stand to pace the living room. "Look, this is her story to tell, but I'm going to tell it anyway, because you need to know what she had to overcome just to let you close enough to *touch* her, man.

"That fucker smacked her around regularly. Not usually in the face to leave bruises, or when I was in town, because he's a spineless asshole. But then she got pregnant."

I swallow hard, hating the words about to come out of his mouth, and feeling so fucking helpless it's almost crippling. I also stand and pace, unable to sit.

"She thought the baby would make him change." Rhys shakes his head. "Men like that don't change."

"No. They don't."

"So, she pissed him off one day. I don't know how. Sometimes all it had to do was rain for him to hit her. He knew she wanted that baby." Rhys stares at me, blinking hard. "All I know for sure is that he kicked her in the stomach, repeatedly, then threw her down the stairs. He made her miscarry, at fifteen weeks. It wasn't an easy miscarriage. She was in the hospital for a week."

*Once.*

"Please tell me that fucker is in jail," I say through the hot, burning rage boiling in my gut. "Because, if he isn't, I'm going to fucking kill him."

"He is. For now." Rhys's smile is cold. "And when he gets out, you'll have to get in line. So, I'm going to ask you, right now, what your intensions are with Kate, and you'd better be brutally honest with me."

"I love her. I'm not leaving here without her."

"Not good enough."

I raise a brow. "Love isn't good enough?"

"No." He shoves his hands in his pockets. "It isn't."

I mirror his stance, hands in pockets, in a stand-off with the man protecting my girl.

I like him.

"She scares the fuck out of me."

"Now we're getting somewhere." His lips quirk. "If she didn't scare you a little, she wouldn't be the one for you."

"I will take my own life before I ever even *think* about hurting her in any way. I'm not saying I won't be an idiot and say things that I'll regret, but I would never intentionally hurt her, Rhys. I'd never touch her in anger. She's…*everything.*"

He studies me for a long moment, and then finally nods. "Okay. I like you."

"They didn't have the milk and cookies ice cream flavor, so I got chocolate chip cookie dough," Kate announces, as she comes in the house through the entrance to the garage, lugging plastic grocery bags. "And you can stop judging me right now, Rhys O'Shaughnessy, because I deserve ice cream." She sets the bags down on the kitchen island, then looks up, and her eyes go wide when they land on me.

Fuck, she looks amazing.

"Someone came to see you," Rhys says.

"And you can show him out," she says to her cousin, and turns to march out of the room. "I don't have anything to say to him."

"Looks like this is going to be a challenge," he says, and claps his hand on my shoulder. "And something tells me few things are a challenge for you these days."

I smile and walk after her.

"I love a challenge."

# CHAPTER 21

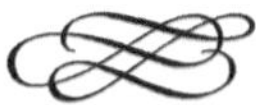

## ~KATE~

*Earlier that day...*

"Seriously? Weren't you in this exact spot, doing exactly this, when I went to bed last night?" Rhys is standing over me, hands on his lean hips, frowning down at me. I'm lounging on the couch, eating stale popcorn.

"What? I'm in the middle of a season of *Vampire Diaries.*"

"How many seasons have you watched in the past three days?"

"Four." I scowl up at him. "I finished with *Orange Is the New Black.*"

"Kate, you haven't eaten real food in days. And you smell...*ugh.*"

"Then don't come in here." I stick my tongue out at him and return to my show. "By the way, Damon is hot in this show. Why are the hot guys always the jerks?"

"I'm a jerk?"

"You're not hot." I smirk and then squeal when he takes my popcorn away and sits at the opposite end of the couch with it. "Give it back!"

"No." He shoves a handful in his mouth, and then spits it back out again. "This is disgusting. When did you pop it?"

"I don't know." I shrug and reach for the Twizzlers. "Two days ago?"

"Now you're just being gross."

"I'm being lazy," I correct him, and cringe inwardly. I am gross. I do smell. I haven't washed my hair in a week. I don't remember what my own bedroom looks like because I haven't left the downstairs since I got home.

Not that I'm going to admit that to *him.*

"So, what's up with that chick, Elena?" he asks, pointing to the screen. "She's hot for a vampire."

"She's not a vampire. Well, her doppelganger is." I catch him up on the show, giving him the highlights, and sigh when the credits roll. "This is seriously good TV."

"Kate?"

"Yeah?"

"I'm worried about you."

"Why? Because I love the *Vampire Diaries?*"

He raises a brow and stares at me like I'm stupid. And I'm not stupid.

"There's no need to worry. I'm just taking some lazy time between jobs, that's all."

"You're sad," he says softly. "I can't stand it when you're sad. Have you talked to him at all?"

I shake my head no. "I don't want to hear from him."

"Maybe you should call him," he suggests.

"Maybe not," I reply.

"You're being stubborn."

*He fucked another woman while I was right next door, pining for him!* I'm so not telling Rhys that. Talk about humiliating.

But the most humiliating part? I *know* this. I know it, and I still miss him so much it hurts.

Because I'm a stupid girl.

And I'm sick of being stupid. And sad. And…smelly.

"You know what?" I say and stand, stretch, and ignore him when he winces at the smell of me. "You're right. I'm done sitting on the couch. I'm going to go take a shower and go to the grocery store."

"Good, you could use some sun. You're as pale as those vampires on that show."

"You know, you used to be nice to me. You used to love me."

"You used to smell good," he replies with a grin and crosses his arms as I saunter by. "Take a shower, and I'll love you again."

"Conditional love." I tsk tsk as I walk by. "There aren't supposed to be strings attached to love, Rhys. Maybe that's why you can't keep a girlfriend."

"I don't want to keep a girlfriend," he replies with a laugh. "Girlfriends expect stuff from you."

"Yes," I agree sarcastically, "like kindness and cuddle time and sex."

"Hey, I can handle those things. Especially the sex."

"Ew."

"But not the other strings like *commitment* and all of my time and nosing into my financial business."

"And monogamy."

He just smiles and I make puking noises as I walk upstairs to my room. I love Rhys. He always makes me feel better.

The shower feels amazing. I stay in long enough to wash my hair three times, shave my legs, and drain all of the hot water.

When I step out, I actually take the time to style my freshly washed hair and put on a bit of makeup; I pull on a cute pair of red capris pants and white button-down sleeveless shirt.

I feel almost human again.

My bedroom is a shambles. I never unpacked my suitcases when I came home from New Orleans. I quickly do that, throw some dirty clothes into the laundry, vow to burn the clothes I've been marinating in over the past two weeks, then bounce down the stairs to find Rhys in the kitchen, making me a list.

"Thanks, *dear.*"

"You're welcome." He grins and checks his list. "I need some things. Don't get any junk food. We've had enough of that to last the rest of the year."

"Yes, sir." I give him a mock salute and take his list. "Since when do you eat parsnips?"

"I'm going to put them in smoothies. They're good for you."

"What *are* they?"

"A vegetable, smart ass."

"I'm getting extra Oreos, just to even it out. Yuck."

"No junk!"

"Whatever."

~

"THEY DIDN'T HAVE the milk and cookies flavor of ice cream, so I got chocolate chip cookie dough." These bags are so dang *heavy.* I seriously need to go to the gym once in a while. "And you can stop judging me right now, Rhys O'Shaughnessy, because I deserve ice cream." I pile the bags on the kitchen island, let out a sigh of relief, and look right up into the whiskey-colored eyes of Eli Boudreaux.

"Someone came to see you," Rhys says.

"And you can show him out," I reply, and turn to rush out of the room. I can't feel my feet, and I pray I don't fall on my ass. "I don't have anything to say to him."

I can hear their voices, but can't understand what they're saying over the rush in my ears. My skin is hot. I can't breathe.

*Damn it!* I was doing so much better today.

I walk straight through my bedroom to the balcony that overlooks my backyard. The sun is warm on my shoulders as I lean on the railing and take a deep breath, fighting tears.

*Why is he here?*

"You'll get burned out there in the sun, *cher.*"

*I will not turn around.* But, oh, God, the sound of his voice is the most amazing sound I've ever heard.

"Look, Kate, I know I should have called you—"

"Why?" I ask without turning around. "Why would you call? The job was done. I came home. There's nothing to say."

"There's a lot to say."

"You're right." I turn now, and will myself to keep myself together until I throw him out on his arse. "There is one thing to say. Fuck you, Eli. All I wanted from you was respect and honesty. To be monogamous until I left. And you couldn't even do *that.* So, fuck you. Now, please leave."

"I didn't fuck anyone!" he exclaims with frustration. "Declan told me what you saw the morning you left, but she wasn't with me, Kate. I didn't go home that night at all. I haven't been home since I left you that night."

"Wait. What?" He advances, but I flinch, so he stops abruptly and shoves his hands in his pockets.

"I haven't been with Cindy, or anyone else, since the minute I met you. I have no idea what she was doing at my townhouse that morning."

"Why haven't you been home?" I whisper.

"Because you aren't there," he replies, almost reluctantly. "And I miss you."

"Look, thanks for clearing that up for me, Eli, but you didn't have to come all this way to tell me that. You could have just sent me an email."

"I'm in love with you," he says, his face intense, jaw ticking. He looks nervous. Unsure of himself.

And that kills me, because Eli is the most self-assured person I've ever met.

"Excuse me?"

"Fuck it," he whispers and takes me in his arms, clutching me to him almost desperately. His nose is in my hair, breathing deeply, his hands rubbing up and down my back.

And I'm not hugging him back. Not yet.

"I remembered something," he murmurs. "Remember when I told you about what my dad said to me when he was dying?"

I nod, and can't help but take a breath, inhaling Eli's strong, spicy scent. God, how I've missed him. My hands grip onto his arms as he continues.

"All I've focused on was the disappointment in his eyes, his voice. The *bad* things he said that day, and I've done everything in my power to make sure that he would be proud of me now."

He grips my shoulders and pushes me away, looking me in the eye.

"But something Declan said reminded me of what Dad said about what's important. That the love of one good woman is worth more than all the casual sex put together. That what matters is being in love, having a family.

"Kate, I thought I didn't deserve you because I work *so hard* to make Bayou Industries something my dad would be proud of, and I thought that in doing that, you'd always take the backseat to my career. But that's bullshit. I can have both. My parents did it effortlessly, because they *made* each other the priority."

"What are you saying?" I ask breathlessly.

"I'm saying," he says and swallows hard, "that you mean the world to me. I've been looking for you my whole damn life. I'm uninterested in a life without you. Not having you with me over the past few weeks has been a hell I don't wish on anyone."

"You hurt me," I whisper, as tears roll unnoticed down my cheeks. He sweeps them away with his thumbs.

"I hurt both of us," he replies softly. "I fell into such an easy love with you, I didn't even realize it was happening, until one day, it was everything."

"You don't do love," I reply.

"I didn't," he agrees with a half-smile. "But you made the man who was incapable of love fall in love with you."

I frown and tilt my head. "You said that to me in the hospital."

He nods solemnly.

"Eli, I don't know if I can do marriage and forever with *anyone* again. I don't know if I have that in me."

"Oh, baby." He kisses my forehead and hugs me to him again. "You do. But we can take this one day at a time. As long as you're with me, every day, nothing else matters, *cher*. We don't have to jump into anything."

My arms clutch him now, wrapping around him and holding him tight.

"I missed you too," I whisper into his chest.

"You're going to burn," he says and leads me into the bedroom. He lies next to me on my bed, turning us so we're facing each other, and I can't help the tears that spring to my eyes. "Don't cry."

"I thought you'd—"

"If I'd known you'd thought that, I would have called and told you differently right away. I had no idea. I'm so sorry."

I shake my head and close my eyes, then lean in and press my lips to his lightly. His hand drifts down my side to my hip, and he lets me take the lead, nibbling his lips, kissing his cheek. I pull my fingertips down his chin as his hand makes its way up my shirt.

"I missed your skin," he whispers.

"I might have missed your abs," I reply softly.

He raises a brow. "Might have?" He pushes me onto my back and unfastens the buttons on my shirt, nudges it aside and kisses my chest, over to my already puckered nipple, pulling it into his mouth through my bra.

"Probably." My hand drifts down his back to his butt. "And this too."

He chuckles and works his way down my stomach. "I think we should make a list. The first on mine is this sexy as hell piercing."

"A list of things I love about you?" I ask with a giggle. He raises his head, his eyes wide, and pushes back up to look me in the eye.

"Do you love me, Kate?"

"I love you very much," I reply sincerely. "All of you."

His eyes close and he tips his forehead against mine, then sends me that sexy, naughty grin of his. "Let's make those lists."

∼

*Two Weeks Later...*

"I would have hired people to unpack your things," Eli says, as he wraps his arms around me from behind and kisses my cheek.

"That's silly," I reply, and hang the last blouse in the closet. "Besides, the thought of having strangers touch my clothes and underwear is not appealing."

"Well, when you put it like that," he agrees with a smile, and turns me to face him. He kisses me softly. "Welcome home, *cher.*"

"Thank you." I smile widely, happy to be here in *our* townhome in the French Quarter. "I love this place."

"I love you."

I smile up at him. "I know."

He swallows and cups my cheek in his hand. "Kate, Rhys told me about the baby you lost, and I've been meaning to find the right moment to tell you that I'm so very sorry for your loss."

I feel tears fill my eyes, but his words are a balm to my heart. "Thank you."

He kisses me softly, gently, his thumbs making circles on my cheeks, and I can't help but hope that there will be other babies.

Lots of babies.

"Is the family here?" I ask.

"We are." Eli's mama's voice comes from the bedroom, and when we step out of the closet, she's smiling widely. "Hello, sweet girl."

"I'm so glad you all came for dinner." I hug the petite woman before walking toward the door.

Just before I leave the room, I hear her say, "Your daddy would be so proud of you, Eli."

I grin and leave them alone, joining the others in the kitchen.

"Are you really living with Uncle Eli now, Miss Kate?" Sam asks excitedly.

"I am." I smile at the sweet little boy and smooth his unruly hair down, then snatch a fried potato out of a serving tray that the caterers brought.

Eli had this gathering catered. He didn't want me to have to deal with cooking dinner *and* unpacking my things.

God, I love that man.

"Are you okay?" Eli asks, as he wraps me in his arms and hugs me tightly, joining us in the kitchen.

"Why wouldn't she be okay?" Beau asks, as he uncovers the shrimp gumbo. "She doesn't start work until Monday, so you haven't had a chance to be a hard ass with her yet."

"How did your boss take it when you quit?" Van asks.

"He was fine when I explained that I didn't want to travel around so much, and that Bayou Enterprises offered me a position."

"I don't want to think about the positions Eli offers you," Charly grumbles, earning a glare from her mother.

Eli simply raises an eyebrow at me, a half-smile on his sexy lips.

"I'm great."

"You're amazing," he whispers in my ear. "And all mine."

I smile up at him, in the middle of the hustle and bustle of his family, laughing and talking, in our home, and know that I'm exactly where I'm supposed to be.

"All yours."

# EPILOGUE

## ~RHYS O'SHAUGHNESSY~

*Three Months Later...*

"It's fine," I insist with a growl, glaring at the doctor. My coach, team physician, even the fucking *owner* of the team are all here in this meeting. "I can play."

"No, you can't," the doctor insists grimly. "You'll tear that rotator cuff again in a heartbeat."

"I've done the therapy," I insist. "I've done everything you've told me to."

"Yes, you have. Rhys, you and I both know that this happens to players every day."

"Not to me." I lean forward. "Not. To. Me."

"He's not saying you're out for good," Reggie, my coach reminds me. "You're just out for the season, and it's almost over anyway."

I'm staring at the doctor, who's looking back at me with tired, sad eyes. He and I both know the truth: the chances of me coming back are slim.

"What do I need to do?" I ask.

"Keep doing what you're doing. Keep up with the PT, get it worked over by a massage therapist regularly to keep the muscles supple. Exercise." He spreads his hands wide, as if to say, *what else can I say?*

"I'll be back next season," I promise the room, and I can't help but wonder who I'm trying so hard to convince, me or them?

"And we'll be excited to have you back," Mr. Lyon, the owner, replies. "Get yourself well, Rhys. That's the most important thing."

We all leave the boardroom, and I walk briskly to my car, anxious to get out of here. Summer is hanging onto Chicago like a pit bull with a bone. It's fucking hot.

I take off down the interstate, ready to be back in Denver, wishing Kate would be there to talk to. And, at just the thought of her, I know I need to hear her voice.

"Hello?" Her voice is full of smiles as she answers.

"Hey, kiddo."

"What's wrong?"

"I'm out for the season," I reply, and check my blind spot to switch lanes. "Doc just

377

confirmed it. They made me come all the way to fucking Chicago to tell me that I can't play."

"I'm sorry. I thought you already knew that."

"I was trying to get back in before the postseason."

"What are you going to do?"

"Keep working on it. Exercise. Get it healthy."

"Do you have to be in Denver to do that?" she asks.

"No, I suppose not."

"Then get your butt to New Orleans. I have the perfect place for you to stay."

I HOPE you enjoyed Easy Love! If you'd like to read more in this series, you can get more information here:

HTTPS://WWW.KRISTENPROBYAUTHOR.COM/BOUDREAUX

# Charming Hannah

*A BIG SKY NOVEL*

New York Times and USA Today Bestselling Author

## KRISTEN PROBY

Charming Hannah
A Big Sky Novel
By
Kristen Proby

CHARMING HANNAH

A Big Sky Novel

Kristen Proby



Cover Art: Kari March Designs

# PROLOGUE

## ~BRAD~

*Three years ago...*

"Would you like another glass of champagne?" I ask Hannah, the tall red headed doctor standing next to me. We're at an exclusive party on Whitetail Mountain, with the owner of the ski resort and all of my closest friends.

"One is enough for me," she says with a smile, showing off her dimples. I can't help but wonder if she has dimples above her ass as well. I've seen her around town since she moved here, taking a position as a doctor, and each time I see her the lust is swift and hard.

She's sexy as fuck.

And I want her.

But I'm also a gentleman. Seeing her here was an unexpected treat.

I pass her a bottle of water and then walk with her out onto the deck where a fire is going to keep us all warm. The torch light parade is over, and people are beginning to leave. But I stand here with Hannah, leaning on the railing and watching people bustle between the two bars in the ski village.

"It's beautiful up here," she murmurs.

I nod and sip my bottle of water. "Do you like Cunningham Falls?"

"It's paradise," she murmurs and then smiles up at me. "I know it sounds corny, but that's what I think of it. The mountains, the small town, the people. I couldn't love it more."

*I feel the same way.*

But I've lived here all my life, so maybe I'm biased.

"How long have you been a cop?" she asks.

"Almost fifteen years. My dad is the police chief." I shrug. "I never wanted to be anything else."

"Do you think you'll be the police chief after he leaves?"

I shrug again. My application is already in for it, but who knows if I'll get hired?

"We'll see." I hook her red hair behind her ear. My sister Jenna walks over to us, her coat wrapped around her shoulders.

"I'm ready to head out, Hannah. How about you?"

Hannah glances up at me. "I rode with Jenna. Looks like we're ready to go."

"I can give you a ride," I offer and Jenna's eyes widen with surprise.

"Oh, you don't have—" Hannah begins but Jenna cuts her off.

"That's a great idea. I have some work to do this evening anyway, so if Brad can give you a lift, that's perfect. I'll talk to you later!" And with that, she waves and leaves Hannah with a stunned smile on her beautiful face.

"Looks like you're stuck with me."

"Are you sure you don't mind?"

I shake my head and lead her inside to gather our coats and say our goodbyes to Jacob and Grace, the hosts of the party. Once in my truck, Hannah gets comfortable in the leather passenger seat and sighs.

"Are you okay?"

"I'm tired," she confesses. "I was at the hospital all last night, but I didn't want to miss this party. I'm glad I came."

"I am too."

I concentrate on the slippery road that winds down the mountain to town. Once we're on the main, better travelled street, I feel more comfortable. It's been snowing heavily, and the mountain road is always tricky. But about a mile later, we come upon an accident.

"Two cars," I mutter and slow to a stop. I immediately reach for my phone to call it in, and Hannah has leapt from the truck, moving quickly toward the car with the most damage.

Thank God it's no one from the party.

"Over here," Hannah calls after I shove my phone in my pocket. She's standing by the driver's side of a small sedan, the door open, and the young woman driver is passed out against the steering wheel. "She's unconscious, but she's alive. I don't want to move her until the paramedics get here. I don't know what her injuries are. Will you stay with her while I check the other car?"

"No need," someone says from behind us. "I'm fine. My God, I couldn't stop the car when I went into a full spin."

"It's okay," Hannah says, turning around and immediately taking her scarf off and pressing it to a bloody gash on the man's forehead. "Hold this to your head. You have a small laceration there."

"I do?"

"He's in shock," she says to me, just as we hear the sirens coming in the distance. "Paramedics are on the way," she says to him and urges him to sit on the snow bank, holding the scarf to his head.

The young woman is coming to, and when she looks around, she starts to cry.

"It's okay," I say and rub my hand up and down her arm soothingly. "You've been in an accident, but help is on the way."

The next ten minutes are a blur as the ambulance arrives. Hannah rattles off a quick report of what happened and the paramedics load both of the injured drivers inside, then heads to the hospital. I stay an extra five minutes to help the officers on scene, and when Hannah and I are back in my truck, she says, "Take me to the hospital."

She doesn't look tired now, and watching her on the scene was amazing.

"Are you sure?"

"I want to check on them before I go home," she says. "I know I'm an OB/GYN, but they're mine now."

I nod and pull into the emergency bay behind the ambulance. Hannah jumps out and I see her give a quick report to a doctor that walks up – one she appears to know – and it's amazing to see her in her own element.

I've never been more turned on in my life.

She's stunning, her blue eyes bright and red hair around her face. She's a force to be reckoned with.

After all of her reports are given to the doctors on staff, she blows out a breath and returns to me with a shy smile. "Sorry, I just needed to see this through."

"No need to be sorry." I can't keep myself from dragging my finger down her cheek. "Are you okay?"

"Of course."

"Hannah!"

Both of us turn at the sound of her name. A tall doctor, Drake I believe his name is, rushes to her and cups her face in his hands.

"Are you okay?"

"I'm fine. I wasn't in the accident."

"Thank God." He pulls her in for a hug, and it's clear that they're close. Intimate.

Together.

So while they're hugging and she's telling him all about what happened, I slip out the door to my truck.

The sexy doctor isn't available.

Fuck.

# CHAPTER 1

## ~HANNAH~

"*I*'m going to die."

"I'm one hundred percent sure that you're not going to die today," my best friend, Drake, says with a smirk.

A freaking *smirk.*

"How do you know?"

"I'm a doctor," he says and reaches over to steal a donut hole from my plate. "I went to school for a really long time so I could tell hypochondriacs like you that you aren't dying."

I narrow my eyes and watch him, sitting all smug like across from me. We're at our favorite café in town, Drips & Sips, sitting outside for the first time this summer, now that the weather is finally nice enough to allow it.

It's a breezy seventy degrees, yet there is still some snow clinging to life at the top of the ski mountain that's directly in my view.

It doesn't suck to live here.

"You can't tell just by looking at me that I'm not dying."

"Okay," he says and takes a big bite of his scone. "Why do you think you're dying?"

"My low back has been *killing* me," I reply. "I have twinges in the ovary area. I'm pretty sure I must have ovarian cancer."

"Or, you have a back ache and you're ovulating," he replies, and I want to slap him for being so flippant about it all.

"Drake—"

"Hannah Banana, I love you, more than you'll ever know. But I'm going to say this to you, again, and it probably won't be the last time. You're an amazing doctor, but you never should have gone to medical school. You know too much. A twinge here and there isn't cancer."

I try to speak, but he holds a finger up and keeps talking.

"It *isn't.* You're a healthy thirty-five year old woman with a great career, ridiculously attractive friends, and you make enough money to buy yourself a pretty condo pretty much anywhere in the world. Stop buying trouble with the whole dying thing."

"You're not *that* attractive," I reply and fidget with the silverware on the tabletop, trying not to sulk.

"Yes, I am," he says and flashes his annoyingly perfect teeth at me.

"I have been on my feet a lot lately," I concede and pop a donut hole in my mouth. "Lots of babies decided to show up this week."

"There you go," he says. "Not cancer."

I sigh and nod, feeling stupid. "Why do I do this to myself?"

"Because you've seen first hand what illness can do. It's scary."

"Also, being a doctor means that we're confronted with our mortality all the time."

"True."

"I don't think this is unusual."

"It's not."

"So I'm not crazy."

"I didn't say that," he replies with a grin, and I finally laugh.

"You're supposed to be my best friend and make me feel better." I kick out with my foot, connecting with his shin.

"Ouch." He laughs and rubs his shin. "You're a violent woman, Hannah."

"Yeah, well, you can take it."

Suddenly Drake's phone begins to ring.

"It's the hospital," he says grimly. "This is Dr. Merritt."

He listens quietly for a moment, then tosses his napkin on the table and I know our breakfast is over.

"I'll be there in ten." He ends the call. "Gotta run. Appendectomy."

"Good luck." He reaches for his wallet, but I shake my head. "Go. I've got this. You get it next time."

"Thanks." He smiles but his head is already in the surgery. He jogs over to his brand new Land Rover and speeds away, leaving me here in downtown Cunningham Falls to enjoy the morning sunshine and to eavesdrop on the couple who just sat down at the table next to ours.

It's not going well.

"I can't believe you're doing this in public," the brunette woman says with tears in her voice.

"At least it wasn't by text," the man replies, and I frown, then hide my face behind my almost empty coffee mug. What a jerk.

"So, why now? I thought it was going well."

There's a long pause, and then the douchebag replies with, "I'm going to be brutally honest here. The sex just isn't doing it for me."

"We haven't even *had* sex yet," she hisses, and he has the audacity to simply nod.

"Exactly."

"You said you understood when I told you that I wanted to get to know you better first."

"Yeah, I thought you meant that you had a stupid three date rule or something. But it's been a month, Penny, and *nada*."

"I'm relieved I didn't have sex with you, and I regret the blow job."

"That was a delightful evening," he says with a wink, and I silently will the woman to punch him in the throat.

But she does something *so much better.*

She stands, and says in the loudest voice possible without shouting, "No, Nick, your limp dick issue isn't normal. You should see someone about that. Not to mention, you couldn't find a woman's g-spot with GPS *and* written instructions. You should probably see someone about that, too. Your inability to please a woman is embarrassing, and I need a *real* man in my life."

With that, she turns and stomps away, chin up, not a tear in sight. And I can't help but stand and give her a slow clap, then turn and glare at Mr. Douchenozzle. He's not smirking now, is he?

He curses and rushes away in the opposite direction, and I sit back with what's left of my coffee, ready to enjoy the last few moments before I have to go to the office.

I tip my face back to soak in some sunshine and revel in the mountain views. The fact that the snow is still holding on at the top is surprising for this late in the year.

It was a particularly snowy winter, and by the time it started to melt, I'd seriously questioned whether I made the right choice in accepting the position here five years ago. I'd originally wanted to settle in a city, delivering a dozen babies a day. I *love* my job, and after putting in my time at big city offices, I didn't know if that was for me, either. I want to develop a working relationship with my patients, not just shuffle them through the office, one after the other, as fast as I can.

When Drake told me there was a position open here, I brushed it off, still not convinced that this was for me. I'd been here to visit, and while it's beautiful, I didn't think small town life was the answer.

I'd left that behind when I was eighteen and finally able to escape the home life from hell for college. A *full ride* scholarship, for the first four years, followed by a mountain of loans that I've thankfully been able to pay down quickly. I don't owe anyone anything, and I earned everything that I now have.

But Cunningham Falls, Montana, is nothing like Wamego, Kansas. There are mountains here. Fewer bugs. More people. And that's saying a lot, given that Cunningham Falls has fewer than ten thousand full time residents.

This is also the biggest and bluest sky I've ever seen, when it isn't winter anyway.

And most importantly, there is no Randall Malone here. No, I ran far from that man and his liquor.

His self destruction.

No child should bear the burden of an alcoholic father. I don't know if he's dead yet. Part of me hopes so. I could do a search. With social media and Google being what it is, it probably wouldn't be hard to find out.

But I haven't looked because honestly, it doesn't matter. He's not even a spot in the rear-view mirror anymore.

"Hello, Hannah."

I turn and shield my eyes from the sun, delighted to see Lauren Cunningham. Actually, Lauren Sullivan now that she's married to Ty.

She rests her hand on her gently rounded belly and grins.

"Hi, Lauren. Wanna have a seat?"

"Are you alone?" she asks and sits in the chair that Drake just vacated.

"Drake had to run off to a surgery. I thought I'd enjoy the sunshine for a minute."

"It's beautiful today," she says with a grin. "It's about time summer showed up."

"How are you feeling?"

"Great." She pats her belly again. "I had no idea that pregnancies could be so different. This isn't anything at all like my first."

"They say no two babies come into this world in the same way, and from what I hear, that's the truth."

She nods and tips her head back so the sun beats on her face. "I'm on my way to see Ty. I thought I'd take him an early lunch."

"That's romantic."

She grins. "And a great excuse to procrastinate. I'm supposed to be writing."

"It'll still be there later."

"And my editor will be happy to remind me."

Her name is called inside, and she stands. "That's me. Enjoy your sunshine, Hannah. I'll see you next week."

"Have a great day."

She leaves, and I check my phone for the time. I need to get to the office. My appointments for the day started late, which I like because sleeping in is my jam. Most babies think it's hilarious to make their grand entrance in the middle of the night, so I take as many mornings as I can off. I also agreed to go to a party this evening for some leggings that are supposed to be the most comfortable thing in the world.

I have no idea why I have to go to a party to buy them, like Tupperware, instead of just buying them in a store, but nevertheless, I agreed to go.

I'm regretting that now.

If it makes me a bad person to secretly hope and pray that someone, *anyone*, goes into labor so I don't have to go to that party, well, then I guess I'm a bad person.

I toss my trash in the garbage and get in my car, already thinking about my first appointment. I back out of my parking space, and *bam!*

I'm rear-ended.

I lay my forehead on the steering wheel. I don't have time for this. I wasted all of my extra time drinking coffee with Drake and basking in the sunshine. I whip my seatbelt off and jump out of my car, ready to survey the damage.

And stepping out of his red truck is Brad Hull.

Tall, broad, soft-spoken Brad Hull, who also happens to be a cop in Cunningham Falls.

Not just *any* cop. No, he's the newly appointed chief of police.

And sexier than just about any man I've ever seen.

And trust me when I say, I've seen a lot of men. Not necessarily intimately, but I've seen them just the same.

"Are you okay?" he asks.

"I'm fine. You must not have been going very fast."

His lips twitch, making me wonder what's so funny.

"I was stopped dead," he replies. "You ran into me."

"Uh, no, I didn't." I prop my hands on my hips and do my best to glare at him. It helps that the sunshine is so bright.

"You did."

I frown and look at our vehicles, relieved to see that there's no damage.

"I definitely didn't run into you. I looked in my mirror and no one was there."

He nods twice. "Or, I was there, but you were thinking of other things."

"Are you calling me a liar?"

"No, ma'am," he says immediately. "I'm not on duty, and there's no damage. But I am not lying either when I say that I was not moving when you hit me."

I narrow my eyes and take a long, deep breath. "Are you going to handcuff me?"

His eyebrows climb in surprise, and I can't help but laugh.

"I don't mean like that."

"Well, that's too bad."

I laugh again and brush my hair over my shoulder. "Am I in trouble?"

"No."

"I'm not going to be arrested?"

"No, ma'am."

I nod. "Great. I have to get to work."

"We should exchange numbers," he says with a smile. "That's the customary thing to do when you're in an accident."

"We weren't—" I shake my head. "Fine." I reach in my car and grab a card out of my purse. "Here's my number. Let me know if I need to cover any damage done to your truck."

"Will do," he says. "Drive safely."

I wrinkle my nose at him and climb back in the car, late for my first appointment. Starting the day already behind doesn't bode well. Just as I pull in the parking lot of my practice, my phone pings with a text.

*We should have dinner tonight to discuss our accident.*

I laugh out loud as I reply.

*I already have plans tonight.*

As I reach for the door, it pings again.

*Tomorrow night, then. You can't say no. I'm the law.*

I bite my lip, thinking it over, and decide what the hell.

*Fine, but you're buying me dinner.*

*Deal.*

~

NOT ONE BABY in this whole town decided to save me from the leggings party this evening. Which means that rather than go home and change into something comfy so I can binge watch a whole season of Scandal on Netflix, I'm sitting in my dear friend Grace's living room, watching other women I don't know browse through racks and racks of not just leggings, but also tops, dresses, and kimonos as well.

I'm standing in the corner with a Coke in my hand, chatting with Grace.

"This house still makes my jaw drop," I inform her as I stare up at her cathedral ceiling. Grace and her new husband, Jacob, live in a multi-million dollar home on the lake, complete with boathouse and slip. Jacob is a real estate mogul from England who happened to purchase the ski resort, along with several local restaurants, in the past few years. But the most important thing is, no matter how much money Jacob has, he makes my friend ridiculously happy.

"It's pretty," she says with a nod. "I told Jacob that I didn't need anything this fancy, but he says it's an investment, and he likes to give me nice things."

"Well, no one can fault him for that." I clink my glass to hers and then stare at all of the clothes in this room. "Have you worn any of this before?"

"I have lots of leggings," she says with a nod. "They're super soft and I like to wear them around the house. But I haven't worn any of the other things. I just wanted to give Penny a chance to grow her business a bit."

"Penny?" I scan the room, and sure enough, there she is. The woman who got dumped and then castrated the moron with words. "Is that her?"

"It is. Do you know her?"

I shake my head and tell her about this morning outside of Drips & Sips.

"Oh, that sucks," Grace says with a grimace. "She really liked him."

"How do you know her?"

"She's a teacher at the school."

I nod. Grace teaches at the local middle school.

"Well, she handled herself very well."

"Sounds like her. She's smart."

Grace gets pulled away to mingle with the other women. I recognize Cara King and her best friend Jillian King, who married brothers about three years ago. I've met them before, but I wouldn't say we're close friends.

In fact, aside from Grace, Drake, and my cousin Abby, I wouldn't say I'm close friends with *anyone*.

And I'm not sure if that's entirely normal or healthy.

"Why are you all by yourself over here?" Jenna Hull, Brad's younger sister, asks. She's smiling as she passes me another Coke.

"I'm really an observer," I reply with a grateful smile. "Thanks for the refill."

"No wine for you?" she asks as Grace joins us again.

"I don't drink. I'm pretty much always on call, unless I'm on vacation, so it's best if I stay sober."

"Wow," Jenna says with a frown. Even with the frown, she's probably the most beautiful woman I've ever seen. With light blonde hair and bright blue eyes, she's a dead ringer for Kristen Bell. "I guess it never occurred to me that you're on call 24/7."

"There are only four obstetricians in town," I remind her. "And I know that my patients prefer to have me deliver their babies if at all possible, so I make myself available to them."

"I'm sure they appreciate that," Grace says with a nod. "But you should take some time for yourself, too. I've been nagging you about this for years."

"I do," I lie.

"She just lied to you," Grace informs Jenna, who nods in agreement.

"I *do*," I insist.

"Really?" Jenna asks. "What was the last thing you did just for you?"

"I agreed to have dinner with your brother tomorrow night," I reply before I can stop myself, and take a gulp of my soda.

*Damn it.*

"Seriously?" Grace asks and does a little excited jig, then almost falls over. I love Grace like a sister, and one of the things I love most about her is her clumsiness.

"You don't say," Jenna says with a grin. "Good for you. Brad's a nice guy, and I'm not just saying that because I'm biased."

"You're totally biased," I reply with a laugh.

"True, but aside from the sister bias, I still think he's a great person."

"And, he's hot," Grace says with a nod.

"I wouldn't say *hot*," Jenna says, wrinkling her nose.

"That's because he's your brother," I reply with a laugh. "And I have to side with Grace. He's a handsome fella."

"Where are you going for dinner?" Grace asks.

"I have no idea. We didn't get that far. I'm assuming he'll just pick me up and take me somewhere."

"How fun," Grace says. "A first date with someone new. It's so romantic."

"Yeah, unless I choke on something or say the wrong thing." I shrug. "It could be a nightmare. But he's nice. And he offered to buy me dinner, and let's face it, a girl shouldn't pass that up."

"Absolutely not," Grace says. "Free dinner with a handsome date, who just happens to be the new chief of police? That doesn't suck at all."

"You'll have fun," Jenna agrees. "Despite being a cop, my brother is pretty laid back. There's no pressure."

"Well, that's good because I haven't been on a date in—" I check my watch "about a year and a half."

"That's a long time," Jenna says with wide eyes. "Don't you miss having sex?"

"Who has time?" I ask with a laugh.

"Trust me, when it comes to sex, you *make* time," Grace replies and pats my shoulder as if in sympathy. "And as hot as Brad is, the sex is going to be off the charts."

"Ew," Jenna says, wrinkling her nose again. "Don't ever say those words again."

"He's your brother, not a eunuch," Grace reminds her.

"I'm not having sex with him on the first date." *Probably.*

"Good," Jenna says. "Make him work for it. Too many women throw themselves at him because he *is* a cop and, rumor has it, hot."

"Super hot," Grace adds with a nod.

"I'm not throwing myself at him. Why would anyone do that?"

"Exactly," Jenna agrees. "I mean, women need to have more self respect. Like any guy who has his shit together is going to want to be with someone who throws themselves at them."

"Guys like a chase," Grace adds. "It's good that you're not going to be slutty."

I can't help but cover my mouth and giggle. "I can't believe we're having this conversation."

"I'm *ecstatic* that we're having this conversation," Grace says. "You deserve to do something just for you, and going on a date is a huge step for you."

"Are you a virgin?" Jenna asks, and if I'm not mistaken, there's a thread of mortification in her voice.

"No." I laugh again. "Definitely not a virgin. I just don't have time to date. People around here keep having babies."

"I get it," Jenna says. "I don't date much either."

"Are you still running the bed and breakfast on the mountain?" I ask, relieved that the conversation has diverted from me.

"I still own it, but I hired a manager to run it for me. I purchased a few other vacation rentals last year that I take care of, and I have a new secret project."

"Spill it," Grace says.

"Well, keep this between us. Brad, Max, and I have bought some property up near the ski resort, and we're building tree houses to use as vacation rentals."

"Will renters have to bring sleeping bags and know the password to get in?" Grace asks.

"No, not that kind of tree house," Jenna says with a smile. "High end, super fancy tree houses. There will be three of them, and I'm hoping to start renting them out this winter."

"Well, I can't wait to see this," I say.

"We will host a viewing party when they're done and invite our friends to come see them before we open them up for rentals."

"*So* cool," Grace says. "Jacob mentioned to me that he sold a large lot just off of one of the ski runs."

"That's us," Jenna says. "I can't wait to show them off."

Thankfully, the subject turns to work and we trade stories. Grace has hilarious student stories, Jenna has all kinds of tales about horrible renters, and I always have fun tidbits from the babies I've delivered.

It's fun to spend time with friends and laugh. I don't remember the last time I did this.

And, of course, my phone rings with a call from the hospital.

"Looks like someone is having a baby tonight after all."

"Do you have to go?" Jenna asks.

"I do. But thanks for hanging out with me tonight. It was fun."

"Here's my number," Jenna says and presses her business card in my hand. "Text me and fill me in on your date with my darling brother."

"Make it a group text," Grace says with a sassy smile. "I want to hear all about it, too."

"If more babies decide to come, I might have to cancel."

"Don't cancel," Grace says. "I will punch you in the throat if you do. You *need* this."

"You're quite violent," I reply and reach for my handbag. "Stop threatening to assault me."

"Stop threatening to cancel your date with Chief Sexypants."

"I'm *so* going to start calling him that," Jenna says with a laugh.

"I won't cancel," I say, laughing with them. "I mean, who doesn't want a date with Chief Sexypants?"

"Exactly," Grace says.

# CHAPTER 2

## ~HANNAH~

*I* made it out of the office on time, and so far, none of my patients are in labor.

It looks like the Fates have decided that this date is a for sure thing, and I'm actually really excited about it. Brad and I have known each other for a while, and I'd be lying if I didn't admit that I'm attracted to him. Chief Sexypants is an accurate name for him. He's tall and broad, with wide shoulders and kind green eyes.

And a really, *really* great ass.

I can't believe I'm finally going out with him. All day today I felt like I was having heart palpitations and giant eagles in my stomach from the nerves. It's not that I'm shy, I'm just out of practice.

And I wasn't terribly good at dating before either. Add that to being out of practice, and only bad things can result from this.

I'm standing in the middle of my bedroom, naked, looking around blindly because I don't know what to do next.

I pick up my phone and call my cousin, Abby.

"Are you ready for your date?" she asks when she answers.

"I'm naked."

"I didn't think you were a first date sex kind of girl, but whatever floats your boat, sweetie."

"Funny." I roll my eyes. "I don't know what to wear. Abby, I only have clothes that I wear to work. And I haven't done laundry in about three weeks, so all of my good underwear are dirty. I *can't* wear period underwear on a first date."

"No. You can't. So go commando."

"That's seriously not sanitary," I reply and frown at the phone.

"Why? You're wearing clean pants."

"I'm an underwear person," I reply. "And all of mine that are clean are ones I wear when it's shark week."

"Well, you're not planning on letting him see your underwear anyway, right?"

"True. And if by some miracle our clothes *do* come off, I'll just have to make sure it's in the dark so he can't see my panties."

"I don't think he'll really care about your panties if you're letting him get inside of them," she says reasonably. I step into my panties and then frown at my feet.

"I haven't had a pedicure."

"Does he have a foot fetish? Jesus, Han, he sounds really pervy."

"This is the first date," I remind her. "I don't know if he has a foot fetish. But my toes are *not* polished."

"Are you wearing flip flops?"

"No, it's still chilly in the evening here. I think I'll wear flats."

"Awesome. We've solved the pedicure debacle. What are you wearing?"

"He didn't say if it was fancy or not."

"Do you have a pretty sun dress that can be either fancy or casual?"

"I have *work clothes*, Abby."

"I gave you a red summer dress last year when I was there."

"Your ass is smaller than mine," I remind her, but shuffle through my closet, looking for the dress. "I found it."

"Try it on."

I pull it over my head and turn to look in the mirror. "Not bad. This will work. I'll take a denim jacket, and that will dress it down a bit if need be."

"Excellent," Abby says. I can hear the smile in her voice. "Makeup?"

"I'm still wearing makeup from work."

"Which means you applied it twelve hours ago. You need to freshen it up."

"I didn't have time to take a shower," I inform her. "I hope there's no blood in my hair."

"Oh God. Ew. And you're worried about your period panties? Honey, your priorities might be a little skewed."

I chuckle and freshen up my eye makeup, then run a brush through my red hair and shrug one shoulder. "No blood."

"Thank goodness. I'm sure you look great, and you'll have so much fun, Hannah."

"I think so," I murmur. "Unless I choke or get food poisoning or something. Also, I've been having these palpitations today. Maybe I should make an appointment with the cardiologist."

"It's called nerves," she says. "You're not having a heart attack, Hannah, you're nervous about a first date with a cool guy. It's normal."

"But you're not a cardiologist. You don't know."

She takes a deep breath, and I picture her closing her eyes, trying to keep her irritation in check.

"I know," I say at last. "I always do this, and I'm stupid."

"You're not stupid. Take a deep breath."

I breathe in deeply through my nose and let it out through my mouth and feel a little better.

"When will he be there?"

I check the time on my phone.

"Ten minutes."

"Okay, here's what I want you to do. Take some more deep breaths, drink some water, and look at your schedule for tomorrow."

I frown, thrown by that last one. "Why?"

"Because you'll be thinking about tomorrow and not worrying about tonight."

"You're pretty smart."

She snorts. "I know. Have fun and text me when you get home because I'll want to hear how it went."

"Okay." I nod, even though she can't see me. "You're right, I'm just going to enjoy myself and *not* wish that I was at home watching Stranger Things."

"Oh my gosh, have you started season two yet?"

"No, I'm only halfway into season one because instead of watching it I'm going on a date tonight."

"Well, just wait until you get to season two. So good."

"Season one is kind of freaking me out," I admit. "I don't like the scary things."

"It's not that scary. Stick with it. You won't regret it. And look at that, you only have seven minutes now."

"Okay, I'm ready. I'm going to go look at tomorrow's schedule."

"Awesome. Have fun, Han. I mean it."

"I will. Talk to you later."

I hang up the phone and blow out a breath. There's no need to be nervous. He's just a man. A human.

I mean, sure, this human is better looking than most others, and the chemistry I feel when I'm in the same room as him is like nothing I've ever felt before.

But he's still just a man.

I throw the load of laundry I put in the washer this morning into the dryer, flip it on, then walk into the kitchen to rinse a few dishes and put them in the dishwasher.

I bring my schedule for tomorrow up on my phone just as the doorbell rings.

"Those were a quick seven minutes," I mutter. I run my fingers through my hair before opening the door to Brad.

He's leaning on the doorjamb, a crooked smile on his mouth and his green eyes are happy. I let myself take him in from head to toe, admiring the grey sweater and dark blue jeans, and the way they showcase his hard, lean body.

"Hi," I say and step back so he can come inside, ignoring the knowing smile on his lips.

"Hello, beautiful," he replies and passes me a bouquet of pink roses. "These are for you."

"Oh, how nice." I bury my nose in them and smile up at him. "Thank you. I'll put them in water real quick before we go."

He nods and follows me into the kitchen. "Your home is nice."

"Thanks." I wrinkle my nose at him. "I'm not here much, so it doesn't get very dirty. I don't know why I told you that." I fill a vase with cold water and quickly clip the ends of the blooms before fussing over them.

"Because it's the truth," he says and brushes my hair over my shoulder. "How are you today?"

"Nervous," I admit. "That's the truth, too."

"No need to be nervous, Hannah. It's just dinner."

I nod and take a deep breath, then smile up at him. "Okay. I'm ready."

He laughs and takes my hand, then surprises me by raising it to his lips and gently kissing my knuckles. "It's going to be fun."

"I know."

He watches me for a moment, then, still holding my hand, leads me through the house to the front door. My arm is on fire from the electricity running through it. Jesus, if just the touch of his hand causes this kind of reaction, I can only imagine what would happen if we were naked.

Not that we will be naked tonight.

I grab my jacket and handbag, lock up behind us, and follow him to his truck.

Once we're settled and headed down the street, he smiles over at me. "I thought we'd head over to *Ciao* for some Italian, if that works for you."

"That's my favorite place."

He grins. "Mine, too."

It doesn't take long to get anywhere in Cunningham Falls, and before long we're seated at a table in the back corner. When the waitress arrives, she writes her name in crayon on the white paper covering the table.

"I'm Natasha," she says with a smile, "and I'll be helping you out tonight. Can I offer you some wine, or something else to drink?"

"Just a Coke for me," I reply.

"I'll have the same," Brad says. Natasha nods and bustles away and I turn my attention to the menu, even though I already know what I want.

I never change what I order here.

"What looks good?" I ask Brad and glance up to find him looking at me with heated green eyes.

"You look amazing."

"I meant the menu."

"I know what you meant," he says and tilts his head to the side, watching me. "Let's get this out of the way right now. What is it, exactly, that makes you nervous about me?"

I blink as Natasha places our Cokes in front of us.

"Are you ready to order?"

"We need a minute," Brad says without looking away from me. He reaches out and takes my hand, and the same electricity hits me again, and I bite my lip. "Let's talk about this, Hannah."

"I'm not sure what to say."

"Is it the cop thing? My height? Have you heard something through the rumor mill?"

"What would I have heard?"

"Who knows?" He chuckles. "It's a small town."

I shrug. "Honestly, it's not *you* that makes me nervous. I'm not intimidated by you in the least."

"Excellent."

"I guess it's just first date jitters."

"Okay, we can work with that." He winks at me and nods at Natasha as she approaches the table. "I think we can order now."

"I'll have the bow-tie pasta with alfredo sauce, chicken, artichoke hearts, and mushrooms." I pass her the menu and smile at Brad.

"I'll have the lasagna," he says. Someone waves at him from across the room and he nods politely.

"It must be hard for you to be out in public when it's your day off."

He tilts his head in surprise. "What makes you say that?"

"Well, I'm *always* on call. Babies don't know what office hours are. But you're the chief of police. People know you, and I'm sure they feel like they can approach you to ask questions, complain, what have you, no matter if you're on duty or not."

"Sometimes," he says with a nod. "I finally had to have my personal cell number changed because I kept getting calls. I have an official cell because I have to be able to be reached any time of day. But I don't need the townspeople to be able to call me whenever they see fit. I am a public servant, but I finally had to set some boundaries."

"Good for you," I reply. "Setting boundaries isn't easy."

"It is when an old lady calls you at two in the morning to complain about how bright her street light is. She doesn't like closing her blinds at night."

"Oh my."

"She wanted me to come out and unscrew the bulb in it so she could get some sleep."

I can't help but cover my mouth and laugh. "What did you tell her?"

"To close her damn blinds and I gave her the correct department to call the next day. She wasn't happy."

"I'm sorry," I say and lean back when our food is delivered. "It must be difficult to have a personal life when you're under a microscope."

"Not really," he says with a shrug and salts and peppers his food. "My father was the chief of police for about twenty years. He and my mom had a pretty normal life."

"Do they still live here?"

"Part time," he says with a nod. "They go south in the winter."

"I can't blame them for that. It was a snowy one this year."

He nods. "Where do your folks live?"

"My mom died when I was seventeen." I take a bite of food. "I have no idea where my dad is."

He's chewing and watching me. *Don't apologize.* That's the worst.

"That's tough," he says, surprising me. "Do you mind telling me what happened?"

"She and my dad were on their way home from a New Year's Eve party, and he hit a tree. Killed her instantly. He was incredibly intoxicated. It was my senior year of high school."

"Jesus."

"I miss her. She was a good mom, despite being married to an alcoholic. He was sent to prison for third degree manslaughter, but by the time he got out, I was long gone, in college. I've never seen or spoken to him since that day."

"You're quite nonchalant about it."

"I did the therapy thing, Brad. I've mourned. I still mourn her because she was wonderful. But he was a piece of shit, and I'm better off without him." I grab a piece of bread slathered in chunks of garlic and take a bite. "My aunt and uncle took me in for the rest of my senior year, and they've really become more like parents to me. Their daughter, Abby, has always been one of my best friends. I do have family."

"I'm glad," he replies. "Family is really important to me."

I nod. "I saw Jenna last night."

"She told me." He laughs and shakes his head, also taking a bit of bread. "She called this morning to tell me to be extra nice to you because she likes you."

"She's sweet."

"She's a meddler, but she's my only sister, and she tells me that's her job."

"And you have a younger brother as well, don't you?"

"Max," he says with a nod. "He's recently moved back to town as well. We're both busy, so I don't see him much, but it's good to have him nearby."

"That's how I feel about Drake."

"Drake Merritt?"

"Yes. He's one of my best friends. I met him in medical school."

"I thought for a while that he might be your boyfriend. That's why it took me so long to ask you out."

I feel my eyes widen in surprise. "Three years long? Brad, that's a long time. And no, he's never been my boyfriend. He's just a dear friend, and he's the reason I decided to move here."

"I'll have to thank him," Brad replies.

"You're quite charming." I sit back in my seat, stuffed full of pasta and bread, and cross my arms over my chest.

"Just honest." He finishes his food and wipes his mouth. "So, you have Drake and Grace nearby."

"I do. Grace is wonderful, and I still see her all the time, despite not being roommates anymore. And Abby and her family come to visit at the holidays."

"Is there anything else I can bring you?" Natasha asks as she comes to clear away our plates. "Dessert?"

"I mean, you can't come to Ciao and not get the tiramisu," I say and look to Brad for confirmation.

"We should absolutely share the tiramisu," he says with a nod.

Natasha leaves, but another person walks over to talk about the potholes in the street in front of their house, and how their neighbor keeps playing music late into the night.

Finally, after five minutes, Brad says, "I understand your frustration, Paul. Just give the city a call tomorrow and they'll talk to you about the potholes."

"What about the music?"

"You're always welcome to call the non-emergency line and an officer will come out and talk to them."

Paul grumbles, but walks back to his own table and Brad reaches around the untouched tiramisu to take my hand. "Sorry about that."

"Like I said before, I'm sure that happens all of the time when you're out on dates."

"I don't go out on many dates," he says with a smile.

"No?"

He shakes his head and passes me a clean fork, then loads his own fork with the fluffy dessert and offers me the bite.

Of course I take it, and close my eyes in absolute happiness as the coffee flavor hits my tongue.

"So damn good."

"Hannah," he says, his voice gruff. I open my eyes and meet his gaze. "You're so damn sexy."

"Enjoying dessert is sexy?"

"When you make those noises and close your eyes? Hell yes. Because I want to make you do those things for purely other carnal reasons."

I swallow hard and set my fork down, licking my lips. "Not tonight."

"Excuse me?"

"I'm not a sex on the first date kind of girl."

"I wasn't suggesting it," he says and takes another bite of dessert. "Doesn't make me want it any less."

We finish our meal, Brad pays the bill, and the next thing I know, we're on our way back to my place. It's after nine, but it's still light outside.

"I love summer," I say and roll my window down. "I love that it gets dark so late, and the warm weather. I always have the best of intentions to take a week off of work in the summer, just to enjoy it. But it never happens."

"I love it too. Do you ski?"

I laugh and shake my head. "No, I never have. We don't have mountains in Kansas, and since I've moved here, I've been too busy to ski. Also, I don't love to be cold."

"You live in Montana, sweetheart."

"Hey, I can stay inside where it's warm. I do, however, love to hike. I plan to go this weekend, in fact, barring any babies making their debut."

"I hike as well. I also love to boat, kayak, and ride my bike."

"You're outdoorsy." I turn in my seat so I can watch him as he drives. His jaw is square, his hands big and sure on the wheel. "Summers are so short here, I'd rather never go inside."

"Mind if I join you on your hike this weekend?"

I grin, enjoying the thought of hiking up the mountain with Brad. "Of course. I was just going to walk to the top of the ski mountain."

"That's a four mile hike," he says with surprise.

"Too far for you?"

He glances at me, a small smile tugging his lips. "No, sweetheart, I was wondering if it's too far for *you.*"

"Psh, that's nothing."

He pulls up in front of my house, and I'm suddenly sad. I don't want to end the night yet.

"Do you watch Stranger Things?" I ask him.

"Yeah, I'm almost done with the first season."

"I'm halfway into the first season. If you don't mind rewatching a few episodes, would you like to come in and watch some of it with me?"

He immediately climbs out of the truck and around to open my door. "I'm in."

"I'm not getting naked," I remind him.

"So noted." He locks his truck and follows me to the door. "I also will not be getting naked."

*Too bad.*

I nod. "So noted."

# CHAPTER 3

## ~BRAD~

*H*er house smells just like her, like cinnamon and vanilla. Her red hair falls in loose curls around her shoulders as she leads me into her living room and queues up the TV, getting the next episode of the show ready.

"Do you want something to drink?" she asks. "I have Coke and bottled water. I might even have a Snapple if you want it."

"A water would be great."

She nods and hurries out of the room and back again, carrying two bottles of water. She's so full of nervous energy I want to pin her to the wall and kiss the fuck out of her, just to smooth out the nerves.

She passes me the water, and I set it on the coffee table, take hers from her and set it down as well, then take her hand in mine and pull her to me.

"Hannah."

"Yeah?" She looks up at me now, her big blue eyes wide. She licks her lower lip, and it's almost my undoing.

"You've got that nervous thing happening again."

"Oh." She clears her throat, and I draw her closer to me still. "I haven't had a man here in a long time." The words are a whisper and her eyes are pinned to my lips now.

"Good," I whisper in return and let my hands glide up her arms to her shoulders. "I'm going to kiss you."

"Okay."

I can't help but smile at the absolute eagerness in her voice, and the way she boosts herself up on her toes, getting ready for me.

God, she'd be so fucking responsive beneath me in bed.

But that's not for tonight. I push that thought from my brain and tilt my head down to hers, allowing my nose to brush back and forth against hers, enjoying the warmth of her skin close to mine and the way she takes a deep breath, making her chest rise.

"You're beautiful," I murmur against her lips.

"So are you," she replies. Her hands are moving over my shoulders and up into my hair, and I can't hold back any longer. I sink down into her, covering her mouth with mine, finally allowing myself to taste her, to soak her in. She's the sweetest thing I've ever seen, and her reaction to me is exactly what I imagined in my dreams.

She pushes up further on her toes, trying to get closer to me, gripping the back of my hair tighter in her fists. My hands drift down to her ass and squeeze her firmly. She's pressed against me now, we're breathing heavily, and I have two choices: I either carry her to her bedroom, strip her naked, and fuck her into the mattress. Or, I stop this now because if I wait, I won't be able to stop.

And she already set the boundary of no sex tonight.

So, no sex it is.

"Hannah," I murmur and pull back, brushing my fingers through her hair. Her eyes are still closed and she's biting her lip. "Open your eyes, sweetheart."

"Hmm?" She complies, and then frowns. "We're stopping?"

"Oh yeah," I say with a nod and step away as soon as I'm sure she can stand under her own power. "If I don't stop now, I won't want to stop at all."

She seems to struggle with this information, but then sighs and nods. "Right. Sorry, Slutty Hannah took over there for a second."

"Don't do that." My voice is sharper than I intended, but the irritation is swift. "You're not a slut, Hannah. We're fucking attracted to each other. Jesus, the chemistry has been off the charts every time we're in the same room together since we first met. That's not being promiscuous."

"You're right. Again." She pushes her hair back. "If you want to go, I understand."

"Hell no, I want to watch this show." I sit in the middle of her couch so she has no choice but to sit next to me. "And I want to feel you next to me for a few hours."

She tilts her head, watching me for a moment, then shrugs and sits next to me after reaching for the remote. "Let me check my phone."

She pulls the device from her pocket, but there have been no calls.

"No babies so far tonight," she says with a grin. "I'm not expecting any of my patients to go into labor this week, actually, but you never know." She sets the phone aside and presses play on the show.

"Jenna said you got called out last night."

"Yeah, it was unexpected," she says and looks up at me with sad eyes. "The baby was stillborn. He was too premature, and we couldn't save him."

"I'm sorry."

"It happens."

"I'm sorry just the same," I reply and tug her against me. She fits perfectly in the crook of my shoulder, her head leaning on my chest.

"Shall we watch this?" she asks.

"Let's do it."

She snuggles up to me and we stay here, snuggled up together, as one episode, then another plays. Finally, she stretches and checks the time on her phone.

"I hate to kick you out, but I should get some sleep. I have appointments first thing tomorrow."

"I have to be in the office early, too," I reply and stand. But rather than walk to the door, I pull her into my arms, hugging her tightly. I hold her for a long moment, then pull away and smile down at her.

"What was that for?" she asks.

"I needed it." *You needed it.* I wink and walk toward the front door. "When would you like to go for our hike?"

"Saturday morning," she says. "Before it gets crowded up there. I like to hike up and then ride the chairlift down."

"How does nine sound?"

"Perfect," she says with a nod. "It'll be fun."

"I think so, too."

I take one more long look at her, her blue eyes sleepy, her red hair mussed up now, and am already anticipating being with her on Saturday.

"Have a good night, Hannah."

"You too."

I walk to my truck, start the engine, and head toward home with the windows rolled down and my sunroof open. It's a warm night. There are a million stars in the sky, and I know if I drove up into Glacier National Park, just forty miles from here, I would be able to see the Milky Way.

That's something I can take Hannah to see another night.

Spending the evening with her was everything I'd hoped it would be. The chemistry is still there like a fucking freight train. It just rolls over us. But more than that, I enjoyed her company.

I plan to spend as much time with her as our schedules allow.

Once home, I secure my truck in the garage and walk into the house, greeted by my white lab, Sadie.

"Hey, girl." She whines a bit and presses her face into my hand, then goes directly to the back door, needing out. My back yard is fenced for her, so I let her out and walk through the house double checking locks and alarms. It's habit. I have to make sure the house and garage are always secure to protect myself from anyone who may be angry and want to take it out on the chief of police.

It happens.

Sadie scratches at the back door, and I let her in. We walk upstairs to the bedroom and she settles on her bed in the corner, ready for sleep.

But despite being tired, I'm restless. I take a long, hot shower which helps to calm me down. I slip into bed and think of a sexy redhead as I fall to sleep.

"Come in," I call when there's a knock on my office door. I've been doing paperwork all damn morning, and the distraction is welcome. I'm surprised when it's Max who walks through the door.

Sadie immediately jumps up from her bed by my desk to greet him.

"Hey, gorgeous girl," Max says and kneels to rub her head and give her kisses. "Aren't you the prettiest girl?"

Sadie falls on her back in elation, exposing her belly.

"You'd think she never gets any attention," I say and lean back in my chair. "Did you come to love on my dog?"

"Yes. And to see what you're up to."

"Just maintaining law and order," I reply. "What are *you* up to?"

"I have to go back to LA," he says with a frown. "I have some work that needs to be done in person."

Max is a highly successful software engineer. So successful that he's sold a few things to Google for a shit ton of money.

"How long will you be gone?"

"A month maybe," he says with a sigh. "Which sucks because this is my favorite time of year here."

"You don't have to work," I remind him. "You have more money than God."

"Probably not," he says with a laugh. "I mean, he's God. And maybe I don't have to work for the money, but I have to work for the sanity. What am I going to do, Brad, retire at thirty-two? And do what?"

"I don't know, it would drive me nuts too," I say and offer him a shrug. "When do you leave?"

"This afternoon."

I just raise an eyebrow, and he cringes. "I know, it's last minute. Jenna's dealing with the tree house architect. I was supposed to be there for the meeting, but I don't think she needs me. She's awesome at this, and can handle herself."

"Agreed," I reply. "Did you give her a heads up?"

"Yeah, and she said she'd be okay. But I told her to call you if she needs you."

"Okay, sounds good."

"Her meeting with them is Saturday morning. That's the only time they could meet this week."

"I'm not free Saturday morning," I reply.

"Why? Are you working?"

"No, I have a date."

He's quiet for a moment, and then he leans forward and I know I'm about to catch hell.

"With whom?"

"Hannah Malone."

"Nice. I like her."

"Do you know her?"

"It's a small town, big brother. Of course I know her. Not well, but she's hot as hell and seems nice."

"Don't make me break your arm again."

He smirks. "Don't worry, I'm not hot for her. Jenna probably won't need you, but if you could be in cell range just in case, I'd appreciate it."

"Not a problem," I reply and pet Sadie when she sits next to me and rests her head in my lap. "Need anything else?"

"Just keep an eye on my house for me."

"I'll have my guys drive by throughout the day."

"Thanks. I'll try to get home sooner. We'll see how it goes."

"Taking your jet?"

"Yeah, it's convenient." He watches me for a second and then smirks. "Hey, you're the one who said I have more money than God. What's the use if I don't spend some of it?"

"I didn't say anything," I insist. "Spend it all, I don't care."

"Let me pay off your house."

"Fuck you."

It's the same argument about every four months. Max wants to help. To share what he's built with those he loves, and I get that. But I don't need him to pay off my fucking house.

"This tree house project is going to cost you plenty."

"And I'll make the money back when Jenna puts her magic on it," he replies with a nod. "Okay, I'll see you in a few weeks."

"See you."

He leaves my office, and I immediately call Jenna.

"Oh good, you called to tell me about your date."

"No, nosy girl, I called because Max just left my office. He's leaving for LA today."

"I know. I told him I'd get his mail for him."

"He said you have a meeting with the architect on Saturday?"

"Yeah, but I told him from the beginning that he didn't have to be there. This is a preliminary meeting where they'll show me what they have so far and I'll hate it, and then they'll have to rework it."

"You sound so optimistic." I smile and glance outside to see one of my officers talking to a kid with a skateboard. It's getting heated.

"It's just how it works. So it's really not a big deal that Max can't make it."

"I'll have my phone on me that morning, so just call if you need me."

"Yes, sir," she says, the way she does when she rolls her eyes at me. "Hi, I'm Jenna and I'm thirty-four years old. I've got this, Brad."

"Yeah, yeah. Call me if you need me."

I hang up on a deep sigh and stand to go to the window and watch the kid argue with my officer. Finally, the kid walks away, his skateboard under his arm. He turns back to flip the bird, and then jogs away.

My officer, Jacob, just hangs his head and sighs. Dealing with kids like that isn't fun, but Jacob is a good cop.

I glance back at my desk and frown at the paperwork I still have to do, then decide *fuck it.* I slip the leash on Sadie and walk out of my office.

"Patrice, we'll be back. I'm on my phone if you need me."

She just nods, not looking up from the computer. That's one of the things I like about Patrice; she doesn't say what isn't needed but she gets stuff done and doesn't take my crap.

This place wouldn't run without her.

It's another beautiful summer day, and sitting in my office isn't how I want to spend it. Sadie sits happily in my police-issue SUV passenger seat, her head out of the window letting the wind blow over her face.

I don't have a destination in mind, so I make a loop through town, passing by my place that sits near the lake, then up past Jenna's B&B and Max's house. The tourists haven't started to rush into town yet for the season, so the traffic isn't bad.

I head back through the older residential section of town, and past Hannah's house. I slow down because her front door is standing open, but I don't see a car in her driveway.

"Stay," I tell Sadie and walk to the door, my hand on my weapon. "Hannah?"

There's no answer. I walk around to the side of the house and look in a window, but I don't see anyone. I don't want to go in the house if she's there.

"Hannah," I call out again.

"Yeah?"

I spin around, caught off guard by the redhead herself who is sweaty and wearing little shorts and a tank top.

"Your front door is open."

"I know," she says and leans over to brace herself on her knees. "Good God, I hate to run."

"Why *were* you running?"

"I'm trying to get into summer shape," she says. "I'm super lazy in the winter." She swallows hard. "I mean, it's cold and I don't like that."

"Yes, you mentioned that last night."

She nods, still catching her breath. "But I love to be active in the summer, and I'm trying to get in shape for it."

"Why was your door open?"

"Because I forgot to shut it," she says with a shrug. "I ran in really fast to use the bathroom because all that running made me have to *go*."

I grin and cross my arms over my chest.

"You look really intimidating with that whole cop stance you have going on there."

"I'm on duty," I remind her.

"Yeah. It's hot." She grins. "Am I allowed to flirt with you when you're on duty, or is that too cliché?"

"You can flirt with me any time you like."

She laughs and wipes the sweat from her forehead with the back of her hand. Sadie lets out a bark and whimper, reminding me that she's there.

"Who's this?"

"Sadie," I reply and walk ahead of Hannah so I can let Sadie out of the vehicle.

"Can I pet her?"

"She'll be disappointed if you don't."

"Hi, Sadie," Hannah says and holds her hand out for the dog to smell. "You're so pretty. What a good girl you are. You're so brave, too."

And just like that, Sadie is nuzzling Hannah's leg and soaking up the attention.

"I didn't know you have a police dog."

"She's a retired police dog. I bring her with me when I'm going to be in my office most of the day."

"What brought you by my house?" she asks.

"I needed to get out of the office for awhile, so I thought I'd drive by here to make sure everything was okay."

"And my door was open."

I nod and watch as she continues to pet Sadie's head, putting the dog into a happiness coma.

"Thanks for checking on me. It was a bathroom emergency."

"Why aren't you in the office today?"

"I had morning appointments," she says with a smile. "I take one afternoon and two mornings off during the week because I inevitably end up working several evenings and weekends throughout the month. It all comes out in the wash, and I can catch up on sleep if I need it."

"I see. Well, we'll let you get back to your workout."

"Oh, I'm done. I'll be good until Saturday." She sits on the ground and lets Sadie fall into her lap. "This is the sweetest dog ever."

"And she knows it." I check the time, and then hear my radio go off in the car. "Hold on."

I jog over and listen to a report of an accident just south of town. Multiple cars, injuries.

"I have to go. There's been an accident." I stare at Sadie. "Damn it, I shouldn't have brought her along."

"Leave her with me," Hannah offers. "We'll hang out for a couple of hours."

"You don't have to—"

"Go," Hannah says. "I have this. Be safe."

I nod and hurry away, my head already in the accident scene I'm rushing to.

# CHAPTER 4

## ~HANNAH~

*J* didn't sleep. Not much, anyway. One of my colleagues was out of town yesterday, and of course that's when two of his patients decided to go into labor. I was at the hospital late into the night.

I should call Brad and tell him that I'll have to take a rain check on the hike today. That's the responsible thing to do. I should sleep. If a bear runs out onto the trail and tries to kill me, I'm way too tired to run away.

I'm just trying to save my own life here.

I roll my eyes and stare at myself in the mirror.

"You don't want to cancel. You like him. Not to mention, his dog is the cutest ever."

Sadie is maybe the sweetest dog I've ever met. She hung out with me all afternoon the other day, following me around the house and then jumping up on the bed with me and sleeping until Brad came to pick her up.

Maybe I should get a dog.

My doorbell rings just as I finish tying my hiking shoes, and I rush out to open the door, only to stop dead in my tracks and stare in the rudest way possible at the man standing in front of me.

He's not wearing sleeves. So, his muscles are just hanging out all over the place. And dear God, the muscles! He could probably just lift me over his head.

It's almost ridiculous.

"Hi," he says with a grin and holds a to-go cup from Sips out for me. "This is for you."

"Oh, thanks." I take a sip and feel my eyes go wide. "This is exactly the drink I always order."

"I know," he says with a grin. "I asked them to make your usual."

"Are you real?"

"Excuse me?"

"I mean, you have the sweetest dog ever, you bring me coffee, and have you *seen* you?"

He laughs now and leans in to kiss my forehead. "You look tired."

"I didn't sleep much."

"We don't have to go."

"Oh yes we do," I reply and back away from him before I humiliate myself and jump him here in my living room. "I have to go."

"Why?"

I just shake my head and grab my backpack. I have fresh water in the bladder, a few packs of jerky and nuts, and my bear spray, which I check twice.

"You probably won't need the spray."

"We have the highest concentration of grizzly bears in the lower 48 states," I inform him and feel my heart already pick up speed at the thought. "I need the spray."

"I just mean that I'm always carrying, so if something happens, we'll be safe."

I stop and glance at him. "You always carry a gun?"

"Yes, ma'am."

"Why?"

"I'm the police chief. You never know what might happen."

"Huh." I shrug, but keep the bear spray where it is, reach for my coffee, and lead Brad out of my house. "You brought her!"

I hurry to the truck, toss my bag in the back seat, and hug the beautiful Sadie.

"She got a warmer hello than I did," he says when he gets into the truck and starts the engine.

"We're friends," I inform him and kiss Sadie's cheek. She's grinning.

"You and I aren't friends?"

"Are you really jealous of your dog?"

"Never thought I would be," he mumbles and pulls away from my house, making me smile.

"Thank you for the coffee." I reach out and touch his thigh, feeling the way his muscles tighten up at my touch. I'm relieved that it's not just me. That I'm not the only one who tenses up when we're together.

The things this man does to my body are ridiculous, considering we've never been naked together.

"When was the last time you did this hike?" he asks me.

"Last fall," I reply. "You?"

"Oh geez, it's been a long time. I was probably in high school."

"Cool." I grin at him and sip my coffee. "It'll be new for you then."

We're soon parked near the bottom of the chair lift. There's a whole village up here of uber-expensive homes, condos, and the ski village itself with a lodge and small convenience store. Almost everything has begun to open up again for the summer tourist season, when people will come up here to hike, bike, zip line, and a whole bunch of other outdoor activities. But it's still early in the season.

That doesn't mean the trail isn't busy. The locals love the outdoors, too, so we won't be alone on the trail, which makes me feel better.

The more people there are, the fewer the bears.

Once we have our backpacks on and Sadie is on her leash, we set off to the trail head, which is just about a hundred yards from the chair lift. It's not an easy climb. Four miles of walking steadily uphill is strenuous, but it's also incredibly beautiful.

We climb out of some trees and onto one of the ski runs, currently covered in grass and flowers, and take a moment to look down onto the valley below.

"Holy shit," Brad murmurs. We stand side by side and take it all in. We can see about fifty miles south, over three different towns. And to the west is Glacier National Park, which we'll be able to see even better from the top.

"It's stunning, isn't it?"

"That's a good word for it," he replies, looking down at me. "How did I forget about this?"

"I think we often take what's in our backyard for granted," I reply as we begin to walk on the trail again. We walk over a log bridge that covers a rushing creek, the water high with snow run-off.

My heart is beating at a ludicrous pace. It's dumb, I'm not going to die on this mountain, but I can't help it. I'm terrified.

"How are you doing?" Brad asks.

"I'm fine," I reply. The hike isn't taxing me at all. I reach down and feel the bear spray on my hip, which makes me feel a bit better.

"That's the fourth time you've reached for that bear spray, and we're not even a mile up yet."

"It's habit," I say. "You know, you don't have to follow me. I can walk behind you."

"Not a chance," he says and I roll my eyes so he can't see.

"Are you trying to be chivalrous?"

"I'm learning you," he replies. "Tell me about this bear phobia."

"Why do you think that?"

"Because you just reached for the spray again."

My heart is hammering, and I can't stop looking around me, listening for any tiny sound. We've passed several people hiking down. They're the go-getters, who come up here super early, hike up, and then have to hike back down because the chair lifts aren't running yet.

I'm not quite that ambitious.

And not one of them was running down the trail for their lives.

"I do have a bear thing. I'm absolutely terrified," I admit and feel my throat burn with tears that want to come, but I swallow hard. I will *not* cry over a fucking bear that isn't even here.

"Why?"

"Because we have the highest concentr—"

"Yes, I know that part," he says.

"Every summer since I've lived here, at least one person has died from a bear attack. Two were injured last year. They love the huckleberries, and there are berries all over this mountainside."

"Then why hike here?"

"Because I love it." I shrug and then shake my head, laughing at myself. "Maybe I have this stupid thought in my head that if I face the fear, I can make it go away. But so far, it isn't working."

"I've never responded to a grizzly fatality on this mountain."

"So you weren't there when that poor man and his daughter were attacked last year?"

"Neither of them died."

I stop and turn around, petting Sadie when she leans on my knee. "You're missing the point, Brad. It's an irrational fear for you. You have a weapon and you know how to use it. You also have Sadie, who I'm sure would go ballistic if a bear was nearby.

"I'm just me." I hold my hands out to my side. "Me and bear spray. But damn it, I live in this beautiful place, and I'll be damned if I won't explore it once in a while. My anxiety can bite me."

"Good girl," he says with a smile. I don't respond, I just turn to keep walking, but just then a cyclist coming downhill way too fast turns the corner and bumps me, hard. "Hannah!" Brad yells, as I stumble down the side of the goddamn mountain, stopping myself on a tree trunk.

"Ouch." I cringe and brush some leaves some my hair.

"Are you okay?" he says from beside me, bracing himself on the tree, digging his feet in so he doesn't slide down the mountainside, and assessing the damage. Sadie is with him, whimpering.

"Is she sad?"

"She wants to work," he says. "She's waiting for commands."

"What a good girl."

"Are you okay?" he asks again.

"My ankle hurts." I take a deep breath, trying to keep my anxiety at bay. "It's probably just a sprain."

Or, you know, broken.

*It's not broken.*

Except, what if it *is* broken? I'm on a fucking mountain and my ankle could be broken. Shit. Shit shit shit.

"Let's get back up to the trail." Brad takes my hand and helps me to my feet. I refuse to put any weight on my hurt ankle, so I'm horribly off balance. "How bad is the ankle?"

"How am I supposed to know?"

His lips twitch. "You're a doctor, sweetheart."

"Oh. Right." I glance up the hill and feel my eyes widen. "Holy fuck, did I fall that far?"

"You did," he says grimly. "And we're going to get you back up there."

"Oh my God. Brad, if this is broken, I won't be able to get up there. I'll be stuck here. I'll die." I reach for my bear spray, but it's gone, probably unclipped from my backpack in the fall.

And just like that, hysterics decide to set in.

"Hey," Brad says, but I don't hear him. I can't breathe.

I'm going to die on this damn mountain.

Why didn't I stay home?

The next thing I know, Brad has slung me over his shoulder, and he is carrying me back up to the trail, where he finds a tree stump and sits me on it.

"Hannah."

I'm breathing too hard to reply. Sadie lays her head on my lap, but rather than finding it sweet, I want to push her away.

I want to push *him* away.

"Hannah." He takes my face in his hands and makes me look at him. "Listen to my voice. Just listen to me."

"Bear spray," I manage, but he shakes his head.

"Shh. Listen to me. Hannah, you're okay. I'm not going to let anything happen to you. No bear is going to get you."

"I'm dumb."

"No." He wipes his thumbs over my cheeks and continues to talk so soothingly. "I need to know how bad that ankle is."

I shake my head and lean on his shoulder, breathing deeply and fundamentally mortified.

This is not how I planned to spend date number two.

"Can you put your weight on it for me?"

"No."

He leans in and presses his lips to my ear, erasing all thought of my ankle.

"Hannah, you're badass. I know you had a bad moment down there, but you've got this."

His hands are rubbing up and down my arms, and I take a long, deep breath. He's right, I do have this, and it's because just being with him and listening to his voice has calmed me, which is new.

I pick my head up and look him dead in the eye, then plant my sore foot on the ground and stand.

"It's not broken."

"Good." He's still touching me, grounding me. "Can you get down the mountain?"

"I can get *up* the goddamn mountain," I reply and raise my chin. "I'm sorry you saw that."

"Don't be." He gives Sadie a hand gesture and the dog falls into line next to him. "We can go down to the car."

"I came to hike." I step away from him and cringe inside when there's a slight twinge in my ankle. But it's not broken, or even sprained.

"I don't want you to hurt yourself."

"I'll take it easy." I look back at him and offer him a smile. "Honest, I want to hike this mountain. I'll take it slow, and I've got you with me, so I'm safe from bears, right?"

He tilts his head to the side, and I can see the wheels turning in his head. I'm sure he's wondering if he should make me go back.

I mean, he could try.

"You're safe," he confirms.

"Great, let's walk up this mountain."

~

"It never gets old," I say and take a long, deep pull of the fresh mountain air. "I mean, look at these mountains."

"You're right," he says and takes a drink of water, then pulls a bowl out of his pack and pours some water for Sadie, who eagerly drinks it down. "This was worth the four miles."

"Right?" I turn to him, excited. The wooden platform we're standing on is at the summit of the mountain, and we're looking into Glacier National Park and on into Canada.

It feels like we're at the top of the world.

Brad drags a finger down my cheek and hooks a stray piece of hair over my ear. "How's your ankle?"

"Fine." Sore. Swollen.

He leans in and presses those lips to my ear again. "You don't ever lie to me, Hannah. I thought we already had that worked out."

"It's sore."

He kisses my cheek. "Let me take you home and put your feet up."

I back up an inch and raise an eyebrow at him. "To your house?"

413

"My house."

"You want to take care of my sore ankle."

"I want to be with you. I don't give a rat's ass in what capacity that is. Hiking, grocery shopping, watching TV, or having you naked and moaning under me."

He's still whispering, but he makes me blush.

"Okay."

"To what?"

"Your house."

He grins and kisses me chastely, then motions for Sadie to come to the chairlift line with us. Because we have her with us, we have to ride in a gondola, rather than on the chair, which is fine with me.

The view is the same.

I press my face to the window and watch the valley coming closer and closer. We pass over people hiking the trail. A deer and her fawn are lazily eating in a meadow.

"I wonder who that kid was that tried to kill me?" I wonder out loud.

"He was going too fast for me to see," Brad replies grimly. "He did yell *sorry*."

"Well, that's something."

We come to a stop at the bottom of the lift, and I hobble out of the gondola. Sitting for only twenty minutes has made the ankle swell more and get stiff.

Damn it.

We begin to walk to the truck, but Brad stops me. "Wait here, I'll go get the truck."

"You can't drive back here."

A cocky smile slides over his lips. "Honey, I can drive wherever I want. And you're injured. Sadie, stay with Hannah."

Sadie sits at my side and we wait while Brad, still wearing the sleeveless shirt, jogs to the truck and returns with it a few minutes later.

He helps me inside, and begins the descent down the mountain.

"I live not too far away," he informs me. "We'll get some ice on the ankle."

"It's too nice outside to spend it indoors," I reply with a slight pout. "Dumb ankle."

He smiles. "I think we can work something out."

He's right, it doesn't take us long to get down the mountain and to his house. He has a nice sized lot with a tall white fence surrounding it. The house is grey and not too big. Well cared for, and new.

"Did you have this built?"

"Yeah, about three years ago," he says as he pulls into the garage, cuts the engine, and closes the door behind us. "Stay here for a minute."

It's not a question, and he doesn't give me time to ask why. He's out of the truck, along with Sadie, and inside before I can blink. I'm waiting for maybe five minutes when he comes back into the garage and opens the door for me.

"Sorry about that, I wanted to make sure everything was still locked up tight and there was no danger before you came in."

"Why do I think there's a story behind that statement?"

He shrugs and takes my hand, helping me out of the tall truck. When I limp inside his house, he simply lifts me into his arms and walks into the kitchen.

"How about a tour?"

"Are you going to carry me through the whole house?"

"I hope so."

I laugh and nod. "Okay. Give me the grand tour."

There's a white and gleaming stainless steel kitchen, living room, and three bedrooms, one of which has been made into an office. The master bedroom is spacious enough for his king bed, a dog bed for Sadie, and a sitting area. French doors open to a patio in the backyard.

The master bath is what dreams are made of with marble floors and countertops. There's a huge walk-in shower, and a large, free-standing soaking tub.

"I could swim in that tub."

"Be nice and you might get the chance," he says with a wink. He carries me back to the living area, but rather than set me on the couch, he walks out of another large set of French doors to the backyard, and my mouth drops.

"Okay, this is my favorite part of the house."

"Mine, too," he says with a grin and lowers me to an outdoor sofa. He kisses my forehead, then turns and walks back into the house.

The patio is covered, with a fireplace in the corner. It's truly an outdoor living space, with plush cushions and a dining room table, along with a grill and outdoor kitchen on the opposite side.

A waterfall runs behind me, making me sleepy.

"Did you do all of this landscaping yourself?" I ask when he returns with a towel and a bag of ice.

"Most of it," he says. "Jenna helped some. She has the green thumb. I like to be outside in the summer, and I wanted a beautiful outdoor space."

"Well, you got it." He rests my foot in his lap and covers it with the towel and ice. "Oh, that's good."

"You probably shouldn't have hiked the rest of the mountain."

"I'm going to be fine," I assure him. "I'll rest for the weekend, and be good as new in a couple of days."

"Have you always had anxiety?" he asks, throwing me off.

"For as long as I can remember." I nod, keeping my eyes on my foot. We said we'd always tell the truth. "I can remember waking up in the middle of the night as a little girl and needing to throw up. I wasn't sick. And once I did that, I'd go back to sleep and feel better.

"My dad wasn't mean. But he liked to drink, quite a lot actually. No one likes to be around a drunk, even if he is happy go lucky."

"No, they don't."

"I used to call it stress. I can stress out about stress that hasn't happened yet. I over think. I imagine the worst."

*I always think that I'm going to die.*

"But sometimes, it'll just come out of the blue, and I freak out. It doesn't last long. Are you scared off yet?"

"Should I be?"

"I'm a mess, Brad. I worry about things that aren't happening."

"You're not a mess. You have anxiety."

"Yeah, well, sometimes it feels like they're one and the same. So if you want to take me home and forget all about this, I'd understand."

"I'm a cop," he says and massages my calf. "I work *all the time*. I see shit that no one should ever see, even in a small town. I've been known to have an occasional night terror. I'm not prince charming, Hannah. We all have shit that we're dealing with."

"Yeah. We do." I reach out and take his hand in mine, squeezing it hard. "I'm sorry."

"I'm okay," he says. "It could be a lot worse."

"Do you have night terrors all the time?"

"No, but often enough. You should know that if we move forward because I don't want to scare the piss out of you. I'll never hurt you. But I might yell. Get restless."

"What helps?"

He stops and looks at me as if he's confused.

"What helps calm you down?"

"I don't know."

I nod, understanding completely. Until this afternoon, I didn't know either.

"So, the same goes," he continues. "If you'd like to go, I get it."

"I can't walk very far," I reply. But I let the ice fall to the floor and scoot into his lap, wrapping my arms around his neck. "I'm not going."

"Thank Christ."

# CHAPTER 5

## ~BRAD~

It's the end of the work day and I'm ready to head out. I have a date with Hannah that I've been looking forward to all day, but just as I'm about to reach for my keys, I get a call on the work cell.

I send it to voice mail.

And then twenty seconds later, I get a call on my personal cell.

"Hell," I mutter and answer.

"I know you're done for the day, Chief, but I think you're going to want to know about this," Officer Thomas, a long time friend and cop says.

"What's up?"

"I need you to come down to the city beach."

"I'll be there in ten."

I hang up and hurry out to the truck, calling Hannah on my way.

"Hey there," she says with a smile in her voice.

"I might be a little late," I say. "I'm sorry, I just got a call."

"If anyone understands, it's me. Just keep me posted. Do you want me to go look in on Sadie?"

I grin, wondering how in the hell I got lucky enough to find this sweet woman. "She'll be okay. She was with me until lunch time."

"Sounds good. Be safe."

She hangs up just as I'm getting close to the city beach, or the swimming area at the head of our lake where people can swim and launch their boats.

There's an ambulance, two squad cars, a fire truck, and a crowd gathered around one of the boat launch docks.

"What's going on?" I ask Thomas as I approach. "And why are these people standing around?"

"We haven't had time to shoo them off," he says with a grim frown. "It's bad, Chief." He leads me to the ambulance, which is angled away from the onlookers. Sam Waters, the head EMT with the department is standing inside next to a gurney with a body covered with a sheet.

"Chief," Sam says. "We worked on him for thirty minutes, but there was nothing we could do."

"Why aren't you on the way to the hospital?"

"He won't be going to the hospital," Sam says. "You didn't hear the call?"

"No, I turned the scanner down while I finished some paperwork. Who is this?"

Sam and Thomas share a look.

"Who the fuck is it?"

"Kendall Reardon," Sam says and rubs his fingers over his mouth. "Kyle's oldest."

"Fuck," I mutter and dig my thumb and forefinger into my eyes. "How?"

"From what we can tell, he dove into the water from a boat and was electrocuted."

"What?" My head whips up.

"There was an underground electric box that surfaced, and it killed him."

"No more swimming." I yell over at the other officers who are managing crowd control. "Teller! No more swimming or boating until we get this figured out. Get all of the boats off this lake, and I want a team patrolling to make sure no one is swimming. Have the owner of the boat take you to where this happened, and call the damn electric company to get this taken care of."

"Yes, Chief," Dan Teller says and moves into action. I get on the radio and call in all of the men I have that are currently off duty. I need all hands on deck for this.

"I didn't think you'd want just anyone to talk to Kyle," Thomas says. "I know you guys go way back."

"You're right." I nod and make another call for my chaplain. "Get Kendall to the morgue, and make sure no one sets foot in that water."

"Yes, sir," both Sam and Thomas reply at the same time. I run to my truck and take a call from the chaplain on duty.

"What's going on?" Matt Nichols asks. He's been a chaplain for five years, but he's lived in Cunningham Falls all of his life.

"We need to visit Kyle Reardon," I reply before clearing my throat. "Kendall was killed this afternoon."

"Damn," Matt mutters. "Is he home this time of day?"

"I fucking hope so, because I don't want to have to go to the school to deliver this news. School just got out for the summer, so the chances are good he'll be home. Meet me at his place and we'll go from there. I want to get to him before someone else calls him."

We hang up and I'm at Kyle's house within five minutes. Matt pulls up right behind me. I take a deep breath and stare at the small, well kept house that I've spent many mornings in having coffee with my friend after his kids have gone off to school. Kyle lost his wife to cancer just a couple of years ago, and now I have to deliver the news that his oldest son isn't coming home.

Matt waits for me on the sidewalk, and I join him, then walk with him to the door. Kyle's car is in the driveway.

He's home. He opens the door, and the second he sees both me and Matt, his eyes fill with sadness and he gestures for us to come inside.

❧

I SHOULD GO HOME. I should absolutely *not* go to Hannah's tonight. My emotions are raw. I would not be good company right now. But I can't seem to stay away. I shoot her a quick text and ask her if it's too late to drop by, and she immediately answers not at all.

Kyle only lives about four blocks from her, so I'm there quickly. She answers the door with a sunny smile, lifting my heavy heart just a bit.

"I'm so glad you texted," she says as she steps back, letting me inside.

"I shouldn't have," I reply honestly and shove my hand in my hair, pacing her living room. "I should have gone home."

She cocks her head to the side and props her hands on her hips. She's in shorts and a simple T-shirt, but I've never seen anything so beautiful in all of my life.

"Why didn't you?"

"Go home?" She nods. "Hell, because I'm not good company for myself either, and being with you sounded much better than pacing my house while Sadie watches with sad eyes."

"Why are you upset?"

I rub my fingers over my lips, not wanting to put what I did today in her head.

"Dead babies," she says and walks right to me, wrapping her arms around my waist and looking up at me with shining blue eyes. "I deliver dead babies. I have to tell women that they have cancer. Or that their child will have Down's syndrome. Or a deformity. I have had a twelve year old girl in my office, pregnant, and terrified to tell her parents.

"I can take this. I can hear whatever it is that you have to unload."

I drag my fingers down her soft cheek and enjoy the way her arms feel around me, then take a deep breath.

"Do you know Kyle Reardon?"

She frowns. "The principal?"

"Yes."

"I don't think I've met him personally, but Grace has always had nice things to say about him."

"His oldest son died today."

The words sound hollow to my own ears.

"Oh, Brad."

"Seventeen years old," I continue and pull away from her. Not because I don't love her touch, but because I have to pace. If I'm going to tell this, I don't want her to touch me until it's over.

"I've known Kyle all of my life. He was a little older than me in school, but we're friends. We ski together in the winter. I've known all of his kids since they were born, and I mourned with him when he lost his wife two years ago to cancer."

"Oh no," she says, but I keep talking.

"And today, I had to show up at his doorstep with a chaplain and explain to him that his son was electrocuted in the water and was killed instantly. That there was nothing *anyone* could do, and that it wasn't anyone's fault. It was a stupid, horrible accident, and it took his son's life."

"I'm so sorry."

"Before I could tell him *anything*, I had to call his sister to come get his other three children, and then I held him while he wept. My friend, who has been through hell and back in the past few years, and was finally pulling it back together. How do you do that?"

I stop and narrow my eyes, barely seeing her now, lost in my own head. "How do you do that, Hannah?"

"You just do," she says softly. "You do what you have to do, and you're strong for them, and then you go home and you fall apart."

"It's so fucking unfair," I growl and shake my head. "Kendall was going to be a senior this year, and he was a phenomenal football player. And not just for a small town. For any town."

"He sounds like a special kid."

I nod and swallow hard, trying to keep it together. "He is. Was."

"Do you need to go be with Kyle?"

"Not tonight. We stayed for a couple of hours, and then his sister and mom came back with the kids. There will be visitors and lots of food delivered when news spreads through town, as it always does. I was so damn worried that someone who was at the lake would call him before I got to him."

"They didn't?"

"His phone started ringing just as I walked in the door, and I told him to turn it off." I shake my head again, still not fully grasping it all.

And Hannah walks back into my arms again, hugging me fiercely, her face pressed to my chest. I hug her back, holding her tightly, and bury my nose in her hair, breathing her in. She's the calm in the storm for me.

"Thank you for listening," I murmur. She tilts her head up, and I want to kiss the fuck out of her. I want to haul her to her bedroom and strip her bare and have my way with her until we've both forgotten our names.

But not tonight. My emotions are raw, and I refuse the first time I sink inside her to be when I'm upset.

"I have an idea," she says, oblivious to my thoughts.

"What's that?"

"How about ice cream?"

I frown down at her, thrown off course. "What about it?"

"It always makes me feel better. Let's walk down to the ice cream place and get a scoop."

"We could drive."

She shakes her head and pulls away. She shoves a twenty-dollar bill in her pocket along with her keys and pulls her hair up in a messy ponytail. "It's a beautiful evening. Let's walk. It's less than half a mile."

"How do you know that?"

"Oh, I checked. If I walk, I can get two scoops." Her blue eyes are still full of worry, but she's trying to take my head out of the horror of today, and damn if it isn't working.

After a couple of blocks of walking on the uneven sidewalks, the trees above us on the boulevards swaying in the slight early summer breeze, I pull her hand up to my lips and kiss her knuckles.

"You're right. It's a beautiful night."

"I know." She grins. "This place changes out the flavors all the time. Maybe they have some summer flavors."

"You're really serious about your ice cream."

She laughs. "Ice cream is serious business."

It's past seven in the evening, so there's a line, but we wait patiently, reading the board of flavors. When it's our turn, Hannah gets a scoop of huckleberry and a scoop of cinnamon vanilla, surprising me when she passes on the coffee ice cream.

It all sounds great, but I get the same as Hannah and before I know it, we're on our way back to her house. Our steps are slower this time, as we eat and enjoy the evening.

"Wait. Did you pay for my ice cream?" I stop and stare down at her in surprise.

"Sure did."

"Not cool, Doctor Malone."

"Why, Chief Hull? A girl can't buy a guy ice cream?"

"Not this guy. If we're on a date, I'm paying."

"That's quite chivalrous, and cave man, of you," she says with a laugh. "I'm happy to splurge on some ice cream once in a while. I promise not to make a habit out of it."

"Now you're mocking me."

I take the last bite of my cone and wipe my mouth with the napkin.

"Of course I am," she agrees. "You're being ridiculous."

"It's ridiculous for a man to take care of his woman?"

This makes her pause, as she eats the last of her ice cream as well, and then tucks her napkin in her back pocket.

"A couple of things," she says at last. "First, I can, and do, take care of myself."

"And what's the other thing?"

"Who says I'm your *woman?*"

"Me." We stop on the sidewalk and I turn her to face me, my hands gripping her shoulders. "I'm sure as fuck not sharing you with anyone."

"Well, I didn't suggest that either," she says, shaking her head, then continues walking. About ten feet away, she looks back at me over her shoulder. "Are you coming?"

"That's all you have to say?"

"You answered my question. But you need to know that I'm an independent woman, Brad. Not because I'm trying to prove anything to anyone, but because that's just who I am. I don't need to be saved."

"Not trying to save you," I reply reasonably. I've never wanted to fuck anyone so bad in my life. "Just letting you know that when we're together, I'll be buying you dinner."

"And dessert, apparently."

We've arrived at her house, but I don't follow her up to her door. She walks back down to the bottom of the steps. "You don't want to come in?"

"I do." I cup her cheek and she leans into my touch. "So I'd better not."

She looks disappointed, but nods. "I don't have to be at the clinic until noon tomorrow," she informs me. "In case you need anything."

I lean in and cover her lips with mine, tasting the sweetness from the huckleberries and the cinnamon she just ate. Tasting *her.*

"Have a good night," I murmur against her lips and turn to leave.

When I start my truck and drive away, she's still standing on her sidewalk, her fingers on her lips, watching me go.

～

*I'M IN THE WATER. I'm an excellent swimmer, but I can't move. It's like I'm trudging through wet cement. My legs are heavy, and I can't get through the water fast enough.*

*I look up and see Kendall floating in the water, face down, just twenty feet away from me. If I can just get over to him, I might be able to save him. What's he doing in the water?*

*Suddenly, I'm surrounded by floating bodies. My men. My sister and brother. Hannah. All just out of my reach.*

*I can't save them.*

*The water is rising around me, no longer just around my legs, but up to my chest now. Then my chin, and over my head.*

*I'm completely submerged, my feet still held in the bottom of the lake. I look up and see faces staring down at me. Faces of those I love. Their eyes are wide open, glaring at me in accusation.*

You didn't even try to save us.

*I'm fighting to swim. To dislodge my feet, but it's no use. I can't get free.*

I wake up, sitting the bed, screaming. I'm covered in sweat, and Sadie is standing beside me, whining in worry.

I still can't breathe. I tip my face up, gasping for air and trying to push the terror away.

I haven't had an episode like this in over a year, but it's not surprising after yesterday. The sadness is here again, but the guilt is gone.

There was nothing I could do about what happened. I couldn't save him.

But my friend is hurting, and that makes me sad. A kid who had a bright future ahead of him is gone, and that's the biggest tragedy of all.

I push my hands through my soaked hair, then pat the bed, inviting Sadie up. She's not usually allowed on the bed, but I could use some companionship right now, and Hannah is clear across town.

Hannah.

She calmed me down yesterday. She seemed to understand, and I don't think I've ever known anyone except my dad who could really understand what this part of the job is like.

She's a special woman, and now that I have her in my life, I'm not going to fuck it up.

Sadie finally lays her head down to sleep, and I leave the bed for a shower. I'm gross, as if I'd been in the ring at the gym for an hour. Once clean, I put on clothes for the day and brew a cup of coffee.

It's only four in the morning, but I'm up for the day. I'll never go back to sleep now.

I want to go to Hannah's and climb into bed with her, but she's asleep, and we aren't quite there yet. Soon, I hope.

Sadie pads out of the bedroom, her eyes sleepy.

"You don't have to get up," I tell her, but she sits next to me, always loyal. I let her outside and set some food down for her, which she appreciates when she comes back in. Finally, I sit in my living room with another cup of coffee and Sadie at my feet and wait for morning.

Four hours later, I walk into Drips & Sips and nod at Anna, the owner who happens to be working behind the counter today.

"Are you taking coffee to a certain doctor again today?" she asks. Anna might be the nosiest person in town, which is saying a lot because Cunningham Falls has its share of nosy people.

"I am," I reply with a nod. "And I'll take my usual as well."

She gets busy making our drinks.

"Heard about that poor Reardon boy," Anna says, shaking her head. "Do you have anything you can tell me?"

"No, ma'am," I reply and grit my teeth. "It's an ongoing investigation."

"It's just so horrible. Poor Kyle. He must just be devastated."

"I'm sure." *Just make the fucking coffee.*

Anna keeps chirping about Kendall and his mom, then finally passes the coffees to me, which I throw a bill down for and tell her to keep the change, just wanting to get the hell out of here.

Sadie is waiting patiently for me in the car. When I turn down Hannah's street, Sadie gets excited. She already knows where Hannah's house is.

Seems I'm not the only one falling for her.

# CHAPTER 6

## ~HANNAH~

Someone is ringing my fucking doorbell. I was at the hospital until the wee hours, I was finally in a deep, lovely sleep, and someone is ringing the bell.

All I know for sure is, this had better not be the damn door-to-door people trying to sell me a vacuum. Or a magazine. Or Jesus.

I wrap my robe around me, stumbling toward the door. I pull it open and am surprised to find an excited Sadie and a ridiculously sexy Brad standing at my door.

"Is that coffee?" I ask.

"For you," he confirms and holds it out to me.

"Come to mama," I mutter and take it from his hand, taking a grateful sip. Sadie brushes past my leg, into the house, and curls up on my couch.

"She's not supposed to be on the furniture," Brad says.

"My house, my rules," I reply and take another sip of the one thing in this world I'm addicted to, and give him a once over from head to toe. "You look like you got about as much sleep as I did."

"Rough night?" he asks without confirming or denying.

"Babies," I reply with a shrug. "You?"

He just shrugs. "Are you going to ask me in?"

"Sure." I back up and gesture him into the room. "Sorry, I was sleeping pretty good. My energy level is about equal to a sloth on Xanax."

"I can leave and let you go back to bed."

His eyes roam up and down my body, reminding me that I'm just in a robe and nothing else. His green eyes are hot, and every muscle in his body is tight.

Even sleep deprived, I can tell when a man is in the mood.

"You've brought me coffee. I'll never kick you out when you've done that."

"I'll remember that," he says with a chuckle.

"Besides, I have plenty of room." I turn and walk into my bedroom, glancing behind me to see that he's following me. He makes a hand gesture at Sadie, which I assume means *stay*. "We can take a nap," I suggest.

His lips twitch, but he doesn't say anything when he joins me next to the bed. He takes my coffee and sets both of our cups on the bedside table.

"Is that what you want, Hannah?" he murmurs and skims his fingertips down my arms.

"Eventually."

He hitches his finger in the belt of my robe. "What do you have on under here?"

I'm staring at his mouth. His lips are just... *wow*. I want them on me. All over me. Every fucking inch.

"Maybe you should just take it off and find out," I whisper, unsure of where my voice went.

He takes a long, deep breath, his finger is moving back and forth under the belt. He leans in and kisses my forehead and pulls the belt loose, letting the robe gape open down the middle.

I expect him to step back to watch it fall away, but he doesn't. He slides his large, warm hand under it, gliding against my skin at my waist, then back to cup my bare ass.

He takes a sharp breath and whispers, "You're naked."

"Yeah."

"Are you always naked when you sleep?"

"Unless I just fall down in my clothes, yes."

"I didn't bring condoms," he says, disappointment hanging heavy in his voice.

"I do this stuff for a living," I remind him with a grin. "I've got pregnancy covered, and I'm as clean as a person gets."

His lips twitch. "Me, too." He kisses my forehead again, then my cheek, and he's pushing my robe off my shoulders to pool around my feet. He lays his lips over mine, not moving them, just resting as his hands move from my shoulders to my breasts. Rather than grope, his fingers lightly skim my nipples, making them pucker in readiness, wanting his lips.

But his lips are still on mine, and now they begin to move. Slowly, lazily, fitting the mood perfectly, his soft lips brush over mine, back and forth. He nibbles the corner, making my skin break out in goosebumps.

He guides me onto the bed, but before he can settle in, I pull at the hem of his T-shirt, tucked into his jeans.

"You're way over dressed."

He smiles against my mouth, and then he's gone to quickly discard his clothes. He went from lazy and slow to The Flash in 2.1 seconds, and now he's standing next to me, all six-foot-five-ish of him, tanned and muscular and *hard*.

Hard everywhere.

"You can come back here now."

He smiles and covers my body with his, but rather than kiss me all over, he braces himself on his elbows on either side of my head and holds my gaze in his.

"Hannah."

"Yeah."

"You're sexier than I ever imagined, and I can't wait to sink inside you."

I can only smile at him.

"But if you think you're running this show, you're sorely mistaken, sweetheart."

His lips are on mine again and his hands are buried in my hair, and I'm already lost to him. To his hands and body and mouth, and he's only just started.

He kisses my jawline to my ear, then down my neck to my collarbone. My legs are restless, scissoring in anticipation, as he pulls one nipple into his mouth and tugs gently, then harder. He's worrying the other with his fingers, and it's like there's a line directly to my pussy, making it pulse with every tug of his lips.

My fingers are in his hair, fisted, holding on for dear life. Jesus, I'm ready to come and he hasn't even touched me farther south than my tits.

How am I going to survive this?

But then he drags his nose down my tummy, over my navel, and spreads my legs wide, and all rational thought flies right out the window.

*Holy hell on wheels.*

My wish from earlier is being granted as his mouth travels over me. My thighs, biting and licking his way up to the crease where my leg meets my core. He brushes his nose over my clit, then goes to work on the other thigh, making me writhe and curse, fisting the sheets.

"Do you have something to say?" he asks and looks up at me with blazing green eyes.

"You're killing me," I grind out through gritted teeth.

"You don't like this?" He bites my tender inner thigh gently and makes me moan in pleasure. "Are you sure, because it sounds like you like it."

"Dear God, I like it."

"What about this?" His fingers stroke my outer labia, just enough to spread the wetness around, and make me about come out of my skin. "Do you like this?"

"Oh yeah."

He chuckles and reaches up to cup my breast, flicking his thumb over the nipple. "Your breasts are perfect."

"Small."

"Perfect," he says again, and with his hand still covering said breast, he holds my gaze as he lowers his mouth to my core, sucking my clit between his lips, and my whole world shatters around me, sending me into another dimension. My head falls back, and all I can do is arch my back and moan as he makes me feel things that I didn't even know were possible.

Like shivers and contractions and my legs shaking uncontrollably.

He's a wizard. This is fucking wizardry.

He moves his mouth off my clit and down to my lips, licking and nibbling, and the next thing I know, he pushes two fingers inside me as he moves back up my body, covering me fully.

"Look at me."

I open my eyes to find his face hovering over mine.

"I'm going to see this happen this time." His fingers are moving, twisting, inside me, brushing against a spot that's making every hair on my body tingle.

I bite my lip and close my eyes, but his voice is firm. "Open."

I comply, and he presses the flat of his hand against my clit, and I fall apart, crying out as he watches me in maybe the most intimate moment of my life.

Before I float all the way back down to earth, Brad moves between my legs, pushing my knees up, and presses his cock against my sopping wet core.

"You're sure?"

"Please, God, don't stop now."

That's all he needs to hear. He sinks inside me, balls deep, and rests there, breathing hard and watching me closely.

"You're so fucking tight," he growls. He falls to his elbows and buries his face in my neck, kissing me there as his hips rear back and then push against me again, picking up a pace that's steady and sure, but not hard or too fast.

I feel so full. On fire. And when he lifts his head and smiles down at me, I feel adored. As weird as it sounds, that's exactly the way I feel right now.

Like he just can't get enough of me.

He holds my gaze as he moves a bit faster, pushing just a little harder, and finally succumbs to his own release.

"Holy shit," he whispers, trying to catch his breath.

"Yeah," I agree and drag my fingers down his face. "Holy shit."

∼

"CAN'T you call in sick today?" Brad asks me about two hours later after we've cleaned ourselves up, then got messy again before eating some eggs and bacon.

Sexy mornings should happen more often. They're highly underrated.

"I don't think so," I reply and bite my lip in disappointment. "But we have two more hours before I have to be there. Don't you have to go into work?"

"I should," he says with a sigh. "After yesterday, I'll have some paperwork to see to, and I need to get reports from everyone regarding the electricity in the water."

"Are people able to swim and boat yet?"

"Yeah, I lifted that ban late last night when I got a call saying all power that runs under the lake has been shut off for now while they figure out what the fuck went wrong." He sighs and rubs his hand over his face, and I'm sorry that I asked. He was finally relaxed.

"I'm sorry," I say and straddle his lap. We're on the couch, lounging with Sadie now curled up on my recliner. I cup his face in my hands and kiss him sweetly. "You're not supposed to be thinking about that right now."

He cups my ass, gripping firmly, and smiles up at me. "What should I think about?"

"Well, there was some pretty impressive sexy time this morning."

"We could keep that trend going," he suggests as I unzip his pants and set him free, already hard again. I'm in a sundress, with no panties, so it's easy to slide right over him, making us both sigh in lust.

"God, you're fucking amazing," he says, pulling my dress up over my head so he can get his hands on my breasts. "Beautiful."

"You feel *so good.*" I'm moving faster, riding him and glorying in how he feels from this angle. "So deep."

"God, babe." He takes my nipple into his mouth, and I can't help it. I fall apart at the seams, bearing down on him so hard that he has no choice but to come with me. I collapse against him, breathing hard.

"Hannah. You asked me before what helps, remember?"

"I do."

"It's you." He cups my face and kisses me softly. "It's just you."

∼

"Is it weird that the hospital has better food than some of the restaurants in town?" I ask Drake the next afternoon. I've been running back and forth between the clinic and the hospital all day because I have a patient carrying twins who went into labor this morning. She's still in labor, six hours later, but there's no distress and she's laboring well. Now that my appointments are finished for the day, I can hang out here at the hospital to be close by, just in case.

So, I'm having a quick late lunch with Drake while my patient takes a break, catching a quick nap.

"I've been in a few hospitals with good food," he says and sprinkles pepper over his avocado salad.

"I guess I always expect it to suck." I shrug and watch my friend, who has a frown on his handsome face. "So what's been going on with you? Are you dating anyone?"

"Hell no," he replies and licks a drop of lemon dressing off his thumb. "Women are trouble."

"How so?"

"They start to get clingy and hint that they want a ring on their finger. And by *hint* I mean state it under no uncertain terms, and by ring I mean a sixty-thousand-dollar rock."

"Like I said, women are trouble."

"True story," I reply with a nod, and then giggle.

Drake sits back and watches me closely. "You're dating someone."

"True story," I repeat and take a big bite of a chicken tender so I don't have to answer his next question right away.

"Who?"

"Bffd mmm."

He raises a brow and waits for me to swallow my food.

"Try that again."

"Brad Hull."

"The police chief?"

"Do you know of another one?"

He looks genuinely surprised. "I actually like Brad."

"Did you think I'd decide to date someone you don't like?"

"I'm surprised you're dating at all. You're usually too much of a workaholic like me."

"I'm still a workaholic, but so is he." I shrug. "So we only see each other a couple of times during the week, but it's nice to find a guy who understands the long hours, you know? Who doesn't complain about it. I mean, he did ask if I could call in sick yesterday, but that's just because the sexy time was off the charts."

"TMI," he says and takes a bite of his salad. "Is he nice to you?"

"Yes, he plays nice." I roll my eyes. "Plus, Sadie is such a sweetie."

"This is a threesome situation?" he asks, blinking rapidly.

"What are you, twelve?"

"On a scale of one to ten, yes." He grins. "Who's Sadie?"

"His dog."

"You've fallen for a guy's dog?"

"She's a super sweet dog," I reply defensively. "She's a retired police dog."

"You know, you could just adopt your own dog. You don't need a man for that."

"Ha ha." I throw a french fry at him and then laugh. "I like both him and the dog. He knows about the anxiety, and he's actually really understanding."

"Wow," Drake says with surprise. "You're serious about this one."

"He gets me," I reply. "So yeah, I want to see where this goes."

"Good for you, Han. Maybe we'll go on a double date sometime."

"I thought you said you're not dating anyone?"

He raises a brow again, and I dissolve into laughter. "Okay, I get it. Sure, we can do that."

My phone rings. "This is Dr. Malone."

"This is Siobhan," my nurse says. "Your patient wants to see you."

"I'm on my way."

I hang up and sigh. "Lunch is over for me. I'm being summoned."

"Take it with you."

"Oh, I am. I'll hide in my office and eat the rest later." I wink at him and turn, but he calls me back. "Yeah?"

"You look happy. I like it."

"Thanks." I smile and hurry away, wondering what's up with the patient. She might just be nervous and need another pep talk. That happens all the time, and is perfectly normal.

I stow my half eaten lunch in my office, wipe my mouth off, grab my stethoscope and hurry into the patient's room.

"What's happening in here?"

"Something's wrong," Jennifer, my patient says. Her husband is holding her hand and looks at me with desperation in his eyes.

I immediately look at the monitors, and everything looks normal.

"There are no warning signs here," I reply, but I lay my hand on her belly, and she writhes in pain.

"It feels like my whole body is being squeezed by a giant hand."

"Well, you're having a baby. You're having *two* babies, and it's going to hurt. Did you go to birthing classes?"

"We did," Trent says with a nod.

"Great. Remember your breathing."

"Right." Jennifer nods. "Breathing." She begins to breathe quickly, pursing her lips and staring at Trent in concentration. The fetal monitor begins to move up, indicating another one, and she squeezes his hand even harder, making him wince.

"See?" I get her attention, pointing to the monitor. "You can see here when a contraction is coming, when it peaks, and when it's coming back down. If it helps, watch this and breathe with it. I'm going to check you real quick."

I turn away and wash my hands, then reach for the gloves. Jennifer is still breathing, and I expect to find that she might be already dilated to about an eight, if she's in this much pain already.

I take a deep breath, telling my brain to shut off. I've delivered hundreds of babies, and I wouldn't do this for all of the money in the world. No way. I'm not going to turn my body inside out like this.

Nope.

But I put a smile on my face, and urge her to spread her legs so I can reach in to see how ready her body is to give birth to these babies.

*Two centimeters.*

That's it?

I pull away and throw the gloves away, then wash my hands again.

"Well?" she asks. "Something's wrong, isn't it?"

"Not at all," I reassure her. "Jennifer, you're dilated at two centimeters."

"Only two?" Trent asks, reading my mind.

"I'm afraid so. I know you're uncomfortable, and if you want to elect for a cesarean section, we can still do that."

"No, I want to have them naturally," she insists.

"Are you sure you don't even want some medication?" I ask. "There are two babies here, Jennifer."

"No meds." She shakes her head and I sigh. She's at a two, which tells me she has many hours ahead of her to labor, and she doesn't want the drugs.

*Take the drugs!*

Always take the drugs. I know, many people would frown at that philosophy, but I've seen a lot of natural births. I'm *never* birthing anything, but if I did, I'd take all of the drugs.

"Okay, that's your choice," I reply, calm as can be. "I recommend getting up and walking around a bit. Up and down the hallway. That sometimes helps. After you've done that for a while, we'll put you in the bathtub. A nice bath will sometimes help your muscles relax."

"Let's do that now," she says, but I shake my head.

"There's no speedy way to do this," I reply. "Babies come when they're ready. I think we're going to be here most of the night, but you might surprise me. Let's get you up walking, and we'll go from there."

She nods and gestures for her husband to pass her the pink terrycloth bathrobe over the reclining chair.

She also brought bunny slippers.

"I like your hospital style," I say with a smile.

"I figured I should be comfortable. Well, my feet anyway."

"Absolutely. Oh, and have Trent massage your feet, too. That will help you relax."

"What helps me relax?" Trent asks.

"You're not pushing two babies out today, my friend. It's all about helping Jennifer relax."

He sighs, but smiles at his wife. "We've got this."

Jennifer doubles over in pain and starts to breathe, leaning on Trent's arms.

*Yeah, no. No babies for me.*

# CHAPTER 7

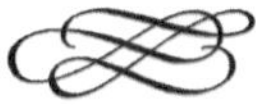

## ~HANNAH~

"Thank you," Jennifer says twenty-three hours later through tear-filled eyes. "Thank you for staying with me all night."

"I wasn't going anywhere," I assure her and smile down at one of the babies in her arms. "I'm sorry we had to deliver them by cesarean after all."

She shrugs and smiles at her daughter. "They're here, and they're safe, and that's all that really matters."

"My colleague is here now, and I'm going to do a few things to finish up and head home. I want you to rest today. I know your family will be excited to be here, but I want you to limit visitors today. I'll give instructions to your nurse. Let her be the bad guy, Jenn. All of you need rest, and I mean it."

She nods. "I know. I'm pretty tired."

*That makes two of us.* I close my laptop and walk out the door to the nurse's station.

I'm still in my scrubs. I'm so damn exhausted I'm surprised I'm still walking. I want to curl up somewhere soft and warm and sleep for about four days.

Maybe five days.

I'm going to finish up my notes and go home. I'm not going to talk to anyone because I'll get stuck here for longer. Do *not* make eye contact with anyone at the nurse's station. Just keep walking to the office.

But when I approach the nurse's station, everyone is grinning at me, sipping coffee and munching on bagels.

And my stomach immediately growls.

"If you tell me none of that is left, I might throw a temper tantrum here and now."

Lucy, a nurse that I've worked with since I moved here, grins and passes me a coffee and a note.

"This was delivered," she says with a wink. "All of this is for you, but it's for all of us, too."

"You're speaking in riddles," I reply, my exhausted brain not able to keep up. So I open the note and feel everything in me soften.

*Hannah,*
*You have to be exhausted and running on empty. Here is some fuel. Call me later.*
*Brad*

"He brought me coffee from *Sips* and bagels from *Little Deli.*"

"And thank the good lord for it," Lucy replies. "Because he brought enough for everyone."

"And then some," another nurse, Betty, says.

"He was here?" I ask.

"No, Mrs. Blakely delivered them."

"I've always liked Mrs. Blakely," I murmur, speaking of the owner of *Little Deli.* "And he got my usual coffee."

"You should call and thank him," Lucy says.

"Do you guys even know who *he* is?" I ask.

"Honey, this is a small town. We've all known for a few days now that you've been dating Chief Hull." Betty takes a sip of her coffee. "And I'd like to say, you should keep dating him if he's going to bring us treats."

I shake my head and laugh, walking toward my office. I need to call and thank him.

"Hull," he says into his phone, sounding distracted.

"I'd like to report a disturbance at the hospital amongst the nurses over a bagel delivery," I say and smile when he chuckles in my ear. "Thank you, Brad."

"You're welcome. I figured you'd need something."

"I do." *I could use you.* "I'm almost wrapped up here, and then I'm going to go home and sleep, then wake up and eat another bagel for dinner."

"Don't eat a bagel for dinner, sweetheart. I'll bring something."

I rub my chest, just over my heart and the slight ache I have there whenever he speaks to me in this soft voice.

"I'll be so out of it, it won't matter."

"If it doesn't matter, then I'm coming over," he says and I just smile, already excited to see him.

"Okay. There's a key under the flowerpot in the corner of the porch. Just let yourself in because I probably won't hear the doorbell."

"Are you okay to drive home?"

"Yeah, it's not far." I yawn and then take a sip of my delicious java. "And I have coffee to sustain me until I get there. Thanks to a handsome police officer I know."

"Who is he? I'll kill him."

I snort. "You're no killer."

"This has turned into an odd conversation." He pulls the phone away from his face to talk to someone in the room with him and then comes back. "Sorry, Hannah, I have to go. Be careful getting home and I'll see you later."

"Thank you for all of this. Sincerely."

"You're welcome."

And with that he's gone and I'm left sitting in my office, barely able to keep my eyes open, despite the caffeine kick.

I need to go crash.

After quickly finishing up a few last notes, I gather a few bagels, a tub of cream cheese, and my personal things and then head toward home.

When I pull into my driveway, someone pulls in right behind me.

"Hey," Grace says when I get out of my car. "I saw you drive past me at the four-way stop a few blocks back, and thought I'd stop by for a second. How are you?"

"Exhausted." I lead her up my porch and into my house. "I haven't been home since yesterday morning."

"That's a long shift," she says and peers inside the bagel bag. "Are you willing to share one of these bagels from Mrs. Blakely?"

"Sure. Let's do it. I'm starving."

I reach for a knife to spread the cream cheese. "What are you up to today?"

"Well, that's the other reason I came by. Jacob and I are leaving later today for New York. I guess he has a couple of meetings, and a swanky party to go to. I have a dress and shoes, but I don't have a pretty clutch, and I know you have that Gucci one that Drake got you for Christmas a few years back."

"Never been used," I confirm. "You're welcome to borrow it."

"Thanks." She grins and takes a bite of her bagel. "How are things with you and Brad?"

I smile, the thought of Brad waking me right up. "Really good." I nod. "Like, really, *really* good. He's such a good guy. He's sweet and strong. He cares deeply about his friends. His dog is the *best*."

I take a sip of my now almost cold coffee, thinking of him. "He's a gentleman. And I mean he's a *gentle man.* Sometimes they're not the same thing."

"Agreed."

"I don't think I've ever met anyone like him. The sex? Holy shit, Grace."

"Wow," she says, watching me avidly. "That good?"

"I didn't even know some of the things he's done to me were possible, and I'm no virgin."

"Atta girl," she says, holding her fist out for a bump. "I don't care what anyone says, sexual chemistry is super important."

"Absolutely. And he also likes to hold me. He's always touching me. And he recently told me that the only thing in the world that calms him down is me."

"Jesus, Hannah, you're in love!"

I stop and stare at her, blinking rapidly.

"Well, no."

"I've only ever talked this way about the man I love," she says reasonably. "And I think it's fantastic. I'm so excited for you."

"Wait." I stand and pace the kitchen, thinking about this. "Maybe this is too good to be true. I mean, I haven't really known him that long."

"Only a few years," Grace says with a smirk.

"I mean *really* known him. What if he's not at all what I think he is? What if he's an alcoholic?"

"He's not your dad," she reminds me and I shake the thought off.

"You're right. Besides, I don't think he could function at his job as well as he does if he was drunk all the time."

"Definitely not."

"But what if he's secretly a serial killer? Or has other wives? Am I going to be a sister wife?"

"I haven't heard any talk about *any* wives, and I don't see a ring on your finger, so I'm going to say no."

"He could have kids. I've never asked him if he has kids."

"No kids," she says and tilts her head to the side. "What are you trying to do here?"

"There has to be another shoe that's going to drop," I reply and sit across from her. "Everything is too perfect. *He's* too perfect."

"Is he really perfect? Does he never have bad breath? Maybe he leaves his socks on the floor? Certainly he must fart."

I smirk. "I've never stayed at his house, so I don't know if he leaves his socks on the floor. He's a human being, so I'm sure there are faults in there somewhere that I just haven't found yet."

"Right, because you're still discovering each other. This is the best part of the relationship, when all of the butterflies happen and you can't stay away from each other. It's exciting."

"Are you saying you don't feel this anymore with Jacob?"

"Hell no, the man still gives me butterflies after a year of marriage," she says with a smile. "And, would it be weird if I'm your patient?"

"Why?"

She just sits there and smiles, and I feel like I'm missing something. Finally, she rolls her eyes and points to her stomach, and I feel my eyes widen in surprise.

"Oh my God! Really? You're pregnant?"

"That's what the stick said," she replies and pats her belly. "But we're not talking about me. We're talking about you and the perfect Brad."

"He's probably flawed," I say and frown. "Maybe."

"It sounds like you're deciding whether to stay with him, or run."

"Why would I run? I don't want to run."

"Good, because that would be really stupid. So maybe you're just, I don't know. What are you?"

"I'm dumb."

"No, you're not," she says with a giggle.

"I can't describe how I feel. It sounds weird to my own ears, but it's like I already know him. It's a connection that I can't explain, and when I'm with him, I feel so calm. It's scary."

"If it wasn't scary, it wouldn't be real," she says with a shrug, and I narrow my eyes at her.

"You're smart."

"I know."

"And if you think anyone but me is delivering that baby, you're on crack."

She laughs and reaches out to squeeze my hand. "Good. Because I don't like strangers looking at my hooha."

"It's a vagina."

"Hooha."

"Repeat after me." I grab her face in my hands. "Va-gi-na."

"Hoo-ha."

We dissolve in giggles and then I take a deep breath and push my hair over my shoulder. "I'm glad you came by. Since we don't live together anymore, I miss you."

"I miss you, too. Did I mention that we're having a big party at the lake house for the fourth of July?"

"That's a month away."

"But do you work?"

I check my calendar, and smile with excitement. "I don't! So unless someone has a baby, I'll be there."

"Cool." Grace smiles. "I've invited Jenna and Max too, so bring Brad with you."

"Yes, ma'am. Who else is coming?"

"Not anyone else I can think of. It's going to be on the smaller side. I invited the King family, but they have their own traditions for the holiday. We'll go out on the lake and eat a ton of food and we have a great view of the fireworks from our deck."

"Sounds like fun."

She checks her phone when it pings. "This is Jacob. I'd better go."

"Oh, I'll grab the clutch for you."

I hurry back to my closet and pull the small handbag out of its protective covering and take it out to my friend. "Have tons of fun, and send me photos."

"I will." She hugs me tightly. "And stop stressing out about this Brad thing. Just enjoy the super hot sex and being with someone nice to you. One day at a time."

I nod and then hide my smile behind my hand when she runs into the doorframe.

My sweet Grace is anything but graceful.

She rubs her shoulder where I'm sure she'll get a bruise, and waves from the car.

I should go crash, but now that I've talked about Brad and finished my coffee, I'm surprisingly not sleepy. Exhausted to the bone, but not sleepy.

Damn it.

I glance around my small house, wondering if there's something to clean, but my housekeeper was here yesterday and it's all done.

I can't exercise. It might kill me.

I could read, except my eyes are tired.

Why won't my brain shut off?

"I need a pet," I mutter. "Something to talk to and snuggle up to when Brad's not available."

And then an idea forms in my head. I reach for my phone and dial Brad's number.

"You're awake," he says with surprise.

"I am and I'm wondering if I can borrow your dog."

There's a pause. "Is everything okay?"

"Yeah, I just want some company and all of you normal people are at work. So can I please borrow Sadie?"

"Sure, she's here at my office. I can bring her to you."

"I'll come get her. It's not far."

"You're sure?"

"Yes. See you in a few."

Excited at the idea of seeing not only Sadie but her sexy as hell owner as well, I grab my keys and bag and hurry out to the car. The police station is only a five minute drive from my house.

When I pull into the parking lot, Brad is standing on the sidewalk with Sadie on her leash.

"Hey," I say when I climb out of the car and join them. "Thanks for letting me borrow her."

"I'm beginning to think you're just with me for my dog."

I'm feeling sassy, so I reach up and fist my hand in the back of his hair, pulling him down to kiss me. It's quick, but it's hot, and when he pulls away, I lick my lips.

"Well, I guess as long as we understand each other," I say and he frowns, as if he doesn't understand what I mean. "About Sadie. I'm just sticking around for her."

"Right." He passes me her leash and Sadie nudges my leg, ready to be petted.

"Do you want to go home with me, sweet girl?" She smiles up at me sweetly. "I think that means yes."

"I'll bring some food for her when I bring you dinner," he says. "She's done her business not long ago, so you're good to go."

"Great." I smile up at him and turn away, leading her to my car. I open the door and she happily jumps in, settling into the passenger seat. "She's done this before."

He laughs. "Go get some rest. I'll see you this evening."

I nod and take us both home. Sadie is excited when I open the front door for her. She runs for the couch, but I stop her.

"No, girl, we're going to bed." Her ears perk up and she turns her head to the side, listening. "Follow me."

I walk to my cool, dark bedroom, strip out of my clothes, and collapse onto the bed, pulling my big, heavy comforter over me. I have an extra heavy comforter that is supposed to help with anxiety.

So far, it works.

I also have blackout shades for the windows because I work at night so often, and I keep the AC low. I need a cold bedroom.

Once I'm settled in, I pat the bed next to me and Sadie jumps up with me, laying her head on my arm. "Thanks for hanging out with me today, sweet girl."

She whines happily, and I decide to send Brad a selfie of us. We both smile at the camera and I shoot it off to him.

Several moments later, he replies with, "Wish I was there with you."

I just send back, "Soon" and snuggle up to this sweet dog.

"Did you know you're very cuddly?" I ask her, petting her super soft head and ears. "You are. And your fur on your head is so soft. You're such a good girl."

Sadie's eyes are blinking heavily, and I can feel mine starting to get heavy too. Finally, the exhaustion is catching up with me and I can sleep for a long while.

But I can't help but continue to murmur to the dog in my arms.

"Your daddy is pretty great. I'm sure you already know that. You're quite loyal to him. I think we have that in common already. Can I tell you a secret, Sadie?"

She just snores, oblivious to the serious conversation we're having.

"I'm falling in love with him. Grace is right." I pet her belly, my mind on the man across town. "I don't know how he's stayed single all this time. And the anxiety in me wants to tear that thought apart, pondering if he has mother issues, or daddy issues, or any other issues that have sabotaged all of his relationships before me.

"But I don't think I'm going to do that this time. I trust him, Sadie, and that's big for me. I admire him. And my God, I love him."

I kiss her head and close my eyes, letting the heavy blanket and snoring Sadie lull me to sleep.

# CHAPTER 8

## ~BRAD~

The key is where she said it would be, under the planter in the corner of her porch. I should talk to her about the dangers of having a key in such an obvious place. It's not safe.

I have lasagna from Ciao in my hands, along with a bag of food for the dog, which I'll leave here.

I have a feeling Sadie will be spending a bit of time here.

And frankly, that's okay with me. She may seem like a big teddy bear, but if there's danger nearby, Sadie is a fierce protector. If I can't be here with Hannah, it makes me feel better knowing that Sadie is.

The house is quiet as I walk through. I set the pan of lasagna in the oven and set it to low to keep it warm, then go in search of my girls.

The bedroom is dark, even though it's still perfectly sunny outside. The light from the hall casts on Hannah's sweet face. Sadie immediately sees me and jumps off the bed to greet me. I kneel to pet her and kiss her head, then point for her to go to the living room, which she does without hesitation.

I step to the bed and look down at Hannah. I should leave her be. She has only been asleep for about four hours, and I know she needs more. And I will leave her alone, but first I want to feel her.

I slide into the bed with her and pull her to me. Her eyes open, and she blinks in confusion.

"Brad?"

"Yes, ma'am."

"I'm sorry, I'll wake up."

"No," I scoot onto my back and she snuggles up to me, her head resting on my chest. She wraps her slender arm around my midsection, holding on tightly. "Stay asleep, beautiful girl. I just want to hold you for a while."

She sighs and drifts immediately back to sleep. I kiss her forehead and hold her to me for a long moment. I haven't seen her in a few days, and I missed her. Her laugh, her voice, her body.

Everything.

It hasn't been long, but she's wiggled her way into my life and now I don't know what it would look like without her in it.

I don't want to know.

I can hear Sadie getting restless, so I slip out from under Hannah and smile when she snuggles up to her pillow, burying her face in it. I pad out to the kitchen and pour Sadie's dinner for her, then let her outside to do her business. While she's out in Hannah's fenced backyard, I run out to my truck and fetch my computer and cell phone.

Sadie joins me back inside, and she gives me the side eye when I won't let her lay on the couch, insisting she lay on the floor.

"Hannah is spoiling you."

She huffs in disapproval, but before long she's snoring. I turn the TV on and let a baseball game play in the background while I work for a while. There's always paperwork to do, calls to make, things to follow up on. If I'd still had Sadie with me, I would have stayed at the office well into the evening.

But this was a great excuse to leave. I can work from here just as well, and I want to be here when Hannah wakes up.

The reports from the electric company are in regarding the Reardon accident. That's exactly what it was, an accident. No foul play and no one's fault. A power line had surfaced at the bottom of the lake and Kendall paid the price.

We're lucky more weren't killed.

The funeral was yesterday, and I stood by my friend as he buried another person he loved more than anything. I can't imagine the pain of losing a child, and I hope to God I never do.

But I was honest when I told Hannah that she calms me. She clears the demons away, and brings lightness to my heavy heart that I haven't felt in a very long time.

Maybe never.

Sadie yawns and turns over on the floor, exposing her belly. I'm tired myself, my eyes heavy from hours of computer work. I close the computer, intending to just take a small break.

"Hey."

Someone is running their hands through my hair, scratching their nails against my scalp.

It feels fucking amazing.

I open one eye to find Hannah standing next to me, smile down at me. I'm surprised I didn't hear her approach. I'm a light sleeper, hearing every noise around me.

"Hi." I drag my hand down my face and frown at the time. "I must have fallen asleep."

"Looks like it."

I reach out, wrap my arm around her waist, and pull her into my lap, nuzzling her neck. "You smell so fucking good." She's citrus and a touch of something else that I can't put my finger on.

She's Hannah, and she's still touching me with those magical fingers, running them through my hair, over my face.

"I thought I dreamed you," she says and kisses my cheek. "But I'm so glad I didn't."

"You didn't. I brought dinner."

"I can smell it. That's what woke me."

"Are you hungry?"

"Starving."

I smile against her neck and then let her squirm out of my grasp. She holds her hand out to help me out of the chair, which I accept.

"I guess I should feed you if you're starving."

"Yes, you should."

Her eyes are still heavy and there are dark circles under them. She's not going to be awake for long.

"Does lasagna sound good?"

"Everything sounds good," she replies and sits in a chair at the table while I dish us both up a good-sized helping. "I would even settle for a leftover bagel at this point. Which were delicious, by the way. Is this from Ciao?"

"Yep."

"Mmm." She sniffs it when I put it in front of her, and then digs in. "I've never had this before. Oh my God, so good."

I nod in agreement, and we're both quiet as we make our way through our meal. When she's finished, I carry both of our plates to the sink, and when I turn around, I can't help but laugh.

Hannah is sitting with her chin propped in her hand, eyes closed.

"Are you sleeping?"

"No."

"You look like you're sleeping."

"Not yet. I just can't keep my eyes open. I hope I don't have narcolepsy."

"Narcawhaty?"

"Narcolepsy." She smiles. "It's that condition where you fall asleep all the time."

"I don't think you have that."

She still doesn't open her eyes. "You don't know. You're not a doctor."

"You're exhausted because you delivered a baby."

"Two. Two babies. And I can't tell you their names because of the law."

"I *am* the law, sweetheart."

"You know what I mean." She yawns, still not opening her eyes, and I can't stand it anymore. I scoop her up in my arms, and her fingers immediately dive into the hair at the back of my head, making my dick stand at attention.

It seems this woman has found my Achilles heel. And it's nowhere near my feet.

When I reach her bed and set her down, she leans in to press her lips to my ear.

"Stay," she whispers.

"Baby, you're exhausted. You need to sleep."

"I will sleep. After."

She smiles up at me and lets her robe fall away, revealing her gorgeous naked body, and it takes everything in me not to pin her down and fuck her into the mattress.

Not that I won't do that, and soon.

But not right now.

Not tonight.

"Hannah—"

"Please stay," she says again and scoots over, making room for me on the bed. "If you're not in the mood for sex, that's okay. Just stay for a while."

"I'm always in the mood for you," I reply and hastily remove my clothes. "I can't stop thinking about you, daydreaming about you."

I slip into the bed next to her and pull her against me, tipping my forehead against hers. Her hand glides up my arm, over my shoulder, and into the hair at the back of my head, and I go cross-eyed.

"Your hair is so soft here," she whispers.

"I'm glad you like it."

"Why do you have goosebumps?"

"Because you're running your fingers through my hair." I smile and kiss her lips softly. "Seems that's a thing for me."

"Interesting." She kisses my chin. "I want to find some of your other *things*."

"You're welcome to go on a scouting mission anytime."

I feel her smile against my neck, and suddenly she rolls on top of me, straddling me and rubbing her bare pussy against the length of my cock.

"Yes, that's one of the things," I say, sarcasm dripping from the words, and she laughs, then bites my nipple, not at all gently. "You have a sudden burst of energy."

"Imagine that," she replies. She has one hand planted on the bed next to my head and the other is flat against my stomach, headed south. She scoots down as well, kissing my hot skin where her hand has been, and settles between my legs, my cock gripped firmly in her hands, her tongue making circles along the ridge around the head.

"Fucking Jesus," I groan and grip onto the sheets.

"No, you're fucking Hannah," she says and then sinks down over me, sucking and licking. She's making noises, which only intensifies the heaviness in my balls and electricity moving through me.

I'm going to fucking come, and I don't want to do that yet.

"Hannah," I warn her, but she shakes her head and keeps going, gripping me hard and I have to take her by the shoulders, pull her off of me, and switch our positions, tucking her beneath me.

"I'm not going to come in your mouth," I growl before sinking slowly inside her. "Not today."

"Another day then?" She moans and hitches her legs up around my sides, gripping my ass in her strong hands and pulling me more tightly against her.

"Maybe." She cocks a brow and I smirk. "Some women don't like that."

"I'm not some women."

"No, you're not." I drag my fingertips down her cheek and cup her neck and jaw, just able to see her eyes from the glow of the hallway. "You're fucking amazing."

"You're good for my ego."

I pull my hips back and then push in again, deeper than before and watch her eyes widen in lust and pleasure.

"I'm not feeding your damn ego. You're magnificent." I kiss her lips, nibble the corner of her mouth and then sink into her, tangling our tongues, tasting her. She's moaning against my mouth, and her fingers have tangled in my hair again, and that's it. I can't stop myself from picking up the pace, pushing harder, and cursing under my breath when she bears down and squeezes me as she comes around me.

I bury my face in her hair and follow her over; the world falls away and I'm lost in her.

There's no going back.

I'm hers.

∽

"So, you've never been kayaking?" I ask Hannah about a week later as we drive the forty miles or so into Glacier National Park.

"No, it's always scared me. I know how to swim, but you always hear of people rolling over in their kayak, and I don't want to do that. Ever."

"Well, I have sit-on-top kayaks, and they're less likely to tip over." I smile over at her and squeeze her hand in mine, feeling the tension in her. This makes her nervous, but she's willing to give it a try, and that says a lot about her. "And if you hate it, we can just hike a bit."

"Okay." She nods and looks in the backseat at her backpack.

"You grabbed the bear spray."

"I know, I'm just checking." She fidgets. "I know it's weird to you that I have this fear, but I can't turn it off. I can't describe it, I just have it, and I can't make it go away."

"You don't have to describe it," I assure her and turn on the road that leads up to Bowman Lake, a lesser-known lake that tends to be less rull of tourists this time of year. "You're right, I don't understand it, but I have other quirks that I can't explain either."

"Like what?"

"Remember when I took you to my house that day that you hurt your ankle, and I made you stay in the truck while I checked the house?"

"Yes."

"It's habit, anxiety now that I think about it, to walk through the entire property when I get home to make sure nothing is disturbed. I lock up tight, and I have alarms and cameras, but I have to do a sweep before I can settle in."

"And you don't know why?" she asks.

*I know why.*

"Actually, when I was a kid, and my dad was chief, we had been out as a family around Christmas time. I don't remember where we'd been. But we came home and there was a man in our house, drunk and pissed off and he came to the chief's house to confront him about it."

"Oh my God."

"It was scary. Dad had a weapon on him, and I don't think we were ever in danger. I don't remember what the man was upset about. Maybe his wife had kicked him out for beating her, I'm not sure. But I remember that he was *so pissed off.* Dad lured him outside and Mom rushed us into a back bedroom and called for backup, which came quickly. But I don't think I'll forget walking into the house and seeing a stranger there."

"No. I wouldn't forget that either."

"I didn't check the house before," I continue. "And I don't think it ever occurred to me that that's why I do it now. As soon as I became chief, I started the routine, and now I realize that's why."

"It makes sense," she says with a nod, and then points to the red building of the small bakery in a town of only a couple hundred people. "Best pastries in the state."

"Let's stop."

The bakery is also a small convenience store for people who may need water, batteries, or other supplies. This is just a day trip, and we're prepared, so we each just choose a bear claw, check out, and get back in the truck.

441

"The road to the lake is bumpy and twisty," I warn her.

"Okay." She smiles and takes a bite of her pastry. "Thank the good lord for these nuggets of deliciousness. I'm gonna work the calories off on the lake."

I nod and concentrate on the road. Despite being a popular destination among locals, the road is dirt, full of potholes, and incredibly windy. About two miles up, Hannah lays her hand over her stomach.

"Maybe I shouldn't have eaten that."

"I'm sorry, I'm trying to take it easy. I can't go fast, but there's nothing I can do about the road."

"It's not your fault," she says and rolls the window down. "Are you sure we're going the right way? This looks like it's never travelled."

"It's travelled," I assure her. "But it'll never be paved. The locals like that it's not swarming with tourists."

"I like that, too," she says with a smile. "How much longer?"

"About six miles."

"Jesus," she mutters and pushes her nose out of the window, breathing in the fresh air. "This had better be worth it."

"It is," I say and smile at her, still holding her hand. "It's stunning up here. You'll love it."

She nods and I will the road to shorten so I can get her there faster, but it's still another forty-five minutes before we arrive.

The parking lot is half full, and I find a space near the path that leads to the lake.

"There are people up here," she says with surprise.

"But not a million of them," I reply and help her out of the truck. We pull the kayaks and oars out of the truck, along with our backpacks, and I lock it up, then turn to her. "If you don't want to haul one of these down there, I'll have you stay here with one of them and I'll take one, then come back."

"Oh please." She rolls her eyes, hitches her backpack on her shoulders and reaches for her kayak and oar, then sets off to the trail. "I work out for this, remember?"

*I'm going to marry her. Today.*

"Impressive," I say behind her and hear her smirk.

"I'm just carrying a kayak."

"Like a badass," I reply. The lake shore is only about thirty yards away, and when we reach the water, she sets the kayak down beside her and just stares at the mountains, the glassy water, and then looks up at me with tears in her eyes. "What's wrong, sweetheart?"

"It's *so* beautiful." She shakes her head and looks around once more, her hands on her hips. "I get to live here."

"Well, close to here." I kiss her cheek and get busy showing her how to maneuver the kayak. "What do you think?"

"I think it looks easier than it is," she says with a laugh. "But I'm going to give it the old college try."

"Good girl."

I help her onto the water craft, get her settled, and watch her paddle away as if she's been doing this for years.

I quickly get my gear ready and paddle behind her, enjoying the way she's smiling and looking around her. I catch up to her and grin over at her.

"What do you think?"

"I think I need to do this more often," she says. "Are there fish in here?"

"Some," I reply. "A few salmon, trout. We might see some eagles snacking today. But this is glacier water and snow run off, so it's really too cold and sterile for there to be a lot of fish."

"You know a lot about this," she says.

"I used to volunteer up here in the summers. I thought I wanted to be a park ranger when I grew up."

"And here you are, protecting people rather than wildlife."

"Yes, ma'am." I rest my oar across my body and take a drink of water. "But I still love it here, more than almost anywhere."

"I can understand why. This lake goes on forever."

"About seven miles," I reply with a nod. "And it's a mile wide in some places. I love that the mountains change as we move down the lake."

"It's stunning, really. I know there's so much of the park that I haven't seen yet, but it always surprises me."

We paddle in silence for a while, enjoying the quiet and the beautiful day. I glance to my right and see a grizzly lazily eating berries on the shoreline, and keep it to myself. I don't want to scare her.

"I see it," she says without even looking my way.

"See what?"

"The bear. And I know they can swim. And my heart is probably going to seize, but I'm okay."

"Are you sure?"

"Yes. I'm in their house, so I have to deal with the fact that I'm going to see them. But I'm glad he's way over there, and that he's more interested in berries than me."

"She," I reply.

"She?"

I point to the two cubs playing on the rocky beach and Hannah smiles.

"They're adorable. And far away."

I nod, proud of her for putting on a brave face. I can see her hands shaking, but she doesn't immediately turn around or freak out. She's breathing deeply, and keeping an eye on the wildlife on shore.

"How many bears do you think are in this park?" she asks.

"I don't think we should talk numbers. I don't want to freak you out."

"Facts calm me," she says and raises a brow at me. "How many do you think?"

"Three hundred, give or take," I reply and watch her swallow hard. "But that's over more than a million acres, Hannah. *A million.* The odds of having an encounter that's anything other than what we just had are *so slim.*"

"I know." She shrugs one shoulder. "Like I said, I can't change it. She was beautiful, and her babies are adorable. I'm glad I saw her from a safe distance. And I don't care if I never see another one."

"You're brave."

She snorts and rests her oar on the kayak. "I'm not brave, Brad. But I'm enjoying this kayak ride. I'm so glad you brought me."

"Me too. Are you ready to turn back?"

"Is that the other head of the lake?" she asks, pointing ahead of us.

"Yes."

"Well, then I guess we should turn back, since there's nowhere else to go."

I show her how to turn around, and she's mimicking my movements. But then a bee flies by her face, and she shakes her head, flailing with her hand, and rocks the kayak too hard to recover.

She falls into the water with a shriek, and before I can jump in and help her, she's grabbed the side of the kayak and pulled herself out of the water, panting and laughing at the same time. She's soaked through.

"Are you okay?" I've paddled over to her and am holding her kayak to mine. She's started to laugh.

"Good God, that's fucking cold!" Her nipples are pressed against her soaked tank top, and she's shivering a bit, wringing her hair out. "No wonder fish don't live there. *Nothing* could live there."

"You'll warm up quickly. It's ninety today. Probably eighty on the lake."

"Whew, I'm awake now," she says and laughs again, turning her face to the sun, soaking in the warmth. "Beginner's luck."

"You're stunning."

"I'm a mess." She turns that smile to me. "If I lean your way, can you kiss me without dumping us both back in this water?"

I don't answer, I just lean toward her slowly and she follows, kissing me with not a little heat. Her lips are cold. She backs away and then her eyes widen in fear.

"Fuck! I lost the oar!"

"I saved it," I assure her and pass it to her.

"You're my hero."

I laugh and tuck her wet hair behind her ear. "Are you ready to go back?"

"Yes. I have to paddle to get my body heat back up."

"I should have brought a sweatshirt or something, just in case."

"I don't think we have the cargo space for that," she says. "I'm fine. I might just paddle faster this time."

# CHAPTER 9

## ~HANNAH~

*I*'m not going in that water. Not today, not ever.

I stare down into the lake, not even hearing the voices around me. It's the Fourth of July, just three weeks after being on a different lake with Brad up in the park. But this is different. This lake killed a young boy this summer, and I will *not* touch the water.

We all gathered at Jacob and Grace's house on the lake a few hours ago. And by *we all*, I mean Brad and me, Jenna, Max, along with Grace and Jacob of course.

And let's not forget Brad's *parents*.

They just arrived in town for the remainder of the summer, and I'm meeting them for the first time today, on a pontoon boat.

On killer water.

"I've heard a lot about you," Mary Hull says with a smile and takes a sip of her cold can of Coke. "I'm so happy that we get to spend the day with you."

I nod and force a smile, trying desperately to calm down. But some of our group is on a ski boat, tubing and water skiing, *in the water*, and I just can't breathe.

I'm terrified.

Not that I'll let anyone else here know that.

"Hannah?" Grace asks, frowning.

"I'm sorry, what?"

"I asked you what kind of medicine you practice, dear," Mary says. "Are you okay?"

"I'm fine." I clear my throat and try to focus, ignoring the fact that Brad is currently water skiing in the water. "I'm sorry, my mind wandered. I am an OB/GYN. I share a practice here in town."

"How lovely," Mary says with a smile. "It must be wonderful to deliver babies into the world."

"It's hard work, and sometimes sad, but I wouldn't change it for the world."

"The guys are having fun," Grace says, pointing to the boat whizzing by about a hundred yards away. Max is in the water now, with Brad, Jacob, Jenna, and Bruce, Brad's dad, in the boat. "I can't water ski. I'd drown."

"No, you wouldn't," Mary says with a laugh.

"Oh, I would," Grace assures her. "I'm as clumsy as they come. My name is not appropriate for me."

We all laugh and I finally start to relax. I decide to go up to the roof of the pontoon boat so I can sit in the sun for a little bit and just be calm.

Just *be*.

"If you ladies will excuse me, I'm going to soak in some sun."

"Won't you burn?" Mary asks.

"I'm the only redhead I know who tans," I reply with a shrug. "But I won't stay out for long."

They both nod happily and I can hear them chatting away as I climb the ladder to the top of the boat. This is an impressive watercraft. With two levels, a slide off the back, and seating for twenty, it's huge. Even this upper deck has an umbrella I can open for shade if I get too hot.

I could live on this boat.

And the best part is, there's no chance of falling into the water the way I did when we went kayaking. That was humiliating, but we laughed it off and had a great day.

I don't want there to be *any* chance that I could fall into this water. I know that Brad made sure the electrical issue was fixed, but it still happened. Someone died.

I don't want to chance it.

*You're being unreasonable.* And I know that. It's the anxiety. The rational side of me knows that there's nothing to be afraid of. The irrational anxious side of me doesn't give even one shit.

I'm going to over think it anyway.

I can't watch the other boat without my stomach dropping, so I turn my lounge chair in the opposite direction and sit back, breathing deeply. I'm in a bathing suit with a cover up, but I'm not too hot. It's always about ten degrees cooler on the lake. The chair is soft and plush, and before long my anxiety has calmed down and I could easily drift to sleep.

But I don't. I'm watching the shoreline off in the distance, floating by lazily. We took the boat out in the middle of the lake, directly in front of Grace and Jacob's house. From way out here, their house still looks massive. It's just been the two of them in that big house, but soon there will be three.

I'm happy for her.

"You're up here by yourself," Jenna says and sits next to me, surprising me.

"I thought you were on the other boat?"

"I had the guys bring me back here. There was a lot of testosterone on that boat." She laughs and passes me a fresh Coke. "We could go in Grace's house and make iced coffees."

"How did you just read my mind?"

"Friend, your mind is always on coffee."

"True. Maybe in a bit, the sun is so nice right now."

Jenna is in a turquoise bikini, showing off her curves. Her natural platinum blonde hair is tucked up in a sun hat, and she's wearing huge sunglasses.

"You look like a starlet today."

She smirks. "Sure."

"You look like a starlet every day. You must hear that a lot."

She shrugs one shoulder and then links her fingers over her flat belly. "Maybe I shouldn't dress nice in front of my crew."

"What do you mean?"

"You know I'm building the tree houses on the mountain, right?"

"Yes, and I'm *dying* to see them."

"I'm so irritated. My brothers are co-owners with me, but *I'm* the brains behind the operation. They're my vision, my heart, my project."

"Gotcha."

"But I guarantee you, every single day when I go to the job site and speak with someone, they either dismiss me altogether, or tell me to have my *husband* come talk to them."

"What the fuck?"

"Right?" She pats my arm and nods. "When I explain that they'll have to talk to *me*, they shake their heads and look frustrated. It pisses me off."

"It would piss me off too."

"So I've told Max and Brad to stop coming to meetings. They're all going to learn to deal with me and me *only*. I've been in real estate for over ten years. I've run my own vacation rentals, including a super fancy B&B, for almost that long. I know what I want, and I have the money to get it.

"But now they've decided to go over budget already and we're only half way built."

"Not acceptable."

"No," she agrees. "So I just fired my contractor yesterday, and now I have to find someone new. I would just do it myself, but it's three buildings, thirty feet off the ground. It's not a normal house."

"It sounds incredible."

"It will be," she says with a smile. "I can't wait for you to see them. I also have my eye on a piece of property in the park that just went on the market."

"As in, *inside* Glacier Park?"

"Yeah," she says with a nod. "There are about a dozen private residences inside the park. This one is on Lake McDonald, and it's gorgeous. I know I could rent it out most of the year."

"Absolutely. You should do it!"

"I'm sinking a shit ton of money into the tree houses right now," she says and wrinkles her nose. "But I may never have the chance to own property in the park again."

"Exactly. Do it. I'm serious. I'll go in on it with you."

"You're a good friend." A slow smile slides over her perfect lips. Jenna looks annoyingly like Grace Kelly. If she wasn't so wonderful, we might all hate her. "I'll just get another loan for it. I *know* it would pay for itself in less than three years."

"Sounds like a no brainer."

She claps her hands excitedly. "Now to get those tree houses finished and rented out so they can start paying for themselves, too."

"Do you mind if I fold out the awning?"

"Not at all," she says as I stand and roll out the awning, casting us in blessed shade.

"That's better. I was starting to sweat, and no one wants that."

"No," Jenna says with a laugh. "My mom likes you."

"I feel bad because I was nervous and I've hardly said three words to her."

"She likes you," she says again. "And I *know* my brother likes you."

"I should hope so. He's naked with me a lot."

"Ew," Jenna says and then laughs. "But good for you guys."

"Am I missing good stuff up here?" Grace asks and joins us. "Also, side note, be *very* proud of me for climbing that ladder and not dying."

"Very proud." I smile as Grace sits opposite of us, so she can see us and takes her sunglasses off.

"I don't know how I'll get down. Me going down a ladder doesn't sound like a good idea."

"You can slide down the slide," Jenna suggests, and just like that my anxiety is in high gear again.

"I'll help you down the ladder," I offer immediately.

Grace just laughs, oblivious to my inner turmoil and changes the subject.

"Did you hear that Louise Summers sold her clothing boutique in town?"

"I did," Jenna says with a nod. "Didn't she retire?"

"Yes, and Willa Monroe bought it. She's doing some remodeling, and I saw her in the grocery store last week, and she said she's going to update it, make it super pretty and trendy. Bring in some higher end clothing lines. I'm excited to see what she does."

"I always liked Willa," Jenna says with a smile.

"Who is Willa?" I ask.

"Willa and Max used to date in high school," Jenna replies and shakes her head. "My stupid brother let her get away. She's widowed now, with a little boy, Jack."

"He's adorable," Grace says. "Has Max seen her since he's been home?"

"I doubt it," Jenna replies and looks around to make sure her brother isn't in ear shot. "I told him to call her, but he's a stubborn ass."

"Well, she's having a fun grand opening party next Friday evening, and I think we should go."

"That sounds fun," I reply. "I'm in."

"Me too," Jenna adds. "Cunningham Falls can use a trendy new clothes store. Let's plan a night of it."

"Are you guys up there?" Jacob calls out from the lower deck.

"We are," Grace calls back.

"We have food down here. I'll come get you, love."

Before Grace can reply, he's scaled up the ladder and scoops her up in his arms, kissing her sweetly.

"How are you?" he asks.

"I'm just fine. I wasn't going to try to go down the ladder without you."

"Good girl." He nuzzles her neck, then walks to the ladder and sets her down, wedging her between him and ladder, helping her down.

"He's sweet," Jenna says. "And hello, British accent."

"I know, it ups the hot factor," I reply with a laugh. "Let's go eat. I'm hungry."

We shimmy down the ladder to find everyone back on the pontoon.

"There you are," Brad says and pulls me to him for a kiss that makes my toes curl. "You look beautiful in this suit."

"Thank you. What is there to eat?"

"Sandwiches, salads, and cookies for dessert. Oh, and some fruit."

Max and Brad give each other a hard time about their water skiing adventure, Jenna, Jacob, and Grace are chatting in a corner, and Mary and Bruce are eating, watching us all with content faces.

"Are you happy to be home?" I ask them.

"Always," Bruce says with a wink. "We hardly left for thirty years because I always worked so damn much. It's been good to see some of the world with my bride."

I smile, watching how sweet Brad's parents are with each other. What must it have been like to grow up in a house that was functional?

I glance at Brad and Max, both still shirtless and in their drying swim trunks, chatting and laughing while eating their sandwiches. It's clear they all get along well, that they care for each other. The wealth that Max has come into in the past few years hasn't changed his dynamic with his family.

And let's be honest, the two Hull boys standing shirtless together is a sight to behold.

"What are you thinking over there?" Brad asks, pulling me out of my own head.

"I'm just sitting here," I reply and grin when he takes my hand and pulls me into his lap, nuzzling my ear with his nose. "That tickles, and your parents are right there."

"They've done this many times," he says and winks at me. "Are you having fun?"

"Absolutely. It's the perfect day to be on the lake."

"Do you want to go for a run on the tube after lunch?"

"No, thanks." I wrinkle my nose, feeling the anxiety rush up inside of me, but I act calm and collected in front of his family and my friends. "I don't think I want to get my hair wet."

"Seriously?"

"Seriously."

He frowns, watching me closely. "You brought a bag that has stuff in it for if you swim."

"I just decided I don't *want* to swim today."

*Please drop this.*

"But you can go if you want to. I'll watch," I continue.

"You're being silly. You're a great swimmer. Just last month, we went kayaking up at Bowman Lake, and she fell in," he tells the others, making us all laugh. "But she pulled herself right out. You're not afraid of the water."

*Not that water.*

The next thing I know, he's standing with me in his arms, walking to the edge of the boat.

"Don't."

"I'll go in with you."

Before I can react, he's jumped in with me in his arms, and I'm completely submerged in the water, kicking and swimming back to the surface. I immediately swim to the ladder and pull myself out of the water, on the verge of tears.

"There," he says, still treading water. "Now you're wet."

"Get out of the lake please," I say, my teeth chattering. Someone wraps a towel around my shoulders. I'm so scared, so *angry*, that I can't see anything other than Brad pulling himself out of the water.

"Not cool, man," Max mutters, but my eyes are pinned to Brad.

"What?" Brad asks. "I was just having fun with you."

"I told you I didn't want to swim."

He cocks his head to the side, narrows his eyes, and props his hands on his hips. He's not going to ask me questions in front of the others, which is a relief because I don't want to have to explain in front of the others that he just took ten years off my life.

I climb the ladder to the top deck, and hear the engine roar to life, the boat pointed to the dock.

Great. They probably want to dump me off, and I don't blame them. I'm such a downer! Not to mention, this is *not* the impression I wanted to give his parents.

What a mess.

"Hannah, will you please come inside with Jenna and me?" Grace calls. "We want coffees and need to use the bathroom."

I sigh in relief, and climb down the ladder, not looking at Brad, and follow the girls into the house. When they head to the kitchen, I find the closest bathroom, close the door, and let myself have a meltdown.

*Oh my God.* I could have died. Not because of the swimming thing, but what if the electricity thing had happened again? And what if it happened when Brad was in the water and it killed *him* and I had to watch him die?

I can't do this. I can't do the relationship thing because he's going to die eventually, whether that's today or thirty years from now, and I just don't think I'm relationship material.

At all.

I'm trying to calm myself down, but now the thought of losing Brad is stuck in my head, and my heart is beating so fast I'm pretty sure I'm having a heart attack.

I take a deep breath and stare at myself in the mirror. I look ridiculous with wet red hair, pale skin, scared eyes.

Why am I always so fucking scared?

There's a knock at the door.

"Han, let me in."

I close my eyes and pray for strength. Of course Brad would follow me.

I swallow, ignore my pounding heart, and wrap myself in strength I *don't* have before opening the door and looking up at him.

"Hi. Sorry, I'm coming."

I try to brush past him, but he grips my shoulders and gently pushes me back into the bathroom, shuts the door, and cages me in against the vanity, making me look him in the eyes.

"Talk to me."

"About what?"

"You're pissing me off, Hannah."

"Yeah, well, that seems to be going around today. I need to get back to the girls."

"Fuck that, you're going to tell me what in the hell happened on that boat."

"Well, I was thrown in the water against my will and my hair got wet. No means no, Brad. I figured the chief of police would understand that."

His eyes narrow, and look a little hurt, and that just makes me feel guilty.

He didn't deserve that, and I can't look him in the eyes anymore.

"Bullshit," he says at last and tips my chin up. "This isn't about your hair. You're lying to me, and you know how I feel about that."

"Well, that's the only answer you're going to get."

I push out of his arms and march for the door, but when I turn the knob, I pause, lowering my head in shame.

This isn't who we are.

"I'm scared," I whisper, then latch the door again and turn to face him. "I was so scared."

"Of what?"

"Of the water."

"You can swim."

*"You're not listening to me."*

"I'm sorry." He looks genuinely baffled, which I understand. I'm baffled by me all the time. "Tell me. Make me hear you."

"I don't give a shit about my hair. And of course I can swim. It's not that I'm afraid of water, I'm afraid of *this* water. *This* lake."

I step to him, needing him to understand.

"I've been terrified all day. Actually, I've been afraid since Grace mentioned that we'd be on the boat today. All I can think about is, someone is going to dive in and get electrocuted."

"Oh, sweetheart."

"I know you said that it's okay, and I believe you. I know that you would *never* put anyone at risk, but I'm afraid of it anyway."

"Why didn't you just say something?"

"Because it's ridiculous." I feel a tear fall on my cheek, and I'm just mortified. "And I'm meeting your parents for the first time, and I want them to like me. I don't want to feel different. I know that I'm safe with you, always, but I can't get it out of my head. I do *not* want to be in that water. On the water? Fine, I can do that, but not in it. And it scared the shit out of me when you were in it because if something were to happen to you—"

"Shh," he says and pulls me against him hard, holding me so tight I don't know when I end and he begins. "Stop thinking that way. I'm not going anywhere, sweetheart. I'm right here. And if you don't want to go into the water for *any* reason, you don't have to. I'm sorry I didn't listen."

"It's not your fault. I shouldn't have said that."

"No, you're right. No means no. I don't think you're different or weird. You feel the way you feel, and that's okay."

His hand is circling firmly over my back, soothing me, and it's the best feeling in the world. I'm calmer now; the giant butterflies in my stomach are gone.

And I was in the water and survived.

"Do you want to go home?" he asks.

"Do you want me to go home?"

"Hell, no. We have prime seats for fireworks." He smiles and brushes his thumb over the apple of my cheek. "I want you to stay with us, and I want to enjoy the rest of the day with you."

"I want that too. Grace said something about iced coffees."

He chuckles and kisses my forehead, then my nose and finally my lips.

"You can have whatever you want as long as you stay."

# CHAPTER 10

## ~HANNAH~

"You cheated!" Jenna yells below us. I'm sitting on the upper deck of Grace's house, my second iced coffee sitting at my elbow, and Brad and I are listening to the others battling it out over ping pong below us.

"I had no idea that people put ping-pong tables outside," I say and laugh when Max swears ripely.

"Did you see that patio? It's huge." Brad slips his hand over mine and gives it a squeeze. "Do you feel better?"

"I do," I reply truthfully and lean in to kiss his arm. "Thanks."

"Brad!" Jacob yells up. "You need to come down here and try to beat Grace. She's beat everyone else."

"I'm fine up here," Brad calls down, but I shake my head.

"You should go play. I'm seriously great. I'm enjoying the view and my coffee."

"You're sure?"

"Completely sure."

He kisses me quickly and then hurries down to play.

"Okay, Grace, it's on," I hear him say and I smile at the sound of his voice.

I *do* feel much better. Talking to Brad helped. I should have just told him how I felt this morning, and the whole embarrassing episode never would have happened. I live too much in my own head. I overthink and it gets me in trouble.

I need to trust. To loosen up. To go with the flow.

I smirk because going with the flow is probably not something I'll ever do. But I am learning to trust.

I check my phone to make sure I haven't missed any calls from the hospital just before Mary joins me on the deck.

"Do you mind if I sit with you for a while?" she asks. I gesture to the seat that Brad just vacated and offer her a smile.

"I'd love it if you joined me."

"It's sure a beautiful day today," she says and takes a deep breath, watching the boats zip around the lake. "And this is a wonderful view."

"It sure is," I reply. "Are you from here?"

"Born and raised," she says with a nod. "I remember some Fourth of Julys that had snow."

"No way."

"A flake or two, yes. Nothing that stuck, of course. Plenty of rainy days. You just never know what you'll get around here. Where are you from, Hannah?"

"Kansas," I reply and frown. "It's very different from here."

"Yes, it is. I have a friend from Kansas. How long have you been in Cunningham Falls?"

"Just about five years." I point out a bald eagle that's swooped over the lake, looking for his dinner. "A friend of mine took a position here a few years before that, and I'd been to visit. I never considered practicing in a small town until the position came open here and Drake called me about it. And then it seemed like the best idea I'd ever heard."

"This town gets under your skin," Mary agrees. "Of course, there are pros and cons to living in a small town."

"Of course, but the pros far exceed the cons."

"I'm glad you think so," she says with a warm smile. After a quiet moment she says, "I like the way Brad looks when you're around."

"How does he look?"

"Happy. Content." She blinks rapidly, as if keeping tears at bay. "I don't know that I've ever seen him look at anyone the way he looks at you."

And, cue the butterflies again, but in a great way this time. Every woman wants to hear that the man they're in love with looks at her in a special way.

"Of course," she continues, "being married to a cop isn't easy. And being married to the chief of police is as challenging as they come."

"Oh geez," I say and laugh her off easily. "We aren't anywhere near marriage."

"Still, you're with him, and I can tell you from experience that it's a job all in itself. His hours are erratic. He sees horrible things. Some he'll tell you about, and others it's best for both of you if he doesn't. He will be tired and moody, and there will be times when it feels like he's more married to the job than he is to you.

"I know, you're not married, but I see the way you look at each other, and I know love when I see it. You haven't said it yet, have you?"

I shake my head no and she keeps talking.

"That's okay. It's good to take it easy and let your relationship progress naturally. But you need to know going into it that you're not just in a relationship with a man. He's an important man, and in this town in particular, they will feel like they own him. You'll share him.

"The statistics for marriages lasting for cops aren't good."

"Mary, I mean no disrespect, but I'm going to interrupt you for a moment." I hold my hand up and when she stops, I shake my head. "I know who he is. And I would like to add that as a doctor, my schedule is just as erratic. I see horrible things. And my patients do believe they own me, and that I should be at their beck and call. I get it. I like to think that I get it as much as anyone who isn't a cop can."

"You're right," she says, watching me carefully. "You would, wouldn't you? You know, my Bruce's daddy was also an officer here in Cunningham Falls, and his mom tried to warn me about these things right before we got married. I didn't listen to her. I was so in love with that man I couldn't see straight."

"And it seems to have worked out well for you," I point out.

"Forty years of marriage," she says with a nod. "Forty years, and only the past three of them have been somewhat normal. But I wouldn't have traded it. What he did was important. He kept people safe, and he saved lives. I'm so proud of him. When Brad told us that he'd applied for the chief position when Bruce announced his retirement, I tried to talk him out of it. I knew that if he wanted a family it would take a toll. But he's so much like his father." She shrugs as if to say, *what are you going to do?* "He's doing a good job, and we are so proud of him."

"I am, too."

Her head whips around to stare at me for a moment and then she smiles. "I think you mean that."

"Of course I do. He's an amazing man. I'm damn proud of him, and I'm enjoying spending time with him very much. I don't know what the future holds for us, but I'm going to continue to enjoy him, for as long as I can. No relationship is easy, and we both chose professions that are harder than most, but I also think that means that we're dedicated. I don't see why that wouldn't also include being dedicated to each other."

"I like you, Hannah." Mary is smiling now, almost smugly.

"Really? Because it sounds like you're trying to warn me away from your son."

"Not at all. I just wanted to see what you're made of. I think you can stick up for yourself just fine. Not just to me, but more importantly, to the townspeople. You'll need that backbone where they're concerned."

"They don't scare me," I reply honestly.

"Good."

"Don't scare her off already," Brad says as he joins us. "I defeated Grace, but it wasn't pretty."

"He did not," Grace yells up to us, making us all laugh.

"When are the fireworks?" I ask, looking at the time. "It doesn't get dark here until after ten."

"They wait until then," Brad says. "I have to have my radio on, just in case. I have sheriff deputies helping my guys tonight, but if anything major happens, they might need to reach me."

"I get it," I reply. "What do we do in the mean time?"

"Eat," Jacob says from the doorway. "I've just had more food brought in."

"I'm going to gain twenty pounds today." I laugh and jump up from my chair. "But I'm not complaining. Also, I think I'll go down and kick some ass at the ping pong."

"You think you can beat me?" Brad asks with a sexy brow cocked.

"Hell, yes, I can beat you. And Grace, too."

"Let's do it," Brad says and rubs his hands together. I follow him down to the patio below where everyone else is hanging out, eating fresh Mexican food from a local restaurant.

"How did you have this delivered on a holiday?" I ask Jacob, immediately reaching for a plate.

"I own the restaurant, darling," he replies smugly and steals a chip off of his wife's plate.

"That'll do it." I load my plate with tacos and chips, gratefully accept a Mexican Coke from Max, and take a seat next to Jenna. "This smells *so good.*"

"Sm gmmf," Jenna says with her mouth full, making me grin.

The food isn't just *good*, it's to die for, and I eat more than my share. When I can't shove another bite into my mouth, I stand, stretch my arms over my head, then saunter over to the ping-pong table and pick up a paddle.

"Let's do this, Hull."

He's sitting on the couch, watching me with hot green eyes. The kind of hot that tells me he wants to bend me over this table and do things to me that are definitely *not* appropriate for mixed company.

I toss him a sassy grin. "Well? Are you coming?"

"I'm coming," he says, his lips twitching with humor. "I just worry about this."

"Why?"

"I don't want to embarrass you in front of our friends."

"Aww, aren't you sweet?" I stick my lower lip out in a pout, bat my eyelashes. "So chivalrous."

"Just looking out for you, sweetheart."

"Thanks, but I've got this."

I serve the ball perfectly, and he volleys it back, but he's no match for my backhand, and he misses my next shot. He whips those hot green eyes up to mine and looks genuinely surprised.

"You're good."

"I know."

I serve again, and before long I win, not even giving him a chance to score on me.

"Who's next?"

"Me!" Grace jumps up, stretches her arms across her body, and takes the paddle from Brad, who is scratching his head and watching me like he doesn't know me at all.

Which only makes me laugh.

"How did you get so good at this?" Grace asks as she serves the ball and I volley it back to her. We volley back and forth more than a dozen times before she gets the point.

Grace is *good* at this.

"College," I reply. "I didn't play beer pong, I played ping pong."

After a ferocious match, I win by just two points.

"You are a worthy opponent," Grace says, bowing before me.

"As are you," I reply, bowing in return, and then we dissolve in a fit of giggles, hugging each other. "How did *you* get so good?"

"I practice a lot. I may be clumsy, but this seems to be one of the things I'm good at."

"I'll play with you anytime." I give her a high five and then head straight for the food again. "Ping pong makes me hungry."

"I have dessert coming down soon," Grace says as I take a bite of a chip. "Cheesecake."

"Good lord," Jenna moans, covering her belly. "Give me thirty minutes to get this food baby to settle."

"Same," Max says. "And then bring it on."

The rest of the evening is full of laughter, ping pong, and food. Stolen kisses. Conversation.

I notice both of Brad's parents watching us closely, but kindly, throughout the hours that follow. It's a relief to know that his mother likes me. I mean, we're grown adults, but having their approval means a lot.

Suddenly, just before ten, Brad's radio goes off.

"They're going to start the light show," Brad says.

"Let's go up to the deck," Grace says with excitement. We follow her up and all lean against the railing.

Brad walks up behind me and wraps his arms around me, caging me against the railing. Just as the first fireworks burst into the sky, he lays his lips against my ear.

"Thank you," he murmurs as the others ooh and aah over the lights in the sky.

"For what?"

"This. All of this."

He kisses my cheek, and then we're silent, watching the sky light up, surrounded by those closest to us.

It's been the best day that I've had in a *very* long time.

Maybe ever.

∾

"THE BOSS MAN WANTS A WORD," my nurse, Melissa, says. She's poked her head around the doorjamb of my office. We had a long one today, and it's only late morning.

"You look tired."

"I am," she says with a shrug. "I hate it when the fourth falls on a week day."

"I know." I smile, feeling the effects from being up late last night myself. "Thankfully our patient load is light today."

She nods and offers me a grin. "You have a patient in room four, and then you're done until after lunch."

"Cool." I grab my stethoscope and my computer. "I'll go talk to Jim and then see my patient. This shouldn't take long."

She nods and I walk to Jim's office. He calls me inside.

"Hi there," I say and sit in the chair in front of his desk.

"Good morning," he replies with a kind smile. Jim has been an OB/GYN in Cunningham Falls for forty years. He's no longer delivering babies, but he's still the head doctor in this practice, and I respect him immensely. I've learned so much from him since I came on. "Hannah, we need to talk."

"Okay."

"I've decided that it's time for you to stop taking call 24/7."

I sit quietly, blinking at him, sure I've heard him wrong.

"Did you hear me?"

"I don't think so."

He repeats himself, and I frown. "I don't understand. Have I done something wrong?"

"Not yet," he says and takes his glasses off, rubbing his eyes. "But you work too much, Hannah. There will be no more taking call on your nights off."

"My patients hire *me* to be there when their babies are born, Jim. It's important to them that I follow through with their care from beginning to end."

"I get it," he says, raising his hands in surrender. "I know what you're saying. But Hannah, we have five perfectly capable doctors in this clinic who can all deliver babies. It's too much for you to work twenty-four, sometimes forty-eight hours in a row, and then show up here to take appointments as well. You'll burn yourself out before you're forty, and I won't allow that."

"I didn't realize that being dedicated to my job was punishable," I reply, feeling my whole body tighten defensively.

"I'm not punishing you, Hannah." He sighs and watches me for a moment. "You're a wonderful doctor, and having you on staff has only strengthened this clinic. I value your education and your knowledge. But you put in too many hours. One day, it won't be *safe*. You'll miss a step out of pure exhaustion, and I have to think about the welfare of you and our patients. I'm not telling you that you can't work. I'm telling you that you can't work on your days off."

"Which is kind of the same thing," I reply. "I love this job. This is who I am."

"No. This is what you do." He smiles kindly and leans back in his chair. "In fact, I've been looking back over your schedule, and it's come to my attention that you haven't taken vacation time in two years."

"I was going to last summer, but Dr. Preston had her car accident and I had to fill in for her."

"I remember." He nods. "And it was appreciated. I want you to make up for it this year."

"Okay."

"Today."

"Excuse me?"

"Beginning today, I want you to take that week's vacation, paid. In addition to the other vacation time you have coming this year."

I frown. "Jim, I have two patients ready to have babies in the next few weeks."

"And if they go into labor, there are doctors here to do that, Hannah."

"So, I have to take a week off of work."

He laughs. "No, you *get* to take a week. Starting now."

"I have a patient in a room."

"Already been taken care of," he says. "We help each other around here. We're cool like that."

"I'm sorry, are you sure I haven't done something wrong?"

"No." He shakes his head and holds my gaze with wise grey eyes. "You're an excellent doctor, and I want you to be here for many years. The rest of your career, if I can manage it. And to do that, I need to protect you from burning yourself out."

"What am I supposed to do with all of this time?" I ask.

"That's up to you," he says and laughs when I just stare at him, dumbfounded. "Hannah, this is a good thing. You'll have more time to live your life."

"Huh." I narrow my eyes on him. "If you're really trying to squeeze me out of here, I'll put up a fight."

"I hope so. Now, you don't have to go home, but you can't stay here. Not until next Wednesday."

"But it's Tuesday."

"Exactly. You'll be off from this Tuesday until next Wednesday. A whole week."

"I guess I could hike," I reply, thinking out loud.

"Yes, that sounds great. Take a trip. Go hike. Go camping. Hell, go to Europe, I don't care. Just don't come here."

"You're going to miss me," I promise him, and he rolls his eyes.

"It's a week, Hannah."

*Might as well be a month.*

# CHAPTER 11

## ~HANNAH~

"*I*'m sorry to bug you at work," Abby says on the phone twenty minutes later just as I walk in my house, "but I have a question."

"I'm not at work."

"What? Why?"

"What's your question?"

"Right." She clears her throat. "I have an extra pair of concert tickets to see Maroon5 next month, and I'm wondering if you'd like to go?"

"Is this really a question? Of course I want to go."

"Cool. Now, why are you not at work?"

I sigh and pull a bottle of water out of the fridge. "Because I was sent home." I sit and tell her everything that Jim just said. "I mean, what am I supposed to do for a whole week?"

"Are you kidding me?"

I frown at the phone. "No, I'm not kidding. A whole week? What the hell?"

"Hannah, you're supposed to *relax*. Have fun. I've wanted you to do this for *years*. I can hear how tired you always are. I think it's awesome that Jim wants you to have a normal life."

"I'm a doctor," I remind her. "We don't have normal lives."

"Well, now you can."

"It's a lot of time to fill. I don't know what to do."

"I can think of a dozen things. Go to the movies, a short road trip, get a massage. Get your nails done. Schedule happy hours with your friends. But first, I think you should go buy lunch for that sexy police chief of yours and take it to him. That would be fun."

"That's not a bad idea." I turn the idea over in my head, and feel a grin spread over my face. "I'm actually kind of hungry."

"See? You'll find things to do. If you can't think of anything, text me and I'll help."

"Okay." I laugh, and grab my handbag. "Thanks for inviting me to the concert. Send me the details."

"Will do. Now, go feed your cop, and then maybe have sexy time in his office."

She hangs up, and I'm suddenly excited to be off of work for the day. I swing into *Little Deli* and chat with Mrs. Blakely while I wait for our sandwiches to be made, and then drive over to the station.

As I'm walking inside, a moment of doubt creeps in. I didn't call ahead. What if he's not available? Or not here at all.

I should have called.

But when I walk inside, I see Brad standing by his assistant, giving her a folder, and he glances up, smiling when he sees me.

"Hey," he says as I approach.

"Hi. I brought lunch."

"Really? I'm starving. No calls, please."

He shows me into his office, closes the door behind us, and pulls me in for a long, hot kiss. The kind of kiss that makes me forget about everything else.

The kind of kiss that makes a girl's panties wet.

"What was that for?" I whisper when he pulls away.

"Lunch." He winks, then takes the bag from my hands and leads me to a sitting area in the corner of his office. There's a loveseat, a chair, and a coffee table. "I thought you worked today."

"I thought so too."

For the second time in less than an hour, I relay the conversation with Jim and then bite into my turkey on rye, moody all over again.

"I think it's fantastic."

"Everyone thinks it's fantastic except me. I don't need a week off."

"Maybe it'll feel good," he suggests and pulls the tomatoes off of his sandwich. *No tomatoes.* This whole learning someone else thing is way more complex than I ever imagined.

"I just don't know what I'm supposed to do with so much down time," I reply and then shrug. "I guess I can repaint my bathroom or something."

"You'll fill the time," he says with more confidence than I feel. "And you can spend this evening with me."

"I can't." I shrug when his eyes whip up to mine. "It's grand opening night at the new dress shop downtown, and we're making a girls' night out of it."

"Grace and Jenna?" he asks.

"Yep, and I'm actually excited for it. We don't do it often."

"Cool," he says and keeps eating his sandwich. When he's finished, I straddle his lap and kiss him hard, wrapping my arms around his neck. His big hands slide over my sides and to my ass. "I'm not fucking you twenty feet from my guys," he says, breathing hard.

"I just want to cuddle," I reply. "Get your head out of the gutter."

"Sweetheart, you've pressed that sweet pussy of yours against my cock. My head is squarely planted in the gutter until you move. Not that I want you to do that."

"I just wanted to feel you," I say and hug him close. "And to thank you for being so laid back. So calm. So *steady*."

"That's sexy." I can hear the smile in his voice.

"Actually, it is sexy." I pull back to look in his eyes. "You always keep it together, and you don't get angry over silly things like girls' night out."

"I would be an asshole if I did that."

"I've known some assholes," I reply. "And I'm just glad that you're *not*. So thank you."

"You're welcome."

"Also, I'd like to come to your house later after time with the girls, if you don't mind."

"I don't mind," he replies and pulls me down for a long, sweet kiss. His lips are soft, but they know exactly what they're doing as they take command of mine in a lazy, sexy dance. "In fact, I'd very much enjoy your company tonight."

"It's settled then." I grin and climb off of him, then gaze around his office, looking for something specific.

"What are you looking for?"

"Handcuffs."

I glance down at him, catching the raised eyebrow.

"I think you should bring some of those home with you."

"Do you?"

"Oh yeah. That would be fun."

A smile spreads over his sexy lips, and I can't help but lean in to kiss him again, enjoying the smell of him, and the way his face feels in my hands.

But if I keep this up, we really will fuck twenty feet away from his guys.

So I back away and gather the mess from lunch, toss it away, and retrieve my handbag. "I'll see you later, then. I guess I'll go clean my closet."

"See? You're already getting projects done."

"I'd rather be delivering babies."

I shrug and wave, then leave his office. Maybe he's right. Maybe it'll be a good week. It sure was nice to be able to bring Brad lunch in the middle of the day.

And I have girls' night out tonight, without being on call, so that's a bonus. I can relax and enjoy without worrying about being called in for a delivery or an emergency.

I don't remember the last time that happened.

And, just for shits and giggles, I'm going to take Abby's advice and schedule a massage for this week.

Maybe everyone's right. Maybe this week won't be so boring after all.

~

"This place is so great," Jenna says shortly after we walk into *Dress It Up*, the new clothing boutique owned by her friend, Willa. Jenna is perfectly dressed today in a short sun dress with a fun hat and strappy heeled sandals. She looks like she walked out of a freaking magazine.

"She has beautiful things," I agree and smile when a beautiful, tall brunette comes walking toward us. She pulls Jenna in for a big hug.

"I'm so happy you're here," Willa says. "I was afraid no one would come."

"Why? This is the *best*," Grace says, also hugging Willa. "And this is our friend, Hannah Malone, who is also the best."

"I've heard your name around town," Willa says, shaking my hand. "It's nice to finally meet you."

"You as well," I reply. "Your shop is lovely."

And I'm not just being polite. The place is *magical*. She's gone with a grey, white, black, and pink theme. The floors are reclaimed barn wood. Chandeliers dripping with crystal hang above us. It's the epitome of fancy, stylish, and just flat out *pretty*.

"Thanks," she says with a smile and glances around. "It's been one big project, but I'm happy with it. I have clothing lines from New York and London, as well as some smaller labels that I love. And let's not forget the shoes."

"No, let's not," Jenna says with a laugh. "Shoes are my love language."

"Do you have flats for those of us who might kill ourselves otherwise?" Grace asks hopefully.

"Of course," Willa replies. "There's something in this store for everyone. There's wine floating around, along with some light appetizers. Help yourselves, and have fun. That's the most important thing. And let me know if you have any questions." Willa waves at another group of women who just walked in. "Excuse me, ladies."

"She's nice," I say as I watch her walk away. "Why did Max dump her?"

"Because he's stupid," Jenna says, handing me a can of Coke. But I surprise her by shaking my head and reaching for the wine. "You never drink."

"I do tonight. I'm not on call, so guess what? I can." I take a sip and enjoy not feeling guilty about having fun. "Let's browse, ladies."

"Let's spend some money," Grace corrects me, and we begin to wander through the shop, enjoying the beautiful things Willa has for sale.

"I love living in a small town, but it's so hard to shop," I say and pull a summer dress off the rack. "It's nice to have a trendy place in town."

"You're *so* right," Jenna replies and points to the garment in my hand. "That dress is a must buy."

I nod and drape it over my arm.

Over the next hour, we drink more glasses of wine, and make piles of clothes that we're going to buy.

It's fucking amazing, and so damn fun.

"This bikini is *everything*," Jenna says, showing me a turquoise two-piece.

"It will look amazing with your hair," I agree, then show her a T-shirt that says *Coffee Before Talkie.* "I need this."

"Oh yes, that's completely you," Jenna replies with a laugh. "And look at this one!"

*I Don't Trip, I Do Random Gravity Checks.*

"That's Grace," I say, adding it to my pile. She has to have it.

"She needs this one too," Jenna says, showing me a T-shirt that says *Rocking The Spoiled Wife Life.*

"Yes, perfect."

"Hannah," Grace says loudly, rushing from across the store, holding something in her hand. "You have to smell this."

But before I can, Grace trips on her feet, falling right into me, and knocking her head against my cheek, making me see stars. On my way down, she grabs my arm, trying to keep me up, but we both end up on the floor, a tangle of arms and legs, and glitter falling from the air.

"Oh shit," she says, snorting. "I hope I didn't ruin any clothes."

"You just ruined me," I reply. We're both giggling like crazy.

"Did I hurt your face?"

"I don't think so." I touch around my eye with my fingertips. It's a little sore, but not bad. "Are you hurt?"

"Nah." She shakes her head, and glitter falls out of her hair. "That was a bath bomb, by the way."

"It exploded."

We look at each other and dissolve into giggles again.

"Willa's going to be *pissed*," Grace says.

"No, I'm not," Willa says from behind us. "Just don't touch anything else with all of that glitter all over you."

We look at each other and laugh some more. We laugh so hard that I can't catch my breath. My sides ache, I can barely breathe, but I can't stop laughing.

We look ridiculous.

Finally, once we've all paid for our things, and left *Dress It Up*, we stand on the sidewalk, wiping the tears from under our eyes.

"That wine was *strong*," I say, once I catch my breath.

"And you never drink, so your tolerance is low," Jenna replies. "You probably shouldn't drive."

I stare at her for a moment, and realize there are two of her.

"No, definitely no driving for me. I'll walk."

"It's raining," Grace says. I glance around and then rush out from under the awning, letting the rain fall on me.

"Oh, it's nice."

"She's so drunk," Jenna says to Grace, making me laugh.

"I'm not *that* drunk."

Okay. I am.

"We can take you home."

"I'm not going home." I shake my head and turn a circle in the rain, but then I'm dizzy so I stop and just let the water fall on me.

"Where are you going?"

"To Brad's." I smile at Jenna. "I know you don't want to hear this, but I'm going to have some seriously hot sex with him tonight."

"Good for you," Jenna says and then wrinkles her nose. "Ew."

"Nope, it's not *ew*. It's *wow*. It's *holy shit, I didn't even know my pussy did that*."

"Holy shit, she's funny drunk," Grace says, laughing. "Come on, drunk girl. We'll drive you to Brad's."

"Actually, I really do want to walk," I reply. "Don't look at me like that. I'll be fine. I'm really not that drunk, and it's not cold."

"I don't know," Jenna says. "Brad would kill me if he knew I let you walk to his place when you're like this."

"I won't let him kill you. I swear." I hug them both, then wave as I begin my walk to Brad's house. It's only about a mile from downtown. I can certainly walk a mile.

But when I get about halfway there, the sun decides to go down. So now I'm walking in the rain *and* the dark.

But I don't care.

I love it here. I love my friends, and I love my boyfriend.

And I love the rain.

The rain that is currently falling even harder. So hard that it's difficult to see in front of me, so I duck under the branches of a big maple tree and wait for a few minutes, hoping it'll die down a bit.

It doesn't rain a whole lot in the summer in Montana, so when it does, it's warm and fast. This will pass.

"Are you okay out there?" Someone yells out from their house.

"I'm fine, just waiting for a break in the rain," I call out in return. This must be a good answer because they don't say anything more.

Finally, the rain calms to a heavy sprinkle, so I set out to Brad's house again. Rather than just dusk, it's pitch dark when I make it to his house. The front windows are lit from inside, with the shades pulled. His porch light is on.

I wander up the sidewalk, climb the two steps to his porch, and then sit in his porch chair, breathing deeply.

I'm almost sober now, but I want to be all the way sober when he opens the door. I don't need to make an ass out of myself in front of him.

No way.

After three deep breaths, I stand and knock on his door, excited to see him. I'm not prepared to see the expression of horror on his face when he swings the door open.

# CHAPTER 12

## ~BRAD~

*I*'m pathetic.

I've spent all evening doing my best to stay busy, waiting for Hannah to ring the doorbell, trying to keep my mind off of her and on other things. I paid bills, I finished hanging some cabinets in my garage, and I gave Sadie a bath.

Much to her dismay.

I've had music playing through the house as I putter around, pretending that I'm not thinking about Hannah and her beautiful blue eyes. Her perfect skin. The way she laughs when we're being silly, or the way she moans when I'm making her crazy.

But as soon as I'm distracted by something, my mind wanders back to her, and I can't help but wonder what she's doing and why in the hell she's not here yet.

Just as I finish folding a load of laundry, there's a knock on the front door. I grin and hurry over, swing it open, and standing before me is Hannah.

Soaking wet.

Covered in glitter.

A black eye.

Anger, swift and hot, surges through me, but before I can ask who the hell did this to her, she smiles brightly and says, "Oh my God, I had *so much fun.*"

She walks past me into the living room, drops her shopping bags and purse on my couch, and greets an excited Sadie, giving the dog pets and kisses, transferring the glitter to the clean animal.

"Hannah."

"Yeah?" She swings around to look at me. "Oh, sorry. I should have done this first."

She launches herself in my arms and kisses me soundly, twisting her fingers in the hair at the back of my neck.

"You smell good," she murmurs.

"You... *don't.*" I laugh and set her down. "Have you been drinking?"

"Oh yeah," she replies with a snort. "I didn't have to work, so I had some wine."

"And you drove here?"

She immediately scowls. "Hell no, I don't have my car. I walked here. I'm not my father."

"Oh, I'm sorry. Of course." I'm completely thrown. This is so unlike Hannah, I'm not sure how to react. But she looks happy, so there's that. "Who the fuck had their hands on you?"

"Huh?"

"The black eye."

She frowns and feels her face, and then laughs again. "Oh, that was Grace. She likes it rough." She snorts again, dissolving in laughter. "It doesn't hurt."

"I can't believe Jenna let you walk here," I mutter, but Hannah shakes her head.

"I insisted. It felt good." She shivers. "But now I'm getting cold."

"You need a hot shower." I take her hand and lead her into my bathroom. I turn on the water to heat up, then turn to her and have the pleasure of stripping her bare. "You even have glitter in your navel."

"Now I don't have to have it pierced."

She's grinning from ear to ear. "I'm glad you had fun, sweetheart."

"I had more than fun." She grips onto my shoulders to steady herself as I pull her wet panties down her legs. "I had a blast. We shopped a ton, and I met some new people. How is it that I've lived here for five years, and there are still so many people I don't know?"

I guide her into the shower and shut the glass door, still listening to her talk.

"I should know more people," she continues. "But I work too much. It feels good to finally feel like I'm part of this community."

"You *are* a part of the community."

"You're sweet." She clears the fog from the glass and smiles out at me. "Brad?"

"Yes, Hannah."

"Can you please come in here and help me wash this glitter off?" She bats her eyelashes, making me grin. "Pretty please?"

I'll never say no to getting naked with her. Ever.

"If I come in there, it may not stop at washing glitter."

"Oh good."

I hurry out of my clothes and join her. "What do you need?"

"Besides you?"

"Yes." She passes me the washcloth that she's soaped up.

"I think my back is dirty." She spins around, and she's right. There's glitter everywhere, so I get to work, washing it off, then rinsing the cloth, over and over again until it's gone. She turns around and points to her breasts, not saying a word. I lather fresh soap on the cloth and wash her chest, her belly and sides, and then she bites her lip and points to her neck.

"I don't see any glitter there."

"It's there," she replies. Her breathing is faster as I drag the wet cloth over her neck. I push her out of the water and against the wall, and she surprises me by resting her foot up on the bench and points to her inner thigh. "Right there."

Wordlessly, I wash her inner thighs, up to the crease of her legs, not touching her pussy.

"Brad," she says.

"Mm hm."

"Right here." She points to her center, and I immediately lower to my knees, staring in awe at the beauty of her. Her clit is swollen with desire, as are her lips, and I've never wanted someone so bad in my damn life.

Rather than use the washcloth, I lean in and lick her, from pussy to clit and back again, before pulling her lips into my mouth and sucking.

"Harder," she says, panting. I comply, using my teeth a bit as well, and she's writhing against the wall as she grabs my hair in a death grip. I push her leg up higher, sure to keep her balanced with my other hand and go to town on her, licking and sucking, biting and nibbling until she cries out in absolute pleasure.

I stand and boost her up against the wall, then push inside her. "You're so fucking wet."

"Turned on," she mutters and squeezes herself around me. "You turn me the hell on, Brad Hull."

I grin against her neck and pound her against the wall, unable to go slow or soft. Slow or soft doesn't fit our mood tonight. We're ravenous, and I'm going to take and take until neither of us can stand it anymore.

"Can't get enough of you."

"Good."

She bites my shoulder, and that's it. I can't do this against the wall anymore, so I flip off the water, and carry her, dripping wet, to my guest room, lay her down and continue to feast on her. Her tits, her pussy, every bit of her.

And she's giving it back just as fiercely. Her hips buck, her hands grab, and she's kissing and biting every piece of flesh she can find.

It's like we're crazy animals, unable to stop consuming each other.

I pull out and flip her over, slap her ass, and plunge inside again, fucking her until we're both crying out, coming hard.

And when we're done, I carry her back to my bed, tuck us both in and begin again, unable to keep my hands off of her.

"I'm sober now," she says with a lazy smile and opens up for me beautifully. "And thank goodness. I definitely want to remember this tomorrow."

⁓

"WE SHOULD SLEEP at some point tonight," Hannah says a few hours later. We're in the kitchen, making pancakes.

"You said you're hungry."

"I am." She grins and passes me the eggs. She's sitting on the counter, wearing one of my CFPD T-shirts, her hair a riot of red. She's adorable. "But you have to work in the morning."

"I've survived on little sleep before."

Once the batter is mixed, I set to work pouring it on my skillet. While I wait for it to be ready to flip, I settle between her thighs at the counter and kiss her soundly. "You're damn gorgeous, Hannah."

"I must be a mess," she says, wrinkling her nose. "I don't think we got all the glitter off."

"I'll be cleaning glitter out of my house for weeks."

"I'm sorry."

"It's okay. It'll bring back happy memories every time."

She drags her fingertips down my face and her expression is suddenly serious.

"What is it?"

She shakes her head and breaks eye contact, looking at my hair as she runs her fingers through it.

I take her hand in mine and kiss her palm, then lay it against my cheek.

"Talk to me, Han."

It's quiet in the house. Dark, aside from the lights under the cabinets, setting the room in a low glow.

"You need to flip the pancakes," she says and kisses my forehead before I move to the skillet and give them a flip. But before I can return to her, she jumps off the counter and retrieves two plates, the butter, and syrup, and the moment from a few moments ago is lost.

"I can't believe how hungry I am," she says.

"These three are ready."

"Gimme."

I put the pancakes on her plate and then pour two more for me, and turn to watch her slather butter and syrup all over her middle of the night snack.

"These are so good," she says after taking a big bite. "Who knew sex could make a girl so hungry?"

"I'd better stock up on pancake mix."

She winks at me, her mouth full.

"I plan to keep you *starving*."

"Right on."

When mine are finished, I turn off the skillet and join her at the table to eat with her. It's a simple thing, having an after sex snack with her, but it's intimate. It makes me feel closer to her.

I glance up in time to see her eyes are heavy.

"I think we've finally worn you out."

She smiles softly. "Yeah. I'm tired."

"What's wrong?" I ask when she frowns.

"I have a bit of a headache. I hope I'm not developing migraines."

I just shake my head and take my last bite. "You drank too much, that's all."

"Hmm."

We put our dishes in the sink and I lead her to my bed, anxious to feel her skin on skin again.

"Why do you always think that something's wrong?" I ask softly.

She thinks about it for a moment, her eyes closed.

"Because I know too much. About medicine. That's what Drake says, anyway."

"What do *you* think?"

"I think that it's part of the anxiety. I worry." She yawns. "I don't think I've ever talked about this with anyone except Drake, and even he only knows a little of it."

"I want to know everything about you," I reply honestly. "Not to judge you, but to learn you."

"I know. I feel the same." She turns on her side and looks up at me. "Why does it always feel safer to talk about things in the dark?"

"Because we feel hidden here. Safe."

"I guess so." She scoots closer to me and threads her leg through mine. "I've always been a worrier. I don't remember a time when I wasn't. It's probably a chemical imbalance. The anxiety, I mean. And there are meds I can take, but it's been there for so long, I'm pretty good at managing it."

"Hiding it," I correct her.

"Tomato, tomahto," she says with a smile. "Either way, I don't feel like I need medicine. But there are going to be times that I'll think I'm sick. Or that I have a disease. I'll always wonder. I've asked colleagues to do full body scans before, just to give me peace of mind, but they usually laugh me off."

"Sweetheart," I murmur and kiss her forehead. "You're a strong, healthy woman."

"I know. The rational side of me *knows* that. I have no reason to believe otherwise. It's like the bear thing, or the lake thing the other day. I *know* better, but I can't change the thoughts."

"I see."

"No, you don't. And that's okay. I'd rather you didn't understand. But I appreciate you asking and not judging."

"Can you tell me more about your parents?"

She frowns, but then shrugs. "Sure. What do you want to know?"

"You just didn't say too much, other than your father killed your mother in an accident, and you haven't seen him since."

"That's pretty much it."

"But that doesn't give me much information."

"You could run his record," she replies.

*Oh, I have.*

"That's not personal either," I remind her.

She sighs. "I honestly don't think of him. Ever. I know that sounds heartless, but he wasn't a great father, or even a nice person. At least, not that I remember. I remember him being drunk most of the time. He didn't work because he couldn't hold a job. Mom stressed out about money and me and everything else, and he just drank.

"I spent a lot of time with Abby and her parents, or at my friends' homes. I preferred it, actually. He never hurt me. He didn't hit me, or yell at me. He ignored me."

"Sometimes that's just as bad," I reply, wanting to wrap her in my arms and protect her.

"I agree. I didn't really consider him at all, until the accident. I didn't think of him as dangerous. He was more of a pain in the ass.

"My mom was pretty great. She was soft spoken. I have her hair and eyes, and I'm grateful for that. I don't know what it would be like to look in the mirror and see *him*."

"I'm sure she was beautiful."

"She was." She smiles sweetly. "And she made the best cookies. She was a great cook. I didn't inherit that ability."

"Too bad."

She wrinkles her nose in that adorable way she does. "Yeah, too bad. Her name was Vivienne, and she wasn't even forty when she died."

"Did she often ride with your dad after he'd been drinking?"

"Not that I know of. They didn't do much of anything together. I wasn't home that day. I decided to spend most of the winter break with Abby, and we were having a New Year's Eve party at her house with some of our friends. Mom had called earlier in the day to say hello and to check in, like she usually did. That's the last time I spoke to her. I was impatient to get off the phone so I could help decorate for the party.

"At about three in the morning, a few cops came to my aunt and uncle's house, and they sat us all down and told me that my mom was gone."

"I've had to go on too many of those calls."

She nods. "It must suck."

"It does."

"I miss her. She would have been proud of me, and she probably would have moved to Montana with me."

"And you never heard from your father after that?"

"Why would I? He never paid attention to me before, there's no reason that I would after. I didn't go to the trial. He plead no contest, so his sentence would be more lenient."

"Thank you for sharing all of this with me."

"You're welcome. And now we don't have to talk about it again."

She yawns and snuggles into me, burying her face in my neck. Before long, she's breathing with the even, steady breaths of sleep, and I'm still turning the story over in my head. I don't feel bad for her; she wouldn't want that. But I wish she'd had a better father in her life.

It's amazing to me that she's as healthy as she is, given the circumstances of her childhood.

She's strong. And brave. And she's mine.

∼

SADIE MEETS me at the door at lunchtime. I walk inside and find a glassy-eyed Hannah sitting on the couch, staring at nothing in particular. She's wearing my T-shirt again, and Sadie returns to her side.

"Hi there," I say, and she looks up at me and offers me a small smile.

"Hi."

"Are you just waking up?"

"Yeah." She pets Sadie's head. "Don't judge me. I haven't had a hangover since I was twenty-one."

"You had a lot of fun last night."

"Yeah, and then I was up fucking for the rest of it." Her eyes light up when she sees the coffee in my hand. "Is that for me?"

"Of course." I pass it to her. "This is too. It's a breakfast sandwich."

"You're really good to me." She takes a sip of her coffee, closes her eyes, and smiles. "This is nice. Thank you."

"You're welcome."

"Were you on time for work this morning?"

"Of course," I say and scoop her up in my arms, then sit and settle her in my lap. "I'm never late."

"You were up all night, too." She sips her coffee and then lays her head on my shoulder. "Should I feel guilty?"

"For what?"

"For your lack of sleep."

I chuckle and kiss her head, smelling her hair. "No. It's my own fault for not being able to keep my hands off of you."

"You always say sweet things. And you do sweet things. You're just a sweet man, Brad."

"Don't let it get out. I have a reputation to protect."

"Ah yes, your badass Chief Sexypants reputation."

"Sexywhat?"

"Sexypants. It's your name when you're not around."

I stare down at her in surprise. "That's what you call me when I'm not around?"

"Only to Jenna and Grace, and not all the time." She grins and kisses my chin. "Don't be mad. It's a complimentary nickname."

"If you say so."

"I'm glad you're here. It's easier to wake up when you're here rather than by myself."

"Well, you have me for about twenty more minutes. Then I have to go back to work."

"Already?"

"It's noon, Hannah. I can't take the rest of the day off."

"What am I going to do all afternoon?"

"Take Sadie for a walk."

She sips her coffee, giving it thought. "I do need to go get my car."

"I can drive you to your car."

"Nah. Sadie and I will walk to get it. I'll do the walk of shame." She smiles. "I've never done that before."

"I guess there's a first for everything."

She laughs and settles against me, and it feels like heaven to just hold her in my arms for a moment, enjoying the calm.

"How is work today?"

"Busy. There was a home break in last night, and a car accident this morning, with one fatality."

Her arm squeezes my shoulder. "I'm sorry."

"Me, too. So, I'll be busy this afternoon."

"What do you have planned for this evening?" she asks.

"I'm open."

"Good. I'd like to treat you to dinner."

"We've discussed this. I buy dinner."

She rolls her eyes. "Fine, I'd like to go out for dinner."

"Done."

"You're difficult."

"You just told me yesterday that I'm easy going and steady."

"Until you're difficult."

# CHAPTER 13

## ~HANNAH~

I've cleaned the house. Sadie and I walked to town to get my car.

I even cooked dinner.

Brad should be home any minute, and I feel about as domestic as I ever have in my life. I'm not sure how I feel about it. I mean, I feel good about it, but it's new. Should I be wearing an apron? Should I be naked *except* for the apron?

That would make him smile.

But then dinner would go cold because I'm quite sure he'd fuck me against the kitchen counter. I'd be disappointed if he didn't.

So I'll keep my clothes on for now.

Also, why am I overthinking this? It's dinner. And by dinner, I mean chicken enchiladas that I slapped together because like I told him last night, I'm not a great cook.

It's not a big deal.

The door to the garage opens, and Brad comes in, smiling, carrying a baby carrier.

I do a double take, and then frown.

"I knew it."

"What?" He sets the carrier on the table and begins pulling blankets off of it, unearthing an adorable, dark-haired baby girl.

"I told Grace that I was sure that you had a secret baby somewhere."

He just laughs and shakes his head as he pulls the baby into his arms and turns to face me. His eyes are soft, almost dewy, as he looks down at the little one. "She isn't mine."

"That's a relief. And she isn't *mine* because I definitely haven't had a baby. So whose is she?"

"My detective's little girl. Her name is Megan." He smiles at her and she reaches for Brad's nose.

"She's cute." I cross my arms over my chest, keeping a safe distance between me and them. "Why is she with you?"

"Her daddy wanted to take his wife out for dinner, but the babysitter cancelled, so I volunteered to take her."

"It's like I don't even know you," I reply and laugh. "This might be the very last thing I would expect."

"She loves me," he says in defense. "Look."

At that moment, Megan stretches her arms out to me, whimpering.

"Or, she's trying to escape."

"You can take her," he suggests, and I freeze.

"That's okay."

"She's asking for you."

I walk to the oven and open it, retrieving the enchiladas. "I'm finishing dinner," I reply, not making eye contact. "And I'm not good with babies."

"Why?"

"Why am I not good with babies?" I turn and stare at him. Megan smiles, a toothless smile and then sticks her fist in her mouth.

"Yeah. I mean look at her."

"She's beautiful."

Brad's phone rings in his pocket, and when he checks the caller ID, he frowns and holds the baby out to me. "Please take her, I have to take this call."

He plants Megan in my arms and walks into his office, shuts the door, and I'm left with a baby.

"How old are you, Megan?" I ask, holding her stiffly. She's watching my face, and then her own face crumples and she starts to fuss. "Oh no. Don't do that." I hold her closer to me and sway back and forth, hoping I'm doing this right. "You don't have to cry. See? It's okay."

I'm swaying and patting her back, and Megan lays her little head on my shoulder, quiet now.

Thank goodness.

With the baby on my arm, I do my best to cover the enchiladas with foil and set them back in the oven on warm. They'll keep for a while.

Five minutes later, Brad comes out of the office, looking preoccupied.

"Sorry about that," he says and stops short when he sees me. "Well, look at you."

"I admit, she's pretty cute." I'm still swaying her back and forth, and she's tucked her little face in my neck. "Is she sleeping?"

"No, she's just hanging out." He grins and walks to us, pats Megan on the back, and then kisses me softly. "You look beautiful."

"Barefoot in the kitchen with a baby on my hip?"

"No, just beautiful," he says, then snorts out a laugh. "But that's quite the description."

"I *am* barefoot," I point out.

"But not pregnant, so there's that."

"Never," I reply, shaking my head emphatically. Megan lifts her head and looks me square in the eyes. "But you are a pretty little thing, aren't you?"

She smiles widely.

"One day, you'll get some teeth. And then, look out, because everything is delicious."

She giggles.

"That's right. All of the food is delicious."

"Speaking of food," Brad says, pulling a bottle out of a bag. He pours some formula in it, mixes it with water, and then passes it to me. "She's probably hungry."

"You feed her."

He just smiles and shakes his head no. I roll my eyes, take the bottle, and settle into his rocking recliner.

"I don't know if I'm doing this right?"

"Haven't you ever been around kids?" he asks as he watches me settle her against me and offer her the bottle, which she greedily takes, holding my hand and watching me with sleepy brown eyes.

"Not really." He passes me a rag so I can wipe up the drip on her chin. "I didn't have siblings, and I didn't babysit. I've never really felt like I'm a maternal person."

She starts to cough, choking a bit, and I immediately put the bottle down, and pull her forward, helping her airway to clear. I wipe her chin again, then settle her in to eat some more.

"Yeah, not maternal at all," he says. He's smiling when I look up at him. "I wouldn't have known how to do that."

"I'm a doctor," I remind him. "And she wasn't choking badly."

I run my fingers over her soft, fine hair and her eyes flutter closed. "She's so soft. How old is she?"

"About five months," he replies quietly, petting Sadie.

When Megan has drunk the rest of her bottle, I settle her against my shoulder to burp her. "I think I saw this in a movie."

"You're doing great. Also, you deliver babies."

"Yes."

"You don't hold them?"

"I pull them out and hand them to their mom or a nurse, and then I go about the task of making sure Mom doesn't die."

"That's important," he says, nodding. "I had no idea that babies make you nervous."

"Well, I'm not as nervous as I was when you first arrived. Thank goodness she's not your secret baby."

"I couldn't have a secret baby in this town."

We both laugh. "True. There aren't many secrets around here."

"She's asleep," he says and drags his fingertip down her cheek. "She's a sweetie."

"I'm surprised she's not more fussy. You always hear of them crying all the time unless they're asleep. That doesn't sound fun. I always wonder, why would anyone willingly put themselves through that?"

"Is that why you don't want kids?" he asks.

I pause, thinking about it. This baby is definitely adorable. She's small, fitting against my chest perfectly, and she smells *so good*. I could bury my nose in her and stay there all day.

"I mean, she's going to wake up, right?"

"If all goes well, yes," he says, laughing again.

"And she'll cry. And probably need a lot of attention."

"She's an infant, so I'd say that's a safe assumption."

I nod, still thinking it over. "I guess that doesn't sound too bad. But I know without a doubt that I don't want to be pregnant. It goes back to me knowing too much. Most pregnancies are normal, but I see way too many that aren't. It's not something I've felt the need to experience for myself."

"Interesting," he says, sitting back on the sofa and watching me. "I guess I'd never really thought about that."

"You're a man. You don't have to worry about the changes to your body, or how well your body will even deal with being pregnant. And that's only the beginning. There can be so many different complications, diseases, disorders, and problems that it would take a month to list them all."

"And you'd worry the entire time."

"Every minute of it," I confirm. "And I know, it sounds—"

"Don't say dumb. You're not dumb, Hannah."

"Well, it sounds dumb to me," I reply with a shrug. "But it is what it is."

I pull the sleeping baby off of my chest and into my arms, so I can see her sweet face. Her lips are pursed, as if she's sucking on a nipple in her dream. "Her eyelashes are long. They're always wasted on babies and men."

"She looks like her mom," he says, just as there's a knock on the door. "Speaking of which, there they are."

"So soon?"

He tosses me a wide smile and answers the door. "She's sleeping."

"Oh, good," Dan says as they come inside. His wife, whom I immediately recognize, rushes over to check on her.

"Dr. Malone," she says with a happy smile. "What a surprise."

"Hi Alice," I reply and nod to Dan. "I didn't realize this little bundle belonged to you."

"You mean you didn't recognize her?" Dan asks with a smile.

"She was a little smaller and a lot bluer that day," I reply and smile kindly at Alice. "She's beautiful and healthy, and I'm so happy for you."

"She's here because of you," Alice says with tears in her eyes and wraps her arms around both of us, hugging us. "You saved us."

"That's the job," I say and pass the baby to her mama. "And I have to tell you, this might be the first time I've spent time with a baby that I delivered. It was fun. I had no idea this tiny baby was that Megan."

"Well, thanks to both of you for taking her so we could have an uninterrupted dinner out," Dan says, shaking Brad's hand. "It was nice."

"My pleasure," Brad says. He runs out to the garage to get the car seat base, and when they've left with the baby, he turns to me with a raised eyebrow. "I didn't know that you were the doctor who delivered her."

"I was."

"That was a shit show."

"It was." I nod, not allowed to talk freely with Brad about the medical history. "But as you can see, it all worked out."

He frowns and looks down, and then without looking me in the eyes, he just pulls me in and hugs me tightly.

"Dan would have lost both of them if it hadn't been for you, and I just want to say thank you for saving them both. Dan's a good friend."

"It's the job," I repeat, but hug him back fiercely. "And I'm happy that it all worked out for the best."

He kisses me head, breathing me in.

"Me too."

~

MY CAR SMELLS like heaven the next morning.

474

The aroma of coffee and donuts fills the space around me, and I want to just pull over and eat and drink it all myself.

That's not possible, but it doesn't make me want it any less.

I park in front of the police station and carry four dozen donuts and a gallon of hot coffee inside, then I run back out for the special individual coffee for Brad. As I walk back inside, Brad is approaching the desk with the donuts, where at least six other men are already loading up on sugar and caffeine.

"This one is for you," I say and hand him the cup. "The lady at *Sips* said this is what you usually order."

His eyes intently watch me as he takes a sip. "She was right. What's all this?"

"Well, I know it's a cliché, but I thought everyone might enjoy some coffee and donuts."

"You thought right," Dan says with a grin. Several other uniformed officers nod in agreement. "And these are the best donuts in town."

"I know." I reach out and snatch up a maple bar. "So good."

"Come into my office," Brad says, but I shake my head no.

"I have errands."

"Do you have two minutes?" he asks. The look on his face says he needs to talk to me, so I nod and follow him into his office, munching on my donut.

"What's up?"

He doesn't answer. Instead, he sweeps me up into a passionate kiss. He doesn't even care that I have maple glaze on my lips.

"You're sweet," he murmurs against me.

"It's the donut."

He grins and kisses me one more time, then sets me away from him. "No, it's you. You didn't have to do that for my guys."

"I know. It was fun." I smile and take another bite of my donut. "I might as well take advantage of this whole week off thing and spoil us all a little bit."

"Don't spoil them too much. They'll get soft."

"Yes, sir." I offer him a mock salute and open the office door. "I'm going to get a massage now."

"Good for you. And then?"

"I think I'll wander around downtown and look for a birthday gift for my cousin, Abby."

"Have a good day, sweetheart."

I smile and close his door behind me, waving to the guys who are smiling at me as I walk past.

I've made some friends this morning.

~

I'M LOADING up on way too much huckleberry stuff. Syrup, jam, pancake mix, even chocolate. I can't help myself. I've turned into a tourist in my own damn town.

I've wandered my way through just about every shop on Main Street in downtown Cunningham Falls. Not only did I find the cutest outfit and pair of earrings for Abby, but I found all of this huckleberry stuff, a painting for the living room of my house, *and* I might have splurged on ice cream.

Okay, I totally did.

I feel fantastic after my massage. It's a warm eighty degrees outside, perfect for roaming around without getting too hot, and it's the middle of a weekday so the tourists aren't as obnoxious as they would be on a Saturday.

Just as I'm about to walk into *Dress It Up*, I hear my name being called from across the street.

"Hannah!"

"Hey," I reply, happy to see my friend and patient, Jillian King, as she pushes her stroller across the street to join me. She has her twins with her, and her face is glowing with happiness as she joins me. "How are you?"

"I'm great," she says, panting a bit. "I took the afternoon off to take the kids to the park. It's too pretty out to waste it."

"I agree." I kneel in front of the stroller and smile at the little girl and little boy who stare back at me with curiosity. "Hello there, Sarah and Miles."

They grin and Miles offers me a high five.

"They're adorable," I say as I stand to talk to Jillian. "I can't believe how big they are."

"They'll be three soon," she says, sighing. "And I'm going to have to come see you soon as well."

"Check up?"

She shakes her head no and gives me a happy smile. "We're expecting."

"I think at least eighty percent of the people I know are pregnant," I reply with a laugh. "Congratulations."

"What are the odds that it's twins again?" she asks nervously.

"Not high," I assure her. "Even though your husband is a twin, the odds are low."

"Thank God. I love these two, but they're a handful. Having just one infant will be a walk in the park."

"That's the way to look at it. How is Cara?"

Cara and Jillian are best friends, and each married twin brothers a few years ago. They live out at the King brothers' ranch, in separate homes, of course. The Kings own thousands of acres just west of town.

"She's great. I think she and Josh are finished having babies. Two are enough for them."

"Well, I'd love to see you all soon," I reply. "And I'll look for you on my schedule."

"Thanks," she says with a smile. "And now we're off to the park."

She walks away, in the direction of the city park down the street, and I walk into *Dress It Up* to see if I can find something new. I've shopped like a pro today, I might as well keep it going.

"Hannah," Willa says with a smile. "It's nice to see you. Can I help you find anything?"

"I'm just out shopping today," I reply. "I know I said this the other night, but I have to say it again. This store is *so pretty*."

"I know. My inner girlie girl went crazy when we were decorating. And I just can't be sorry."

"You shouldn't be. It makes me want to buy pretty things, and I would think that was the intention."

"Absolutely, and it's good to hear that it worked," she says, nodding. "Plus, when you're a single mother of a little boy, it's nice to be around girlie things sometimes."

"I'm sure. You have a son?"

"I do. He's eight." She reaches behind the glass display case that she uses for the cash register and grabs her phone, pulling up a photo. "Alexander, but we call him Alex for short."

A brunette boy with dimples and a mischievous grin stares back at me. "He's a cutie."

"He's a terror," she corrects me and tucks her phone away. "But he's eight, and he's a boy, so I'm told that being a terror is normal."

"I think so."

"So, you're dating Brad?" she asks without apology. Her chin is up, her eyes on mine, and I respect her even more. She's not trying to gossip, she's asking for information.

"We've been dating for a few weeks. Geez, more than that now, I guess."

"I've known the Hulls for a long time, and I can tell you, they don't get better than Brad."

"I'm glad you think so."

"Don't worry," she says, waving me off and straightening a shirt on a hanger. "I don't have a crush on him. If anything I feel sisterly toward him. I dated Max for a while a million years ago."

"I heard," I reply and then shrug when she raises a brow. "Small town, Willa, and I'm friends with Jenna."

"That's right." She nods and then laughs. "Max was a long time ago, but I still have a soft spot for his family. They were nice to me."

"They're nice people."

"Exactly. So, I just wanted to let you know that Brad is what you see. He's a good man, hard worker, handsome fella. And good for you for snagging him."

"Dating in this town is hard," I reply and she emphatically nods her head.

"Tell me about it. I'm either related to half the town, or I know too much about them. Or they're only here on vacation. Not to mention, I have a kid, and he comes first. Always."

"As it should be."

"A lot of men don't get that."

"A lot of men aren't worth your time then."

She stops and smiles at me. "I like you."

My phone pings with a text from Brad. *Meet me at your place at 5:00?*

"Speak of the devil," I murmur and reply with *sure.*

"Enjoy him," Willa says. "Make him loosen up a bit. He's so stuffy."

I nod and wave as I leave her store and decide to head home for a shower before Brad arrives.

Funny, he's not stuffy with me.

Hot. Sexy. Funny. But not stuffy.

# CHAPTER 14

## ~BRAD~

"*This* is… intimidating." I'm standing next to Jenna and Max, staring up at the tree houses that are currently under construction. They are about thirty feet in the air, supported by metal beams that will eventually be hidden by faux bark, making the supports look like trees.

"Tree houses," Max murmurs and then smiles down at Jenna. "Only you would come up with something like this."

"It's been in my head for years," she replies with a shrug. "And it's going to be *so cool*. If I can get the contractor to stay on budget. This is the second one I'll have to fire in less than a month."

"The budget is a million," Max reminds her with a frown.

"I know. And he's almost reached it already and we're only half way there. I would take over and just do it myself, but these buildings are off the ground. I need an expert for this."

Max and I share a look of concern, and then we go off in search of the contractor together. We find him, sitting on the circular staircase in the biggest of the three houses, sipping coffee and laughing with a colleague.

"Oh, hi there, Max and Brad."

He doesn't acknowledge Jenna at all, which has me balling my hands into fists.

"We need to talk," Jenna says, but he won't make eye contact with her. "Mr. Jefferson, we need to discuss the budget."

"Oh, no need to worry," he says, but Jenna sets her hands on her hips and glares at him.

"You've almost reached my top budget and you're only half way finished with the project."

"Well, that can happen sometimes, especially when the woman in charge likes expensive things," he says and winks at me, but I just narrow my eyes at him and he loses his smug grin, clearing his throat. "Brad, I'm sure you know—"

"I don't," I interrupt. "This is Jenna's project, and you clearly don't respect that."

"The budget is the budget," Max adds. "And you don't respect that either."

"You're fired," Jenna says.

Jason Jefferson's eyes bulge and he starts to sputter. "What do you mean?"

"Fired," Jenna repeats. "Out. Canned. Done. I want you off my property in twenty minutes."

"You can't use my guys," he says nastily. "If I go, they go."

"Fine," Jenna replies, not looking at him. "I'll find someone else."

"I'll spread rumors," he begins, but I walk forward and push my nose into his face.

"You'll what?"

"I'll spread rumors," he repeats, not backing down. "I'll tell everyone that she sleeps with the crew and her brothers try to intimidate us."

"I'm not trying," I say and lean in further, not touching him. "I'm *doing*. Despite it being a dick move, I understand that in a small town a man doesn't want to take orders from a woman. But it's the goddamn twenty-first century and this is Jenna's work site. It'll be run the way she sees fit, and she wants you gone."

"Fine," he snarls and nods to his employee. "Pack up. Let's get out of here."

"I'm an independent contractor," the young man says and turns to Jenna. "He's not my boss. I'd like to stay."

"You're welcome to stay, Bubba," she says with a smile. "Anyone else who wants to stay, and work for *me*, is welcome to do so."

Bubba nods and leaves the house, walking out to talk to the others.

"You need to leave," she says to Jason, who's seething. "And if you try to spread rumors about me or my brothers, I'll start telling the *truth* about your work ethic and ruin your business. I don't want to do that. I think this project was just too big for you, and that's okay. But it's time to call it quits."

"You're a bitch," he snarls and stomps away, gathering his tools.

"I hope he doesn't come back here to destroy what we've already done," she murmurs.

"He won't," Max says, shaking his head. "He can't chance jail time and ruining his business. He's just butt hurt."

"Who are you going to hire?" I ask her.

"I have a few calls out," she replies. "I'll get someone new right away. This project is too fun and too different. Someone will want it. I'm also going to showcase it in the Parade of Homes later this year, so they'll get exposure there as well."

"Man, Jason is a stupid son of a bitch," I reply. "But I'm glad he's gone. You don't want someone here like that."

"He wasn't always," she says and walks into the area where the kitchen will be. "He was excited in the beginning, but I meant it when I said that it got to be more than he could handle. I wish he had just been honest about it from the beginning. Male egos are fragile."

"That they are," Max says with a grin. "I can put up more money if you need it."

"I will," she says with a sigh. "Thanks to Jason. But I know that this place will pay for itself in the first three years, even with the added budget."

"I agree," Max replies with a nod. "Now that I see it in person, I know it's going to be impressive."

"Just wait," she says with an excited grin.

"Mr. Hull?" Bubba comes back into the house with a smile. "I've discussed it with the other guys, and they'd also like to stay and be a part of the project."

"It's not my project," Max reminds him. "You all need to talk to Jenna. Always."

"Of course," Bubba says and offers Jenna a chagrined smile. "Sorry about that. We'd like to stay if you'll have us."

"Let's have a quick meeting," she replies and walks outside. "Everyone who wants to stay on this project, I want you to report inside now, please."

She has her boss hat on now, and I admit, it's impressive. I'm proud of my little sister.

Once everyone has gathered inside, about eight men, she smiles at them, and then gets to business.

"I'm thankful that you'd all like to stay on the project. It's important to me, and it's going to be wonderful when its finished. But you all need to understand, *I'm the boss.* Always, every day. My brothers are investors, but that's it."

Max and I both hang in the back, our arms crossed over our chests, and watch her take the lead.

"If you have any issues with that, you're welcome to leave now."

She pauses and waits, but no one leaves.

"Great. I'll be hiring another contractor this week, and he will also be a point of contact for you. We will continue with Friday lunches being brought in, as we have been. I want you to be happy and productive."

"I don't have any issues with you at all," one of the men says. "You're fair, you're firm, and you're kind to us. Jason is a dick."

"Yes, well," Jenna says with a laugh. "I think we all agree with you. Thanks for being here, guys. We are behind schedule."

"We'll pick up the pace," someone else says. "It'll get done on time."

The rest of the men nod in agreement, and a few moments later, they go back to work and Jenna lets out a big sigh of relief.

"That could have gone very badly."

"They respect you," Max says.

"And they like you," I add. "It goes a long way."

She nods and then runs off out of the house. "Sorry guys, I remembered something I have to do in the other house."

Max and I shrug and wander out onto the large balcony that looks out onto the ski slopes, green now with summer grass and bright flowers.

"It's a good spot," Max says.

"I had my doubts, but she has something special here."

"Speaking of something special," Max begins, "tell me about Hannah."

"Touch her and I'll kill you."

He laughs and shakes his head. "No, asshole, tell me about *you* and Hannah."

"I like her." I shrug, as if it's no big deal, and lean on the railing, not meeting his eyes with mine.

"And?"

"What are you, a woman? Do you want me to tell you all about our first kiss?"

"Sure." He laughs. "You've always been the quiet one. You don't talk about personal things often."

"They're personal."

"And you're difficult."

"What do you want to hear? That I'm in love with her? That I can't imagine what life was like without her?"

"That's a start."

"It's too soon," I mutter and shake my head in frustration. "It's been less than two months."

"So?" I jerk my gaze to his. "Who gives a fuck about how much time has passed? You're not strangers, and you've spent enough time together to know how you feel about her."

"She's amazing," I reply simply. "She has the next few days off of work, and I'd like to do something special for her."

"Can you take some time off work?" Max asks.

"Yeah, I have plenty of paid time off coming."

"I have an idea," he says. "Take her to my condo in Laguna Beach. Use the plane."

"Impress her," I reply, not hating the idea.

"Treat her," he counters. "Go live it up a little."

"I don't like taking advantage of you."

"Jesus Christ," he mutters and pushes his hand through his hair. "I understand that you don't want me to pay off your house. But for fucksake, Brad, I own these things out right, and I'm not using them. *You* should use them. Take your girl for a romantic weekend at the beach."

"Okay."

He looks up, his eyes wide with surprise. "Yeah?"

"Yeah, that would be fun. Thank you."

Max lets out a sigh. "I thought you'd never agree to it."

"I'm proud of you," I say and turn to face him. "I couldn't be more proud. You've made more money than you can ever spend on your own, and you did it with grit and determination. You're smart. Of course I'm proud of you. But those things are *yours*, not mine. I like making my own way."

"I know, and I respect that. But using some of the things I've made or bought isn't freeloading. I *want* to share all of this with my family. Otherwise, what's the fucking point?"

I blink, not thinking of it this way before. "Thanks for that."

"You're welcome. Now go soak up some beach time with Hannah. Have vacation sex. Laugh. I think you both could use it."

"That's the truth. I need to make arrangements at work, but is the jet available this afternoon?"

"It's ready when you are."

"Can you keep Sadie?"

"Of course. That dog loves me more than she does you."

"Whatever."

"I'll call down to the condo and tell them you're coming. Everything will be ready for you."

"I owe you."

"No. You don't. That's the whole point."

~

WORK IS SQUARED AWAY. I was surprised by how easily they all agreed to look after things for me while I'm gone.

I guess it's been a minute since I took a vacation.

Sadie is safely with Max, my house is locked up tight, and I've called the airport. The plane is ready.

481

Max has owned it for a few years, but I've only ridden in it once before. It feels odd. Indulgent. Ridiculous, honestly. I mean, why would I need to ride in a private plane?

But Hannah will get a kick out of it. I've seen photos of Max's condo in southern California.

We'll both get a kick out of that.

I haven't been excited for a trip like this in a long time.

I pull up to Hannah's house and see her car parked in the drive. She's at her computer when I walk inside, her gorgeous red hair piled on her head, and she's only wearing a tank top and panties, her legs pulled up under her in the chair.

She's a fucking wet dream.

But we don't have time for me to live out the dream right now.

"Hi, sweetheart."

She smiles and looks up, offering her lips for a kiss, which I gladly accept. I sink into her, kissing her much more deeply than I'd planned, and I have to tear myself away from her if we're going to leave the house today.

"I have a surprise for you."

"Really?" Her smile widens. "Flowers?"

"Better."

"Coffee?"

"Better."

She lifts a brow. "Better than coffee?"

"Oh yeah. I want you to pack a bag."

She frowns now and stands up out of the chair, and my semi-hard on is now at full alert.

"Where are we going?"

"It's a surprise. You'll also need pants."

"Will I need a passport?"

"Not this time." I grin and cup her cheek, unable to keep myself from touching her. "We're just going away for a few days."

"Warm or cold climate?"

"Why?"

"I need to know what to pack, Chief Sexypants."

I cringe at the horrible nickname. "Warm. Think beach."

"Oh, the beach!" She claps her hands and jogs to her closet. "How fun. I'll take lots of flip flops, a few bathing suits." She pokes her head around the doorjamb, her hair falling in her eyes. "Will we need to dress up for anything?"

"Possibly."

She narrows her eyes and then shrugs. "Okay. I'll pack a sundress. Shorts. Tanks. Maybe a sweater in case it's cold in the evenings."

"We're only going for a few days," I remind her as she rushes past me to the bathroom.

"I know, but you just never know what I might need. All the makeup, hair stuff." She gathers all the girl products in the world into her arms and tosses them into her suitcase, then proceeds to organize everything just so. "Okay, I think I have everything. Do I need to do my hair and makeup for the plane?"

"No." I take her shoulders in my hands and turn her to me. "You look beautiful just like this."

"I'm a mess."

"I don't think so."

"And I'm not wearing pants."

"That doesn't bother me either."

She chuckles and kisses my chin. "When do we have to leave?"

"In about thirty minutes."

Her eyes go wide. "Brad! We won't make the plane in time!" She rushes to pull on shorts, slips into sandals, and zips her suitcase closed. "We have to hurry."

# CHAPTER 15

## ~HANNAH~

*I* don't know why he's so calm. We have *minutes* to get to the gate in time. There's no way they'll let us through security now.

Is this what I'm destined to deal with all the time if I stay with him forever? Because I have to be honest, I can't do that. I'm way too organized for that. I get to the airport *at least* an hour before the flight takes off.

I mean, who shows up with only a few minutes to spare?

"It's going to be fine," Brad says with a smile as he turns toward the airport.

"Do you want to just drop me off and I'll run in and check us in?"

"No."

I stare at him and then shake my head, completely knotted up inside. But, I should calm down. This is *his* show, and if the plane leaves without us, that's not my fault.

Yeah. That's it.

Rather than pull into the parking lot, he takes a turn on what looks like an employees' road that winds behind the airport, back where the planes are parked.

"We're going to get in trouble," I mutter, but he just chuckles next to me. "Who *are* you? You're acting very weird."

"Relax. I know that's not easy for you, but I've got this. We're not getting in trouble."

I sigh, not believing him in the least, but decide to take both our advice. What's the worst that will happen? We won't go on this trip?

Hell, an hour ago I didn't even know there was a trip.

He turns away from the commercial airliners and drives over to a smaller plane that has the main door open, the stairs pushed against it like it's waiting for passengers.

"This is our ride," he says casually and parks about ten yards from the plane.

"This?"

"Yes, ma'am." He winks before getting out of his truck, talks to a member of the ground crew, and opens my door for me. "Your carriage awaits."

"We're taking a *private* plane?"

"We are."

I hop out of his truck and stare at the gleaming white and black jet, completely shocked.

"Wow."

"Hi, Chief." A man steps out of the plane and shakes Brad's hand. "We're ready when you are, sir."

"Great, thanks. We're ready any time. Hannah, this is Jeremy. He's the pilot today."

"It's a great day for a flight. Smooth sailing the whole way." He smiles and walks back inside the plane and disappears.

"I requested that we not have a flight attendant today," he says with a smile and leads me inside the jet. It's bigger than I thought it would be. There are at least a dozen plush leather seats, all comfortable recliners that swivel. "There's a bathroom in the back, and there's a galley with snacks and drinks if you want anything."

"I'm fine," I reply, completely shocked. "This is gorgeous. How did you manage this?"

"It's Max's plane," he says and helps me fasten my seatbelt. The pilot quickly comes back to go over safety features and introduce us to the co-pilot, and then he disappears behind the door leading to the cockpit and I hear the engines start. "We're using all of his fun toys over the next few days."

"That's pretty cool." The seat feels like a big hug, wrapping around my body and cradling me. "This might be the most comfortable airplane seat I've ever been in."

"I'm glad you like it."

"What's not to like? It's a super fancy treat. Max seems nice."

"I like him," Brad replies with a shrug. "He's generous, and he hasn't let all the money go to his head."

"That's good." I nod and watch as Brad takes a seat across from me, swivels to face me, and clicks his own seatbelt closed. He crosses one ankle over the opposite knee and rubs his fingers over his mouth, watching me with hot green eyes.

"What's wrong?"

"There's no fucking loveseat or couch on this plane," he says immediately. "As soon as we're airborne, I'm pulling you into my lap."

I laugh, but electricity is zinging through me at the intensity of his voice. "I guess I've been warned."

He doesn't reply, and we're quiet as the plane picks up speed down the runway and takes off. I glance outside, surprised that the plane ride isn't bumpier as it climbs away from the green trees and blue lakes below into the sky.

"A smaller plane usually means more turbulence," I comment and turn to find him still watching me.

"This plane is pretty steady."

I nod and squeeze my legs closed, completely taken off guard at the sexual tension in the air. If I thought it was there earlier at my house, it's nothing like right now.

I'm going to have sex in an airplane.

That's new.

We sit, staring at each other, until there's a ding over the speakers that signals we're at cruising altitude and we're safe to move about.

Within seconds, Brad is out of his seat and next to me, unclipping my seatbelt and lifting me into his arms.

My hands dive into his hair as his lips find mine, and it's like we're starved for each other, like we haven't been together in ages rather than just this morning.

Rather than sit with me in his lap, Brad quickly strips us both out of our clothes, and guides me down to sit in my seat, scooted forward so my ass is at the very edge of the chair.

The next thing I know, he pushes my legs up, spreads them wide, and buries his face in my core, making me bite my lip to keep from crying out.

I don't need to alert the pilots to the show happening twenty feet behind them.

"You're so damn sweet," he growls, watching me as he licks and nibbles, then pulls my lips into his mouth and makes a pulsing motion, succeeding in puckering my nipples.

I'm quite sure I'm going to have a bloody lip by the time this is over.

And I couldn't care less.

"You can make noise," he says.

"No way." I have to grip the arms of the chair for dear life, not worried in the least that I might pierce the leather with my nails. "They can hear."

"No, they can't." He grins and pushes a finger inside me, watching me almost leisurely. "They have headsets on to talk to air traffic control. They're in their own world."

I gasp when he pushes a second finger inside and makes a *come here* motion, making me quiver and see stars all at once.

"Oh God."

"That's right."

"I can't even."

"Oh yes. You can." He lowers his mouth to my clit, and that's it. I explode into a million pieces. Without missing a beat, he wraps his arms around my back and picks me up, settling in the seat and me on top of him, straddling his hips.

I lower myself onto him, and when he's buried as far as he can go, I lean in and kiss his mouth, loving the smell and taste of me on his lips.

"You make me crazy," I whisper.

"Not nearly as crazy as you make me," he counters, gripping my ass and urging me to move up and down in a long, quick motion. "I couldn't wait to get airborne so I could have my way with you."

"I have to admit, this is a first."

He fists his hand in my hair and pulls me down to kiss him. "You make me want things I never have before, Hannah."

"Like what?"

I bear down and squeeze, making him clench his teeth.

"This. Sex where someone could hear."

"You said they *can't* hear."

He grins. "Well, they probably can't."

I pause, momentarily mortified, and then throw caution to the wind and move faster, bearing down harder.

"Trying to make me come?"

"Hell, yes," I reply and bite his neck. "And I want you to be loud."

His fingertips dig into my hips and every muscle in his body tightens as I continue to nibble and bite. And when I sink my fingers into his hair again, he cries out and comes apart, leaving me with a very satisfied smile.

"You look like the cat that ate the canary."

"Or the girl who made you come," I counter. "I'll have bruises on my ass later."

He frowns. "I'm sorry."

"Don't ever apologize for that," I reply as I stand and walk, naked, to the back of the plane. Once I've cleaned up, I return to find Brad already dressed, my clothes laid out on the chair we just had wild plane sex on.

I watch him as I pull on my clothes, fluff my hair, and sit opposite him, the way we started this trip.

"Would you like something to drink?" he asks casually, his voice calm.

"You sure do switch gears quickly."

"I always want you, Hannah. I could take you again right now. But we'll take a break. In the meantime, I'm thirsty."

"Me too." I smile gratefully, my nipples puckered all over again. "A Coke would be great."

"Done." He stands to go fetch our drinks, but pauses to lean in and kiss me thoroughly. "I'm going to fuck you frequently over the next few days."

"Thank God."

~

"Jesus." I drop my handbag on the table by the doorway of the condo and stop to stare straight ahead. It's all beautiful, but the view is already my favorite part.

And I'm barely inside.

We're on the top floor of an owners' building of this resort on the beach in southern California. Laguna Beach, to be exact. I've never been any farther west than Montana, and never to an ocean.

This is just spectacular.

"The penthouse has three bedrooms," Brad begins as he carries the luggage into a bedroom, and then returns to look at me, then the view, and back at me again. "Hannah?"

"Yeah?"

"Are you okay?"

The ocean is bright blue, and disappears into a sky just as blue as the water. There are palm trees and brown sand and a pool with a sunshine embedded in the tile below us.

I turn to stare at Brad, and then launch myself into his arms, kissing him crazy.

"I take it that's a yes," he says with a smile when I pull back.

"I've never seen anything like this."

"Is this your first time to the ocean?"

I nod and when he sets me on my feet, I make a beeline for the sliding glass doors that lead out to a covered balcony, big enough for a dining table that seats six, a gas fire pit and a sectional sofa.

"This is *amazing*."

"Max chose well when he bought this place," Brad replies as he joins me at the railing. "He says it's a good investment, and while I'm sure that's true, he also spends quite a bit of time here."

"Why would he ever go home to Montana?"

"Have you seen his house there?"

I shake my head no and he grins.

"It may not have this view, but it's pretty great as well. Come on, I want to show you the condo and then we can do whatever you want."

He takes my hand and leads me inside, pointing out five bathrooms, three of which are attached to bedrooms, a formal living space, and a dining room off of a gleaming white gourmet kitchen.

When he takes me into the master bedroom and shows me the adjoining bath and closet, all I can do is laugh.

"You've got to be kidding me. This is a *vacation* home?"

"I know, it's crazy."

"Brad, this closet is my dream closet."

I turn in a circle, taking it in. It must be two hundred square feet, with floor to ceiling shelving and built in dressers. There's a vanity area, and a chandelier hanging from the ceiling over an island with more drawer space.

"It's mostly empty," I murmur.

"Max is single," Brad reminds me. "And he's here about six months out of the year."

"A woman should be using this closet. I need to set him up with someone."

He laughs and tucks my hair behind my ear. "He does fine by himself. We'll take the smaller master suite on the other side of the condo. It also has a sweet bathroom and an ocean view. I'm not going to have sex in my brother's bed."

"Ew. No." I laugh and follow him back to the living room. "This is just amazing. Thank you for bringing me here."

"There was no way you'd survive a whole week off at home," he says with a laugh.

"I've taken weeks off before."

"Not unplanned," he points out and I have to nod in agreement. "This way, you're really on vacation. No need to feel guilty for being lazy or indulgent."

"You're good to me."

He simply smiles and kisses my forehead. "What would you like to do first?"

"I'm putting my bathing suit on, grabbing my iPad, and parking my ass by the pool to read a book."

"Excellent," he says with a smile. "Let's do it."

~

"I can't believe I fell asleep by the pool," I grumble later that evening at dinner. It's a bit early, but I woke up starving, so Brad took me back to the condo to change clothes so we could eat at one of the resort restaurants. Our table is by the window so I can look out at the water. "Thanks for pulling the umbrella over me."

"I know you say you tan, but that much sun can't be good for a redhead." He spreads some butter on a piece of bread and passes it to me. "Here. Eat."

"Yes, sir." I take a bite and close my eyes in happiness. "Oh, it's fresh out of the oven."

"Keep making that face," he says quietly.

My eyes fly up to his in confusion.

"I'm already hard," he says and takes a bite of his own bread. "You're about three seconds from me carrying you out of here."

I smirk and take another bite. We ordered pasta, and I can't wait. If it's half as good as this bread, I'll be in heaven.

"Did I miss anything good during my nap?"

"No," he replies with a smile. "And you looked sexy as hell with your sunglasses on, your iPad resting on your chest."

"What did you do?"

"I got a little work done. I took a call and sent an email on my phone."

Our food is delivered, smelling absolutely delicious. I take a bite and decide on the spot that I want to live here all the time.

"This is so good."

"Delicious," he agrees, but I shake my head no.

"All of it. The plane, the condo, the ocean. Being here and doing it all with you. It's amazing. And I know that you didn't have to take time from work, and that doing so at the last minute was probably stressful, so thank you. I won't complain or say you shouldn't have because frankly, it's all too fantastic. I'm so happy that you did. But I know it wasn't easy."

"I haven't taken time away in a long time myself," he admits. "Too long, honestly. My crew was happy to see me go, and I know they have everything handled. I just had a few things to wrap up, and you napping gave me the opportunity to do that. But you're welcome. It was a spur of the moment idea. I'd been up on the mountain at the tree house project with Jenna and Max, and after our meeting, I was talking about you with Max."

"What were you saying?" I smile innocently, bat my eyelashes, and take a sip of my water.

"That's classified," he says. "But then it occurred to me that Max is always offering the plane and condo to Jenna and me and we never take him up on it. You have time off, and it's not hard for me to take off for a couple of days. So here we are."

"Was Max surprised?"

"Oh yeah. But pleasantly so. I mentioned earlier that he's generous. It's true, he is. He's paid for our parents' winter place, so they didn't have to sell the Cunningham Falls house to pay for it. Now they have both."

"That's awesome."

"He's funding the tree house project, but that'll pay him back within a couple of years. Jenna's vision for it is amazing. She won't have any issue with drawing in tourists."

"She's so smart."

He nods. "So while my brother is a pain in the ass a lot, he's also a good man. And he's generous with his family."

"He's a pain in the ass because he's your brother."

"Of course."

I laugh and sit back, finished with my dinner. "This was *so good*."

"I've heard the dessert menu in this place is ridiculous."

"Well, we're going to have to sit here for a minute so I can hold it. Because I'm totally getting some."

He grins and then looks up when the waiter approaches.

"I have binoculars for you," he says and sets them on the table. "There seems to be some whale activity."

He points outside, and I immediately reach for the binoculars, in complete awe of the enormous humpback whales that are jumping out of the water.

"Seems it's dinner time for them, too," Brad says.

"Is that what they're doing?"

"I don't know, it sounded good."

I pass him the binoculars so he can see them too. He watches for a moment, then hands them back to me, and I watch while he settles the check with the waiter.

"I have an idea," Brad says. "Let's go down and walk on the beach for a while, let our dinner settle, and watch the whales. We can always come back later for dessert."

"You're a smart man, Chief Sexypants."

He rolls his eyes and stands, holding his hand out for mine.

"Are you ever going to stop calling me that?"

"Nope."

# CHAPTER 16

## ~HANNAH~

"I hope I don't step on a jellyfish."

We're on the sand, walking down to the water. I have the binoculars hanging around my neck for whale watching, we stepped out of our shoes at the beach entrance, and we're both in shorts, so there's no need to roll our pants legs.

"I'll keep an eye out for any rogue jellyfish," he says. He's holding my hand, our fingers linked. The sun is just starting to set on the horizon.

"I read somewhere that when they sting you, it hurts really bad and the only way to take the sting away is to pee on it."

"Well, that's a delightful thought," he says. "I'm not really into that sort of thing."

I push his arm, making him splash in the water. "I'm not either, perv."

"I will defend you against all jellyfish and the threat of pee."

"And they say chivalry is dead."

He stops in front of me, his back to me. "Hop on."

"I'm not gonna pass that up." I hop onto his back and he catches me around the knees. I wrap my arms around his shoulders and lean in to kiss his ear. "This is nice."

He doesn't say anything for a while as he carries me down the beach. I'm watching intently for whales and laughing at seagulls who have flown over to see what we're up to, and to see if we have a hand out.

He finally sets me down, and I plant my feet in the sand, ready for the water to wash over them.

"Oh, it's like bath water."

"It's warm in the summer," he agrees and watches me with happy eyes. "You look beautiful like this."

"Like what?"

"Happy. Playful."

I stop and tip my head back, take a deep breath and smile. "I feel happy. And you were right, I've been able to relax, and that's a huge gift."

"And it's only day one," he reminds me.

"That's right." We're walking further down the beach. The sky is a riot of orange, blue, and purple. The sand is getting rockier, so we turn back toward the resort. "We walked further than I thought."

"It's easy to do on the beach."

"Have you been here often?"

"I've actually never visited this resort before, but I love the ocean. When I was a kid, my parents would bring us to the Oregon coast every summer. It's colder up there, but still fun."

"I love it. I didn't know what I was missing." I glance up at the resort, all lit up in the twilight. "It's beautiful."

"And quieter than I expected. I thought it would be flooded with tourists."

"It's mid-week. Maybe that has something to do with it." He nods, and I keep rambling. "You know what else I'm enjoying?"

"What's that?"

"We don't have to share each other. Neither of us is in danger of being called in to work, and we're not putting in odd hours. I get to spend a block of time with you, uninterrupted. That might be the best vacation of all."

"We should do it often. Just schedule it and make it happen."

"I would do that." I actually *love* that idea.

"Or, better yet, you should just move in with me."

I trip on my own feet, surprised at the suggestion, and Brad catches me before I fall on my face.

"Easy. Are you okay?"

"I'm fine."

*Holy shit!* I'm not fine. He just asked me to move in with him as casually as asking me to go to the movies.

We've never said the L word.

I've almost said it once or twice, but that's not the same as saying it. Not even close. How can he ask me to live with him if he doesn't love me?

"What do you think?"

"About what?"

Okay, that was lame. But I don't know what to say.

"Moving in with me." He smiles down at me and tucks a strand of hair behind my ear.

"Well, I guess I'll have to think about it."

"Makes sense," he says with a nod, and then he completely drops the subject. So now I don't know if he regrets mentioning it, or if it's really that casual of a thing for him.

And of course I'm going to spend forever overthinking it. I wish I had my phone on me; I'd text Abby.

I'll text her when we get back. She'll know what to say.

"You're suddenly quiet," he says.

"I think I'm just tired," I lie, feeling guilty about it. I'm all pumped up with adrenaline now. "It's been a long day."

"So should we skip dessert and go up to the condo?"

"I think that's a good idea."

He nods and leads me up to our condo, and once inside, I make a beeline for the bathroom. I lock the door and stand in front of the mirror, staring at myself.

I look not a little scared.

Because I am.

"He just asked you to move in with him and you clammed up," I whisper to myself and shake my head in disgust. What does that mean? That maybe I don't love him? That I should break up with him?

I frown and shake my head, dismissing that idea. There's no need to be rash.

"Hannah?"

"Just a minute."

I take a deep breath, push my fingers through my hair, and glare at my reflection in the mirror.

*Pull it together.*

I open the door to find Brad leaning against the wall, waiting for me.

"There are other bathrooms," I point out and walk into the living room with Brad on my heels.

"What's going on?"

"With whom?"

"With you." He grabs my arm to stop me from pacing. "Talk to me. I can hear the wheels turning in that gorgeous head of yours."

"You threw me," I reply and pull out of his grasp. "How can you just toss those words out so casually, like it's nothing? It's not nothing, Brad. It's not a little thing."

"Moving in with me?"

"Yes." I roll my eyes and pace away from him. "*You should move in with me.* Like you're asking me to hike in the park."

"I may not be good at words, Hannah, but you're right. It's not a little thing. It's the biggest thing in my life." My eyes fly to his bright ones. His jaw is tight, his hands fisted. "I hate that I only get to see you a few times a week because of the responsibility of our jobs. I don't want to see you when we can both squeeze it in."

"So, it would be convenient then."

"Yes. No. Fucking hell." He shoves his hands through his hair and stomps away from me and then back again. "You're infuriating, you know that?"

"Back at you."

"I love you, goddamn it." He grips my shoulders and pulls me closer to him. "I don't want to live without you. I can't focus on anything *but* you, Hannah. When I'm not with you, I'm thinking about you. I want you to move in with me so I can see you more, spend more time with you, sleep next to you every night."

"Brad."

But he doesn't let me finish. He scoops me up and hauls me into the bedroom, lifts my sundress over my head and tosses it carelessly on the floor, then guides me onto the bed. He shimmies out of his clothes and covers me completely.

"You always make me feels so small when I'm under you."

"You are small," he murmurs and kisses my cheek. "But so fucking strong. Brave. Funny." He kisses down my neck to my breast and plucks my nipple in his teeth. "Sweet."

"Oh my."

"Listen to me."

"I'm listening."

I glance down to find him smiling up at me. "I love the hell out of you, sweetheart."

I swallow hard and let my head fall back, staring at the ceiling.

*Don't cry. That would be so damn embarrassing.*

"Look at me."

"You're bossy." But I do as he says. He looks mighty pleased with himself.

"This." His hand covers my core. "You." He kisses my navel and then higher on my breast bone. "Are mine."

I cock a brow and watch as he lays open-mouthed kisses all over my torso, leaving heat and electricity in his wake.

"That's right," he continues, not waiting for me to respond. "Your body and your heart belong to me, Hannah."

"Awfully sure of yourself, Chief Se—"

"Now isn't the time to be funny," he growls and covers me again, his face even with mine. "I'm serious, Hannah. You're mine, goddamn it, and I want you with me."

"If I'm yours, you're mine too. It works both ways."

He frowns as if he's confused. "Of course. Haven't you heard what I'm saying to you?"

"Yes. You're claiming me, and telling me, but you haven't said anything about being mine, and that's the only way this is going to work."

"Baby, of course I'm yours. I told you, I don't see anything *but* you." His fingers gently glide down my cheeks as he sinks inside me, making me gasp in pleasure. "I'm yours completely. *That's* why I want you to move in with me. Everything I am, and all that I have belongs to you."

"I just want you," I whisper and moan when he begins to move in earnest. "Because I love you too. I've wanted to say it for a while, but I thought it might be too soon."

"If it's how you feel, it's not too soon."

I smile and lift up to kiss him. "You're not so bad with words, you know."

He tips his forehead against mine and moves in a steady, even rhythm. He's not fucking me now. He's making love to me more beautifully than ever before.

He's strong and masculine and brave. And with me he's gentle and sweet. I trust him. I enjoy him.

I love him.

"So what do you say? Are you going to move in with me?"

"Of course."

He grins. "You had me worried there for a minute."

I cup his face gently. "I'm yours, remember? No need to worry."

~

"You slept late," I say the next morning as Brad comes stumbling out onto the deck. He's rubbing the sleep from his eyes. "Do you want coffee?"

"Please." He drops onto the couch next to me and curls into me, snuggling closely.

"I can't pour the coffee with you on me."

"Coffee after this."

I smile and run my fingers through his hair the way he likes. We were up most of the night, making plans and just talking. One thing about Brad and me is we never run out of things to talk about.

The sun is up and the world is awake, and I didn't want to miss it.

"How long have you been up?" he asks.

"About an hour. I ordered room service, and I've been out here soaking in the ocean."

"I'm glad you love it here," he says and sits up. I reach over and pour him a cup of coffee, fix it up the way he likes, and pass it to him.

"You're usually the one making me coffee. This is kind of nice."

"I don't remember the last time I slept this late."

"You needed it." I set my iPad aside and take a bite of my bagel with cream cheese. "Do you feel rested?"

"Yeah. And ready to get busy making plans."

"For today?"

"For when we get home and we move you into my place."

I laugh. "We have plenty of time for that. You don't have to spend our vacation worrying about it."

"I want it done ASAP. What are you going to do with your house? I assume you own it?"

"I'll rent it out for a while. It's a great investment, and I don't see a reason to sell it right away."

"Are you keeping it as a way out if things don't work out for us?"

I frown and take another bite of my bagel. "I don't like to think that way, Brad. I don't think that things will go badly. But I'd be a fool if I didn't have a back up plan."

He watches me for a moment, his eyes cool.

"Come on, if it were Jenna, would you suggest she sell her house tomorrow and go live happily ever after with some guy?"

"If that's what she wants." I give him the *whatever* look and he shrugs. "Okay, no. I'd recommend she keep her house and that she be careful. But I would wish her well if the guy was as fantastic as I am."

I laugh and scoot into his lap. "Well, that goes without saying. And I'm not bullshitting about the investment thing. Owning property in our little resort town is lucrative."

"You're right. Rent it out, sell it, hell, do whatever you want with it. It's yours, after all." He pulls his phone out of his shorts pocket and opens the messages. "I'm going to text a few guys I know to get some movers reserved. I figure with your schedule, you'll need help with packing and stuff."

"I hadn't thought of that, but it's a good idea. I'll want to be on hand when they're in my house, though."

"We'll both be there." He's typing out quick messages, and my own phone pings with a text.

*Where the fuck are you?*

"Oops. I forgot to tell Drake that I was leaving town."

I bite my lip and type out a quick response and attach a photo of Brad and me at the pool yesterday.

"Is he angry?"

"Probably worried," I reply. "He'll be shocked when I tell him I'm moving in with you."

"Why?"

"Because I've always said that I probably won't ever do the commitment thing. Who wants to deal with a doctor for a girlfriend?"

"I don't seem to mind it," he replies, his attention still on his phone.

"You know, it's impressive that you're able to text and still hold a conversation with me at the same time."

"I'm a man of many talents."

I grin and there's a response from Drake.

*You scared me. We're supposed to let each other know when we go out of town.*

"See? He's just worried."

*I know. I'm sorry. It happened really fast! It was a surprise from Brad. But all is well and I'll tell you all about it when I get home.*

"I have movers coming next Tuesday."

"That's in four days."

His eyes find mine. "Is that a problem?"

I just laugh and shake my head. "When you decide you want something, you don't waste any time."

"Not when it comes to you, sweetheart. What do you want to do today?"

"I want to walk on the beach again. Or better yet, go for a run on the beach. And then I want to be lazy at the pool for the rest of the day."

"We can do those things." He leans in and kisses me sweetly. "Thank you."

"For what?"

"For all of it."

# CHAPTER 17

## ~HANNAH~

"I've hardly seen you since you got home," Grace says a week later. We're packing up my house, or what's left after all of my important personal things were already taken over to Brad's just a few days ago.

"I know, it's been a whirlwind." I sit back on my heels and push my messy hair out of my face, then decide *fuck it* and tie it up on my head. "I went back to work, and we started moving my stuff all around the same time, so we've been busy *and* exhausted."

"I can't believe you took the plunge," Drake says, who's busy stacking boxes. "You're sure it's what you want?"

"Yes." I stick my tongue out at him. "I'm happy and in love. Just be happy for me."

"I'm happy for you. I just want to make sure you weren't pressured into anything. It feels sudden."

I shake my head and go back to stacking books in boxes. "It's not sudden. We've been dating for a few months, and we know that we love each other, so why not live together? You know how crazy our hours are, and Brad's can be just as hectic. We want to be able to spend as much of our downtime together as possible."

"I think that makes sense," Grace says with a shrug. "Although, I'm not a good judge of that sort of thing because I moved in with Jacob after knowing him for a week."

"*That's* fast," I say and look at Drake as if to say, *see?* "And even though it was fast, it worked out wonderfully for you."

"It did," she says with a happy smile. "And I have no doubt that this is going to work out for you and Brad. I can see the way you smile when he walks into a room. It's adorable."

"Adorable," Drake agrees, propping his hands on his hips.

"Yes, I can see that you're happy for me," I reply.

"I'm cautious," he replies grimly. "Because I love you and I *know* you. I'm protective."

"Like a pesky brother."

"Exactly," he says with a smile. "Someone needs to be. And I do want the best for you. I want you happy and in love and all that happy crap."

"He's so romantic," Grace says.

"And I want you to be smart," he continues without acknowledging Grace. "Because while falling in love is fun, it's also sometimes blinding."

"I'm not blind," I reply, not angry with Drake in the least. "Honestly, I'm not. He's a human being, and he's not perfect. But he's pretty wonderful anyway, and he loves me. I love him, too. That's a good reason to want to live together."

"Okay then," Drake replies with a nod. "You know I support you. Always. But I'm also going to be the pesky brother who watches over you."

"How sweet." I pat his cheek, and then give it a little squeeze, making him cringe. "You're the best brother a girl could have."

He rolls his eyes and gets back to work packing boxes.

"Why do I have so much crap? I've only lived in this house for like four and a half years."

"That's what we do," Grace says. "We gather things. And then they fill up our house and we wonder why we have so much of it."

"I haven't cracked these books open in years."

"And yet," Drake says, "you're piling them in boxes and I'm hauling them around."

"I mean, your muscles are impressive when you lift heavy things," I say helpfully, but he just glowers at me. "Also, you love me."

"That's why," he says, shaking his head.

"So, you and Brad had a romantic time at the beach?" Grace asks with a grin. "Tell us everything."

"It was *so beautiful,* you guys. You both should go sometime. The resort is just stellar, with amazing food and views. I haven't been that relaxed in… hell, I don't remember the last time I was that relaxed."

"That's awesome." Grace smiles as she rubs her little belly. "I told Jacob that I want to go sometime, and he said he'd make it happen. What a great place to spend some of this pregnancy, when I'm big and uncomfortable."

"You should do that," I reply with a nod. "You can lay by the pool with a book and just relax. It would be perfect. But I don't want you to fly after you hit the eight-month mark."

"Yes, Dr. Malone," she says with a smile. "And speaking of me being pregnant, Jacob has also said that he's going to wrap me from head to toe in bubble wrap so I'm sure not to hurt me or the baby."

"You'll be fine," I reply and then cock my head to the side, thinking. "Actually, we should just put you in a bubble all the time."

"Probably," she says. "Drake, this box is full."

"So, I'm basically just the slave around here today," he grumbles.

"You're the brawn of our operation," I agree. "You like feeling needed and you know it."

"Maybe." He tapes Grace's box shut and then carries it to the growing pile against the wall. "So what did you decide to do with all of this?"

"Well, not all of it will fit in Brad's house. So, I took over what's most important to me already. Clothes, toiletries, electronics. You know, all that stuff. Now we're packing up the rest of my personal things to go to storage until I have time to sift through it all and decide what to do."

"What about the furniture? It's practically brand new," Grace says.

"Well, I was talking to Jenna the other day, and she suggested rather than making this place a monthly rental, I make it a vacation rental. I hadn't thought of it before, but I looked at comps in the area for what the income potential could be, and it just made sense. So I'm going to move out the personal stuff and spruce up what's already here and rent it out to tourists."

"Jenna's smart," Grace says. "That's a great idea. And around here the earning potential has to be fantastic."

"Yeah, and the potential for asshole tourists is fantastic too," Drake says, scowling. "They'll wreck the place."

"Not all of them," I say. "What the hell is wrong with you today? You're so moody."

"I'm always moody."

"You're particularly sunshiny today," Grace says, batting her eyelashes innocently.

"There's nothing wrong with me," he says. "But if I'd known I was going to be moving all of these damn boxes, I wouldn't have gone to the gym this morning."

"You don't have to be here," I remind him. "I have a dolly that I can use to move stuff around."

"I don't want either of you moving this stuff," he says and I just cock a brow, watching him.

"You get this way when you haven't gotten laid in a while," I say, tapping my lips with my finger. "Is that it?"

"To be fair, I get testy when I haven't gotten laid in a while," Grace adds, making me smile. I nod in agreement, and Drake rolls his eyes. He's the king of the eye-roll today.

"There's absolutely nothing wrong."

"Bullshit," I reply. "I've known you for a dozen years, and there's something bugging you."

"I lost a patient last night." He leans against the wall and wipes the sweat from his brow. "It was a fluke, and it was during surgery. Routine gall bladder removal. It shouldn't have happened."

"I'm sorry." I stand and walk to him, wrap my arms around his waist and hug him close. This is the hardest part about what we do because eventually we're faced with the reality that we're human, and we can't save everyone. "I'm very sorry."

"I'll be okay," he says and squeezes me tightly. "And I'm sorry I'm an asshole."

"It's okay." I pull back with a smile. "You're only an asshole part of the time."

His lips twitch just as the doorbell rings. I open the door and freeze. There are two Montana Highway Patrol officers standing on my porch.

"Brad." I reach blindly for Drake's hand. If something's happened to Brad, I don't know what I'll do. I can't lose him. I just found him. "Please tell me it's not Brad."

"No, ma'am."

I sigh in relief, adrenaline coursing through my body. "Thank God."

"I'm patrolman Peterson, and this is my partner, patrolman James. Can we please come inside?"

"Sure." I step back and allow them in. "I'm moving, so the place is a mess."

"We won't be long. You'll want to sit down."

My eyes fly to both Grace and Drake, who are both watching the officers with suspicion. Grace has her phone gripped in her hand.

"What's this about?"

Both men, in their forties with grim faces, look at each other. Patrolman Peterson says, "Would you rather we talk in private?"

"No, I'd rather you tell me what's going on."

He nods and takes a deep breath. "I'm sorry to inform you that Randall Malone was killed yesterday morning in a motor vehicle accident just outside of Billings, Montana."

"What?" Suddenly both Drake and Grace are flanking me, each holding one of my hands, and the blood is rushing in my ears. "That can't be possible. He doesn't live in Montana."

"No, ma'am. But he was driving through Montana, for what purpose we can't be sure."

"But I live in Cunningham Falls," I whisper and close my eyes. "That asshole was coming here."

"He was in a multiple vehicle accident yesterday," he repeats, "and he was the only fatality."

"Well, at least there's that." Drake squeezes my hand and I just shake my head. "Thanks for letting me know."

"That's not all," he continues. "It seems you're the only surviving relative of your father's, so we need to know where you want the body to be transported to."

"Excuse me?" I scowl and pull my hands free so I can fist them. "I *don't* want him."

"Well, you can choose to not claim him," the patrolman says. "But in that case—"

"Can she think about it?" Grace asks, interrupting him. "Is there a number she can call you at once she's had the chance to think it all through and take it in. This is a lot of information."

"Of course," he replies and pulls out his business card, passing it to me. "You have a few days to decide what you'd like to do. You just give me a call if you need anything. I'm very sorry for your loss."

With that, they both tip their hats to me and leave, and I just stand here, staring at nothing.

"Did that just happen?"

"I'm afraid so," Drake says from beside me. "I'm sorry, Hannah Banana."

"I'm not sorry." I turn to face him, fierce anger burning through me. "It's just a blessing that he didn't kill anyone else this time. What the fuck was he doing in Montana anyway?"

"I don't know," Drake says. "Hannah—"

"No." I shake my head and stomp away. "I'm so damn pissed. How *dare* he come to my home? *My home.* What did he think he would do when he got here? That we'd have a great reunion, and break out some pictures and reminisce about the good ol' days? Because there weren't any good ol' days, Drake. None. And now they want me to claim his body?"

I laugh and pace around the living room.

"And do what with him? I don't give a rat's ass what happens to that body. And why shouldn't I abandon him?" I continue, seeing red and feeling palpitations begin in my chest. "He abandoned me my *whole life.* And then he killed my mother."

My breathing is harsh, and I can feel tears wetting my cheeks.

"Hannah, you need to sit down," Grace says, but I shake my head. I'm too wound up.

"I don't understand why he couldn't just stay in Kansas, in his pathetic life. I am fine without him. I'm better than fine. I'm fucking fantastic."

I stop to breathe, and realize that I'm having chest pains.

*Fuck.*

"I've worked myself up into a heart attack."

"What?" Grace demands and rushes to my side. "What's happening?"

"Chest pain. Short of breath." I look to Drake, but he's just watching me intently, not saying anything. "You're never this stoic."

"I'm letting you be angry."

"I'm not angry, I'm fucking furious. I don't need this." I let my head fall back. "I can't die. I just found the love of my life. This isn't fair."

"You're not dying," Drake says. "You're having an anxiety attack."

"Fuck that," I retort and glare at him. "I'm having *chest pain and shortness of breath.* You went to med school."

"I did, and I also know those are symptoms of an anxiety attack."

"That's not what this is," I insist and sit on a chair, holding my chest.

"Maybe I should call 911," Grace says, but I immediately shake my head.

"No, if you do that, they'll tell Brad. I don't want him to see me like this."

"Hannah, he's the love of your life as you just put it," Grace says. "If I didn't call Jacob at a time like this, he'd spank my ass red, and not in a fun way."

"Kinky," Drake murmurs, trying to make me laugh, but it's not working. "Hannah, take a deep breath."

"I can't." I push my head between my knees and bury my face in my hands, completely mortified. This is how I'm going out. Of a heart attack in my early thirties because my father decided to kill himself on a highway in Montana.

Someone presses a cold rag to the back of my neck, momentarily making me feel better, but then the pain shoots down my left arm and I'm officially freaked the fuck out.

"I have left arm pain." I stare up at Drake, truly scared now. "Drake, this isn't normal."

He sighs and nods. "Okay. I still don't think it's a heart attack, but we should take you in to be checked out, just to be sure."

I nod and stand, letting the business card I've been clutching in my hand fall to the floor. I don't bother with my handbag or phone, or even my keys as I follow Drake out of my house to his car.

"I'm going to call Brad," Grace says, but I turn on her and point my finger in her face.

"No." I shake my head. "*No*, Grace. Do not do that."

# CHAPTER 18

## ~BRAD~

"Wow, you've done a lot since I was here last." I'm standing with Jenna at the tree house project, our hands on our hips, staring up at the structures that finally look like a tree house. The siding is cedar shingles, and they look like they've been here all along. Like they belong on this mountain.

"It's amazing what you can get done when you fire a deadbeat and have someone on staff who knows what they're doing." She smiles sweetly, and motions for me to follow her into the biggest of the three buildings.

I'm stunned to see kitchen cabinets already installed and workers bustling about, measuring for the countertops that will be delivered in the morning.

"Blue cabinets?"

"I know, aren't they great?" she says with a big smile. "The countertops will be white, and it's really going to pop."

"If you say so."

"I do." She picks up a clipboard and starts reading through her checklist. "So you and Hannah had fun at Max's place?"

"We did. Have you ever been down there?"

"No, I keep meaning to, but something always comes up with one of the rentals." She shrugs. "I'll get there eventually."

"You should hire a management company to help you." This is an argument that's been happening for about two years now, ever since Jenna decided to branch out from the B&B and add other vacation rentals to her list of properties. "How many properties do you have now?"

"Twelve, if you include these," she says. "And yes, it's a full time job, but I love it. I have a manager at the B&B now, so that pretty much runs itself. I trust Maggie completely with it. So, I oversee the building of the homes, the design, and the rentals. I have house-keepers."

"I should hope so," I reply and shake my head at her. "You know, just hiring a management company to oversee the housekeeping and scheduling the rentals would be a huge help."

"I know." She sighs and rubs her forehead. "I know I'm being stubborn. But I *love* this stuff. Real estate is my jam, and greeting guests when they check in is a kick. They're excited to be there. And the personal touches I put on everything is what keeps them all coming back."

"There's no doubt that you're great at your job, Jen. You absolutely are."

"I'm going to see how it goes with these," she says, gesturing to the tree houses. "If they're as high maintenance as I think they will be, I'll have to hire someone to at least oversee the properties in Whisper."

Whisper is a neighboring town, only ten miles away, that is much bigger than Cunningham Falls and houses all of the amenities that our little town just can't, such as chain restaurants and department stores.

"How many are over there?"

"Six," she says. "So, I might need help down there. We'll see. For now, I'm content."

"That's the important thing."

"And now that you've distracted me from talking about your trip, spill it. Don't tell me about the sex."

"There's not much of anything else to tell." I grin when she wrinkles her nose and makes a gagging sound. "I mean, there was a *lot* of sex."

"Ew, really?"

"Well, there was, but there was other stuff too. We walked the beach a few times, watched whales. There's a great pool area, and the restaurants are great. We didn't leave the resort the whole time we were there."

"That sounds like the best vacation."

I nod and raise an eyebrow. "Maybe it's time for you to take a vacation."

"I don't have anyone to take a romantic vacation with," she reminds me.

"It's not like you put yourself out there, Jenna. You work and you go home."

"I'm not discussing my dating life with you."

"Fine." I sigh and then smile when she passes me a paper bag. "What's this?"

"I went to *Little Deli* earlier for sandwiches for the guys, and I got too many. You might as well take them for the guys."

"I'll take them over to Hannah's. She has Grace and Drake there to help her pack up the rest of her things."

"Why?"

"I told you that she moved in with me."

"No." She frowns. "You told me she was *going* to move in with you, and I assumed that meant in the coming months, not ten minutes later."

"Is this a problem?"

She blinks, thinking it over. "No. It's not a problem. You know I love Hannah, and I think she's good for you. I'm just surprised at the speed that you made it happen. You're usually more... laid back."

"I want her with me." I turn to leave. "Thanks for the sandwiches. I'll take them over to her now."

I saw her four hours ago, and I feel like I'm going through withdrawals. My friends would say I'm whipped.

And they wouldn't be wrong.

I enjoy her more than I ever thought I could. Spending time with her is the highlight of my day, and when we're apart, I count down until I get to see her again.

She's the best part of my life, and I'm relieved that she agreed to move in with me. Spending every night with her has been amazing.

She's at her old place today with Grace and Drake, finishing up with some packing and clearing out so we can get it ready for vacation rentals. I park at the curb in front of her house, pleased to see her car in the driveway. I reach for the brown bag full of lunch and climb out of the truck. It's quiet as I approach the house. The front door is open, with just the screen door shut, but maybe they're busy packing and aren't talking.

That would be unusual for Hannah and Grace, but not impossible.

"Hello?" I step inside and frown. Boxes are half packed, packing tape is sitting about, but no one is here. I call out again and walk to the back of the house, through the kitchen to the backyard, but still no one.

"What the hell?"

I dial Hannah's number and feel my heart start to beat faster when I hear it ring in the living room.

She doesn't have her phone. The house is open, her car is in the driveway.

What the fuck is going on?

I stalk into the living room to get her phone. No calls or texts that would give me a clue as to where she is.

I glance down and see a business card on the floor.

"Montana Highway Patrol, Vern Peterson."

For the first time in my life, my palms are starting to sweat as I dial Peterson's number and wait for him to answer.

"This is Brad Hull, the police chief of Cunningham Falls, and I'm looking for Hannah Malone. I found your business card in her home."

"I spoke with her today," he confirms.

"About what?"

"I can't tell you that, but I can tell you that when I saw her an hour ago she was fine."

I scowl. "She was here an hour ago? Do you know where she went?"

"No, Chief. Sorry. She was there when we left."

I thank him and hang up, more frustrated than before. What the hell is happening? And why did the highway patrol need to speak with her?

I try calling Grace's number and curse a blue streak when she doesn't answer.

I don't like not knowing where she is. Not like this. Something is very wrong.

I'm pacing the living room when a number I don't recognize calls my phone.

"Hull."

"This is Drake. I think you should know that I'm with Hannah at the emergency room."

"Is she hurt?"

I'm already running out to my truck and driving toward the hospital, which is thankfully just ten minutes away.

"No," he says. "Let me know when you get here."

He hangs up and I toss my phone on the seat, run my hand over my face, and pray for patience. I run into the emergency room, stopping at the nurse's station.

"Fran, I need to get back to see Hannah."

Fran, a woman I've known most of my life, just frowns. "I'm not at liberty to give you any information on who may or may not be here."

"Don't fuck with me, I know she's here. Drake called me. I need to get back to her."

"I can't do that," she repeats. "It's family only, and you're not her husband."

"Neither is Drake."

"He escorted her here."

"I'm the chief of police."

Fran smiles, but I can see that I'm getting nowhere. "That doesn't matter here. This isn't a police matter, and I'm not letting you back there."

"I'll push my way through."

"I'd love to see you try. I've stopped men far bigger than you, Brad Hull." She props her hands on her hips, her chin the air, standing firm.

"Damn it, Fran."

"Go find a seat, and I'll come find you when and if you can go back."

I turn away just as Drake comes out to the waiting room.

"Thank God," I say when he approaches. "Nurse Ratchet here wouldn't let me back."

"I heard that," Fran says, but I ignore her.

"Hannah is safe and unharmed," Drake begins and pushes his hand through his hair.

"You're not making me feel any better."

"She doesn't know I called you, and frankly, she'll punch me in the balls when she finds out I did."

"Why?"

He shrugs. "I suspect she's embarrassed, but you should be here. The highway patrolmen showed up at the house to inform her that her father died."

"Shit."

"He was in Montana."

My eyes meet Drake's grim ones. "In Montana."

He nods. "I think she should tell you the rest because it's not my story to tell, but she's pretty upset. Not that her dad died, but it triggered some anxiety, and—"

"I get it."

"She doesn't look great, so I want you to prepare yourself for that. I haven't seen her this bad before."

I nod. "Understood. Now take me back there."

Drake leads me through the doors, despite a glaring Fran. I walk into a room to find Grace sitting next to Hannah, who has deep purple circles around her eyes, her red hair a riot around her, and her face blotchy from crying.

"Hey, sweetheart."

Rather than get angry, or order me out, she just breaks down in tears. She covers her face and cries, and I simply sit next to her and pull her into my arms, holding her close.

I should be hurt that she didn't want me here. I should be angry.

But all I feel is love, and relief that she's okay.

"Someone is about to come get her for a chest x-ray," Drake says as Grace stands. "We'll be in the waiting room if you need us."

I nod and hold Hannah against my chest, letting her cry it out.

The door closes, and she says, "I'm dying."

I frown and pull her away from me so I can look into her blue eyes. "Excuse me?"

"Heart attack," she says, and my world falls away.

"You're having a damn heart attack?" I press the call button for the nurse and stare blindly at the monitors. "Drake said you're okay."

A woman bustles into the room. "How can we help?"

"If she's having a heart attack, shouldn't someone be in here?"

"We don't think that's what's happening," she says with a smile. "We have labs drawn, heart monitor going, and she's about to get a chest x-ray. Right now, in fact."

A young man comes in and ushers me off the bed so he can wheel her out to a nearby lab. He doesn't ask her to get up, but instead does all of the work with her lying on the bed. After the x-ray is taken, he asks if we'd like to see the images.

"Yes," Hannah says immediately and stands so she can see his monitor.

"This looks pretty standard, although I'm no radiologist."

"No, look." She points at a spot where her lungs are. "This is a tumor."

"I think those are blood vessels," the tech says. "I've done hundreds of these, and those are blood vessels."

Hannah just shakes her head and gets back on the bed, looking defeated. "Please take me back to my room."

She's wheeled back, and hooked back up to her monitors. After a few moments, the doctor comes in and sits at Hannah's bedside.

"I have good news, Dr. Malone. Your labs have all come back normal so far. I'm waiting on one more enzyme lab, but I expect that to be normal as well. Your EKG and chest x-ray are both in normal limits."

"I don't know how that can be," Hannah says with true confusion on her face. "I saw the tumor on the x-ray. Didn't you see it?"

The doctor frowns and opens her laptop, bringing up the x-ray in question and turns the computer so Hannah can see it. "Where?"

"Here." She points to the cluster in the center of her lung.

"Those are blood vessels."

"Bullshit," Hannah mutters and shakes her head. "It's cancer. I'm having a goddamn heart attack and I have cancer and you're doing *nothing*. I want a second opinion."

"Hannah, I promise you, you're not dying."

Tears are streaming down her sweet face, and it makes me ache. She's devastated. She's convinced.

And it doesn't matter that she's a doctor. All of her training and common sense are gone, replaced by the reactions of a scared woman.

I don't know what to do for her, but I know I'm not going anywhere.

Not now, not ever.

She looks up at me with tears rolling out of her blue eyes and says, "I don't know what to do. What do I do?"

# CHAPTER 19

## ~HANNAH~

"*H*annah, listen to me," Dr. Linderman says, catching my attention. "This is *not* a tumor. And I'm watching the monitor right now. Your heart is steady and just fine. I'm not lying to you."

"It's fluttering right now," I reply, so fucking frustrated that no one believes me. And even more frustrated that I can't stop the nonsense running through my head.

I can't remember any of my medical training. None of it.

"Flutters happen with anxiety," she replies, and I just stare at her in horror. I've spent the past two hours here for *nothing*. All because of this stupid anxiety.

"I'm so sorry," I whisper. She pats my hand and smiles kindly.

"You don't have anything to be sorry for."

"My left hand feels weird."

"You're tense. I'm quite sure the nerves to your arm are being pinched, and that's causing the discomfort."

"So, I'm *not* having a heart attack."

"No. You're not. I'm going to wait for that last lab, and then you're free to go."

She smiles and leaves the room, and I can't look Brad in the face.

I'm humiliated.

"Baby," he says. "Look at me."

"I'm so embarrassed."

"You don't need to be." He sits on the bed with me again and pulls me into his arms, which makes me feel better. "It sounds like all of the symptoms felt like a heart attack. I would have been scared myself."

I nod, but then take a deep breath and swallow hard.

"Here's the thing, Brad. I can't turn this off. I can't make it stop. I'm a trained professional, but when this starts, all of my training goes out the window and rational thought goes with it. I'm *sure* that something is wrong. Everyone thinks it's funny. Or cute."

I wipe a tear off my cheek.

"Drake will make a joke, or brush it off, and I'll play along. But it's not funny." I lift my eyes to his now and have to bite my lip so I can pull myself together, even a little bit. "It's not funny. It's scary. I will go a long time without anything like this happening, but it's always, *always* in the back of my mind that something is wrong. Headache? I must have a brain tumor. Lower abdominal pain? Ovarian cancer. I'm a hot mess, Brad, and I wouldn't blame you in the least if you bailed now. I would."

"No, you wouldn't," he says quietly.

*Okay, I wouldn't.* But I wouldn't blame him if he did.

He kisses my temple and then reaches to grab a stethoscope off the countertop.

"Here, put these in your ears."

I do as I'm told and wipe my nose on a tissue. Brad holds the other end over his own chest and I immediately hear his heart, strong and sure in my ears.

"Do you hear that?"

"Of course."

"Close your eyes." I do as I'm told, and he begins to talk. I'm swept up in the sound of his deep voice, his strong arms wrapped around me and his heart beating in my ears. "This is the heart of a man who loves you more than he ever thought he could. I didn't know what I was missing until you came into my life, Hannah. This heart believes in you, admires you, and takes so much joy in you."

Tears continue to fall down my face, but I don't care. I press my cheek to Brad's shoulder and keep listening.

"When I thought my heart would break earlier this summer, when I had to tell a friend that his child was gone, you were there to help me recover from that. You held me, and you soothed the pain, Han. This is a grateful heart."

He pauses and kisses my temple.

"This heart is strong. Listen to how steady it beats, how sure it is. It's brave and true, and it always does the right thing, even when it's hard. It's healthy, Hannah. So healthy. It's going to beat for many more years to come."

I open my eyes and am surprised to discover that at some point he moved the stethoscope to my own chest. The strong, healthy heart I've been listening to is my own.

"You always manage to make me feel better. You bring so much to my life, Brad."

"Do you still want me to bail?"

"No. I might trip you if you try to leave."

He kisses me again and sets the stethoscope aside. "You are not broken, sweetheart. You're not a hot mess. You're a human being, and sometimes life is just hard."

"Yeah. I feel bad for Drake and Grace. They were there when the patrolmen came."

"I'm glad they were," he admits. "I'd hate to think what would have happened if you'd been alone."

"My dad died."

He nods, and I assume that Drake told him.

"He's been dead to me for a long time. I'm not terribly sad that he's gone. Does that make me a bad person?"

His lips twitch into a smile. "No. You're not a bad person."

"They said that I'm the only surviving relative, so I'm responsible for his body." I swallow hard. "I don't want to deal with that."

"You don't have to. There are options." He cups my face in his hand gently. "Is it that he was in Montana that triggered all of this?"

"Probably," I admit, feeling angry about that again, but not willing to throw myself into another episode. "He was coming here to try to get something from me. It wasn't any other reason. He was probably broke. But I would have told him no and sent him packing.

"I hate that he was so close to my home. I made a place for myself here, far away from him and all of the chaos he caused. I made a way for myself in this world without him. He wasn't welcome to invade the safety of the life I've built."

"That makes sense," Brad says. "We'll deal with it, together. Just like we dealt with this together."

"I didn't want you here," I admit, and he cocks a brow. "Grace said if she pulled something like that, Jacob would spank her ass red."

"I'm considering it," he replies, and my eyes whip up to his. "You scared me. And when I arrived, they wouldn't let me back to see you because I'm not family."

"I didn't think of that. Grace wanted to call you, but I wouldn't let her. It goes back to what I said earlier, I didn't want you to have to see me like this. It's embarrassing."

"If I were in an accident, and cut my leg open, would it make sense to you that I wouldn't want you in the emergency room with me because I was embarrassed about the way it happened?"

"How did it happen?" I ask, playing devil's advocate.

"You're missing the point."

"No," I confess. "It wouldn't make sense and I'd be tearing the place apart to get to you."

"I was about to try that, but Fran says she can take me and I'm inclined to believe her."

I laugh at the thought of the little nurse going up against Brad.

"I'm glad you came."

~

"Sadie hasn't left my side since we got home."

It's several hours later, and I'm curled up on the couch with Sadie's head in my lap. She's snoozing and I just can't stop crying. She wakes up now and again to check on me, whimpers a bit, and then falls back to sleep.

"She loves you," Brad says just as the doorbell rings.

"That hasn't been good luck today." I lay my head back on the couch, fighting off the crying-induced headache.

"It's pizza," Brad says as he comes in the room. "From Drake. There's a note on the box that says he hopes you're feeling better."

"That was sweet." My stomach growls, and I realize I'm hungry. "I guess it's good timing."

"Do you enjoy pineapple on your pizza?" Brad asks after opening the box.

"Oh yeah."

"Maybe we have to rethink this whole living together situation."

"You mean, you *don't* love pineapple on pizza?"

"It's too sweet," he says, but then smiles. "But it's just on half. Drake's not stupid."

I grin and watch him walk into the open kitchen to get us plates, and wouldn't you know it, the tears start again.

I can't fucking turn them off.

My eyes are ridiculous. They're puffy and purple, and I look like I went a round with a heavyweight champ. I keep rubbing them because I can't turn the tears off.

It's a vicious circle.

"I don't even know what I'm crying about anymore."

"It's your body cleansing itself," Brad assures me and passes me a plate. The aroma wakes Sadie out of a dead sleep, and she's immediately ordered onto the floor.

"Are you the doctor now?" I ask.

"No, just guessing." He takes a bite and watches me. "I don't like seeing you like this."

"I know, it's pretty bad."

"No, I just don't like to see you cry."

We're about halfway into our pizza when the doorbell rings again.

"This time it's flowers," Brad says, carrying them into the living room and setting them on the table next to me. I pull the card out and open it.

*"Hannah,*

*By the time you read this, we hope you're feeling much better!*

*Love,*

*Grace and Jacob"*

"That was nice." I wipe the tear from under my eye, and then the doorbell rings *again.* "I can't take much more of this."

He laughs and goes to answer it. He's gone longer this time, but then returns with a bag from my favorite ice cream shop and a card.

"Huckleberry?" I ask.

"Of course."

I read this card.

*Hannah,*

*Just a reminder that I love you!*

*Jenna*

"Is everyone trying to make me cry today?"

"I don't think that's hard to do, sweetheart." He sets the ice cream in the freezer and returns to his pizza. "I think your friends are just worried about you."

"It's amazing. I've always known that I belong here. I don't know how to describe it, other than I knew I was home when I got here. But over the past few months, I've finally begun to feel like I'm a part of the community. I have an amazing network of friends, and your family makes me feel welcome."

"They all care about you."

I nod and take another bite of pizza, then set it aside and crawl into his lap. "I think that at first they cared about me because they love *you.* But now they love me too, and it's a really good feeling."

His arms tighten around me. The fear and anger from earlier are gone now, and I'm left with so much gratitude.

Love.

I straddle him and settle against him, feeling him harden.

"I love you," I whisper.

"I love you back," he whispers in return, making me grin. I wiggle out of my sweatpants, unfasten his jeans and set him free, then lower myself onto him, making us both sigh in pure delight.

"You make me feel things, Brad. Big things."

"It is impressive, isn't it?"

I blink at him, then let out a big laugh. I wrap my arms around his neck and ride him, enjoying him. Soaking him in.

"Yes, perv, it's impressive."

# CHAPTER 20

## ~HANNAH~

*Two Months Later*

"How was your day, dear?" Brad asks as I walk in the house from work. He beat me home today, and if my nose isn't deceiving me, he's made spaghetti for dinner.

*Good God, I love this man.*

"It was pretty good. I had two hysterectomies today, and I thought I was going to have to stay a bit late for a delivery, but it came about an hour ago."

"That baby knew that you had a sexy guy to go home to."

"Yes. That must be it. And then I saw my therapist for an hour, and I'm glad I'm going. He's helping a lot." I giggle and turn my face up for a kiss. He takes it from an innocent peck to a hot, searing make out sesh in about one-point-six seconds. "Mm, I missed you, too."

He winks at me and returns to his work station, chopping up vegetables for a salad.

"I grabbed the mail on my way in," I announce and sort through it, setting his mail to the side. There's an envelope from the school of medicine that I graduated from, and I immediately open it. "Wow."

"What is it?"

"A thank you letter," I reply and read it out loud.

*Dr. Malone,*

*It is with great respect and appreciation that I write this letter to thank you for your donation to the Yale School of Medicine. For generations, taking anatomy classes has been a rite of passage for medical students, and this integral part of becoming a physician would be lost without the opportunity that donors such as yourself have given us.*

*We take great pride in knowing that you believe that we can make great changes in the future of medicine. The donation of your family member is something we hold near and dear to our hearts and use the greatest care as we use them to teach future generations of physicians.*

*On a personal note, you were one of my students in your second year here at Yale, and I wanted to offer my sincerest condolences and personal gratitude.*

*Sincerely,*

*Matthew T. Murdoch, M.D., Ph.D.*

I FOLD the letter and return it to its envelope as Brad walks around the island to wrap an arm around my back.

"Are you okay with this?"

"Yes. Absolutely." I nod and smile up at him. "I know that I did the right thing in not abandoning him and instead donating his remains to science. I finally have a reason to be proud of my dad, and he's *finally* a productive member of society."

Brad smiles and returns to his vegetables.

"I think your dad would be happy with that."

"I don't know if he would, but my mom would be, and that's something too. Now, I'm starving, and that smells fantastic."

"It's a family recipe."

"Spaghetti?"

"That's right."

I glance at the empty jar of store bought spaghetti sauce and snort. "Are you a descendent of Ragu?"

"No, smart ass. You use that as the base, and then add other things to make it more delicious."

"If you say so. Gimme."

"You're very demanding." But he smiles and dishes up a helping of the steaming sauce and pasta. It does smell fantastic. "Here you go."

I take a bite and chew slowly as he watches, knowing that he wants me to offer him a reaction.

I swallow and shrug a shoulder. "It's pretty good."

"Just pretty good?"

"Okay," I say with a smile. "It's *really* good. I hope there will be enough for leftovers."

"I made a ton," he says and dishes up his own plate.

"I have a favor to ask."

"Anything."

"After dinner, do you mind taking me down to the lake? It's a nice day and it's not anywhere near dark yet."

"Of course." He takes a bite of his own dinner. "We can go anywhere you like."

"Just the lake."

We're both hungry, so dinner disappears quickly. We stack our dirty dishes in the sink for later and head out in his truck for the public access beach.

"It's so nice since most of the tourists have gone home," I remark, enjoying the way the sunlight bounces off the water.

"Even OPTS is over."

"OPTS?"

"Old people tourist season. Haven't you noticed that about the time that school starts and the families go home, that's when the old people come in for the last half of September?"

"No," I reply with a giggle. "Is this really a thing?"

"Hell yes, it's a thing. I can't even begin to tell you how many elderly people we pull over in the early fall. It's ridiculous."

"I've never heard of such a thing," I reply as he pulls to a stop by the boat launch dock at Whitetail Lake. "Let's go sit on the dock."

He gives me a weird look, then says, "Okay."

He follows me down the long dock over the water to the very end. I sit down, careful to not put my feet near the water, and he joins me.

"It's a beautiful evening," I say again, grappling for conversation.

"Yes. Did you bring me here to break up with me?"

My gaze whips up to his, but he's smiling down at me.

"No. Not even close."

"Good. What's up, Hannah?"

I swallow hard and look down at the water. "I think I need to put my feet in this water."

He's quiet beside me for a moment, and then he reaches over and takes my hand in his, linking our fingers.

"Why?" he asks softly.

"Because I'm afraid of it, and I don't need to be." I lift my chin and look at him. "Because you've helped me conquer so many fears this year, and this is one that I need to be gone so I can enjoy our lake again. I want to be able to kayak and boat and swim in it next year with our friends without being afraid.

"I'm so fucking tired of being afraid."

"Okay." He nods and looks down at the water, then back at me. "How do you want to do this?"

"I don't have any idea." I blow out a breath with a humorless laugh. "When I'm hiking in the woods, afraid that I'll get attacked by a grizzly bear, I just march fast ahead, intent on getting through it alive."

"Well, you could just take the plunge, literally, and put your feet in there."

"I don't think it's that simple." I chew my bottom lip for a moment, thinking it over. "Tell me again about how they decided that it's safe."

"Well, first they turned off all of the power that runs under the lake, and then they used a grid to methodically comb the lake, diving down to see where the power lines were exposed."

"Why are there lines that run under the lake?"

"Because there are homes all around the lake, but not necessarily roads that access it all. The city is currently working on approving a road that would completely circle the lake, but we don't have that at this time. So, to make it more cost effective to feed power to all of the houses, they ran the lines through the lake, under the bottom of it where it's the most shallow, at the most narrow points."

"I see." I nod, looking out at the lake before us. The sun is just beginning to set, casting the mountains in pink. It's breathtaking. "And you believe that it's totally fixed, without any chance of it happening again?"

"I do believe that," he says, squeezing my hand. "Not only did they fix the problem, they spent weeks surveying every foot of the lines, making sure they're secure and safe. Hannah, I wouldn't let my townspeople near anything that could harm or kill them."

"I know that," I reply. "Remember, this isn't rational."

"It's okay." Most of the beach is deserted, except for a family walking their dog about two hundred yards away. The little girl has taken her shoes off and dips her feet in the water, giggling at how cold it is.

"A toddler can do it," I murmur and then look back out at the water again. "Will you put your feet in with me?"

"So if we die, at least we die together?"

"Not funny." But then I laugh, unable to help myself. "Okay, it's funny. Yes. If one of us dies, we both die."

"I can do that." I slip out of my flip flops and he takes his shoes and socks off and looks at me. "Are you ready?"

"Hell no."

"We don't have to do this."

"Yes, we do." I purse my lips and dip my big toe in, then pull back fast. "Not even a zap."

"All right, the whole foot now. Let's do this."

I nod, and we both sink one foot into the water. It's cold and feels good on my skin, between my toes.

And I didn't die.

I sigh, feeling like a huge weight has been lifted off of my shoulders. I sink the other foot in with it and let them dangle, swishing around.

"I'm still here."

"Thank goodness," he says, still holding my hand. I don't feel foolish, I feel powerful. "I'm *so* proud of you."

I look up to find his green eyes happy, full of pride, and sexy as hell, just as they always are.

"You know what? Me too. Let's go home."


I HOPE you enjoyed Charming Hannah! If you'd like more information about the Big Sky series, you can click here:


HTTPS://WWW.KRISTENPROBYAUTHOR.COM/UNDER-THE-BIG-SKY

# SHADOWS

A BAYOU MAGIC NOVEL

# KRISTEN

*New York Times* and *USA Today* Bestselling Author

# PROBY

**Shadows**
**A Bayou Magic Novel**
**By**
**Kristen Proby**

# A NOTE FROM THE AUTHOR

Dear Reader,

If you've read me for any length of time, you know that I love a love story. Telling love stories is what I'm most passionate about. Over the past couple of years, I've wanted to dabble in a little suspense, a little paranormal romance. I love to read this genre, and I thought it would be fun to write it. I touched on it with Mallory's story in Easy Magic, and I think you'll be pleased to see a glimpse of Mallory in this story as well.

Shadows is two years in the making. It seemed I always had other deadlines, other stories that came first. So when it was time to plot Shadows, and I sat down to write it, I was ecstatic.

And let me just tell you, it didn't disappoint.

I would like to point out that this story is darker than what I'm known for. The love story is there, of course, but there is also a quest involved that had me on the edge of my seat. Some of what's here may disturb you, as it should. We're talking about a serial killer, after all.

I hope you enjoy these sisters, their gifts, and the men who love them. This is the first of three books.

So sit back, make sure the lights are on, and let me tell you a story...

Kristen

# PROLOGUE

## BRIELLE

"*D*on't touch that!"

Daphne, my youngest sister, recoils from the rocking chair in the corner. It's dark under the stairs, but I know it's there.

I can see the shadow sitting in it.

The shadows are everywhere.

"Come on," I continue, gesturing for my sisters to huddle under our blanket fort with me. Shut out the shadows. The noises.

The house.

"I don't like it under here," Millie, the middle daughter says. She points her flashlight away from her face, illuminating our little haven, reflecting the quilt above us and casting everything in a red glow. We managed to sneak lots of pillows and old, ratty blankets under here. There's a storm raging tonight, and that's when it seems to be the worst.

For all of us.

We're what they call *sensitive*.

I've read books that I keep at school so our daddy doesn't see. It makes him the maddest of all.

And when Daddy's mad, we get punished.

I'm the oldest. At thirteen, I'm the one who protects my sisters from the house. From all of the bad things around us. It's always been this way. Our parents don't know. And even if they did, I'm not sure they'd care. Not really.

Because they don't believe me when I tell them about the shadows in the house.

And they don't believe Daphne when she says she sees things when she touches the old furniture.

A clap of thunder rocks the house, and Daphne lays her head in my lap, whimpering.

"I hope we don't get caught," Millie whispers. "Last time—"

"We won't," I assure. "Dad's not here, and Mama's passed out."

But, suddenly, there's a loud banging on the back door, and we all stare at each other in horror.

That entrance is only a few feet from where we're huddled under the stairs.

"She won't wake up," I whisper and pull Millie into my arms. "Please don't let her wake up."

But she does.

A few seconds later, we hear loud footsteps stomping through the house.

"I'm comin' already!" Mama yells to whoever's pounding on the door.

Soundlessly, we turn off our flashlights. Being in the dark is its own horrible torture.

But getting caught?

I don't want to even think it.

"What are you doin' here?" Mama demands after yanking open the front entry. I can feel the whoosh of air slide under the thin door of our hiding spot.

"Checkin' on you," a man says. "Storm's a doozy."

"We're fine," Mama replies. "You woke me out of a dead sleep."

"Where is he?" the man asks. I'm pretty sure it's Horace. He lives nearby and helps Mama and Daddy with things around the house.

"Gone," Mama says. "And he ain't comin' back."

I feel Daphne stiffen.

*He's not coming back?*

"That means you and me can—"

"It don't mean nothin'," Mama interrupts him. "Now, git. Git outta here, 'fore'n I sic the cops on you."

There are no more voices. Just a slamming door, and then Mama's feet stomping back down the hall and up the stairs to her bedroom. I hear the floorboards creak as she gets back into bed.

"Can we turn the light back on?" Millie whispers.

"Not yet," I mutter back to her. I need to make sure Mama's asleep before we turn on the lights or make any noise.

We're not supposed to be under here.

But it's the safest place in the house.

We're quiet for a long time. I run my fingers through Daphne's hair as she lays on my lap. Millie rests her head on my shoulder.

Our arms are looped around each other as the storm rages, and the house settles— more alive than ever.

"Do you hear it?" Millie asks.

The chair is rocking in the corner now, squeaking with every back and forth motion.

Footsteps upstairs. And they aren't Mama's.

"Can you tell if she's asleep?" I ask Millie.

"I don't want to reach out," she admits. Millie's psychic abilities are off the charts, even for a ten-year-old.

"Just real fast, then shut it down."

She sighs next to me and then is quiet while her mind searches the house.

"She's asleep," she whispers. "And he's here."

"Who?"

She whimpers. Daphne stirs and sits up.

"I saw him," Daphne says. "In my dream."

"Who?" I ask again and flip on my flashlight.

I don't have to ask a third time.

A new shadow is suddenly sitting with us.
"Daddy."

# CHAPTER 1

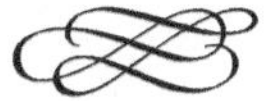

## BRIELLE

"*H*ello, everyone, and welcome to my tour. I'm Brielle Landry, and I'll be your guide today. Now, I know there are roughly eleven thousand ghost tours in the French Quarter, so I thank you kindly for choosing mine."

I smile at the crowd that's gathered on the sidewalk before me. We have a group of all ages this evening, from young teenagers to middle-aged folks. There are those who want to be in the front, listening raptly. And then, of course, there are the drunk ones, who will likely be the hecklers.

"I have just a couple rules for y'all. No walking in the street. If you've been here for twenty minutes, you've already learned that drivers don't slow down, and I won't lose anyone to vehicular homicide on my tour."

The group laughs, and I continue, my eyes roaming the crowd and taking stock.

"We won't be going inside any of the beautiful buildings we'll be talking about tonight, but halfway through, we will stop at a bar to soak in some A/C and have a refreshment or two."

"Or five," Heckler Number One says, elbowing his friend.

"I'm always happy to answer questions, so don't be shy, y'hear? Now, let's get started."

I point to the big, gray building behind me. Most tours save this one for last, but not me. It's the most haunted of the group, and I want to get it over with.

Not that the rest of the tour *isn't* haunted. Ghosts are literally everywhere.

But this one? It's sinister.

I hate it.

Tour groups love it.

"This building behind me is the LaLaurie mansion," I begin. "Well, a rebuilt version of the original house, anyway. Like most buildings in the Quarter, it suffered a nasty fire. Delphine LaLaurie lived here with her third husband, Louis. She had two daughters from previous marriages. Both of her earlier husbands died early deaths."

I swallow hard as I look over at the façade. More shadows than I can count stare back at me.

"Delphine and Louis had a love for torture." The drama is thick in my New Orleans accent as I relay stories of torment, and the horrific atrocities done to the hundreds of slaves that once lived in the building behind me. "And these stories I just shared are the less horrible ones."

Several pairs of eyes whip to mine in surprise.

Including a pair of green orbs the same color as the malachite pendant I wear around my neck for protection.

I instinctively reach up and fiddle with the stone as I continue.

"Who haunts it?" someone calls out.

*Who doesn't?*

"One day, Delphine chased a twelve-year-old slave girl up to the roof of the building with a bullwhip. The young girl had been brushing Delphine's hair and hit a snag. She ran from the whip, and it's said she jumped to her death out of fear.

"Leah, the slave girl, is buried on the grounds of the mansion, along with countless others. When renovations were done years after Delphine and Louis fled to Paris, skeletons were found in the walls. So much death has happened here, that it wouldn't surprise me if dozens of spirits haunt the house.

"It was once owned by Nicolas Cage, but it has a different owner now. They don't offer tours."

I gesture for the group to follow me, and we continue down Royal Street.

My route through the Quarter is deliberate. I take the same path every day. There are no surprises that way.

Surprises for me are never fun.

Yes, I see shadows, but they're the same ones every time. I know where they lurk.

My hecklers turn out to be fun rather than ruining the tour for everyone else, and before long, we've stopped for our refreshments. I grab myself two bottles of water, one to drink now, and one to stow away in my bag for later.

"How do you know all this stuff?"

I turn and see those green eyes from before smiling down at me.

"I studied," I say with a grin of my own. The man is handsome as all get out, with a dimple in a cheek covered by dark stubble. But it's those eyes that draw me in. "I was a history major in college, and since I'm from this area, I've always been fascinated by local history."

"You tell a hell of a story."

"Thank you." I take a sip of my water, watching him. "Where are you from?"

"Savannah, originally."

"Another haunted city."

"They claim to be the most haunted in America."

I feel my smile turn colder. "While I've never been there, I'm sure Savannah is beautiful. But we have more dead in New Orleans than we have living. And while it's not a competition, I'd bet this city would stand up to yours any day of the week. At least, for hauntings."

"Maybe you need to visit."

*Not a chance in hell.*

"Maybe one day."

"I'm Cash." He holds out his hand to shake mine. His palm is warm, his grip strong.

"Brielle. But you knew that."

"You're a beautiful woman, Brielle."

"A complicated one." I wink at him, pull my hand away, and round up the troops. "Let's go, everyone. It's time for more ghost walking."

Once we're back on the sidewalk, I point to the building behind me. "This was once a boys' school. The original building burned down in the seventeen hundreds, and the boys perished in the building. It's said they still live here."

I glance back and see several small shadows looking out the windows.

"It's a hotel now, and guests have reported hearing laughter and children playing. Do you remember back in the day when we had regular film cameras?"

The older members of my group smile and nod.

"Well, back then, people would take their vacation photos. When they got home, they'd take the film in to be developed. Several vacationers reported that as they were sifting through their memories, they saw photos of them. Asleep. From above."

I glance over to see Cash raise one dark eyebrow. His dimple winks at me as he crosses his arms over his impressive chest and listens intently.

He would be less distracting if he were in the back of the group.

"So, while harmless, the boys *are* mischievous. They like to turn the channels on the TV."

"We're staying there." A woman looks up at her husband. "I'll never sleep tonight."

I laugh and, just as I turn to lead the group to the next point of interest, I falter and stop in my tracks.

A new shadow.

A new *shadow.*

About my height, standing on the sidewalk. I can never make out faces, but I can tell this one is turned toward me. It's a feminine spirit.

I blink quickly and try to recover so I don't alert my group to anything amiss.

*A new shadow.*

It's rare, even in the Quarter.

But I clear my throat and walk past the shadow to our next stop.

"THAT WAS *AMAZING*." A college-age girl smiles broadly and bounces on the balls of her feet. The tour ended fifteen minutes ago, but I always stay after to answer questions. "I'm Tammy. I just *loved* all of the stories. It's so interesting."

"I'm glad you enjoyed it."

"I was wondering about that Laurie house?"

"The LaLaurie?"

"Yeah. That one. Where can I learn more about her? I mean, I know it sounds sick, but I'm fascinated by that stuff."

"Torture?"

She blushes. "History stuff. I guess it does sound awful, doesn't it?"

"There are lots of articles about Delphine online. Just Google the name, and you'll have more information than you can read. But I'll warn you, it's graphic."

"Thanks." She smiles at me, then hurries to catch up with her friend.

"People are morbidly curious," Cash says, joining me. He hung back, waiting for everyone else to ask their questions. Now, it's just the two of us.

"Always." I shudder. I know exactly what was done to those slaves.

Sometimes, the shadows talk.

"Did you have more questions, Cash?"

"One." I start to walk down the sidewalk, and he joins me. I expect him to ask about places that I didn't cover in my tour. Or maybe about the cemeteries.

Everyone always wants to know about those.

But I can't do tours there. It's too much.

Although I do have companies I can refer him to.

"What did you see?"

I stop and frown up at him. Cash is tall. Way taller than my five-foot-six height.

"Excuse me?"

"After you told the story about the kids dying in the fire, which is creepy as hell by the way, you turned, and then you stopped and went white as a sheet. You looked like you saw a ghost."

*Well, I did see a ghost, Cash.*

But I can't say that.

"It was great having you on the tour this evening." I smile at him and pat him on the arm. "Have a fantastic vacation. Be careful."

And with that, I hurry away, headed to the one place in the city that I'm absolutely safe.

"HELP ME PUT these chairs up, will you?"

Millie flutters around her little café, stacking chairs on tables so her night crew can come in and mop the floors.

Witches Brew will be three years old this spring, and so far, it's been a success for my younger sister. And it should be. This café is perfect for the French Quarter, from its fun name to the quirky décor and delicious menu.

Coffee served in a cauldron? Sure thing.

Want a love potion? You can order one up.

She'll also read your tarot cards if you ask nicely.

I know that tourists come in here and think it's just a fun, silly café.

But it's as real as it gets.

Millie is a gifted witch. A crazy, amazing psychic. And those love potions? Well, they're real.

She's a hedgewitch.

Or, in layman's terms, a kitchen witch.

And she's as scatterbrained and fun as she is a little scary.

I couldn't love her more.

"Whatcha doin'?" she asks as we place the chairs on the little, round tables.

"Just finished a tour. Figured I'd come in and see how business was today."

"Off the hook," she says and wipes the sweat off her brow with a towel. "And we're not even in the full swing of tourist season yet."

"Same." I smile at her. We're as different as can be. I'm dark-haired with blue eyes, and Millie is blond, tall, and has chocolate-brown eyes.

She's stunning.

"How many men did you have to chase out of here today?"

"Only one," she says, grinning. "If they'd stop ordering the love potion, I wouldn't have to chase them out at all."

"You know, you don't have to actually *give* them the potion every time. They'd never know the difference."

"I charge an extra three dollars for that brew," she says, raising her chin in the air. "And *I* would know the difference. I just need to remember to tell them not to drink it until they're outside."

I laugh and walk behind the counter that's lined with stools to help her fill the napkin dispensers.

"Aren't you exhausted?" Millie asks. "Why aren't you headed home?"

*Because I saw a new shadow, and it freaked me out.*

"Because I wanted to see my little sister."

"Uh-huh." She watches me closely. "I'm psychic, you know."

"You can't read me."

It's true. She can't. I have my shields up, and I'm shut down so tightly, there's no way she can read my mind. If I don't guard myself, I get inundated with spirits. Once upon a time, I thought I could escape it by moving somewhere else.

Two months in Colorado Springs proved that isn't true.

So, I came home and learned to build my walls and protect myself. Millie gave me the malachite.

So far, it's all working.

But I still see them.

"I met a guy tonight," I say casually.

"Spill it."

"His name is Cash." I wrinkle my nose. "I mean, who names their kid *Cash?*"

"Is he hot?"

"Yeah. Tall, dark, and handsome, with green eyes."

"Nice. Did he ask for your number?"

"No."

She sticks out her bottom lip in disappointment.

"He might have, but I blew him off before he could."

"Wait." She holds up a hand, her bracelets jangling. "Why would you do that?"

I take a deep breath and round the counter so I can sit on a stool. "Because he noticed something."

She raises a brow.

"I was finishing up at the Andrew Jackson Hotel."

She nods.

"As I was about to walk down the street, I turned, and there was a shadow on the sidewalk. Just standing there. I've never seen her before."

"*Her?*"

"Yeah, she was about my height. Very feminine."

"Did she say anything?"

"Not that I heard. It just threw me because you know how careful I am about my route. I don't like surprises, especially not like this. It's creepy as hell. And, yes, I know I should be used to it by now, but—"

"It's creepy, like you said." She leans on the counter and bites her lip, thinking. "It probably means that someone recently died there."

"I know that."

"And now it's a new spirit on your tour. Too bad she didn't say anything. If she did, you could add it to your show. Could be fun. *'Lucy was killed in this building three days ago, and her spirit now wanders the sidewalk in front of her former home.'*"

"Talk about creepy."

I sigh and run my fingers through my hair. "Did you sweep this area recently?"

"Is the floor dirty?"

I look at her as if she's being obtuse on purpose. "You know what I mean."

"It's been about a week."

"You need to do it again."

Millie frowns, looking around the space. Her shields are as strong as mine, maybe stronger because she doesn't just see the dead, she *feels* them, and that's much more dangerous.

She fiddles with the amethyst around her neck.

"What do you see?"

I narrow my eyes. "I shouldn't tell you."

"I don't want to look, Bri. I dropped my guard for just a second earlier and was slammed with the pervy thoughts of a nineteen-year-old college kid who couldn't take his eyes off my ass. So, just tell me. Is it the little girl again?"

"Yeah. And she brought a friend." I reach over to take my sister's hand. "Don't drop your shields anymore, Mill. Not for a minute. *Ever.* I know we live and work here in the Quarter because it's where we make our living, but it could really hurt us."

"I know."

"I couldn't bear it if I lost you, too."

She shakes her head. "You didn't lose Daphne."

"She's not speaking to me."

"Because you're both stubborn as hell, and you need to get over it."

"You always were the peacekeeper."

"That's what being the middle child does for you, it literally puts you in the middle. I love you both. Now, snap out of it and just call her."

"I will."

"Liar."

I laugh and then frown when a third shadow appears. It looks just like the one from the sidewalk.

"What is it?"

"You need to cleanse this place. I think all of the different auras coming in and out of here all day is leaving some residual energy behind."

"I'll do it tonight before I leave. I'm also going to make you something special, so don't move that butt from that seat."

"You're bossy."

"And sassy." She winks as she fills a stainless-steel shaker with all kinds of things that I don't recognize.

This is not my area of expertise.

I can talk about the history of New Orleans all day.

My sister, however, mixes potions and casts spells.

She's gifted. She learned with some of the most powerful witches in the world, right here in New Orleans.

"How is Miss Sophia?" I ask, making Millie smile.

"She's amazing. She said to tell you hello. And to guard yourself." Millie frowns. "I forgot to pass that along. But she also said that you need to be strong regarding what's to come."

"What's that mean? What's coming?"

"She didn't say."

"She always leaves the most important parts out."

Millie pours the concoction into a glass and slides it over to me.

"No love potion, right?"

"No. It's a shielding potion. For protection."

I sniff it. "Smells like strawberries." I take a sip and smile in surprise. "Wow, it's like a milkshake."

"Helps it go down easier," she says with a wink. "Come back tomorrow, and I'll make you another."

"I'll gain ten pounds." I take another sip. "But I don't think I care. Wait, can you just do some kind of spell to take the calories out?"

"Sorry." She giggles and drinks the rest of the drink herself. "If I could do that, I'd be super-rich."

I finish my drink, and after I help Millie wash my glass and tidy up from the impromptu beverage, I wave goodbye to her.

"Be careful," she says before closing the door.

I'm always careful.

I take the same path from her place to mine, every single time. So far, I haven't seen any shadows on this route, and that makes me happy. The bars and clubs are hopping, full of tourists drinking and dancing. The French Quarter hums with energy, no matter the time of day.

I glance to my right just before I cross the street that leads several more blocks to where my apartment is, and am surprised to see Cash standing on the sidewalk, leaning against a pole.

"Are you following me?" I ask.

"No, ma'am," he says with an easy smile. "It seems I'm just destined to run into you. Can't say that I mind."

I smile back at him, regretting the way I brushed him off earlier.

"Well, then, perhaps I'll run into you again."

"I do hope so." He winks, and I hurry along to my apartment.

I round the corner of my block and stop in my tracks.

"Who are you?"

There's no answer, but I know it's the same shadow from the sidewalk and from Millie's café.

No shadows have ever followed me before.

Why now?

# CHAPTER 2

*"Where do you think you're going?"*

~Ted Bundy

$S$he's perfect.

He's been looking for the right one. It's been a few weeks since he last took someone, and he finally got rid of that toy this morning. Having just one subject at a time isn't really his style.

He likes having several girls in his lair at once. They talk to each other. They conspire. Hearing their chorus of pleas, their cries, gives him great joy. It arouses him far more than sex ever could. Women aren't to be used as sexual partners.

They're his prey.

They think they can escape him. Go back to their pathetic little lives.

Why are women so fucking stupid? Don't they know he has something far better waiting for them?

He grins as he watches from his usual spot under the streetlight. His shoulder leans against the pole as he watches Brielle finish up her nightly tour.

He comes every night.

She's never seen him.

He'll have to teach her to be more careful. More watchful. Bad things could happen to her, and he needs her whole, so she's hale and hearty and ready for what he has planned for her.

But that's for later. Right now, he needs someone new. Someone fresh.

And he's looking right at her.

"I'm Tammy. I just *loved* all of the stories. It's so fascinating."

*Well, hello, Tammy.*

She could be a mirror image of Brielle.

And that just can't be, can it?

Brielle finishes talking with Tammy, then moves to take more questions. He approaches the young woman.

"I just heard you ask about the LaLaurie mansion."

She turns to him with wide, blue eyes. Oh, yes, she's perfect. Those eyes with the dark hair. She's the right height, too.

Tonight's going to be fun.

"Yes, do you know more?" she asks.

"I know plenty, and I have a friend who can give us a private tour," he replies kindly. "In fact, we can go back there now, if you like."

"Oh, I don't know," Tammy says, looking around. "I came with friends, and they'll be pissed if I ditch them."

"You'll be back here before you know it," he lies easily. "Don't you worry."

She bites her lip, considering her options, but curiosity gets the best of her, and she nods.

"All right, then. But I have to hurry."

"No problem. Come with me."

He's always calm, and this is no different. He guides her through the crowds of the French Quarter and down the street toward the house she's so interested in.

But instead of approaching the door to knock, he turns to his car.

"Aren't we going inside?"

"I just have to call first since they're not expecting me."

"Oh, right." She offers him a tentative smile and nods. "That makes sense."

He can see the nerves starting to set in. She's wondering if she made the right choice.

Before she can flee, he reaches for the syringe he has ready, resting in the cupholder of the front seat. She doesn't see it coming when he turns swiftly and jabs the needle into her arm. Within seconds, she's drooping against him.

"Too much to drink tonight, darlin'," he says with a smile and guides her into the backseat. "Let's go sober you up. You don't want to miss the fun."

# CHAPTER 3

## CASH

"*I*'m going to gain about sixty pounds while I'm here." I lean back in my chair and rub my flat stomach. "You keep bringing me to amazing restaurants."

"Would you rather we take you to crappy ones?" my brother, Andrew, asks with a grin.

"Touché." I take a sip of my water and blink rapidly when I see Brielle walk through the door.

"What?" Andy's wife, Felicia, says and turns to see what I'm looking at. "Do you know her?"

"Sort of."

I grin when Brielle's eyes scan the room and then catch mine. Recognition sparks, and then pleasure moves over her beautiful face.

I'm embarrassed to admit that I'm relieved.

If she'd been disgusted and turned to leave, my ego would have taken a hard hit.

"Are you following me?" I ask her when she walks up to our table.

"I could say the same thing for you, Mr. Stalker," she says, grinning, and turns to my family. "Hi. I'm Brielle."

"This is my brother Andy, and his wife, Felicia."

"Pleasure," Brielle says and nods. "I see you found my favorite restaurant in the Quarter."

"It's ours, too," Felicia says. "Would you like to join us?"

"Join us," I agree, gesturing to the chair next to me.

"Oh, thanks for the invitation, but you've finished your meal, and I ordered mine to go." She winks at me, and I feel it all the way to my gut. She pats my shoulder. "Y'all have a good day."

She walks away to collect her meal from the counter and then sashays out of the restaurant and down the street.

"How do you know her?" Felicia asks. She leans in, avidly awaiting every detail.

Felicia is a busy-body from way back.

"I don't know her well," I reply. "She was the guide on the ghost tour I took the other night. You know, when you guys ditched me for date night, and I had to fend for myself?"

"You went on a *ghost tour*?" Felicia's eyes dance with excitement. "How was it?"

"Interesting, actually." I sip my water again. "She has a way with telling a story, that's for sure."

"And, at the risk of getting slapped by my gorgeous wife, she's not bad on the eyes," Andy adds.

"She's beautiful," Felicia agrees, nodding. "You should ask her out."

"She might not be single."

"No ring," Felicia says immediately. "Trust me, girls look for that stuff."

"That doesn't mean she's not—"

"He might never see her again," Andy adds.

"I want to go on a ghost tour," Felicia announces. "I've always wanted to do it but never made the time. We've lived here for two whole years, babe. It's time we go."

"It just so happens, I know a guide," I say with a grin, the idea of seeing Brielle again sparking immediate joy.

"That's handy."

We both look at Andy, who just sighs. "Fine. I'm in. But I don't believe in any of that haunting, ghostly, voodoo shit."

"So noted," I reply.

"And after the tour, Cash should ask Brielle on a date."

"Wait, what?"

Felicia claps her hands. "It's perfect. It can't hurt to *ask*. If she's taken, she'll say so. No harm, no foul. But she was looking at you with interest, brother mine."

"She won't stop nagging until you ask the hot girl out," Andy says. "So, just save us both the headache."

"I love you, too."

Andy grins. "Let's go ghost hunting."

～

"THANKS FOR COMING on the tour with me this evening, everyone," Brielle says, smiling at the group. It's a larger one than the other night. "I'll hang around in case anyone has any questions. No pressure, though. Have a good night."

"Now," Felicia says in a loud whisper. "Go ask her now."

"You're pushy," I say calmly and watch as several people huddle around the gorgeous brunette to ask their questions. "I'll let the others talk with her first."

"Smart," Andy says on a yawn. "But I'm not waiting around. Let's go home, babe."

"I want to see Cash ask her out," Felicia says, frowning. "This is the best part, and that's saying a lot because that tour was *awesome*. I wonder if our house is haunted."

"Let's go see," Andy says with a wink. "Give the man some space. It's creepy to hover when he's about to make his move."

"Is it creepy?" she asks me.

"No, I don't think you're creepy, but you guys go ahead. I don't know how long she'll be."

Felicia's hopeful expression falls, but she nods. "Okay. But I want all of the details later."

535

"Of course, you do." I laugh as I wave them off, then turn to listen as Brielle talks about other legends and ghosts in the French Quarter.

"Thanks for your time," an older blonde says with a smile before walking away and leaving Brielle alone.

"So...I swear I'm not a stalker," I say as I approach her. She turns and smiles at me, but it doesn't reach her eyes. The carefree woman from earlier is gone.

Suddenly, I want to scoop her into my arms and protect her.

And she hasn't even said that anything is wrong.

"I was surprised to see the three of you join the tour tonight," she admits.

"After you left the restaurant this afternoon, Felicia announced that she'd always wanted to go on a ghost tour. She talked us into coming."

"I hope she had a good time."

"She did." I shift from foot to foot, suddenly nervous.

And I'm never nervous.

"I have a question."

"Sure."

"Are you involved with anyone? Husband? Boyfriend?"

The smile reaches her eyes now. "No. I'm not involved with anyone."

"Well, that's good, because I'd like to ask you out for some coffee."

"Right now?"

I glance around and then turn back to her. "Sure. If you're free."

"Have you been to Café du Monde yet?"

"I can't say that I have."

She smiles and motions for me to walk with her. "Then you're in for a treat. The fastest route is through Jackson Square, but I'd like to go another way if that's okay."

"Is it so you have more time with me? It's all right, you can admit it."

She laughs loudly. When I take her hand in mine, she doesn't pull away. "I just have certain routes that I prefer to take through the city. It's an OCD thing. A quirk, if you will."

"I don't mind quirks that keep me in your company."

We're quiet as she leads me down the dark streets full of loud people. Music pours from the doors of bars and restaurants. It's a symphony of noise.

Even if I wanted to chat with her, it would be difficult. But I'm fine just walking together, holding her hand.

I can't explain it. I barely know her, but I crave her company.

It was as if I recognized her the second I saw her.

With my background in psychology, I could probably tear into the whys and hows of that and make it incredibly *not* romantic.

Or, I could just enjoy it. Relax.

That's what I'm supposed to be doing in New Orleans anyway.

"It's just down here," she says loudly, pointing to the end of the block. She leads me to the front of the line, and we're offered a little, round table that has a napkin dispenser on it and nothing else. "The menu is here."

She points to the side of the dispenser.

"But, if you trust me, I'll order for us. Just tell me if you want hot or cold coffee."

I cock a brow, watching as she tucks a dark strand of hair behind her ear. "Cold."

She nods, and a woman approaches to take our order.

"We'll have two frozen café au laits, and a family order of beignets," Brielle says. I pay for the order, and the woman hurries off to fill it.

"So, tell me more about you," I say.

"Actually," Brielle says, crossing her legs and watching me closely, "why don't you tell me about *you*? All I know is your name. Cash. Is that short for something?"

"It's short for Cassien. What else would you like to know? You know I'm from Savannah."

"What do you do for work?"

I fidget in my seat. "I work for the FBI."

Her brows lift. "You're an FBI agent?"

"I am." I nod and lean back when two frozen drinks and a large plate of beignets are set before us. "I've been with them for about ten years."

"What do you do for them?"

"I'm a profiler."

"Wow, that's fascinating," she says and takes a bite of a donut. "Do you profile murderers? Like serial killers?"

"Sometimes." I nod and watch as she licks some powdered sugar from her lower lip.

I want to lick that lip myself.

"Okay, that's pretty cool, Cash. I can honestly say I've never met a profiler before."

"That you know of."

She nods. "True. Do you work out of Savannah?"

"I'm actually based in the Dallas field office, but I travel frequently, going wherever I'm needed."

"And what are you doing in New Orleans?"

I sigh and suddenly wish the coffee were whiskey.

"I'm on mandatory leave."

She tips her head to the side. "Did you kill someone in the line of duty?"

"No." Not this time. "I just came off a pretty intense case. I haven't taken a vacation in a long time, and my boss pretty much pushed me out the door. I'm not welcome back for a few weeks."

"That's quite a vacation."

"Too long." I sigh, still frustrated. "I'm not used to being idle. That's how I found you. Andy and Felicia wanted to go out on a date the other night, and I didn't want to sit at their place alone, so I went out and found your tour."

"I'm glad you did," she says quietly. "Is it weird that I feel like I've met you before? I barely know you. You're a stranger. Yet, here I am, hanging out with you like we're old friends."

"It's not weird, I was just thinking the same. Maybe we met in a former life or something."

She doesn't laugh at that. She just narrows her eyes and taps her lips, seeming to give it some thought.

"I was joking."

"I know you were, but I suppose it's possible."

"Do you believe in past lives?"

Her eyes meet mine. "I believe in a lot of things, Cash. And I'm going to tell you, right here and now, even when I barely know you, that if you'd like for us to simply go our separate ways, I won't hold it against you."

I frown. "That feels a little dramatic."

"It's not." She wipes her hands, finishing the last of her treat. "I told you the other night, I'm a complicated woman. I wasn't kidding."

"I suppose we're all complicated, in our own ways. You haven't scared me off."

"Yet," she whispers.

"Okay, tell me what you think would send me running?"

"I see dead people," she says with a straight face. "It's why I'm so good at my job. I don't just know the lore because I studied it. Much of what I know has been told to me by the souls who experienced it themselves."

I blink at her. I honestly don't know what to say.

"See? Complicated."

"How long has it been that way for you?"

"Since my earliest memories," she says. "And, yes, it's scary. I don't know if I'll ever get used to it entirely, but I've learned to live with it."

"Being in the French Quarter must be unbearable for you."

She tips her head to the side. "Huh. You haven't run off yet."

"I see no reason to go anywhere."

"To answer your question, no, the Quarter isn't super fun for someone like me. But I make my living here. And I take precautions."

"What kind of precautions?"

"I think I've talked about myself long enough. Tell me more about you. Why the FBI?"

"Well, I got my Ph.D. in psychology and then decided to go through the academy. I always knew I wanted to work for the FBI. Maybe I read too many thrillers when I was a kid. It was a lot of studying and training. As I mentioned, I've been an agent for about ten years, and a profiler for five, meaning post-training."

"Good for you. Do you enjoy it?"

"Despite some of the things I've seen, you mean? Yes. Because, at the end of the day, we put monsters in cages."

"I bet you've seen a lot of horrible stuff."

*More horrible than you can imagine.*

"You said you're originally from the area?" I ask, changing the subject. She smiles and stands, motioning for me to follow her.

"I'll tell you about my sordid past while you walk me home."

"Deal."

"I grew up out in the bayou, about an hour from the city. I have two sisters, both younger. My parents were pathetic and horrible excuses for human beings."

"That good, huh?"

"Abusive." She shrugs one shoulder, and I feel immediate and intense anger. I want to hurt anyone who would dare abuse this woman. "Neglect. Not to mention, we lived in the most haunted house in Louisiana, and that's saying a lot."

"Wow."

"Do *you* believe in ghosts, Cash?"

I frown, thinking it over. "I think I like a good story. But I don't know if I believe, to be honest, because I've never experienced anything paranormal."

"Never?"

"Not that I'm aware of. I know I've never seen a ghost."

"Have you ever been somewhere and, suddenly, all of the hairs on your body stand on end, and you don't know why?"

"Sure."

"Or walked into a room that suddenly feels a lot colder than any other part of the house?"

"Everyone's felt a chill."

She smiles up at me. "You've experienced things, Cash. You just didn't know that you were experiencing them."

"Huh."

"Or are you one of those people who thinks things like this don't exist?"

"I've seen evil," I reply honestly. "And I'm not so close-minded that I can say there's not something out there that we can't see. I can't say I'm a believer, but I think *you* believe it, and sometimes, that's all that matters."

"That's a good answer."

"Do you live here in the Quarter?"

"Yes." She nods and leads me around a corner. "I have an apartment just down the street here."

"Is it haunted?"

"Everything's haunted. But the spirits there are calm and don't bother me much."

I take her hand once more, and when her fingers clench hard on mine, I frown down at her.

She stops short, staring straight ahead.

It's like watching her the other night all over again.

"Brielle? What's wrong?"

"This has never happened before," she whispers, and I can see she's starting to shake.

"Hey. Hey." I tip her face up to mine. "I'm right here, and I won't let anything hurt you. But you have to tell me what's happening."

"We have to go inside," she says. "Will you come with me?"

"Of course."

She's walking fast now, almost pulling me along the sidewalk. She turns to the side as if she's slinking past something she doesn't want to touch, then hurries up the stairs to her apartment.

She fumbles with the lock, so I take the key from her, unlock the door, and walk in with her. She immediately slams the door, leans against it, and looks up at me with round, glassy eyes.

"*Now* you're scaring me," I inform her.

"I need my sister," she says, pulling her phone out of her pocket. "I'm going to call for her, and while she's on her way, I'll tell you everything."

"Deal."

Her eyes are on mine as she holds the phone to her ear. "It's me. I need you right now. I'm at home. Okay, but Cash is here, and I haven't told him yet. See you soon."

She hangs up, but instead of talking, she just walks right into my arms and hugs me tightly as if she's holding on for dear life.

As if she's pulling strength from me.

"Brielle," I whisper and kiss the top of her head. She smells like lavender. "Talk to me."

She pulls back and paces to the window, staring down at the street. "She's still there. Both of them are."

"Who? I didn't see anyone."

"I can't be sure who the first one is," she says and turns to me. "But the other one? It's Tammy. From my tour the other night.

"She's dead."

# CHAPTER 4

## BRIELLE

*I* can't find my center.

Hell, I can barely breathe.

This hasn't happened since I was a child.

"Talk to me, Brielle," Cash says. His hands are strong on my shoulders, his green eyes concerned but not disgusted.

"Like I said earlier, if you want to go, I understand. Because it's about to get weird, Cash. I wish I was like normal girls, but I'm not, and I'm telling you now, you should probably go."

"I'm not going anywhere."

I swallow hard, fighting back tears of relief and joy. If one of my sisters told me that they already trusted their life with a man they only met days ago, I'd tell them they were nuts.

But here we are. I can't explain why or even how, but I *know* him already. I can feel it down in my bones that I can trust him—with even my deepest secrets.

"I told you, I see dead people."

"Let's sit."

"No, I'd prefer to stand. I need to pace a bit." I walk away and look out the window again.

No shadows.

Apparitions.

"I always see shadows," I continue. "I've never been able to make out the features of the spirits I see, though."

"Until now?" He guesses correctly.

"Until now," I confirm. "And let me just say, it'll scare the hell out of a girl."

"I can only imagine."

There's a knock on the door, startling us both.

"It's me!" Millie yells through the door, and I rush over to open it. "What's wrong? Wait. Hi, I'm Millie."

She holds out her hand for Cash to shake, which he does immediately.

"Cash."

"I know." Her eyes narrow as she examines him, and I know she's sweeping his thoughts. It's intrusive as all get out, but she's my sister, and that makes her protective. "I like you."

"I feel like I was just given a test that I didn't prepare for."

"You were," Millie confirms. "You passed. Now,"—she turns to me again—"talk to me."

"So, I saw that new shadow the other night."

Millie nods.

"Well, just before I called you, I saw something else that's new. Not just a new shadow. An apparition."

She blinks rapidly. "As in, you saw their *features?*"

"Yes." I nod and then start pacing the living area again. "For both of them. The first one, the one I saw the other night, isn't a shadow anymore. Now, there are *two*. Girls. And one is from my tour the night I met Cash."

Millie slowly lowers herself to the couch, perching on the edge of it, watching me with wide, brown eyes. "They must be trying to communicate with you."

"Their mouths were moving." It comes out as a whisper, and a shiver slithers down my spine. "But I couldn't hear what they were saying."

"Wait." Millie holds up her hand, her eyes wider than before. "This means they're *following* you, Bri."

"Yeah." I sigh and rub my fingertips over my forehead. "Yeah, that started the other night."

"You didn't say anything," Millie says.

"To either of us," Cash adds, his hands balling into fists at his sides.

"Well, to be fair, this is our first date," I remind him, but he doesn't laugh. He just narrows his eyes at me.

"It's a hell of a first date," Millie mumbles. "I mean, most people just get naked and have sex and then regret their life choices in the morning. This is on a whole different level."

I smirk and then shrug. "The night's not over yet."

"This isn't funny," Cash says, slowly shaking his head. "You're being terrorized by the dead, Brielle."

"Sometimes it's either laugh or cry, and I don't want to cry," I admit. "Trust me, I've cried over crap like this all my life."

"There has to be a way to shut it off," he mutters as if he's thinking aloud. "Hypnosis? It's not my area of expertise, but I have friends—"

"I'm thirty." I prop my hands on my hips. "Trust me, we've tried everything to at least tone it down. It just is what it is, and I've learned to deal with it. That's why I have certain routes I take through the Quarter. No surprises. I chose this apartment because the spirits here are quiet. I don't travel much. I have a routine, Cash, and it's worked well for me."

"Until today," Millie says softly. "We need to find out what these girls want and send them on their way so you can get back to a somewhat normal life again. You know what happened the last time."

"Wait, this has happened before?" Cash demands. My eyes are pinned on my sister's.

"Not the apparitions. This is brand new," I reply. "But the following has happened before. I'll tell you about it later." I turn back to my sister. "I need for them to go away," I agree. "Because I'm afraid I can't give them what they want. Whatever it is they need."

"We don't know if we don't know," Millie says. "I can open myself up and feel them for you if you want, since you can't hear them."

"No," I say immediately, rushing to her and taking her shoulders in my hands. "Do *not* do that, Millicent. I'm not giving you permission to do that."

"Okay, I won't."

"Promise me."

"I promise."

"I'm missing something."

We both turn to Cash, who watches us intently.

"If she opens herself up and crawls into the mind of a spirit, there's a good chance she won't walk back out again," I inform him. "Millie is a powerful psychic."

"I'm a witch, too," she says proudly.

"Does everyone in the family have these,"—he waves his hand in the air—"gifts?"

"Just the sisters," I reply. "Daphne is the youngest, and she's psychometric. She touches objects and sees the past through them."

"Fascinating," he says.

"Honestly, I'm shocked he hasn't run away screaming yet," Millie says to me. "Or called the cops."

"He *is* the cops," I say with a shrug. "FBI profiler."

"A *profiler*?" She stands and walks to him. "So, you're a psychiatrist?

"I am," he confirms.

"May I?"

"Sure."

She takes his hand, looks deeply into his eyes, and after about fifteen seconds, leans in to give him a gentle hug.

"I'm so sorry."

"It's okay." He hugs her in return and smiles when she pulls away. "I'm not running, Millie. I'm confused, intrigued, and completely entranced by your sister. I'm worried, as well. And, frankly, I want to hurt anyone that would even dare to try and hurt *her*."

"Really like him," Millie says to me with a grin. "If you don't scoop him up, I will."

"He's not meant for you."

"No." She shakes her head. "No, he's not."

"So, what now?" Cash asks. "What do we do now?"

"There's nothing to do yet," I reply. "I freaked out a bit because this is all new, but we don't have anything to act on."

"Two women are dead," he reminds us. "We have to call the authorities and get an investigation underway. I have contacts here, I can call—"

"But we don't know the circumstances," Millie says, interrupting him. "They might have been in an accident together. They might have died of natural causes. They could have died years ago and are just now reaching out—though that doesn't make sense with you talking to the one girl the other night."

"We wait," I add, nodding. "And in the meantime, I'll just have two creepy girls following me around. Oh, and one more thing. They didn't die of natural causes, that much is clear."

No, the torture marks on their skin weren't anything *normal*.

They were killed; after they were put through inexplicable horrors.

～

"Was that your first sage cleansing?" I ask after Millie leaves for the night. She stayed and helped me sweep my apartment for anything that made its way inside. It should also tone down the resident spirits for a while.

"It was," Cash says. He leans on my kitchen counter, watching as I tidy up, trying to keep my hands busy for a little while longer.

He's ridiculously handsome. Hot, even. Tall and broad with muscles and tanned skin. His lower front teeth are just a little crooked, which only makes his smile more interesting.

But I could get lost in those green eyes.

"What are you thinking?" he asks.

"That you should probably go. I've kept you here for far too long."

His eyes narrow on my face. "I'm not going anywhere."

"So, I know I joked around earlier about sex on the first date, but I'm not getting naked with you tonight. Sorry to disappoint."

"Funny." He chuckles and reaches out to drag his knuckles down my cheek. "I'll sleep on the couch. I don't want to leave you alone tonight. What if they haunt your dreams?"

"Sleep's always been my safe place." I can't hold back from wrapping my arms around his middle and hugging him. "I appreciate you thinking of it, but I've never had sleeping issues, thank goodness."

"Well, that's something, then." He kisses the top of my head. "But I'm still staying. We've already established that, although this is new, it's strong. And if you think I won't be here to protect you, you still have a lot to learn about me."

"I don't think you can protect me against this," I whisper into his chest. "But having you here is soothing, so, thank you. You don't have to sleep on the couch. I have a guest bedroom. I don't get many visitors, but I have it anyway."

"I'll take it," he says. "Where's your room?"

"Second door on the right."

"Come on."

He takes my hand and leads me to my bedroom. He turns down the bed and then faces me. "I'll go make you some hot tea. Your sister pointed out the one I should use."

"She's helpful."

"You get ready for bed, and I'll be back in a few minutes."

"Cash." He stops in the doorway and turns back to me. "Thank you."

"You're welcome."

I can hear him puttering around in my kitchen as I change into yoga shorts and a loose tank top, then pad into the bathroom to brush my teeth and my long, dark hair. I wash my face, and just as I walk out of the bathroom, Cash walks into the bedroom with two steaming cups of tea.

"Thank you again," I say as I sit on the bed and accept a mug. "I'm glad you made yourself a cup. I was going to suggest it. It'll protect you, too."

"Am I in danger?"

I frown. "I don't think so. I know that nothing here can hurt you. Or would want to. Trust me, I wouldn't live here if that were the case. But, just in case, the tea can't hurt."

He nods and sits in the rocking chair across from the bed, watching me. His brow lifts when we hear footsteps in the living room.

"That's normal," I say with a grin. "It'll calm down in a few minutes."

"Do you just live your life in fear, every single day?" he asks, surprising me. I think back to the three of us huddled under the stairs of the god-awful house we grew up in.

"For a long time, we did. The three of us. Our childhood wasn't fantastic, Cash, and only half of that was due to our gifts and not understanding them. The other half was our parents."

"You mentioned them earlier."

"My father died when I was thirteen." I take a sip of tea and guard my mind, reinforcing my personal shields and grounding myself. He's been truly gone for a long time, but I don't want to take any chances. "I'm pretty sure my mother killed him, but I can't be sure."

"You're kidding."

"I wish I were." I shrug a shoulder. "He haunted the three of us for a decade. He's the only spirit that's ever followed me. Before this week. He was a bastard when he was living, punishing us for the smallest things. He took a lot of joy in inflicting pain."

"Fucking hell, Brielle."

"And it didn't stop after he died. So, yes, our childhood was full of fear. Then, once the three of us were all out of the house, Millie started studying with Miss Sophia, a very powerful witch, not far from our childhood home. She told her about our father, and Miss Sophia was finally able to create a spell to get rid of him forever. Without her help, I'm sure he'd still be around."

Cash's jaw clenches. "And your mother? Is she dead, too?"

"No." My smile turns cold. "But if I had my way, she would be."

"You can't tell an FBI agent that you wish your mother was dead."

"Yes, I can." I raise my chin. "While my father inflicted punishment and pain, she simply ignored it. Ignored *us*. I raised my sisters, not our parents. In fact, when I turned eighteen, I moved out and took them with me, filing for full custody. She didn't fight it. She still lives in that godsforsaken house in the bayou, by herself, slowly dying.

"She didn't believe us when we told her about what we saw, what we felt. And she would beat us with the belt if we talked about it."

"Christ."

"So, when we left, I immediately called other people in the area that were like us. And I started to ask questions. Built a community around us. We learned, we grew stronger, and after a while, we healed."

"I'm so glad. I hate that you went through that."

"Maybe we're all stronger because of it," I reply honestly. "We learned to control ourselves out of necessity, so our gifts aren't messy or frivolous now."

"That's a positive way to look at it."

He blinks slowly, watching me.

"What about your family? Tell me about them."

"Does it sound weird for me to say that I feel guilty that I had the exact opposite of you?"

"You shouldn't feel guilty at all."

"Andy is my only sibling. He's a couple of years younger than I am, and he works for the New Orleans PD."

"Lots of law enforcement in your family."

"My dad was a cop," he says and nods. "He was killed in the line of duty when I was eighteen."

"Oh, Cash. I'm sorry."

He nods and drinks the rest of his tea, then sets the mug aside. "It was tough. Mom never remarried. She still lives in Savannah. She's been sick lately."

His eyes hold mine.

"Cancer."

"Why aren't you there with her?"

"I was," he says on a sigh. "I went there first, and she's doing much better. She basically shooed me out the door and told me to go spend some time with my brother."

"She sounds wonderful."

"She is," he says with a nod. "But, to be honest, I was ready to go. All she does is lecture me about working too hard, and that I need to find a nice girl to settle down with."

"She loves you." I set my empty mug aside and lie down, facing Cash. I pull the blankets up around my shoulders and smile at him. "I swear, it's not the company making me tired."

"You had a busy day," he says, letting out a small laugh. "And an emotional one. If you need me, I'll be next door, okay?"

"Okay."

He crosses to me and kisses my forehead, then turns off the light and leaves the door open just a crack. I hear him walk to the kitchen, set our empty mugs in the sink, and then into the guest room. His feet shuffle around as he gets ready for bed, then the bedsprings squeak a bit as he climbs under the covers. And then it's quiet. Even the spirits have settled down.

My eyes droop, and before long, I sink into sleep.

*This is new. It seems today is the day for it, whether I'm awake or asleep.*

*Have I mentioned that I don't like surprises?*

*I'm walking through the Quarter on my usual route to work. I nod at people I know and ignore the shadows that lurk in the corners. I'm used to them. Some don't know I'm here, and some try to get my attention, but I always keep my eyes straight ahead.*

*Focus. Focus is always the key. Stay centered. Grounded. Keep my mind calm. If I let the fear sink in, I'll make myself vulnerable, and that's not good.*

*The sun is up and bright in the sky, but suddenly, a shadow covers it, sending everything into darkness. I stop and blink, trying to let my eyes adjust to the dim surroundings. When I can see at least some things again, they're right in front of me.*

*The two women.*

*The two apparitions that have been following me for days.*

*"You have to help us," Tammy, the one from my tour group says. "You have to find us."*

*"Find us," the other agrees. They reach out for me. Both are covered in blood, and wounds still seep all over their bodies. The girl I don't know has a slit throat, and one eye is missing.*

*Tammy doesn't have any fingers on her right hand.*

*"Who hurt you?" I ask, but no sound comes out of my mouth. "Tell me who hurt you."*

*"There are more," Tammy says. "So many more. We need you. You have to find us."*

*"Who did this?" I ask again, frustrated when no sound emerges. Damn it! I need to communicate with them. "Please, tell me how to find you."*

*"Help us," they say in unison. "Please. You have to help us."*

"Holy shit."

Suddenly, I'm sitting up in bed, gasping for air. Cash holds my shoulders firmly.

"Brielle, wake up. You're safe, baby. Wake up."

"I'm awake," I gasp and lean in to rest my forehead on his chest.

"You were having a nightmare."

"No." I look up into his green eyes. They seem brighter in the dim light. "I was dreamwalking. The girls are talking, Cash."

"What did they say?"

"They asked me to help them. Find them." I feel a tear slide down my cheek. "Horrible things were done to them."

"They told you?"

"I could see it." I swallow hard. My mouth is so dry. "He tortured them."

"Where are they?"

"I don't know." I shake my head in despair. "I don't know."

# CHAPTER 5

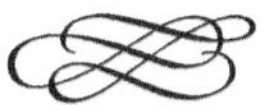

## BRIELLE

"**G**ood morning."

I smile at Cash as I walk into the living room and sit on the couch next to him. He passes me his coffee, and I take a sip.

"Good morning."

I think I could get used to having him here like this. After he comforted me in the middle of the night, he stayed with me, holding me until I fell back to sleep. And this morning, when I woke up, he was no longer in bed with me, but I could smell the coffee.

"How do you feel?"

"Tired." I shrug and take another sip of his coffee, then pass it back to him. "I guess dream-walking will do that to a person."

"You guess?"

"This week is full of firsts."

Cash frowns and takes my hand in his, linking our fingers. "I'm worried about you, Brielle. And I barely know you."

"Thank you." I lean my head on the couch and watch him thoughtfully. "I'm seriously shocked that you haven't escaped yet. Why are you still here?"

He blows out a breath and sets his mug aside. "I was asking myself that this morning. It's not that I feel bad for you, or even that I feel an obligation."

"Good."

"I'm drawn to you in ways I can't explain. Like I said before, it's a…recognition. Like, I was looking for you and didn't even know it."

"Same," I whisper.

"I've never believed in soul mates or that sort of thing," he says. "And I'm not sure I do now. But there's something here, and I'm going to stay for as long as you'll let me."

I smile just as a knock comes from the front door.

"Are you expecting someone?" Cash asks.

"It's probably Millie." I walk to the entry and look out the peephole, then open the door and smile at my sister. "I thought you'd be working this morning."

"I have employees for a reason," she says as she walks into the room carrying three coffees. "I brought goodies."

"Bless you," I mutter, reaching for the paper bag she's carrying. "Fresh croissants make everything better."

"For you," she says to Cash, passing him a coffee. "There's a protection spell in there."

"Does it have eye of newt?" he asks, flashing a smile.

"Not this time," Millie replies with a wink, making Cash's smile slide from his face. "And I might have put a little spell on the pastries, as well. We can't be too careful. We don't know what we're dealing with here."

I'm already sitting on the couch, my legs crossed under me, happily eating my way through the bag's contents.

"I'm so damn hungry," I say with my mouth full.

"Probably all that walking you're doing in your sleep," Cash says calmly.

"What?" Millie's eyes fly to mine. "Where did you go?"

"I didn't physically go anywhere. I wasn't sleepwalking, I was dream-walking."

"Oh, I've *always* wanted to do that," Millie says with excitement. "I didn't know you could."

"I didn't either. And, trust me, it wasn't nearly as fun as it sounds."

"I'm going to let you two talk while I go get my things from Andy's house."

I frown up at him. "You're moving in?"

"I told you, I'm here for as long as you'll allow it. I can't protect you from my brother's home." He leans in and kisses my head. He hasn't kissed me on the lips yet, and it's killing me. "Since you have Millie with you, I'll run over there now. I'll be back shortly."

"I don't need to be babysat, you know."

"There's strength in numbers," he says, his handsome face completely sober. "And until all of this is resolved, I'd rather you weren't alone."

He hurries out of the apartment, and Millie watches him walk down the street through the window.

"He's hot."

"I know," I say and reach for another croissant. "I should probably have some protein with this."

"That one has turkey and cheese in it," she says, watching me carefully. "Where did you go in your dream, Bri?"

"I was walking in the Quarter." I take a deep breath. "Toward work. Everything was normal until it went dark. Suddenly, the two women were standing before me."

"The sun went down?"

I frown, thinking about it. "No. More like something covered the sun."

Millie leans forward. "A cloud?"

"A shadow." I blink rapidly. "A *shadow* covered the sun."

"Okay, keep going."

"I could hear the girls. They kept saying that I needed to find them. Help them. But when I tried to ask questions, no sound came out of my mouth."

"Fascinating," Millie says. "Did they say where they are?"

"No. They didn't give me any other information. It's so damn frustrating."

"I wonder what happened to them?" Millie asks.

"They were tortured."

It's her turn to blink rapidly in surprise. "Excuse me?"

"You heard me."

"How do you know?"

"Because I could see it." I swallow hard and tell her what I saw. "It was awful. I wish they were still just shadows."

"I'm so sorry you had to see that," Millie says softly.

My phone rings. "Holy shit."

"Who is it?"

"Daphne." I hold Millie's gaze as I answer the phone. "Hello?"

"Hi." My sister's voice is quiet. I've missed it so much. I feel tears spring to my eyes. "I know we have our issues right now, but I've been dreaming, Bri. I feel like you need me."

"I do." *And not just for this.* "How are you?"

"I'm fine, but those girls aren't."

"You've seen the girls?"

"And you," she confirms. "Last night, I saw you talking to them in my dream."

"I didn't see you."

"I kept trying to get your attention, but it was no use. It was damn frustrating."

"Come over. Millie's here, and we can talk about it all."

"I'm working today," Daphne says with a sigh. "But let's go out for dinner. We can talk then."

I agree, and we end the call.

"It's not just you," Millie says.

"No, she says she had the same experience I did last night." I shake my head in disbelief.

"That means I'm next." Her smile brightens. "And I'll be ready."

~

"SHE'LL BE HERE," Millie assures me. We're at our favorite restaurant in the Quarter, Café Amelie.

"She's ten minutes late. Daphne is never late."

"She'll be here," she says again as she reads the menu.

"Maybe she changed her mind. I could tell she wasn't thrilled to be talking with me."

"One of the things we need to clear up tonight is this stupid fight y'all have been having for more than a *year*. It's ridiculous."

"I—"

"Sorry I'm late." Daphne hurries to the table and sits in the empty seat next to Millie. She looks *amazing.* Her red, curly hair is weaved into a simple braid, and her golden eyes look tired.

She's a sight for sore eyes.

"I've missed you—" I begin, but she holds up a hand, stopping me.

"I'm not here to talk about the issues we have," she says. "Let's get that straight right now."

She moves to shove a piece of paper into her bag, but I stop her.

"Where did you get that?"

She frowns and glances down at it. "A lady on the street gave it to me. Asked me if I'd seen her before."

"Let me see."

She passes it to me, and I stare down at a photo of Tammy. Her last name is Holmes. She was only twenty-four, visiting New Orleans from Wisconsin.

549

"This is one of the girls."

"I didn't recognize her," Daphne says, looking at it again. "Of course, I wouldn't. She didn't look like this last night."

I swallow hard. "No. She didn't."

"Two things need to happen tonight," Millie announces, taking control of the conversation. "One, you *will* figure out a way to get past this stupid fight."

Daphne starts to argue, but Millie shakes her head, shutting our baby sister up.

"And two, we need to figure out what's happening to these poor girls and decide what we're going to do about it. Where's Cash?"

"Who's Cash?" Daphne asks.

"He's a new person in my life," I reply. "I told him I was going out for dinner with my sisters, and that I'd see him later."

"So, you've already moved on from Jackson, then?" Daphne asks, glaring at me from across the table.

I reach over and hold Daphne's hand in mine. "I need you to talk to me, Daph. We can't get past things if you keep shutting me out. I did *not* do anything inappropriate with Jackson."

Her eyes fill with tears at the mention of his name. Jackson was Daphne's high school sweetheart. They broke up when he went into the military, and when he returned, he asked me to meet up with him for lunch.

Daphne walked in on us and immediately assumed the worst.

"I saw it with my own eyes."

"You saw us having *lunch*."

"He had his damn hand on you!"

"You acted like a child," I counter, completely frustrated with my little sister. "You threw water in his face and stormed out as if you'd found us in bed together."

"Oh, trust me, I'm relieved that I was spared that much."

"Ew." I lean back and stare at her in horror. "Jack has always been like a freaking *brother* to me, Daph. I would *never* do that, no matter what. He's for you, and I'm not the least bit attracted to him. How could you even think that? We've gone more than a *year* without speaking, all because you assumed I jumped into bed with your boyfriend?"

"He's *not* my boyfriend," she whispers and dabs at the tears on her cheeks. "And even if it was just a simple lunch, it doesn't matter. He came back, and rather than reach out to me, he reached out to *you*. Do you know how horrible that feels?"

"It wasn't the right time," Millie says calmly.

"For the love of the stars, Mill, just let me be a woman for five minutes, okay? It hurt me, and I'm entitled to feel that way."

"Sure, you are," I agree, surprising her. "You feel betrayed. But you let it fester all this time and wouldn't even let me explain. You *assumed* I was bouncing all over the man you love, and that's pretty harsh, Daph."

"I'm not sorry," she says softly. "You should have called me right after he asked you to meet."

"He's my friend."

"He's my *everything*."

I sit back and study her. If the tables were reversed, and we were talking about Cash, how would I feel?

Hurt, certainly.

But I like to think I'd give them both the chance to explain.

"So, even though we didn't do anything inappropriate, you're going to continue taking your anger out on me? That's not fair."

Daphne pouts for a moment, then sighs and wipes the last of her tears away. Daphne's always been the most dramatic of us, but she's never behaved like this before.

"You're right," she says at last. "It's not doing any good. And, frankly, being angry all the time is exhausting."

"I can only imagine. I don't want you to be mad at me."

"Let's table this for now," Daphne says.

"Wait. Does that mean you're speaking to her again?" Millie asks.

"Yes, I'm speaking to her." Daphne rolls her eyes. "Now, let's get to the real reason we're all here." She points to the paper still sitting on the table.

"I'll fill you in on what's been happening so far." I go back to almost a week ago when I first met Cash, and tell her everything, from the moment I first saw him, to seeing the new shadow, and then the apparitions last night.

Has it really been less than a day?

It feels like months.

"And you haven't experienced anything?" Daphne asks Millie.

"No, not yet. But my shields are strong, and I'm super careful to center and ground myself. I have to."

"I know," Daph says and pats our sister's shoulder. The waitress arrives to tell us about the specials and take our orders. Once she's gone, Daphne clears her throat.

"So, there's something else I should tell you guys." She glances at each of us, then ducks her head as if she's embarrassed or ashamed. "I went to see Mama."

"What?" Millie and I bark in unison.

"Why would you do that?" Millie asks.

"She called me," Daphne says.

"I didn't know she had electricity, much less a phone," I say.

"She went to Horace's house to call," Daphne says. "She sounded real bad and made me feel guilty, so I agreed to go."

"No," Millie says, shaking her head emphatically.

"I wasn't there long," Daphne says. "The inside of the house is awful."

"What did she want?"

"I don't know." Daphne shrugs. "Once I got there, she said she didn't remember calling me. It was weird. She was mean. And you know as soon as I stepped inside…"

She shivers, and Millie and I both put our hands on her, giving her our strength—both literally and figuratively.

"We'll go to the café after this," Millie says. "I have potions for you to take."

"I appreciate it," Daphne says, adding a nod. "We can't ever go back there, guys. Not ever."

"And we never will," I assure. "Now, what do we do about this?"

I point to Tammy's missing person poster.

"We talk to Cash," Millie says.

"Why?" Daphne asks.

"Because he's with the FBI," I reply. "And he's a profiler."

"Wow. You snagged yourself a cool boyfriend, Bri," Daphne says.

"He's hot, too," Millie informs her. "And has a good heart."

"You looked?" Daph asks.

"Of course, I did. She's my sister."

~

"YOU'VE MULTIPLIED," Cash says with a smile when we walk into my apartment an hour later.

"I'm the youngest sister," Daphne says, sending Cash a little wave. "Daphne."

"Cash. Pleasure to meet you."

Cash turns to me and pulls me in for a lazy hug. "How are you, darlin'?"

"Not too bad, actually. Sorry we're later than I thought. We had to swing by the café to get some protection potion for Daphne."

He narrows his eyes as he glances at my sister. "What's going on?"

"It's quite a story," I say and gesture for him to have a seat with me on the couch. Millie sits in one chair across from us, and Daphne takes the other.

"Whoa," Daphne says in surprise.

"What?"

"Someone had sex in this chair."

Cash's head whips around to me, and I hold up my hands in surrender. "It wasn't me. I haven't had sex in…well, we don't need to go there."

"Not you," Daphne confirms and then laughs. "I don't know where you got this chair, but I like it. Whoever owned it was happy and quite playful."

"Well, that's fun," Millie says, grinning. "You should re-christen it later. After we leave."

"Thanks for the pointer," I say with a laugh.

"It's not a bad idea," Cash says, making me grin.

"Focus, please."

"I had the same dream that Brielle did last night," Daphne begins. "And when I was on my way to dinner, a woman stopped me on the street and gave me this."

She pulls the missing person flyer from her bag and passes it to Cash. He reads it, then looks at me with sad, green eyes.

"I remember her from the tour," he says.

"So do I. It's the same girl I see."

"Can you see them now?" Millie asks.

"They're outside," I inform them. "They don't follow me inside. Probably the wards or the crystal grid."

"Are they on the sidewalk?" Daphne asks.

I stand and peek outside. Sure enough, the two women are on the sidewalk, staring up at my apartment.

Talk about creepy.

"Yep."

"So, we know now that Tammy at least has been reported as missing," Cash says thoughtfully as I sit with him.

"She's dead," I say.

"We know that," Cash replies. "But the authorities don't. I'd like to consult with my brother on this."

"He's a cop here in New Orleans," I inform my sisters, then turn to Cash. "But what kind of cop?"

"He works in robbery," he admits.

"We have another contact," Millie says. "We just need to ask Miss Sophia. There are a couple of detectives who have worked with psychics in the past."

"Mallory Boudreaux's grandmother," I reply, remembering. "I need to go into Mal's shop this week anyway. I'll ask for her contacts then."

"If she doesn't know, Miss Sophia will," Millie says.

"I don't want to sit on this," Cash says. "There could be more girls missing."

"Cash, I don't have any proof, and I don't have any information aside from knowing she's dead. And, trust me, most people—especially cops—don't believe in psychics. They'll blow me off for sure. At least until I have more information or some proof."

"This is damn frustrating," he mumbles, rubbing his fingers over his lips. "In the meantime, I'm going to run searches in my database to see if other women with similar descriptions are missing."

"They do look alike. And they look like someone else," Daphne says thoughtfully.

"Who?" Millie asks.

"Brielle."

All eyes turn to me in surprise at Daphne's statement.

"You're right," Millie says. "At least, Tammy does. We don't know anything about the other girl."

"She resembles her, too. At least from what I could tell in my dream." Daphne shakes her head.

I stand to pace. I think better when I'm moving.

"Is that why they're coming to me? Because they look like me? Maybe they're trying to warn me or something."

"It's possible," Millie says as I walk past the window and glance outside.

"Shit," I mutter. "Guys? There are now three girls."

# CHAPTER 6

*I*t's possible that he went overboard this past week. But after such a dry spell, and once he got the taste of the woman he took from Brielle's tour, he just couldn't help himself.

"Hello, dear," he says to one of the five girls he currently has tied up in his room of fun. She's the most recent, and she hasn't stopped crying since she woke up this morning.

Of course, he doesn't find the show of emotion attractive in the least.

It's a weakness.

And that means this one won't last long once he starts playing with her.

Pity.

"Now, Brielle, there's no need to cry."

"I'm not B-B-Brielle," she whimpers. "I'm Ally."

He backhands her across the face, making her lip immediately bleed.

"You'll learn."

But she doesn't stop crying. No, she just sobs louder.

If he were a less patient man, he'd just slit her throat right now.

But that won't do. No, he went through too much trouble bringing her here, taking her out of a bar with plenty of people around to see.

She was too perfect to pass up.

He'll just have to listen to her cry.

Unless...

"Here, Brielle, this will help." He grabs a bloody rag from his workbench and stuffs it into her mouth to muffle her cries. "There, now. Much better."

He ignores the other three tied to their beds, some slipping in and out of consciousness, and one weeping quietly into her bare mattress, and then turns to the girl strapped to his chair. He clicks his tongue when he sees the blood running down her thigh from where the leather has bitten into her innocent flesh.

"Oh, this won't do. You've been trying to get away, haven't you?"

Her eyes are glassy as she shakes her head, denying her own struggles.

"I'm the only one allowed to make you bleed, Brielle. I told you that before."

He reaches for the woman's hair and surprises her when he pours warm water over it, then begins to wash it with shampoo that smells like apples.

"It has to be clean," he says, his voice soothing and even. "Nice and clean."

Once the soap is rinsed, he painstakingly braids the long, dark hair, securing it with a black hair tie.

Then, once it's just the way he likes it, he reaches for the scissors and cuts off the braid at the nape of her neck.

"I'm keeping this," he says, his face stretching in a sinister smile. "It's my little trophy. You don't mind, do you?"

She shakes her head, making him chuckle.

"Of course, you don't. You're such a good girl, Brielle. Always so sweet and nice."

He returns to his workbench and hangs the braid above the window, joining the other twenty-nine plaits.

"Thirty," he mumbles. "The same as your age!"

He turns to her triumphantly, ignoring the cries and whimpers coming from the others, completely focused on the woman in his chair.

"Oh, that calls for something special. Something very special, indeed."

He flips on the switch of the car battery charger next to the chair, parts her legs, and reaches for the cord.

"You're going to love this."

# CHAPTER 7

## CASH

"There have to be more missing persons reports," I mutter as I power up my laptop. Brielle and her sisters sit nearby, talking about the new girl that's joined the other two apparitions.

My brother pointed out to me this morning that this could all be a scam. And I can't exactly say his hypothesis is wrong. Brielle could be making up everything she supposedly *sees*, all for the sake of being dramatic.

Or, she could just be plain crazy.

And, frankly, I don't know her well enough to say for certain that he's not right.

But it feels like she's telling me the truth. And my intuition is rarely wrong.

I've seen the scared look in her eyes when she sees something new. That fear isn't a lie.

So, until I can say for certain that they're all whacko, I'm in this for the long haul.

"It's cool that you have access to the Fed's files," Millie says and smiles.

"I'm hoping it helps us figure out at least a pattern," I reply, entering stats into the search engine.

Dark hair.

Blue eyes.

Average height.

New Orleans.

And then hit *go.*

I glance up to find Brielle's bright blue eyes focused on me. She's quiet, but her face is tight with worry. All of this is taking a toll on her.

How do I know that?

How is it that I just met her a few days ago, and yet I feel as if I've known her for ages?

"How are you, darlin'?"

She shrugs a shoulder. "I'm okay."

"Holy shit," Millie mutters, pulling me back to the task at hand.

"What?" Daphne asks, hurrying over. Brielle doesn't join us.

She knows.

"Dozens," I mutter, paging through the names, the photos. "I only put in a five-year time span."

"Extend it," Brielle says. "Go back ten."

I do as she asks and feel my stomach drop. "There are more, but not many. It seems the number is far less until six years ago. At least girls missing from New Orleans. I'm going to look through each one to get more information. We'll look for girls taken in the French Quarter to start, and then we'll expand from there."

"With that list, it'll take you all night," Daphne says.

"You guys can go home," Brielle says quietly. "Get some rest. Maybe we'll have more information in the morning."

"This is going to take time," I agree and nod. "Brielle's right. Get some rest, ladies."

"I'm exhausted," Millie admits. "And I need to look in on the café before I head to bed. But I'm a phone call away."

"Same," Daphne says. "I don't live as close as Millie, but I can be here quickly."

Both sisters flank Brielle, all of them wrapping each other in hugs. They quietly whisper something in unison, like a prayer, and then once they've said their goodbyes, it's just Brielle and me.

"How many do you think?" she asks.

"I haven't dug around—"

"Ballpark."

"A couple dozen, at least. Some of these cases will have likely been solved. But once I narrow it all down and weed through it all, there will still be a couple dozen unsolved, I'm sure."

She blows out a breath and scratches her nose. "What do you need from me?"

"Coffee. This is going to take a couple of hours at least. You should get some sleep."

"I'm afraid to sleep," she admits softly. "And that pisses me right off, Cash. I told you, sleep has always been my safe place."

"And it will be again," I assure her. "As soon as we figure this all out."

"I hope it's sooner rather than later."

She pads into the kitchen, and I watch as she brews me a cup of coffee, adding just the right amount of sugar and cream.

I've never told her how I take my coffee.

When she delivers it to me, I set my computer aside and pull her onto my lap, cuddling her close.

"How did you know how I take my coffee?"

She opens her mouth, then closes it again and gives me a shy smile. "I don't know. I just knew."

"It'll be handy having you around." I smack a kiss on her cheek and then set her next to me on the couch.

"For my coffee-making skills?"

"Among other things," I say absently while I sip my coffee and gaze at the computer screen.

"You've never kissed me."

I glance over at her. "I kissed you just a moment ago."

"On the cheek."

Ah, here we are.

"Does it bother you that I haven't kissed your sweet lips yet?"

She shrugs that shoulder again and blows out a breath. "Maybe."

"Once I start kissing you, I won't want to stop there. You're a game-changer, Brielle, and we're a little busy right now. I don't want to fuck it up. Do I want to put my hands on you? My lips? Hell, yes. Who could resist you?"

She blushes and opens her mouth, but I press my finger against her lips, shushing her.

"I want many things with you, and we'll get there. But in the meantime, I need to figure out how to get these damn dead people to stop tormenting you so I can have you all to myself. Is that what you wanted to know?"

She puckers those lips still pressed to my finger and kisses the tip of it lightly, then smiles.

"Yeah. That's what I wanted to know."

My computer beeps, drawing my attention.

"Okay, I've sorted out the unsolved cases, including the cold ones."

"Cold cases?"

"Don't you watch TV?"

"Not much."

I smile and answer her question. "Cold cases are those that are old and never solved, ruled to be unsolvable."

"Gotcha. That makes sense."

She leans against me, pressed to me from shoulder to knee.

Once I've weeded through the remaining results, I'm left with forty-two.

"Forty-two?" she asks, reading the tally at the top of the screen.

"Yeah, that's what we're left with. That doesn't mean he's killed all of these girls, though. They're just the ones that fit the general description. Some of the bodies were found, but the cases were never solved."

She swallows hard, then points to a photo in the middle. "She's the first one I saw."

I jot down the name and keep paging through, but it's not until we get to the more recent listings that Brielle points again. "There's Tammy."

"Do you see the most recent girl?"

She frowns, examining each of the women again, and then she points to the last girl on the list. "This one. That's her."

"You're sure?"

She nods and bites her lip. "Yeah. They don't look much like those photos now given what was done to them, but that's them."

"What do they look like, Brielle?"

"You don't want to know."

"I've worked on some horrendous cases. There's not much that can surprise me."

"It's not just that they've been beaten. One definitely was because her whole face is swollen and bruised. But it's more. They've been...tortured. Tormented." She stands to pace again. She seems to think better when she's moving. "One of the girls, the one who was beaten, was also eviscerated. Slit from throat to pubic bone. Her torso looked empty of organs."

"Christ."

"Yeah, I don't see them as they were when they were alive and happy. I see the horror. Every detail."

"I'm so damn sorry, Brielle."

"Me, too. It was way better when they were just shadows and they'd tell me what happened to them. I didn't have to *see* it." She plucks at her lip, thinking. "One of the other girls had a slit throat. And the third one was burned."

I swallow hard, hating that she's had to see all of that.

"So, here's what we know," I begin, all business-like, my voice full of authority. "He's consistent. He likes one type of girl and doesn't deviate from that type. Dark hair, blue eyes, average height. Maybe he has a mommy complex, and he's killing his mother over and over again. Or, he's a jilted lover. There's something about these women that makes him comfortable and turns him on."

"Turns him on?" she asks incredulously.

"Oh, for sure. He most likely gets an enormous amount of sexual gratification from killing these women. From the actual *act* of torturing and killing them. He's definitely a sexual sadist."

"Sick son of a bitch."

"Absolutely. He probably has a mental illness of some kind. He's likely a psychopath, at the very least a sociopath, and absolutely a narcissist. He doesn't see what he does as wrong. He's proud of it, but he understands right from wrong, and laws, and he's very good at covering his tracks so he doesn't get caught."

"He's a serial killer," she says, surprise lighting up her face.

"Of course, he is. This isn't new for him. He's been killing for many years, most likely longer than the six we know about. These are just the people with a missing person report. He probably started at a young age, brutalizing animals, then progressed to experimenting with the homeless and other people that he thought wouldn't be missed. He may not have killed right away, but it likely didn't take him long to progress to that."

"How do you live with all of that in your head?" she asks.

"I could ask you the same thing."

She shakes her head, glances outside, and then sits next to me again, leaning her head on my shoulder. "They're still out there."

"I suspect they're not going anywhere for a while."

She nods. "Sleep with me tonight. I don't want to be alone. Please don't leave me alone."

"I'm right here. I'll stay with you."

"Thank you."

~

"No dreams last night." She smiles up at me as we walk through the French Quarter. She's leading me to her friend's store, where she claims the owner will be able to direct us to the correct police officer to talk to.

I'd rather just call my brother and ask for a contact.

But I'm not the one seeing dead people. So, for now, I'll do things her way.

"I'm glad." I squeeze her fingers. "You hardly moved."

She was pressed to me all night, and I wanted to make love to her more than I've ever wanted anything in my life.

But it's not the time for that yet.

We'll get there.

"It's just around the corner." Brielle guides me down the sidewalk, and we stop in front of a store called Bayou Botanicals. "I absolutely *love* Mallory's shop. It smells good and feels amazing. Let's go."

I open the door and follow Brielle into a lovely store full of oils and soaps and other things I can't identify.

"Brielle." A redhead smiles and hurries over to hug Brielle. "It's so good to see you." I assume this is Mallory, and her face changes when she touches Brielle. Tightens. "Oh, friend."

"I'm okay," Brielle assures her. "I want to introduce you to Cash."

"Hi, I'm Mallory Boudreaux," the woman says, shaking my hand. Her eyes narrow on mine, and just like when I first met Millie, I assume I'm being scrutinized in ways I can't begin to understand.

"Do you need more frankincense?" Mallory asks Brielle.

"Yes, actually. And we came for another reason, as well."

"I know," Mallory says with a small, sad smile. She turns to me. "I'm psychic."

"It seems everyone I meet lately is."

"Fascinating," Mallory says. "And probably disconcerting."

"Very."

Mallory reaches for a bottle and sets it on the counter. "You need Miss Sophia."

"Well, I was hoping *you* would know who your grandmother used to work with at the police department."

"I was too young and way too angry," Mallory says. "I hated that she worked with them. So, I don't have any names for you, but Miss Sophia might. She's here."

"*Here*-here?" Brielle asks in surprise.

"She brought me some tea this morning. I thought it was a casual visit, but I suspect she knew you'd be in today." Mal winks and disappears into a room marked *Employees Only*, then returns with an older woman. The woman is small, but her face is free of wrinkles. She has shiny, blond hair, and when she sees Brielle, her eyes fill with tears.

"Oh, my sweet girl."

"I'm okay," Brielle insists as she's pulled in for a firm hug. "A little unsettled, but I'm fine."

Sophia cups Brielle's face in her hands and stares into her eyes, keeping perfectly silent for a long moment.

"There," Sophia says, "that should help for a while."

"Thank you. Miss Sophia, I'd like to introduce you to—"

"Cassien Winslow," the older woman says and crosses to me, her shrewd, blue eyes fixed on mine. "We've been waiting for you, haven't we?"

"You have?"

She steps closer. "You don't know?"

"I have no idea what you're talking about."

She takes my hand and closes her eyes. Suddenly, electricity shoots through my arm and down my spine. A quick movie of still images flashes through my mind. Brielle and I together, naked. Tears. Fear. Fire. Joy.

Holy shit.

"What was that?" I ask.

"A taste of what's to come," she says and leans in close to whisper words meant for only my ears. "You need to be clear of mind and strong of will for what's coming for you, Cassien Winslow."

"What's coming?"

"I can't tell you that. I know you're confused, but you were made for this. Literally. You're one of the six."

I frown, but she doesn't continue. She turns to Brielle. "What were your questions, dear?"

"We need to go to the police," Brielle says. "Cash is with the FBI, but we need local law enforcement, and I don't know who to go see that might actually believe what I have to say and not just blow me off as a loon."

"The police that worked with Mal's grandmother are all retired," Sophia says.

"Oh, that's too bad," Brielle replies.

"I'm sure we can ask to speak with whoever is in charge of missing persons and go from there," I suggest, then find all three pairs of eyes on me. "What? We have information about missing women. That's how it works."

"Not for us," Sophia shoots back. "Not everyone trusts the words of a witch, Mr. Winslow."

"Is that what you are, Miss Sophia?"

She flicks one finger, and suddenly, I'm in the center of a strong wind, swirling around me. Just me. I go from hot to cold and back again until she flicks that finger once more and everything calms.

"Point taken." I smile at the older woman. "I meant no offense."

"Oh, none taken, dear. That was just a friendly demonstration."

Mal and Brielle laugh.

"I suggest you talk to a man named Asher," Sophia says.

"Have you worked with him before?" I ask.

"No, I've never met him." Sophia's calm eyes meet mine. "I know things. Asher will help you. And, Cassien, you need to call your mother."

My eyes widen. "What do you know of my mother?"

"Just call her," Sophia says, then she turns to Brielle and kisses her cheek. "They'll keep talking. Listen carefully."

"Yes, ma'am."

∼

"She didn't answer?" Brielle asks when I shove my cell into my pocket and hold the door of the NOPD headquarters open for her.

"No. I'll try again when we're finished here."

Now I'm worried. My mom has battled health issues for the last several years. I text Andy and ask him if he's heard from her today. Hopefully, he has.

"How can I help you?" a uniformed woman asks from behind bulletproof plexiglass. Her name tag reads *Lewis*.

"Is there an Asher that works here?" Brielle asks. "I'm sorry, I don't know his last name."

"Lieutenant Smith," Lewis says and nods. "I'll call back and see if he's in his office."

"Appreciate it," I say with a smile, and we wait while Lewis makes the call, talks into the phone, and then nods.

"He'll be up to get you in just a moment."

"Thank you," Brielle says, her smile forced as she walks to the other side of the small waiting area with me.

"What's wrong?"

"Lots of shadows here," she says with a sigh. "But they're all shadows. Not apparitions. She has one looking over her shoulder."

"Wow."

Brielle nods. "This building is two hundred years old, so it's not unusual for there to be lots of activity. It's just not part of my usual routine, and—"

"You don't like surprises," I finish for her.

"Hello."

We turn at the man's voice. He's tall with jet-black hair and tanned skin.

"Asher?"

His eyes narrow on Brielle. "Yes, I'm Lieutenant Asher Smith."

"Lieutenant, I'm Cash Winslow. I'm with the FBI, but I'm here in an unofficial capacity. Also, I'm armed."

I show Asher my badge and my gun, much to Brielle's surprise.

"I didn't know you carried a *gun*," she hisses.

"Thanks for the heads-up," Asher says. "I'll ask you to leave your weapon with Lewis. We'll give you a receipt for it and give it back when you leave."

"Understood," I reply. It's standard procedure.

Once my gun is locked away and I have my receipt, Asher leads us back through the bullpen to his office. He shuts the door and gestures for us to sit.

"How can I help you?"

Brielle licks her lips and glances over at me. "I don't know where to start."

"Start at the beginning," I urge her. "That's always the best route."

She nods, looks at Asher, and starts her story.

"I see the dead."

Asher's brows climb into his hairline, but he listens quietly as she walks him through all of the events, step by step, from the night I met her until now.

Before he can reply once she's finished, there's a knock on his door, and a woman pokes her head in. "The body found this morning has been identified. Tammy Holmes."

"Thanks."

The female officer nods and shuts the door behind her.

"I think we're going to have to come back to this," Asher says. "I have a full plate right now—"

"I know what happened to her," Brielle says, her voice taking on a hint of desperation now.

Asher's eyes narrow on Brielle. "Go on."

"She was beaten severely. Her face was almost no longer recognizable." Brielle shakes her head, then describes the way the victim was cut open, and all of the other atrocities done to her.

When she finishes, Asher sits back in his chair, staring across his desk silently.

"You don't believe me," Brielle whispers.

"This is New Orleans," Asher says. "I've seen a lot of things in this town. But we haven't released any of that information to the press."

"I don't need you to," Brielle says, raising her chin.

"Okay, then tell me how you can help. Were you there? Did you *see* him do those things to her?"

"No, I see things after the fact. As I said, I see dead people. The girls came to me, but they haven't told me how to find them yet, just that I *have* to find them. I already told you that."

"Listen. I have a dozen missing girls, all with the same MO. We finally found one in the bayou this morning, which just confirms my worst suspicions. I need more to go on. The fact that they're simply *dead* doesn't help me. I need to know where, how, when."

"I know," Brielle whispers.

"What do you do for the FBI?" Asher asks me.

"I'm a profiler."

He looks between Brielle and me, then slides his card over to me. "Keep me posted. In an official capacity, I'm not ashamed to admit that I could use you on this case, Cash."

"I can ask to be assigned to it," I offer.

"Let me request it, officially," Asher says. "I'll put that through this morning."

"You're going to let us help?" Brielle asks.

"Him," Asher says, pointing to me. "Because he has a badge and the knowledge I need. But I want to know if and when you know more."

"Okay."

We stand to walk out of the office. Brielle walks out first, and Asher asks me to hang back.

"I also want you to keep an eye on *her*," he says quietly. "For protection, and to make sure she's not dicking with us."

"She's not," I assure him. "And I know you're bringing me on so you can keep an eye on us. This isn't my first rodeo."

"As long as we understand each other."

# CHAPTER 8

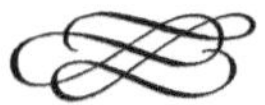

## BRIELLE

"At least he didn't look at me like I'm crazy," I mutter when we walk out of the police station, Cash tucking his gun back into its holster under his pant leg. "Why didn't I know you've been carrying that?"

"You never asked me," he says with a crooked grin. He pulls his phone out of his pocket and frowns down at it.

"What's wrong?"

"Andy says he hasn't heard from our mom today. I'll try to call her again." He holds the phone to his ear, listening to it ring. "Mom! I've been trying to reach you all morning."

His shoulders sag in relief, and I slip my hand into his free one, giving it a supportive squeeze.

"Are you feeling okay?"

I tune out the conversation and glance behind me. There are only two girls following me now.

Tammy's gone.

Is it because they found her body and now she can be at peace?

Is *peace* what they each want?

I wish I could talk to them, understand what in the world is going on.

I wonder if the only way to figure this out is to allow myself to dream-walk again. To ask questions and be more present in the moment and less afraid.

To be fair, it was a surprise last time.

But if I'm more prepared, I might be able to make it work in my favor.

"I'll talk to you soon."

Cash hangs up and sighs in relief.

"How is she?"

"Tired," he says. "She says she's just tired, but I talked her into going to the doctor."

"I'm glad. I suppose we should stop in to see Millie at the café. And I should call Daphne."

"No."

I stop on the sidewalk and stare up at Cash. "What? Why?"

"No, we're going to take a few hours just for us."

I'll admit, I was embarrassed last night when I blurted out that he hadn't kissed me yet. I'd like to chalk it up to exhaustion and sexual frustration.

But it's probably more about me being socially awkward.

"Say something," he says.

"What do you want to do?"

"Anything, as long as it's with you, we're not talking about murder or death, and I can get to know you better."

"You want to go on a date? At eleven in the morning?"

"Dates happen at any time of day," he reminds me. "And, yes, that's what I want. Let's take a break. We've done everything we can for now. Until Asher or my boss calls to let me know I'm officially part of the investigation, there's nothing more for us to do."

He brushes his knuckles down my cheek.

"I'd like some time alone with you."

"Death follows me wherever I go," I warn him, but he just smiles.

"Yes, but we don't have to dwell on it, do we?" He kisses my nose and leads me back to my apartment and his car, which he parked at the curb yesterday. "I want to take you somewhere."

"Okay." I sit in the passenger seat. Once he's started the car, he pulls away and heads across town, away from the French Quarter.

"I asked my brother to tell me where his favorite restaurant is away from the Quarter," Cash informs me. "I think we need a little break from there. We'll have a nice lunch, then go from there."

"It's not part of my usual routine, but I admit that it sounds nice." I settle back against the leather of the seat and take a deep breath. It feels good to let someone else make plans. "I work tonight."

"No."

My head whips around so I can stare at him. "Excuse me?"

"Don't you think you should take some time off until we get a handle on this?"

"No, I don't." I shift in my seat to face him fully. "First of all, you don't get to tell me what I can and can't do, Cash. Second, I have to work. I have bills to pay. And trust me when I say it's not cheap to live in the Quarter."

"This sicko's taking girls, torturing and killing them, and they look exactly like *you*."

"I'm well aware."

Two of them are sitting in the back seat of his car, but there's no need to tell him that.

"Give me one week," Cash says as he guides the vehicle into a parking space and turns to me with beseeching, green eyes. "Please, just give me a week. I'll pay your rent this month. Hell, I'll pay for everything."

"That's not—"

"I'm scared," he admits and reaches for my hand. He kisses my knuckles and then looks back at me. "If he were to take you, I would never forgive myself."

"One week," I confirm. "I'll give you that. I'll make a call once we're inside."

"Just like that?"

"I don't know many men who would freely admit that they're afraid," I reply. "Most give an order, stomp their foot, and expect the little woman to fall in line."

"I'm not an asshole."

"No. You're not. So, yes, I'll agree to a week. You don't have to pay my rent, though. I'll be fine."

"Thank you," he whispers, then gets out of the car. He opens my door and leads me inside a new building that houses a Mexican restaurant. "New construction. Not remodeled, *brand new.* No ghosts here."

I smile, touched that he put some thought into choosing the place. Of course, there are ghosts everywhere, no matter when the building was built.

But I won't tell him that and rain on his parade.

"I hope you like Mexican food."

"It's actually my favorite."

~

"I ate my weight in chips." I pat my belly as he drives back toward my apartment. We agreed to head over because his boss called while we were having fried ice cream. Cash is officially part of the investigation. "Why can't you stop eating them once you start? They're like crack."

"It's the fried ice cream that does me in," he confesses. He pulls up in front of my building and follows me upstairs.

"When do you have to go report in?"

"Tomorrow morning," he says with a smile. "I can get most of the information remotely. And I'm not leaving you today."

"I don't—"

"Need to be babysat," he finishes for me. "I know." He shuts the door behind us and advances on me, prowling.

The look in his amazing green eyes is hot as fuck.

"I'm not here to babysit you," he says as his hands slowly loop their way over my hips and around my back.

"No?"

"Nope." He kisses my forehead. "I have other things in mind that don't involve sitting."

"No sitting."

He smiles and kisses my cheek. His body is warm and firm, and his hands rub delicious circles over my back.

"Not unless we decide to rechristen that chair Daphne talked about," he says. His hands glide over my butt, and he suddenly lifts me effortlessly, supporting me with his palms under my ass, carrying me to the bedroom.

"Are you ever going to kiss me?"

"Eventually." The lips that I want so desperately on mine twitch into a sly smile. He lays me down in the middle of the bed and crawls over me, dragging his nose over my clothes, sending shivers down my spine and causing goosebumps to rise.

My back instinctively arches off the bed in invitation.

"God, you're amazing," he whispers against my neck. He places a wet kiss there, then drags his lips up to my ear. "Sexy as hell. Keeping my hands to myself for a whole week has been complete torture."

"But not keeping your lips to yourself?"

He smiles down at me. "Now I feel a lot of pressure to do this right. What if I'm really bad at it, and you're expecting fireworks?"

"You're not bad at it."

566

"You don't know." He kisses the apple of my cheek. "I could be a dud in the kiss department."

He kisses the corner of my mouth, teasing me relentlessly.

Finally, *finally*, he presses those hot lips to mine and sinks in.

This man doesn't merely kiss and call it a day.

No, he kisses like it's his damn job. Like kissing me is the only thing in the world he can think about.

As if he's wanted to kiss me for decades.

I sigh, push my fingers through the hair at the nape of his neck, and hold on as my body comes to life under him. His hand cups my breast over my shirt, his thumb brushing over my puckered nipple.

We're fully clothed, and I've never been so turned on in all my life.

"So sweet," he whispers before changing the angle of the kiss and diving in all over again. I'm drowning, and it's the most intoxicating thing I've ever experienced.

"Am I a dud?"

I lick my lips and narrow my eyes as if I'm thinking it over.

Honestly, I just can't make coherent thoughts form yet.

"Brielle."

"I like the way you say my name."

He quirks a brow. "How's that?"

"Like it feels good on your tongue."

"Your name isn't the only thing that feels good." He licks along my jawline. "You make me crazy, you know?"

"No, I didn't know."

"Well, you do now." His lips cover mine again, and his hand tugs my shirt out of my pants. He kisses and undresses me as if it's effortless.

As if he does it every day.

The air is cool against my naked skin.

"Goosebumps," he whispers before suckling my nipple, then blowing on it.

I had no idea it could get harder than it was.

But it can. It does.

And he's still dressed.

"If I'd known you were hiding all of this talent, I would have attacked you days ago."

He chuckles and lets me pull his shirt over his head so I can get my hands on his warm, smooth skin.

He's tanned.

Toned.

Has muscles for days.

And for now, he's all mine.

"You look like the cat who ate the canary," he says.

"Oh, I'm pleased for sure." And in just a mere ten seconds, I have him naked, his heavy cock resting on my belly as he kisses me silly.

I work him over, gently at first, and then with more aggression as he hardens more in my grasp.

"Condoms," he mutters.

"Drawer." I point to the table beside the bed and grin when he finds an unopened box.

A girl should always be prepared.

Even girls who never get laid.

You just never know.

I take the little packet from him, tear it open, and with my gaze glued to his, I roll it down his length, enjoying the way his jaw clenches from the pleasure.

"Keep touching me like that," he mutters, pinning both of my wrists over my head with one of his big hands, and positioning himself at my slick entrance, "and I'll blow this before we even get started."

"Oh, I'm having a good time so far."

"Just good?" He pushes inside of me and seats himself, pausing. "We can do much better than *good*, sweetheart."

Before I can retort, he covers my lips with his again and starts to move, rendering me completely thoughtless.

All I can do is feel.

Him. Us.

And how this seems familiar.

~

"PAST LIVES," Millie suggests the following morning. "That would explain it."

I just finished telling her about the day before. Sex for hours. Sighs and laughter.

More orgasms than should be allowed in any twenty-four-hour period.

And how it all felt like we'd done it before.

"I don't even know for sure if I believe in that."

"I do," Daphne says. "It's written somewhere, isn't it?"

I frown at my baby sister. "What, past lives? Like in a book? I mean, people have been telling fictional stories about it for ages."

"No." Daphne shakes her head impatiently. "It's on the edge of my memory, but I swear we've seen it somewhere before."

"The book," Millie says, snapping her fingers. "Remember that old book we found when we were kids?"

"Oh, yeah. Where is that?" I ask, shocked when Millie shrugs. "What do you mean you don't know?"

"Mama took it away from me when I was sixteen and refused to give it back. It was just a few weeks before we all moved out of there."

"You never told us that," Daphne says.

"I was afraid you'd get mad at me for getting caught," Millie admits. "I don't have it, guys."

We look back and forth between us, dread settling in.

"We said we'd never go back there," I remind them.

"That was before," Daphne says. "We *need* that book. Grandma wrote it for us."

Our grandmother was a witch, and she wrote a book of spells and prophecies and random magical knowledge that she hid in the house. We found it when I was about fifteen, and we all pored through every page.

We didn't know Grandma practiced the craft.

No one ever told us.

Then again, our parents mostly ignored us.

"How are you able to make your potions?" I ask Millie.

"Lots of practice. I memorized most of them, and whenever I have a question, I just ask Miss Sophia and add it to my own grimoire."

"I can't believe you never told us." I rub my stomach. It's already full of butterflies—and not the exciting kind—at the idea of going back there.

That house almost killed us all once.

"We have to go together," Daphne says.

"Mom won't let us in," I remind them. "She's crazier than ever, and mean on top of it. She certainly won't willfully give us that book."

"It's ours," Millie says. "I never should have given it to her."

"It's not like you had a choice back then," Daphne reminds her, patting her shoulder. "Sometimes, you got the worst of it."

Millie is the spitting image of our mother. Tall and blond and absolutely beautiful. Once upon a time, our mom was, too.

Not anymore.

"We don't necessarily need the book right this minute."

My sisters stare back at me.

"Past lives, apparitions, evil things happening," Daphne says, ticking off the items on her fingers. "Sure would be helpful to have a handbook right about now."

"Okay, I get it." I sigh deeply. "I don't like it, but I get it."

"When should we go?" Millie asks.

"Tomorrow." I square my shoulders as if I'm preparing for war.

Because I am.

"I want to go with Cash. There's strength in numbers, like he said."

"Are you sure you want to show Cash where we grew up?" Daphne covers my hand. "It's not pretty. No one would blame you if you wanted to keep him as far away from that as possible."

"He won't leave me because we grew up poor." I shrug. "I don't know how I know that, but I do. I'm not proud of where we grew up or how we did, but I'm proud of what we've accomplished since we got away from there. I think Cash would prefer to go with us than have us go alone."

"She's right," Millie says. "He should go."

"Tomorrow it is, then."

# CHAPTER 9

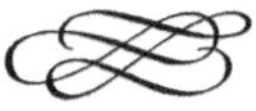

*"I was born with the devil in me. I could not help the fact that I was a murderer, no more than the poet can help the inspiration to sing."*
~H. H. Holmes

"Y ou weren't there!" He slaps her across the face, disgusted when she cries out in pain. "You think that hurts? You wait. Just wait, you little piece of shit."

"Please," she cries, begging. She's beseeched him for days, pleaded with the monster to let her go. "I won't tell anyone, mister. Honest. I just want to go home."

"Shut up!" He hits her again. Rage is a beast roaring through him. It's Tuesday. Brielle *always* works on Tuesday. She has Monday off, and that's when he rests and plays with his toys.

On Tuesdays, he goes back to following her.

But she stood him up tonight.

She'll pay dearly for that.

"I was going to go easy on you," he mutters as he assembles his tools. "I was in such a good mood, Brielle. I was going to make it sweet."

The smell of urine and blood hangs in the air, still fresh from late last night when the electricity finally took the life of that last one. She moaned in pleasure for hours, screamed his name as she came.

She loved it, just like he promised her she would.

But it was eventually too much for her.

It always is.

"Let her go, you sick fuck!"

He spins and pins the girl he took two hours ago with a look that has made others piss themselves in the past.

But not this one.

No, she's feisty.

She shrugged off his medicine, and she's been fighting against her restraints the whole time.

He'll break her, just like the wild horse she is. He'll remind her of her place, and who's in charge.

And when the life finally leaves her filthy body, he'll celebrate.

"Now, Brielle, that's not polite."

"I'm Sarah Chandler, you sick son of a bitch. And I'm going to kill you."

This makes him smile. Oh, he loves a challenge. Secretly, he sometimes enjoys it when they fight back just a little.

He can't let them know that, though. No, he has to maintain his standards.

She's going to be fun.

But first, he has other plans. He turns back to the whiny little bitch on his table and snarls.

"You made me mad tonight, Brielle. Do you know what happens when I get angry?"

"Please," she whines. "I swear, I didn't do nothin' to you, mister."

"You're not so innocent." He hits her again with the leather belt he keeps by the table, just for fun this time. Her flesh immediately welts and turns bright red. "Now that's a pretty sight."

There's crying and mewling behind him. Six women can make more noise than a barn full of pigs.

"No one can hear you." His calm is back as he turns to look at each of them. "You can scream and cry all you want, Brielle, but no one will ever hear you. You're never going to leave here."

He breathes deeply, satisfied that his little toy has soiled herself.

He reaches for the hacksaw.

"Here we go, Brielle. Now, be a good girl."

The work is messy. It's a good thing he bought the heavy rubber aprons years ago to keep his clothes clean.

And, of course, he covers his hands, hair, mouth, and eyes so there's no chance he can contaminate his toys with DNA.

That wouldn't do.

The blood spatters and sprays as he cuts. Piercing screams rend the air. Thrashing ensues.

And then, her blue eyes focus on his as, little by little, the life slowly drains from her.

"Ah, that's a good girl."

He's hard. Killing always leaves his cock pulsing, but he never gives himself the pleasure of release.

Not for this one.

Or any of these.

But soon.

# CHAPTER 10

## BRIELLE

"It's bad." Cash and I are sitting in the backseat of Daphne's car. He holds my hand tightly. "Like, whatever you consider to be bad, multiply it by about a thousand, and it's still not bad enough."

"I'm sure it's fine," he replies and kisses my hand.

"No, it's not fine," Millie says from the passenger seat. "B's not lying. In fact, it could be worse than what she's describing."

"It is," Daphne confirms, and my stomach clenches.

Maybe they were right. Perhaps bringing Cash to my mom's house was a bad idea.

Except, that place is a house of horrors for me, and Cash seems to ground me. Maybe he can steady all three of us. I know that's asking a lot, but when it comes to this, I'm asking.

And I'm not sorry.

Daphne turns off the freeway and points the car deep into the bayou.

"Did y'all grow up in this house?" Cash asks.

"Until Daphne was about fourteen," Millie says. "Then Brielle was old enough to move out, and she took us with her."

"Mama didn't try to stop her," Daphne adds.

"Bri saved our lives," Millie says quietly.

"That might be a bit of an exaggeration," I reply, but both of my sisters shake their heads emphatically.

"You know it's true."

"Are you saying you would have died from neglect?" Cash asks.

"Psychological and spiritual warfare," I say calmly.

"Jesus."

"Pretty sure Jesus and the rest of the deities out there helped keep us alive," Daphne says. "Pastor Cliff spoke with us. Prayed for us, often. I might have gone crazy without him."

"Witches who believe in Jesus?" Cash asks, a smile on his face.

"Don't overthink it. We're complicated women," Millie replies. "I forgot how damn creepy it is out here in the middle of nowhere."

"Live oaks are beautiful *and* creepy," Cash agrees, watching the bayou pass by. "And this looks like it belongs in a horror movie."

We all go silent as Daphne navigates onto another smaller road, and then it turns to dirt.

"You just went white as a ghost," Cash murmurs to me.

"I've never hated a place more." I take a deep breath. "You ladies know what to do."

We're reinforcing our shields, protecting our minds and our hearts from the horrors we're about to see. Millie casts a spell of protection around Cash, as well, and I'm grateful for not only that but also the protection potions she put in our coffees this morning.

We need all the help we can get.

The lane narrows even more, the path overgrown with low-hanging limbs and Spanish moss. It clearly isn't traveled often, if at all. With the exception of Daphne visiting the last time she came here.

"A part of the road washed out during a storm at some point, so it's going to be extra bumpy here in a minute. Hold on," Daphne says as she slows down, taking it easy over the ruts. She turns another tight corner, and there it is.

"Holy shit," Millie whispers when Daphne stops the car. We all sit in silence for a moment, staring at the house we grew up in.

It doesn't look habitable. Actually, it's *not* habitable, but Mama lives there anyway.

It was once a grand, three-story plantation home with a deep, wrap-around porch. Gas lanterns hung from the porch, along with a swing on either side of the red front door.

It's no longer grand.

The porch has separated completely from the main structure and caved in on itself in several places. The space around the front door looks to be intact, but I'll suggest we go up one at a time when we approach, just in case.

"Someone lives here?" Cash asks quietly. "Has it always looked like this?"

"No. Not when we were kids, at least. But this is what the bayou will do to a building if it's not maintained. It reclaims the land."

"Every single window is broken out," Millie says. "And in the stifling heat of summer. How does she not get heatstroke?"

"Who cares?" Daphne asks. "Let's get this over with."

"You three are with me, at all times," Cash says. "I'm armed."

"We can't fight what's in there with a gun," I inform him but squeeze his hand gratefully. "But, yes, we'll stick with you."

We climb out of the car and make our way gingerly up the dilapidated front steps.

I pound on the door.

There's no movement for a while. Just the sound of cicadas and frogs and whatever animal is rustling through the bushes.

I pound again.

"This was a bad idea," Millie says and turns to me. "What do you see?"

"The usual. More shadows than I can count, all staring at us. Walking the grounds, sitting where that old swing used to be over there."

"Just standing here gives me the heebie-jeebies," Daphne says. "I will *not* touch anything inside. I'm sorry, guys, but even the doorknobs—"

"Agreed," I interrupt and then pound on the door again.

"Go away!" Mama yells from inside.

"Well, we know she's alive," Cash mutters.

"Mama, it's us," I yell back. "We need to talk to you."

The door is yanked open, almost coming clean off the hinges.

"What the fuck do you want?"

I don't know who this woman is. The tall, beautiful person who raised us is gone. She's hunched over, her blond hair gray and stringy. Her teeth are missing. Her eyes are cloudy, the pupils dilated as if she sits in the dark all the time.

From the stench coming through the door, I'd wager that she hasn't seen a bar of soap in years.

"We need to ask you some questions," I reply. "Do you know who we are?"

"Don't matter who you are," she says. "Don't care."

"We're your daughters," Daphne reminds her. For a moment, it looks like her eyes might clear and that she'll remember, but then she just frowns.

"Don't got no chillins."

"Yes, you do," Millie says kindly. "We won't take up too much of your time. We just have some questions."

"Don't know nothin'," she mutters but moves back away from the door to let us in. All four of us cover our mouths and noses with our shirts, overwhelmed by the smell of filth and death.

"Mama, are there dead animals in here?" I ask.

"Hafta eat, don't I?"

We look at each other and follow after her as she shuffles through garbage and insects. Where the dining room used to be is a pile of debris from the old bedroom—*my* bedroom —above it. The ceiling collapsed at some point. My old twin bed, such as it is, lies on the top of the heap.

The mountains of garbage are horrifying as we move through the old living space toward the kitchen. But it's the stench that I'll never forget.

I'll have to burn these clothes later.

I'll never get the smell out of them.

"Where do you sleep?" Cash asks, and Mama rounds on him.

"Who the hell are you?"

"This is my good friend, Cash," I say. I bet most girls don't introduce the guy they're hot after to their mom that way.

Lucky me.

"I don't talk to no mens," Mom says.

"It's a good question," Millie says. "With the second floor collapsed, where *do* you sleep, Mama?"

"Oh, where'd my manners go?" I frown as I watch our mother smile and push back her hair as if she has unexpected company. "I meant to clean up 'fore'n you came by, but I must've got busy with the chillins."

"Your home looks fine," Daphne says as if she's talking to a stranger, and I immediately take her cue. My youngest sister has done her best not to touch anything, but I can see the strain on her face.

"I agree," I say. "You keep a lovely home."

"Well, thank you kindly," Mama says with a toothless, satisfied grin. "Hasn't been easy to keep up with them girls since I done killed their daddy."

She winks, to my horror, and gestures for us to follow her to the den off the kitchen.

I trade glances with the others and follow her, surprised at what we see.

Where the rest of the house is utterly condemnable, this room isn't so bad. She keeps the door closed from the rest of the house. She has a simple twin bed made neatly with old blankets that I recognize from my childhood. There's an oil lamp and a rocking chair in the corner.

The chair that used to be under the stairs.

The one where a shadow still sits, rocking back and forth.

"That thing never stops movin'," Mom says and shrugs. "Probably uneven boards or somethin'."

"Or a ghost," Daphne whispers, catching Mama's attention.

"We don't talk like that in this house, young 'un," she says sternly. "There be no ghosts here, y'hear me?"

"Yes, ma'am," Daphne says quietly.

"These girls, always carry'n on about ghosts and goblins." She shakes her head as if it's all nonsense. "Now, what can I do for you?"

"Mama, do you remember a book that you took away from Millie when she was a teenager?"

Mom narrows her dull eyes as if she's thinking.

"Can't read," she says simply, surprising me.

I didn't know that.

"It was a book that *I* was reading, and you took it away from me," Millie adds. "I really need it back."

"I burn all the books here so I have heat," Mom replies with another shrug. "Probably burned that up, too."

"Do you mind if I look around for it?" Millie asks.

"You're plum stupid if you think you should wander around through this house. It's full of evil spirits," Mom says, shocking all of us.

One minute, we don't talk of ghosts.

The next, the place is full of evil spirits.

I mean…she's not wrong.

But her mental illness has clearly progressed so much that it's hard for her to make any sense.

"I'll be careful."

"Don't matter to me." Mom waves her off.

"Go with Cash," I say instantly. "None of us goes alone."

Cash squeezes my shoulder, then follows Millie out of the room.

"Y'all can sit," Mama offers, pointing to the bed as she sits in the rocking chair, right on the shadow. "We're not too fancy in this house."

"I'm fine," Daphne says immediately but smiles to soften the rejected offer. "How are you doing?"

"Same as always," Mama replies. "Ain't nothin' change 'round here."

Except the number of spirits. I don't know why, but they seem to have multiplied considerably. Doubled, maybe even tripled. Everywhere I look, another shadow lurks.

No wonder she's crazy.

I would be, too.

"You know, if you ever want to leave this place, there are people who can help you."

Mama narrows her eyes at me. "Tryin' to run me outta my own house?"

"No, ma'am," I say immediately. "It was just an idea."

"This place is nice enough. My girls never complain."

"Your daughters are all grown," Daphne reminds her. "We're your daughters, Mama. Remember? We all grew up and moved away."

She frowns as if she's confused. "But I talk to y'all every day. You visit me here all the time."

One of two things is happening here. Either Mom is simply certifiably nuts, or the spirits here are taking our shapes to mess with her.

At this point, it could be either.

Or both.

"I haven't set foot in this house in more than a decade," I remind her.

"Who are you?"

"I'm Brielle."

"Brielle's dead. He killed her."

My skin prickles. My heart skips a beat.

"Who killed her?"

"Killed who?"

I sigh in frustration. She can't focus on a conversation long enough to make a logical statement.

"What do you do here all day with no electricity or running water?" Daphne asks.

"There's water out back," she says, pointing over her shoulder toward the swamp. "I wash my clothes in there."

She washes her clothes in swamp water.

It's a wonder she hasn't been eaten by 'gators or died from a bacterial infection.

"I just talk to my friends, an' I keep a pretty garden outside. Did you see it?"

"No, ma'am. There's a garden?" Daphne asks. Our mother did like to garden when we were kids. We spent a lot of time out there with her.

"I'll show you."

She pulls herself out of the chair, and we follow her through the house to the back entrance, right next to the door that leads to the storage space under the stairs.

I spent the majority of my childhood under there.

I wait for Mom and Daphne to go outside before I open the little door really quick to poke my head in.

It hasn't changed since the last time I was in there with my sisters. It's as if Mama never went in there, but she must have at some point. She pulled the rocking chair out.

I close the door and join Daphne and Mama outside, just around the corner of the house.

Mom's smiling.

Daphne's face is white.

"Can you please tell Brielle what you told me?" Daphne asks her.

"Oh, is Brielle here?" Mama glances over at me and frowns. "I thought you were dead, Brielle. That's what he told me."

"Who told you that?"

"Don't remember." She rubs her nose with the back of her hand. "Anyway, he's buried right here."

"Who?"

"Your daddy." She rolls her eyes. "Never liked him. Mean son of a bitch."

"He was mean," I agree with a nod and stare at all the blooming roses. There must be twenty bushes, a riot of beautiful color. "You must spend a lot of time out here, taking care of your roses."

"Nah, he just keeps fertilizing them. Mean old man." She shakes her head. "Told me I was crazy. Can you believe that?"

"No, ma'am," Daphne and I reply in unison.

"Kept callin' me that over and over again until I showed him just how crazy I could be. Buried him right here."

Daphne swallows hard, her hand hovering over a bloom.

I need to get her out of here.

"We found it," Millie says as she and Cash come around the side of the house. "We saw you out here."

"You have a beautiful garden," Cash says.

"Who are you?" Mama demands, her face immediately scrunching in rage. "I don't like the mens around here. Git outta here. Y'all leave, now."

"Gladly," Daphne says as we hurry around the house to the car. She starts it, and once we're all inside, she peels out of the driveway, watching Mama in the rearview. "Brielle."

I look back, shocked to find the shadows joining Mama, huddling around her. They're pouring out of the house, coming around the sides, and they cover her, wrapping their arms around her.

It's the creepiest fucking thing I've ever seen in my life.

"You can see that?" I ask Daphne.

"We all can," Millie says and sighs.

"I can't," Cash says.

"You're lucky." I rub my hands over my face. "But at least we have the book. Where was it?"

"Upstairs, in her old bedroom," Millie says.

"It's still intact?"

"If you can call it that," Cash replies. "We looked around the entire house, just to check everything out."

"I wrapped us both in my shields," Millie says. "And it's a damn good thing I did. Did you guys notice how out of control the activity is there?"

"It's like a hotspot for paranormal activity," I say, thinking it over. "I never considered that before, but that might be the case. Perhaps the house is built on a burial ground, or something so horrible happened there in the past that the ghosts are drawn to."

"And because we're sensitive, it fucked with us as kids," Daphne says, nodding. "It makes sense."

"Now that we're gone, along with our spells and potions of protection, there's nothing there to protect Mama from the activity," Millie says. "You guys, I know she was a bad mother and, honestly, she's a bad *human being*. But no one deserves that kind of torment."

It doesn't surprise me when the dreams come. After spending the morning doing my best to deflect the atrocities in my mother's house, I figured I'd have a difficult time in my dreams.

*"Come on."*

*Now, there are four. When I went to sleep, there were still only two spirits following me, but now there are four.*

*"I want to help you. Tell me what to do."*

*"You have to follow us," one of the girls says, and relief immediately sets in. They can hear me. This one's new. She has a slit throat, but aside from that, she looks whole. "Come on."*

*The next thing I know, I'm standing in a room. It's good-sized, sectioned off into different areas. In one corner, there's what looks like a workbench with shelves above it, lined with tools.*

*A chair sits in another corner. It looks like an old-timey electric chair with leather straps on the arms and legs.*

*In the third corner is a door, presumably leading to the rest of the house.*

*And then there's the fourth corner, where there are currently four women tied to what looks like toddler beds. The tiny mattresses are bare. Some have blood and pee stains.*

*The smell in the room is as bad as my mother's house, but lingering with the stench of feces and urine is the metallic scent of blood.*

*So much blood.*

*And fear.*

*The girls can't see me. I try to talk to them, to get their attention, but they can't hear me. I need to ask them questions.*

*Where are they? How did they get here? Who brought them here?*

*Without those answers, this is pointless.*

*"Who are you?"*

*I'm surprised when another girl glances up and talks to me.*

*"I'm Brielle."*

*Her eyes widen, and her lip quivers. "He's going to kill us. He's going to kill all of us. And then he's going to kill you."*

*"Who is he?"*

*She shakes her head. "He's the devil."*

# CHAPTER 11

## CASH

"I dreamed," she says as she walks into the kitchen from the bedroom. Her hair is a mess of dark waves around her beautiful face, her blue eyes look sleepy and tormented.

I've only known her a week, and yet I miss the happy look she had in her eyes before all of this started. She was quick to smile. To flirt.

Now, it seems she's wrapped in an invisible, heavy blanket.

I'm going to do my best to get her back to the happy woman I first met.

"Talk to me." I pull her onto my lap, and she reaches for my coffee, making me smile. I don't mind sharing it with her. Hell, I'll share my life with her if she'll have me.

That thought shocks the hell out of me.

My job is too intense to have a family. It's best to be single, without ties to anyone.

But now that Brielle's in my life, I can't imagine it without her.

"More walking," she says with a sigh and leans her head on my shoulder. "But this time, I was in the room where he holds them."

"What?"

"He has four right now. One saw me, but I didn't get much information out of her."

"So, you don't know where he's holding them?"

"No. And it pisses me off, Cash."

"Well, it doesn't make me happy, either. I have to be in the office in about an hour."

"I'm coming with you." She kisses my cheek, then hops off my lap and sets to work making her own cup of coffee. "I need to talk to Asher."

"You don't want me to talk to him?"

"No. I have questions, and I need to prove to him that I'm not a whack job."

"I think if that was the case, he wouldn't have asked for my help," I remind her as I slide my hands over her hips and around her waist to hug her from behind. "You smell good."

"Neroli oil," she says, smiling up at me. "It's good for anxiety. And, I'll be honest, this whole thing has me more than a little anxious."

"You wouldn't be human if it didn't." I kiss her hair, then turn her in my arms so I can pull her in for a strong hug. "Maybe you need a break. I'll see if Andy and Felicia can join us for dinner."

"A distraction might be nice, especially after being in the bayou yesterday."

It was an experience I *never* want to repeat. I was honest when I told her that very little surprises me.

And yet, I was shocked as hell.

The living conditions were foul. The woman who birthed the three girls I've come to care about was…sick. That's the best word I can use for it. She is mentally ill for sure, and that's probably the root of the neglect of her children. But the fact that she admitted to killing her husband means that I'm under obligation to have her arrested.

Though it wouldn't matter.

She's already locked up, undergoing a far more brutal punishment than the government could ever throw at her.

"My sisters warned me not to take you there."

"Why?"

She leans back to quirk her brow. "Come on. You know you want to dump me after seeing where I came from."

"Dump you? No. I don't want to do that." I kiss her forehead and make slow circles on her back with my palm. "I have about a billion questions, but I don't want to lose you."

"I can probably answer your inquiries."

"I think the one person who could answer the bulk of them the best is too mentally ill to do so. She belongs in an institution."

"I know." She rubs her face and then leans her forehead on my chest. "I know she does. But she'll never willingly leave that house. It has its claws in her."

"She admitted to killing your father."

"She did kill him." She looks up at me again. "And he continued tormenting my sisters and me for the better part of a decade afterwards. Speaking of him, I need to know what Daphne saw when she touched the roses yesterday. Whatever it was, it freaked her out."

"What made him stop tormenting you?"

"Millie met Miss Sophia, and she helped us get rid of him. He beat us repeatedly when he was alive, and then he taunted us from beyond the grave."

"A lovely man."

"He probably deserved much worse than what Mama gave him."

"Do you know how she killed him?"

"No, she never said. In fact, until yesterday, she never admitted to killing him—that I know of anyway."

"But you knew she did?"

"One day, he was there, being an asshole of epic proportions. Hours later, he was gone, she said he was never coming back, and we had a new shadow in the house. I was old enough to put two and two together."

"I see." I nod and back away from her. "I won't make any calls to have her picked up. But if I did, and they put her in an institution, it would be better than where she is now."

"Let's get through this, and then we can worry about my mother," she suggests. "One thing at a time."

"Deal."

∼

"So, you're telling me he's currently holding four more victims," Asher says, observing Brielle carefully.

"Yes."

"Because you saw it in a dream."

She blows out a breath and starts to pace. "There are now four girls following me. They came to me in the dream and told me to follow them. Then, the next thing I knew, I was in a room with four *living* girls. It looked like a torture chamber."

"How so?" He starts taking notes. "Tell me what it looked like."

"It was a big room." She closes her eyes and begins to describe a workbench with tools, an electric chair, and the beds where the girls were tied up. "It's filthy. They soil themselves there, and there's so much blood by the workbench. Mostly dry, but there was some fresh blood, as well."

"Look on the walls," I instruct her as if I'm talking to a hypnosis patient. "Are there photos? Is anything written there?"

"Nothing's written," she says quietly. "But above the workbench, he has a bunch of things pinned in a line."

"What is it?"

She opens her eyes and looks right at me. "Hair. Braided hair."

"How many?" Asher asks.

"Thirty-two."

I take a deep breath. "He's killed thirty-two girls since he started this phase of his hunt. The braids are his trophies."

"I hope you're right. Because if I can get my hands on that hair, I can positively identify the victims and give the families some answers," Asher says, then turns back to Brielle. "I need you to do this again, but I need more information. I need you to walk through that door and tell me who he is. And, most importantly, *where* he is."

"I don't know how to do that," Brielle says in frustration. "I don't know how it's happening in the first place, Asher. This is not one of my gifts. I'm a medium, and I have some psychic abilities, but dream-walking isn't something I know anything about. I've never done it before."

"Hey," Asher says, holding up his hand, his voice softer. "Brielle, I get it. This is scary, and…well, just plain shitty. I hate that it's in your head. But I have faith that you can do this."

"Why do you suddenly believe me?"

"I didn't *dis*believe you before," he says. "But we haven't told anyone that the bodies show evidence of electric shock torture. Or that their hair has been chopped."

She blinks, thinking it over.

"How many bodies have you found?"

"Six."

"Six out of thirty-two," I say calmly.

"You're the profiler," Asher says, turning to me. "Why aren't we finding all of them?"

"He doesn't want you to find the ones you have," I reply. "Where did you find them? The bayou?"

He narrows his eyes, and I keep talking.

"He's a sick fuck, but he's highly intelligent. He's dumping the bodies in the bayou because he knows they'll likely get eaten by critters and there won't be anything left of them. So, if you found them, it's because they didn't have time to get eaten."

"The most recent was found by a swamp tour group. They saw her floating in the water and fished her out."

"That's horrible," Brielle says softly. "I'm going to let you two do your jobs. I'm headed over to Millie's for the day. She and Daphne are already there poring through the book we fetched from Mama's yesterday. Maybe there are instructions in there for dream-walking."

"I'll take you."

She shakes her head no. "It's not far. I'll text you when I get there."

She kisses me, and then she's gone.

"Watching someone you love go through something this horrible is its own kind of torture," Asher says, watching me.

"I didn't think I was made for it. Love." I sit down again and sigh. "But she's it for me. And I've only known her for a week. It's fucking crazy."

"Not too crazy," he says, flashing a smile. "I didn't know my wife much longer than that when I knew she was it for me. And she was held and almost killed by a serial killer."

"Jesus. I'm sorry."

"It was a few years ago, and she's doing great now. But I know what it's like to be afraid for the woman you love. We're going to catch this bastard if it's the last thing I do. Now, the profile."

"He's intelligent," I continue. "Most of the bodies are long gone. Sadly, you'll never recover them. He isn't the type to bury them in the backyard or anything like that. But the braids are interesting. It tells me that it's likely the hair that draws him to his prey. The color, the length. What a killer chooses as his trophies is quite telling."

"Long, dark hair. Why that?"

"It's usually one of two things. Either he's killing his mother over and over again, or he's a jilted lover, and he's killing the woman who scorned him."

"That seems a bit dramatic." Asher rubs his fingers over his mouth in agitation. "They all look like Brielle."

"I know."

"That has to be the connection between her and the victims. Do the girls know, after they've died, that she's susceptible to being taken? Are they trying to warn all of the brunettes in town, but because Brielle has gifts, she's the only one who can see them?"

"All of those are great questions. But, honestly, I don't know. That could be the case, *or* it's Brielle that he's killing over and over again."

"Do you think it could be one of *her* jilted lovers?"

I didn't before. I hadn't considered it because what man likes to think about the dudes that have boned his girl before him?

But it does make sense.

"It's the only thing I can think of," I reply. "And, yes, I'll be asking her for a list of her former boyfriends tonight."

"No man likes to ask his woman for a list of the guys that she used to have sex with. I don't envy you."

"Yeah, it fucking sucks. But so does thirty-two dead girls, with at least four more being held. My ego can take it."

"I like you, Cash."

∾

"Are you asking me for a list of the men I've slept with?" Brielle asks. We're standing in Witches Brew with Daphne and Millie sitting nearby, all of them gawking at me.

"Hear me out."

"I mean, most men just ask for a number," Millie says to Daphne. "Like, *how many have you slept with?*' They never ask for a list of names."

"He's taking their hair as a trophy," I say, my eyes still on Brielle's. "They look like *you.* The spirits are coming to you as a warning. Or a plea for help."

"So, you think the killer is an ex-boyfriend?" Daphne asks. "Talk about a bitter dude."

"There are two," Brielle says simply, surprising me. "Devon Price and Simon Harp."

"Ew, you did it with Simon?" Millie asks, scrunching up her nose. Brielle rolls her eyes.

"Neither of them was jilted. Devon was a guy I dated briefly in college, but he moved on to my roommate, so that breakup was pretty self-explanatory."

"And the other?"

"He used to own the ghost tour company," she says. "I found out *after* the fact that he was married."

"I'll have Asher run a check on them," I mumble as I shoot the man a text, seething inside at the idea of Brielle being with men who clearly didn't care about or respect her.

"Anything else you want to know?" she asks tightly. "Favorite positions? Number of times, that sort of thing?"

"Now you're pissing me off."

"We're even then," she says. "I get that you're being a cop right now, but you're my… well, my something, and I don't feel comfortable with this conversation."

"Aww, isn't that sweet?" Daphne asks. "She called him her *something.*"

"Super sweet," Millie says, resting her chin on her hand.

"We're right here," I remind them both. "This isn't a show for your entertainment."

"You should have asked us to leave then," Daphne says with a shrug, not apologetic in the least.

"I need to find him," I say and reach for Brielle, pulling her to me. "I need to find this asshole so we can move on with our lives. I don't care who these idiots are. They were stupid enough to let you go. They're meaningless."

"Unless they're killing girls," Brielle says with a nod. "Okay. I'm hungry."

"Let's go eat, then."

❧

"I'm gonna go stay with your mom, Cash," Felicia says as we finish up some pecan pie for dessert. Brielle and I met up with Andy and his wife for a casual dinner, and it was the perfect thing to take our minds off everything going on.

"Really?" I frown. "Did she ask you to do that?"

"No, but when I spoke to her this morning, she said she was tired."

"That's what she told me the other day, as well," I say, nodding.

"I know it's almost impossible for Andy or you to go see her right now, so I'm gonna go check it all out. See how she is and find out if she needs anything. I wish we could talk her into moving here with us."

"She's a stubborn woman," Andy says, patting his wife's back. "And we appreciate you going to check on her."

"He's right, on both accounts," I say with a nod. "I've been worried about her. I'm glad you're going to check on her. Please let us know if she—or you—needs anything."

"Oh, I will."

I pay the tab, and the four of us walk through the Quarter together. The restaurant isn't far from Brielle's apartment, so Andy parked there, and we walked over together.

"This building," Brielle says, pointing across the street, "used to be called Lafitte's Blacksmith Shop. The original owner, all the way back in 1722, was Jean Lafitte. He was a privateer and used the shop to cover up his illegal activities. It's now a bar. Patrons have said, after a drink or two, they see Lafitte in all of his pirate garb."

"I mean, I see a lot of things after a drink or two," Felicia says with a chuckle.

"Well, there's that," Brielle says, smiling. "But I can say, and I'd never put this in my tour, that Lafitte is certainly still in residence. In fact, he's currently standing in the window, watching as we walk past."

"And now it's creepy," Felicia says with a shudder. "You really *should* put this stuff in your tour."

"No way," Brielle says. "I would get too many questions, and the hecklers would be off the charts."

"You're probably right," Andy says. "So, you can take us on private tours and tell us all the extra-scary stuff."

"Trust me when I say, the French Quarter has seen atrocities you don't want in your head," Brielle says, carefully selecting her words. "Sometimes, the scary stuff, as you put it, is entertaining. But there are times that it's more than that. And if you feed into it, it'll follow you home."

"I don't want to know more," Felicia says, shaking her head. "No more for me."

Once at Brielle's apartment, we say our goodbyes, and I lead Brielle upstairs. While she puts her leftovers in the fridge, I walk into the bathroom and draw her a hot bath.

"I didn't know you were a bath man."

I turn to find her leaning her shoulder on the doorframe, watching me with a smile.

"This is for you. I think you could use a little pampering tonight."

"Are you just trying to suck up after asking me about my former lovers?"

"No." I kiss her nose. "I'm just taking care of you because I'm worried about you."

"Well, that's lovely." She kisses the palm of my hand, then presses it against her cheek, leaning into my touch. "Thank you."

"You're welcome."

She crosses to the medicine cabinet and pulls out a bottle of bath salts.

"Here, you can use these."

"Do they have a special spell on them for protection?"

Her lips quirk into a smile. "No, they have lavender in them, which is good for relaxation."

"Just lavender?"

"I know, it's boring. But if you really want something magical—"

"No, this is fine." I pour the salts into the bath and gesture for her to climb in.

"You know, I was thinking about the killer this evening, and—"

"No. We're not talking about it tonight. We're going to rest and let our minds reset. There's nothing we can do tonight anyway."

She sighs as she strips out of her clothes, not self-conscious in the least to be naked in front of me, and steps into the steaming water.

"You know what, I can live with that."

"Me, too."

# CHAPTER 12

*"I don't feel guilty for anything."*

~Ted Bundy

hat a pity.

He stares at the lifeless body on the small bed in disappointment.

He'd had plans for this one. So many wonderful ways he was going to play with her. He wanted to make it last with her, let her go for *hours* before he finally killed her.

She was special.

Of all his toys, she was the one who cried the least. She didn't really make any noise at all, and he was excited to see what it would take to hear that voice.

But instead, she found a way to hang herself with the ropes he used to tie her hands.

She didn't try to get away, which was interesting. She didn't untie the others.

No, instead, she used the rope to simply hang herself.

And if he were honest, that made him like her even more.

Though it was a pity that he couldn't play with her more.

"Ah, Brielle. Look what you did," he says as he untangles her from the rope. Her blue eyes are bulging, her face an interesting shade of purple.

But her hair is still long and soft.

So he lays her on the table and washes her hair, braids it, and cuts it for his collection. Even though he wasn't the one to finally end her life, he was ultimately the cause of her death, so he deserves the satisfaction of seeing her hair in his collection.

Brielle would want that for him.

He smiles in satisfaction as the hair joins the others, and then he carries the lifeless body outside and throws her over the railing to the swamp below.

She'll sink within minutes.

Either that or a 'gator will come for her.

He should really be considered a conservationist, given how much food he provides for the critters of the bayou.

With that thought in his head, he grins and walks back inside. He really prefers to have more than three girls at a time, but since that one killed herself, he's down to just three.

That won't do.

"I'll have to go hunting this evening," he says with a sigh and sets his hands on his hips. "If I'm careful, I could take two. That's tricky, but I've done it before."

Neither of the remaining girls is crying. The one he's had the longest is sleeping. He checked her vitals earlier and verified she's still alive, just tired.

That's understandable.

He made one of the other girls rape her with a broomstick for about an hour this morning, and that'll tucker a girl out.

He turns to one of the other remaining girls and smiles.

"Hello, Brielle."

"Sarah," she responds coldly. "I'm Sarah."

He doesn't reply. Not at first. The anger is swift and hot, but he doesn't want to hit her. At least, not yet. The fire burns so fiercely in this one. He wants to draw it out a while. He needs to see how long it'll take before he finally breaks her mind, *then* he'll mutilate her body.

He's looking forward to it.

So, he simply leans in until his face is just inches from hers. He can smell the stink of her. If he put her outside, the bugs and rats would have a field day.

"You should thank me," he whispers. "I could make it so much worse for you than this."

She doesn't reply, just turns her head away in disgust.

He leaves her be and walks back to the sleeping girl. He pushes his fingers through her hair, enjoying the way the strands feel against his skin.

He's already getting hard.

"Brielle, wake up. We're going to have some fun."

# CHAPTER 13

## BRIELLE

*"*$C$*ome on!"*

*It's happening again. Six girls gesture for me to follow them, and then suddenly, I'm back in the horrible torture room. It's daytime. Light filters through a dirty window, catching on the dust floating in the air.*

*There are still three girls, including the one who saw me last time, but the other two are different.*

*The ones who were here before are dead.*

*They helped to lead me here.*

*Knowing that he's already killed them makes my stomach sink. He's killing these girls so quickly that it seems he will make his way through many more before we find him.*

*Light shines under the door that leads to the rest of the house. I can hear he's listening to music.*

*Hello by Adele blares through the room, barely muffled.*

*I used to love that song.*

*Not anymore.*

*I need to get through that door so I can see who he is and where I am. I need to go back with information so we can catch him before he kills these poor girls.*

*I start to walk toward the door, but a voice stops me.*

*"It's you again."*

*I turn to find the girl from before staring at me. The same one from last time.*

*"You can see me?"*

*She nods and swallows hard.*

*"I never let him see that he scares me. My brothers always taught me to stand my ground, to never let them see you sweat." She sniffs. "I'm never going to see them again, am I?"*

*I don't know.*

*I hope she does.*

*"Sure, you will," I say and try to smile at her. It's only been a day since I last saw her, but I can see the fight leaving her. The fear, the torture, the torment are taking their toll. "You have to stay strong. You have to keep fighting back."*

*"It makes him mad. I talk back to him. I bit him when he tried to touch me."*

*"Good for you."*

*She turns, showing me her bare back where whip marks weep with blood. "I was punished."*

*"Please tell me your name. Tell me what he looks like."*

*"He calls us all* Brielle."

*My heart stops.*

*"What did you say?"*

*"Brielle," she says again. "Like you."*

*Before I can ask more, someone tugs on my arm, and I turn to see one of the spirits beside me, her eyes wide. "You have to wake up. Right now. Wake up, Brielle."*

The phone rings beside Cash. He grunts sleepily as he reaches over and answers his cell.

"This is Winslow." He listens, and sleep leaves his face entirely as he looks over at me. "We'll be right there."

"What's happening?"

"The bastard tried to take someone tonight, but he fucked up. She got away."

"Oh my gods." I jump from the bed, and we hastily dress, then hurry from my apartment to Cash's car. There's no traffic at this time of night, and we arrive at the police station moments later.

"Cash and Brielle for Lieuten—"

"He's expecting you," the receptionist says immediately. She doesn't even ask Cash for his weapon as she buzzes us through, and we hurry through the bullpen to Asher's office.

Before he opens the door, Cash turns to me. "Let me do the questioning."

"I will."

He opens the door, but when we step inside, the office is empty.

"Over here," Asher says from behind us, gesturing for us to follow him. "She's in a more comfortable office. She's scared shitless."

"Catch us up," Cash says as we follow Asher down a long hall.

"She came in, crying and asking for help. She was out with friends and said a guy dragged her out of a bar on Bourbon. You can ask her some questions, as well. I don't know much more than that, she's only been here about fifteen minutes."

Cash nods, and we follow Asher into a small lounge. There are several comfortable chairs, one sofa, and a kitchenette that boasts coffee and little else.

It's definitely more comfortable for a scared girl than Asher's official office.

"Hi, my name is Cash." He approaches the girl with authority but does so gently. He squats in front of her, not too close, and doesn't try to touch her. The girl cries softly. "What's your name?"

"Shelly," she whispers. "Shelly Diaz."

"You're a brave woman, Shelly," Cash says, surprising her. "I'm proud of you. I'm sure you've already told Lieutenant Smith what happened tonight, but I'd like for you to tell me, as well. Take a deep breath and think it through. We need you to be as descriptive as possible so we can find this person."

"This all feels really extreme," Shelly says with a frown. "I mean, I thought I'd give a statement, but I don't know much. Drunk dudes must assault girls on Bourbon every single night."

"I'm sure they do," Cash says, nodding at the girl as he shifts the chair next to hers to face her, then sits in it. "But there's someone out there kidnapping and killing women."

Her eyes round, her hands clench, and all of the blood drains from her face.

"Holy shit."

"You might be the one person who can help us figure out who this bastard is, Shelly. So, we really need you to be as descriptive as possible."

"Holy shit," she says again and takes a deep breath, letting it out slowly. "Well, I didn't get a good look at him. The place was dark, and I was standing at the bar, waiting for a drink. Some guy came up to me and asked if I was having a good time. Told me I was pretty. It happens all the time, and that's not my ego talking, it's just the truth. Like I said, guys hit on girls in bars every night."

"I understand," Cash says. "Keep going."

"So, I didn't reply to him, just nodded. I didn't even look at him because I wasn't interested in being friendly with some strange dude. I have a boyfriend back home."

"Are you on vacation?"

"Yeah." Her lip quivers. "I'm here with some friends from Dallas. We drove over because I'd never been here before, and we wanted to have some fun."

"Go on," Cash urges.

"I didn't say anything, I just nodded. Then, this guy kind of pulls on my elbow, I guess to get my attention, I don't know. So I said, '*Look, mister, I don't want to talk to you.*' Sometimes, you just have to be blunt to make them go away, especially if they've been drinking. And, well, you know how it goes."

"Sure," Cash says.

"The next thing I know, he's tugging me through the bar to the exit. He's got a vise-grip on my arm, and he's just yanking me." Her lip quivers again. She lifts the sleeve of her top, revealing bruises just above her elbow. "I was yelling, but it was *so loud* in there. And crowded. There were people all around, but he told them we were just having a fight, and that he was taking me out where we could talk rationally."

"What a jerk," Asher mutters, catching Shelly's attention.

"He was more than a jerk," she says. "I've taken self-defense classes, and I knew that the worst thing I could do was let him get me alone or leave that bar."

"Good girl," Cash says. "You're absolutely right."

"I didn't think he was trying to *take* me, I thought he was trying to rape me. I've been raped before, at a party in college, and let me tell you, he didn't scare me so much as he pissed me right off. No man is ever going to do that to me again. Ever. So I fought back. But he was really strong. Like, way stronger than he looked."

"What did he look like?" Cash asks.

"He's not really that tall," she says, thinking it over. "Not much taller than me, I'd say. He has gray in his hair, and he's a white guy."

"A middle-aged white guy," Asher says. "Can you narrow it down a bit? Did he have any scars or tattoos?"

"Not that I saw," she says, plucking at her bottom lip as she seems to think it over. "I don't really know what his face looks like because I was trying to get away from him. I didn't stop to memorize it."

"You'd be surprised what you might have noticed," Cash says. "Did he have a big nose?"

"I don't think so."

"Wrinkles? Was he overweight?"

"He was average." She shrugs. "And I didn't see any wrinkles. He smelled, though."

"Like what?"

"Like a cat box." She wrinkles her nose in disgust. "Like a dirty cat box."

"How did you get away?" I ask, speaking for the first time. Her eyes find mine as if she didn't realize I was there until now.

"I kneed him in the balls and planted my elbow in his jaw, then ran inside. He'd shifted to turn the corner, and I saw the window of opportunity and took it."

"Wow, that's awesome."

She smiles at me. "You look just like my older sister, Lisa."

"What did he do when you got away?"

"He called after me, but I was already hurrying back into the bar. I went right to the bouncer and told him what'd happened. He stayed with me while I found my friends, and then they all convinced me to come see you."

"You did the absolute right thing," Asher says. "Everything you did tonight saved your life. You should be damn proud of yourself."

"I'm scared shitless," she says. "Do you really think he would have killed me?"

"Yes," Asher says simply. "I know your friends are waiting for you, but do you want a police escort back to your hotel?"

"No, we're driving right back to Dallas after this. I don't want to stay in New Orleans. It's safer at home."

"Just let us know if you change your mind," Cash says kindly. "And if you think of anything else, something he said or even the color of his eyes, call us right away."

"I have a question," I say, surprising them all. "Did he introduce himself when he approached you? Did he say, '*Hi, my name's Dave,*' or anything like that?"

"No." She sighs, frowning. "But he did call *me* a strange name. I never told him my name, and he kept calling me something. So, at first, I thought he had me confused with another person."

"What did he call you?"

"Brianne or something—"

"Brielle?" I offer, and her eyes light right up, confirming my worst nightmare.

"Yeah, that's it. It's different. Pretty. But not my name."

"Okay, thank you," Asher says and leads Shelly out of the room.

Cash and I stare at each other, not saying a word until Shelly is gone, and Asher returns.

"He's after *you*," Cash says.

"I just remembered that the other night when I dream-walked, the girl he's holding told me the same thing. She said he calls them all Brielle. I completely forgot."

"Now we need to interview *you*," Asher says, dropping into the sofa across from me. "Who the fuck is this guy?"

"I have no idea."

"He knows you," Asher counters. "And he's killing you, every fucking day."

I swallow hard as bile rises into the back of my throat.

"That's enough." Cash's voice is hard as he turns to me. "I checked out both of your ex-boyfriends. The guy from college lives in Arizona with his wife and two kids. The guy who used to own the tour group moved to Miami and got married last month."

"Good for them."

"So it's not a past lover," Asher says with a sigh. "A friend? A brother, cousin, child-hood friend?"

"I don't have any brothers." My mind is whirling with possibilities. Who the hell could be doing this? "My father's dead. I don't have many male friends. Or friends in general, actually. They usually think I'm too creepy."

"Why?"

My smile is thin. "There's a shadow sitting right next to you. It has one ankle crossed over the other knee, and his arm is resting on the back of the couch as if you two are on a date."

Asher jumps up and rushes over to the kitchenette.

"There's a shadow standing to your left, right in front of the coffeepot. It's been moving back and forth from that spot to the sink and back again since we came into the room. It's as if he's making coffee over and over again. Which he very well might be doing. He could be stuck in a ten-second loop, repeating it over and over again for all of eternity like an echo. I don't know about you, but that sounds like its own kind of hell to me."

"Jesus Christ," Asher mutters, rubbing the back of his neck as if all of the hairs there are standing on end.

"I could keep going. I told you, I see dead people. It's who I am. So, if I'm going to be close to someone, they have to not only accept that fact, but they also can't be faint of heart.

"When I was younger, I tried to hide it from friends at school or boys I liked. I mean, who wants a creepy Debbie Downer around all the time, right? I know I don't. But, sooner or later, we'd be somewhere, and it would come out."

"Keep going," Cash says. When Asher frowns at him, he says, "This could lead to a light bulb moment."

Asher nods. "True. Keep going."

"Well, like one time in high school, I went to the movies with this guy I liked. Jeff Anderson. He was nice, kind of geeky. Anyway, he asked me out, and I said yes. We get to the theater, and it's an old one. There were so many shadows wandering around, it scared the hell out of me, and it takes a lot to do that.

"But I was young, and I *really* liked Jeff, so I just took a deep breath and sucked it up. We got our popcorn and Cokes, and when we walked into the auditorium, Jeff led me to seats in the middle of the place. But there were shadows already sitting there."

"What did you do?" Asher asks.

"I said, *'let's sit somewhere else.'* At first, Jeff was fine with it, but everywhere he went, there was a shadow sitting in the seat. Maybe it was the same one dicking with me. I don't know. That's happened before.

"So, finally, I said, *'this place is too haunted for me.'* He laughed, but when he looked at my face and saw that I wasn't kidding, he said some hurtful things, and we left. He refused to take me home. Said he didn't want a devil worshiper in his car. I had to walk home."

"All the way to that house in the bayou?" Cash asks.

"Yeah. It was horrible. The bayou is horribly haunted. I got home well after midnight, and my sisters were worried sick."

"What about your mom?" Asher asks.

"She slapped me across the face when I walked through the door."

"She's a lovely woman," Cash assures Asher. "So far, what I've learned from this is: I need to kick Jeff Anderson's ass, and your mom is a grade-A bitch."

"I won't disagree." I shrug a shoulder. "I know it's not Jeff doing this. The people who leave my life because of my abilities do so because it scares them. I don't have to be a shrink to know that. It's never made someone so angry that they wanted to kill me or anyone who looks like me. That would make them—"

"Psychotic," Cash finishes for me. "And, yes, it could happen. But I'm inclined to agree that it's unlikely. I'm also sorry that you had to deal with so many jerks."

"Everyone does."

"Are there any more shadows lurking around here?" Asher asks.

"Dozens," I confirm. "But those are the only two in this room. There's one that stands behind the receptionist. It looks over her shoulder as if its checking her work."

"My office?" Asher asks.

"None in there."

There *is* one in there, but there's no need to scare him.

"Well, thank Christ for that. And I'm at a loss for what to do now. The bastard failed tonight."

"That's going to make him angry," Cash says. "He'll strike again. If he hasn't already. And it'll escalate. He'll increase the speed in which he kills them."

"He's going pretty fast already," I say. "When I was there tonight, two of the girls were gone, and he had two more in their place."

"Wait, you were there tonight?" Cash asks.

"Yes. One of the dead girls alerted me to wake up."

"Were you able to ask questions? Walk through the house?" Asher asks.

"I was interrupted before I could walk through the door, but I was able to talk to the other girl again. The one who told me the killer calls them all by my name."

"What else did she say?"

"That she fights back, and she doesn't let him see that she's afraid of him. She has older brothers. That's really it."

"You have to do it again," Asher says. "Right now."

"I'm not able to *make* myself do it," I remind him. "I don't know what triggers it, aside from the girls being desperate for me to find their bodies. But Millie has been asking around and poring through the book. I'll go to her in a few hours and see if she's made any headway."

"I want to catch this son of a bitch before he kills anyone else," Asher says. "He's going down."

# CHAPTER 14

## BRIELLE

"*I*'m dead on my feet."

"That's not funny," Millie says, frowning at me from behind the counter. We're at Witches Brew, and she's filling an order while I read through our grandmother's book.

Meme didn't have the best penmanship.

Some of it is hard to read. Either that or it's in another language, which is entirely possible.

"I want to add the love potion," Millie's male customer says, winking at her. "Let's roll the dice and see if it works."

"All I ask is that you take it outside before you drink it," my sister says, laughing. "If I had a dollar for every man who's fallen in love with me after drinking this, I'd be at least fifty dollars richer."

"I might fall in love with you without the potion," Flirty Customer says with another wink.

"Sorry, you're not my type," Millie says and flashes a sassy grin as she builds his vanilla chai latte and adds the love potion.

"What, you don't like devastatingly handsome, rich men?"

"I don't like *married* men," she replies smoothly, stirring his drink.

"How did you—?"

"I don't call it Witches Brew for nothing." She winks, and when she moves her hand away from the drink, it continues to stir without her, making the customer swallow hard. "I suggest, if you drink that, you do it while looking at your wife so you fall in love with *her* since you promised to do so until death do you part."

She passes him his change, offers him a friendly wave, and once he's through the door, she blows a loud raspberry through her lips.

"Dudes like that are disgusting," she says as she leans over the counter toward me. "Have you found anything good?"

"Not yet. Most of it is gibberish to me."

"That's because you don't speak witch." She frowns when her eyes drop to my neck. "Where's your pendant?"

"Oh." I reach for it, but it's not there. "I must not have put it back on after my shower. I'll text Cash and ask him to bring it with him when he comes this way for lunch."

I pull my phone out of my bag and shoot off the message, then frown down at the book.

"What if this doesn't work, Mill?"

"There isn't another option," she says and waves at another customer who just walked through the door. "Go ahead and sit anywhere. I'll be right over to take your order."

"I love your café."

Her grin is wide and proud. "Me, too. How does it feel in here today?"

I let myself look around the space. "No shadows."

"I smudged last night, and it should hold for a while. Are the girls still around?"

"There are six, but they stay outside. I don't know why they can't come in."

"Let's be frank here, I'm glad they stay on the sidewalks. It would just be awful if you had to stare at mangled bodies all day."

"You have a good point."

"Miss? We're ready to order."

Millie hurries over to the couple at the table in the corner, and I stare down at a yellowed page of the book.

The thing is huge. I've always seen big, magical tomes full of spells and recipes for potions in movies like *Practical Magic* or even *Hocus Pocus*, which always makes me laugh because my sisters and I look just like the Sanderson sisters—if we were evil witches, of course.

But I never expected these books to really exist. Not until we found this one in the house under floorboards in the little storage room where we hid.

"It has to be a hundred and three degrees outside," Millie says as she hurries behind the counter to fix the customers' drinks.

"Feels like it," I agree.

"How can people drink hot coffee on a day like this?" She shakes her head and starts up the steamer. "It perplexes me."

"I'm sorry I'm late," Daphne says as she rushes inside, carrying a large tote bag full of notes and books. "I've been at the library doing a little research."

"Wait, *you* went to the library?" I stare at her in shock. "Daph, that place must wreak havoc on you."

"Not fun," she agrees. "I can't tell you how many people have sex in libraries. It's disgusting. Not to mention, there were some books that people used to try and figure out how to kill someone and get away with it."

"Our killer?"

"Not that I could tell. No, mostly, they were people trying to off their spouses. It's just sad. Anyway, my shields are up, and I'm careful. Millie and I didn't find much in Grandma's book about dream-walking. Yet, anyway. There are some passages written in Cajun and a couple of others in what looked to be Latin that we couldn't decipher, and Millie's going to ask Miss Sophia what they say. In the meantime, I did some digging on dream-walking."

"Is there an instruction manual?"

"I wish." She digs around in her bag and slaps some books and loose papers on the counter. "Hey, Mill? Can I please get an iced chai? I'll love you forever."

"You'll love me forever anyway. But, yes. Do you want anything, Bri?"

"I'll have the same as Daphne, thanks."

"I'm adding some—"

"Yes, yes. Of course, you are," Daphne says, waving our sister off. "Now, as I said, there is no manual on how to do it. Unfortunately, like most things that are part of our reality, it's not really something that's been studied, and therefore, we don't understand exactly how it works."

"We already know all of that."

"But there *are* some interesting meditations and incantations in here that might help." She thumbs through the book until she arrives at the page she wants. We both accept our drinks from Millie.

"I have a call out to Miss Sophia, but there was an emergency with a coven up in Shreveport, and I don't know how long she'll be gone," Millie says.

"She'll get back to us soon," I say and sip my drink, then frown. "What's in this?"

"Two potions this time. It makes it a little bitter, sorry."

"You take all the fun out of lattes," Daphne says but sips her own drink. "Okay, it says here that you need to breathe deeply as you lie in bed and close your eyes. Think about the place you want to travel to or the person you want to talk to. Or both, I guess. Have an imaginary conversation or think about the landmarks along the way from where you are to your final destination."

"Basically, literally go there in your head," Millie says.

"Yes, exactly." Daphne takes another sip of her drink. "Do it over and over again until you fall asleep."

"That seems too simple."

Both sisters glance up at me.

"Right? I mean, if it were that simple, people would have arguments with other people in their sleep all the damn time."

"Not everyone is psychic," Daphne reminds me. "And, maybe they do, but they just don't remember it the next day."

"Or they just chalk it up to a weird dream," Millie adds. "Most civilians pass off dreams or mystical encounters as something explainable. A bump in the night? The house is settling. They think they hear a voice? Must be the neighbor's TV."

"I get it," I reply with a sigh. "Okay, so don't make it hard. Simple is good. I need to lie down and breathe and think about that horrible place."

"I hate this so much," Millie says, covering my hand with hers. "I hate that you're the target and that you have to see these unspeakable things. It's not okay. None of this is."

"We've dealt with *not okay* since birth, my sweet sister," I remind her.

"It's your turn for okay," Daphne says, sighing. "Yes, I know I've been a bitch in the past about the whole Jackson thing, but you don't deserve this, Bri. I don't understand it."

"I don't either. I just wish I could see who he is."

Daphne turns to Millie. "You're psychic. Can't you see?"

"She can't reach out, Daphne. You know—"

"I can't see him," Millie says quietly. "I've looked, but I can't see him."

"Wait. You *looked*?" I sit back and stare at my sister in horror. "Millie, if you'd seen him, if you'd crawled into his head—"

"I didn't," she interrupts. "And you're my sister, Brielle. Of course, I looked, the consequences be damned. You'd do the same for me."

"I wish I'd known the girl was at the police station," Daphne says. "I might have been able to touch her and see him that way."

"Damn, it didn't even cross my mind." I shake my head. *Why didn't I think of that?* "She's long gone back to Dallas now."

"The dream-walking is the best bet for now," Millie says on a sigh and watches as her customers finish their coffees and leave the café.

"Should we talk quieter? This will creep the hell out of your customers," Daphne says.

"They can't hear us," Millie says with a smile. "And don't ask me how. You don't want to know."

"Speaking of creepy," I mutter and take a sip of my chai.

"I DON'T LIKE IT," Cash says quietly. "The investigator in me understands that this has to happen, but the man in me wants to say, '*hell no*' and take you out of here altogether."

"I know." I cup his face and let the warmth of him seep into me. It makes me feel comforted. Treasured. Safe. "But we have to finish this."

"Let me take you somewhere when it's all over," he says and kisses my palm. "Anywhere. An island somewhere. Or we can get lost in Europe."

"Europe might kill me." I smile and lean in to kiss his cheek. "But the island sounds lovely."

"An island it is, then." He clears his throat. We're lying on the bed, and I've told him how I go about trying to dream-walk intentionally. Both of my sisters are in the living room, on hand in case I need them to pull me out.

I don't know how they'll know if I need them, but Millie assured me that she would know.

I have to trust her.

And I do. There is no one in the world that I trust more than the three people in my apartment with me right now.

I swallow hard, close my eyes, and begin taking long, slow breaths.

In through the nose.

Out through the mouth.

I don't know the way to where I'm going, so I can't think about that, but I do know what it looks like when I get there, so I imagine those details. I picture the dirty room, the blood on the floor, the dingy window. My nose wrinkles as I think of the stench. The heaviness that hangs in the room from the death and despair.

I wonder how many girls there have been. I know we think there were a few dozen at least, but I have a feeling there have been many more than that. I don't have to be a profiler to know that this isn't something he just started doing over the past six years.

He likes it way too much for it to be that new.

And if he's middle-aged, like Shelly seemed to think, he's likely been at this for decades.

I think of the girls. The six who continue to follow me, and the three in the room the last time I was there in my dream-walk.

I imagine the one who can see me, who talks to me.

I hope with everything in me that she's still alive.

*"You're back."*

*It worked. I'm here! I glance at the girl and feel immense relief that she's still alive.*

"*And you're still here.*"

"*He was mad tonight,*" *she says, and her eyes flick to her left. Two more girls have joined the ones already there, making it five young women being held now. There are only three toddler beds against the wall, so the new girls sit on the floor, awkwardly tied to the bedposts.*

*They're both crying and shaking. He's stripped them naked, but aside from that, it doesn't look as if he's hurt them.*

*Yet.*

*And they can't see me.*

"*What's your name?*" *I ask the girl.*

"*Sarah,*" *she whispers.* "*Sarah Chandler. But he calls us all Brielle.*"

"*I know. But I won't call you that. You're Sarah. I want you to remember that. Hold onto your name, do you hear me?*"

*She nods quickly.* "*I'm Sarah. I have three older brothers, and I am a veterinarian.*"

"*Wow, that's amazing.*"

*A ghost of a smile tickles her lips.*

"*I'm going to look around, Sarah. I need to gather more information for the police. I need to know how to find all of you, okay?*"

*She nods again, and I walk away, headed to the door.*

*It's locked.*

*Frustration is swift and all-encompassing, but I turn and try to find other clues.*

*Maybe there are papers on the workbench. I walk that way and look around, disappointed to find it recently cleaned. There's not even any blood on it now. No papers on the shelves either.*

*I glance around the room. There are no photos on the walls. Only the braids hang on the walls, and the roman numeral IV written in blood beside one of the small beds. Four.*

*Did someone cut themselves and then count the days until they died?*

*The thought sends a shiver through me.*

*I hear footsteps.*

*The girls whimper as the steps grow louder, approaching the door.*

*I'm going to see him! I'm finally going to see his face, and then I can tell Asher and Cash what he looks like, and we can find out who he is. We can put him away. We can make all of this stop.*

*The doorknob rattles.*

*The girls cower.*

*Sarah stares at me in horror.*

*But he doesn't come inside. There's a long pause, and then the steps fade away again.*

*The girls sigh in relief.*

"*He does that all the time,*" *Sarah says.* "*It's just another way to fuck with us. Scare us. He taunts us mercilessly. Constantly. That's the worst part of all. Death would be a welcome escape from this hell.*"

"*No.*" *I rush to her and reach out, but my hand moves right through her.*

*I can't touch her.*

*I can't help her.*

*I've never been so damn frustrated in all my life.*

*The sun glints off something under Sarah's bed.*

"*There's a knife right under you.*"

*Her eyes grow wide, and she struggles to see over the side.* "*I can't reach it.*"

"*I have to get that knife into your hands.*"

*I try to pick it up, but I can't grasp it.*

*Damn it!*

*Sarah looks at the girl sitting on the floor. "Hey, do you see a knife under my bed?"*

*The girl is crying.*

*"Stop crying and listen to me." That gets her attention. "I need you to pass me that knife."*

*The girl sees the weapon and uses her toes to pick it up and drop it on Sarah's bed. Sarah palms it in her free hand.*

*"You keep that hidden, and you use it," I say strongly. "You're going to live through this, Sarah."*

*"I hope you're right."*

I WAKE with a start and blink rapidly, both of my sisters and Cash hovering over me.

"Are you okay?" Millie asks. Her face is lined with concern.

"I still didn't see him," I say and sit up to brush my hair off my face. "He's playing with them. Taunting them. He has five girls now. And there was a knife that he must have dropped. Sarah has it now, so if he tries to hurt her, she'll hurt him back."

"Sarah?" Cash asks.

"The one that can see me. Her name is Sarah. Sarah Chandler. She's been there a while, Cash. With the rate he's been killing these girls, the clock is ticking for her. And she knows it. But she's smart, and she's strong."

"She needs to be," Daphne says, her face pale.

"What's wrong?"

"She held your hand," Millie says quietly.

"You could see?" I ask.

Daphne nods and swallows hard. "It's something out of a horror movie."

"It's worse than that because it's real," I reply and reach out to give her a hug. "You didn't have to go with me. I wish you hadn't."

"We had to know if you needed help," Daphne replies. "But you're getting stronger."

"I'm getting madder," I say, barking a short laugh.

"That will fuel the strength," Millie says, taking each of our hands.

"I still don't know how to find him."

"In your dreams," Cash says. "And if that's what it takes to find him, we keep doing it."

"I need a break. But I can try again later."

"You deserve the break," Cash replies and kisses my forehead.

"We're not leaving here until this is over," Millie says. "Daphne and I will sleep here. We need to stick together. It's going to get more dangerous now. I don't know how I know that; I just do."

"Agreed." I nod and take a deep breath. "It's going to be dangerous. And fast."

Cash links his fingers with mine. "We're ready."

# CHAPTER 15

~Albert Fish, AKA The Brooklyn Vampire

His balls feel heavy and swollen. They throb. That dumb bitch thinks she can hurt him, kick him, and then run away from him?

Fuck that. He'll teach her a lesson.

He'll teach them all a fucking lesson. She's losing her manners. Her respect for him. And he will not stand for that. No, he'll remind her just how important he is, how much she *loves* him.

Maybe she's forgotten how she used to look at him. How she played coy and hard to get. But he knew that was her way of flirting with him. He's stayed in the background for too long, given her too much independence.

It's time for that to change. Soon.

He paces his little house, back and forth, with throbbing balls and a bruised jaw. He showed her, didn't he? He took *two* women after she tried to hurt him, and he'll hurt them far more before he's done with them.

The anger fuels him. He stomps back to his room of pleasure and marches through the door, startling all five of his toys.

He knows it's not their fault. And taking *her* indiscretions out on them doesn't seem entirely fair, but he has energy to burn, and this is his favorite way to do that.

And…someone has to pay.

Someone *will* pay.

Dearly.

"Come here, Brielle."

He passes by the one that's been feisty. He doesn't have it in him to engage in a cat and mouse game tonight, and when he decides it's her time, he'll need more energy.

No, instead, he walks to one that he's only had a day or two and smiles into her sweet, precious face.

"You made me real mad tonight, Brielle."

Her face crumples, and she starts to cry, spit dripping down her chin as she begs and pleads with him to let her go.

"Oh, do you honestly think I will do that? That I will let you go? Tsk tsk." He unties her from her restraints. "I won't let you go yet. You're still alive, silly girl."

She hiccups and keeps crying. She soils herself, which brings him great joy.

Yes, great joy, indeed.

"I don't think we'll play at the bench today." He kisses her cheek as he pulls her across the uneven wood floor to the chair. He saves the chair for special occasions.

Revenge feels like the perfect occasion.

He gets her situated, her hands and legs secured in the leather straps. Her mouth gapes soundlessly now, her despair palpable.

"You have to breathe, Brielle. It won't do to have you pass out on me now. That will only anger me. You don't want to anger me any more than you already have, do you?"

She shakes her head, but still, no sound emerges.

He grips her throat in his hand, squeezing slightly.

"I said breathe."

She takes a deep breath, her blue eyes pinned to his.

"Please don't kill me."

"I'm sorry, I'm going to have to disappoint you there."

He reaches for his favorite knife, but it's gone. Just one more thing to displease him today.

One more disappointment.

He chooses another blade, one not quite as sharp, and then turns back to her. Without a word, he slices her flesh from hip to knee.

She keens in pain as the blood runs down the side of the chair.

"That will teach you not to run from me."

# CHAPTER 16

## CASH

"It's good that I came," Felicia says into my ear. She arrived in Savannah this morning to check on my mom.

"What's going on?"

"Well, she hasn't been out of the house in a while," she says, speaking low. "And she's clearly not able to get around like she used to. The house hasn't been cleaned. Honestly, she needs help."

"We'll get her anything she needs. A housekeeper, a home nurse. Whatever she needs."

"Andy feels the same way, of course. And I agree. I just wanted to make sure I have your permission to make decisions and get things set up for her."

"Felicia, you know I trust you. Just keep us posted. And please tell Mom I love her."

"Will do. I'm going to take her to get her hair done and out for lunch today. We're having a girls' day."

"She'll love that. Thank you."

"Are you kidding? This is a vacation. Talk to you soon."

She ends the call just as Brielle walks out of the shower, wrapped in a fluffy, white towel.

"Was that Felicia?" she asks.

"Yes, she's at Mom's. It's good she's there. She will take care of things."

"She'll be great," Brielle says with a smile, but it doesn't reach her eyes. Her hand clutches her chest, and she scowls. "Why do I keep forgetting my pendant?"

She stomps back into the bathroom and calls out to me, "Have you seen my necklace?"

"You had it on this morning."

She pokes her head into the bedroom. "I know, and I took it off for my shower. Now, it's gone."

"Did you ask your sisters?"

She disappears again, and I hear her talking with her siblings.

"They haven't seen it," Brielle says as she bustles back into the bedroom and starts tearing the bed apart. "Maybe it came off while you were rocking my world."

"So, you're saying I rock your world?"

She rolls her eyes and looks at me like I'm ridiculous. "Maybe."

"On a scale of one to ten, where would I rank on the world-rocking scale?"

"Your ego is big enough without me feeding it, you know."

"Is my ego the only *big* thing I have?"

She barks out a laugh, the levity finally reaching her eyes. "You're silly."

I tug her to me and kiss her long and slow, reveling in how she fits against me as if she were made just for me.

"You two are disgusting," Daphne says from the doorway. "Millie and I are going to check out our respective businesses to make sure the sky hasn't fallen in either of them."

"We'll be back later," Millie calls from the hallway.

I kiss Brielle on the nose, and Daphne rolls her eyes then disappears down the hall.

"Bye!" Brielle calls with a laugh. "If I didn't know better, I'd say you enjoy taunting my sisters."

"Oh, I enjoy it very much," I confirm and nod. "I don't have to be in the office until around one today. Asher's working on a different case this morning."

"Perfect. Mallory called and asked if we'd like to have lunch with her and her husband, Beau."

I quirk a brow. "Beau Boudreaux? The tycoon?"

"One and the same." She nods and wanders to the closet to choose some clothes. "I haven't seen him in a long time. He's a busy guy."

"What with being a billionaire and all."

"And the owner of a massive company. He also has a big family. He's a nice guy. You'll like him."

"Okay," I reply and take her hand once she's dressed and ready to go. "Lead the way."

〜

"I ADMIT," Beau says an hour later as we wait for our lunch to be served, "I'm fascinated by your career."

"It's not always as exciting as they portray it in the movies," I reply. "A lot of it is boring deskwork."

"But a lot of it isn't," Mallory replies. "And, I will say, I can't imagine having that much knowledge of how horrible human beings can be is an easy job. It must weigh heavily on you."

"Sometimes," I agree. "It depends on the job, of course. But you're right in that I don't necessarily work with the best of society."

"And now you're here, on your vacation, doing it again," Brielle says, taking my hand in hers and linking our fingers. "I'm sorry about that."

"I think I'm in the right place at the right time."

"That's a lovely way to think about it," Mallory says with a wide smile.

Our meals are served, and right after I've taken the first bite of my shrimp gumbo, my phone rings.

"I'm sorry. It's my boss in Dallas. I'd better take this."

I step away from the table, move out to the sidewalk, and accept the call.

"This is Winslow."

"It's Peters," he says, his voice brisk and all business. "I have news that you're not going to like, Cash."

I narrow my eyes. "What's up?"

"Simpson won't be going to prison."

There are moments in movies when the protagonist receives bad news, and the camera spins around them quickly as if everything is spiraling out of control.

This is that moment for me.

My stomach roils.

"Why the fuck not?"

"He's been found not guilty by reason of insanity. So, instead of a cage in prison, he'll be in a mental hospital for the rest of his life."

"Unacceptable. He's not fucking insane. I'll sit on the stand and testify."

"Too late," Peters says.

"Why wasn't I notified that this was going to trial? And how in the fucking hell did it happen so fast?"

"Your guess is as good as mine. I smell something dirty, but I can't prove it, and what's done is done."

"All of that work. For nothing?"

"He's going away," he reminds me. "Just not where you want him to go."

"I want him fucking dead." My voice is low and hard. "And I'd like to be the one to do it."

"I'm going to pretend I didn't hear that," Peters says. "Any news on the case you're working?"

"Nothing significant. I'll keep you posted."

"Do that."

He hangs up, and I squeeze the bridge of my nose, take a deep breath, and pull my shit together before walking back into the restaurant.

"Everything okay?" Brielle asks when I sit next to her.

"Fine." I clear my throat and reach for my water, wishing for something much stronger. Mallory's eyes narrow on me from across the table.

She's probably reading my mind. I have no idea how this stuff works, but I expect her to call me out on my lie.

Instead, she says, "Do you have siblings, Cash?"

"One brother. He's a cop here in New Orleans."

"Oh, that's awesome," she replies.

"My sister-in-law Kate's best friend is married to a cop," Beau says. "Asher Smith."

Brielle and I look at each other in surprise.

"Do you know him?" Beau asks.

"Actually, yes. We're working with him on a case," I reply.

"Well, he's a good man," Beau replies. "I trust him implicitly."

"I agree," Brielle says, surprising me. I actually got the feeling she didn't like Asher much. "I don't know him well, but he seems like a decent person and a good cop."

"How's that all going?" Mallory asks.

"Slow," I admit. "Frustratingly slow."

"It won't always," she says.

"If you know something about this, Mallory, I need you to tell me."

"I don't," she says, shaking her head. "I wish I did. I wish I could see it all clearly, but I only see flashes of things. Like Brielle, I see the dead. I'm a medium. And if I touch a person, I feel what they feel, and I can see their thoughts."

"That must be inconvenient," I say to Beau with a grin.

"I can't read him," Mallory says, leaning her head on Beau's shoulder. "It's one of the reasons I knew he was for me. But I assure you, if I knew the answers you seek, I'd tell you right away. What he's doing is pure evil."

"Thank you," I reply.

We spend another hour with small talk and finish our meals. After we've said goodbye to the other couple, Brielle and I set off for the police station. It's time for me to check in with Asher.

"What happened?" Brielle asks.

"To what?"

"You took that call, and when you came back, something was different. You covered it up well, but I know you well enough by now to see that something's off. What happened on that call? Is your mom okay?"

"It wasn't Felicia," I reply, taking a deep breath. It's time Brielle knew the truth of what happened before. Of the demons I carry. "It was Peters, my boss in Dallas, like I said."

"Do you need to go back to Texas?"

Her hand tightens on mine at the thought.

"No, he doesn't need me there. Do you remember when I told you that I'm here on a forced vacation?"

"Sure."

"I was assigned to a particularly difficult case in Maine six weeks ago. There was a killer up there, Rodney Simpson. He was taking men and sexually assaulting them, killing them, and then burying them in his backyard."

"Holy shit," she whispers.

"Statistically, a male serial killer who kills other men isn't that common. Yes, there are some out there—Dahmer, Gacy, the Candy Man, to name a few—but it's more commonly women or children, for many reasons that I won't bore you with right now. All we knew was that we had six men missing in Maine, and most likely a serial killer on our hands.

"The interesting thing was, he didn't just take men who were vacationing or on business from out of town. Yes, he did take a few of those, but he also snatched men who lived right there in the small town. When *that* happened more than once, it clued us all in that we likely had a multiple murderer.

"My unit was assigned, and we dug right in, finding more clues than local law enforcement had uncovered. Not because they did a bad job, we just had more experience and more tools at our disposal. I mean, a tiny town like that in Maine can rarely boast even a single murder, let alone something of that magnitude.

"It was frustrating, though, because he kept eluding us. He was too calm and too detached to make a mistake."

"But he eventually made one, right?"

"Yes. Well, no, but he did get arrogant. He decided to start playing with us. He made us part of the game. He sent letters threatening the members of the team. Said he was going to take one of us and make an example of us. Of course, we took the threat seriously, but—"

"He *took* one of you?"

"Carlson," I confirm, feeling sick to my stomach. "He was forty-six, had been with the bureau for more than twenty years. A good man with a wife and five children. He went out to get us all coffee one morning and never came back."

"Oh my gods."

"He sent us video of what he was doing to Carlson." I swallow the bile and try to push the mental images from my mind. "I'll spare you the details. After four days of torture, he finally killed Carlson and left him strung up in the middle of Main Street in the dead of night."

"Didn't they have cameras?"

"Not before, no. This town was like going back in time thirty years. They didn't have any kind of security or surveillance before we got there. But it was one of the first things we did. The killer didn't know that we'd had them installed, and his public display cost him dearly. We got his identity."

"Who was it?"

I swallow again and stop when we get to the police station. We sit on a step, and I finish the story.

"Rodney Simpson. The chief of police."

"No way!"

"Yes, way. He was under our noses the entire fucking time, and we didn't know it. God only knows how many people he killed over the years. Maybe dozens. I spoke to him every single day. *Worked* with him. So did Carlson. And that's the really fucked-up thing. I don't know how I missed it. I don't know how I didn't figure it out sooner. *Six weeks,* Brielle, and that bastard didn't even trip my radar *one time.*"

"It's not your fault."

She takes my face between her hands and makes me look into her eyes.

"The fact that that man is a sick bastard is not your fault. He's a monster, and he took a great deal of pleasure taunting all of you. I don't have to be psychic to know that. And you don't have to be a shrink to know that I'm right."

"Carlson died because I didn't do my job well or fast enough."

"No, he died because a person who swore to protect and serve turned out to be a psychopath, Cash. You know that as well as I do. You can't beat yourself up for that anymore, or it'll eat you up inside. Trust me on this."

"I don't want you to blame yourself for those girls' deaths, Bri."

"Any more than I want you to blame yourself for your friend's death. Sometimes, monsters walk among us, and there's just nothing we can do about that."

I kiss her hand and pull her to her feet.

"Let's go catch this particular monster, shall we?"

"Absolutely."

We walk into the building and go through the process of checking in at the reception desk. When we reach Asher's office, he jumps out of his chair and slides his phone into his pocket.

"You're just in time," he says. "We have another body."

We rush to the morgue in the basement of the building. Brielle's body tightens. I'm sure there are many spirits down here, ready to taunt the hell out of her.

"Are you okay?"

She nods stiffly. "I'm all right."

Asher opens the door to a cold room lined with freezers that hold bodies on rolling trays.

In the center of the room is a table holding a body with a sheet covering it.

"Pulled her from the swamp this morning," the medical examiner says. "Another swamp tour."

"He's getting sloppy," Asher says.

"Impatient," I reply. "He's working faster now. He's starting to make mistakes."

The ME glances at Brielle and then back to Asher. "She might not want to see this."

"I'm fine," Brielle says again.

"It's not pretty," he says as he grips the sheet and peels it down the corpse's torso.

"Oh," Brielle whispers, leaning over the body. "She wasn't tortured."

"Strangled," the ME confirms, pointing to the ligature marks around her neck. "She was definitely dead when she hit the water, though. No fluid in her lungs."

"That's unusual." Asher turns to me. "It doesn't follow the killer's MO."

"You're right." I narrow my eyes. "She does have dark hair, and it looks like she's about the right height."

"Sixty-seven inches," the ME says. We all look at him. "Five foot seven," he clarifies.

"But there are no other marks on her," Asher says. "Our guy is way angrier than this."

"Agreed." I glance down at Brielle. "Do you recognize her?"

"She's not one of the girls who's been following me," she says, shaking her head slowly. "I don't think I've seen her before."

"I'm not ready to rule this as a homicide," Asher says. "She might have killed herself."

"If she hung herself, how did she end up in the swamp?" I ask and notice Brielle pull her phone out of her purse. "What are you doing?"

"I want Daphne to touch her."

All of us turn to her in surprise.

"Who the hell is Daphne?" Asher asks.

"My sister," she responds. "She's psychic and psychometric, meaning she knows and sees things by touching objects. It works with people, too." Her attention turns to the phone call. "Hey, Daph? Can you come to the police station? It isn't going to be a fun visit. I need you to touch a dead body. I know. Are you sure? Okay, see you soon."

"I'm not sure I want a civilian touching my vic," Asher says.

"If she's not a victim, Daphne will know. And if she *is*, Daphne might be able to see the killer."

"I'll call up and tell them to escort her right down," Asher says immediately, making us both smile.

"Oh. While we wait, I should let you both know that I'm going back to work," Brielle says as casually as if she's talking about going to the grocery store.

"Negative, ghost rider." I shake my head emphatically. "Now that we know you're his target, you are absolutely *not* going to work."

"Cash, I need to try and lure him out. If he's really after me, if I'm his sick end game, I need to be somewhere that he can easily take me."

"No way."

"Actually, she's not wrong," Asher says. "And she won't be alone. We can have undercover officers on her tour. Hell, *you* can be on her tour. I'll go one night and take my wife and kids. We'll rotate. There will be eyes on her at all times."

"And eyes on everyone *around* me," she says. "If he's lurking nearby, there's a better chance that someone will notice him. I mean, he must be watching me, right?"

"What if this all blows up on us?" I ask desperately. "What if we do everything right, and he still manages to take you? I will not lose you to this sick asshole, Brielle. I'll protect you, no matter what it takes."

"I'm not Carlson," she says softly. "This is not the same thing. There are cameras in our town."

"Trust me, we've tried using them to find him," Asher says in disgust. "He must know where they are and has figured out how to evade them."

"He's smart," Brielle says. "But you said yourself, he's getting impatient. We need to end this. And doing that might just mean me putting myself out there as bait."

"This is a bad idea," I whisper. "And there will be rules. Strict rules, Brielle, I mean it."

"I won't do anything stupid," she says immediately. "Trust me, I don't want to get caught. But I do want to catch *him*."

Asher's phone rings. "Excellent. Bring her down."

"Is Daphne here?" Brielle asks.

"She's here."

# CHAPTER 17

## BRIELLE

"I can honestly say that no one's ever invited me to touch a dead body before," Daphne says when she walks through the door. She hugs me tightly before being introduced to Asher and then turns to the covered form on the table. "Let's get this over with."

"I want to reiterate what Brielle said," Cash says. "You don't have to do this."

"Are you kidding? I might see this bastard. Of course, I have to do this."

"Do you need her to be uncovered?" Asher asks.

"Yes, please." Daph takes a long, deep breath. She links her fingers with mine, and we silently recite our protection spell, the one we've used since we were small girls. When we open our eyes, the body is uncovered. "She wasn't tortured."

The surprise in Daphne's voice mirrors my own from earlier.

"That's why you're here," I say softly. "We need to know for sure if she was his victim."

"Lucky me," she whispers and licks her lips. She reaches out, her palm hovering over the girl's arm. As she touches her, skin to skin, she inhales sharply. "Oh, she was absolutely his."

"What do you see?" Cash asks.

"A lot, actually. Let me make some sense of it." She frowns, taking it all in. It's always been fascinating to watch Daphne *see*. Her eyes cloud over, her pupils dilate. "Okay, she was there a couple of days. She watched what he was doing to the others. She listened to them cry out, beg, sob. She didn't react much. And she knew that she wasn't going to let him do what he did to the others to her. So, when she was able to get her hands free of the ropes, she looped them over the bedpost and hung herself."

"Christ," Asher mutters, rubbing his hand over the back of his neck. "Can you see him?"

Daphne scowls. "Yes. I can see him. His back is to me, and he's sawing up a victim on his workbench."

"Has he turned around?" Cash asks.

"Not yet." Daphne pauses, and her breath hitches. "He's going to turn around. There he is. But…"

"But what?"

"I can't see his face. He's wearing a mask and something over his hair. Goggles."

"A disguise?" Asher asks.

"No, it's a surgical outfit," Daphne says. "Like he's protecting a patient from his germs. It's so fucking creepy."

"Can you look for a different time?" I ask her. "Maybe when he took her?"

She shakes her head mournfully. "She's not showing me. She keeps showing me how she fell into the water. He dragged her by her arm. It dislocated her shoulder, and then he threw her over a railing into the water below."

"So he *lives* over water?" Asher says. "This is new information."

"I don't know if he lives there," Daphne replies. "But he's definitely holding the girls there. Because he just dragged her from the bed, outside, and hitched her over the rail, like I said. She's fading now."

"Fading?" Asher asks.

"Her spirit is weakening. She's leaving," Daphne says. "Everything loses its intensity over time, especially people, although I've never touched a corpse before. I usually get my information from *things*. Tables, chairs, a letter, a child's ball. I've never done this before. It feels like the end of a song when it fades away to nothing."

"So interesting," I whisper. "Thank you."

"I didn't do anything," she says as she backs away from the body and accepts a towel from the ME. "But I do know her name. Kathy Sikes. She was a mother. On vacation with a girlfriend just before her thirtieth birthday. She lived in Chicago."

"I'll find a way to reach her family," Asher says quietly. "We may have a missing person report on her."

"You did a lot," I inform my sister. "You just helped Kathy rest peacefully. That will mean a lot to her and her family."

"I want to find this bastard," Daphne says, her voice strong with conviction. "I'm sick to death of his bullshit. Of him killing all these women. And why? Because they look like you? It's not fair."

"No, it's not," I agree and wrap my arm around her shoulders. "I wish I knew who the fuck this guy is, so we could find him and stop him."

We walk out of the morgue and take the elevator up to the first floor before stopping at the exit.

"I'm going with Daphne," I inform Cash and lean in to kiss his cheek. "We'll go find Millie. Daphne's shields are down now, and we need to get them restored, and I'm going to read through Grandma's book again. There *has* to be something in there that can help us stop this."

"I'll let you know when I'm done here," Cash says. "And, Brielle, don't you dare go back to work until I'm with you."

"I promise, I won't."

Daphne and I leave the police station and turn toward Witches Brew.

"You're going back to work?" she asks casually.

"I have to. I have to lure this fucker out."

"That's probably dangerous."

We walk a full city block in silence before she speaks again.

"He doesn't hate you," she says, surprising me.

"Who?"

"The killer. He's not doing this because he hates you."

I stop on the sidewalk and turn to her. "How do you know that?"

"Because *he* touched *her* and I could feel that. He doesn't think he's acting out of anger. In fact, he loves you. Or at least he believes he does."

"That's beyond fucked-up, even for a serial killer."

"Hey, I'm no profiler, and it was a super brief impression, but when he took her, when he touched her, he felt happiness. Affection."

"I don't have many men in my life." The frustration hangs heavily in my voice. "I have Cash. That's pretty much it. On a regular basis, anyway."

"Well, he knows you. And, no, I don't know how or why. If I did, I would have said so back there. It's so damn frustrating."

We walk into Witches Brew and stop short.

"You're kidding," Daphne says as a smile spreads over her face.

"A little help?" Millie asks, trying to control a coffee machine that seems to be going crazy, all by itself.

"What in the world?"

We hurry behind the counter and start flipping knobs and switches, but it doesn't help. Finally, I crawl under the bar and unplug the machine entirely, and everything goes quiet.

"Thank you," Millie says. She's wiping her brow when I shimmy out and sit on my ass, right there in a puddle.

"What did you do?" I ask.

"It was just a little spell I've been working on," she says with a shrug. "I thought it would be nice if the machine worked a little faster, but I must have said something wrong because—"

"Because it went crazy like something out of *Beauty and the Beast*?" Daphne asks, her hands on her hips.

"Well, yeah." Millie sighs. "Sorry, guys. I'll clean this up."

"We'll help." I stand, and the three of us mop up the milk and water as Daphne and I fill our sister in on the happenings of the past hour.

"You've been busy," Millie says softly. "I'm sorry, Daph."

"It could be worse," Daphne says. "I could have dead people following me around the city."

Both of them turn to me. "How many now?" Millie asks.

"Six." I sigh and glance out the window to the sidewalk. "He killed someone last night. They just follow me. Sometimes, their mouths move like they're speaking, but I can't hear them. It's frustrating as hell."

"The answer is in the dream-walking," Millie says.

"How do you know?" I ask.

"Because you never dream-walked before this. It's new. And because no one is going to find him without you seeing where he is or *who* he is. It's up to you, and I hate that for you, but I also kind of think it makes you a serious badass."

"I mean, I *am* a badass," I agree with a grin. "And I hate that it's up to me because I feel like I'm failing."

"I don't even want to suggest this," Daphne says, "but I think you need to fully surrender yourself to it. Let your shields down completely when you go to sleep."

"No," Millie says, horrified.

"It's the best way," I agree, thinking it over. "If I keep protecting myself, it's less likely that I'll see everything I need to. I'm missing things. Daphne's right."

"We'll be with you, as always," Daphne reassures us.

"Right now." I stand and reach for my bag. "I want to do it right now."

"You're just going to force yourself to go to sleep?" Millie asks.

"You can give me something to make me sleep."

"It makes you so damn groggy, we'll be lucky if you wake up by Thursday."

"It's only Monday," Daphne says in surprise.

"Exactly," Millie agrees.

"So, give me a smaller dose." I shrug. "But whip it up fast because we're heading back to my apartment."

"You'd better give Cash a heads-up," Daphne warns. "I don't want to be on his shit list."

"Are you afraid of Cash?" I ask, surprised.

"No, but he's going to be around for a long time, and I want him to like me." She smiles smugly.

"How do you know that?"

"Oh, please," Millie says as she measures something with a special spoon. "We don't have to be psychic to see that the man is completely in love with you."

"It's weird, isn't it? We were thrown together because of a serial killer, and we're falling in love."

"There are weirder ways to fall in love," Daphne points out. "It could be in prison or something."

"You're not helping."

~

*"You're back."*

*Sarah's sitting on her little bed.*

*"You're still here."*

*"Damn right, I am." She smiles thinly but it doesn't reach her tired eyes. "It's happening faster now, though. So many girls...gone."*

*"Why hasn't he hurt you?" I wonder aloud.*

*"Because I fight back, and I think that scares him. Or excites him." She hitches a shoulder. "And I'm gonna keep fighting back."*

*"Do you still have the knife?"*

*"Yep. He was mad when he couldn't find it. Sick fuck."*

*I nod and glance around. At least one more girl I don't recognize. Maybe two.*

*"He's taking so many now."*

*"And killing them faster," she agrees.*

*"I'm going to try to go out there now. I have to see him. I have to figure out where we are so I can bring the police here. We're working really hard, Sarah. I promise."*

*She only nods as I walk to the door and try the knob.*

*This time, to my utter surprise, it gives.*

*I can walk out the door!*

*It opens to a hallway, with the smell of pine hanging in the air. As if someone came through with a cheap can of aerosol air-freshener and doused everything with it.*

*He must be covering the smell from the room.*

*I gingerly walk down the hallway. Nobody should be able to hear or see me, but Sarah can, so I'm not taking any chances.*

*I can hear music playing. Soft strains that sound like something from the '40s. Big band-style, but slow. It's the only nice thing I've seen or heard in this place.*

*The floor creaks under my foot, and I stop, waiting to see if anyone comes running around the corner.*

*No one does.*

*I pass one open doorway and glance inside, then have to fight off the urge to throw up.*

*It's a shrine. A fucking shrine with candles and flowers and incense burning.*

*And a picture of ME in the middle.*

*He's made a shrine to me.*

*Who the hell is this sick bastard?*

*I back away and keep going down the hall. On the left is another open door with another shrine.*

*But it's not my photo in the center.*

*It's Millie.*

*The air whooshes out of me as I back away and come to another room, this time with a shrine built around a photo of Daphne.*

*So, it's not just me he's after.*

*It's all of us.*

*The living room is neat as a pin. The furniture is old with holes and faded fabric, but the pillows are placed precisely in the corners. The green shag carpet has recently been vacuumed.*

*Footsteps in the kitchen grow louder as someone walks my way, and I stiffen, hoping with all my might that I recognize him and that he doesn't know I'm here.*

*He doesn't look at me as he walks past, so close that I can smell him. I can feel the heat coming off his body.*

*Suddenly, I realize I do know him. I do recognize him.*

*I didn't even know he was still alive.*

*"Oh, hello," he says as he looks at me and gives me a happy, wide smile. "Brielle! You're here. I'm so happy to see you."*

*I look around, wanting to escape, forgetting that I'm in a dream.*

*It's a dream.*

*"Yes, I can see you. I can always see you." He smiles kindly. "Did you see my room of fun?" He gestures to the back of the house where the girls are. "Isn't it great? I've been doing all of this for you, of course. I just knew you'd love it. I've been waiting for you because I wanted to have enough practice to make everything perfect for you.*

*"You're special, Brielle."*

*He laughs and looks around his house.*

*"I'm so glad I cleaned up this morning so the house was nice for you. Now, I know what you're thinking..."*

*He holds up his hands in surrender and sits in an old chair in the corner. I haven't said a word yet, haven't even confirmed that I am, in fact, here.*

*"You're wondering why I would do such special things for you and not your sisters. After all, fair's fair, right? Well, I have so many wonderful things planned for them, too, don't you worry. But you're the oldest, Brielle, so it just made sense to start with you. They'll understand, won't they?"*

*I don't reply. I simply tilt my head, watching him quietly. I remember him well, but I don't ever* remember him speaking this much. I didn't even know he could *talk* this much. I always assumed he was stupid. I never liked him. He always gave me the heebie-jeebies.

Guess I was right to listen to those instincts.

"Brielle?" He frowns as he watches me. "Aren't you going to say anything?"

"I don't know what to say." And if that's not the truth, I don't know what is. I don't want to set him off, to send him into an angry tirade and have him go off and kill all of the girls in that room.

But I also don't want to encourage him.

I'm no psychiatrist!

"Brielle." He stands and walks to me, taking my shoulders in his hands, and I want to throw up again. I do not want his hands on me.

I never did. Just a brush of his hand on my shoulder when I was a kid made me shiver.

And I'm not sure why he can touch me in this dream when I can't touch anything.

"I'm sure you're so overwhelmed with excitement that you don't know what to say. I understand. You've always been such a sweet girl."

"You barely know me," I whisper.

"I admit, it's been a while, but I know everything, Brielle. I've watched you on your little tour. You're such a smart woman, aren't you? I know you've decided to date that man. Now, I admit, I didn't like it. I wanted to just cut his head right off his body the first time I saw you two together. But I also knew it was just a matter of time until you came around."

"Came around to what?"

"Well, that we're all meant to be together, of course. Just the way it was supposed to be all along."

"You're crazy."

The words are out of my mouth before I can stop them. His expression falls. The look in his eyes hardens. But before he can do anything else, I smile.

"You're crazy to think that I wouldn't want that too, of course."

"There now," he says, satisfied. "That's a good girl."

I wake with a start and run to the bathroom, then hover over the toilet and throw up until my body is wracked with dry heaves. I can't stop it. Someone rubs my back while someone else sets a cool rag on my neck.

Finally, I sit on my haunches and look up to find Daphne, Millie, and Cash all staring down at me with concern.

"I know who he is."

# CHAPTER 18

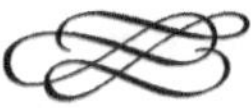

*"After my head has been chopped off, will I still be able to hear, at least for a moment, the sound of my own blood gushing from my neck? That would be the best pleasure to end all pleasure."*
~Peter Kurten, AKA the Vampire of Dusseldorf

He hasn't been this excited in a long time. Brielle finally knows what his plans are, and despite it coming earlier than he anticipated, he's pleased.

Yes, they will have to decide what her punishment will be for jumping the gun. The timeline is there for a reason, and she ignored it. That displeases him, so there will be consequences for that.

Should he cut out her tongue? He ponders that for a moment as he sharpens his second-favorite knife in the corner of the room of pleasure. No, cutting out her tongue would mean he could no longer have wonderful conversations with her, and that would be a pity.

Perhaps he should just take her toes. They are pretty little digits, but she has displeased him, and that means she needs to be punished.

Losing those pretty little toes will be a great punishment indeed.

Satisfied with his plan, he turns to the girls. The new ones are too fresh. Their fear too raw. They certainly won't do for today's fun. He needs one of the seasoned girls.

His eyes move to the one on the end, the one he's kept the longest of any of the girls he's taken. He's not sure why he decided to draw out the inevitable for her. She still has a lot of spirit, which he admits, he admires.

He's enjoyed having her here, but it's time for her to have some fun.

She's earned it, after all.

"Oh, Brielle, today has been such a treat." He whistles to himself for a moment as he gets his workstation ready for her. He's decided to treat himself even more today and play with the disemboweling again. He so enjoyed it the last time, although he got too excited and his toy died before he was able to fully detach her anus from her body.

It really was disappointing. But this time, he'll be more careful. He's been practicing in his head, running it over and over, and he's certain he won't make the same mistakes again.

The table is freshly cleaned, and his tools are ready when he turns to the girl with a smile.

"Today is very special indeed, Brielle. We are going to have *so* much fun. Now, I'll wait to put my gear on until after I get you situated. I know that's not how I usually go about things, but I honestly enjoy the way your little body feels against mine without the rubber apron. And soon, not today, but very soon, we're going to be together in the *most* special way, so I'll let myself feel you today."

She doesn't flinch. She's not breathing hard. She looks calm and collected and resigned to what's about to happen.

It's the most beautiful thing he's ever seen.

It's as if she loves him as much as he loves her.

Finally!

"Okay, Brielle." He leans over and unties her hands, then helps her to a standing position and starts to turn toward the bench. Suddenly, the unthinkable happens.

His knife, his favorite knife, is suddenly plunged into his side, right into his stomach. He stares at her, pain rushing through him.

"I told you I was going to kill you, you sick fuck."

He slaps her hard, sending her to the ground, and pulls the knife out of his side. Blood spurts over his hand covering the wound.

"Brielle," he keens. "How could you?"

He starts to cry, shaking his head.

So much blood.

And he's so sad. She hurt him! She tried to kill him.

No. Not his Brielle.

She wouldn't do that.

This one is no good.

He has to stop the bleeding.

"Ruth," he mutters as he hurries out the back door and down the stairs that lead to solid ground. "Ruth can stop it."

He hasn't seen her in a while, but she wouldn't turn him away, not when he's like this. She'll help him stitch up the wound, and then he'll go back and kill that little bitch.

How could she?

How *dare* she?

He trips and falls to the ground, his shoe falling off in the process. He stares down at it.

Should he try to put it back on? There are so many things in the swamp that could hurt his feet.

His mama always told him that.

But there's no time. Too much blood.

He wrestles his way back to his feet and shuffles along. The house is only a mile from his. He could get there blindfolded.

Yes, this is the right thing.

Ruth will help.

But he's sweating in the heat, and he's lost so much blood. Too much. It's running down his side, his leg. Everything is going dark around the edges of his vision.

Why is he so cold?

He needs Ruth to put a blanket on him, that's all. She has lots of blankets.

But maybe he'll stop in this old shed and take a break. Just to catch his breath, then he can make it the rest of the way to Ruth's house.

He hobbles inside and slides to the ground.

Critters have made this their home over the years. The roof is gone. He can't escape the hot sun.

And as he closes his eyes, he knows he won't make it to Ruth's.

Suddenly, he's hovering over his body. There's so much blood. There's no way he can survive.

But that doesn't mean he can't finish the job he's set out to do. It's still the most important thing, after all.

And now that he's free of that worthless, aging body, he can work even more diligently.

He soars over his old house, past the driveway, and onto the road leading to the highway.

Then he floats down to the road.

And waits.

# CHAPTER 19

## CASH

"Who is he?" I demand, my heart hammering in my ears.

"Horace."

The girls all stare at each other. "What?" Daphne asks at last.

"It's Horace," Brielle repeats and stands to walk back to the bedroom. "And he's a fucking psychopath. Call Asher."

"On it." I dial the other man's number and as soon as he answers, I start talking. "She knows who he is. First name is Horace. What's his last name?" I ask.

"I have no idea," Daphne says with a frown. "He was always just Horace."

"We know where he lives," Millie says. "Right by Mama."

"Jesus. Did you hear that?"

"I heard it," Asher says, "but I don't know what it means."

"I'll send you the address of their mother's house. If Horace is nearby, he can't be far. We're headed there now."

"We're leaving, too. Give me that address. And, Cash, follow protocol. We don't want anything to mess up this bust."

I text him the address while we hurry down to the car. I'm driving, with Brielle in the passenger seat. "Now, who the hell is Horace?"

"He was a man who lived near us growing up," Brielle says. She pulls on her bottom lip, watching the city speed by. "Our parents hired him here and there to help around the house. He did yard work, painted the house, did some plumbing, electrical. Really, he was the family handyman."

"Creepiest handyman ever," Millie mutters from the back seat. She grabbed their grandmother's book on the way out of the apartment and is now reading it in her lap. "I never liked that guy."

"None of us did," Daphne agrees.

"Why? What made him so creepy?"

"He was just always *there*," Brielle says. "If we were outside playing, he was nearby, trimming hedges or pruning flowers. If we were inside watching TV, he was just beyond the window, looking in."

"Did he ever approach you? Touch you?" My stomach turns at the thought of some sick fuck putting his hands on these women when they were girls.

"No, he never touched us," Daphne says. "In fact, he avoided touching us. I remember one time, he was sitting at the table in the kitchen having coffee with Mama, and I walked past him and innocently brushed his arm. He recoiled as if I'd burned him."

"He and Mama had an affair for years," Brielle adds. "She played with him. I was a kid, and still I knew it. She used to laugh when he left the house."

"They weren't quiet," Millie says. I glance at her in the rearview and watch her wince. "And she humiliated him. Even back then, I knew it. Why in the world would he come back for more of that nonsense?"

"Could be a pattern for him," I reply, thinking it over. "If his mother humiliated him, and then *your* mother did the same, he might think that that's how women behave. That it's normal."

"Well, that's just fucked-up," Daphne says.

"I mean, he's a serial killer," Brielle reminds them. "So, pretty much everything he does is fucked-up."

Lights flash behind me just as my phone rings.

"Asher," I say into the phone.

"We're behind you. I have four more cars behind *me.*"

"Excellent," I reply. "Just follow me. The road in there is rough, so it'll be slow going once we're off the main road. I'd say we're about twenty minutes away."

"Copy that. Once we get to the house, you do *not* go inside."

"I know the procedure," I reply and hang up. "I'm with the FBI for fuck's sake."

Brielle reaches over and takes my hand in hers, giving it a squeeze. I glance her way and smile.

This is almost over.

I'm so fucking relieved. I want to be with her in a normal setting when I'm not constantly worried about her well-being. I just want to *be* with her.

"We're almost there," Daphne says, pointing to the lane that turns off the main road. "Turn there. After we go over that part that was washed out, turn right. His house is about a half a mile from the turn."

"Got it."

We have to slow down more than I'd like, but there's no choice with the lane in the condition it's in.

Just when I round a bend, Brielle holds up a hand.

"Stop the car."

"What?"

"Stop the goddamn car."

I slam on the brakes and turn to stare at her. "What? What is it?"

"Do you see him?"

She's staring straight ahead. I follow her gaze and about come out of my skin.

Standing maybe ten feet in front of the car is a shadow.

A man.

"I fucking see him," I mutter in surprise.

"He's dead," Brielle says.

"Do you see a shadow or a man?" Millie asks. "Because I see a shadow."

"Me, too," Daphne says.

"That makes three of us," I add.

"I see a man. I see Horace," Brielle says. "Drive through him."

"Are you sure?"

"Oh, yeah. Fuck him."

I nod once, put the car in drive, and step on it, plowing right through the shadow. It dissipates around us, and I gingerly drive over the washed-out area, then turn onto Horace's driveway.

Sure enough, about a half-mile later, a small house comes into view. The back side of it butts up to the swamp and has a rickety porch suspended over the expansive water beyond it. The house is small, and it leans to one side. But the roof has been recently patched.

I stop the car and wait while Asher and his men jump out of their vehicles and surround the house, all of them armed.

Less than three minutes after they break down the door, Asher comes out and gestures for us to follow him.

"He's not here," he says as we walk through the front door. "But we found the women, all still alive."

"Whoa." Millie's eyes are wide as she stands in the living room and stares at the photos on the walls. "It's all three of us."

"He told me that we were all part of his stupid plan. I was just first because I'm the oldest," Brielle says and takes Millie's hand in hers. "He had plans for you and Daph, too, but he didn't say what they were."

"I killed him." The girl's the first to be escorted out, wrapped in a blanket. "At least, I think I did. I stabbed him, and then he hit me and ran away. But there's no way he could survive that. I stabbed him in the gut."

"Get men out to the swamp," Asher orders one of his men. "We're going to find that fucker."

"Sarah." Brielle approaches the other woman carefully. "Do you remember me?"

Glassy eyes turn to Brielle, and then Sarah starts to cry.

"You found us," she says and wraps her arms around Brielle. "I did what you said. I stabbed him."

"You are a fucking badass, Sarah Chandler. I'm so damn proud of you."

"We all are," Daphne says, joining in on the hug. Millie wraps her arms around all of them, and they stand for a long moment, giving each other comfort and strength.

And if I know these girls at all, they're adding a little magic to the mix right now for Sarah, as well.

Once all the abducted girls are loaded into ambulances and taken to the hospital, I join Asher back in the killer's playroom.

I stop at the doorway and take it all in. I've seen other lairs, and I've seen more blood, but I don't know if I've seen this level of absolute *evil*.

Three toddler-sized beds line one wall, each with a bare, soiled mattress. An electric chair is in the corner, and the opposite wall boasts the biggest workbench I've ever seen in my life, with tools of all shapes and sizes lining shelves above the bench. They've all been cleaned, but forensics will lift blood samples from the tools and the counter. And, most likely, the floor, beds, and chair.

"Fucking hell," Asher says, his hands on his hips as he stares at dozens of brunette braids hung on the wall. "Thirty-six."

"He's killed far more than that," I reply as I join him.

"Why didn't he keep more trophies?"

"Oh, he most likely did. We'll probably find them all somewhere in this house. These are just the trophies he was admiring for killing Brielle."

Asher turns to me. "How are you able to stomach this?"

"I won't lie to you, this one isn't easy because it *is* Brielle, and she's mine. No case is a walk in the park, but this one makes me want to kill him with my bare hands. That doesn't happen often."

"We're searching the house as we speak, so we'll discover anything else there is to find. Did you see the shrines in the bedrooms?"

"Yeah." I swallow hard. "He's apparently been obsessed with them since they were kids. They grew up in a house about a mile from here, and Brielle told me he used to be their handyman and that he had an affair with their mother."

"Sick fuck," Asher says.

"We found something!"

Both Asher and I hurry to the master bedroom where a team has been searching.

"I pulled up this rug, and sure enough, there was a hole cut in the floor," Officer Thibideaux says. "And I found this."

He points to the box sitting on the bed. It's made of wood and has something sculpted into the lid.

"It's a star," I say, staring down at it.

"It's a pentagram." I spin at Brielle's voice behind me. "I couldn't figure out why he could see me when I was dream-walking, or how he could touch me in the dream. I'm pretty sure Sarah's sensitive and may not know it, and that's why *she* could see me. But him? I couldn't figure it out at first.

"But after being here, in his house, and having my own shields down somewhat, I know. Not only is he psychic, but he's also a witch. That's a pentagram. I don't know how long he's been practicing. I don't know how powerful he was or where he learned his craft. I don't know if he comes from a line of witches. But I'll start doing some research and ask around. But you all need to know before you open that box that it most likely has a protective spell on it, and it may have a booby trap hex, as well."

"A *booby trap hex*?" Asher asks, a smirk appearing. "Is that the official term?"

"No, the official term is it could burn your hand off if you touch it. Does that help?"

Thibideaux shakes his head and reaches for the box. When a bolt of lightning shocks his hand, he backs right off in surprise.

"How do we open it, then?" Asher asks.

Millie walks into the room, takes a deep breath, and smiles. "Because the one who cast the spell is dead, I can break it. Give me some room, please."

We all stand back and watch with rapt attention as she splays her hands over the box, looks up to the sky, and begins to chant.

"Lord and Lady working for me and through me, assist me in breaking the spell cast on this object. The wielder has passed beyond the veil and no longer holds sway over this object or its contents. For the good of all, according to free will, grant me access, and—"

I don't really hear all of the words she says after that. The room grows warm, and light fills the space, and then it's gone in a flash as Millie sighs deeply.

"There, it's safe."

Asher reaches for the box, and nothing happens to his hands when he removes the lid.

"Cash."

I join him and feel my jaw tighten at what's inside.

"Looks like he had a thing for eyeballs," Asher says quietly.

There must be a hundred eyeballs in the box.

"Get this to the ME," Asher says. "I want to know how many there are. If he took both of his victims' eyes, or just one. I want to know *everything* about this son of a bitch."

I walk out of the room and lead all three sisters out of the house. They all look exhausted.

"They haven't found his body yet," Millie says and turns to Daphne. "Were you able to pick anything up on him?"

"I touched things in there," Daphne says, her voice trembling slightly. "All I saw were echoes. Memories. Nothing from the present."

"He's here," Brielle says, looking down at her feet. "He's been following us through the house, grinning. He's proud of his work."

"If that isn't the creepiest thing I've ever heard, I don't know what is," Millie says.

"I mean, there *were* at least a hundred eyeballs in a box, so there's that, too," Daphne reminds her. "I don't want him following Bri for the rest of her life. We need to get rid of him."

"He's not going to stay," Brielle says in surprise. She's looking at something, or someone, in front of her. "He just said goodbye."

"Just like that?" Millie asks and turns to me. "What are the chances that a serial killer would be like, '*well, you got me. Peace out!*'?"

"Slim to none," I agree with her. "But I won't complain if that's his plan."

"Me either," Daphne says, just as two of the men who set off to look for the body come running back to the house.

"What do you have?" I ask.

"We found his shoe and a large pool of blood on the ground right next to the swamp."

"We think he collapsed there and was dragged away by a critter," the other officer says.

"Keep looking," Asher says from the doorway. "We'll keep searching for his body until dark, and then we'll look again tomorrow."

"He's dead," Brielle says.

"You and your sisters keep saying that, but I don't see a body, and without that, I can't confirm that he's gone. I can't tell all of those families that my psychic consultant assures me he's dead, so it must be true."

"I know," Brielle says with a shrug. "I get it. But he can't hurt anyone anymore, and that's the most important thing."

I wrap my arm around her shoulder and pull her against me so I can kiss her temple. "Proud of you," I whisper in her ear.

"I want all of you to go home," Asher says, pointing to us. "Cash, I'll need you at the office this evening for a full debriefing, and possibly the news conference. Reporters will ask questions I may not be able to answer."

"Just let me know when and where you need me," I assure him.

"I want to go to the hospital to see the girls," Brielle says. "They need some strength today."

"We'll all go," Daphne says. "Millie, let's stop by the Brew and make them some potions."

"Excellent idea," Millie says, heading for the car. "Let's go."

Once the girls are in the vehicle waiting for me, I turn back to Asher.

"I have plenty to say about this animal, but I didn't want to say it in front of those three. He's not a typical psychopath. I'll brief you more later."

"Agreed," Asher says and nods. "I've never seen *anything* like this, and I've been in homicide for a long fucking time. I'd like to hear your thoughts. Go take care of the women, and I'll see you in a few hours."

I nod, and once I'm in the car and headed back toward the city, Brielle turns to me.

"What did you say to him once we were out of earshot?"

I take her hand and kiss her knuckles. "That, darlin', is none of your business."

"Well, he told you," Millie says and laughs. "I can't believe I can laugh after what we just saw. He had *shrines*. With photos and everything."

"Where did he get the snapshots?" Daphne wonders. "They're pictures even Mama wouldn't have because they were clearly taken after we left."

"Unfortunately," Brielle says with a sigh, "I think we're going to have to go to Mama's at some point and ask some questions."

"Why?" Millie asks.

"Because she's his *neighbor* and has known him for as long as I can remember. She'll know something more than we do."

"She doesn't know who *we* are these days," Daphne says. "How do you expect her to know anything about Horace killing innocent women?"

"It's worth a try," Brielle insists. "But not today. We've all been through enough. I'm just relieved that it's over. He can't hurt anyone else."

"Is he still following you?" Millie asks.

"No, and the murdered girls are gone, too. They were gone as soon as we stepped out of my apartment after my dream. I'm telling you, it's over. We can all go back to living our lives."

"Well, thank the goddess for miracles," Millie says. "Now, let's go take care of those girls."

# CHAPTER 20

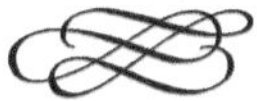

## BRIELLE

*N*o one follows me around for the first time in weeks, and I'm ridiculously happy about it.

No creepy dead girls.

No Horace.

Just the usual shadows of New Orleans here and there. Surprisingly, they don't scare me like they used to. There are more shadows in the hospital, which is to be expected.

I'm easily able to ignore them.

"I hope they let us in soon," Millie says, holding a tray of hot chocolates, each containing a spell of protection and healing. "I don't want these to get cold."

"You can come back," a nurse says from the doorway leading to the ER rooms. "All of the ladies are awake and would like to say hello."

"Are you sure?" Daphne asks. "They've been through something pretty horrible."

"They have family with them and will be here for a couple of days. But, yes, they agreed to see you."

We stop at each room, offering a cup of hot chocolate and lots of hugs.

"I look like you," the one named Megan says softly. "You're so lucky he didn't take you."

"I know I am." I nod and push away the sudden guilt that pierces my heart. It's not my fault, and I know that, but I can't help but feel responsible for the suffering that these girls endured.

I can't imagine the fear, the horror.

I purposefully save my visit with Sarah for last. My sisters don't join me when I walk into the room. Sarah's face lights up when she sees me. "Hey!"

"Hey, yourself." I sit on the bed near her hip. "How do you feel?"

"A little better now that they're pumping some fluids into me," she says, pointing to her IV. "I'm happy to have all of my brothers here. I might not let them out of my sight again."

"The feeling's mutual, squirt."

I turn to look at Sarah's brothers and feel my eyes widen. They're all big men, well over six feet, with broad shoulders and meaty hands.

I wouldn't want to piss any of them off.

"It's nice to meet you all."

"Sarah says you came to her sometimes and talked to her," one of the brothers says with a frown. "How is that even possible?"

"I don't know for sure." I shrug and shake my head. "I was dream-walking. And if I told you everything, you'd think I'm crazy."

"No, I think the dick that did this is crazy," he replies. "I'm grateful to you for helping Sarah escape."

"Sarah did that because she's a badass. She has older brothers who taught her how to take care of herself. I was just there at the right moment when a knife had been left on the floor and pointed it out."

"Either way, we're grateful," another brother says. "We're going to go get something from the cafeteria while you two talk."

"Thanks."

Sarah sighs. "It feels like a nightmare. I mean, I know I'm starving and dirty and my muscles hurt from sitting on that fucking bed, but part of me feels like it was all a long, drawn-out night terror."

"Worst nightmare ever," I reply softly. "So, you remember seeing me?"

"You were standing in that room as clearly as you're here right now," she says. "It confused the hell out of me. I thought I was imagining things at first, but then you talked to me. I figured, even if I was going crazy, having someone to talk to was kind of nice."

"Have you ever considered yourself sensitive to paranormal things?" I ask, watching her carefully.

"Sure. I grew up in a haunted house. Nothing too crazy, just footsteps here and there. I don't see dead people, like that movie, but I've checked into hotels and asked to have my room changed because the one they gave me felt off. That sort of thing. Is that what you mean?"

"That's exactly what I mean," I confirm. "I think that's why you were able to see me, and the others weren't. Sarah, I'm so sorry for what you went through, what you must have witnessed in that place."

"I closed my eyes a lot of the time," she admits on a whisper. "And I feel like a damn wimp for it, but I think I would have really gone out of my mind if I'd watched, you know?"

"Absolutely."

"He was a monster."

"The worst kind there is," I agree. "But he's gone. You got him."

"Did they find his body yet?"

I frown and check my phone. There's no message from Cash. "I don't know. They hadn't yet when we left the scene earlier, but I haven't heard anything since then. They might have."

"What if they don't? What if I didn't kill him after all, and he's off somewhere getting stitched up?"

"He's not." I clear my throat. "Sarah, I'm psychic. A medium. I *do* see dead people. And I saw him. He's dead, and that won't change whether they find his body or not."

"Wow." She swallows hard. "Well, that sucks for you."

We're quiet for a moment, both lost in our own thoughts, and then it's like a light bulb goes off in her head.

"Wait. Does that mean that you could see the others? The other women?"

"Yeah. I could see them. That's how I knew something was going on. They came to me to warn me, and to tell me to find them. But now that he's gone, they're gone, too."

"Well, I think that sucks just as much for you as it does for the rest of us." She reaches for my hand and grips it fiercely. "You're a victim, too."

"We're not victims, Sarah. We're still here."

"Damn right, we are. Can we stay friends? I mean, I know it sounds weird, and if it's too off the wall for you, that's okay, I just—"

"We're totally friends," I say, interrupting her. "I'd like that very much."

I DON'T THINK a shower ever felt so good. I bet that's how the others felt today once they knew they were safe and were able to wash away the filth from their time in that horrible room.

Best shower ever.

I hope that all the girls get the best counseling there is, and that they're able to heal from their ordeal.

I towel-dry my hair then twist it up into a bun and dry off the rest of my body. When I reach for the lotion, I see my necklace, sitting right there by the sink as if it was there all along.

I searched high and low for it this morning and couldn't find it.

"Must be going blind in my old age," I mutter as I smooth lotion on my legs and loop the chain over my neck. "Apparently, thirty is when it all goes downhill."

I smirk and pad out of the bathroom. My sisters both went home tonight, ready to get back to their lives. Part of me misses them already. We've always been close—except for my spat with Daphne—and it's been nice having them nearby these past couple of weeks.

Having Daph speaking to me again is the best thing ever.

But I know they're not far away, and I'll most likely see one or both of them tomorrow.

I pause at the doorway of my bedroom and smile when I see Cash sitting up in bed, waiting for me.

Speaking of the best thing ever.

"Hey there," I say as I walk to the side of the bed and slip between the covers next to him.

"Hey, yourself."

"How are you?"

"I think this might be the most tired I've ever been in my entire life," he says with a gusty sigh. "But it feels good to know *he's* gone and not coming back, and that everyone's safe tonight."

"Yeah." I cozy up next to him, enjoying the way it feels when he wraps his arm around me, and I fit right under his shoulder. I can hear his heart beating. "I like that, too. The whole thing is weird, don't you think?"

"The fact that you saw murder victims and we tracked down the killer, only to discover that he had a thing for you and your sisters? Whatever do you mean?"

"Smartass." I snort. "There are some holes that need to be filled, though."

"I don't want to talk about this tonight, Brielle."

I look up at him. "You don't?"

"No. We've been talking about it for weeks, and now that it's over, I want to take one night to just enjoy you. We can talk about it tomorrow."

"I mean, I'm right here, just waiting to be enjoyed."

He pushes me onto my back and takes a tour of my shoulders with his lips. Tingles float over my skin, making me feel more alive than ever before.

Each time we're together, it's better than the last. I don't even know how that's possible.

"I love your skin," he murmurs before catching a nipple with his lips. "So soft, so pink."

I push my fingers through his hair, happy to let him lazily work his way across my flesh. He's not an impatient man when it comes to sex. He likes to linger, enjoy, and it makes my toes curl.

I've never met anyone like him. And I know that there will be no one like him ever again.

So I lie back and enjoy the lazy, sexy ride.

~

"THIS IS THE ANDREW JACKSON HOTEL." I point behind me and smile at my group. Oh, my goddess, it feels good to be back at work. I didn't realize how much I loved this job until I couldn't be here for a while. "This was an all-boys school, way back in the day."

I talk about the school burning down, and how the boys are said to still be there, haunting the halls.

This group has been lively, with a few more hecklers than usual, but a few quick-witted comebacks from me seems to have calmed them down for the most part.

"We're staying there," a man says, making me smile.

"Someone on my tour always is." I wink and lead them farther down the street, giving them little details about specific buildings. Not all of them are haunted, some of them are just interesting because of how old they are and what may or may not have taken place there once upon a time.

The best part of the tour this evening is that there are no new shadows. Nothing different at all tonight, and that makes me happiest of all. The girls are truly at rest, and we're ready to get on with our lives.

To go back to *normal*. Whatever that is.

"How do you know all this stuff?" a guy asks as we walk down the sidewalk. "Are you psychic or something?"

"What would you say if I told you that I *am* psychic?"

"I would say you're full of shit," he replies bluntly.

"Well, I'll just say this then, I went to college to study American history, with an emphasis on Creole history, here in Louisiana. I'm from the area, and I love the folklore here. Most everything I tell you on this tour can be verified in history books."

"Only *most?*" he asks.

"Well, the rest of it depends on whether you believe in the paranormal or not, doesn't it? No one can *prove* the existence of ghosts. Even spirits caught on film can usually be explained away. Double-exposure, reflections, weird lighting, that sort of thing. And, yes, people have their own experiences, but that's just hearsay, right?"

"Do *you* believe in ghosts?" he asks me.

"Sugar, you can't live in New Orleans and *not* believe in ghosts. They're all over the place. So, yes, I do believe they exist."

"So, you're saying spirits are just roaming around, trying to dick with all of us?"

"No, not at all. In fact, not all ghosts are intelligent."

He blinks at me blankly.

"There are theories that some spirits are caught in a loop. Like…an echo. They do the same things over and over again, whether someone is there to see it or not. They don't know that anyone is there. They may not even know they're dead. It's like a recording.

"And then there are spirits that do know they're dead, and they haunt. Maybe they haunt a place or a thing or a person."

"Whoa." He holds up a hand and stops walking. "A person?"

"Sure, it's happened. For whatever reason, a spirit attaches itself to a living person, and no matter where the person moves or where they go, the spirit goes with them."

"Creepy AF," he says and grins at his friend, who's been standing by, listening silently.

"Now it's time to talk about more dead people," I say and wink as I stop in front of the LaLaurie mansion and reinforce my shields. Even though things have been routine on tonight's tour, this is the one place that still makes me uneasy.

Maybe because the woman who owned it—and still haunts it—was as evil as the man we just caught.

Maybe more so.

I'm only about thirty seconds into my speech about the mansion and its history when there is a loud pop and sparks fly everywhere from above.

We all duck out of the way and look around in confusion. Are we being shot at? Did a bomb just go off somewhere?

"The streetlight exploded!" someone exclaims, pointing to the light directly above me. I look up and, sure enough, smoke streams from where the bulb once was, and the filaments are still glowing from the explosion.

That's new.

At least there's no shadow hovering over it.

"Wow, is everyone okay?" I ask the group, looking everyone over. "Did anyone get hurt?"

"Just scared us," someone said.

"If that's part of the show, it's effective," someone shouts, making me laugh.

"No, that's definitely not part of the show. That was a freebie, just for you guys. Okay, well, now that your heart rate is up, let's talk about Madame LaLaurie…"

# CHAPTER 21

~Richard Ramirez, The Night Stalker

*ust look at her down there*, he thinks to himself as he floats above the streetlamp that he successfully blew up. She's laughing and wandering through their city with her little group of idiots, who all want to know about the paranormal things that plague the French Quarter.

He always understood that Brielle needed to make a living, and that sharing her gifts with others was an efficient way for her to do so.

She does the best she can.

But she's capable of so much more.

He didn't realize that it would take him a while to figure out his new way of life. That he wouldn't slip easily between his physical body to the spiritual one and carry on the way he was before.

It seems there's a learning curve.

That displeases him. He's been following Brielle all week, trying to communicate with her, but she can't see him. Or, if she can, she's ignoring him. That's something he'll have to punish her for later.

But he's chosen to trust that it's not Brielle's fault. He simply has to work harder. Which is fine. Hard work has always come easily to him. He enjoys it.

He floats above the group as Brielle leads them through town. From his vantage point, he can see the other spirits she talks about, trapped in their own afterlives of torment.

He doesn't pity them. They earned what they got and where they are.

Just as he did.

But he's not trapped, he controls his destiny. And as soon as he figures out some things, he'll be right back on track.

He watches as Brielle smiles and says goodbye to a customer. She's so beautiful, his sweet girl.

*Don't you worry*, he thinks. *You haven't lost me, Brielle. I can't wait to show you what I have in store. You're going to be so happy. So excited. It won't be long now.*

# CHAPTER 22

## CASH

"It's been a week," I say to Asher as I sit across from him in his office. I just arrived, and I want some answers.

And a conversation with a colleague.

Something's eating at me.

"How is Brielle?" Asher asks.

"She's doing well, actually." I rub the back of my neck and sigh. "She's gone back to work and says nothing strange has happened. The spirits of the girls are gone. Millie and Daphne have gone home. Everything seems to be back to normal."

"And you don't trust it," he guesses correctly.

"It's ridiculous, but you're right. I don't trust it. Catching him or discovering who he was wasn't an easy task, as you know. But then it was over and wrapped up so quickly it just seems…unfinished to me. Please tell me you found his body."

"We did," Asher confirms, and I feel my stomach loosen for the first time in a month. "He crawled into a ruined shed about a quarter-mile from his house. He bled out there. We're still waiting for an autopsy, but there was a huge amount of blood. As Sarah said, he was stabbed in the stomach."

"I'm surprised he made it a quarter of a mile. I wonder why he went that way instead of calling for help?"

"You know why. There's no way he could have called 911. He would have been caught."

"In which direction was the shed?" I ask. Asher reaches for a map, unrolls it on his desk, and we lean over it.

"Here's his house," Asher says and points to a red dot. "This is where we found him."

"I think this is Brielle's mother's house," I say, pointing to a property less than a mile away from the shed. "I wonder if he was headed there for help."

"Could be," Asher says. "My men stopped by there and tried to ask questions."

I lean back in the chair. "I bet that went well."

"She's crazy, Cash."

"I'm a licensed psychiatrist, and I can confirm that statement. She also killed her husband roughly twenty years ago."

The other man's eyes narrow. "Come again?"

"You heard me." I stand and pace the office. "I don't have proof, just the word of a crazy old woman and my girlfriend, who was only a teenager at the time."

"The house needs to be condemned. She needs to go to a mental hospital."

"I know." I turn to look at him.

"I'm reporting it to the proper authorities."

"Understood."

"Now, I have a whole slew of things to talk to you about regarding this case. I hope you don't have any plans for a few hours."

"I'm all ears," I reply as I return to my seat. "I have plenty to say, as well, but I'm anxious to hear what your team found in the house."

"More creepy shit than I like to think about," he says, shaking his head. Asher looks bone-tired. "He kept meticulous journals, dating back to when he was young. And he stored them in chronological order."

"That was thoughtful of him."

"Everything in that house was spotless. Tidy. Precise."

"Makes sense."

"Does it?"

"Oh, absolutely. He thrived on control, and that included his home. Everything had a place. He was clearly a planner. The girls he took may have been random in the heat of the moment, but he knew *when* he would take them, and he had a very particular type. He planned what he would do to them. Most likely, he practiced the same techniques for many years."

"You're right," Asher confirms. "He was fifty-four years old when he died. The first journal dates back to when he was sixteen. That's almost forty years of killing."

"Surely, he didn't start with humans."

"Animals," Asher says. "The family dog. A neighbor's cat. It escalated from there. He documented names if he knew them, so we have lists of his victims. Many families will have answers to the disappearances of their loved ones because of this."

"That's something, I guess. What else?"

"My team has spent the better part of this past week poring through every journal. They took notes on what they read. We counted one hundred and seventy-four victims, starting with his mother when he was eighteen."

"Christ Jesus."

"Those are just the human victims. We didn't count the animals, but there were a lot of those, as well. And, Cash, he wasn't just after Brielle."

"I saw the shrines for her sisters. He was going after them, too."

"He'd already started." Asher fishes out some photos and slaps them on the desk for me to see. "The eyeballs we found in that box? He said in a journal that he was collecting those for Daphne. Because she has the *sight*."

"There were almost a hundred eyes in that box. They're with the ME to determine if they're from ninety-six different victims, or if he took both eyes from each victim."

"He most likely took both," I say and move to the next photo. "Is this blood?"

"Thirty pints of it," Asher confirms. "It said in his notes that he was collecting it for Millie, because she's a kitchen witch, and he thought she could use it for potions."

"For fuck's sake, what kind of potions could she make with human blood?"

"I don't even want to guess," Asher says, sighing loudly. "He took the hair for Brielle, simply because he had a thing for her brunette hair. In his notes, he says that he didn't think he could take anything to help her gift of seeing shadows, but he could make sure no other women had hair nice enough to rival hers."

"Sick fuck," I whisper.

"So, he had trophies for each of the girls. The blood and eyes, he said, were the *practice* toys he'd played with to get ready for the main show. But he'd mastered his craft for Brielle and was nearing the end of the show. He'd planned to take her next week."

My head whips up in surprise. "He had it *planned?*"

"That shouldn't surprise you."

I shake my head and try to detach from Brielle, remove myself as her lover, and think of this from a professional standpoint.

"You're right. It shouldn't. And now that I think about it, it doesn't surprise me. What was the last entry in the journal?"

"Here."

He flips to the last page of the journal and passes it to me.

*April 23,*

*She came to me. Finally! I've heard her in the room of fun, talking to the girls, and hoped that she'd come to me, and she finally did. She saw everything. I've kept the house spotless in hopes that she'd arrive soon. She seemed very pleased and didn't even mind when I touched her. I don't think it occurred to her that I could touch her during her dream-walking.*

*Brielle and the others always underestimated me. They didn't know that I understood their gifts. That I share them. I could teach them so much! And I will, very soon.*

*Just a few more days, and Brielle will be here. In our home. I have to finish playing with the other toys first, but that won't take long. I have a couple more experiments to run on them before I feel comfortable using the techniques on my Brielle. I want to give her the best experience of her life. I want to provide her with things that no one else ever has.*

*It's going to be so beautiful!*

I toss the book on the desk and swallow hard.

"When will the autopsy be done?"

"Sometime this week," Asher says. "The morgue's been a little busy the past few weeks."

"Yeah. What happens to him when it's done?"

"Well, this is where it gets weird."

"*This* is where it gets weird?"

He pulls out another document and passes it to me. "That's his will. He left everything to Brielle and her sisters."

My eyes scan it. "He had it done through an attorney and everything."

"He wasn't a stupid man. An evil one, but not stupid."

"So now they own the property and all of his personal effects."

"Yes, and as next of kin, they get to decide what to do with his remains."

"Well, that's pretty fucked-up, Asher."

"Oh, trust me. This is the weirdest case of my career, and like I told you before, I've seen some shit. This rivals some of the most extreme serial killer cases I've heard of."

"Same here, and I've also seen some shit. But there's something that I can't put my finger on that tells me this isn't entirely over."

"He's on ice in the morgue," Asher reminds me. "It's pretty much over."

"Yeah." I stare at all of the evidence on Asher's desk. "Yeah, I guess you're right. How in the hell am I going to tell the girls that the sick fuck who wanted them all tortured and dead left all of his worldly possessions to them?"

"I can tell them," Asher offers.

"No, it should come from me." I sigh again and stand. "How soon do you need to know what they want to do with his remains?"

"No rush at all."

"Good. I'll be in touch."

I'm on my way out of the police station when my phone rings.

"Hey, Felicia. How's it going over there?"

"Well, we're at the ER," Felicia says. I can tell she's trying to sound like nothing's wrong, but something's wrong. "I didn't want to worry you, but I thought you should know."

"What's up?"

"I just didn't like the sound of your mom's breathing. She says it's nothing, that she always wheezes like that, but she didn't sound this way when I arrived. So, I brought her in just to get checked out."

"Good idea. Please keep me posted. I need to call Andy. I haven't talked to him in a few days."

"You've been a little busy," she replies kindly. "But he'd like to hear from you. I think he's getting a little lonely without me."

"I'll get in touch with him today. Thanks, Felicia."

"You're welcome. Talk soon."

Before I can put my phone into my pocket, my brother calls.

"Did you just talk to my wife?" he asks after I answer.

"Just hung up with her."

"I'm worried about Mom. The last time she had pneumonia, she almost died."

"We don't know that she has pneumonia. She could have allergies."

"Yeah." I can hear the strain in my brother's voice. "You're right."

"Why don't I come by and take you out to lunch? Are you free?"

"I have some time."

"I'm still at the police station. I'm sitting on the steps out front."

"Be right there."

He hangs up, and I shoot Brielle a text.

Me: *Hey, babe. Gonna grab lunch with Andy. Need anything?*

I grin when I see the dots bounce as she replies.

Brielle: *Have fun! I don't need anything. I'm at Daphne's store, having lunch with the sisters.*

Me: *I'll text when I'm done.*

I've never been to Daphne's store. We always meet at either Brielle's apartment or Witches Brew, but Brielle told me that Daphne owns an antique shop.

I bet there are a lot of antiques in New Orleans.

"I didn't know you were still working on the case," Andy says as he approaches.

I stand and join him on the sidewalk. "Yeah, there are still things to tie up. That man was on a level of evil I've never seen before."

"I'm glad you were here to help with it," Andy says. "I don't know how you do what you do. I think it would drive me insane."

"I put the cases in boxes," I say as we walk into a restaurant nearby. We're quickly shown to a table. "I have to compartmentalize it all. Because you're right, it messes with you. The last case, losing Carlson—"

"Which was *not* your fault."

"That one got under my skin. And, frankly, you wouldn't be human if they didn't get under your skin a little bit. But you have to put it all in boxes, or it will consume you.

"I don't know how I'm going to make a relationship with Brielle work."

"Why?"

"Because what I do takes me all over the damn world, Andy. I haven't seen the inside of my apartment in Dallas for at least two months. I don't even know why I have it. Not to mention, you said yourself that I see some horrible shit. That'll bleed into any relationship."

"First, I want to know how *this* case has affected you."

"It messed with me," I admit, knowing I can trust my brother. "Because it was less black and white than any other case I've worked. I've never had to deal with the paranormal. I didn't think I believed in it before."

"And now?" We pause as the waitress approaches and takes our orders.

"I've seen it," I say bluntly when she leaves. "At first, I humored Brielle. *She* believed it, so I just went along with it. But what she described, and what she's able to do? That's not a hoax, man. And it's not anything I can explain, even with all of my years of education and training. It just *is*. So, yeah, I believe it. Not to mention, I saw a friggin' ghost myself, so…"

"Whose ghost?"

"The killer's. He was standing in the middle of the goddamn road, I shit you not."

"Whoa." Andy sits back in his chair, his eyes wide and pinned to mine. "You're kidding."

"I wish I was."

"And how do you feel about Brielle?"

"I'm completely and irrevocably in love with her."

A slow smile spreads over my brother's face. "It finally happened."

"Not sure what I can do about it, though," I repeat. "My job doesn't lend itself well to marriage."

"I didn't say anything about *marriage*."

I laugh and shrug. "Yeah, well, that's usually what happens when you decide you can't live without someone, right? She's it for me, and I don't know how to make it work."

"I know the NOPD would hire you in a heartbeat. Not to mention, there's an FBI field office right here. You can transfer. You have options."

"I most likely wouldn't be a profiler anymore, though, and I worked my ass off to get here. You know that."

"Profiler, or be with the love of your life?" He holds up his hands at his sides as if he's weighing something on scales. "I mean, I think it's a no-brainer, man."

"I know." I sigh. "Now, let's get back to you. How are you doing?"

"I miss my wife," he says with a frown. "She needs to get home."

"We're just a couple of lovesick fools."

"Ain't it great?"

～

I'M glad I had lunch with my brother. He always gives me a different perspective on things, and I feel better after talking with him.

He's not wrong.

634

If I move here permanently, not only would I have Brielle, but I'd also have Andy and Felicia.

It's damn tempting.

More than tempting.

Let's be honest, it's probably going to happen.

I push through the door of Reflections, Daphne's store on the edge of the French Quarter, and smile when I see all three sisters sitting in a corner, drinking coffee.

"There he is," Brielle says with a grin and leaps up to offer me a kiss. "I missed you today."

"Same here." I lay another deep kiss on her before we join the others. "I love your place here, Daph."

The pretty redhead grins and glances around her store. "Me, too. I could sure tell you some interesting stories here, Cash."

"Yeah? Like what?"

She stands and places her hand on a tall, yellow vase. "This was made in 1923 by a man who lived in the bayou. He made it for his wife, who was about to have their first baby. Yellow was Mildred's favorite color, and he had to do something to keep his hands busy while they waited on the child. He was so excited."

Daphne's face turns sad.

"But when Mildred went into labor, something went wrong. Both she and the baby died. So, he gave this vase to his cousin, who lived here in New Orleans."

"That's horrible," Millie whispers.

"You can do that with every piece in here?" I ask.

She nods and sits in the chair again. "I can do that with literally *everything*. I see the thoughts of the people who sat in airplane seats before me. I see pretty much everything, Cash."

"That has to be exhausting."

"I'm able to block a lot of it because I've learned to build my shields of protection, and Millie makes me potions for strength. It takes a lot to surprise me these days."

I turn to Millie. "And you're proficient in potions and spells and such?"

"Yes, I'm a hedgewitch," she confirms. "I've studied for years. I'm also psychic, but not in the same way these two are. I don't see the past or dead people. I read people's minds. I can touch someone and see their thoughts, feelings, things like that. So, I try to avoid skin-on-skin contact most of the time unless I take precautions."

"Fascinating," I mutter. "You're all remarkable and more interesting than I can say."

"I like your boyfriend, Bri," Daphne says, grinning. "He hands out compliments. He can stay."

"I'm glad you approve," Brielle says with a laugh. "Now, tell us what you found out today."

"You're not going to like it."

# CHAPTER 23

## BRIELLE

"**W**hat's going on?" I ask Cash. I don't like the concern in his green eyes at all.

"First of all, they found his body," he says, and all three of us slump in relief. "He was in an old shed between his house and your mother's."

"He must have been trying to get to Mama, to see if she could help him," Millie says.

"As a sidebar," Cash continues, "speaking of your mother, the police visited her house while they were canvassing the area, looking for his body. They're going to recommend she be institutionalized, and the house condemned."

I blink at him, then look at my sisters. "It's for the best."

"Then why does it feel...*not* for the best?" Daphne asks.

"Maybe they can help her," Millie says. "Maybe getting out of that haunted house and being among professionals who can treat her will help. It won't make her a nice person, but it has to be better than how she's living now."

"Agreed," I say and nod. "So far, this isn't awful."

"Yeah, well, buckle up," Cash mutters. "I spoke at length with Asher today. They've been gathering all of the evidence from his residence, cataloging and poring through it all. His team has worked very hard on this."

"Of course, they have," I agree.

"Horace was an intelligent man. Do you mind if I pace, Daphne?"

"Of course not, pace away, just keep talking."

Cash stands and walks back and forth, speaking as he thinks. "He kept journals. From day one."

"How long?" Millie asks.

"Nearly forty years," Cash responds. "I'm going to be brutally honest with you all because you deserve to know the truth, but it's not comforting information."

"We need to know," I say firmly. "And after what we've all recently gone through, I think we can take it."

"Agreed," Daphne says, as Millie nods enthusiastically. "Just tell us everything."

Cash swallows hard and then starts to tell us about the journals. The eyes, the blood, and the hair. Horace's past and plans for the future come rushing out of him in a tidal wave, leaving us all breathless and wide-eyed.

"He eventually wanted *all* of you," Cash says at the end. "And he was moving down the line, one at a time. But for years, he practiced, honing his skills, perfecting his plans."

"Why us?" I wonder aloud. "I mean, it's not like we knew him that well. He was just some guy that lived nearby and used to help our parents from time to time. Sure, he may have been sleeping with our mother, but it's not like we spent holidays with the man or called him *Uncle Horace* or anything."

"Well, I have theories on that," Millie says, surprising me. "I remember when I was young, like maybe ten, Mama told me that I was Horace's daughter."

Daphne and I gasp in horror.

"Don't freak," Millie says, holding up a hand. "She was lying. Mama *always* lied. She thought it was fun to dick with people's minds, remember? I'm absolutely *not* related to that man in any way. But I wonder if she told Horace the same thing, and he believed her?"

"What if she told him that we're all his children?" Daphne asks.

"And so he wanted to kill his supposed daughters?" I ask. "That doesn't make sense."

"Serial killers aren't rational," Cash reminds me. "Just because they're smart, it doesn't make them sane. So, if what Millie says is true, it's absolutely possible that he believed you were his kids, and that's where the fixation came from. We can only speculate on why he turned to sexually sadistic torture and murder versus requesting a simple DNA test."

"Well, that's some messed-up shit," Millie says with a sigh. "Not that it wasn't already. Thanks for telling us."

"I'm not done," Cash says. "There's more."

"*More?*" I ask.

"Oh, yeah. This is where it gets bad."

"*This* is where it gets bad?" Daphne says, letting out a half-laugh. "Great. Give it to us."

"The three of you are his next of kin."

We sit silently, watching as Cash stops pacing and turns to the three of us.

"Did you hear me?" he asks again.

"So you *know* that he's our father? Pretty sure that was a horrible joke," Millie says.

"I wish it were," he replies gently. "And I don't know about the DNA, but Horace had a very detailed will. It's legal, and he names the three of you as equal beneficiaries, inheriting all of his property."

"Burn it," I announce angrily. "Burn it all to the fucking ground."

"Great idea," Daphne says.

"And that means," Cash continues, "that as executors of the estate, you have to decide what to do with his remains."

"Burn them with the fucking house," I reply.

"I'm quite sure you can do that," Cash says with a nod. "Though maybe not *with* the house." He grins. "No decision needs to be made at this time. The house is still a crime scene, and no autopsy has been done yet, so there's no need to make a decision today."

"I say burn it all," I repeat and stare at the teacup I have resting in my lap. I scowl as, right before my eyes, the warm liquid splashes over the rim and onto my leg. "Hey! What the hell?"

"Did you spill?" Daphne asks.

"No. I was just sitting here, and it just…sloshed over the side."

"By itself?" Millie asks.

"Yes. By itself."

"You're upset," Cash says reasonably, and I turn my scowl on him.

"I'm not an idiot. I'm telling you, I didn't spill it."

"Okay." He holds up his hands in surrender. "I believe you."

"I don't know what to believe anymore," Daphne admits with a sigh. "Everything is just so…odd."

"Well, at least the worst of it is over," Millie says.

"Don't jinx it," I reply.

~

"Cash?" I wander through my apartment later that night, after I return home from work.

"Back here," he says. I find him in the guest room, where he's set up a makeshift office. "How are you?"

"Tired," I admit, a small smile forming as I climb onto his lap and nuzzle his neck. I love how strong his arms feel wrapped around me. "I'm sorry I snapped at you earlier today."

"I'd snap at me, too," he says and kisses my hair. "It's been a lot."

"A lot of what?" I raise my head so I can look him in the eyes. I absolutely love his green eyes.

"Just a lot," he says, leaning in to kiss my lips lightly. "And I haven't really asked you how you're holding up."

"I'm actually doing pretty well, all things considered." And it's true. I feel good. I feel relieved more than anything. "I guess today's news threw me for a loop."

"Me, too."

"I thought we were done with all of it, and then to find out that we're not, it's just like he continues taunting us even though he's long gone, you know?"

"I know. It's not fair."

"Can we refuse to be the next of kin?"

"I don't know the laws and regulations surrounding that," he says as he brushes his fingers through my hair. "I suppose you could, but then I imagine the estate would go to the state, and God only knows what they'll do with it."

"True." I nibble my lip, enjoying the way his fingers feel in my hair. "I guess we'll end up doing something about it."

"You don't have to think about it today," he reminds me. "So, set it aside for now. There's no need to worry."

"You're right."

He frames my face, his long fingers cupping my chin as he lays his lips over mine, consuming me with passion and lust.

There's always so much lust where Cash is concerned.

Suddenly, I pull back and stare at him in horror.

"What is it?"

"Your hands are on my face."

"Yes?"

"Who the hell is brushing my hair?"

It stops. I scratch my scalp and shiver.

"What do you mean, Brielle?"

"Someone was brushing their fingers through my hair. I thought it was you."

"No, I was holding you, and then I was kissing the hell out of you."

I stare at him, then stand and shake my hair out. "Do I have bugs in my hair?"

"Not that I can see." He joins me, and it's his hands brushing through my hair now. "No, I don't see anything at all."

"That's so creepy." I shiver again. "I mean, I know I have spirits in this apartment, but they've *never* touched me before."

"Have spirits *ever* touched you?"

"No, I just see them," I reply. "And it's all back to shadows now, which is a relief."

I move to clutch my stone pendant, but it's not around my neck.

"What's wrong?" Cash asks.

"I keep losing my damn necklace." I walk over to my bedroom and sigh when I see it lying on my pillow. "I don't know how it got here, but at least it's here. I'll put it on later."

"Look, I think you've had a lot on your mind," Cash says, wrapping his arms around me from behind. "I suggest you take a long, hot shower, have some tea, and then I'm going to make love to you for the rest of the night."

"The *whole* night?"

"Do you think I can't do that?"

"I mean, that's a pretty bold offer, but I'll take it." I spin in his arms and grin as he kisses me deeply, those amazing hands cupping my ass and pulling me against the length of him. I can feel his already firm cock against my belly. "Maybe we should do some sex stuff before my shower."

"I can wait." He kisses my nose. "Come on."

He leads me into the bathroom, where he proceeds to turn on the water and adjust the temperature. He helps me out of my clothes and holds my hand as I step over the side of the tub into the hot spray of the shower.

"Okay, you were right. This is nice."

"I love it when I'm right," he says, making me grin.

"Why don't you come in here and wash my back?"

"If I come in there, darlin', you won't get clean." He pokes his head around the shower curtain. "Take your time. I'll brew you some tea."

"You're handy to have around," I call after him and listen to him chuckle as he walks out of the bathroom.

I do enjoy having Cash around, and it's not just for his tea-making skills or even the intense sex we have almost every day. It's so much deeper than any of that.

There are times that I feel like he's an extension of me, and vice versa. We haven't talked about what will happen once his vacation time is over, and he has to go back to his life from before.

I don't want to think about the possibility that he'll leave, and that this will just be a fond, sexy memory mixed in with the scariest time of my life.

We've shared so much together over the past month. How in the world will I ever go back to being without him, as if he were never here?

I turn and get my hair wet, then reach for the shampoo, thinking it over.

I suppose I could ask Millie to make me a potion to forget he ever existed. But that seems even sadder than the thought of not seeing him anymore. At least, this way, I'll have the memories of us, even if they make my heart hurt.

I don't want him to go.

But I can't go with him.

And I can't make him stay if that's not what he wants.

I don't have any additional answers once my hair is rinsed of both shampoo and conditioner. One thing I do know is that he's here now, and I'm going to enjoy every moment I have with him, no matter what.

I push back the curtain and reach for a towel to wipe my face and wrap it around my wet hair. Then I grab a second towel to dry my body as I step out of the shower. I wrap the terrycloth around me and frown when I see my necklace sitting on the lip of the sink.

It was on my pillow. I left it there earlier. I know I did.

Cash must have brought it in for me. He's so thoughtful. I reach for it and pull the long chain over my head, then see movement on the fog-covered mirror.

A chill runs down my spine.

An invisible finger is marking up the fog on the glass.

*I'm still here. H.*

I back up and reach for the doorknob.

"What's wrong?"

I hear Cash in the other room, and there's pounding on the door now, but I can't get the knob to turn.

"Brielle, what's wrong in there?"

"I can't open the door!"

"Let go of it."

I do as he asks and glance back to see the writing still there. Cash gets the door open and rushes in.

"Why did you scream?"

"I screamed?"

"A blood-curdling one."

I simply point to the mirror. "He's still here, Cash."

"He wrote that?"

I don't have time to speak before another word is written on the glass.

*Yes.*

# CHAPTER 24

*"I can't stand a bitchy chick."*

~Gerald Stano

*Burn it all down?*
If he could hit her, Brielle would be lying in her own blood right now.
The rage is all-encompassing but stronger than it ever was when he was still alive. The emotions in the afterlife are intense.

Brielle, one of only three people he's loved his whole life, just said that she'd like to burn down everything he worked for. And her sisters didn't stand up for him. They didn't even bat an eye!

How could they? How *dare* they? Don't they know how hard he worked, day in and day out, to make something beautiful for them? It's clear they're nothing but three entitled, spoiled, horrible girls. He needs to teach them a lesson.

He won't be making anything wonderful for them anymore. No, that time has passed. They've ruined that with their ugliness.

Instead, he's going to punish them in ways they never imagined. The ways he killed his toys will pale in comparison to what he has planned for his daughters.

He didn't raise them to be this way, did he?

If Ruth had given him the chance to discipline them more, maybe things would be different. Perhaps he would have had an opportunity to make it good for his girls.

But, no. She taunted him with them. Though that's what women do, isn't it? They tease, and they condemn, and they open their legs to get satisfied, and then they flick you off like an annoying fly.

Ruth.

Maybe he should make a trip to her house to punish her, as well. She deserves it.

They all do.

He wandered away from the girls after Brielle talked about burning his things. Not just his things, *their* things. Everything he did, he did for them.

But now that it's theirs, they don't want it.

He was so blinded by rage, he was able to spill the tea, but that wasn't nearly satisfying enough.

He wishes he were at full strength so he could take care of matters correctly.

But he's getting there.

He spilled the tea.

He moved the necklace several times.

And, tonight, he ran his fingers through Brielle's glorious hair. It calmed him for a moment until she started speaking about him again.

He was wrong.

She doesn't love him.

And now she's in the shower. He can see her naked body, the way the water runs over her breasts and her tight nipples. She washes herself—*down there*—and he feels himself harden, even though he no longer has a physical body.

How?

How can he get sexually excited after death?

It makes no sense.

Once she gets out of the shower, he sets the necklace on the sink and laughs when she spies it and frowns in confusion.

*That's right, little girl. I'm playing with you.*

She mumbles to herself.

He wants her attention so badly, needs to make her understand that he isn't gone.

He focuses on the mirror and, with a great deal of effort, writes a message on the glass.

He's even able to reply to a question.

But the effort is too much for him, it drains him, and he fades away.

He needs to regroup and grow stronger so he can use his power when he needs it the most.

# CHAPTER 25

## CASH

"I'll call Asher." I reach for my phone, but Brielle lays her hand on my arm, stopping me.

"I told you before, this isn't something you can kill with a gun. I'm afraid the police can't help us with this."

I've never felt so helpless in all my life. Even the Carlson case didn't frustrate me like this.

"What *can* help us, then?"

She bites her lip, fiddling with the stone around her neck. Finally, she moves past me and into her bedroom, where she simultaneously drops the towel and reaches for her phone.

"I have to call my sisters," she says, absently dialing a number and pressing her cell to her ear as she reaches for clothes to toss on. "He's still here. Yeah. I'll tell you all about it, but I'm scared, Mill. We have to figure out how to get rid of this bastard for good. Uh-huh. Okay."

She hangs up and tosses the phone on the bed.

"What did she say?"

"She's calling Miss Sophia, and then she'll call me back. I'm going to call Daphne in just a sec."

I quirk my brow as she launches herself into my arms and clings to me, her nose pressed to my chest.

"Hey, it's okay, darlin'."

"No, it's not." She tightens her grasp. "But it will be. And I have a feeling the next few days are going to get scarier, and maybe super weird. So, I want to take a second to say thank you. Thank you for not running away, and for being a rock in the middle of all this chaos."

"There's nowhere else I'd rather be." I kiss her hair, breathing her in. "We're going to get rid of this asshole, once and for all."

"You're right." She smiles up at me, just as her phone lights up. "I have to take that. But when this is all over, *again,* I want to curl up in bed with you for a few days without leaving it. I want to snuggle and watch bad movies and eat junk food."

"Can we be naked?"

"Sure," she says with a laugh.

"And why do they have to be *bad* movies? Let's watch good ones."

She laughs in earnest, holding her phone in her palm. "Deal. Good movies and nakedness. Any other requests?"

"As long as you're there with me, I'm good to go."

She winks at me as she answers the phone and presses it to her ear. "Yes. Oh, that's so nice of her. Okay. Did you call Daph? Awesome, we'll meet you there in thirty. Thanks. Love you, too."

She hangs up and turns to me.

"Millie talked to Miss Sophia, and she wants all of us to come to her house right away. This is good news, Cash. She's powerful and knows *so much.* She can help."

"Are you sure you want me there?"

She grabs my hand and presses it to her face. "Yes. I want you with me."

"Let's do this."

The drive to Miss Sophia's takes longer than the drive to the women's mother's house. Miss Sophia lives even deeper in the bayou. Her cabin is warm, even from the outside and in the dark. Smoke billows from a chimney. Plants and flowers line the porch, hang in boxes under the windows, and cover every available surface.

It looks like something out of a fairy tale.

But Miss Sophia is the good witch, not the one that eats little children.

"Come in," the woman says from the doorway, ushering us in. "Your sisters are already here. I also called in some help."

I feel my eyes widen in surprise when we cross the threshold. The house doesn't look big enough from the outside to hold this many people.

I recognize Mallory. The rest are strangers to me.

"This is my granddaughter," Sophia says, gesturing to a beautiful, blond woman sitting at an old, wooden dining room table. "Lena, this is—"

"Cash," Lena finishes for her with a smile.

"Are you psychic, too?"

"Absolutely," she says, her pretty smile widening. "But also, Mallory and Grandmama have told me about you. It's nice to meet you."

"Likewise."

I'm introduced to other men and women of different ages and races, and then I finally sit by Daphne and let out a sigh.

"It's a lot to take in," Daphne says with a nod.

"Am I sitting in the middle of a coven?"

Daphne grins. "Several, actually. Don't look so surprised. This is Louisiana. There are a lot of people here."

"And a lot of witches, apparently."

"That, too," she agrees. "Millie's over there with a woman named Harmony, still poring through our grandmother's book."

"Why is it taking so long?"

"Because a good chunk of it is written in languages we don't understand," Daphne explains. "But Harmony does, so she's helping Millie."

"Who's the guy on the opposite side of the table? He looks...angry."

"That's Lucien. He's not angry, he's brooding. He's a brilliant warlock. He's only thirty-five but has the wisdom of an old man who's been studying his whole life. Magic comes naturally to him, but then again, it should. His family has been in the lifestyle for hundreds of years."

"Interesting." I watch as Lucien glances up from the book in front of him and takes a couple of seconds to study Millie, and then, as if he catches himself, he looks back down at the pages on the table. "He has a thing for Millie."

"Oh, absolutely," Daphne agrees, nodding. "He's for her. She won't admit it, though."

"Why?"

"I don't know if you've noticed, but we tend to be stubborn women."

I chuckle and shrug a shoulder. "I will admit to no such thing."

"Smart man." She laughs as she watches her sister and Lucien. "They'll figure it out when the time is right."

"Now you sound like your sister."

"What a lovely compliment." She pats my arm. "I like you, Cash. And I like you even better for my sister. Speaking of which, I'd better see what she and Miss Sophia have cooking over there."

She stands and leaves me, and I watch her cross the room to Brielle and Miss Sophia. They're not just cooking up ideas, they're literally *cooking* in the kitchen.

I glance around the room again and realize that I don't have anything to offer these people in way of help. At least, not right now.

And I'm antsy.

And more than a little angry.

It's in my nature—and training—to investigate. So, that's what I'll do.

"Brielle," I say as I approach her. "I'm going to call Andy and see if he can go over the crime scene with me tonight."

"Tonight?" She turns and stares up at me as if I'm nuts. In fact, the whole room has gone quiet. "But it's almost midnight. It's *dark.*"

"Andy will be with me," I remind her. "No one is there, Brielle. Aside from some wildlife, there's nothing there that can harm us."

"But, I—"

"Let him go," Miss Sophia says, watching me. "But please, take these. And ask your brother to drink his. It'll protect you both."

She passes me two bottles, cold from the fridge. I don't even ask what's in them.

I've learned to just do as asked without asking questions. And, most of the time, it's delicious anyway.

"Please be careful." Brielle clings to me. "Be very careful."

"We'll be back here before you know it." I kiss her hair. "I have to do something while y'all work. I have to *work.*"

"I know." She smiles bravely. "It's fine. Everything's going to be fine."

"You'll be safe," Sophia assures us all. "Please return here when you're done. And bring Andy with you. I'll cleanse you both."

Once again, I don't ask questions. "Yes, ma'am."

∾

"Wʜᴀᴛ ɪɴ ᴛʜᴇ hell are we doing out here in the dark?" Andy demands as we get out of our cars and meet at the porch. The light is on. The last investigators out here must have left it on.

"I want to do some digging," I reply simply. "And I didn't want to do it by myself."

"It's creepy as fuck out here," my brother grumbles as I slice through the police tape over the front entrance with my pocketknife and open the door. I flick on the lights inside.

"You've seen way creepier than this," I assure him as we slip inside, and I shut the door behind us.

"Uh, I don't think so. I don't spend much time in the bayou. Especially at night."

"So, the bastard's dead, but he's not *gone*."

"What does that mean?"

"It means his spirit is still dicking with my girl, and it's pissing me the hell off. Brielle and her sisters are currently with the rest of their witchy friends, trying to find an answer to the billion-dollar question of how to get him gone for good."

"And you decided to bring me out here."

"I wanted to look around, yes. Maybe there's something here the investigators missed."

"It looks like they took everything," Andy says, looking around the small cabin. He's right, it doesn't look anything like it did last week when we were here. Even the furniture is gone, most likely taken into evidence.

We walk the space, using the flashlights on our phones to light up the areas under the sinks, and in the cabinets.

"Damn it, my phone died," Andy says with a scowl. "I had a full battery when I got here."

"Odd," I murmur, checking my phone. I'm down to ten percent.

I also arrived with a full battery.

I turn the flashlight off to save power.

"Come on. This is the really fucked-up room." I lead Andy to the back of the house, where Horace used to hold the girls.

I flick on the lights.

"Jesus Christ," my brother breathes as he walks in behind me.

"They took the beds." I gesture to the wall opposite us. "There were three toddler-sized beds there where he tied them up. Over there was the workbench and all of his tools, and in that corner was an electric chair."

"The blood on the floor," he whispers. "Jesus, Cash, there must be *gallons*."

I nod, taking it all in. I don't know why we're here. I don't know what I expect to find. The police took *everything* to test for blood and other bodily fluids, and to discover hairs…*anything*.

"The smell is still rank," I say as we pace the space. "I would think that after they took out the girls and all of his tools, the smell would lessen."

"It should," Andy agrees, then stops and sets his hands on his hips.

I walk toward him, and then he holds his hand up. "Stop."

"What?"

"Walk that path again."

I do as he asks, and when I turn around, I see him eyeing the floor.

"Do it again."

I walk back and forth several times.

"What do you see?"

"It's not what I see, it's what I hear. I think there's something under us."

The hair stands up on the back of my neck. "You're kidding."

"No, I'm not."

We walk to the door that leads out of the room then out to a tall deck that hovers over the swamp.

"It's water," I point out when I turn on my flashlight and shine it on the swamp below. "No door to a basement. I don't think there could *be* a basement."

"I'm telling you, it sounded hollow in one spot when you walked over it."

"This is an old house," I remind him as we go back inside. "It's bound to sound weird. Make odd noises."

He shakes his head and walks back and forth. He's pushing against one board with his toe when, suddenly, the board pops up as if it's loose.

"Bingo," Andy says triumphantly.

We pry the board out and reveal a trap door. It fits so seamlessly into the floor of the room that there's no way anyone would know it's there unless they *put* it there.

"Do you have enough battery in your phone for this?" Andy asks me.

"I hope so, because I'm not going down there in the dark," I reply, just before we pull up the door, revealing a ladder that descends into a deep, wide room.

"There's a switch." He flips it, and lights come on below. "Cash."

"I see it."

"My God."

We're both lying on our stomachs, staring into the room below.

"It has to be lined with iron or something strong that keeps the water out," I murmur. "And I'd love to know how he got all of those freezers down there."

"Dozens of them," Andy says then looks up at me. "You get *zero* guesses as to what's in them."

"Looks like we're going down."

I put my phone in my pocket and head down first. The ladder is sturdy, not creaking in the least as we make our descent.

The freezers run along the perimeter of the room, side by side, on all four walls.

I haven't even thought about what could possibly be in the cupboards above the freezers.

Once Andy's beside me, I flex my hand and then reach out for a handle.

"You've got to be kidding me."

Bodies? Yes, but cut up into parts in this one. It looks like this is a freezer full of hands. The next one is legs. And then heads.

Dozens of heads, staring forward but missing their eyes.

In one massive chest freezer, we find three intact stacked bodies.

"Cupboards," Andy says with a grim sigh. "The smell is worse."

"You open it."

He shakes his head but does as I ask.

Jars of hearts. At least, that's what they look like. One cupboard has nothing but intestines.

Not in jars.

Another cabinet has rows and rows of containers of blood.

"It looks like when someone's mom cans tomatoes to get through the winter," Andy says. "Blood-style. Was he a fucking vampire?"

"No, he was collecting the blood for Millie. At least, that's what he said in his diary."

"Sick fuck."

I open another cabinet, but there are no body parts. There's nothing but a huge, black book.

I take it off the shelf and pass it to Andy.

"Don't open that. I don't know what's in it, or if it's spelled. I'm going to take it back to Brielle and Miss Sophia. Maybe it's something they can use."

"I wouldn't know what to do with it even if I did open it," he says with a laugh.

"I have to call Asher and get the teams out here again. Tonight."

I pull my phone out of my pocket to call, but it's dead.

"Son of a bitch."

"Why did our phones die?" Andy asks.

"Well, some people say that ghosts can suck the battery life out of electronics," I reply and shrug.

"Are you saying this place is haunted?"

I look at him like he's crazy, and then glance around this room of horrors. "Look around you, brother. More people have died in this house than maybe in any other in the world, aside from perhaps a hospital. I'd be shocked if it's *not* haunted."

"Yeah. You're right. Let's go up so you can plug it in and call. You'll have a better signal anyway."

I nod, but as we move toward the ladder, the lights go out.

The door slams shut.

"What the fuck?"

I try to turn on my phone, but it stays black.

"Shit. My phone died, remember?"

"Are you telling me we're stuck down here in the dark with no cell?"

"I don't know that we're stuck."

I fumble in the dark until I find the ladder, then climb it. I find the switch, and when I flip it up, the lights come back on.

"Ghosts fucking with us."

"Let's get the hell out of here."

~

"Get that out of my house," Miss Sophia says, pointing at Andy. "That grimoire will not stay."

"I'm sorry," I say immediately, and Andy takes the book back to his car. "We found it at the house and thought it might be something you could use."

"I know your intentions were good, but that thing is pure evil."

Andy returns and apologizes.

"Come in, both of you," Sophia says, calmer now. "It's time you learn more about Horace."

We join the others, sitting at the table.

"We've spent the past few hours reading and studying everything available to us," Sophia begins. "And we know how to defeat him, but it won't be easy."

"Horace is the son of Babette Jarreau. The Jarreau family has been immersed in magic for hundreds of years, perhaps longer than your family, Lucien. All of our families were friends of theirs, and all was fine. Until Babette."

"I've heard stories," Lucien agrees, standing. "Do you mind?"

"By all means. I suspect you may know more about this."

Lucien nods. "My great-grandmother, Adelaide, was Babette's grandmother's sister," he says. "It's said that Babette was born with evil inside her. She gravitated to the black arts, insisted that they practice on the dark side, despite the teachings and beliefs of her family. She was banished from her coven and from her family, and she seemed to be fine with that.

"I don't know who fathered Horace. Babette was a mean, strict mother, who manipulated her son to do her bidding. She was also a jealous woman because Horace had more skill when it came to the craft. But all she gave him was black magic. Never the benevolent kind. That's all I know, or at least what's been told to me."

"As far as I can see, it's the truth," Sophia says with a nod. "And that book you found substantiates the tales. That book carries evil within it."

"Can't say I love the idea of it being in my car," Andy says, shaking his head.

"We will cleanse you and the vehicle," Sophia assures him. "But first, you have a phone call to make, yes?"

"Yes. Our phones died. Brielle, can I please borrow yours?"

"Of course."

# CHAPTER 26

## BRIELLE

"*W*as your phone low when you got there?" I ask him, trying to keep the urgency out of my voice. The answer to this question is vital.

"No," he says flatly. "We both had full charges. Both phones died within fifteen minutes of being there."

I glance at Millie, who slowly shakes her head back and forth.

That means there's a ghost, or ghost*s*, sucking the electrical charge out of any equipment on site.

It means the place is haunted.

I don't know how many spirits we may be talking about.

Cash speaks into the phone, and I notice the whole room goes quiet once again, everybody listening.

"Dozens," Cash says and finds my eyes with his bright green ones. "It's a room under the torture room. There are freezers filled with bodies, cupboards filled with organs and blood. The team needs to be out there now, gathering everything. I don't know. Yes, I can meet you there."

"No," I say immediately and reach for his hand. "I don't want you to go back."

"I'll see you soon," he says into the phone and then hangs up and passes it back to me.

"It's not safe there."

"Brielle, I'm part of the investigation, and trust me when I tell you, what we found needs to be catalogued and taken *tonight*."

"I'm not disagreeing. Wait...*dozens?*"

"More than that," Andy confirms, his face grim. "He's been hunting for a long time, Brielle."

"I assumed he was just throwing all of the bodies into the swamp," Cash adds. "That would make sense. But he wasn't. He stored many of them right there in the house."

I cover my mouth with my hands, staring at Cash in horror. "Oh, my goddess."

"We're going to put a stop to all of this," Sophia assures us all. "But we have to work together. He's too strong for the three sisters to do it alone, and the six aren't ready."

"What six?" Cash asks.

"Not ready," Sophia repeats, putting an end to the discussion.

"We have to burn it all," I say to Cash. "The house, the body, that book. Everything. Under the full moon."

"And when is the full moon?" Cash asks.

"Tomorrow night."

"Handy," Andy says with a grin. "We can just get it all done and over with."

"Even more reason for me to get over there and meet Asher so those bodies can be taken out and given proper burials."

"He's right," Sophia says. "He's safe from the evil there. We've made it so. And we have plenty of work to do to get ready for tomorrow night."

I nod, take Cash's hand in mine, and lead him out the door and to his car.

"I need you to wear this." I take off my necklace and loop it over his head. "Don't take it off. It'll protect you."

"You need it," he says.

"Not here, I don't. I'm safer here than anywhere else in the world. You take it. Promise me you won't take it off."

"I promise." He leans in and presses his lips gently to mine. "Are you okay, sweetheart?"

"No. I'm scared, and I'm worried. As long as you stay safe, I'll be okay."

"That's my line," he says against my lips. "Just keep thinking about that day in bed. I'm going to cash in on that very soon."

"See that you do."

*I love you.*

I want to tell him now more than ever. So, I lean close and press my lips to his ear.

"I love you more than anything, Cassien Winslow. Please stay safe tonight."

I could feel he was about to pull away, but instead, he tugs me hard against him, crushing me in a hug. "You can't get rid of me so easily. Love like this doesn't come along very often."

He kisses my forehead, and then he and Andy are gone, headed back to the house that chills me to the bone.

"Come on, child," Sophia says from behind me. She doesn't startle me; I felt her approach. "Let's get to work."

"He didn't exactly say it back to me," I remark as we climb the stairs.

"If you can't see the love in his eyes when he looks at you, you're as blind as Stevie Wonder, my sweet girl."

~

"IT'S TIME."

I turn to see my sisters waiting for me on the threshold of the guest room at Miss Sophia's house. We all worked well into the night. All of the others went home to rest, leaving just the three of us with Miss Sophia.

She wanted to keep us here last night, to protect and watch over us.

I nod and swallow hard. I'm not nearly as nervous as I was last night. Somewhere around three in the morning, a calm washed over me, leaving me feeling confident and secure in the knowledge that although tonight will be a fight, we will win.

Everything *will* be okay.

I have to believe that.

"Have you heard from Cash?" Daphne asks as we walk into the kitchen and drink the potions Miss Sophia set out for us.

"Yes, he's meeting us over there. They got that basement room cleared out early this morning, and we've been given full ownership as of about an hour ago."

"And the body?"

"It'll be there," I confirm.

Miss Sophia left before us, so the three of us drive to Horace's house together. I don't even glance down the road to Mama's. I've barely spared her a thought since all of this began.

We pull in behind another car and get out. The building is already surrounded by all of the witches that were at Miss Sophia's house throughout the night, along with others I don't know.

"She called in reinforcements," I mutter.

"There can be no mistakes on this one," Miss Sophia says as she joins us. "I need a word with just the three of you before we begin."

"What's wrong?"

She looks worried. "I shouldn't tell you this. Giving you information about what's to come isn't safe and isn't what I normally do. But I also don't want to give you false hope. What we do here today is important and will extinguish this evil one's light for a while."

We glance at each other.

"For *a while?*" I ask.

"Yes. His spirit is stronger than any other I've seen. His will is unmatched. So, yes, we will break him here today, but in order for it to be permanent, there will be steps that can't be taken at this time. That's all I can tell you."

"The six," I murmur. "Are not ready."

Her eyes hold mine. "That's right."

A truck pulls in right behind us, interrupting us, and Cash hops out of the passenger seat. He rushes to me and holds me close, and I immediately feel more at ease.

"How are you, babe?"

I smile against his chest. "I'm much better now. Did you get any rest?"

"I'll rest tomorrow." He kisses my cheek, then motions to Andy. "The boys are going to set the body in the house. Is there anywhere specific you want him?"

"I'm in charge of that," Daphne says. "The answer is *yes*, and I will be able to feel where is best."

Daphne joins Andy and the others, and just as I turn to the house, the front door opens, and we all pause.

"Git outta here!"

"Mama?" I frown, not believing my eyes. "Mama, what are you doing here?"

"Y'all needta git!" She hoists a broom with one hand, and in the other, she holds...a hand.

A shadow's hand.

"Everyone stop," I order, raising my arm. Miss Sophia joins me.

"He has her, child," she says softly.

"I see him." Before my eyes, he changes from a shadow to an apparition. He holds Mama's hand and smiles in that evil, sick way of his. "Does he think he can hold her hostage?"

"Ask him," Millie suggests.

"Horace, I don't know what you're doing with my mother, but it won't work."

He doesn't reply. He simply moves behind her and wraps his arms around her chest. Suddenly, hundreds of shadows pour out of the house, flanking him, joining him as they wrap my mother in evil. She cries out as if she's in pain.

"That's enough," I yell. "You're acting like a child who didn't get his way!"

"Circle the house," Miss Sophia instructs everyone. "Get in your places! The moon is rising. It's time."

I turn to Andy. "Put him on the porch. Uncover him."

Andy nods. He can't see Horace and the shadows, he can only see Mama, shrieking in pain. Andy sets Horace's body on the porch, uncovers it, and hurries back down the steps.

Shadows try to follow him, but Sophia circled the house with salt before we arrived, and it serves as a barrier, holding the evil inside.

The chanting begins from the side of the house and then spreads around the structure counterclockwise. The witches behind the house sit and stand in boats, linking themselves together by holding hands.

The shadows cover the house now, a spectral pile of death.

The chanting grows louder.

The wind picks up, swirling through our hair, tugging at our clothes. The chanting is loud so it can be heard over the wind, fueled by magic and might.

Lightning strikes the house, setting it ablaze. I watch as Horace's face distorts into rage and fear, and my eyes hold his.

"You're going to hell, you son of a bitch."

The fire engulfs the house, and the shadows shriek, retreating as quickly as they appeared.

"Don't break the circle!" Sophia yells to me, but I shake my head.

"I can't let her burn to death!"

I run over the salt, and immediately feel the heat of the fire. The shrieking gets louder.

Suddenly, I'm pulled inside, held by meaty arms with the face of the devil snarling at me.

"I've got you, you little bitch. I may not get your sisters, but you're mine. You think you can hurt me?"

He slaps me, sending me to the floor.

It's so hot.

I'm going to burn in here.

"I can't believe you're such an ungrateful little bitch." He kicks me, making me cough in pain. "I'm going to kill you. I'm not going to make it beautiful like I planned before."

He fists my hair and lifts me high off the floor. It feels like my skin is melting off my body, the air is so hot.

"Brielle!"

*Cash!*

"You ruined everything," Horace says and slams me to the floor again. It's hard to breathe. I can't see. But I can hear Cash calling my name.

"You're not going to kill me." My voice is a croak. Suddenly, Cash is standing next to me, his hand around mine. "We're going to destroy you!"

I begin my own chant. I can hear the others, their voices rising up around us, and as the words leave my mouth, Cash carries me out of the house. He grabs Mama's hand as we pass her and drags her with us.

Once we're on the other side of the salt barrier, the flames turn red, then blue, and rise up to the night sky, almost blinding us with their light. The explosion is fierce and bright, and then, as quickly as it started, the wind is gone, and the shadows shriek one last time before evaporating into the air. The black particles float up into the sky and disappear.

"She's burned," someone says, and I glance around, wondering who they're talking about.

"Brielle." I turn to look at Cash. "Honey, you're burned. We need to get you to the hospital."

"What about you?"

He shakes his head. "I ran in and out."

"It felt like you were in there forever." I swallow and turn to find my mother sitting not far away, looking around as if she's just woken from a dream.

"Brielle?" she asks. "Where are we?"

I look at Cash and frown.

"We're at Horace's house. Or what's left of it."

"Horace?" She frowns, and then her eyes fill with fear. "He's a bad man. A bad, bad man."

"He's not here."

Millie and Daphne join us. Miss Sophia, Lena, and Mal are close by. The others are still chanting, casting spells and cleaning up.

"Don't know how I got here," Mama says. "The voices stopped talking."

"The voices?" Daphne asks.

Mama nods, and then her eyes fill with tears. "You're all grown up. When did you grow up?"

"We grew up a long time ago," Millie reminds her.

"She's confused," I say as Miss Sophia joins us, but she shakes her head.

"I don't think so. Not in the way you mean. Ruth, what's the last thing you remember?"

"Well, I don't know. I remember their daddy hitting me. Harder than the times before."

I feel my eyes go wide.

"And then he was gone. Everyone was gone. And I was left in the house. Every time I tried to leave, I went away again."

"Oh my gods." I stand and reach for her. "They kept you there."

"Who?" she asks, then frames my face with her frail hands. "Oh, you are a beauty, aren't you?"

"I wish I'd known," Miss Sophia says. "Ruth, I'm so very sorry. I had no idea that you were a prisoner in your own house."

"There was a woman, in the rocking chair." Mama's eyes are blue and clear as day as she smiles. "She kept me company."

*The rocking chair.*

Could it be that the one spirit that wasn't evil was the one in that chair?

Was she protecting her?

"Let's go, ladies," Cash says, wrapping his arm around my shoulders. "We need to get these burns checked out."

I nod but keep my mother in sight all the way to the hospital.

～

"So, let me get this straight," Millie says in the morning, sitting next to my bed at the hospital. "Our mother *isn't* an evil human being, but it was the evil spirits in the house that made her that way? And kept her there? And, Horace, along with his terrible mother, were behind it all?"

"Well, we can't prove that they were behind it," Millie says. "But I know because I dropped my shields long enough to look. Horace helped. He kept the bad spirits there, to keep an eye on us. He had a thing for Mama, and she *did* play with him a lot, so she's not completely innocent."

"Well that's...disturbing," I whisper. My throat hurts from the heat and smoke I inhaled in the house. "What happens to her now?"

"She'll be in the mental hospital for quite some time," Cash says as he walks into the room. "I just spoke with her doctor. He'll be in soon to talk to all of you."

"You know, I've said it before, and I'll say it again," Millie says. "She may not be the salt of the earth kind of mother, but no one deserves that kind of torment."

"I wonder if she was possessed when she killed our father," I say, frowning. "I mean, she doesn't even *sound* the same, right? Her accent, the way she phrases things, it's so different from how she sounded when we saw her just a couple of weeks ago."

"It honestly could be," Daphne says. "I'm sure we can ask Miss Sophia more questions later. She went home to rest."

"Everyone sure supported us," I say. "The whole thing was just amazing."

"Witches aren't always scary," Millie says with a wink. "And they look after their own."

# CHAPTER 27

## BRIELLE

"It's about time we took this day," Cash says as he passes me a bowl of freshly popped corn and cozies up with me on the couch. "I mean, you're not naked, but it's close."

"I can't be naked all the livelong day," I remind him and push a handful of popcorn into my mouth.

"You're such a lady, darlin'," he says on a laugh, so I toss a kernel his way, which he eats.

"You can get me naked later." I haven't said anything to him yet, but there's a new shadow in my apartment today. It's not malicious. On the contrary, actually.

But it's not my place to say anything.

So, I've steered him away from sex and instead suggested that we curl up on the couch with a Marvel movie, while we wait for the call that's about to come.

We don't wait long.

"Hello?" he says into the phone. "Hey, Felicia. How are things?"

He sits up and sets the bowl aside before pushing his hand through his hair. I rub his back in big, soothing circles.

"I see. No, I know there's nothing you could have done, sweetheart. I'm so grateful that you were there, and I know Andy is, too. He'll be happy to have you home soon, but I'll talk to him today, and he and I will come to you tonight or tomorrow. No, you don't have to do all of that by yourself, we'll be there. Thank you, Felicia. We owe you big time. Love you, too. Okay, bye."

He hangs up and sighs deeply. "My mom passed away today."

"Yeah." I lean in to kiss his shoulder. "I know."

He frowns down at me. "How do you know?"

"I, uh—"

"Right." He nods once and scratches the back of his neck. "Is she here now?"

"She is. I can't see her face, she's just a shadow. But I can tell it's her."

He bites his lip and then stands to pace the living room.

"Mom, I have some things to tell you. First of all, I'm sorry that I wasn't there these past few weeks. I know you enjoyed having Felicia with you, and she loves you a lot, but it should have been me, and I apologize for that."

"She's shaking her head at you."

Cash laughs. "Yeah, she would." He turns to me, his green eyes suddenly alight with humor. "Mom, I have to tell you about something else. I met this girl, and you'd like her a lot. She's funny. She's close to her family, so that's nice, and she has some quirks, but hell, who doesn't, right?

"She has blue eyes that just reach in and grab hold of your heart. I was hoping to introduce you to her in Savannah, but this'll do, I guess. Because you see, Mom, I love Brielle, and I'm going to ask her to marry me."

My heart stills in my chest, but I don't say anything. I just watch him as he tells his mom all about me.

"She doesn't know yet, of course. I know it means that some things will have to change with my job, and where my home base is, but I like it in New Orleans, and it'll be nice to be close to Andy most of the time. I think you'd approve of that."

I clear my throat. "She nodded."

"I just don't think I can go through life without her, Mom. She's incredible. So, I'm going to stay here, marry her, and have some babies. Who would have thought? I certainly didn't."

"She just raised her hand." I can't help but laugh.

"Of course, you knew." His eyes fill with sorrow now. "Man, I'm going to miss you, Mom. I wish I'd said these things when you were still here, but I guess this'll have to do. I'll take care of Andy and Felicia. And Brielle, too. You don't have to worry about anything. I love you, Mom."

I brush at a tear on my cheek. "She blew you a kiss, and she's gone."

He nods. "Wow, this is weird. But good. Thank you for that."

"You're welcome."

"I meant it. Every word of it."

He scoops me into his lap and buries his face in my neck. "You're my home, Brielle. You have been since the first moment I laid eyes on you. Marry me. Have a family with me."

"Yeah." I kiss his cheek. "I think that's a good idea."

He grins.

"It's a damn good idea."

"I can't wait to tell my sisters. We get to plan a wedding!"

"Let's keep it just between us for a little while."

"For how long?"

"Just an hour." He grins and lifts me, headed for the bedroom. "Maybe two."

# EPILOGUE

## MILLIE

"*A* spring wedding." I take a deep breath and let it out slowly, grinning like a loon. "Oh, that sounds so lovely."

"Especially in New Orleans," Daphne agrees. "Do you have a venue yet?"

"I haven't even started thinking about it," Brielle replies. "I mean, he just asked me yesterday."

"I'm sure sorry about his mama," I say. "That's so sad. But you gave him an awesome gift of getting to talk to her before she moved on."

"He seems pretty at peace with it all," Brielle says. "Sure, he's sad, but that's to be expected. I think she was sick for quite a while. That's why his sister-in-law was out to check on her."

"That makes sense," I say. "Still sad, though. I'll whip them up a soothing potion to help them feel better."

"You're sweet," Brielle says. "Thank you."

"Well, they're family now," I remind her. "What kind of flowers are you going to have? I think you should have some wisteria. And lilacs. Camelia is a must."

"No roses," Daphne says, shaking her head. "If I never see a rose again, it'll be too soon."

"I always meant to ask and kept forgetting," Brielle says to our sister. "What did you see when you touched the rose at Mama's house that day."

Daphne frowns and swallows hard. "Nothing."

"Lies," Brielle and I say in unison.

"We're talking about your *wedding*," Daphne says. "I don't want to talk about creepy, horrible things. I'll just confirm that the man who fathered us is buried in that spot. And it was his spirit that haunted the hell out of us for years."

"Well, we knew that." I bite my thumbnail the way I always do when I'm deep in thought. "Do you think the evil spirits in that house made him mean? Or do you think he started out that way, and the spirits fed on his cruelty?"

"Maybe both," Brielle says with a shrug. "I don't think Mama started out mean, but she was a victim of the evil in the house. As for him? Who knows? It could have been a combination of the two."

"Have either of you been to see her?" Daphne asks.

"I went," I say, surprising them both. "She recognized me, and she seems to be doing better. But she has a long road ahead."

"Okay, enough about that," Daphne says. "Who's going to be your maid of honor?"

"What do you mean?" Brielle frowns. "I have two. Both of you will do it. I could never choose between you."

"That's sweet."

"And we accept," Daphne adds, laughing. "Millie, we should toast with some champagne."

"I have the perfect bottle," I say as I stand and head for the kitchen. "I got it a couple of months ago. And, no, I haven't put any potions inside it. Yet."

"Shocker," Brielle says with a laugh. "I think we can be without a potion just this once. Hey, speaking of, you didn't give a love potion to Cash, did you?"

"Nope, he loves you all on his own. He didn't need me for that."

I open the fridge and reach for the bubbly, then stop cold.

There's a small cup of blood sitting right in the middle of the center shelf.

"Hey, guys?"

"Yeah?" they say in unison.

"Where did this come from?"


I HOPE you enjoyed this paranormal romance! If you'd like more information on the Bayou Magic series, you can click here:


HTTPS://WWW.KRISTENPROBYAUTHOR.COM/BAYOU-MAGIC

# Underboss

A With Me In Seattle *Mafia* Novel

*New York Times* and *USA Today* Bestselling Author

# KRISTEN PROBY

Underboss
A With Me In Seattle MAFIA Novel
By
Kristen Proby

UNDERBOSS

A With Me In Seattle MAFIA Novel

Kristen Proby



Cover Design: By Hang Le

Cover photo: Wander Aguiar

Paperback ISBN: 978-1-63350-081-5

# PROLOGUE

## ~NADIA~

*I hate* these parties. Papa says I have to be here because it's a family duty, and I'm expected to be on my best behavior. Behave like a lady. Be alert, kind, passive.

I'm always alert.

I don't think I'm always kind, but I wouldn't say I'm mean, either. I mean, the other girls at the private school my parents send me to all seem to like me. I'm not like that mean girl, Shannon, who makes fun of the girls who haven't gotten their boobs yet.

I don't have boobs yet, either.

But I can't wait for the day I get them. Then maybe I won't hate coming to these stupid weddings the family is obligated to attend. They're so *boring.* But, someday, my boobs will grow, and the boys won't ignore me anymore.

*No one* will ignore me.

But back to my behavior. I'm not passive. And I'm not meek, even though I'm sure my father would prefer that I was. I talk too much. I ask too many questions. But I want to know everything there is to know about my family and the business we're in.

I take a sip of my Shirley Temple and scan the crowd. My parents are laughing with a bunch of other people—all old, like them. Papa puffs on a cigar. He doesn't usually smoke, but Mama doesn't mind if he does at events like this, in celebration.

The bride, in her white dress with its puffy sleeves, twirls around the dance floor with the groom, who doesn't look nearly as nervous as he did at the ceremony.

I thought he might pass out. He was green and shiny, and someone had to pass him a tissue to clean up the sweat on his forehead.

It was awesome.

I've seen most of these people before—usually at other weddings or funerals. I've heard Papa and Mama talk about the *families* and how it's important to maintain peace during these functions.

Whatever that means.

My big brother, Alex, is off chasing after some girl. I saw him looking her over with hungry eyes, giving her the kind of once-over he seems to do more often now that he's sixteen.

It's gross.

And when I told him so, he said I was just a baby and that I'd never understand.

But I'm not a baby. I'll be thirteen next month, after all. I'm practically a grown-up.

I blow out a breath, and when my eyes land on *him*, I feel my stomach clench. I haven't seen him before. He looks about Alex's age. Tall with dark hair and brown eyes. And he's laughing at something another boy said.

The guy looks as if he could be the dark-haired one's brother.

I smooth my hands down my red dress, square my shoulders, and walk over to him.

"Hi. I'm Nadia," I say and look all three of them in the eyes as I hold my chin high and wish I had bigger boobs. "I don't think I've met you before."

They turn quiet and look at me as if I'm a science experiment.

"Carmine," the most handsome one says. "And this is Shane and Rocco. My brothers."

"*Rocco?*" I snort. "Did your mother not like you very much?"

"It's a nickname," Rocco says with a shrug. "I like it better than Rafe."

"You're wrong." I prop a hand on my hip. "Rafe is much better. I want to talk to you."

I point at Carmine and then take his hand in mine, pulling him away from the others. We walk past the food table loaded down with shrimp and crab and then move around a corner where we can have some privacy.

"Are you always this forward?" Carmine asks.

"Sure. What's the point in being anything else?"

His brown eyes narrow, and he looks me up and down. Once again, I'm reminded that I'm sorely lacking in the boob department.

I should have stuffed this stupid bra with something to make me look...*fuller.*

"What did you want to talk about?" he asks.

"I don't want to talk. I want to do this." Before he can reply, I boost myself up onto my toes and press my mouth to his. He squeaks in surprise, but he doesn't pull away.

I drop back onto my heels and stare up at him. Holy shit, for a first kiss, that was fun. *Really* fun.

And he didn't even use any tongue.

"Look, Nadia—"

"Gotta go."

I turn and hurry away, suddenly embarrassed and not sure what to say. I just wanted to kiss him. To see what it was like.

And now, I know.

*It was freaking awesome.*

I smack into a hard chest. When I look up, my eyes meet my father's.

"What are you up to, little one?" he asks.

"Nothing." I shake my head. "I was just—"

"Do you know who that is?" he interrupts. Of course, he knows. He *always* knows. It's so annoying.

"Who?"

"That boy you were with."

I shrug a shoulder. "Carmine."

"Carmine *Martinelli.*" I feel my eyes round. I've heard my father talk about that family before. "I want you to stay away from him. And his brothers. Is that understood?"

When his voice takes on that edge, I know he's not to be questioned. "Yes, sir."

"Good. Now, come on. They're cutting the cake."

I follow my father but glance back to find Carmine leaning his shoulder against the wall, watching me. A slow smile spreads over his face.

It's too bad he's off-limits.

# CHAPTER 1

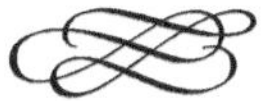

## ~CARMINE~

"When will you be back?"

I sip my whiskey and gaze out the window of the family's private jet, waiting for the pilot to get the go-ahead to take off.

"Depends on how this goes." I cross one foot over the opposite knee. "If it goes well, I don't know. If she tells me to go fuck myself, I'll be back tomorrow."

My younger brother, Shane, snickers on his side of the call. "From what I know of Nadia, she'll tell you to fuck off either way."

"True." I feel my lips twitch just as the pilot's voice comes over the speakers.

"We're cleared for takeoff, sir."

I push a button next to my seat. "Excellent."

"Have a safe trip," Shane says. "Keep me posted."

"Talk soon." I hit end on the screen and blow out a breath. No detail *hasn't* been scrutinized or picked apart. Nadia already knows me. There isn't anything I can do about that.

But she doesn't know what I have up my sleeve, and that's in my favor.

Now, I just have to get down to Miami—literally on the other side of the country from my home in Seattle—and make her fall in love with me.

I blow out a breath and tip my head back against the fine leather seat.

Piece of cake.

IN OPULENCE AND LUXURY, the resort rivals any in any major city of the world. I've stayed in some impressive places, from Monte Carlo to the Maldives, and The Island Resort ranks right up there.

I'll be in the lap of luxury over the next few hours to days, and that doesn't disappoint.

I checked in, settled into my suite, and now I'm on the hunt for my prey.

I don't have to go far to find her.

I keep people on my payroll to give me the information I need the second I ask for it, and they've been on their toes when it comes to keeping track of the Bratva princess.

I walk through the resort spa to the private pool with its white chaise lounges, and sure enough, there she is, soaking up the sun in a pitiful excuse for a black bikini.

It's hardly more than two scraps of fabric, but it showcases Nadia's slim, tanned body to perfection.

At some point, she cut her blond hair into a short style that complements her stunning face nicely. I always forget how gorgeous she is until we're face to face, and it hits me like a punch to the gut.

"Is this seat taken?"

"No," she says without cracking open an eye. She looks serene. Relaxed. Almost as if she's about to fall asleep. She looks like the spoiled daughter of a powerful man.

Which is exactly what she is.

It's a comfortable eighty-two degrees outside as I lower myself onto the chair and stare at the Atlantic Ocean beyond the pool. I take a deep breath of salty air and turn to the woman next to me.

"It's a nice day, isn't it, Nadia?"

The use of her name has her slowly turning her head against the chair. She lowers her Chanel sunglasses down to the tip of her nose and takes me in from head to toe with those blue eyes.

"Carmine." My name sounds like acid on her tongue. "Fancy meeting you here."

"Funny coincidence, isn't it?" I grin and take the fresh glass of whiskey delivered by the waiter. "How's the family?"

Her eyes are cool as she sits up and sips the iced drink at her elbow. The glass is sweaty as though it's been sitting for a long while, ignored. I can't help but watch her plump lips wrap around the straw.

With long, willowy limbs, full lips, ice-blue eyes, and light-colored hair, Nadia is a beautiful woman.

She's also a very dangerous one.

"Everyone is fine. Thank you for asking." She sets the glass aside. "And yours?"

"Oh, they're doing well. What brings you to Miami?"

"Vacation."

"Well, who can blame you? I'm here on a little holiday myself. It's still too cold in Seattle. I needed some sunshine."

"And you've found it."

I nod once, watching her. She looks relaxed. Calm. As if she doesn't have a care in the world. Then again, what could she possibly have to worry about?

Aside from me, anyway.

Because I'm about to chew her up and spit her out.

If I didn't hate her family so deeply, I might pity her.

"Do you have dinner plans?"

Her eyebrows climb in surprise. "Are you asking me out on a date, Carmine Martinelli?"

"A dinner among friends," I reply and shrug a shoulder as if it's the most natural thing in the world. "Our families are very old friends."

Two opposing mob families are hardly buddies.

"Right." She smiles now, and I can admit, my stomach clenches in response. Yes, Nadia is breathtaking.

Fucking her won't be a hardship.

"I'm quite sure I can change my plans. What did you have in mind?"

"Something simple. Quiet so I can talk with you. Catch up. Meet me in the lobby at seven?"

"I'll be there."

I stand to leave, but before I can, her quiet voice calls me back.

"You look better than I remember," she says with a half-smile as her eyes travel down my torso to my swim-trunks-covered dick and back up again. "You grew up well."

"I could say the same for you." I nod and turn to leave, then toss over my shoulder, "Don't be late."

~

SHE STRIDES into the lobby at three minutes after seven, wearing a long, black gown with a dip in front that falls almost to her navel, displaying her cleavage. She's in shimmering silver shoes and carries a small clutch in her hand.

I don't doubt that she has a small pistol strapped to her inner thigh.

"You're late." I lean in to kiss her cheek.

"Am I?" She smiles coolly. "Well, I never was good at taking orders. I'm starved."

"Excellent. We're staying here for dinner."

I lead her into the hotel's steakhouse. The hostess shows us to our table, discreetly located in a quiet corner of the restaurant so we can be alone.

Once the wine has been poured and our appetizers and entrées ordered, Nadia sits back and studies me over the candles on the table set for two. She swirls the wine in her glass. Her mind is clearly whirling.

"What is it?" I ask her.

"How did you know I was here?" She doesn't miss a beat, and she's not coy.

Nadia is a clever woman.

I don't falter as I set my wine glass on the table. "I didn't. It was a happy coincidence."

"Bullshit."

I quirk a brow. "I'm a lot of things, Nadia, but I'm not a liar."

She sneers into her wine glass. "Right. The Martinellis are known for being upstanding citizens."

I laugh and then shrug as if to say: *"What can you do?"*

"I'm not here on behalf of the family. I'm here for some peace and quiet. And I ran into a beautiful woman that I happen to admire and find appealing. It's really that simple."

"Handsome *and* charming," she murmurs. "What a lovely surprise, indeed."

Dinner is lively. We talk about people we both know. We flirt and laugh. And we both drink a little too much wine.

So much that two hours later, once we've consumed the food, and I've paid the hefty check, I don't bother asking her where her room is. I simply take her up to mine.

"Are you planning to seduce me, Carmine?"

"Yes." The answer is simple. And it might be the first truth I've spoken since I saw her at the pool.

"Excellent."

~

"Where are you going?" I catch Nadia's hand in mine and tug her onto my lap as she walks past me to the balcony.

"I need to make a call." Her voice is smooth as silk as she leans in and presses her lips to mine. She takes it further than just a peck, and just when I'm about to grab hold of her and tumble her onto the bed, she pulls away. Wearing nothing but the hotel robe, she saunters through the open glass door to the balcony beyond.

We moved from Miami to St. Petersburg last week. I rented a sexy little car, and we road-tripped across the state and up the west coast of Florida with the top down, enjoying each other's company and the views.

Now, we're checked into the Don Cesar resort, settled in another top-floor suite with magnificent views and top-notch service.

I watch Nadia pace the patio for several moments, her phone pressed to her ear, and then decide to get in a quick shower. We might actually leave the hotel today and do something besides each other.

I've spent the past two weeks with her, and I know our time together is running short. Aside from every inch of her delectable little body, I haven't learned anything about her family's secrets. She's a tight-lipped woman.

It's frustrating as fuck.

And, I can admit with reluctance, admirable.

I just finish washing my hair and turn off the water when she opens the bathroom door and grins when I step out of the glassed-in stall.

"Did your call go well?"

"Not exactly." The smile falls from her face, and her lips turn into a pout.

"What's wrong?"

"Nothing's *wrong*, exactly. I just won't be able to go home tomorrow as I originally planned. It looks like I need to book a room at the Ritz in Paris."

I dry my legs and wrap the towel around my hips. "Why Paris?"

"Paris is always a good idea, Carmine." She laughs and boosts herself up onto the countertop. "My house is being remodeled, and it won't be ready for at least six more months. So, I'll be living out of hotels for a while. And why not do that in my favorite city in the world? I'll shop and take in some culture."

"Come stay with me in Seattle."

The offer is past my lips before I even realize what in the hell I'm suggesting.

"That's ludicrous."

"Why?" I frame her face in my hands and brush my lips across hers. "Why is it ridiculous that I want to spend more time with you? Your home is unavailable, but mine is just sitting there."

"I've never really spent much time in your city," she says hesitantly as if she's actually considering it.

"I'd love to show you Seattle."

She sighs softly and rubs her nose over mine. "Are you sure about this? When your family finds out that you're practically living with a Tarenkov—"

"Let me deal with my family, darling. I'll make some calls right now so the condo is ready."

"You live in a condo?" She tips her head to the side.

"Yes, why?"

"You just strike me as a house man. A big, fancy one."

*I have a fancy house, but you won't be living in it with me.*

"Well, it's a big, fancy condo in the heart of downtown Seattle. Penthouse. So, I'm not exactly slumming it."

Her lips twitch.

"When would you like to go?" I ask as I bring up my assistant's contact on my phone. "Tonight?"

"Tomorrow," she says as she jumps off the counter and tugs my towel away. "I have plans for you today."

I pull the belt of her robe free and feel my dick harden at the sight of her small, firm breasts, already puckered and ready for my mouth. She lets the terrycloth drop to the floor, and when I simply reach out and plant my fingertip against her hard clit, she gasps.

Her body is responsive. And as much as I hate myself for it, I can't get enough of her.

I lift her and carry her back to the bedroom, where we tumble over already-mussed linens. She rolls on top of me, straddles my thighs, and tugs the skin of my neck between her teeth.

The bite stings, but only briefly before she licks me there, humming in delight.

I drag my fingertips up and down her calves. She's so fucking soft, so smooth. *Everywhere.*

"I'm going to ride you hard and fast," she mutters.

"No."

Her blue eyes meet mine in surprise.

"It's not going to be fast."

In one quick move, I have Nadia pinned under me.

"I'm going to take my time with you for the rest of the day. I'm going to make you moan, sigh, and forget your fucking name."

Her pupils dilate, and her breaths come faster with lust and anticipation.

I kiss my way down her torso and then nudge my shoulders between her legs, spreading her wide. I feast until she's a writhing mass of lust, and my cock pulses with need.

I almost forget to reach for the condom but remember to sheath myself just before I plunge inside her. And then I still.

"Move," she insists, but I only grin down at her.

"Is this what you want?" Very slowly, I pull back, letting the rim of my dick glide against the walls of her womanhood. I'm not disappointed when she moans in delight.

"Faster."

"No."

I kiss her lips and slowly slide back in, torturing us both.

"You're not in charge right now, Nadia."

She whimpers, and I pull out again, then slam into her, making her gasp and open her eyes in surprise.

"Jesus, Carmine."

"No, darling. Just Carmine."

I take her on the ride of her life, moving effortlessly from slow and easy to fast and frenzied. Finally, when we're both sweaty and gasping, I let her fall over the edge into oblivion.

Enjoying Nadia has been a pleasure. Making her fall in love with me...seemingly effortless. If her last name weren't Tarenkov, I might let myself feel something for her other than simple desire.

But that's not the case. Because hatred has a pulse, and I have a job to do.

~

"Well, you weren't kidding when you said it was fancy," Nadia says the next afternoon as we step off the private elevator into the penthouse. The truth is, the family owns the entire building. We use the apartments on the lower floors for many different things, such as offices and torture space. The penthouse is a luxury condo that we keep for guests —or for times like these when someone in the family needs to use it. "Look at this view!"

She hurries over to the heavy glass doors and opens them to the balcony. Puget Sound spreads out before us in all her glory, the blue water dotted with sailboats and ferries.

"You definitely can't beat the view."

I walk up behind her, rest my hands on the railing on either side of her, and kiss her smooth neck just below her golden hairline.

Nadia's short hair is sleek and sexy. Just as alluring as the long hair she's been known for.

"What made you decide to cut your hair?" I ask.

"I didn't." She turns in my arms and leans her elbows on the railing as she stares up at me. A slight breeze blows around us. "It was cut for me."

"By?"

She shrugs. "Doesn't matter."

I catch her face in my hand. "Who cut your hair, Nadia?"

She licks her lips. "I honestly don't know. I was ambushed. They cut it, broke a rib, and then disappeared. That's why I was in Miami. I needed to get away."

"Why hasn't your family tracked down who did that to you?"

As much as I hate the Tarenkovs, my blood boils at the thought of anyone laying a hand on this woman.

We don't hurt women. Ever.

"Because they don't know. I didn't tell them."

"Nadia—"

"Don't lecture me."

"Your father and brother need to know so they can protect you."

"*I* can protect myself."

"I don't doubt that for a moment. But someone was able to get to you. Why your hair?"

"I'm known for it. It's just hair, Carmine. It'll grow back. It was the broken rib that really pissed me off. Couldn't breathe right for a month. Now, let's drop it."

"For now. But we'll circle back to it. Now, would you like the grand tour of your new abode?"

"Hell, yes."

# CHAPTER 2

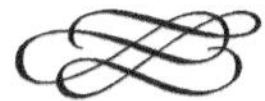

## ~CARMINE~

*Three Months Later...*

"**I** love you." The lie rolls off my tongue easier than the first time I said it, just a few weeks ago. Nadia and I have become inseparable since she moved in with me. We fuck. We laugh. We eat.

And then we fuck some more.

I know her body better than I know mine. Every curve, every erotic inch that makes her writhe in ecstasy.

But it's a shot to my ego and my pride that I still don't know her mind. Nadia is good at keeping her thoughts close to her chest and only sharing bits and pieces of information. But she's loosened up considerably, and our time together has been fun.

So much so that I enjoy having her in my house.

No, not *mine*. I won't have the daughter of the man I hate most in the world living in my home. But she doesn't know that.

I press a kiss to her nape as she fusses with an earring, and then she smiles at me in the mirror.

"I love you, too, darling," she says. Her eyes go wide as I slip the diamond necklace around her neck from behind and fasten it with nimble fingers. "Oh my God, Carmine."

Her hand moves to touch the ice that glitters in the mirror.

"Later, when I make love to you, you'll wear this and nothing else."

Her gaze flies to mine, and she smiles quickly before turning to launch herself into my arms.

"You know I love gifts," she says against my mouth.

"And I love giving them to you." Nadia is spoiled. Selfish. Indulgent—all of the things I expected of her.

It's a pity that she didn't prove me wrong. Part of me wanted to respect her. To discover that she's nothing like the rest of her family.

But that didn't happen. Don't get me wrong, Nadia's been fun, but she's the typical, overindulged daughter of a powerful man; a woman used to getting her way.

She playfully tugs on my lower lip with her teeth, then walks across the room to open her Hermes bag, moving a few small things over to her tiny clutch.

"I hope nothing horrible happens today," she says with a sigh. "It's Annika's wedding day. She deserves to have a happy day without any mafia shenanigans thrown in for good measure."

"Weddings, like funerals, are truce days. You know that." I fasten my cufflinks, the ones with the rubies that Nadia got me for my birthday last month. "Everyone will be on their best behavior."

We've been in Denver for three days, preparing for Nadia's cousin's wedding. Annika's groom, Richard Donaldson, has no ties to any mafia family, and that's the way Annika wanted it. Rumor has it that her family isn't thrilled, but they're permitting the union.

Reluctantly.

My family flew in yesterday. Nadia and I had dinner with my parents, Shane, Rocco, and my cousin, Elena, and her husband, Archer. Elena was raised like my sister. When someone murdered her parents, I took it upon myself to see to avenging their deaths.

Nadia's family *will* pay.

But not today.

Three other family organizations will also attend Annika and Rich's wedding. But there's an unwritten rule for weddings and funerals of mafia families. No violence. No retribution is to be dispensed on those days. They're days of celebration. Community. If beefs or scores need to be settled, it's for another time and place.

We may be brutal, but we *can* be respectful.

"My brother flies in this morning." Nadia checks her lipstick in a handheld mirror, and I school my features.

Alexander Tarenkov will die at my hand. Not today, but one day soon. For his many transgressions.

"I was surprised he didn't come sooner."

"He was in Europe," she says with a shrug. "Doing what, I have no idea. You know he doesn't say much to me."

I smile as she takes one last look in the mirror. "Are you ready, sweetheart?"

"Ready."

~

"A TOAST," Igor Tarenkov says as he raises his glass and gets the attention of the roughly three hundred people at the reception. "To my niece, Annika. My little firefly. You make a lovely bride, my darling. And to Richard. If you fail to take care of my girl, you'll swim with the fishes. Cheers."

We laugh and raise our glasses as Igor sits at the table with his brother—Annika's dad —and Richard's parents, who look a little worse for wear.

"I don't think Rich's parents are used to people like us," I murmur to Nadia, who chuckles and sips her champagne.

"You'd be right. Annika said they're doctors from the suburbs."

"Just like her," I point out as the bride approaches our table.

"I'm so happy to see you," Annika says to Nadia as she leans in to kiss her cousin's cheek. "Are you all having a good time?"

"What's not to like?" Rocco asks.

"Hello, Rafe."

My brother's expression turns to a scowl. "I've told you a million times to call me Rocco."

"I will never do that," Annika replies with a straight face. "Your name is *Rafe*. That's what your mother calls you."

"You're not my mother," my brother reminds her.

"Isn't that fortunate?" Annika replies without missing a beat.

I always liked Annika. Like my cousin Elena, Annika has no interest in the family business. She's a doctor with a business in Denver. Her new husband, Rich, is also a physician.

They'll live a quiet life, making a good living from their jobs, even if Igor uses them from time to time to clean up a mess or two.

Having a doctor in the family is incredibly helpful.

Rocco narrows his eyes on Annika, but she just smiles at us. "Oh, I want you to meet someone. Ivie, come here."

I recognize the maid of honor as she hurries over to our table and offers us all a smile.

"Everyone, this is my best friend since we were six. Ivie Roberts."

"Hi." Ivie waves and flashes a shy smile. She's pretty but not beautiful. Not extraordinary like the other women in the room. "It's nice to meet you."

"The pleasure is all mine," Shane says as he takes her hand and kisses her knuckles. "You're lovely, aren't you?"

Rocco and I share a surprised look.

"Oh, it's just the dress," Ivie says, glancing down at the blood-red gown that fits her curvy body like a glove.

"No, I think it's the woman wearing it."

"How charming," Nadia says. "Ladies, let's make a trip to the champagne table."

Nadia loops her arms through Annika's and Ivie's and leads them away. Ivie glances back and gives Shane a sassy wink.

"Really?" I say to Shane, who just stares back at me blankly.

"What?"

"What do you mean *what?*" Rocco says with a laugh. "You were totally mooning over that girl. And she's not your type. She's not *any* of our types."

"What does that mean?" Elena demands, and Archer suddenly seems fascinated with the silverware on the table.

Smart man.

"She's fucking amazing," Shane replies with a scowl. "Did you *see* her?"

"Yeah." I nod slowly. "We saw her."

Without another word, Shane stands and goes in search of the woman, and Rocco lets out a laugh.

"What's wrong with her?" Elena demands again. "She's pretty."

"She's not ugly," I agree. "But she's hardly Shane's type. He goes for the cold, super-model types."

"Like Nadia?" Elena asks with a cocked brow.

My eyes narrow on her. I don't know why I suddenly feel so defensive of the Bratva princess. I can't stand her.

"You don't understand." The words are clipped. Short.

But Elena doesn't back down.

"You know how I feel about this."

She thinks my mission's futile—is sure that Nadia doesn't have the answers, and that I'm wasting my time.

I think she's wrong.

"Let's dance," Nadia says, suddenly at my side. I take her hand, kiss the palm, and stand at her request.

"That would be a pleasure."

She leads me out to the dance floor. As the Goo Goo Dolls sing *Iris*, I pull Nadia to me, flush against me, and we move around the space.

Her lean body is a temptation that I never stop longing for. It'll be a pity that I won't get to fuck her anymore once all of this is said and done. I don't know that I've met a woman I've been so sexually compatible with before. I may not find one ever again.

The fire in her eyes as she gazes up at me tells me that she's just as fired up as I am.

Without another word, I take her hand and lead her off the floor, down a hallway, and to an empty storeroom that must be used as a maid's closet for the hotel.

I lock the door behind us and yank her against me.

"Did you do that on purpose?" I growl against her neck. "Seduce me on the dance floor so I'd be hard and wanting you?"

"Maybe." Her voice is breathy as her hands immediately reach for my slacks, pulling them open so she can plunge her hand inside to cup me. "Probably."

"Fucking hell." I turn and pin her against a shelving wall of folded sheets. I gather her skirt in my hands until it's up around her waist and then grin when I find her bare.

"I love it when you go without panties, babe."

"I know." She bites my earlobe. "Now, fuck me, Carmine."

She doesn't have to ask me twice. I retrieve the condom from my suit pocket, and when I plunge into her, I'm like a wild animal, unable to stop myself from fucking her hard and fast, punishing us both with the crazy rhythm I set.

"God, yes," she sobs and lets her head fall back against the sheets. "Fuck, yes."

It's over as quickly as it began. Once I dispose of the condom and we right ourselves, I open the door so we can return to the party.

Pandemonium hits.

"Oh, shit, what happened?" Nadia says as she hurries to the dance floor where a crowd has gathered. I follow.

We push our way to the front in time to see Armando, one of my father's men, seizing on the floor. He's foaming at the mouth, his face beet-red, eyes bulging.

"He's been poisoned," I mutter as I stare down at the man.

"I'll call the police," someone offers, but they're quickly taken aside.

We don't call the authorities.

And the fact that this was done *here*, with a mix of families and civilians, makes my blood boil.

I march over to Nadia's father's table, where my dad is already standing, his expression mutinous.

"That drink was meant for *me*," Pop says. "Armondo grabbed it by accident. We laughed about it, and then I flagged down the waiter for another. Moments after drinking it, that"—he gestures to the floor—"happened."

"Are you implying that I ordered your murder at my niece's wedding?" Igor asks, his tone mild. "I'm not the only boss here, Carlo."

"Yours is the only family the Martinellis have an issue with," Pop replies.

Shane and Rocco stand beside me, all of us behind our father. Nadia and her brother, Alexander, stand behind their father.

My gaze holds Nadia's.

"I don't know what you're talking about," Igor says. "I've never done anything to you or your family."

"You had my sister killed," Pop immediately replies.

"I always liked Claudia," Igor says and drums his fingers on the table. "Vinnie, not so much. He was a pitiful excuse for a man and certainly had no business being the boss of your organization. But I suppose that's none of my business."

"So you killed him," Pop says.

"I certainly did not," Igor says and leans forward. "No one in my organization is responsible for Vinnie's or Claudia's deaths. If I was, I would take responsibility for it."

My father nearly vibrates with his fury.

"What good would that do me?" Igor continues. "The Bratva is successful, thriving, without the need for war. Just because I thought Vinnie was a worthless piece of shit doesn't mean I ordered his death. And I certainly wouldn't give the order to have you, my *friend*, Carlo, killed at my firefly's wedding."

"Then what the fuck is going on?" I demand and scan the crowd. Someone took Armondo's body away and cleaned up the floor. The guests murmur quietly. The DJ started the music again.

Only at a mafia wedding could someone get murdered and have the party carry on as if nothing at all happened.

"Clearly, someone has it out for our families," Igor says. "Nadia."

Nadia places her hand on her father's shoulder. "Yes, Papa?"

"I'm assigning this to you."

"Carmine will help you," Pop agrees, and I feel my back straighten.

"I don't need to involve Nadia in this."

"I've just involved her," Igor says. "You've been playing house for weeks, and nothing has come of it so far. Let's change tactics."

My eyes move to Nadia's, and right before me, the warmth I've seen in those blue orbs freezes.

"Did you honestly think I was in love with you?" She smirks. "Grow up, Carmine."

I should have seen it. I should have known that she was double-crossing me. Maybe I did. Perhaps I ignored it.

I'm a fucking idiot.

"It's decided," Pop says. "You two will hunt down those responsible for what's happened here today. And for my sister's death."

With the wave of a hand, we're dismissed. Before Nadia can run away, I corner her and turn her to me.

"What?" She glares up at me.

"What was the end game?" I ask, my voice hard as stone.

"I didn't have one. Yet." Her gaze falls to where my hand rests on her arm. "I didn't give you permission to touch me."

I feel the smile slowly spread over my lips. "So, it's true what they say? You're nothing but an ice princess."

She doesn't even flinch. "And you'd do well to remember that. I don't want your help with this."

"You have it anyway."

"I said—"

"Do you think I give two fucks what you said?" I lean in to her. "We work together. Starting now. No more show. No more lies."

"No more sex."

I chuckle. "Darling, you couldn't keep your hands off me if you tried."

"Watch me."

# CHAPTER 3

## ~NADIA~

"What are you doing here?" Papa asks as I walk into his Denver office. He frowns and sets a pen on the notebook he was scribbling notes in. "You're supposed to be in Seattle with Carmine."

"I'm not going to Washington." I pace to the window and stare down at Coors Field, downtown Denver, and the mountains beyond. I have to admit, it's a beautiful city. Once you get past the high altitude, it's one of my favorite places. But I'm not here to admire the scenery.

"Carmine is in Seattle," Papa reminds me.

"I believe so."

"So, I'll ask again, what are you doing here?"

"I don't need to be with Carmine," I say and watch as a crane works on a skyscraper. "I can work just fine without him. Better, actually."

"You're supposed to be working together."

"Now that the charade is over, there's no need."

"That's not your decision to make."

His stern voice has me turning to look at him.

"We don't trust each other." I cross to my father. "For good reason. The Martinellis think we had their family members killed."

"We didn't."

"You and I know that, but convincing them is another matter entirely. And why would he work with me anyway?"

"Because he's been ordered to do so."

I roll my eyes and then sigh as I sit in the chair opposite my father.

"You've worked hard for your entire adult life to be taken seriously in this family," Papa says thoughtfully. "You don't question orders. Why now?"

"Alex wouldn't want to work with him, either."

"Did you fall in love with him?"

I scowl at the absurdity of the suggestion. "Absolutely not. He's a liar—and not a particularly good one. And he's a Martinelli."

"He's also young and handsome."

*And excellent in bed, but I'm sure my father doesn't want to know that.*

"I'm not young and stupid," I remind him. "I just didn't see the value in following him to Seattle when what we're looking for most likely isn't there."

"It's a place to start," he replies and waves me off. "Get up there. *Today*, little one. And keep me apprised of the situation."

"Yes, sir."

I stand and turn to leave.

"Nadia?"

"Yes?" I spin back to him.

"I love you."

I smile and blow him a kiss. "I love you, too, Papa."

THERE'S a car in his circular driveway. I don't think the older Cadillac belongs to Carmine.

I park behind it just as the front door opens, and Carmine steps out with another man. The unknown person nods and then gets into his vehicle and drives away.

I slam the door of my rented Lexus and send Carmine a sassy grin as I climb the steps of his house.

"I knew you were the big, fancy house type."

"How did you find out where I live?" he asks by way of greeting.

"Oh, Carmine." I pat his cheek and breeze right past him and inside, not bothering to wait for an invitation. "Don't insult either of us by asking stupid questions. You knew plenty about me before you found me in Miami. And I know more about you than you'd probably be comfortable with."

"I just have one question," he says as he follows me into his living room. "Is your house really being remodeled?"

I cross to the mantel and run the pad of my finger over a little owl statue there. "I don't have a house. If you'd done more research, you'd know that."

"Maybe you live in a house owned by your father," he suggests.

"I bounce from place to place," I say without elaborating. I walk over to a painting and touch the name of the artist. "You have a lot of expensive knickknacks."

"Are you going to simply walk through my house and touch everything?" I notice his teeth are clenched, his hands fisted. It fills my heart with glee.

Pissing him off is a pleasure.

"Maybe." I smirk and wander into the kitchen. "I'm starved. I couldn't stomach the crap they served on the plane. I know you have a private jet, but I went ahead and jumped on a commercial flight this morning. Even first class turned my stomach."

I open his fridge and take inventory of the contents. I pull out a cheese and cracker tray and dig in.

"This salami is fantastic. Where did you find it?"

"You'd have to ask the caterer." He leans his hip against the island and crosses his arms over his impressive chest.

Carmine Martinelli is the male version of beautiful. He looks like a fallen angel. With that thick, dark hair, those deep brown eyes, and full lips that could turn a girl inside out, he's an impressive specimen.

No, I didn't fall in love with him.

But I enjoyed him. Every chance I got.

"You look well," I say and pop a cracker into my mouth. "But you have some bags under your eyes. Not sleeping well?"

There are no bags. He looks fucking magnificent. But seeing the spark of annoyance flicker in his eyes is worth the dig.

"What do you want, Nadia?"

"We're working together, remember?" I shrug a shoulder and open a jar of green olives. I didn't lie about being hungry. I'm suddenly starving.

"Given that I haven't heard a peep from you since the wedding, I figured you'd blown that off."

"A peep?" I snicker and chew on another olive. "You're cute, Carmine."

He huffs out a breath of annoyance.

I love ruffling his feathers.

"Anyway, I thought I'd come to Seattle and see you. Find out what you know."

"I'm working on some leads."

I nod slowly. "What kind of leads?"

"Rumors. Making calls."

"The mafia is good at keeping secrets, aren't they?" I shake my head and close the food containers back up, then return it all to the fridge. "Bastards put a lot of bullshit in this world, but when it comes to covering their tracks, they're damn good at it."

"What do *you* know?" he asks.

"I did get a call when I got off the plane," I admit and walk over to him. I brush my finger down the buttons of his white shirt. "I always did like looking at you in these white button-downs."

He catches my hand in his and pushes me away.

"What did the caller say?"

The rebuff hurts my feelings more than expected—and more than it should. But I keep my face schooled in the sneer I've worn since I arrived.

"A new chemical's being passed around," I say casually. "It's lethal. Highly addictive. And in large quantities, can cause seizures and foaming at the mouth."

"Who—?"

"I'm not going to tell you that," I say smoothly. "And you know it. That's all I know for now. I really should go. I'll be in touch."

I march away from him before I do something monumentally stupid, like strip him naked and suck his cock.

Carmine has a grade-A penis.

And it's off-limits.

"Have a good day."

"Wait," he says as he hurries after me. "Where are you staying?"

"Oh, don't worry. I'll be around."

"Nadia."

"Goodbye, Carmine."

I hop in the car and zoom away from his house.

I'm not good at emotions. I'm excellent at keeping myself aloof. Cold, even. I don't mind being called the ice princess at all. Because when emotions get tangled up in business, you die.

And I'm not ready to meet Satan yet. Or, should I say, he's not ready for me?

I don't like that I feel things when I'm around Carmine. It's purely physical.

"Yeah, keep telling yourself that," I mutter as I drive toward the freeway.

I knew the several months I spent with Carmine were a lie. He didn't love me, and I certainly didn't love him. We were merely playing house. Manipulating each other.

But we also had fun. We laughed a lot. We got along well. And the sex...

Well, let's not go there.

I enjoy him. And that's the part that annoys the hell out of me. Because he's a Martinelli, and my father told me when I was thirteen that anyone with that name was off-limits.

Nothing has changed in that regard.

So, I'll do as my father asked and keep an eye on Carmine, but I'll also keep my distance.

For my fucking sanity.

Because I'm going to be the next boss. My brother doesn't have the chops—he's too selfish, too immature.

I can't stand him.

*I'm* the one who studied at my father's knee since I was a child. I'm the one who pays attention and does as she's told.

And I'm often overlooked because I'm a woman.

But that won't stop me.

I'll do my job here and continue proving to my father that *I'm* the one who should step up after he's gone.

～

THE HOTEL just wasn't cutting it. Too many people were in and out. Too many eyes. I know that Carmine has eyes on me, but I was making it too easy on him.

So, I checked out two days ago and secured a vacation rental by owner, a VRBO, instead. I used my father's assistant to make the reservation, so my name's nowhere on the application.

I like being anonymous. Carmine wasn't wrong. My family owns the condo I live in just outside of Atlanta, and my name isn't on that one either. I don't want anyone to trace me back to any holdings. I want to be mysterious.

It's hard for the bad guys to find you if they can't figure out where you live.

*Not that they didn't find me anyway,* I muse, rubbing a hand over the rib that still sometimes gives me fits.

I haven't heard anything on the drug thing for days. I'm basically just sitting in Seattle, twiddling my thumbs. I could do this from *anywhere.*

But Papa wants me here.

I blow out a breath and shut my laptop. I've been calling in favors and making calls, and I'm going nowhere fast. It's like I'm two inches away from getting the information I need, but then it gets tugged just out of my reach.

It doesn't help that I don't know exactly what I'm looking *for.* The simple news of a new drug doesn't give me much to go on. That happens every day in every city, and my family isn't into the drug-dealing scene.

Maybe our fathers have us on a wild goose chase, just to see if they can pull the strings and have us follow along like good little puppets.

I wouldn't put it past them.

I need some air, so I slide my feet into my running shoes, grab my windbreaker, and set off on a jog.

This little neighborhood near the water is beautiful. Full of older homes, it's clearly an established neighborhood with low crime and little drama.

I would generally think of it as boring.

My pace is steady as I climb the first hill. Seattle is nothing if not hilly, but it makes for a good workout so I'm not complaining.

I just hit my stride when something sails over my head, and someone lifts me from behind.

"Let go of me, you asshole!" I'm kicking and flailing about, but it's no use. I can't see who grabbed me.

So I go limp. Deadweight.

The man holding me grunts with the effort it takes to hold me, but throws me onto a seat of a vehicle. And then we're moving.

"Who the fuck are you?" I demand.

No one replies.

I know there are at least two of them. The one who grabbed me and the other who's driving.

Fuck, this isn't good.

They could kill me and dump me. My father would rain hell down on them, but they could still do it.

The vehicle—van?—parks, and I'm jerked out and taken down what feels like a series of hallways. Finally, they dump me onto a chair and tie my hands behind my back.

"What the fuck?" I ask—and am punched in the jaw.

I see stars. My mouth throbs.

"You're asking a lot of questions."

I frantically search my brain to place the voice. Have I heard it before? It doesn't sound familiar.

"And that pisses you off," I guess.

Someone punches me again, in the left eye this time.

"We're going to teach you to keep your questions to yourself, bitch."

The beating is ruthless. By the time they dump me on some random sidewalk in downtown Seattle, I'm bloody, bruised, and quite sure my right shoulder is dislocated.

It's hard to breathe.

I pull the bag off my head but can't see out of my left eye. What I can see is clouded and red because of the blood in my right eye.

Christ, I don't know what to do.

I can't go to the hospital. And I'm never stepping foot in that VRBO again.

*How did they find me?*

I'm going to pass out, and I don't want to do that here, so I stumble to my feet and look around. I'm in an industrial area. People walk about, but they don't look my way.

It's as if women are dumped, bloody and broken, every fucking day.

Whoever grabbed me didn't take my phone, so I pull it out of the sleeve in my leggings and punch in the address for the condo that Carmine and I lived in for several months. I know his family owns the building, and no one lives in the penthouse full time.

I'll crash there until I figure out what to do.

According to my cell, I'm only a couple of blocks away. I hobble toward the building, having to stop and lean on the concrete to catch my breath a few times.

Did they break another goddamn rib?

It takes five times longer than it should to reach Carmine's building. I'm ecstatic to discover that my codes still work on the door and the private elevator that leads up to the penthouse.

When the apartment doors open, I step in and lean against the wall as I listen for any movement inside.

There's nothing.

It doesn't appear as if anyone's been here since Carmine and I were here before leaving for Denver last week.

Has it really only been a week?

The red roses Carmine got me are still on the sofa table, wilting. A pair of my heels lay on the floor next to the kitchen island.

This is the only safe place for me in the city. I need to call my father, but that will have to come later. I'm not even sure what my name is right now.

The adrenaline of the attack is wearing off, and I know I'm going to be sick. Nausea roils my stomach, and dizziness fills my head. I just want to *sleep.* I probably shouldn't. I most likely have a concussion, but I'll be fine.

Everything will be fine.

God, I hurt. More than I ever have in my life.

I swing by the kitchen to grab a bucket from under the sink in case I do throw up, and then stumble to the couch in the living room. The sofa is huge, deep, and so comfortable that Carmine and I took many an afternoon nap here, tangled up with each other.

We also fucked like rabbits on it, but I'll think about that later.

The moment I lie down, I feel exhaustion overtake me. But the rest is fitful—I can't get comfortable. I can't catch my breath.

I really should call an ambulance. My father would *not* be pleased, but I'm alone, and something is very wrong.

I feel the anxiety building in my stomach. I reach for my phone, only to discover that I set it on the counter in the kitchen.

I want to cry.

Everything screams in agony.

And, suddenly, someone looms over me.

# CHAPTER 4

## ~CARMINE~

*I*'m in the middle of my second set of pull-ups when my phone rings.

I ignore it.

I've been pissed for days. Does Nadia think she can just waltz into my home, taunt me, and then breeze out again? That she can smirk at me and act as if I haven't had her in every position imaginable? That I don't affect her at all?

I won't admit to anyone that she got under my skin.

But goddamn it, she did.

My phone rings again. When I drop to the floor, I accept the call.

"What?"

"I'm sorry to interrupt you, sir. You need to come to the penthouse."

I narrow my eyes. "What happened?"

"Nadia's here, sir. And she's going to need you."

"I'll be there in thirty."

I end the call and, without another thought, hurry to grab my keys and wallet, then get into my car and peel out of the driveway, headed toward the freeway.

I like living away from the areas where we conduct business. I like keeping things separate. My grandmother taught me the importance of that.

But in times like these, it's a royal pain in the ass.

Thanks to traffic on the freeway, I make it to the building in twenty-six minutes, park in my reserved space, and take the private elevator up to the penthouse.

What in the hell is Nadia doing back here? Gathering the things she left behind when we went to Denver? That made sense.

But when I step off the elevator, I instinctively know that something is very wrong.

The space is still. The blinds are still closed, so it's mostly dark inside.

I flip on a hallway light to illuminate the area and see Nadia's blond head on the couch.

She's lying down.

And when I approach her, every drop of blood in my veins boils.

"Don't hurt me," she moans. "Can't."

"Nadia." I squat next to her and take in her bruised and bloodied face. "It's Carmine. I'm not going to hurt you."

"Carmine?" She lets out a small gasp through cut and bloody lips. "Didn't know where to go."

"You came to the right place. No one will think to search for you here. I have to call my people to come in and take care of you."

"No."

"Yes." I kiss her bloody hand. "I'll take care of this."

I pull out my phone and call our medical team. After they assure me that they're only minutes away, I hang up and hurry into the bathroom where I wet a washcloth and return to start cleaning her face as best I can so I can see the extent of her injuries.

"Hurts."

"I know." My voice is clipped, even to my ears. It takes everything in me to be gentle.

All I want to do is get my hands on the piece of shit who did this and make them pay. Painfully. Slowly.

Horrifically.

The elevator slides open, and the three men we employ to handle our medical needs come marching in.

"Christ," Malloy says with a hiss. "What did you do to her?"

"If you want to keep your job, you'll never ask that again," I bark as I step back and let them take over. At first, Nadia recoils from their touch, but with some soothing murmurs, she finally relaxes and lets the men examine her.

"I can't tell if her vision's been affected in this eye," Malloy says grimly. "It's swollen shut. I'll need to take another look in a few days."

He stands and pulls me aside as the other two continue working their magic with gauze and antiseptic.

"I've never suggested this before, and I know it's not how we do things..." Malloy begins and then props his hands on his hips. "But she needs to be in the hospital, Carmine."

I shake my head, but Malloy continues.

"She's been beaten so severely; I don't know if she has internal bleeding or a punctured lung. Her shoulder may be dislocated, and we might have to reset it. I recommend leaving the room for that one."

"I won't go."

He swallows and shakes his head. "Whoever did this was obviously given an order to fuck her up and leave her just this side of dead. And that's what they did. I have no idea how she even got herself up here."

"Because she's stubborn and damn smart. I'm not taking her to the hospital."

"Sir—"

"No. We'll take care of her here. Do your damn job, Malloy."

His mouth flattens into a line, and then he nods once. "I'm going to give you a list of things to watch for. If even *one* of them shows up, you need to call an ambulance right away. I mean it."

It's brutal standing back and watching them care for her. I feel helpless. She screams when they move her shoulder, but it's not dislocated—just wrenched badly. She whimpers when they poke and prod to see if anything is broken.

They hook her up to an IV and start pumping her full of antibiotics and morphine to help with the pain. Before long, she's settled back on the big couch with fresh dressings, a blanket, and orders to stay and rest for at least a week.

I'll personally see to it that she fucking obeys that order.

After my men leave, I return to her and gently brush her hair off her face.

"Sorry," she murmurs drunkenly.

"For what?"

"You're mad."

I sigh and lean over to press my lips to her forehead. "Not at you. When I find out who did this, I'll kill them."

"Get in line."

"Do you know who it was?"

She licks her swollen lips. "No. Couldn't see. Water?"

"Of course."

I hurry to the kitchen and fill a glass with crushed ice, and then bring it back to her.

"Here, suck on this."

"Mm." She sucks greedily on a chunk. "Nice."

"I'll be right here, Nadia. I'm not going anywhere. You sleep now and get healed up so you can kick some ass."

"Yeah." She sighs but reaches for my hand. "Stay."

"I told you, I'm here. I promise, I won't go."

"'Kay."

She slips into sleep, and I pull my hand down my face.

What the fuck? An hour ago, I wanted to spank her ass. Now, I want to protect her, fight for her. Keep her safe.

Because the truth is, she *has* gotten under my skin. That doesn't mean I trust her, but she didn't deserve this.

~

"KING ME."

Nadia scowls down at the checkerboard. "You're cheating."

"Negative." I stand and walk into the kitchen to get more chips.

We've been in the penthouse for five days. She slept the first three away, allowing her body to heal.

And now she's up and showered, her arm in a sling, scowling at me over a checkerboard.

"Is there any queso left?"

"No, you ate it all last night. At least your appetite is back."

"Yeah, well, I like food. You know that."

I grin, thinking back on all of the fun meals we'd had together. "I do. Watching you eat isn't a hardship. Where have you been staying? I'll have someone go and gather your things. Bring them here."

"I can go get my stuff soon enough."

"Why won't you tell me?"

"You probably already know."

I do. But she doesn't need to know that.

"Nadia, I think we're in the truce zone here. Think of this like a wedding or a funeral."

"Yeah, well, it almost *was* my funeral. And I don't know that it wasn't *you* who ordered this to be done to me," she blurts and stands to walk to the window. "You got here awfully fast after it happened."

I have to shove my hands into my pockets. Just six months ago, I would have said that nothing this woman could say or do could hurt me.

But things have changed.

And it seems she *can* hurt me.

That's unsettling and something to think about later.

She turns at my silence. The bruises on her face are beginning to fade from black to a sickly purple.

"You won't deny it?" she demands.

"I don't know how your family does things," I begin slowly, "but in *my* family, I've been taught to *never* hurt women. Physical punishment is not tolerated when it comes to women. Ever, under any circumstances."

I remember the day my cousin Elena first showed me the scars on her body she'd sustained at the hands of her father, my uncle. More anger seethes through me.

"Maybe not everyone in your family feels that way."

"They do." Agitated, I pace the floor. "I can say, without a shadow of a doubt, that my family is not responsible for this."

"Maybe one of your brothers—"

"IT WASN'T US!" I shout at her and then swear under my breath. "For fuck's sake, Nadia, no. I may not know what to feel when I'm around you, but I know that I wouldn't hurt you. No one in my family would hurt you. *You* haven't done anything to my family or me."

"Except make you think I'd fallen in love with you. Fucked your brains out. Moved in with you."

"Good sex isn't worth maiming over."

She shakes her head.

"I'm not convinced that your family isn't responsible for my aunt's and uncle's murders. And if they are, they *will* pay. I guarantee you that."

"If my father gave that order, he would cop to it," she says with a sigh. "I admit, I don't know every single order he's given, but he's not one to kill and then deny or deflect. He takes ownership of his decisions without regret. If he was behind those murders, he'd say so."

I can tell she believes what she's telling me.

"But, at the end of the day, we don't trust each other," she continues.

"Do you remember what happened when I found you here?"

"You were *so* pissed at me," she says.

"No." I cross to her, needing to touch her. "I told you then, and I meant it. I wasn't angry with you. I was livid that someone—*any*one—had put their hands on you this way. The fury was, and still is, a breathing thing inside me. I would have been upset to see any woman hurt like this, but the fact that it was *you* made it so much worse. So, no, we may not fully trust each other, but damn it, I care about what happens to you. I don't want to see *anything* happen to you. And we've been given orders to work *together*. To figure this mess out and get it resolved. I don't know what's happening now, with the murder at the wedding and your attack. I don't know if it has anything to do with my aunt and uncle, but I need to find out. I have connections that you don't and vice versa. We're stronger in this together. So, until we resolve this, you're stuck with me."

Her blue eyes slide to mine. "What do you mean?"

"You'll be staying with *me*. I can't protect you the way we've been doing things, obviously."

"I don't need—"

"Just stop talking." In exasperation, I march away from her. "Yes, you're strong and badass, and you can take care of yourself. But right now, people want to hurt you, and I'm partly responsible for that. There's a team of people here to help keep us safe. And goddamn it, that's what you're going to let me do."

"So, I'm being held hostage?"

I grunt but can't help but start laughing. "Yes. Clearly, this luxury penthouse is a horrible situation. I feel for you, Nadia. But keep a stiff upper lip. Suck it up and deal with it."

She snorts. "No sex. I mean it."

"I'm not in the habit of forcing unwilling women to fuck me."

Her face sobers at the steel in my voice. "I didn't mean to insinuate that you'd rape me."

"I need some fresh air."

She nods and glances at her phone when it rings.

"Not gonna answer?"

"I have no intention of speaking to my father. At least for a few more days."

I narrow my eyes. "Why haven't you told him about this?"

"Because. And the reasons are none of your business."

"If you confide in him, you could live wherever the fuck you want. He'd send protection, *and* he'd start his own hunt for the bastards who touched you. Nadia—"

"You have the luxury of trusting your family," she interrupts. "It's not something we share."

I step back, surprised. "You don't trust your family? When it comes to the business we're in, trusting them is of the utmost importance."

"My father, yes. I know he loves me and would do anything to protect me." She swallows hard. "But I don't trust my brother at all."

That's something we can agree on. Alexander Tarenkov is a slimy piece of shit, and it would make my black heart happy to tear him limb from limb with my bare hands.

"Why?"

"Alex is a selfish man," she says simply. "Only concerned with himself and how to manipulate every situation to his advantage. He'd make a horrible boss. The family, the *organization*, would collapse within a year. I don't know what shady deals he has going on the down-low, but I'd guess there are a few of them. No. I shouldn't be telling you any of this."

With a sigh, she lowers herself to the couch.

"I hate your brother with every fiber of my being." My voice is flat as I sit across from her. "There's nothing honorable about him."

"I know."

"Do you think he's behind everything that's going on?"

"No." She smirks. "He's a pussy. He doesn't have the balls to kill anyone. Alex is self-serving, yes, but he's also content to ride just under the radar. I do think he's laundering money that he's hiding from Papa. And when he's found out? Well, let's just say it won't go over well.

"But killing another family's boss? Possibly starting a war? No. He's not smart enough for that."

Unfortunately, I agree with her. He's slimy to the core but also as weak as they come. And not especially intelligent.

"So, in the meantime, you've been attacked twice, and your father has no idea."

"He'll be angry," she admits. "But until I figure out who's behind it and everything else, I'll keep it to myself. Besides, what's done is done. He can't undo it."

"If I kept something like this from my father, he'd be *livid.*"

"You're lucky," she says. "That your family is so close. That it's your safe haven."

"You need that, too. Our business is too lonely to be alone, Nadia."

"I'm not alone. I'm being held hostage, remember? So, what now? What's our next move?"

"We're staying here for another week."

She scowls, but I hold up my hand to stop her from saying anything more.

"You're healing, but you're still fragile. When we get out of here, I need to make sure that you're well and capable of having my back. We're likely going to get into a couple of sticky situations. As long as you're feeling up to it, we'll go to New York next week."

"Have you called the Sergis?"

"I'll call Billy when I have a solid date." No mob family travels to another family's territory without alerting them and asking for permission. It's a code we all live by and respect.

So, the fact that someone was in Seattle to hurt Nadia only intensifies my anger.

No one should have been here.

"They hate me there."

"*Hate* is a strong word," I remind her.

"And accurate."

"You'll be with me."

"What if they hate you, too?"

I smile thinly. "They don't."

# CHAPTER 5

## ~NADIA~

"*I*'m bored out of my *mind*." I pace the penthouse in front of the windows. "It's been two damn weeks. I feel great. I can even cover what's left of the bruises with makeup, and you'd never know they're there."

Carmine lounges on the couch, reading something on his iPad.

"What are you doing?"

"Reading stock reports." He sips his coffee. "How are your investments doing?"

I cock my head to the side. "Are you some kind of financial advisor?"

His grin is wide and toothy—and cockier than any one man has a right to be.

"I have a master's in finance," he says. "I guess you could say that I'm a financial advisor."

"To your family," I finish for him. "You help them hide money."

There's that smile again. "I assure you, everything I offer is legal."

"Bullshit."

"So, I'll ask again. How are your investments?"

He's evading.

"I don't have any."

His brow knits. "*None?*"

"No."

"Nadia, you're pushing thirty. You should have a Roth IRA, at the very least. You should have stocks. I know you're set to inherit more money than the net worth of several countries, but—"

"Carmine. I don't want to talk about finances. I want to get the hell out of here."

He sighs. "Let's go for a walk."

"Anything." I bounce into the bedroom to snatch up the new shoes I ordered a few days ago. Since blood now covered the running shoes I had on the day I was attacked, I needed new ones.

When I'm dressed and ready to go, Carmine sets his iPad aside, and we step into the elevator.

"We should head to New York tomorrow," I say as we ride down to the ground floor.

"It's Friday, Nadia. Let's go Monday."

"Because the mafia takes weekends off?" I roll my eyes. "You're stalling."

"I told you before; I want to make sure you're healthy."

"I feel great." It's not a complete lie. Aside from a little ache in my shoulder when I raise my arm above my head, and the vision in my left eye still being a little blurry, I feel pretty good. The doctor said I might not get my sight back all the way, though.

That pissed me right off.

But I'm not dead, and that's something.

"I saw you wince this morning when you reached for a mug in the cabinet."

"You're watching me like a fucking mother hen." I scowl as we step outside and then stop to take a deep breath. "I love summer."

"Seattle is nice in the summer," he says. "Less rain, more sun. Not too hot, thanks to the Sound."

"It's a beautiful day." I tip my head up to the sky.

"You might want to pay attention, so you don't faceplant on the concrete."

I laugh and glance up at him. "You would probably catch me."

"Maybe."

These past two weeks have shown me that I can let my guard down around Carmine. Now that it's just *us*—no pretenses, no blatant lies or games—I actually trust that he won't hurt me.

Not intentionally, anyway.

He's the only person in the world that I *can* trust right now, and I just hope that he doesn't do something stupid to betray that faith.

"What's that place?" I ask, pointing across the street. "It looks like a coffee shop. Cherry Street Coffee House. How did I not know that was here all the time we've lived here?"

"I don't think I've been in there," he says. "Do you want some coffee?"

"Yes. An iced Americano sounds awesome right now. Let's do it."

We watch for traffic and then hustle across the street. The café is so cute, and it smells *amazing* when we walk inside.

I order my iced coffee and throw caution to the wind, including an orange and cranberry scone. Carmine gets the same. Before long, we're walking out of the shop again, loaded down with our treats.

"This is the best day I've had in two weeks."

Carmine laughs. "If I'd known that all it took for you to have the best day ever is a coffee and a scone, I would have done this sooner."

"Now we know. This could be a new daily occurrence."

"I overheard the barista telling someone that they have killer cinnamon rolls." Carmine shrugs as he takes a bite of his scone. "Maybe we'll have to check it out for breakfast."

"God, yes." I sip my coffee in happiness. "It feels good to finally feel semi-normal, you know?"

"I imagine that it does," he replies. "And it's good to see you looking like yourself again."

"I think that—*whoa!*"

My toe catches on an uneven part of the sidewalk, and I pitch forward. My coffee flies, and before my face can hit the ground, Carmine's arm wraps around my waist, and he catches me.

It all happened so fast, yet at the same time, it seemed to be in slow motion.

Especially the part where my almost-full coffee fell and splashed *everywhere.*

"Sonofabitch," I growl. "I was enjoying that."

"You can have mine." Carmine makes sure I'm standing upright and offers me his cup, but I shake my head.

"No, you enjoy it. I still have my scone."

"We'll share," he says, and then his eyes narrow on my face. "What hurts?"

I don't want to tell him. I don't want to say it out loud because then it'll be true.

"I'm fine."

His finger gently taps under my chin, and he makes me look him in the eyes.

"Don't fucking lie to me, Nadia."

"My shoulder." I sigh in exasperation. "I wrenched it a bit when my arm flailed. But it'll be fine. I'll just ice it and take an Advil when we get back. It'll be just fine."

He sighs and offers me a sip of his coffee, which I accept.

"Let's head back."

I'm tired. I didn't expect our walk to exhaust me as much as it did. Maybe it was the almost-fall that did me in.

The return trip is more subdued. We're quiet as we sip Carmine's coffee and eat our scones. When we get up to the penthouse, Carmine orders me to sit on the sofa.

"I'm getting you some ice," he informs me. His tone says he's not to be argued with.

I'm not really interested in arguing anyway.

The ice pack feels good on my sore shoulder. "Why don't you sit with me, and we'll put a movie on?"

He nods, turns on the TV, and passes me the remote. Then he sits next to me with his iPad in his lap.

He often works as I watch television. I won't admit it out loud, but I enjoy just being with him.

And that's stupid. But it is what it is.

"How about *Thor?*" I ask. "The third one. It's the funniest."

"I'm game."

I turn it on and then lean my head on Carmine's strong shoulder. Thor and Hulk are in an arena, about to battle it out as my eyes slip closed, and I fall asleep.

～

"Wake up, pretty girl."

I take a deep breath and crack open one eye. It's still dark outside. "Jesus, what time is it?"

"Five," he says. He's already fully dressed in a dark suit, no tie. "I told the pilot we'd be in our seats no later than six-thirty."

"Here's your hat. What's your hurry?" I bury my face in my pillow.

"We'll lose three hours to the time change, and I want to see Mick and Billy this afternoon."

Just the mention of the Sergi family makes me groan.

It's been five days since we took our walk, and I almost fell. My shoulder seems to have recovered, and Carmine called Billy Sergi, the second in command there, last night.

They granted him access to the city.

Of course, Carmine didn't say anything about having *me* with him.

I drag my ass out of bed and stumble into the bathroom. After I've done my business and am in the steamy shower, Carmine magically appears with a cup of coffee.

"You're a god," I say as I take the mug and sip the hot brew. "Thanks."

"You're welcome. Be ready in twenty."

He marches out again, but not before his eyes wander over my naked body.

Carmine hasn't made any moves on me in the weeks we were at the penthouse. He's kept things completely platonic.

And I know that it was *my* insistence that ensured we didn't have sex.

Sex muddies the waters. Clouds judgment.

And sex with Carmine is so fucking good, I would be a quivering pile of sexual need twenty-four-seven if we started something physical.

But damn, I miss the sex. And judging by the look in Carmine's eyes when he walked away, he does, too.

I let the hot water and caffeine wake me up, and thirty minutes later—much to his annoyance—I'm ready to go.

"It's a good thing I packed last night," I say. "Or I would have been late."

His brow lifts, and I can't help but laugh.

I'm back in business-mode, dressed in black slacks, a white silk shirt, and a red scarf. Tall, black Louboutin heels complete the outfit, and when I stand next to Carmine, I'm only a few inches shorter than he is.

"Those shoes do things to me," he mutters.

"I know." I tuck my makeup bag under my arm and follow him into the elevator. When we reach the garage, the driver meets us and tucks our bags into the trunk.

Because it's so early, traffic to the airfield isn't crazy. We don't go to SeaTac. Instead, we're driven to Boeing Field, where many private planes come and go.

The driver parks near the Martinelli jet, and before long, we're tucked safely inside, coffee at our elbows, and a flight attendant at our beck and call.

I don't like the way she ogles Carmine.

Not that he's *mine.* He's not. But I still don't like it.

"Have you fucked her?" I ask quietly.

He frowns down at me. "Who?"

"Her." I don't look up at the flight attendant.

"Look at me."

I don't do as he asks. I won't look at him and show him the vulnerability in my eyes. It pisses me off that it's there in the first place.

"Nadia."

"Forget I asked. Let's talk about how high-maintenance you are, Carmine. Why can't we just take a commercial flight to New York? First class is pretty swanky these days."

"Your father has a jet."

"Yeah, for *him* to use. The only time I'm on it is if I'm traveling with him. I'm okay with a normal flight."

"Must I remind you that you're carrying a ten-thousand-dollar handbag?"

I glance down at my Birkin and smile. "I never forget about my bag. But it was a gift. And a one-time purchase. It doesn't cost me anything to maintain it."

"You're decked out in luxury brands from head to toe, Nadia. You live well. I won't apologize for doing the same. We all have things we're willing to splurge on. This is one of mine. I fund every flight I take on this jet. Not the family. And because I've been savvy with my money, I can afford the luxury."

"Hey, I'm not irresponsible with my money." I poke him in the side. "I just don't have a fancy portfolio."

"I'm going to help you with that."

"Why would you do that?"

"Because it's important to have investments. It only adds to your independence. And after what you told me about your lack of trust with your family, I think it's imperative that you're dependent on them as little as possible."

I stare at him, my mouth agape. "You're *worried* about me."

He rolls his eyes. "Don't be silly."

"You *like* me," I continue, teasing him. "I think you *like me,* like me, Carmine Martinelli. What will people say?"

"Stop talking."

"The next thing you know, you'll be pledging your undying love and proposing. I don't want to have babies, Carmine. I'm telling you that now—"

The next thing I know, I'm trapped against the back of the seat, and he's kissing the hell out of me. This isn't a playful peck to get me to stop talking. It's passionate, full of frustration and lust, and I hear the moan coming out of my throat as I sink my fingers into his dark hair and hang on tight as he takes me on an erotic ride.

"That'll teach you to shut up when I tell you to," he mutters against my lips as the plane taxis down the runway. "And the answer to your question is, no. I've never fucked her."

I clear my throat as he backs away and returns to his seat, settles in.

"It's none of my business."

"Keep telling yourself that, sweetheart."

～

"Maybe I should stay here."

We've been in the suite at the Four Seasons for an hour. The space is decorated in black and white, all modern and clean and completely sterile.

It's beautiful, most likely costs a small fortune, and is not my style *at all.*

But I'd rather stay here than head into the lion's den.

"You're not staying here, Nadia."

"I told you before…the Sergi family doesn't like me, Carmine."

That's putting it mildly.

"What did you do, kill one of them?"

"No. I was supposed to marry Billy but I threw a fit, and my father told them never mind. It pissed them off. You know how it is when a family is supposed to marry into another."

"Elena was supposed to marry Alex," he says dryly. "She dodged that bullet."

"Exactly. I dodged the same one. And they're just not happy about it. They don't trust us now."

"When did this happen?"

"Six years ago."

He whistles between his teeth. "That's a long time, Nadia. If all's been quiet since then, I'd think they've moved on and have other things to be mad about."

697

"Yeah, well, you'd think." I bite my lip. "Still, I'll just hang out here and wait for you."

"No, you'll come with me. But I suggest you change out of those heels."

I shake my head, resigned to my fate. "They're a weapon if I need them. And I can run in them as easily as I can in my sneakers. I also have a concealed sidearm on me."

"Where?"

I smirk. "I'm not telling you that."

He saunters over to me. "Maybe I'll find it for myself later."

"You can try."

His jaw tightens as he looks me over with hungry eyes, but he only swallows and turns away.

"Let's go. The sooner we do this, the quicker we can start asking questions in other areas of the city. This is a courtesy call to say hello and let them know what we're up to."

"Great."

The Sergi's headquarters is located in downtown Manhattan, right in the middle of all the action. The building looks innocent enough.

But I would bet every cent I have in the bank—which is more than Carmine expects, and that I invested just fine, thank you very much—that the things that happen in this building would turn Carmine's hair white.

I take a deep breath as he holds the door for me. We're shown into an office where Billy and his father Mick sit.

Mick's the boss.

Billy does his bidding.

It's all very customary as far as mafia families go.

"It's good to see you, Mick," Carmine says. But, suddenly, Mick flies to his feet, and guns are drawn, all pointed our way.

"What the fuck is she doing here?"

# CHAPTER 6

## ~CARMINE~

"Whoa, whoa, whoa." I hold up my hands and slide to my left, closer to Nadia. Jesus, she wasn't kidding.

They really don't like her.

"You didn't say anything about that bitch being here," Mick sneers.

"She's with me," I say quickly. "Our families are working together because we've recently come under attack. I'm here because we need your help."

Mick's eyes narrow, but he signals for his goons to put away their weapons.

"What's going on?" Mick asks.

Billy hasn't said a word. He only glares at Nadia as we step forward into the luxurious office and sit across from Mick.

I briefly fill the boss in on the attempt on my father's life at the wedding in Denver, the subsequent attack on Nadia, and then remind him of my aunt's and uncle's murders long ago.

"Do you honestly think Vinnie's murder is tied to this now?" Mick asks, doubt hanging heavily in his voice.

"I don't know, but I'm going to find out," I reply. "I need to ask around the city, find out what your men know about the attempt on my father's life—and Nadia's for that matter."

"The Martinellis and the Tarenkovs are working together," Mick mutters and shakes his head. "Fascinating. Well, you can ask around, but no one will tell you anything. Even if they do know what's going on. This isn't your territory."

"Then what do you suggest?"

"Go home," he says bluntly.

"Not without answers."

Mick blows out a long breath. "We should have had this conversation over the phone. If you'd given me a heads-up, I could have asked around before you got here."

"There's a lot to be said for looking into a man's eyes when you talk to him." I clear my throat. "Mick, *you* aren't behind this, are you?"

"No." His lips flatten into a hard line. "It's true, there is no love lost between our family and the Tarenkovs, but my beef isn't worth a war. And Carlo and I have always had an agreeable relationship. But, if you'll give me a couple of days, I'll ask around. On the down-low. I don't think it's wise to bring a lot of attention to this. It might escalate the situation or make those responsible go into hiding. And then you'll never get your answers."

I nod in agreement. He hasn't said anything that I didn't already take into consideration.

"It looks like Nadia and I will spend a few days in your beautiful city. Take in the sights. Maybe see a show."

"Enjoy your vacation," Mick advises. "I'll be in touch when I know something."

"Thank you." We rise and start to leave, but turn back at Mick's voice.

"The next time you request entry into my city, you'd better be fucking honest about who you're bringing with you. I don't like surprises."

"Understood."

"I'VE HEARD great things about this show." Nadia walks out of the walk-in closet off our suite's bedroom and holds the necklace I gave her in Denver out to me. "Will you please fasten this?"

"Of course." I slip the diamonds and platinum around her slim neck and fasten it under her hairline, then kiss the ball of her shoulder. I notice she doesn't have any earrings in. "You're damn beautiful, Nadia."

She grins at me and then does a little spin in her red dress, showing it off. "Thanks. I'm glad I brought this along, just in case. And you look pretty damn good yourself in that suit."

I adjust the knot of my tie and then hold my hand out for hers. "Shall we?"

"Let me just grab my clutch." She rushes to the bed and slips a tube of lipstick into her bag, then takes my proffered hand. "Let's go watch a Broadway show."

The truth is, Nadia takes my breath away. She handled herself well at Mick's office today, knowing when to stay quiet and let me do the talking. She's intelligent. And she's sexy as fuck.

I shouldn't have kissed her on the plane this morning. I was only trying to shut her up, but all I did was remind myself how good we are together in bed.

How much I want her.

How I never *stopped* wanting her.

And she's made it clear that a physical relationship is out of the question.

I'm a damn fool. I need to keep my hands to myself and keep my focus on the task at hand.

She's a colleague who has become a friend. That's all.

But when we step into the elevator, and she leans her head on my shoulder as we watch the floors tick down, all I want to do is pull her to me and kiss her breathless.

Instead, I turn my lips down and kiss the top of her head.

"Tell me about this show." *Before I take you back upstairs and fuck you into next week.*

"The lead actress is London Watson. She's a *huge* name in theater, and she wrote this show a couple of years ago. Still stars in it. I'm excited to finally see it."

"Sounds great."

We walk through the hotel lobby and see our car is waiting. The ride through Manhattan is slow, as always, but before long, the driver drops us off in front of the theater. I bought us VIP tickets, so we bypass the line and are immediately shown to our seats.

"That's Paul Rudd," Nadia whispers and nods to the man several seats down. "Holy shit, I love *Ant-Man.*"

"Tell him so. We have a few minutes before the show starts."

She bites her lip and then shrugs her shoulder and stands to approach the actor. Paul smiles up at her, then stands to talk to her. I can't hear everything that's said, but there are smiles, a couple of laughs, and then Nadia returns to me.

"Oh my God," she says. "He's so nice."

"He looked like a good guy."

She grins. "This is a fun day. Well, aside from having guns pointed at my face, of course."

"Yeah, that was a little intense."

"But the rest of it has been better than expected."

"I'm glad."

She links her arm through mine and leans on me. Nadia has become more and more physically affectionate over the past few weeks, at least since we started staying at the penthouse again.

I don't mind the affection.

But damn if it doesn't make me want more.

"You really do look nice in this suit," she says casually. "I don't think I've seen it before."

"I'm sure you have."

"No, this one is navy. You usually wear black."

I glance down at her. "You pay attention to the color of my suits?"

"You usually wear black," she says again. "I like this on you."

The lights flicker, signaling the start of the show. Through the entire three hours, Nadia touches me—holds my hand, leans her head on my shoulder, smiles up at me.

She's flirting with me.

Blatantly.

Boldly.

Either she's trying to seduce me, or she's playing a game. And I have no patience for that. She has me tied in knots, my dick semi-hard as we leave the theater.

"London was *amazing,*" she gushes as we get into the waiting car. "She's so talented. I absolutely loved it. Man, I'm starving."

She grins over at me.

"Are you hungry?"

"Hmm."

She frowns. "You don't know if you're hungry?"

"I could use something." I turn my head and watch Manhattan pass us by. The traffic is no less frantic at midnight than it was close to four hours ago.

"Let's just order in at the hotel," she suggests. "We can get comfortable and eat all the food. That sounds awesome."

I nod. When the car stops in front of the Four Seasons, a bellman opens our door. I climb out first, then turn to offer Nadia my hand to help her out of the vehicle.

She's in another pair of those mile-high heels she loves. The kind that look damn hot over my shoulders as I fuck her into oblivion.

I remember very well.

"New York just energizes me," she says when we step into the elevator. "Don't you love this city?"

"You're talkative tonight," is my only reply.

"It's New York," she says. "Like I said, it energizes me. I don't come here often enough. For obvious reasons."

She slides her hand into mine, and I glance down at her.

"Why are you flirting with me so hard tonight?"

Her smile doesn't dim, but the light in her blue eyes sparks. "Oh, so you *did* notice?"

"Hard not to." I lead her out of the elevator and down the long hallway to the presidential suite, then unlock the door and walk inside. "You've turned it up."

"Turned what up?"

"The flirting." I turn and look at her as I loosen my tie. She drops her bag onto a table and crosses her arms over her chest. "What's going on?"

"I like flirting with you." She moves to me and brushes my hands out of the way so she can unbutton my shirt. "I like *being* with you."

"You set the rules hard and fast from the beginning of this, Nadia. No sex. I've upheld my end of that bargain."

"I know." There's no flirtation in her voice now as her eyes find mine. "And I also know that it's unfair and just plain ridiculous to muddy the waters. To change the rules."

"But I have a feeling you're going to do just that."

"We're good together," she says at last. "I thought I could turn that piece off. That I could ignore it. But damn it, the truth is, we *are* good together. And we'll be working together for God knows how long."

"Are you saying that you want to reintroduce sex into our dynamic?"

"Well, that just sounds like a business merger." She rises onto her tiptoes and barely skims her lips over mine. "And there's nothing sexy about a business merger. What you and I do to each other is fucking sexy, Carmine."

I sigh, wanting nothing more in this moment than *her*. And in about six seconds, I'm going to have her.

But we need to get something straight first.

"There's no pretense here, Nadia. No act."

"It's just you and me, who we *really* are, enjoying each other, Carmine. I know that."

"Good."

I don't waste any time. I lift her against me and hurry to the bedroom. "If anything hurts—"

"Trust me, this doesn't hurt."

I grin and set her on her feet next to the bed. "Leave the shoes on."

Her eyes are full of pure female satisfaction as she reaches behind her and unzips the dress, letting it pool around her ankles.

"Leave the necklace on, too."

"Any other requests?"

I laugh and urge her back onto the bed. "No. Let me do the rest." I take her right foot in my hand and kiss her ankle bone, right above the shoe. "Do you have any idea what these fucking shoes do to me?"

"Why do you think I wear them?"

She leans back on her hands, watching me as I kiss up her leg, then spread her wide and lick a wet trail from her inner thigh to the pink lips of her glistening pussy.

"You were always good at this."

She sighs and lays back on the mountain of pillows as I take her on the ride of her life —all with my mouth. I lick and suck, then lick some more. I vary the pressure and speed, and when I push two fingers inside of her, she comes apart spectacularly.

"Good girl," I murmur as I kiss up her flat stomach to her breasts. "I love your tits. You know that, right?"

"They never grew in."

"Excuse me?"

She laughs and brushes her hand through my hair. "When I was young, I was desperate for them to grow so boys would notice me. Much to my dismay, they stayed small."

"I see zero things wrong with these." I brush my tongue over a hard peek and then kiss her neck passionately.

I fumble in the bedside drawer, find a little packet, and make quick work of protecting us. But before I can slide home, she pushes me onto my back and straddles my hips.

She always loved this position the best, and she'll get no complaints from me.

She rides me hard and fast and reaches back to cup my already-tight balls.

"Fuck, Nadia."

"Yes, fuck Nadia," she agrees and clenches her core around me.

I don't want to come yet, so I grip her hips in my hands, lift her, then shift our position so I'm behind her. Then, I push back inside. Her round ass is in the air, and I give it a loud smack as I fuck her from behind.

"God, Carmine." She clenches the bedsheets in her fists and pushes back against me. "Yes."

Three more hard thrusts are all it takes to have us both coming apart at the seams, crying out in ecstasy.

∼

"Oh, God, I love this."

She's wearing a white hotel robe and nothing else, and we're sitting on the terrace, a large tray of food on the table between us as she eats her weight in shrimp cocktail.

"I mean, just look at the lights."

The New York lights are stunning. We're not far from the World Trade Center memorial and can even see the lights of it from here.

"It's a beautiful place," I agree and reach for a taco. Tacos aren't on the menu, but they made them for me tonight. "If you love it here so much, why don't you live here?"

"Because I'm a Tarenkov," she reminds me. "There's no way the Sergis would allow that. Especially Billy. That little worm."

She sips her chocolate shake and scowls.

"He did seem a bit angry with you today."

She laughs at that and then switches from her shrimp to the dessert she ordered: crème brûlée.

"He's a baby. Worse than Alex," she says as an afterthought. "I would keep an apartment here in a heartbeat, but it's not possible because of the family drama. The Sergis don't trust us, and we don't trust them either, truth be told. But once a year, I do come shopping. I send Mick an email, and he always replies cordially, giving me a four-day pass to spend some time here. It's the best four days of my year."

"This is still a free country, Nadia."

She turns sad, blue eyes up at me. "Come on, Carmine. You know that isn't true for people like us. Never has been. Men who claim to love us dictate our lives, but they wouldn't hesitate to use us for personal gain if they saw the need arise. It's a game we play every damn day of our lives."

She eats more of her dessert.

"But you know what? I don't want to talk about that."

"What do you want to talk about?"

"I don't want to chat at all. I want to lick what's left of this crème brûlée off your penis."

My eyebrows climb at the suggestion. "I'm not saying no."

"I didn't think you would."

# CHAPTER 7

## ~NADIA~

*I* wake up in the center of maybe the biggest bed on Earth, all of the blankets rumpled and in a pile in the middle, with me draped around them like the big spoon.

Carmine, however, is nowhere to be found.

I sit up and rub the sleep from my eyes. I'm sure I have mascara shadows under my lashes because I didn't bother washing my face before Carmine carried me in here and had his way with me.

I grin and stand, feeling the pull of tender muscles. The soreness feels good, though, not at all like it did as I recovered from the attack. I feel good and sexed.

I pad naked into the living space to see if Carmine is reading the news on his iPad, but he's not out here, either. So, I walk into the half-bath in the hall, use the restroom, and then find the white robe on the floor where Carmine let it fall, wrapping it around myself.

I journey back through the bedroom to the master bath and lean on the doorjamb with a grin.

Lounging in the white porcelain soaking tub is Carmine, up to his neck in sudsy water. He's laid his head back, and his eyes are closed.

I cross to him and let my robe fall to the floor.

"Don't you smell nice?" I murmur. He opens his eyes. They immediately warm, then travel the length of me. "Looks like there's room for two."

"Why don't we find out?"

I grin and climb into the hot water, straddling his hips and rubbing myself against him playfully. "I didn't peg you as a bath guy."

"It feels good to soak now and then."

I sniff the air. "Is that rose oil, I smell?"

"What's wrong with a little rose oil?"

I lean over to bite his neck. "Like I said yesterday, you're just a little high-maintenance."

"I like luxurious things," he says, but his voice doesn't sound defensive. He's simply stating a fact. "Whether that's a private jet or a soak in a tub the size of Manhattan, it doesn't matter."

I push my wet hand through his hair. "I just like to give you shit."

"If you keep rubbing yourself on me like that, I'll give you something, too."

"Oh?" I cock an eyebrow and grind on him. "Like this?"

"You're a vixen," he mutters. "And it would take a saint to resist you."

"I have it on good authority that you're no saint."

He laughs and glides his hands up my thighs to my waist and then around to my ass, cupping the globes and lifting me gently so he can urge his cock inside of me.

"No condom," he growls.

"Still on the pill." My voice is raspy. The water sloshes around us as I start to move. God, I love this position. The head of his dick glides perfectly over my most sensitive places, sending thrilling shockwaves through me.

I never last long when I ride him, and with the water caressing my ass, my sides, and my lower back, I come faster than ever, crying out with each wave that hits me.

"Again," he orders. "Look at me."

His brown eyes are hot as he works me harder and faster. He's sitting up now, guiding me, pushing me until we both succumb to a climax that has us shivering and panting.

"Well, okay then." I swallow hard. "Good morning."

"Yes, it is." He nuzzles my breasts, then leans back against the tub once more. "What shall we do today?"

"Are you kidding me? I'm in New York. I want to go shopping."

His grin is wide and full of humor.

"I was hoping you'd say that."

I stand and carefully step out of the tub. I don't want to fall on my ass, and we spilled a lot of water during our fun time.

"I need a shower, but I'll be ready in an hour."

"I'll order up breakfast," he says as he climbs out of the tub.

"It's handy having you around, Carmine."

He grins, winks at me, and then leaves the bathroom.

Jesus, Mary, and Joseph, that man is sexy. I start the shower, and when the water is the right temperature, I step in and get busy washing my face.

I'm in a damn good mood. Maybe the best I've been in for months. Maybe ever. I'm in my favorite city, with someone I enjoy, and I'm going to spend an obscene amount of money.

"Breakfast will be here in twenty," Carmine calls out.

"Sounds good," I yell back.

Yeah, it's damn convenient having that man around.

~

"THE BAG you just bought looks like the one you already have."

We're eating pizza and sitting by a fountain. The boutiques will deliver our new things to the Four Seasons for us so we don't have to walk around Manhattan loaded down with bags.

"Uh, excuse me Mr. I-just-bought-a-ten-thousand-dollar-watch-that-looks-just-like-the-one-I'm-currently-wearing."

He stops mid-chew and narrows his eyes at me. "It looks nothing like this watch."

"And my new bag looks nothing like the others I have." I shrug a shoulder. "Besides, it's a new style this season. And it's going to look *so* cute with jeans and a sweater."

"I want to look at shoes at Bergdorf."

I grin at him. "I can live with that."

We finish our pizza and walk down the street to the old store, wandering through. Browsing. When we find the men's shoes, Carmine studies some Louboutins that have me salivating.

He's not the only one who appreciates luxury.

"You could wear those with any and all of your suits."

He nods and wanders down the table, picking up a pair of sneakers. Carmine flags down a salesperson and asks to try them on in his size.

"Sneakers?"

"I do wear casual clothes."

I take in his khaki slacks and light blue button-down. "When?"

"I brought out a couple of sizes because you just never know how Louboutins will fit," the salesman says as he returns and sets the boxes at Carmine's feet.

After twenty minutes—and six pairs—Carmine chooses two, and then we're off to find the women's shoe section, just one floor up.

"I need more heels like I need a hole in the head," I mutter as I brush my index finger over a pair of glossy patent leather Chanel heels. "But damn if they're not beautiful."

I try on Dior, Choo, and Hermes, and settle on a pair of Dior slingbacks, Hermes sneakers, and the *cutest* Valentino flip-flops.

Again, they'll deliver everything to our room, so we leave the store and start walking down Fifth, hand in hand, enjoying the afternoon sun.

"I did a lot of damage today," I say with a happy sigh. "But it's so fun. Nothing compares to shopping in New York. Well, aside from Paris. Paris is the mecca, of course. But New York ranks up there. I could have spent all day in the Hermes boutique and bought scarves and all kinds of fun little things. But I won't wear them often, so I need to be strong and cut myself off."

"I enjoy watching you shop. You touch everything."

"I'm a texture girl. I like to feel the leathers, the silks, and cashmeres. It *feels* pretty, you know?"

"Just one of the reasons I enjoy touching you."

I laugh, but when I look up at him, he's staring down at me, and he is *not* laughing. "You're charming, you know that?"

"I'm just telling the truth. I hope you like tea."

"Tea?"

He nods and leads me to the doorway of the Tiffany & Co. We get in the elevator and ride it to the fourth floor, and then he leads me to the Blue Box Café.

"Oh, I've never eaten there."

"We're having afternoon tea," he informs me with a smile.

"Fancy."

A regal woman with perfectly coifed, sable hair greets us. She takes Carmine's name and checks her reservation list, then leads us to our table and sets Tiffany-blue menus in front of us.

"We're having the afternoon tea," Carmine informs her.

"Of course." She nods and backs away. What seems like only moments later, a waiter wheels a cart to our table, piled high with finger foods and hot, steeping tea.

The waiter explains everything on the tray, pours us each a cup, and then leaves us to our own devices.

"I'm sort of shocked," I admit as I reach for a scone, break it in half, and spread real, whipped butter on it.

"At what?"

"This is the last thing I would have expected from you."

"We've had plenty of meals together."

"I meant the *tea*." I chuckle and take a bite of my scone, then close my eyes in happiness. "This is delicious."

"We'd already had lunch, but I wanted to do something different for you."

"This is different. And fun. And fancy."

I watch as his brows knit together.

"It's okay, Carmine. I like the fancy side of you."

We try the finger sandwiches, some fruit, and spend an hour simply enjoying each other's company.

"This place is just so beautiful." I look over at the wall with an enormous clock on it. The wall itself looks as if it's made of gray and Tiffany-blue granite. "And the food was great."

I yawn and cover my mouth with my napkin.

"Am I boring you?" he asks.

"No. Definitely, not." I laugh and run my fingers through my hair. "I think all the walking and shopping is finally catching up with me. Maybe it's time to head back and catch a nap."

"We have one more stop to make first."

I tilt my head. "Where?"

"It isn't far."

He pays the check and then pulls me through the restaurant and back into the elevator, but rather than leave the store, he leads me to a waiting salesperson.

"Hello, sir," the man says with a slight bow. "I'm Dennis. I'll be happy to work with you today."

I frown at Carmine. "Looking for another watch?"

"Earrings," he says as Dennis starts to pull velvet boxes out of the glass cases and sets them on the counter. "You weren't wearing any earrings when we went to the theater last night."

I stare up at him. "Seriously?"

He quirks a brow. "I'm quite sure Dennis would be rather upset if I were kidding." He turns to the other man. "Did you see the necklace?"

"My necklace?"

Dennis nods. "I received your text with the photo. It's a stunning piece, and I'm sure we have earrings here that will match it nicely."

"You want me to pick out earrings to match my necklace?"

I stare at him, blinking slowly, dumbfounded.

"That's why we're here," he says.

"You don't have to do that."

"Give us a moment," he says, and Dennis discretely walks away so we can talk in private.

"Carmine, you don't have to buy me gifts."

"I don't have to do much of anything," he says. "I *want* to do this for you. They'll look beautiful."

"You gave me a lot of gifts when we were fake-dating." I chew my lower lip.

"We're not fake anything now," he says smoothly and reaches out to brush his thumb across the apple of my cheek. "I enjoy you, Nadia. More than I anticipated. And I'd like to buy you something beautiful to remember our time in New York. No strings attached."

*What if I'm starting to wish for strings?*

My heart flutters. What the fuck is wrong with me?

Carmine signals for Dennis to rejoin us, and I turn to the several velvet trays with a sigh.

I know as soon as my eyes land on them.

They're understated, which works well because the necklace is anything but. These earrings won't overshadow the diamonds around my neck but will add just a bit of sparkle to my ears.

"These."

Dennis offers them to me, along with a mirror, and I fasten them onto my lobes, then tilt my head side to side, admiring them.

"Would you like to look at the chandeliers?" Dennis asks, pointing to a gorgeous pair of diamond earrings that probably cost about the same as a small suburban home.

"No, thanks." I turn to Carmine. His lips are tipped up in a small smile. "These will go perfectly."

"I think you're right."

He reaches out and touches my ear with his finger. "Discreet, but beautiful."

"And the necklace is still the centerpiece."

"No." He steps into me and lowers his lips to my ear. "*You're* the centerpiece, sweetheart. The jewelry is just frosting."

He turns back to Dennis.

"We'll take them."

"Excellent, sir."

Dennis is all smiles as he sees to the bill, and I can't stop hearing the last words from Carmine in my head.

*The rest is just frosting.*

Has anyone taken the time to see me for *me*? To see past the designer clothes and accessories to the woman beneath? I feel like I've been constantly trying to prove to my father, my brother, and everyone in our family that I'm smart enough and damn savvy enough to take over the organization one day.

But they always dismiss me.

Not Carmine. He respects my opinions and listens to me when I talk. He acknowledges that I enjoy pretty things but also knows that it's just the surface.

That what's beneath is so much more.

"Ready?" he asks with a smile.

"Yes." I look in the mirror once more, happy to wear the earrings out of the store. "You know, I hope you realize that when I give you shit for being a diva, I don't really mean it."

He glances at me as we walk through the store. "You've never called me a *diva*."

"Not in those words, exactly."

"Does it truly bother you that I like the finer things? Does it emasculate me in your eyes?"

"No." Visions of Carmine and I in bed swim in my head. Of him working out. Of all the ways that he shows, every day, that he's a *man*. One I'm incredibly attracted to. "Not at all."

"Good, because I plan to take you back to the hotel and fuck you blind."

My mouth opens and closes. I'm not sure what in the hell to say to that.

But when we step outside, four men suddenly surround us, all with weapons drawn.

"The boss wants to see you. Get in the car."

I sigh and frown at all four of them. "What in the hell is it with the Sergi organization and guns? Can't you just ask a girl nicely?"

"Let's go," the goon says, ignoring my statement altogether. "You can complain about how we do things to the boss."

# CHAPTER 8

## ~CARMINE~

"*Y*ou do realize that it's not necessary to hold us at gunpoint to get us into your office." My voice is dry as I sit across from Mick and narrow my eyes at him. "We're happy to come in willingly."

Mick smiles, but his eyes aren't full of humor.

"I have no idea what you're talking about."

I just stare back at him until he looks down at the papers on his desk. "I've done some asking around, some talking, and I'm afraid I don't know much more than you do."

"But you know something."

Mick leans back in his chair and folds his beefy hands over his impressive stomach. When you think of the stereotypical mob boss, Mick is the image that comes to most minds. He's a big man—in both stature and weight. He's imposing.

"Turns out, someone approached one of my men about selling something new here in the city."

I sit forward. "A new drug?"

"Yeah, but I don't know who did the approaching. Or what kind of drug."

I scowl. "Come on, Mick, you know everything that goes on in New York."

The other man's eyes flash with anger. "I thought I did. And trust me when I say that I'd be happy to drag my man in here to interrogate him myself."

"Then do it."

"He's fucking dead."

"Goddamn it." I rub my hand over my mouth. "How did he die?"

"I was at that wedding," Mick reminds me. "My man has been dead for a few days, but it looks like he met the same fate your father's man did."

"Poison," Nadia murmurs beside me. "Are they trying to sell poison? Why would anyone take it if the result is death?"

"I don't think it's the poison they want to sell," Mick says. "There've been rumblings of something new on the streets. Something damn powerful, addictive, and cheap to make."

"Hell, you just described meth," Carmine says.

"I'm not a fan of drugs," Mick replies. "I know some of my guys sell a little here and there, but that's not my game. And they know it. My hunch is that my guy told the stranger no, and that answer wasn't the right one. I have no way of knowing who it was that approached him."

"His cell?" I ask, already knowing the answer.

"Gone." Mick hisses out a breath. "Listen, this doesn't sit well with me, either. Someone came, unannounced, into my city and killed my man. I'm damn pissed."

"I know the feeling." I stare at Mick. "What now?"

"I'll keep asking," Mick says. "You keep me posted, as well. Someone's going to pay for this."

"On that, we can agree. I'll keep you informed when and if we find anything. I appreciate you working with us on this, rather than against us."

"It seems someone has decided to wage war with several organizations," Mick says thoughtfully. "They're either very brave or out of their fucking minds."

"Maybe both," Nadia adds, and Mick's eyes slide over to her for the first time.

"We'll stay in touch," Mick says again, dismissing us.

"Thanks for your time." We stand, and before I can walk away, Mick says my name.

"Carmine. Watch your back. This has *conspiracy* written all over it."

"Same to you."

~

"I GUESS THIS WAS A WASTED TRIP," Nadia says as she flops onto the sofa in our suite.

"Not at all."

I sit next to her and lift her feet into my lap. "We had a good few days here. And although it's not the information we were hoping for, we at least know it's not Mick."

"He could be lying."

I stare at her pink-tipped toes as I push my thumb into the arch of her foot. "I don't think so. He's pissed."

"What now?"

I've been running that question through my mind since we left Mick's office. "I think we need to go back to the city where this all started."

"Denver."

I nod and reach out to brush her hair behind her ear just as my phone rings.

"Hi, Shane."

"Hey, what did you find out from Mick?"

I relay the information and hear my brother curse on the other end of the line. "Yeah, that was my thought, exactly."

"This is a game for someone," Shane says. "They're fucking playing with us. But why? What's the end game?"

"That's the million-dollar question," I reply. "Nadia and I are headed to Denver first thing in the morning. I think we need to do some digging there."

"Denver is supposed to be neutral ground for all of the families," Shane reminds me.

"Yeah, well, that went in the toilet when someone tried to kill Pop."

"I'll meet you there," Shane says. "See you at the office."

"See you."

I hang up and turn to Nadia, who's watching me closely.

712

"Shane's going to meet us in Denver. He's been at his place in the mountains for the past couple of weeks, doing some digging of his own."

"Why does he have a place in Colorado?"

I tilt my head to the side. "Why shouldn't he?"

"Denver is neutral ground. We all have offices there, but no one lives there."

"Your cousin and her husband do," I remind her. "Just because your father isn't based there full time doesn't mean he doesn't have connections to the city. Besides, Shane doesn't live *in* Denver. He lives in a small mountain town called Victor, several hours outside the city."

"Shane's been there this whole time?"

I narrow my eyes at her. "He's a grown man and can live anywhere he likes, Nadia. Shane likes solitude. The mountains suit him. And he's within driving distance to several airports and can get in and out easily."

"Hmm," is all she says as the doorbell rings. "Oh, I bet that's our stuff."

She hurries to the door, and sure enough, it's the bellman with all of our purchases on a cart. He unloads them onto the dining table big enough to seat eight, then leaves. Nadia is all smiles as she starts digging into bags and boxes wrapped with ribbon.

"I'm *so* glad I got these shoes," she says as she slips out of her sneakers and tries on her new Dior heels."

"What's your problem with my brothers?" I ask while she's in a good mood and on a new shoe high.

"I don't know them well," she replies. "Oh, I forgot about this jacket. I know it's summer, but it'll be perfect for fall."

"But you don't like Shane having property in Colorado."

She shrugs a shoulder as she checks out her new purchase in a full-length mirror. "It's just all suspect. Shane has a place near Denver. This mess started in Denver."

"Your cousin lives in Colorado," I remind her once more. "All of the families have offices there. Just because Shane spends more time there than most doesn't make him the cause of all of this."

"I know." She sighs and turns back to me. "And I also know that you care about him, and you'd defend him to the ground."

"Every fucking day," I agree, frustration a bubble in my throat. "If we're all going to be judged by our taste in real estate, Annika and her husband could be the cause of all this, too. The first attack happened at their wedding, after all."

"Oh, come on." She turns to me as she lets the jacket fall off her arms and catches it with her fingers. "Rich is an ear, nose, and throat doctor. He's no mobster. And he certainly isn't a drug dealer."

"Annika?"

Her eyes flash in temper and annoyance.

Good, we're on equal footing.

"Annika has worked her ass off to stay out of the family business. She wants no part of it. None of it. She's a damn good doctor. Hell, *I'm* more likely to be the one behind this than she is."

I cock a brow.

"No. It's not me."

"Well, it's not me, either. At least, we've established that. Let's get to Denver in the morning. We can plan what happens next then."

She blows out a breath and reaches for her Chanel shopping bag. "Okay. In the meantime, I'm going to play with my new goodies."

"Play away, sweetheart."

～

"Rocco." I smile at my brother as Nadia and I walk into our Denver offices. "I wasn't expecting to see you here."

"Shane called me last night. I want in on the fun." He nods at Nadia. "Hi."

"Hello. *Rafe.*"

My brother rolls his eyes. I don't know why he doesn't care for his given name, but he's always insisted that people call him Rocco, ever since he was a kid.

Of course, Mom refuses to call him anything but Rafe. She named him after one of her favorite characters in a romance novel.

Maybe *that's* why he doesn't like it.

"I have something," Shane says as he hurries through the door. "And let me just say, it wasn't easy to get."

"What is it?" I ask as he sits at the desk and opens his laptop, then starts tapping the keys.

"The waiter from the wedding." Shane's brow furrows as he searches the screen. "No one knew who he was. I asked the catering company. They had no record of him. I had to bust into the security camera logs at the resort. And let me just tell you, their security is buttoned down *tight.* Took me several days to crack the code.

"But once I did, I was able to find some footage of our man. Here." He points to the screen. "See him? He's floating through the crowd a bit."

"It's grainy and in black and white," I say, squinting to see better.

"Yeah, their security is the bomb, but the video quality sucks. I cleaned it up a bit."

He points to the bigger monitor on the desk, and Rocco, Nadia, and I shift our attention there.

"Carmine and Nadia sneak off," Shane says with a cheeky smile. "You look a little intense there, brother."

I was. I wanted to fuck Nadia like I'd never wanted anything else in my whole damn life. And if memory serves, it was some pretty damn good sex.

Nadia glances up at me with a smirk.

"Okay. Here." Shane points to the screen. "See, he's setting the glass for Pop on the table."

"And looking around while he does it," Nadia adds. "That's definitely shady."

"None of us noticed," Rocco says. "We were all too busy partying."

"Our guards were down because it was supposed to be neutral territory," I say, thinking it over. "Not just in Denver, but at the wedding. We all had our guards down."

"Before Pop can take a sip, Armando takes the glass by accident. He's laughing with someone and just picks it up and drinks."

I watch as Armando does just that. Pop looks over and scowls for a second, then shrugs and laughs, signaling for a waiter to order a fresh drink.

"I'm going to speed this up a bit because it takes a couple of minutes for the poison to kick in." Shane hits a button, and the video runs faster. Then he slows it down, and Armando's face changes. He reaches for his throat, his eyes bulge, and the next thing we see, he's flailing about and ends up in the middle of the dance floor, seizing.

"That's enough," I say, but Shane shakes his head.

"Watch here." He points again. "There's our man. He takes a picture of the scene and then slips back into the crowd. And he doesn't come back. He ducks out."

"You said you found out who he is?" I ask, seeing red.

"Sean Brown," Shane says. "At least, that's the name he's gone by for a while. I found him doing a search for his image. He's also gone by Clark Brown and Rudy Brown."

"Why all the names?" Nadia wants to know.

"He's been in and out of jail," Shane says. "I assume he changes his name so he can get jobs. Have a clean record."

"He's anything but clean. Fuck, he's a contract killer."

"Looks like it," Shane agrees. "I have an address."

"What are we doing sitting here, then?" Rocco pulls his nine-millimeter out of his shoulder holster and checks the magazine. I do the same, and I notice Nadia pulling her small piece from her Hermes bag, checking it, as well.

I laugh.

"What?" she says.

"You carry a concealed in an eleven-thousand-dollar handbag?"

She grins. "Doesn't everyone?"

～

"WE DON'T KILL HIM." My voice is firm with the order. "We question him."

"Maybe break his arm," Rocco says with a shrug as we climb the steps to the upstairs apartment. Sean—or whatever his name is—lives on the second floor of a rundown building in a shitty part of town.

I raise my fist to knock on the door, but it's ajar.

"Not a good sign," Shane murmurs as he pulls his weapon. We all follow suit, and I nudge the door open with my toe. We soundlessly hurry inside.

But we don't have to go far.

"Fucking hell," I mutter and stare up at the man who used to be Sean as he swings from a noose tied to a beam in the ceiling.

"Shit." Nadia circles around him. "He's been up there a while."

His face is purple, eyes bulged, and the rope cut the hell out of his neck. The smell of decay is overwhelming.

"There's a note," Rocco says and begins to read aloud.

*I can't live with what I did. I've done some fucked-up things but killing ain't one of them.*

"That's it," Rocco says.

"Well, damn." I rub my hand over my face and listen as Shane murmurs into his phone. He's calling in a cleanup crew.

The cops won't find Sean.

He won't be found at all.

And we're at another dead end, literally. Back to square one. Which royally pisses me off.

"Look for a phone," I say, already headed back to the one and only bedroom in the flop. His phone is on a charger by the bed, so I pocket it. Shane can dig into it when we get back to the office.

I rummage through drawers but don't find anything else when Nadia pokes her head in.

"You'll want to see this."

I follow her to the bathroom and snarl. "Jesus fucking Christ, this is disgusting."

"Yeah, our boy didn't know what a toilet brush is. But that's not what I wanted to show you." She opens the medicine cabinet. "Look at these."

Bags and bags of little blue pills.

"I'll give you two guesses what these are," she says.

"Given that none of us are pharmacists, it could be anything. Maybe Sean had an Aleve habit."

Nadia rolls her eyes. "Right. It's an anti-inflammatory. That's why he had like five thousand of them in this cabinet."

"We'll take them," Shane says. "Crew's on the way. Let's bail."

We take the bags of pills with us, and I skirt by the body still hanging in the living room.

"He looks like a baby."

"Twenty-two," Shane confirms. "Still wet behind the ears."

"Seasoned enough to kill," I remind him. "I'd hardly call him innocent."

# CHAPTER 9

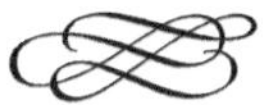

## ~NADIA~

*I*'m fucking tired.

It's late. Carmine and I left New York before the sun came up this morning, and we've been working hard all day.

Carmine's still at the office with his brothers, but I bailed. I need to sleep. I have to get my mind off drugs and death for a few hours.

I need a break.

I fill the tub in the master bathroom of the beautiful Airbnb Carmine rented and add some bath salts to the water. Before I can strip down and sink in, my phone rings.

Why would Alex be calling me this late?

It's midnight in Atlanta.

"Is Papa okay?" I ask in way of greeting.

"As far as I know," he says. "Can't a guy just call his sister to check in?"

"Not usually. No." I lean my butt on the counter and stare at the water in the tub, wondering what he wants. "What's up?"

"I'm wondering how you're doing. Found anything yet?"

"Not really. We're back in Denver."

"Yes, I heard."

My eyes narrow. "How?"

"We have eyes everywhere, Nadia. You know that. You're still with Carmine."

"Yes."

"Are you still fucking him?"

I don't even know this man anymore. When we were kids, we were close. I adored him. But the older he got, the colder he became.

"You realize you basically just called me a whore?"

"Answer the question, Nadia."

"No, Alexander. I won't. Because I'm a grown woman, on a job given to me by the boss, who doesn't happen to be *you*."

"You're such a bitch. Just tell me what's going on there. Keep me in the damn loop. I can't help if I don't know what's happening."

"I don't want or need any help from you," I counter. "I never have before, and I definitely don't need you now. Just keep your nose and your fingers out of this."

"Nadia—"

I hang up before he can say more.

The water has grown cold, so I drain it and think about starting over. But I'm too tired, and I've lost interest.

Instead, I start the shower and get in, quickly washing the day away, and then step into leggings and a sweatshirt.

I stop by the kitchen and pour a glass of Cabernet, then scoop up my laptop and walk into the living room.

The sofa faces a wall of windows. It's dark now, but during the day, you can see the mountains to the west.

Carmine has a thing for beautiful views.

I've just opened the laptop and started going through some unanswered emails when Carmine walks through the front door, also looking tired.

But my eyes zero in on the box in his right hand.

"Is that what I think it is?"

He sets the container on the kitchen island, tosses his keys next to it, and glances at me. "I thought you'd enjoy some donuts for breakfast."

"I'd enjoy some donuts *now*."

I laugh and launch off the sofa with renewed energy at the promise of sugar but stop short when I get a good look at Carmine.

"What's wrong?"

He shakes his head and walks to the fridge, pulls out a bottle of beer I didn't know we had, and takes a long pull from the bottle.

"Did something else happen?"

"No." He swallows another sip and then sits on one of the stools. "It really shouldn't be this hard. I feel like I'm on another wild goose chase, just missing the mark by an inch. It's damn frustrating."

"I know. But we'll figure it out. People are loyal, but I've also found that they like to run their mouths. Someone will fuck up and say something they shouldn't, and we'll find them."

"It's odd for a family to target another and not be bold about it. To stand up and say, '*Yeah, motherfucker, I did this. And I'll do it again.*'"

"The mafia has arrogance down to a science," I agree with a laugh.

"Well, they're not copping to anything now."

I open the box and immediately salivate at the sight of a maple bar. I grab for it like a kid starved to within an inch of her life.

"These are my favorite donuts in the city." I wander over and sit on the couch, chewing happily. "Oh, by the way, we're having dinner at Annika and Rich's place tomorrow."

"We are?" he asks.

"Yep. She called earlier. Your brothers are also invited."

He nods and then wanders to me, leaning in to take a bite of my donut.

"Hey, get your own."

"No." He takes my hand, pulls me to my feet, and leads me to the bedroom. "Now, I want to taste you. You're much more delicious than any donut."

"Lead the way."

~

ANNIKA AND RICH'S home in the Cherry Creek neighborhood of Denver is beautiful. It's an upscale area that professional sports players, celebrities, and the wealthy in general call home.

And I can see why. In addition to a nice golf course with a country club, there is excellent shopping, restaurants, and bars. If I lived in Denver, this is where I'd buy a house.

"Hi, you guys," Annika says with a wide smile as she opens the front door and gestures for us to come inside. "I'm so excited to see you all."

"You're gorgeous," I say as I lean in to kiss my cousin's cheek. But when I pull back, I can see the tension around her gorgeous blue eyes. I narrow mine, but she shakes her head quickly, sending me a silent message that now isn't the time for that conversation.

She greets Carmine and Shane, and when she reaches Rafe, she pauses. "Hi, Rafe."

"Annika." He kisses her cheek, as well, but the look he gives her is anything but friendly.

It's intimate.

How did I miss *that*?

"Come on in, everyone. Dinner's almost ready. Ivie's checking on it right now."

"Ivie's here?" Shane asks, his interests piqued.

"I thought it would be fun if she joined," Annika replies as we all take seats around the large living room. The house is traditional, all of the rooms separate—no open-concept here.

But it's beautifully decorated, and I know that Annika invested a lot of time making this house a home for Richard and her.

"Where's your husband?" I ask, but before she can answer, the man does.

"Sorry, everyone," Rich says as he hurries into the room from the back patio. "I had to take a call."

Rich is tall, slender, and utterly *boring*.

I don't know what Annika sees in him. Sure, he's smart and comes from a good family, but he's as dry as a corpse that's been left out in the sun for a year.

I bet he only likes to fuck in the dark, under the covers, after a shower.

I wrinkle my nose at the thought and then smile when Rich turns his attention on me. "Hello, Nadia."

"Hi, Rich. Thanks for having us over for dinner."

"Oh, it's our pleasure. Annika should get to see her family from time to time."

*What the hell does that mean?*

Before I can ask him, Ivie comes bustling out of the kitchen and almost falls on her face.

Poor Ivie. She's such a klutz.

"Whoa," she says with a laugh.

"Easy there." Shane immediately jumps up to help her. He takes her hand, kisses it, and leads her over to the sofa.

"Oh, thanks. I'm good. Just clumsy. Annika and I decided to make lasagna with garlic bread and salad. It's just about done."

I notice Carmine and Rafe share a look.

There is so much happening here, all unspoken, and all I can do is watch in fascination. There's trouble in paradise with my cousin and her husband. Shane wants to get into Ivie's pants. And Rafe and Carmine clearly find it all comical.

This is the best entertainment I've had in years.

"I'm starved," Annika says with a grin. "Let's eat."

"Not too much pasta for you, darling," Rich says as he pats her shoulder. "Why don't you stick with the salad?"

"Why don't you let your wife eat whatever the fuck she wants since she's a grown woman and everything?" I turn to Rich with a toothy, humorless smile.

It's not returned.

And I give zero fucks.

He simply sits at the table, and we start passing around dishes, filling our plates as Annika pours the wine.

When she reaches Rafe's glass, he shakes his head, and she moves on to the next.

But the glare Rafe aims at Rich would make most men piss their pants.

"How are things at the clinic?" I ask Ivie.

"Great," she says with a nod. "We're busier than ever right now."

"What kind of clinic do you run?" Carmine asks.

"We have a medi-spa," she replies easily. "We offer services from simple facials to botox to reconstructive surgery."

"Plastic surgery?" Shane says.

"Sort of, yes," Ivie says.

"There's a lot of botox happening in this city," Annika says with a wink. "And thank goodness."

"I was thinking of coming in to see you," I say, pointing to the crows' feet around my eyes. "I have a few lines I'd like to take care of."

"You don't have wrinkles," Carmine says, staring down at me in surprise.

"Yeah, I do."

"I can fix you right up," Annika assures me. "And I'd love to spend some time with you."

"Can you fit her into your already busy schedule?" Rich asks, his voice hard.

What the fuck is up with him?

"I always have time for Nadia," she replies. Her voice is just as hard as her husband's. Rich's jaw clenches.

Yeah, I'd say the honeymoon is over there.

And I definitely need to talk to her. Soon. Find out what in the hell is going on. Annika has always been my best friend. My confidante. Sure, I've been busy since the wedding, but that's no excuse.

Whatever she's going through, she won't face it alone.

"Oh, my God, this is so good." I bite into a piece of hot, crusty bread. "Seriously, A, you're an amazing cook."

"Ivie and I did it together," she says with a smile and gazes longingly at the bread. "I'm glad you like it."

"Here, try it." I pass her the basket, and she shrugs, takes a piece, and then passes it back.

Rich isn't happy. The dick. And that only makes me want to offer her another chunk.

I *despise* men who try to control their wives like this.

Carmine and Rafe chat about stocks, and I tune them out because it's all Greek to me.

Shane flirts shamelessly with Ivie, making her blush like crazy, which I think is absolutely adorable. Ivie's shy, a little clumsy—or a lot, depending on the day—and while she's pretty, no one would call her a beauty queen. She's the perfect epitome of the girl next door.

But she's smart and funny, loyal, and also one of my best friends.

I turn my attention to Rich, who's shoveling food into his mouth and doing his best to ignore his wife, who I see is drinking wine like a fish.

And Annika doesn't drink.

I'm going to get to the bottom of this.

"I'm going to put more bread in the oven," she says and stands from the table, pushing her way through the swinging door to the kitchen.

"I'll go see if she needs help," Rafe says and follows her.

Rich just rolls his eyes.

"I need to use the restroom. Is it just around the corner there, Rich?"

He nods and points to the hallway on the other side of the kitchen. There's another entrance to the kitchen on that side, so I stop and lean against the wall, just out of sight, listening to the conversation happening within.

"I've got this," Annika says.

"I can help. Jesus, A, what's wrong?"

"Nothing." I can picture the fake smile on her beautiful face. "Everything's great."

"Bullshit." Rafe lowers his voice now. "You look miserable."

"I—" There's no sound for a moment. "You shouldn't be in here."

"You never should have married that asshole," Rafe says. "You know it should have been me."

"And your father said no," she reminds him, and I stumble back in surprise. Annika wanted to marry Rafe Martinelli? Why would Carlo say no? Our families aren't enemies.

"Yeah, well, your uncle didn't like the idea, either."

Papa knew?

I scowl.

Why am I always the last to know about this stuff? And why didn't Annika confide in me?

I know it's not all about me, but it hurts my stupid feelings.

"Let's get this out to the table."

"Annika."

"Rafe, I can't do this. I'm a married woman whether I like it or not."

"And I'd say that you don't like it very much right now."

"That doesn't matter."

"Oh, yes, it does."

"I'm not talking about this anymore."

I walk around the corner in time to see Annika and Rafe coming out the other door, Rafe carrying the bread for the table.

I look at Rich. He doesn't even raise his eyes from his plate.

I feel like I've just entered an alternate universe.

~

"SHANE GOT IVIE'S NUMBER TONIGHT," I inform Carmine as he unlocks the door of the Airbnb.

"I saw," he says and shakes his head. "I don't get it."

"Get what?"

"Nothing."

"No, you started it. What, exactly, don't you get?"

"Look, if I answer you, I'm going to sound like a huge asshole."

I cross my arms over my chest, raise a brow, and wait.

Carmine sighs painfully, pushes his hand through his hair, and then shrugs. "Okay. I like her. She seems like a nice woman."

"But?"

"But she's just not Shane's type."

"And what type is that, exactly?"

"You know…"—he gestures to me, waving his hand up and down—"he usually goes for the supermodel types."

"You do realize that even supermodels don't look like that in real life, right?"

"You do," he says without even thinking twice, and I have to blink at him.

Then I laugh.

"No, I don't. I think you're a little biased. Which is sweet. Ivie's awesome. She's funny and smart. And, yes, she's pretty. Shane isn't good enough for *her.*"

"I told you I'd sound like a jackass."

"Sometimes the person we fall in love with isn't what we expect."

"He's not in love with her."

"Not yet." I kick off my shoes and walk over to the freezer, grabbing a tub of ice cream. "Something else happened tonight."

"What's that?"

"Did you see how unhappy Annika looked?"

"I saw that she and Rich are most likely fighting," he says. "It doesn't take a professional to see that. He's a douche."

"He didn't used to be." I shove a spoonful of Chunky Monkey into my mouth. "When they were dating, he was sweet. Laid-back. Even a little bit beta."

"*Beta?* What the hell does that mean?"

"You know, not alpha. Not in your face, or the one to put his foot down about things."

"So…soft."

"A little."

"I'm no beta."

I laugh again and wipe ice cream off my chin. "No, you're alpha all the way. I don't like that things seem to be changing for her so soon after their wedding. She looked sad and *scared.*"

"Do you think he hurts her?"

Carmine's eyes darken. I know this is a sore spot for him.

And it's something I respect.

"I don't know." It's an honest answer. "But you can bet that I'm going to ask her. I didn't like that he told her what she could and couldn't eat."

"I caught that," Carmine says. "And he didn't like your response."

"How many fucks do you think I give about that?"

"Less than none."

"You'd be right. Oh, and there was something else."

He opens his mouth for a bite of my ice cream.

"I listened in on a conversation between Annika and Rafe in the kitchen."

"Busy little thing, weren't you?"

I ignore that and keep talking. "Did you know that your brother and Annika had a thing going? That they wanted to marry, but our fathers wouldn't allow it?"

Carmine's face blanks in surprise, and then he blinks rapidly.

"No fucking way."

"I heard it with my own two ears."

"He would have told me."

"And I would have said that she would have told *me*. But here we are, neither of us in the loop, and I know what I heard in that kitchen. He said that it should have been him. And she reminded him that your father said no."

Carmine swears under his breath. "Jesus. Why didn't he say something?"

"I think it's time I catch up with Annika for lunch. Just us girls. We have a lot of talking to do."

# CHAPTER 10

## ~NADIA~

*I*'m loaded down with greasy burgers, fries, and shakes from another of my favorites here in Denver. Yes, I'm going to gain sixty-five pounds if I keep this up, but there's a method to my calorie-filled madness.

This is Annika's favorite meal in the whole world. And if I want to get information out of her, it won't hurt to feed her something extra delicious.

I walk into the medi-spa and smile at Ivie behind the front desk.

"Hey," she says with a bright smile. "You're right on time. The last patient just left, and Annika and I are officially free."

She clicks the mouse on the computer, then hurries over and locks the door.

"Annika is in her office, but we can have lunch in the conference room."

"Perfect. I brought a *ton* of food."

"You always were my favorite," Ivie says as she winks and knocks on Annika's door. "Nadia's here with food. Come join us."

"I'll be right there," Annika calls back.

"She's been in a mood today," Ivie says as she opens the door to the conference room. I set the bags of food on the table. "I've hardly seen her at all, and when I asked her what was going on, she blew me off. Very *not* like her. So, I'm glad you're here. Between the two of us, we'll get it out of her."

"I have plenty to get out of her," I reply and then sigh. "I hate feeling so disengaged from you guys. I miss you."

"You're here. We talk and hear from you. But we miss you, too. We need to be better about seeing each other more often."

"Agreed. I wonder what's going on with Annika." But I know. It's that asshole, Rich.

Ivie and I unpack the bags, and I just start to suck on the straw of my vanilla shake when Annika walks in.

I immediately know that something isn't right.

She doesn't look up as she sits in one of the comfortable chairs and starts unwrapping her burger.

"Thanks for lunch," she says.

"Look at me," I order her.

"Don't be silly—"

"Look at me, A."

She looks up, and I want to punch the wall. "What the hell happened?"

"What do you mean?"

Ivie leans in to examine Annika's face. "How did I miss it? Annika, you have a black eye. You tried to cover it up, but holy shit. What's going on?"

"Oh, it's nothing." Annika tries to laugh and pops a fry into her mouth. "I tripped while walking down the stairs, and—"

"No." My voice is hard and low and leaves no room for argument. "What. Happened. To you?"

With her eyes still trained on her fries, she shrugs a shoulder.

"I've been begging you to talk to me for days," Ivie says. Her voice shakes with emotion. "You can trust us. You know that."

"You're the only two I *can* trust," Annika whispers.

"Tell us the truth. Let us help." I reach over and take her hand in mine.

"I don't know who he is anymore," she begins. "As soon as we got married, everything changed. It was like a switch flipped, and he went from being a fun, laid-back man to the devil himself."

She rubs her forehead in agitation.

"Suddenly, he wants to control *everything*. Even what I eat. When he said last night that I should stick with salad, in front of all of you, I wanted the floor to open up and swallow me. I was *so* embarrassed."

"He said that you should get to see your family once in a while," I prompt her. "What was that about?"

"I've been telling him for weeks that I wanted to go see you or invite you here, and he kept telling me no. No way. He's systematically cut me off from my parents, from everyone I love—except for Ivie because we work together."

"Just let him try to cut me off from you," Ivie says with fire in her voice. "I'll cut his fucking balls off first."

"Down, girl." I smile at an irate Ivie. "Clearly, Rich can't get rid of us. We're here to stay. This all started after the wedding?"

"On the wedding night," she confirms. "We went to the honeymoon suite, and I took a bite of some cake—we had so much wedding cake left—and he took it away from me and tossed it in the trash. Said I'd never eat that garbage again. That I was too fat."

I've never experienced rage so swift and all-encompassing. I wish he was here right now so I could bloody his damn face.

"Since then, he's counted every calorie. I have to keep a log of what I eat and give it to him at the end of the day. If he thinks I'm lying, well…"

She stops talking, and Ivie and I share a look.

"He what, Annika?"

She simply points to her eye.

"He's been hitting you this whole time?" Ivie demands.

"Not often, but more than once is too many times."

"Why didn't you tell us?" I ask. "Why didn't you say something?"

"If I tell, the family will kill him."

"So?"

Annika shakes her head. "I don't want him *dead.* I just don't want him. But I'm married to him now. I'm just…stuck."

"Bullshit."

"No way."

Ivie and I speak in unison.

"Divorce *is* an option," I say. "My father will absolutely approve of that, especially when I tell him about the abuse."

"You can't." Annika grabs onto me, her movements desperate. "You can't tell. You have to promise me that you won't tell *anyone.*"

"Annika—"

"Promise," she continues. "I don't want them to hurt him."

"And why not?" I stand and pace the room, so frustrated that I don't know what to do with myself. "Annika, he's hurting you. Daily. Why shouldn't the family take care of it? Even if it's not death, he should be ostracized. He can go fend for himself. There's no place for him here."

"I agree," Ivie says. "You're not this woman. You're not a punching bag. No one is, and you have the resources to get out of this."

Annika sighs and rests her face in her hands.

"I can't leave him. Not yet."

"What else is happening that you're not telling us?"

"I think he's involved in something bad. I don't know what, but I have to keep an eye on him for a little while longer."

"To what end? I refuse to let you get killed over this, Annika." Ivie stands and leans over toward her friend. "You don't have anything to prove."

"I just need a little time," Annika insists.

I want to rail at her, and I can see that Ivie feels the same. But my cousin has dug her heels in.

"If he hits you again, you fucking call me." My voice is ice. "You call me, and I'll come get you."

"Okay."

I want to ask about Rafe. I want to convince her to leave that pitiful excuse for a man *today.*

But she's had enough.

Ivie and I share a long look. The silent message is clear.

We'll watch, and we'll protect her.

~

TWO HOURS LATER, I can't get to Carmine fast enough. But on my way to the Marinelli office, I call my brother.

"Thought you didn't want my help," he says, and I roll my eyes.

"Don't be a baby. I have a question. When Annika started dating Rich, and when he proposed, did the family do a standard background check on him?"

"Yeah, I ran it myself. He's so clean; he's boring. And his family is the same. Why?"

"I just left Annika."

I hesitate. I don't trust Alex with much, but he and Annika were close when we were younger. I think he'd want to know about this.

"Let's just say that Rich isn't the happy-go-lucky guy we all thought he was."

"What does that mean? Is he hurting her?"

I sigh. "I was at their house for dinner last night, and he was a major ass. The way he spoke to her, the way he looked at her, it was *not* good. And today, she had a black eye."

"What the fuck?"

"It just doesn't make any sense, so I wanted to reach out and ask if you'd run the background. I should have known that it was done, but I needed to double-check."

"If he's a con man, it slipped past me."

*That wouldn't surprise me.* Alex is lazy, and if Papa gave him the task of running the check, it wouldn't shock me if he just looked at the surface and then let it go.

Except this is *Annika.* And Alex has always had a soft spot for our cousin.

"What are you going to do now?" he asks.

"She asked me not to do anything for a little while, so I'll just be here in case she needs me."

That's not the whole truth, but he doesn't need to know the rest.

"Keep me posted, please," he says, his voice softening. "If this continues, we'll take care of it."

"Yeah. We will. Okay, I'll let you know if anything else happens."

He clicks off without saying goodbye, and I hurry into the office to see the three Martinelli brothers all huddled around computers.

They are a sight to behold. Carmine and Shane are both tall, dark, and handsome, with chocolate eyes. Rafe is on the lighter side with blue eyes, but there's no mistaking them for siblings. And just walking into this room would send a normal woman's blood pressure into the stroke-zone.

"I might have something," I say as I walk into the room. All three heads come up to look at me.

"Hello," Carmine says as he stands and pulls me to him for a kiss. Right there, in front of the others. "I haven't seen you all day."

"Don't get mushy in front of your brothers."

"I'll get mushy wherever I damn well please."

I laugh as Shane clears his throat.

"Stop pawing at her and let the woman talk."

"Yeah." I slap at Carmine's shoulder as I pull away. "Stop pawing at me."

"You didn't seem to mind last night."

"Really?" Rafe demands.

"Fine." Carmine lets me go, and I push my hair away from my face.

"Okay, so last night, something seemed very *off* with Annika."

"Clearly, she and the new husband are having issues," Shane says with a nod. "You could cut the tension with a fucking knife."

"Definitely," I agree. "And he just wasn't acting like himself. That jerk isn't the guy we all knew before the wedding."

My eyes are on Rafe as I speak. His face is rigid, and he clenches his jaw as I keep talking.

"So, today, I decided to go see her, take her lunch, and do some digging. After all, Annika and Ivie are my two closest friends in the world, and if Annika is hurting, I want to know why. And I want to make someone pay.

"When I got there, I discovered that she had a black eye."

"What the fuck?" Rafe asks as he comes out of his seat. "The bastard hit her?"

"Yeah." My voice quiets. "He did. And he's done more than that."

I relay what happened during my lunch with my friends. When I finish, all three men are pacing the office, each with mutiny written all over his handsome face.

"I'll fucking kill him with my bare hands," Rafe growls, but I shake my head.

"She wants time. And here's the part that doesn't add up, though I didn't say anything to her at the time. She thinks he's up to something."

"Up to what?" Carmine asks.

"She didn't say, but my alarm bells went off like crazy. I asked Alex if the family did a standard background check before the wedding, and he said that he did it. But my brother is lazy, and I know he didn't dive very deep. He couldn't have."

"I can go so deep, Richard will feel me in his kidneys," Shane says, reaching for the computer. His fingers fly over the keyboard. "Yeah, this first pass is pretty standard. Credit score is seven-fifty. No jail. Really nothing to report at all."

"That's too tidy," Rafe says, his face still set in hard lines. "That reeks of cover-up."

"Agreed. It would be easier if I had fingerprints."

"Be right back." I turn to leave, but Carmine stops me.

"You're not going by yourself."

"Well, then get a move on, and let's go. I'll call Annika from the car. She can meet us there. Let's nail this whole mess on this slimeball."

Carmine and I hurry to his rental. I barely have time to fasten my seatbelt before he's peeling out of the parking lot and merging onto the freeway.

"How could my family let this happen?" I wonder out loud. "How the fuck did Rich make his slimy way into my family and start killing people? And why would he do it at his own wedding?"

"Smoke and mirrors," Carmine says. "If it happened at the wedding, he'd be the last person anyone would look at. Son of a *bitch*."

"Why does a random doctor from Denver want to kill your father?" I wonder out loud. "It doesn't make any sense."

"Shane's still digging. I don't buy this whole boring suburban doctor bit. He's hiding something, and we'll find out what it is. In the meantime, we need to get those prints, and we need to make sure Annika is safe. I don't like her being there with him."

"I don't, either." I shake my head and watch the city zoom by. "It was all I could do not to kidnap her and make her come with me. I don't want that asshole anywhere near her, ever again."

I'm just about to call Annika when my phone rings in my hand. "Hey, I was just going to call you."

"I need you." Annika breathes hard in my ear. She sounds panicked.

"What's wrong?"

"I need you to come to my house."

"Carmine and I are headed there now. That's why I was going to call. Are you hurt?"

"No, but if he gets here before you, I will be. Hurry. Please, hurry."

She hangs up, and Carmine steps on the gas.

"You heard?"

"Yeah." The set of his mouth is grim. "I don't know what I expected when we came to Denver, but this isn't it."

"No. It's not."

I want to thank him. His family is under no obligation to help with this. But I've learned one thing in the months I've known him: Carmine is a man of honor.

All the Martinellis are.

They may be part of a mob family, but they do what's right. And my instincts weren't wrong when I decided to start trusting him.

He's become much more than just a job to me. There are feelings in play that I haven't taken the time to dissect, to just *be* with and figure out.

There just hasn't been time. I need to do some sorting, determine where my head and heart are.

But for now, it's enough to be able to depend on him—and to know that I'm safe.

Carmine drives through the open gates of Annika's drive, and when we pull up to the front door, he cuts the engine, and we're both out of the car like a shot.

Annika opens the door, her eyes wide in shock.

"What is it?"

"Oh, God."

# CHAPTER 11

## ~CARMINE~

"*I* knew it," Annika says as we hurry into the house behind her. "I knew something was wrong. I just found this."

She practically runs into an office at the end of a long hallway as if she has to get there before whatever's in there disappears.

"Is he here?" Nadia asks.

"No." Annika's voice shakes as she points to a trunk on the floor next to her husband's desk. "Look in there. Rich always tells me to stay out of this trunk, that it's none of my fucking business what's in here."

"Lovely way to talk to your wife," I mutter as I open the lid and stare down at what must be a dozen sandwich bags full of pills, a bundle of hundred-dollar bills, and a piece of paper.

"It's an address," Annika says when I pick up the paper. I open it, and sure enough, it's an address.

*449 Oak Ave. 4pm*

"He's a fucking drug dealer." Annika sits on the arm of a sofa and stares blindly ahead. "He's dealing. I want no part of this. I've worked damn hard to stay *out* of the illegal scene, Nadia. You know I have."

"I know."

"Where is he?" I ask as I turn to look at the two women. "Where is he right now?"

"His office, I would guess," Annika replies. "And if you're going there, I'm going with you because I want to give him a piece of my damn mind."

<hr>

RICHARD'S OFFICE is across town, so it takes us a good thirty minutes to get there.

I don't know what kind of pills are in those packages, but I have a feeling it's the same drug that killed Armando at the wedding. I took a bag and the computer mouse from the desk to give to Shane for prints.

The three of us march through the medical plaza and up a flight of stairs.

"His office isn't attached to the clinic," Annika says, pointing to a door next to the clinic. "He likes having a separate entrance."

"How convenient," I mutter and knock once before turning the knob. To my surprise, it isn't locked.

"Well, shit," Nadia murmurs as she holds Annika back. "No, baby. No, you don't want to see this."

"Yes, I do." Annika forces her way through, and all three of us stare at Richard, slumped over his desk, white foam coming from his mouth. "Oh, Jesus."

"Keep her back," I say to Nadia. She nods, and I step closer to the desk. More of the same pills are in piles on the top as if he'd been counting them out to go into bags. Could he have accidentally taken one and killed himself?

Or did he do it on purpose?

Without touching the body, I search the space. I see no note, and nothing seems out of place.

I reach into his pockets and find his phone and wallet.

"Do you know the code to the phone?" I ask Annika.

She just blinks, staring at her husband.

"Annika."

"No. He wouldn't tell me."

"Can I take it to Shane?"

I just keep adding things to my brother's to-do list.

"Yes. My God, he's dead."

"We're going to leave everything exactly as it is," I say and take her arms in my hands. "We're going to sneak out of here like we were never here, and then we're going to call the police."

"Carmine," Nadia says in surprise.

"I could call the cleanup crew, but if I do, he'll go missing. His family will look for him. If we call the police, it'll be wrapped up as a drug situation gone wrong, and Rich's family can bury him."

"And I can play the part of the devastated newlywed," Annika says bitterly.

"It's your call," I tell her. "How do you want to play it? Either way, you have to lie."

"Call the cops. His family will know that he was a drug dealer and a piece of shit. And they can bury him. But I won't act the part of the devastated widow. He didn't earn that."

"Okay, let's go. When we get to your house, you can call the office and ask them to get Rich from his office."

She nods, and we leave the way we came.

~

"I HAVE prints and drugs for you." I toss both items on the desk as Shane looks up in surprise.

"Where'd you find drugs?"

I fill him in on everything that happened over the past few hours.

"So, the fucker's dead?" Shane shakes his head. "Well, without the prints, I can tell you that I found quite a bit that piece of garbage, Alex, missed. Rich never went to college. It was all a front. And he didn't work at that clinic. He rented the office next door and pretended to go there to *work* every day."

"Holy shit."

"I'm still digging into some stuff, but these prints will help. If my suspicions are right, Rich was behind everything all along. He tried to kill Pop, he sent out the feelers to New York, and when that fell through, he had that kid killed."

"But why? It just doesn't make sense." I shake my head, perplexed. "Why start wars with the mafia when he just came into the family?"

"Good question. Maybe he thought he was proving his worth to Nadia's dad so he could start working more intensely for the family. Who knows? How's Annika holding up?"

"She's damn pissed off."

"Yeah, I would be, too."

"Nadia stayed at the office with her. The police are probably there by now."

My brother's brow lifts. "Police?"

I tell him the plan and remind him that we have a few contacts in the Denver PD to make things go down the way we want them to.

"Looks like we have our man," Shane says. "Right here in Denver, all this time."

"It's a hell of a thing," I agree. "I wish he'd been alive when I found him. I'd have liked to break his fingers and then shove a pill down his throat myself."

"Are you sure it was self-inflicted?"

I shrug. "My gut says so. I think he poisoned himself by accident because he was an arrogant idiot. He was counting pills on his desk. No gloves."

Shane clicks his tongue. "All he had to do was lick his finger or something, and it would all be over."

"My thoughts exactly."

"So, what now?"

I shake my head. "I'm not entirely sure. I still have questions. Why would he have Nadia attacked?"

"Because she was digging around, and he didn't want her finding him out."

"You're right. It makes sense."

"I'm still going to keep digging on him. I want to know more, but I have a few other jobs coming up, so it'll take some time."

"He's dead. I'd say there's no hurry. Where's Rocco?"

"He got called back to Seattle. He's probably in the air by now."

I nod. "Thank you. For all of your help. You didn't have to."

"It's what family does," he reminds me. "Now, I'm going to load up and get back to my place in the mountains. The city gives me hives."

I laugh as Shane closes his computer and shoves it into his bag. He's a recluse, through and through.

"I'll lock up behind you."

"Want me to call Pop?"

"Nah, I'll do that, too."

~

IT'S LATE when Nadia finally walks into the Airbnb. She texted a while ago to tell me she was on her way.

Just from her text alone, I could tell she was exhausted.

And sad for Annika.

Nadia may do her best to hide things behind her hard exterior, but she's full of love and compassion, especially for those she loves.

She shuts the door behind her, then turns. Her eyes widen as she takes in the room. I've lit several dozen candles, and I have food waiting in the oven. But first, I'm going to pamper her a bit.

"Follow me." I take her hand in mine and kiss it, then lead her back to the bathroom, where a hot bath waits for her.

"Roses in the bath?"

"That's right."

She doesn't say a word as I help her out of her black shirt and blue jeans. When she's naked, I keep her steady as she steps into the bath.

"I didn't even realize I needed this."

"I did." I kiss the top of her head and let her soak. The wine I bought—Nadia's favorite—is chilled and ready, so I pop the cork and fill a glass. "Sip this while you soak. Just sip it. I don't want you to get drunk on me."

"What did I do to deserve this five-star treatment?"

I squat next to her and tuck her short, blond hair behind her ear. "We've been so caught up in things since we got here that I haven't done enough things like this."

"Is this goodbye?"

The question is a whisper.

"What do you mean?"

"Now that we know who was behind the murder, there's no need to work together anymore."

I lick my lips and watch her face intently. "Is that what you want? To go our separate ways?"

"It's the way it is. We did our parts. It's done. Now, we move on."

I nod and stand, walking out of the bathroom. She didn't answer the question. She didn't say that parting is what she wants.

It's definitely *not* what I want.

I pull out the steaks, potatoes, and salad, get everything plated and ready to eat, then walk back in to check on Nadia.

She's not in the bath.

She's in the bedroom, packing her bag, wearing nothing but a robe.

Excellent.

"What are you doing?"

"Packing, obviously."

I nod once. "Why don't you eat before you do that? I have dinner ready."

"I'm not hungry."

"Just humor me."

I take her hand once more and tug her behind me to the kitchen, where our food awaits. She sniffs and then softens.

"You know I can't resist steak."

"I know." I hold a chair for her, then sit next to her and start cutting into my ribeye. "How is Annika tonight?"

"She was sleeping when I left. We went through some things in Rich's office, but then the police came, and then his family. It was just a mess. I got everyone but Ivie out, fed her, and then poured her into bed. Ivie's staying the night with her."

"She'll have a rough few weeks, but then she'll be able to move on with her life."

"I know. How do you move on from that, though?" She takes a bite of salad, seeming to think it over. "She was convinced that she knew him, was head over heels in love with him, and it turns out he was scamming her the whole time. How do you ever let yourself trust again? Fall in love again?"

"I think it takes a lot of time and healing." I pass her a hot roll. "She may need some therapy. Does your family have access to a psychologist?"

"Yes, my father has one on staff. She'll have a lot of support and anything she might need available to her, of course. I just feel for her."

"You love her." I take her hand in mine and squeeze.

"Yeah, and I can count on one hand the number of people who mean something to me in this world, and she's in the top three."

"Who are the other two?"

She frowns, pulls her hand out of mine, and returns her attention to eating. "How are Shane and Rafe?"

"Shane's back at his place in the mountains, and Rocco was pulled to something in Seattle."

"I can't believe you guys still call him Rocco."

I shrug a shoulder, watching her eat. Her lean throat moves as she swallows her food, her eyes heavy with fatigue.

She's magnificent.

And after tonight, she'll know without a shadow of a doubt that I do *not* want to say goodbye.

"I'm thinking Paris," I say, earning a surprised glance.

"For what?"

"For our first stop." I eat some potatoes. "A week at the Ritz would be nice. And then I think we should spend another week in the south of France, on the beach. There's a lovely resort there that I'll arrange."

"Did you hit your head today?" she demands.

"Not to my knowledge, no."

She takes another bite of steak and watches me. "So, you're going to take a several-week vacation in Europe? Awesome. Have fun."

"Not me." I wipe my mouth on a napkin. "*We.*"

"Who's we?"

"You, my lovely Nadia. And me. Us."

"But I thought you said—"

"I didn't say anything. I asked you if it was what *you* wanted, and you didn't answer the damn question."

"Okay, fine. I don't want to say goodbye. Is that what you want to hear?"

"Yes, actually. It is."

"But I don't see an alternative. I live in Atlanta. You live in Seattle. We're not working together anymore."

"The last time I checked, we're both adults."

"You know that it doesn't matter for us. Our lives aren't ours, Carmine."

"Do you really think our fathers will lose their damn minds if we spend some time together on vacation? I think they have enough to worry about."

She doesn't respond to that.

"So, we'll spend some time in Paris, and then in Cannes. We'll shop, we'll eat, and we'll explore. And I'll make love to you day and night, damn it. I'm going to soak you into every pore of my body. When it's all over, you'll be sick of me."

"Doubtful," she whispers.

"Sweetheart, don't cry."

"I'm not crying. There's an onion in my salad."

I scoop her into my lap and kiss her softly. "Let's enjoy each other for a while. No pretenses, and no tracking down murdering assholes."

"I should stay here for a couple of days to make sure Annika's okay."

"Of course." I kiss her once more. "We'll stay here for as long as you need."

"Carmine."

"Hmm?" I kiss down her neck, unable to resist her.

"I'm not going to fall in love with you."

I can't help but smile against her skin. She's everything I've ever wanted. She's my match in every way. And my opposite.

"No, there will be none of that."

But there already is. And we both know it. We're just too fucking stubborn to admit it.

# CHAPTER 12

## ~NADIA~

"*H*e's in the ground, and it's time to move on."

Annika rakes her hand through her long, blond hair and blows out a shaky breath. She's sitting on the couch, her feet tucked under her, still in her black mourning dress.

Ivie sits next to me. Now that the guests have gone and it's just the three of us, we've kicked off our shoes.

"I didn't think his mom would ever leave," I say, staring down into my wine. "She just kept going room to room, loading up everything she could into her arms like she was on a game show or something."

"I don't even care." Annika turns tired eyes to me. "She can have it all."

"And she'll take it." Ivie's voice is heavy with bitterness. And I can't blame her. "She has no right to any of it. You're his wife."

"Do you think I want it?" Annika demands. "I couldn't care less about the clock he bought in Germany or any of the other *fancy* knickknacks he had lying around. I'd just sell or donate it all anyway. There are some papers that I need to go through myself, and I have my things, of course, but I can't get out of here soon enough."

"Did you say that the realtor is coming tomorrow?"

Annika nods. "I don't know when I'll be able to put the house on the market, but as soon as the lawyer gives me the go-ahead, I'll list it and find something else."

"You should buy one of those fun little condos downtown," Ivie suggests. "Right in the heart of the hustle and bustle. You can shop, eat, go to shows or games."

"I don't even know if I want to stay in Denver," she admits softly.

"What about Seattle?" Annika's mouth firms at my suggestion. "It's a great city, and I'm sure the Martinellis would give you the green light to live there."

"No."

I sigh and tip back my head. I'm done beating around the bush on this one.

"What in the hell is up with you and Rafe?"

Annika blinks rapidly, and Ivie scowls, first at me and then at our friend.

"I don't know what you mean."

"Oh, yeah, you do. I overheard you two in the kitchen when we were all here for dinner."

"It's not polite to eavesdrop, you know."

"Yeah, well, I'm not sorry."

"Wait." Ivie shakes her head and sits forward. "I'm missing something. Annika had something going with *Rafe*?"

"It was years ago," Annika says with a sigh. "We were kids. We'd see each other at things like weddings and such, and we both went to college at Duke."

"Rafe went to college at Duke?" Ivie asks, clearly impressed. "Wow."

"There's chemistry there," Annika whispers. "And, yeah, we saw each other for a while. But you guys, we're in mob families. Opposing ones. My parents would have thrown a fit."

I frown, thinking it over. "We aren't exactly at war with the Martinellis."

"But we're not on the best of terms, either. The betrothal between Alex and Elena fell through, and then they assumed our family had killed theirs for years. All of that happened at the same time. So you can't tell me that they would have welcomed my affair with Rafe with open arms."

I nod and shrug a shoulder. "Okay, so the timing was bad. But we're on better terms now. And if Rafe's who you want, I think you could make that happen."

"I don't want Rafe or anyone else involved in the organization." Annika's voice is clipped. "I never have. I thought I'd found a nice, settled, professional, and we'd live a boring, happy life in the suburbs. Look where that got me."

"It makes sense that you're not exactly ready to get back on the horse, so to speak, right away," Ivie says. "There's no rush."

"I don't know how I can ever trust anyone again," Annika says. "And while I do trust Rafe, I know that he's not the one for me. Not for the long haul."

"Why didn't you tell me that you had a thing going with him?" I ask her.

"Honestly, it was kind of fun to have a secret fling with someone I shouldn't. It felt taboo and reckless. But then I fell in love with him." She whispers the last three words, and I can't help but cross to her and hold her hand.

What is it about the Martinelli brothers?

"But it was a long time ago, and my life has changed. And I still don't want to be involved in the family business. He's neck-deep in it. It wouldn't work."

"I understand what you mean."

"Now, you tell us about Carmine," Ivie says with a smile. "Come on, spill it."

I don't want to hold back, so I tell them everything, from my father asking me to keep an eye on Carmine, to him *finding* me at the resort in Miami, and everything that went down since then.

It just feels so damn good to tell someone I trust what's going on.

"And now he's going to take you to France?"

I nod, thinking it over. "I should talk to Papa before he goes back to Atlanta. Make sure he doesn't have a problem with it."

"How does it feel to be in love with Carmine?" Annika asks.

"I'm not in love with him." I shake my head and stand to pace. "I mean, I *like* him. We have a good time together. The sex is *crazy*. And over the past few months, I've grown to trust him—which surprised me the most."

"But you don't love him." Ivie's tongue is in her cheek, and I glare at her.

"No. I don't love him."

Even I hear the lie.

"We're enjoying each other."

"Enjoy away," Annika says. "You've earned it."

"Right. I discovered that your husband was a killer and a drug dealer. I don't feel like I've earned a posh European vacation."

"I discovered it," she reminds me. "It's not your fault that I fell in love with a liar. Now, you can stop babysitting me because I'm a damn strong woman who can figure this out. And I have Ivie here. Go have crazy amazing French sex."

I giggle. "Is French sex different from regular sex?"

"Go find out," Ivie says. "We've got things handled here. I'll keep Rich's mom under control."

"Oh." I turn to her and prop my hands on my hips. "Did Shane ever call you?"

"Yeah." A smile covers her pretty face. "We've talked a bit. All on the phone. He's… interesting. Intense. Sexy as all get-out."

"What is it about the Martinelli brothers?" I voice the question this time, and we all giggle. "They're too sexy for their own good."

"I'M GLAD I CAUGHT YOU." I walk into my father's office, shut the door, and walk around the desk to hug him. "How are you, Papa?"

"I'm always better when my daughter comes to see me." He grins and kisses my cheek. "What are you up to, little one?"

"I just wanted to talk to you before you went back to Atlanta." I sit on the desk next to him and let my feet dangle, the way I've done since I was a small girl. "I haven't spent much time with you in a while."

"You've been busy," he says, leaning back in his wide leather chair. "I hope you're planning to take some time off now."

"Actually, that's what I wanted to talk to you about." I clear my throat. "Carmine invited me to go to France with him for a couple of weeks."

Something sparks in my father's eyes, but then he blinks, and it's gone.

"And did you accept?"

"Yes, but I thought I should run it by you, in case it's something you'd rather I not do."

"You're an adult, Nadia. You can spend time with whomever you choose."

My eyes find his. "You know that isn't true."

Papa takes a long, deep breath. "It's true. There are men that I would not be okay with you spending time with. Like Billy Sergi."

"*I'd* not be okay if I spent time with him." I wrinkle my nose. "The little worm."

"I hope you enjoy yourselves," Papa says. "There's a restaurant on the Seine that I highly recommend."

"Thank you." I bend down and kiss his cheek again. "I miss you, Papa. When I get back, let's spend a weekend together."

"I'd love nothing more, little one. Be safe. Tell Carmine I'll break both his legs if even a hair is disturbed on my precious daughter's head."

I laugh, but I know the threat is real. "No need to be violent. I'd better go pack. I think we're leaving this evening."

"Nadia."

I turn back to him with raised brows. "Yes, Papa."

"I love you."

"I love you, too."

～

"I THINK THAT'S IT." I walk through the Airbnb, making sure that I didn't forget anything. "I brought more than I thought."

"We shopped in New York," Carmine reminds me as he sets our suitcases by the front door.

"Ah, yes, how could I forget New York?"

He catches my hand and pulls me against him, then nibbles the side of my mouth. I immediately turn to mushy goo.

This man is potent.

"We're trying to leave," I remind him. "Not get naked again."

"I'll get you naked on the plane."

He lets go, and I stare after him. "On the *plane*? But we won't be alone."

"Close enough. And I have a very discreet staff."

And with that, he walks out the door, pulling two of the suitcases behind him, a backpack slung over his broad shoulder.

It's unfair that simply toting luggage is sexy on this man.

I grab my smaller bag, my handbag, and one last roller suitcase and let the door close behind me.

Our time in Denver is over. Now, we're on to France.

Denver International Airport is quite far from the city, so I sit back, expecting at least a forty-five-minute drive, but the driver leaves the freeway sooner than expected and takes us to a smaller airfield closer to the city.

"This is easier," Carmine says simply. He's holding my hand, softly rubbing his thumb over my knuckles.

Now that our attention has turned from finding a killer to just enjoying each other, he's much more physically affectionate than he was. And that's saying something because Carmine's always been handsy.

Not that I'm complaining. A girl could do far worse than having Carmine Martinelli's hands on her.

I'm not typically an affectionate woman, but with Carmine, the rules seem to fly out the window.

"This plane is bigger." I glance at Carmine. "You have *two* private jets?"

"No." He leans over and kisses my nose. "We have two private jets and a helicopter. Rocco flies the 'copter. I usually prefer the smaller plane, but this one is more appropriate for trans-Atlantic travel."

"Oh, right. Yes, it's better for *trans-Atlantic travel*." I press my lips together so I don't laugh. I love teasing him. "You're so fancy."

"And you've just earned your first spanking."

He doesn't even look at me. Doesn't smile. He just steps out of the car and offers me his hand.

I don't bother sputtering a protest.

The ground crew is already loading our luggage onto the plane. We're greeted at the top of the stairs by a man in his fifties, wearing a simple black suit and a red tie. His hair is silver, threaded through with just a few dark strands, and he has a bushy mustache over his top lip.

He looks like someone's grandfather.

"Good evening, Mr. Martinelli. Ms. Tarenkov. It's a pleasure to have you aboard tonight. Please, make yourselves comfortable."

"Thank you, Charles," Carmine says with a nod. "Please let the pilot know that we're ready whenever he's given the okay to take off."

"Of course, sir."

I smile at the polite Charles and follow Carmine down a short hallway to a lounge area on the plane. There are cream-colored leather couches, a faux fireplace with a television hung above it, and a wet bar.

"We'll spend most of the next nine hours or so in here, but there's a bedroom back there." He points and then leads me farther back on the plane to show me a small bedroom with a king-sized bed and little else. "In case you want to sleep. Or...other things."

"I liked the couches," I reply and turn on my heel to return to the lounge. I sit, fasten my seatbelt, and pull my iPad out of my bag.

Carmine sits across from me just as Charles returns with a tray in his hands.

"What can I get you to drink?"

"Just water for me," Carmine says.

"A Coke would be lovely."

Charles nods regally and turns to the wet bar to fetch us our drinks. Carmine holds my gaze with his as Charles fills glasses, delivers them to us, and then walks back to the galley.

"I could have gotten this myself if I'd known it was right there."

"Charles enjoys his job," Carmine replies. "We have lots of food aboard, as well, and he'll serve us dinner. And breakfast in the morning."

"Just like first class."

"Admit it. This is much better than first class."

I smirk into my glass. "It's a small step up."

Carmine's brown eyes are full of humor when Charles returns with menus so we can choose our entrées for dinner, and then the plane begins to move.

Within just a few minutes, we're airborne.

Once we've reached cruising altitude, Carmine unclips his seatbelt and moves over next to me. But rather than kiss me, or hold me against him, he simply holds out his hand.

"Give me your foot."

"Which one?"

"You choose."

I raise my left foot, and he starts to knead my arch with his thumb. I moan and lean my head back, closing my eyes as I enjoy the best foot rub of my life.

"You're good with your hands."

"I'm good with a lot of things," he reminds me. "I plan to spend the next nine hours reminding you."

"I'm so glad I'm getting a refresher course." I snort. "I think I've forgotten everything."

"You're extra sassy tonight."

I don't lift my head off the seat, but I turn to look at him. "I'm sorry. I don't mean to be difficult."

"I'm not complaining. You were tense in Denver. Worried. And as soon as we got on this plane, it was as though a huge weight was lifted."

"That's how it felt." I sigh, letting the tension from the last couple of weeks go. "I'm glad it's over. Still, I hurt for Annika. But we had a great talk last night, and I know she's going to be okay."

"She's going to be amazing. And now it's time for you to rest, relax, and let me take care of you for a while."

"I'm perfectly capable—"

He covers my mouth with his, playfully at first, but then it turns intense, and all I can do is grip onto him and return the kiss.

Finally, he pulls away and kisses my chin lightly. "Just enjoy, Nadia. For once in your life, don't overthink it."

"You talked me into it."

# CHAPTER 13

## ~CARMINE~

"**Y**ou could shop anywhere in Paris," I say to Nadia as she leads me down a little cobblestone street tucked back in a corner off the left bank of the Seine in Paris. "And this is where you want to go?"

"Yes." She tugs on my hand and smiles at me. We arrived in Paris yesterday morning and spent the day in our suite at the Ritz, sleeping and fucking, recovering from jet lag.

This morning, she was ready to explore the city.

After I had my way with her in the shower.

"There's a little shop tucked away back here," she says as we stroll along the uneven sidewalk. "And it's the best. Just wait until you see it."

There are many *little shops* along this street, all selling different things—clothes, jewelry, art. But the store she stops at has me scratching my head.

"This?"

"Yep." She climbs the three uneven steps and tries the knob, but it's locked. "Jean Luc must be on a break. Oh, there he is."

She grins as an older man with little hair, wrinkled, leathery skin, and what's left of a cigarette burning in his mouth walks up with a frown.

"I only come for you," he says gruffly.

They don't hug or even exchange pleasantries, but he unlocks the door, and Nadia steps inside with an excited flourish.

I'm even more confused when I follow her.

The store is no bigger than my bathroom at home, and every surface is covered with things. If I were a claustrophobic man, I'd turn around and leave.

But I'm far too fascinated to leave now.

"Oh, Jean Luc, you never disappoint."

The man simply sits on a stool behind a tiny glass counter and watches Nadia. "I have a new Chanel. Vintage from 1968."

"Let me see it."

He reaches under the counter, pulls the signature black bag out, tugs a handbag free, and sets it on the glass.

"Oh, she's pretty. And the leather has really stood up well."

"It was hardly used, in all these years," Jean Luc replies. "I know you're fond of Chanel."

"Who isn't?" She grins. "I'll be hitting up Angelina tomorrow."

"Such a tourist trap now." He clicks his tongue.

"Yes, but *she* went there. Every day," Nadia reminds him. "And I do enjoy that hot chocolate."

"Who does not enjoy a cup of *le chocolat chaud* now and again?" he says, and unless I'm seeing things, he actually smiles at her. "Eight thousand."

Nadia's brows climb. "That's a little steep."

I want to interject. Eight thousand euros for a *used* handbag?

Jean Luc shakes his head and gives her a morose look as if she's physically hurting him. "Seven, then."

"Five," she counters.

"Nadia, you pain me. You can't find vintage like this, in this condition. I could sell to many others for more than five."

"Then sell it to them." She shrugs a shoulder as if it makes no difference to her, and Jean Luc sighs heavily.

"Six, and no less."

"I can live with six." She nods happily. "Done. Now, do you have a black Hermes Kelly?"

Jean Luc's eyes narrow for a moment as if he's pondering the question, but something tells me the man knows exactly what he has.

"For you? I will show you this."

He walks to a cupboard and pulls out another handbag, setting it on the glass next to the Chanel. A black handbag with a top handle and a gold clasp.

"Oh, she's beautiful. What year?"

"2004," he says. "Also, never used. Sat on a closet shelf for years."

He pulls out a pair of gloves before opening the bag and then showing it off to Nadia.

I'm lost. Who is Kelly, and why does she have a handbag named after her? I start to ask when Jean Luc tells her the price.

My eyes widen at the five figures that just came out of his mouth.

But Nadia doesn't even blink as she looks it over.

"Not even a scratch on the hardware," she murmurs. Her hands lovingly caress the leather as if she's touching a lover.

As if she's touching *me.*

"Jean Luc, you just sold yourself a Kelly. I'll take both."

"I have new jewelry," he begins, but Nadia shakes her head with a laugh.

"I'm going to stop while I'm ahead. But thank you. And thank you for opening your shop just for me. On a *Tuesday* morning."

"The French don't keep American hours," he reminds her, but his eyes are full of humor. "Who is your man?"

"I'm sorry, I got so excited, I completely lost my manners. Jean Luc, this is Carmine."

I shake the other man's hand, surprised by his firm grip. "It's nice to meet you."

"And you. Coming to Paris to fall in love is always a good idea."

*This* makes Nadia blink rapidly and seems to catch her off guard.

"Paris is called the city of love for a reason, no?" he continues as he gets the two new purchases ready for Nadia to take with her. "I thought Nadia would never find her man, but I see I was wrong. You've been coming to see me for how long now? Six years?"

"About that," she says quietly, clearly uncomfortable, but I step forward and take her hand in mine, giving it a squeeze.

"Six years, she always comes alone. Such a beautiful woman. I think she should be with someone. Not me. I am too old. But someone."

He takes her credit card and expertly uses the new machine discreetly tucked to the side.

"So I'm happy you called and came in today and brought your Carmine." He passes the card back and asks her to sign the slip. "I will worry less."

"Jean Luc, you're the sweetest." Nadia leans over and kisses his cheek. "You don't have to worry about me. I'm perfectly fine."

With fondness, he tucks an extra little box into Nadia's bag and walks us to the door.

"Enjoy your time in Paris. You're welcome to come see me anytime."

"My credit card is already weeping," Nadia says playfully. "But you know I'll come see you every time I'm here. Take care, Jean Luc."

He waves us off, and we stroll away. I take the bag to carry and lean over to kiss her temple.

"That made you uncomfortable."

"I've never known that man to talk so much," she says. "He's always so quiet. I assumed he didn't speak English well. Then, I bring you with me, and he's Chatty Charlie. It's just weird."

"No, weird is paying what you just did on used purses."

She gives me the side-eye and then raises her chin defiantly. "You just don't understand."

"Then explain it to me. I'd love to see what you do when you look at those bags."

"Okay." She nods and then offers me a grin. "I'm getting hungry. Let's go to Café Flore for lunch. We can chat about it there. It's not far."

"You've spent a lot of time in Paris," I comment as we make our way to the café.

"I wasn't lying when I told you that it's my favorite city. When I don't have anywhere to be, I come here. I roam the streets, wander the museums, you name it."

"And meet interesting Frenchmen who sell you old accessories."

She smirks as we cross the street to the café. We're seated, and to my utter shock, Nadia orders our lunch in perfect French.

"What?" she says when she turns back to me.

"You speak French?"

"Yeah, but don't tell Jean Luc. I like him thinking I don't so I can pretend not to understand when he tries to upsell me." She winks and takes a sip of her coffee, but her face sobers as I continue watching her. "What is it?"

"There are moments I realize that I don't know nearly enough about you." I reach over and take her hand. "I thought I'd already learned so much, but I realize that I've only scratched the surface with you, Nadia."

"Well, we spent the better part of three months lying to each other," she reminds me. "Then, we had a job to do."

"That's not a good excuse."

"It works both ways, you know. I don't know much about you, either."

"Then, for the next two weeks, we're going to do exactly that. Learn about each other. So, tell me about the bags."

She shimmies in her seat. "My favorite topic."

"What was it about these two bags that you loved?"

"It's two very different reasons. We'll start with the Chanel. Coco Chanel lived here in Paris, at the Ritz, actually, but she also had an apartment above her boutique. She didn't sleep there. She gave parties and worked there. I've never been upstairs, but I've been on *the* stairs, and it's a trip, let me tell you. Anyway, she went to a little café near the Louvre called Angelina. Every single day. She sat at the same table and always ordered the hot chocolate. It's a short walk from the Ritz. We'll go. You'll never feel the same about hot chocolate again. And I think Chanel's quality is insanely good, especially the vintage pieces. And because this bag was made before her death, she may have held it herself. I love the history of it, and it's always in style."

"Fair enough. And the other?"

"That was Grace Kelly's favorite handbag. Hence the name, the Kelly."

"Ah, makes sense now."

She smiles and leans back as our lunch is served. Once the waiter bustles away, she eats a fry and then keeps talking.

"These bags are made by hand, here in France, by artisans. Each one takes a lot of hours to make…"

I sit and watch her perfect face as she talks, using her hands for emphasis, explaining in detail how every product makes its way to a storefront.

Her enthusiasm is contagious. I don't need a bag, but she has me ready to run out and buy the first one I see.

"And here I thought you were all about the family," I reply when her story winds down.

"I am." She takes a bite of her sandwich. "It's always the priority and will be until the day I die. But this is a fun hobby."

"An expensive one."

"Says the man who bought a ten-thousand-dollar watch in New York."

"It wasn't secondhand."

Her laughter is a drug.

"Have you spent much time in Paris?" she asks.

"Not as much as you," I reply. "And I've only really seen the most touristy of places."

"Then we'll avoid those." She chews thoughtfully. "Will you think I'm weird if I suggest a cemetery?"

"Are you planning to kill me, then?"

"No. I've heard about a really beautiful cemetery here in Paris. If you're up for it, we could go check it out this week. The weather's beautiful."

"I'm game."

"Bet you never thought you'd be hanging out with me in a cemetery, did you?"

"Honestly, I never thought I'd be with you at all." I push my finished plate aside.

"Same." She rests her chin in her hand. "I told my father about us coming here."

I raise a brow in surprise. "And what did he say?"

"He didn't seem to care in the least."

"And if he did?"

She sighs and glances down at her empty cup of coffee. "If he'd been angry or forbade it, I wouldn't be here." Her eyes find mine again, and I see the heaviness in them. "We have responsibilities, Carmine. To our fathers. I love him. I respect him. And, at the end of the day, I guess I'm trying to prove something to him. So, as much as I wish I could say that I'd tell him I'm a big girl who can call her own shots, I know that's not the case."

"I understand." It sits like a lead ball in my stomach, but I do understand. Because I'd do the same thing.

I, too, had a conversation with my father before we came to Paris. And if he'd been unhappy with it, well, I'd be in Seattle.

Alone.

"Do you ever wish we weren't...?" She waves her hand in the air, not finishing the sentence.

"Intelligent? Wonderful? Wealthy? Witty?"

"Part of the organization, you moron," she interrupts with a laugh. "And, I should add, modest."

"No." I reach for the check and put my credit card in the leather folder. "I don't wish that. Do you?"

"No. I'm not like Annika. She hates it. Wants to be as far removed from it as she can. But I always found it fascinating."

"Maybe it ties in with your love of history," I suggest, and she nods.

"I think so. Our family goes back generations. To Russia. I used to love sitting on my father's knee and listening to him tell stories from his childhood about his parents—and theirs. My family has been in our line of business for hundreds of years."

"That's something we have in common." I sign the check and reach for Nadia's bags. "Let's go back to the hotel."

"I could use a little rest."

～

WE'VE JUST REACHED our suite when I get a call from Rocco.

"Isn't it the middle of the night there?" I ask.

"Early morning," he replies. "Just giving you a heads-up. Someone broke into Gram's house last night."

I narrow my eyes and watch as Nadia sets her new bags in the closet, then starts taking her clothes off. "What the fuck?"

"What is it?" she asks, but I hold up my hand.

"The alarm went off at about two this morning," he continues. "Our security was there within ten minutes, and the cops came five minutes later. A window was broken. I don't know what they took. If anything. They didn't make much of a mess."

"I wonder if they were looking for something specific."

"If they were, they found it and bailed. No prints. They took out the cameras."

"Damn it."

"Yeah, I know. We're locking it down, and I'm going to live there for a while. It's not good that it's been sitting empty for this long. We need to sell it, Carmine."

"And do what with all of her shit?" I rub a hand over my face. "I'll be home in a couple of weeks. Let me know if this happens again."

"Will do. Have a good vacation."

He clicks off, and I turn to find Nadia watching me with concern. "What happened?"

"My grandmother passed away last year."

"I remember. We went to the funeral."

I nod and recall seeing her at the church. "Her house has been sitting pretty much empty since she died. I went through a lot of stuff because I was trying to find Elena, which is another story. But aside from that, there's ten thousand square feet and sixty year's-worth of shit to sort through."

"And someone broke in."

"Yeah. We shouldn't have left it that long. Rocco's gonna stay there for a while."

"It was probably a professional. Someone who staked it out and knew that it was empty."

"Most likely," I agree and push my finger into the waistband of her jeans. "Now, let's forget about the goings-on more than an ocean away."

"What do you have in mind?"

# CHAPTER 14

## ~NADIA~

"*I* want to be with you," he murmurs as those talented lips take a slow journey down my neck to my shoulder. His hands skim down my arms, over my naked torso, and down to my ass, still covered in denim.

He squeezes, and my core clenches in response. But before I can say anything, his hands grip my thighs, and he lifts me like I weigh nothing. I wrap my legs around his waist, and he carries me to the dining room table.

"I want to kiss you." He unfastens my jeans, and I lift my ass so he can guide them over my hips and down my legs.

The underwear follows, and I'm left lying naked and spread wide for him.

I expect him to dive right in, wrap his lips around me and take me for one hell of a ride.

But to my surprise, that's not what he does at all.

His fingertips barely brush my skin, sending goosebumps all over me.

"You're so fucking soft," he whispers before kissing my inner thigh. "So damn responsive. God, you're getting wetter by the second."

"Come on, Carmine. You're killing me here."

He just shakes his head and continues taunting me, teasing me. His touch is gentle, his kisses wet and carefully placed over my already heated skin.

I arch my back, wanting nothing more than to have him fuck me hard on this table. What's with the gentle shit?

Sex is impatient. Fast and dirty.

It's not *this.*

"Carmine," I breathe when his fingers brush over my most intimate lips. "Jesus, don't be such a tease."

He chuckles and licks up my stomach to my navel and then farther to the underside of my small breasts.

Who knew that little spot was so damn sensitive?

"You're killing me."

"Just relax," he croons. His voice is thick and sounds like melted chocolate. Full of lazy lust and affection, and it does something to me.

Something I don't recognize—or particularly feel comfortable with.

My throat closes, and my core clenches when his lips drag up over one already perky nipple. I don't know what this is. My already raw emotions are even more on the surface, and I don't like it. I don't want to feel vulnerable with him.

"Damn it, Carmine, you're going too slow. Just fuck me already!"

He stills, pulls his hands back, and raises his head to look down at me. "That's not what I'm doing here, Nadia."

"What *are* you doing?"

My breasts rise and fall with my breaths, coming faster now. What is all of this *emotion?*

"I don't have to spell it out for you."

"Yeah, I think you do. You have me tied in knots here. Just *do* it already. What's wrong with you?"

His eyes narrow, and if I'm not mistaken, he looks hurt. But before I can say anything, he quickly unfastens his slacks and pushes into me, hard.

"Is this what you want?" he demands and then slams into me again. And again. "You just want me to fuck you?"

I grip onto the edge of the table and hold on tight, but he suddenly stops and swears under his breath.

"Goddamn it."

"Carmine."

"Just give me a second." He shakes his head, and I can see despair there. Confusion. So, I sit up and take his face in my hands. "A few months ago, I would have simply fucked you until you walked wrong and been content with that. But that's not where we are anymore, Nadia."

I frown as he kisses the palm of my hand. "Carmine, we're enjoying each other. Having a good time together."

"Yeah, we are, but it's more than that. And if you say it's not, that you don't have any feelings for me beyond that, you're lying."

I bite my lip and feel my eyes fill. And that just pisses me off.

"Don't cry, baby."

"I'm not." I clear my throat.

"I can't just fuck you and then go on with my day. Not anymore. I feel more than that, and I'll be damned if I continue denying it—if that's what you're asking me to do."

"I don't know what I'm asking."

"Why is this so hard for you?" He brushes his thumb over my lower lip, his eyes following the movement.

I *want* to give in to my feelings for him. I *want* to fall in love with him.

"Of course, I have feelings for you. Maybe tender sex just isn't my thing."

"You're not a great liar."

"I'm an amazing liar," I disagree and narrow my eyes. "But maybe I'm not lying about that."

"You are. Tell me why you don't want to be vulnerable with me like this. Jesus, Nadia, we've been honest with each other about so many things over the past few months. We've seen a lot and been through more. Why does this level of intimacy scare you?"

I shake my head. I don't want to admit that I'm scared, and I hate him for putting me in this position. Why can't we go back to it being simple?

Why do I find it so hard to do this?

"What if I get my heart set on something that isn't possible?"

There. I said it out loud.

The look in Carmine's brown eyes softens, and he tips his forehead against mine. "We don't know that it's impossible."

"We don't know that it's not," I say and hear the tremble in my voice. "Falling in love with you, *really* falling in love, was never part of the plan."

"No. It wasn't." He kisses me gently. "I hated your guts for a long, long time, Nadia. I wanted to make you hurt. Wanted to make your whole family pay."

I frown. "Well, that's one way to make me feel all warm and fuzzy."

"Smartass." He smiles and kisses my nose. "But then I spent time with you, learned who you are. And I know that not only are you not the one I should hate, but I respect the hell out of you. You're going to make one hell of a Bratva boss one day."

My mouth just opens and closes in surprise. I've never felt more naked. Exposed. Not just physically but emotionally, as well.

He's still inside me, and he just stripped my emotions bare.

"I want that," I whisper.

"I know. And you deserve it. But even more than that, I've grown quite fond of the woman you are. One who enjoys sweets and can kick ass. Who isn't afraid to ask for help when she needs it. A woman who spends more money than some people make in a year on a used handbag."

"You really need to get over that."

He laughs and finally starts to move, slowly, in and out of me.

"You're everything," he says. It sounds so simple but carries *so* much weight. And all I can do is show him how I feel because I can't say the words.

I just can't.

I brush my fingers through his hair and kiss his shoulder as he slowly makes love to me. And after I have the craziest climax of my life, he carries me to the bedroom.

"We aren't done yet."

"You may not be, pal, but I'm exhausted."

He chuckles and kisses my cheek. "We'll wake you up again."

～

OKAY, so there's something to be said for making love.

I've never done it before.

I feel energized the next morning. Satisfied. And oddly…sentimental.

I'm not an overly romantic girl. Damn him for digging his way under my skin when I wasn't looking and making me get all used to him.

"Here we are," Carmine says as our taxi stops next to the entrance of the cemetery. He takes my hand, and we walk over to the towering iron gates.

"This place is huge," I say as I look at a map. "We might be here awhile."

"We have all day."

We walk inside, up a short hill, and then all I can do is stand and gape. The cemetery is enormous. The headstones are old and different, and I can't wait to check them all out.

"Let's go this way and then check out the mausoleums last," I suggest.

"Lead the way," he says, gesturing with his arm. He's dressed casually today in a black T-shirt and cargo shorts, and he makes my mouth water.

How can a man look like that in a shirt and have it be legal?

I have no idea.

I'm in a simple red sundress today because it's summer in Paris and it's warm. Thankfully, I also have a good-sized crossbody bag that holds my concealed carry, and I have a smaller piece tied to my thigh.

Yes, we're on vacation, but you can never be too careful. I saw Carmine slip his handgun into a holster in the waistband of his shorts, above his impressive ass.

"It just goes on and on," I say and point out a statue. "That headstone looks like a woman weeping, and she's holding the hand of someone in a jail cell."

"This whole place is a work of art," he says.

"I hope this isn't boring for you."

"Not at all." He takes my hand in his and kisses my knuckles. "It's fascinating. And I'm with you. How could I be bored?"

"Good point." I wink at him and then glance over my shoulder. It looks like someone is watching us.

I do a double-take, and the person is gone.

Huh. I must just be on edge today. My emotions are all over the place, and I'm keyed up. That's all.

Nothing to worry about.

"Okay, this is…interesting." I stop next to a large concrete casket covered in moss. But coming out of the top are two arms with the hands touching, as if two people are buried here, holding hands even in death.

"I don't think I want to be buried like that," Carmine says thoughtfully.

"You don't think it's romantic?"

He glances down at me. "Do you?"

"I don't know. It's kind of macabre, but it's also kind of sweet."

We wander around some more and see the graves of Chopin, Oscar Wilde, and other artists. The memorials are absolutely stunning.

Then we turn a corner, and behind a chain-link fence is the grave of Jim Morrison.

"It's a shame they had to close it off because of vandals," I say. "But still cool to see."

"Do you like The Doors?"

"Sure." I shrug and glance back.

The same man is there again.

"I think—"

"Yep, I saw him. We'll find a more private spot and confront him."

I nod and, hand in hand, we walk down a road in the cemetery that looks as if it belongs in New Orleans with beautiful aboveground mausoleums.

"These are beautiful."

"It's amazing how different every part of the cemetery is."

"I agree."

I glance back but don't see the man following us any longer. But just as we turn a corner, he walks out from behind a crypt, a knife in his hand.

"Get in here," he hisses. "Now. Don't make a scene."

Carmine squeezes my hand, and we follow him into an open mausoleum. We slip inside, and he shuts the door.

"Who the hell are you?" Carmine asks, but the man strikes out with the knife, and I take out his knee.

He crumples to the ground, but he lashes out with the blade again.

Carmine punches him, then picks him up and holds him by the collar. "Who the fuck are you?"

"You're going to die today," the man growls, but before he can wave the knife again, I bend his hand back and take it from him, then press my gun to his head.

"Answer the damn question."

His eyes jitter back and forth between Carmine and me.

"You're not exactly discreet," Carmine says, his voice perfectly calm but hard as stone. "Either you wanted us to see you, or you're shitty at this job."

"Fuck you."

"I don't think so." Carmine knees him in the stomach, sending him to the ground once more, wheezing. We circle him slowly.

"Who sent you?"

"I'm not telling you *shit*."

I smile sweetly and squat next to him. "Oh, yeah, you are. Because if you don't, you won't leave this place alive. You'll spend all of eternity here with the…"—I check the name on the crypt next to me—"the Bettencourts. I'm sure they're nice people. And there's plenty of room here for you. You like to snuggle with corpses, don't you? I mean, they've been here since…"

I recheck the tomb.

"Since 1928. They're probably nice and decayed by now."

He looks green; like he's about to throw up.

"I won't ask nicely again," Carmine says.

"Richard hired me to follow you," he snaps. "I've been tailing you since you were in Denver. I'm just supposed to keep an eye on you and report back."

My gaze flies to Carmine's, and I stand to talk to him.

"How does he not know that Rich is dead?" I murmur.

Carmine shakes his head and then looks down at the man and curses. "Are you…"—he waves his hands around—"*crying?*"

The man is just sitting there, weeping.

"There's no crying in the mafia."

"Why are you quoting movie lines?"

He turns to me. "Because there's no crying. He's crying."

"Yes, I know."

We both turn back to him and swear.

"Fucking hell."

He's already seizing, foaming at the mouth. "He took a pill."

"He'd rather die than give information," Carmine agrees, and we watch until he stops jerking.

"What now? We can't leave him like this. Someone will find him. A groundskeeper or someone."

"We do what you suggested. Open that crypt and put him in there with the nice Battencourts."

I raise a brow. "Ew."

"I'll do it."

"No, I'll help." First, I poke my head out the door to make sure we haven't drawn a crowd. That would be uncomfortable.

But no one is even about.

"It's clear."

Carmine nods and opens the tomb. We both look down at the man.

"Wow, he looks good for being dead for almost one hundred years."

"The embalming did its job," Carmine agrees. "Nice suit, too."

"Well, this is a nice mausoleum. They had money." We turn back to our stiff. Carmine grabs his shoulders, and I take his feet, and we maneuver him into the burial chamber. "He just fits."

"No one will find him for a long time." We close the lid and have to push down for it to settle. "If ever."

"I don't get it." I straighten my dress and return my gun to its leg holster. Carmine picks up the knife and wipes it free of prints, then opens the other crypt. I walk over to look. "His wife."

"She doesn't look as good as he does."

The skin on her face is mostly gone, leaving her teeth showing. I check the date.

"She's been dead twenty years longer. They didn't embalm then."

He tosses the knife in with her and closes the top.

"You know the most interesting things, sweetheart. You were saying?"

"I don't get it," I continue. "He didn't know that Rich was dead. It wasn't a secret. You and I were at the funeral. If he was following us like he said, he would have seen us there."

"Maybe he was off work that day," Carmine says with a shrug and walks over to the door. "I don't really care. He's not following us now."

He opens the metal gate, and we step out, much to the surprise of a young couple currently walking around through the cemetery.

"Oops." I grin and wipe my mouth, then wink up at Carmine. "Finally checked that one off the bucket list."

Carmine laughs and pulls me away, just as the young woman gasps.

"Never a dull moment with you, is there?"

"Nope. And you're welcome."

# CHAPTER 15

## ~CARMINE~

"**Y**ou really should come in with me," Nadia says as she treads water in the crystal-blue pool. We've been at the resort in Cannes, on the French Riviera, for five days. We went from sightseeing and walking all over Paris to lazy days by the pool and eating all of the food in sight.

It's all about balance.

"I'm happy to sit here and watch," I reply. Nadia just shakes her head and starts swimming back and forth. We're not alone here at the pool since it's open to all resort visitors. But because it's the middle of the week, it's not overly crowded, either.

I'm sitting on a lounge chair, similar to the one that Nadia was sitting in that day that I found her in Miami all those months ago.

But so much has changed since then.

Finished with swimming, she moves over to the infinity wall and stares out at the water beyond.

The view here is stunning. We've spent quite a bit of time on the balcony of our penthouse suite, enjoying the sunsets.

It won't be long before we're back home, immersed in all of the responsibility that comes with our lives.

But for now, we're simply enjoying our vacation. Together.

I take a sip of the fruity drink that Nadia ordered for me and watch as the woman turns from her view and gives me a smile as she swims through the water.

Her eyes widen in surprise, and I lean forward, wondering if she needs my help.

"Oh, crap," she mutters, and as she walks up the steps and out of the pool, her bikini top is in her hands.

And her breasts are bare and on display.

"You'd best cover yourself."

"The damn clasp broke," she says. "And I liked this suit. Oh, well, I brought another one."

"Put something on, Nadia."

She looks up and frowns. "We're in *France*. Trust me, no one cares that I'm topless."

"I care."

She tips her head to the side. "Seriously, it's no big deal, Carmine."

"Put something on, or we'll go to the room."

She simply sits on the chair, leans back, and tips her face up to the sun, her small breasts out for everyone to see.

"No."

I press my lips together in frustration. "Nadia."

"Carmine," she says lazily and reaches for her drink. "I'm a grown woman. It's not illegal to be topless poolside in France. So, I'm going to sit here. Topless."

"For fuck's sake." I grab her black cover-up, toss it over her, and lift her into my arms. I don't miss the man across the pool, watching us.

He'll be dealt with later.

"What in the hell are you doing?"

I don't answer. I simply carry her to the elevator, and when we reach the top floor, I stride into our room.

She's glaring at me now.

I couldn't care less.

"You're such a fucking caveman," she growls. "I didn't do anything wrong, Carmine."

"Stop talking." I set her on the floor and then pin her against the wall. I take her hands in mine and lift them over her head with one of mine. With the other, I worry a nipple between my fingers. "If you think I'll sit back and let you sit out there on display, for everyone to see, you're sorely mistaken."

"*Let* me—"

"I said, stop talking." I drag my nose over the shell of her ear, breathing her in. My fingers pinch the nipple, just a little harder. "This, right here, is mine. Only for *me* to see."

She whimpers when I move over to the other side and pay that nipple the same attention.

"No one gets the pleasure of seeing this but me."

"Caveman," she whispers, but I can tell the anger has left her, replaced by pure, unadulterated lust.

I make quick work of her bikini bottoms and my shorts, and with her hands still pinned over her head, I boost her up and slip right inside of her.

"This is what happens when you defy me, Nadia. You piss me off and make me want to claim what's mine."

"Oh, my God."

"Look at me."

With her blue eyes on fire and pinned to mine, I work her hard, making her come fast. With the second orgasm, I follow her over and lean my forehead against her shoulder as I release her hands, and she wraps her arms around my neck.

I can't breathe.

And I can't let her go.

"Jesus, you do shit to me," I mutter.

"Same." She swallows hard and looks at me as I pull my face back. "It really bothered you, I guess."

"I wasn't playing."

Her mouth quirks into a grin. "I can see that. Fine, I'll wear the suit. But I could say the same."

"I'd look awful in a bikini top."

She smirks. "Do you think I didn't see the waitress flirting with you when she delivered your drinks? Or how the other women watch you when you walk across the pool area, wearing nothing but your shorts?"

"And how do they look at me?"

"Like they want to eat you alive. And I can't blame them." Her hands glide down my chest. "You're a sexy man, Carmine. You have muscles for days. Combine that with this smooth olive skin and that sexy face of yours, and well, you turn heads."

"Thanks for feeding my ego."

"I'm not. It's just how it is. But I don't wrap you in a towel and pull you out of there."

"I didn't like it," I repeat. "And I won't apologize for it. If you want me to wear a T-shirt at the pool, I'll do that."

"Well, that makes me just sound dumb."

"No." I grin and kiss her chin, then set her on her feet. "It makes you sound possessive, and that doesn't bother me so much."

"I'm going back down." She pads over to the dresser and pulls out a clean swimsuit. When she's dressed, she turns back to me. "Are you going to join me?"

"Yes. Would a tank top be too revealing?"

She laughs now and shakes her head. "You don't have to wear anything."

I slip the tank over my head and shrug. "If it makes you more comfortable, it doesn't bother me."

"We're sappy. You know that, right?"

"Darling, what a sweet thing to say."

～

THE CASINO IS loud and bustling around me. I'm seated at a high-roller blackjack table, sipping whiskey and watching Nadia from several yards away.

She's at a poker table, pouting because she just lost five thousand dollars.

"Well, poo," she huffs and gives the man beside her a forlorn look. "I'm really bad at this, aren't I?"

I ask the dealer to hit me and hold at nineteen.

"I've seen worse," her companion says. "Let's try this, shall we?"

His hand is on the small of her back and drifts down to her ass as he leans in to help her with her next hand.

My stomach twists.

He's going to lose that hand. And I'm not talking about the cards.

I win at nineteen and rake in twenty grand in chips as the asshole laughs and nuzzles Nadia's nose.

I sip my whiskey and act disinterested.

She loses again.

"That wasn't quite as bad," he tells her and moves in closer. "Now, for this hand, we'll do things a little differently."

I'm dealt a four of clubs and a queen of hearts. I tell the dealer to hit me and draw the six of diamonds.

I hold, and the dealer goes down the line of other players.

Nadia wins her hand and claps her hands joyfully, then kisses the man on the cheek.

That earns her ass a nice squeeze.

Fucking hell, how long do I have to watch this shit?

Finally, she whispers in his ear, and he rewards her with a wide smile and a nod of acceptance.

They leave the poker table.

I fold my cards, take my chips, and follow them.

"Are you on a good floor?" she asks, loud enough for me to hear her.

"The twelfth is nice and quiet," he assures her as they get into an elevator.

I take a different one and count my lucky stars when I get off just after them and follow them down the hall. He opens their door, and I hurry up, then push my way inside before he can shut it behind them.

"Hey, what's the big deal?"

"We could ask you the same thing," Nadia says, not smiling and flirting now.

He tries to act as if he doesn't know what she's talking about, but the longer we just stare at him, our weapons drawn, he loses the fight. He finally blows out a breath and holds up his hands in surrender.

"I guess you caught me."

"You've been following us for days," I reply. "And you're not very good at it. Just like your associate in Paris. Who's dead, by the way."

He narrows his eyes and then shrugs a shoulder. "He was a shitty operative."

"So are you."

This gets his temper up. "No. I'm not."

"We saw you," I repeat. "And what was that show downstairs? Did you think you could just flirt with her, and she'd jump right into bed with you?"

"And why not?" he asks, his voice bold. "We've all heard the stories about Nadia Tarenkov, fucking anyone who offers."

Without hesitation, I hit him across the face with the butt of my sidearm, drawing blood.

"Wait. Are you *in love* with her?" He laughs and doesn't bother to wipe at the blood on his face. "That's not even funny. It's sad. Pathetic, really. She'll just double-cross you, man. That's what she does."

"Shut the fuck up." Nadia kicks over the desk chair and forces him down into it, and I pull the twine out of my pocket and secure his hands behind his back.

"Why are you following us?" Nadia asks him.

"I don't have to tell you shit. Go ahead and kill me. You're going to anyway."

He's not wrong.

"Rich has been dead for weeks. Why are you still doing his bidding?" I ask.

He scoffs. "You think this came from *Richard*? Come on, Carmine, you weren't born last night. Pull your dick out of your brain and think about it. This comes from way higher up than Richard. That dude was a piece of shit. A total pussy."

"You know, I don't disagree with you," Nadia says as she walks around him. "But I never understood why men like to compare weakness to female genitalia."

She reaches down and grips his dick in a firm fist, making him yell in rage.

"When it's your *dick* that's so weak. So, the truth is, Richard was a dick."

Then she looks up at me and laughs. "Dick is short for Richard."

"Makes perfect sense, then," I agree.

She lets him go and walks over to me, urging me to the side so she can speak to me privately.

"Could it be true that Richard was working for someone else?"

"It could be, but Shane dug around on him and didn't find anything. He was going to keep delving into it in his free time. I'll have to call him and see if he found anything new."

"Yeah, let's do that. Ah!"

The asshole has Nadia pinned to the wall, his hands around her neck in a flash. I have no idea how he got out of the restraints.

"Let her go." I press the business end of my sidearm against the side of his head, but he doesn't let up on his grip. Nadia's face is already turning purple. "I said, fucking let her go."

No response.

I glance at Nadia and see that she won't last much longer.

So I squeeze the trigger and kill the son of a bitch.

"Jesus," she wheezes as he slumps to the floor, and she can breathe again. "Fuck."

"Hey, look at me."

She does as I ask. Her eyes are red. Her throat will be bruised.

I aim and shoot him once again.

"He's dead, Carmine."

"I thought he'd let go when I had the gun to his head."

"He was cocky and arrogant," she says when she finally catches her breath. She pulls an unopened bottle of water out of the fridge, but I shake my head no.

"Don't drink that. We don't know that he didn't poison everything in here."

"You're right. Christ." She drops the bottle to the carpet. "Who's going to clean up this mess?"

My smile is humorless as I pull my phone out of my pocket and tap a series of numbers, then send the text through.

"It'll be handled."

She just stares at me. "In *France?*"

"Anywhere." My answer is simple. "Your family would do the same."

She nods and pushes her hand through her hair. "You're right. I'm just rattled. I'm not used to being choked out like that. I guess it's safe to say that breathplay isn't my jam."

"No." I lean in and press a kiss to her neck where the bruises are already starting to form. "We won't be exploring that. There are too many other ways to bring pleasure. Let's go."

I don't spare the goon on the floor a glance as I open the door and lead her out, keeping an eye on our surroundings in case there's someone else lying in wait.

But as we leave the casino, we're alone. Once in the car on the way to the hotel, she leans her head on my shoulder.

"We need to go home," she murmurs.

"Agreed." I kiss the top of her head. "Vacation is over. We'll fly out tonight."

"Good. Are we going to Seattle?"

"Yes. Unless there was somewhere else you wanted to go?"

"No, Seattle works. I'll need to call my father when we land. I need to fill him in on what's going on."

"I think we should have a meeting with both of our fathers. Do you think yours would come to Seattle?"

She thinks it over. "If your father sends the invitation, I'm sure he will."

"I'll get that ball rolling. We thought what was happening in Denver died with Richard."

"We were wrong." She yawns. "We were very wrong."

And I'm furious.

No one will ever touch her like that again.

"I shouldn't have paused in shooting him," I say when we're in the elevator headed up to our room. "I hate myself for it."

"He might have stopped," she says. "Hey. I'm here, and I'm fine. We're going to figure out who's behind this, and we're going to kill *them*. No hesitation. No second chances."

"No. No hesitation." I pull her to me when we close the door to our suite and hold her close. We're rocking back and forth, clinging to each other, when my phone rings.

I don't let her go as I bring it to my ear. "Yes."

"The plane will be ready within the hour."

"Excellent."

I click off and tip her chin up with my finger.

"Let's go home, babe."

# CHAPTER 16

## ~NADIA~

"*T*hat's your grandmother's house?"

Carmine cuts the car's engine, and we sit in silence, staring at the enormous brownstone home just outside of Seattle, still perfectly manicured and maintained.

"It is." He sighs and then turns to me. "My brothers, Elena, and I practically grew up here. Especially in the summers. The house sits on roughly twenty acres of land. More than sixty years ago, when my grandfather bought the property, he got it for a steal."

I raise a brow, and he laughs.

"No, he didn't *steal* it. But he got a great deal on it. Today, it's worth well into the eight figures."

"I bet someone would love to buy it, divvy up the land into smaller parcels, build, and sell. Make it a nice little neighborhood near the water."

"I'm sure they would. And they'd make a good deal of money off it. But that's not going to happen."

"So, you're just hanging onto it for what? Sentimental value?" I shake my head and get out of the car. "Carmine, this property is prime real estate to make your family money."

"We have plenty of money," he reminds me. "And we're making more every day. Now, let's go find Rocco and see what's going on."

He slips his hand into mine and leads me through an arched, double door entrance and into a grand foyer with a split staircase.

It's a stunningly beautiful home. And it suits what I know of Carmine's grandmother, the matriarch of their mafioso family.

"He's probably in the kitchen," Carmine says and leads me through rooms full of old furniture, artwork, and windows that offer a view of the water.

"I see why you have a thing for beautiful views."

He smiles. "I learned from her."

We walk past a dining room and into the kitchen, where sure enough, Rafe leans on the counter, tapping keys on his laptop as he munches on a sandwich.

"Hey," he says and looks up at us. "Jesus, you look like shit. Aren't you supposed to come home from vacation looking all bright-eyed and bushy-tailed?"

"What the fuck does that even mean?" Carmine asks with a laugh. "We came straight here from the airport."

"Ah. Jet lag. So, I hear you had some fun being tailed over there."

"You heard right," I reply and open the fridge, starving. "You have cream cheese. Do you have bagels?"

"Sure. Here you go."

He opens a cupboard, and I have my pick of everything, cheese, or plain.

I always go for the cheese.

"Want one?" I ask Carmine.

"Sure. I'll do it. You're exhausted. Here." He takes over, and I point to the cheese, then settle back to chat with Rafe.

"And you had a break-in here," I reply, to which Rafe nods.

"Yeah. Fucker got inside by breaking one of the big picture windows in the library. I had them repaired yesterday."

"But not with the original glass," Carmine says with frustration.

"No," Rafe agrees, then turns to me to explain. "Ninety percent of the glass in this house is original. It was built in 1909. Gram was particularly fond of the glass."

"I'm sorry. That sucks. What did they take?"

"As far as we can tell, nothing." He blows out a disgusted breath and paces the kitchen. "I've been through every room. Aside from the window, *nothing* was moved. It doesn't make any sense."

"Unless they were looking for something or *someone* who wasn't here," Carmine replies as he sets a plate full of bagel goodness in front of me and then sits next to me with a plate of his own.

"I thought of that," Rafe says. "Since it's not been a secret that the house has been empty, I'd say it was some*thing* they were looking for."

"If it was a run-of-the-mill thief," I say, licking cream cheese off my finger. "He could have been looking for jewelry, artwork, antiques. But I saw a lot of priceless art and antiques on our way through when we arrived."

"And nothing is missing," Rafe says. "Father took all of the jewelry and any money Gram had lying around here home with him a few days after she died."

"So, someone broke in and was disappointed at the lack of loot," Carmine says with a shrug. "We'll ramp up the security, especially if you don't want to keep living out here."

"I don't really mind it," Rafe says, thinking it over. "It's just so damn far out of the city. By the way, I checked your house the other day. Nothing's going on there."

"We'll head over after we finish here," Carmine says. "But thanks for checking. I have around-the-clock security."

I finish my bagel and sigh in happiness. "Thanks for the carbs."

"You're welcome. Have you heard from Annika?"

I wondered if he'd bring up my cousin. Part of me wanted him to so I could drill him.

But the man standing across from me just looks...miserable.

"Yeah, we text just about every day."

"How is she?"

I tip my head to the side. "Why don't you ask her?"

"I have. She doesn't fucking reply." He drags his hands over his face in agitation. "She's cut me out entirely, and it's more frustrating than I can tell you."

"She's getting by," is all I say, but when he just stares at me, I continue, carefully choosing my words. "She feels foolish. And she's mad."

Rafe nods, and Carmine reaches over to squeeze my hand.

"If you talk to her, just tell her to text me back."

I laugh and then shrug when Rafe sends me a look that's likely made plenty of men piss their pants.

"I'll mention it. But Annika is her own woman, Rafe. And she wants *nothing* to do with the mafia. She's never made that a secret."

"I can't be held responsible for the family I was born into." The frustration rolls over his face as he shakes his head. "And neither can she. She has to stop punishing us both for it."

"Is that what she's doing?" I wonder. "Or is she simply trying to live a simple life?"

"She's stubborn as hell, that's what she is," Rafe says.

"On that, we can agree. I'll pass along your message." I turn to Carmine, who's remained quiet as he listened to the exchange between Rafe and me. "What time are we meeting with our dads?"

He checks the time and then stands. "In a few hours."

"You're meeting with Pop *and* Igor?" Rafe asks with surprise.

"Yes. We need to talk about the men who followed us in France," Carmine says. "And I want to do it in a secure place. Over the phone or internet won't cut it. You're welcome to join us. Is Shane still in Colorado?"

"I'm not sure where he is," Rafe says. "He said something about a job in Colombia."

I raise a brow. "What, exactly, does Shane do for a living?"

"That, we can't tell you," Carmine says but takes the sting out of the statement with a kiss to my head. "Let's go home and freshen up for our meeting. Rocco, we're meeting at three, at the downtown building."

"In the office?" he asks.

Carmine nods and sets our dishes in the dishwasher, then leads me out of the kitchen and toward the front door.

I want to ask for a tour of the magnificent house, but I know that we don't have time. And, at the end of the day, no matter how close Carmine and I have gotten, I'm still a member of the Tarenkov family. There will always be a line. And taking me on a tour of the Martinelli matriarch's house might be crossing it.

We're quiet in the car. So much so that I close my eyes and rest. Neither of us slept on the flight here. We even went and laid on the bed, snuggled up, but couldn't doze off.

We didn't talk, simply lay there. Restless. Uncertain.

Pissed off.

Someone's still after us, and we don't know who. Not to mention, I didn't like leaving bodies behind in Europe. It was supposed to be a *vacation.* We weren't supposed to have to kill anyone or constantly look over our shoulders.

Not that the looking behind you ever entirely goes away, even when you feel absolutely safe.

Because the truth is, being in the mafia means you're *never* truly safe.

I open my eyes when Carmine stops the car and then frown.

"We're not going to the penthouse?"

"No," he says and turns to me. "I want you here. In my home."

"I don't understand."

"When I first brought you to Seattle months ago, I didn't want you here because I didn't trust you. And I was with you for other reasons. It was all a farce. The penthouse was neutral territory, so to speak. But that's all changed."

He takes my hand and threads his fingers through mine.

"I want you here, in my house. Not the penthouse."

"But all of my things—"

"Have been moved here," he finishes with a small smile. "Come on, let me show you."

He hurries out of the car, then comes to the passenger side and opens my door.

"You were here once," he says as he pulls me up out of the car and leads me to the door. "And I certainly didn't trust you then, either. It irritated the hell out of me that you found me here."

"Oh, that was certainly the point," I reply with a laugh. "I wanted to frustrate you that day."

"You succeeded. But today, I'm inviting you."

"So, this is your home. And I see that it's not far from your grandmother's."

"No." He unlocks and pushes open the door and then leads me inside. "I loved spending time with her there. And I came to learn that I liked keeping my personal time separate from work. I like our building downtown, don't get me wrong. But it's not home."

I take in the expansive living space with new eyes. The style is *very* different from the home we just left, but it's no less opulent or beautiful.

"The kitchen is gorgeous," I say as we walk through it. "I enjoyed going through your fridge while you fumed."

He chuckles and leads me past, showing me guest rooms, a workout space, an office, and finally, his master bedroom.

It's big, but he's a big man, so it suits him. "More views," I muse and walk to the door that leads out to a patio and a lush garden.

The master bathroom and drool-worthy walk-in closet are nothing less than what I'd expect of a man like Carmine, someone who definitely enjoys all of the finer things in life. It doesn't escape me that all of my clothes and personal things are in the closet, hung neatly.

"You have a lovely home," I say as he pulls me to him. My voice is sincere. It *is* lovely. "And it suits you."

"Thank you."

"You weren't kidding. All of my things are in that sexy-as-fuck closet. My shampoo is even in the shower."

"We won't be living at the penthouse," he confirms. "I hope that doesn't upset you."

Upset me? No. But I'd be lying if I said I wasn't a little confused as to where this was going.

Then again, maybe I'm just overthinking things. It doesn't have to *go* anywhere.

He kisses me, long and slow, as we stand in the middle of his bedroom. "We have time for a nap."

I smile at the suggestion. "Do we have time for more than a nap?"

His brown eyes narrow with lusty mischief. "Oh, yeah. We can manage that."

THE DRIVE into the city doesn't take long. With an hour of sleep and a round of lazy sex behind us, I feel surprisingly rejuvenated.

And I'm excited to see my father.

I've been in constant contact with him since the incident at the casino in Cannes. He accepted Carlo's invitation to meet in Seattle—much to my surprise and delight.

Carmine parks in the underground lot of his building. Rather than hitting the button for the penthouse in the elevator, he pushes the one for the tenth floor.

I raise a brow.

"This is the office."

"Your father's office?"

"No." He shakes his head. "That's on the twentieth floor. Don't worry, you'll see. It's more comfortable. Less imposing."

When we arrive at what used to be a condo but is now a beautiful office space, I see that he's right.

Rather than a large desk where an authority figure might sit, there are sofas, tables, and workspaces throughout. Someone stocked the kitchen with everything a person could ever need or want.

The decorations, in muted colors, are perfect for making someone feel comfortable and at ease.

Less than a minute after we arrive, Carlo walks in with Rafe right behind him.

His face lifts into a smile as he shakes Carmine's hand. "Welcome home, son. Hello, Nadia. You look lovely."

"Thank you."

"Of course, she does. She's the spitting image of her mother," my papa says from the doorway. "Hello, little one."

"Papa!" I run over and kiss him on the cheek, then take his hand and lead him into the room. "I'm so happy to see you. Thank you for coming all this way."

"For you, I would fly to the end of the world." He cups my face and gives me a wink, then turns to Carlo and his sons. "Hello, my friend. Thank you for inviting me into your city."

"Thank you for coming," Carlo says as the two men shake hands. "My son made it clear that what he and Nadia have to tell us is very important."

"It is," I assure them both as we all take seats. I glance at Carmine, giving him a silent nod to go ahead.

"As you all know, Nadia and I were vacationing in Europe. A little holiday after discovering that Richard was responsible for killing Armando and several others. We thought the situation was settled with Rich's death."

He glances at me, and I pick up the story.

"However, while we were in Paris and strolling through a cemetery, we discovered we were being followed."

I recount the incident with the man in the mausoleum and how we handled it.

Carlo laughs, much to my surprise.

"I apologize. I know it's not a funny situation, but you hid the body in a crypt? That's just priceless."

My father chuckles with him, and I continue.

"A couple of days later, we moved on to Cannes, and within about forty-eight hours, we picked up on another tail. He was at the pool when we were there. At the same restaurants as ours. You get the idea."

I glance at Carmine, and he continues.

"We devised a scheme to catch him. And we did. But this time, when we told him that

Rich was dead and asked why he was following us, he said that Rich wasn't the one who gave the orders. That it went *much higher than that.*"

Papa and Carlo share a glance.

"Do you know what that means?" I ask.

"It means this goes deeper than we thought," Papa says with a long sigh. "And someone tried to kill my daughter. Whoever is behind this will die."

"Who was Rich working for?" Carlo wonders aloud.

"We're going to fucking find out," Rafe says.

# CHAPTER 17

## ~CARMINE~

"*F*or a doctor, your husband sure kept a lot of files at home," Nadia says to Annika. We're in Annika's home, in various areas of Rich's old office, poring over paperwork. He had tons of files, and every piece of paper has to be looked at.

"He wasn't a fucking doctor," Annika snaps back. She's sitting cross-legged on the couch, her dead husband's laptop in front of her as she tries to break the passcode. She sighs and leans her head back on the sofa. "Sorry. I don't mean to sound like a bitch. I wish I could figure out this password."

"For *not* a doctor, there sure are a lot of patient notes here," I muse as I open another file and frown down at medical information on someone named Samantha Briggs. "I would think it's illegal to have patient information at home."

"It is," Annika assures me. "It's also illegal to pose as a doctor when you aren't. I'm so fucking mad at him." She stands and paces the office. "I wish he was alive so I could punch him in that smug face and then kill him myself."

"While I understand—and agree with—the sentiment," Nadia says, "that won't help us today."

"I don't even know what we're looking for," I reply and toss a file on the growing stack.

"Sorry I'm late," Ivie says as she hurries into the office, then promptly stubs her toe on the doorjamb. "Ouch! Son of a bitch."

"I swear, you need to wear Bubble Wrap," Nadia says, shaking her head. "Are you okay?"

"Yeah. That hurt." Ivie sits and rubs her toes. "I tried to get here sooner, but traffic was a bitch. So, how can I help? What can I do? Annika filled me in on the whole mystery at hand."

I turn to Annika and raise a brow, but the woman only shrugs. "She's my best friend, Carmine."

"I'm totally trustworthy," Ivie assures me. "I can help you look through the house or something, but I likely won't know what I'm looking for."

"That makes four of us," Nadia says. "None of us knows what we're looking for, but we'll know it when we see it."

"Something out of the ordinary," I reply. "Names, numbers, notes that are vague or even incriminating. That would be convenient."

"I'm trying to get into his computer, but the fucker locked it down pretty solid," Annika adds.

"How about this?" Ivie says. "I'll make you all a late lunch and help out wherever I can."

"I need a break from this," Annika says and tosses the computer onto the cushion beside her. "I'll help you, Ivie. We'll be back in a few with sustenance. Maybe I'll be more productive if I'm not hangry."

The two women leave the room, arm in arm, and Nadia sighs across from me.

"I guess it's a good sign that she's hungry," she says, still staring at the doorway. "She looks a little better than she did when we left here a few weeks ago."

I want to disagree. I think Annika looks horrible. The anger and hatred are festering inside of her. She has dark circles under her eyes, and she's lost a lot of weight in a very short time.

But I don't say any of that because Nadia is worried enough, and we have plenty on our plates.

"Carmine."

"Yes, sweetheart?"

"We're not going to find anything in these medical records. I don't even know why he has them here or what he used them for. But this isn't the answer."

"I agree." I rub my hand down my face. "I've been trying to reach my brother to see if he's had time to tinker some more. I'd like to have Rich's phone here so I can do some digging, but I can't reach Shane. He won't answer his damn phone."

"Maybe he's still out of the country," she suggests.

"It would help if he'd answer and tell me that."

Annika and Ivie return with a tray full of sandwiches and chips, soda, and water.

"I'm starving," Annika says, taking a sandwich and some chips for herself. "Eat up. There's more in the kitchen if you're still hungry."

"This is enough for an army," Nadia says and bites into a sandwich.

I try to call my brother again, but it goes straight to his voicemail.

"Son of a bitch," I mutter and then pin Ivie with a stare. She blinks and looks behind her.

"What?"

"I know you talk to my brother. Have you heard from him?"

"Shane?"

"Yes, Shane. Where the fuck is he?"

"I don't know." She shrugs and then says it again. "Honest, Carmine, I don't know. I haven't heard from him in a few days. He said he had some work to do and that he'd be in touch. Not to worry."

"Yeah. That sounds like him."

I bite into a turkey on rye and look around the room.

Nadia and I have been back in Denver for three days, and we haven't learned anything that we didn't already know when we arrived.

It's damn frustrating.

"If you hear from him, tell him to call me."

"I can do that."

"So, um, Annika," Nadia begins and smiles at her cousin, "Rafe asked about you the other day."

Annika doesn't even pause in the fast consumption of her chips. "Okay?"

"I told him to ask you, but he said you don't reply to his texts or calls."

"No." She slips another chip into her mouth. "I don't."

Nadia sighs and watches her cousin in exasperation. "Are you ever going to?"

Annika chews her bite, swallows, then looks at Nadia and says, "No."

"Why not?" Ivie asks. "He's a good guy, A."

"This is nobody's business," Annika replies and reaches for another bag of chips. "I'm just not going to, okay? I'm sorry, Carmine. I don't mean to insult you or anything."

"Rafe's an idiot," I reply happily. "I wouldn't reply, either."

"He's not an idiot," she says softly. "He's brilliant and kind and all of the good things that Rich wasn't."

She sets the unopened bag down.

"Then I'll ask again." Nadia's voice is gentle. "Why won't you answer him?"

I figure this must be what it's like to be a fly on the wall during a girls' night. I don't think I want to repeat the experience.

"Because I'm broken, and Rafe is way too good for me."

"That's a pile of bullshit," Nadia says simply. "You're not broken, and *no one* is too good for you, Annika Tarenkov. You're hurting, and you need time to heal. You'll get there."

Annika shrugs a shoulder and reaches for the laptop.

"Let's just get back to work and get this over with."

Time drags. Several hours and two sandwiches later, we're still at square one.

"I officially hate paper," I announce as I push the last folder aside. "And I know too much about all of these people's medical histories."

"Let's call it a day," Nadia suggests. "We can start again tomorrow with fresh eyes. Maybe we'll go to Rich's office."

"It's empty," Annika replies. "I went there to clean it out shortly after you left for Europe, but someone beat me to it. The only thing left was the desk."

"What?" I stare at her, dumbfounded. "Why didn't you say anything?"

"Because you were in France, on vacation. And, frankly, I didn't care. It was one less thing I had to deal with. Somebody did me a favor."

"He wouldn't have kept something incriminating there," Ivie says, shaking her head. "It wasn't secure, and he wasn't there all the time. If there's something that can help point to who's behind all of this, I think it'll be here. Rich was cocky. Arrogant. He felt safe here. Knew that no one would mess with him here."

"You're right," Annika agrees. "And I was *not* allowed to be in here. Especially when he was gone. If there's something to find, it's here."

"We need to stop for today," Nadia announces. "We're all moody and tired. We've been at it since sunrise. We need to get some rest and start again tomorrow, like I said."

I watch Nadia. She looks exhausted. We haven't stopped moving since France. There's been little time to rest and get over the jet lag.

She's not wrong. We do need to rest.

"You're right. We're probably missing something because we don't have our wits about us. Let's pick it up in the morning."

"Thank God." Annika closes the laptop. "I've tried every combination of words and numbers I can think of."

"If Shane would answer his phone, he could get into it without breaking a sweat. I'll keep trying him."

"I will, too," Ivie adds and reaches for her cell.

"It's settled then," Nadia says and stands to stretch. "We'll come back tomorrow."

∼

"I NEEDED to get out of there," Nadia confesses when we pull into the driveway of our rental. "I love my cousin, you know I do, but she was irritating the shit out of me today."

"She's angry."

"She's being a brat," she counters. "And that's not like her. She won't talk to me. All she wants to do is brood and sulk, and it's irritating as fuck."

"Not everyone knows how to handle their emotions after a powerful loss like that."

"I know. And I'm sympathetic. She lost who she *thought* was her husband, the life she imagined they'd build together before he even died. And then he was just...gone. She couldn't confront him. She must have so many emotions going on, and I feel for her. But her attitude is shitty, and I needed a break."

"Fair enough." I park and lock my car, and we walk inside the house. It's the same one we used when we were here a few weeks ago. It's starting to feel like a home away from home.

I wonder if the owners would consider selling it? It would be convenient to have a piece of property here in the neutral city of Denver.

I'll have to make some inquiries.

"I'm taking a shower," Nadia announces, and already has her shirt over her head as she saunters down the hall to the master, her ass swaying in that way that never fails to kick me in the stomach with lust.

I want her.

I always want her.

I've fallen in love with her.

I follow after her and hear the water turn on in the shower. Deciding to leave her alone to wash off the frustration of the day, I light a few candles and then go to the kitchen to arrange some fruit, cheese, and crackers on a tray. It's not fancy, but it'll be a nice snack.

I set the platter next to the bed and turn to find Nadia standing in the doorway, towel-drying her hair.

She's naked and still damp from the shower. I can't wait to get my hands on her.

"Is that for me?"

"It seems that most of what I do these days is for you," I reply as I cross to her and cup her face in my hands. "Better?"

"Yeah, that felt good."

I kiss her lips tenderly. "Come, relax. Have a snack."

"I can think of something I'd like to snack on." Her lips curl up into a flirty smile, and she drops her hair towel to the floor, then reaches for my jeans.

"And what would that be?" The question is playful. "A card game, perhaps?"

"I'd kill you at poker."

"I've seen you play poker," I remind her.

"That was an act. I could have cleaned up on that table."

"Darling, you're just full of surprises."

She yanks my shirt over my head and tosses it to the floor, and then she's on me, raw need pouring from every pore of her body. We stumble to the bed, fall in a clumsy heap, and then it's all groping hands and laughter as we fumble our way to each other.

She's out of breath when I pin her beneath me, but her blue eyes are wild and locked on mine as I nudge her thighs apart with mine and drive home.

I gasp as she moans.

I *need* her the way I need air. I can't be gentle as pure desire fuels me, pushing and pulling, driving us both to the ultimate destination of eruption.

"Christ Jesus," she moans. Her back arches, and she clenches around me, then lets go.

I can't keep my hands off her breasts, my mouth away from her neck, and move up to her lips as I press on, still chasing the all-encompassing need to claim her. To show her how much I *need* her.

Finally, with my jaw clenched and my eyes shut, I fall over the edge and collapse on top of her, heaving and tingling.

I feel fingertips roaming over my spine and shift my face from the pillow to her neck.

"You're the best part of my life. Don't ever forget that."

Those fingertips still for just a moment but then begin moving again.

"I won't forget," she promises. "But you're going to have to move because I can't breathe."

I find the strength to roll to the side and smile over at her. "Sorry."

"It's okay. I'm mostly numb anyway." She giggles and reaches for a strawberry. "And I'm *so* hungry. Why am I so hungry?"

"You've been eating like a mouse since France."

"No, I haven't."

"Yes. You have."

She watches me and reaches for some cheese, then sits up to eat. "I've just had a lot on my mind, you know?"

"I do. And so do I. Don't worry, I'll keep an eye on you and make sure you eat."

"It's handy having you around."

"I'm glad you think so. Because I'd like to stick around for a long while. When all of this is done, I want you to move in with me."

She frowns. "Aren't I basically already moved in?"

"I want to make it official. I want to move all of your things to Seattle."

She swallows her cheese and watches me with those stunning eyes of hers. "To your house?"

"Yes. To my house. If you hate it, I'll sell it, and we'll buy something else."

She stands and reaches for her robe, wraps it around her, and turns back to me. "You'd sell your house for me if I didn't like it?"

Why do I feel like that's a trick question? "Of course, I would. I want to make a life with you, Nadia. I want you to live where you're comfortable and happy."

"In Seattle."

I see where this is going.

I tug on a pair of shorts and stand across the bed from her, my hands in my pockets.

"Yes, I'd like to live in Seattle. Is that a problem for you?"

"I don't know." She moves a piece of wet hair off her cheek. "It's not something I've considered before. Seattle is off-limits because our families—"

"Our families are fine. If you don't like Seattle, don't want to make a home there—"

"I didn't say that." She hurries around the bed and takes my hand in hers, then kisses my chin. "I'm overthinking it. I like Seattle, Carmine. And I like your house. I mean, it could use a woman's touch here and there…"

Hope spreads through my belly.

"It could. You're right. Do you know of a woman who might want to add her touch?"

She smiles and tips her face to mine. "I just might. I'll put out some feelers."

"You're a sassy one."

"And you get to live with me. Lucky man."

Yes. Yes, I am a lucky man.

# CHAPTER 18

## ~CARMINE~

*I* slept like the dead. I don't remember the last time I slept that hard.

I roll over and look at my watch.

9:30 a.m.

I sit up and scowl.

Nine-thirty? What in the actual fuck?

Nadia's already up. I don't know why she didn't wake me. It's completely uncharacteristic of me to sleep past seven.

I drag my hand down my face, then reach for my shorts. Jesus, jet lag is a motherfucker.

I pad into the kitchen and narrow my eyes. The whole house is still.

Where's Nadia?

Just as my phone rings in my hand, I notice the note on the counter.

*C-*

*Ran out for donuts and coffee. You're so sleepy! Be back soon.*

*XO,*

*N*

"Yeah?" I say without looking at the name on the display.

"You need to come up to Victor."

"Shane? What the fuck, Shane? I've been trying to reach you for days. Why don't you ever answer your goddamn phone?"

"I have a life, brother. But never mind that now. I need you to come up to my place to look at some stuff. Rocco's on his way to get you. Should be there any minute. I've been calling you for a few hours."

"I overslept." I sigh and scratch my scalp. "Christ, I haven't even had any coffee yet."

"I have plenty. Get your ass ready to go when Rocco gets there. Oh, and, Carmine, come without the girl."

"Why?"

"Just don't bring her. This is as confidential as it gets."

He ends the call, and I hurry back to the bedroom to get dressed and pull myself together. I usually trim the scruff on my face in the mornings, but there's no time for that today. I clean up a bit, comb my hair, and walk back out to the kitchen.

I look up to see Nadia coming through the door, juggling a box of her favorite donuts and a tray of coffees.

I rush over to help her, gratefully lift a coffee from the tray, and take a long sip.

"God bless you."

"Are you okay? You have sleep marks all over your face."

"I slept hard."

"Yeah, you did." Nadia lifts the lid of the box and sniffs the treats inside. "I bought too many, but I couldn't help myself."

"Thanks for going out to get this." I take her shoulders in my hands and kiss her. "I have to go."

"Huh? Where are we going?"

I kiss her forehead so I can stall and figure out a lie to use. I haven't had to lie to Nadia in months, and it leaves a sour taste in my mouth.

"I have to meet with my brothers. Some business that isn't tied to what we've been working on."

She nods and takes a bite out of a maple bar. "Okay. Are you sure you don't want me to go with you? We could go straight to Annika's from there."

There's a knock on the door.

"That's my brother. You know what? You take the car. I'll meet you there."

"Okay." She frowns, watching me. "Are you sure everything's okay?"

"As far as I know, everything's fine."

Rocco walks into the house and grins. "Mornin'."

"Hi, Rafe," Nadia says. "I didn't get enough coffee for you, but you're welcome to take a donut or two. Actually, here. You might have just saved my life. I'll take two, and you guys take the rest. Now I won't eat them all myself."

"Nice. Thanks."

I take the box and kiss her again. "Thanks. I'll see you later."

"See you later," she says cheerfully as I close the door behind me and follow Rocco to his car.

"What the fuck is going on?" I demand when I climb into the rental.

"No idea," he says and stuffs half the donut into his mouth. After he swallows, he continues. "Got a call from Shane. Thirty minutes later, I was in the chopper headed here."

"Where's it parked?"

"Not far. We'll be at Shane's in an hour."

I feel sick after lying to Nadia.

We arrive at an airstrip where the chopper is waiting for us. Rocco and I climb in, buckle up, and he checks gauges and flips switches. When we have our headsets on, we take off.

The air over the high Rockies is choppy, so the ride is rough, but it doesn't take long before we land about a hundred yards from Shane's house on his property near Victor, Colorado.

As an old mining town in the mountains, Victor used to host more than a hundred thousand people. But now that most of the gold is gone, aside from the last few plots that large corporations own, the town has shrunk to just a couple of hundred people.

Just the way Shane likes it.

How he can live at ten thousand feet, in the middle of nowhere, I have no idea. The air is thin as hell, and it always takes me a day or two to get used to being up this high.

Rocco cuts the engine, and we get out of the helicopter and jog to the house where Shane's standing just outside his door, arms folded across his chest.

"Saved you a donut," Rocco says as he passes the box to Shane. "Your favorite."

"*One?*"

"Better than none," Rocco replies and shrugs as we follow our brother into the big farmhouse.

Shane's property is a fortress. Sitting on a few hundred acres, it's surrounded by state-of-the-art security with cameras and alarms. He has all kinds of toys, weapons, and other equipment that I probably don't want to know about, in addition to the helipad.

He leads us through a honey oak kitchen and the dining and living spaces, which all look completely normal. Fancy, but normal.

Then, he passes through a doorway and procedes down a long flight of stairs. When he flips on the lights, we're no longer in a simple farmhouse.

We're in a headquarters.

Machines beep and computers cover several desks. There are phones, screens, maps.

It's all very James Bond.

Or, Shane Martinelli.

"I got home a couple of days ago and was finally able to start digging into that slimeball, Richard," he begins with a donut in his mouth. "It was right there, in front of our faces the whole goddamn time."

"What was?" I demand.

"Let me start at the beginning." He flips on a screen, and it fills with a photo of Richard. "This asshole isn't Richard Donaldson at all. It's a cover. One that was well crafted, by the way. But it was thin. They didn't add layers, so I didn't have to dig far to discover that he's a phony. If Alex Tarenkov had done his job, it would have been harder to find. But, more on that in a minute."

He clicks a button, and data starts scrolling across the screen.

"Dimitri Lebedev." I turn to Shane in shock. "He's Russian?"

"Oh, he definitely is. But he was born in New York City in 1987. His parents were KGB spies in the seventies and early eighties and came to the US for asylum. The fucking government gave it to them in exchange for some information. You know, we were dealing with the Cold War at that time, and I'm sure they had plenty of secrets to share.

"So, our boy Dimitri was raised here in the US. Went to college at NYU. Smart kid, majored in PoliSci. Guess who his roommate was?"

Rocco and I stare at him. "Who?"

"Alexander Tarenkov."

Shane clicks some keys and some photos of the two men show up on the screen.

"Motherfucker," I mutter.

"So, these two were buddies in college. How Annika didn't know that, I have no idea. Because from what I've heard, Annika and Alex always got along well. Maybe Alex wasn't the type to bring his bestie from college home for the holidays. Maybe he knew if he brought Dimitri around his father, there would be trouble given that Dimitri's parents were KGB agents and all. But that's all speculation."

"We'll have to ask him," Rocco says.

"Wait a minute. If these are his parents"—I point to the couple on the screen—"who were the people at the wedding who claimed to be Rich's family?"

We all look at each other, and then Shane shrugs. "They were hired to act the part. This whole thing was a cover. But not for Dimitri."

"For Alex," Rocco finishes.

"Bingo. Whatever this jerk's into, it goes deep, and it's been going on for a long time. He had one arrest in college for dealing, but it was just some weed. Those records were buried. I assume thanks to his father."

"But the Tarenkovs don't deal," I say, shaking my head. "Nadia told me herself that drugs aren't their game."

"And I buy that," Shane says, continuing. "Igor has always been adamant that their family isn't into the drug game. But that doesn't mean that *Alex* isn't."

"I need to ask Nadia—"

"Look, I know you're in love with her. Jesus, it's all over your face. But you need to tread carefully here," Shane interrupts, turning to me. "Because I have reason to believe that she's in on it with him."

No. Absolutely not. Everything in me wants to rail at him in anger, punch him in the fucking face for even *suggesting* that the woman I love is connected to this.

But I don't.

I wait.

Shane clicks more keys, and the photos on the monitor shift to ones of Nadia and Alex.

"These were taken just six months ago in Atlanta," Shane says.

The two of them are walking down the street together, laughing.

"The Tarenkovs are based in Atlanta," I remind him, but my gut is still in knots. Nadia hates her brother.

So why then is she in all of these photos with him, looking as close as two siblings can be?

"The point is, we don't *know*, Carmine. She could be playing you. She could be double-crossing you."

I remember what the goon in Cannes said: *"She'll just double-cross you, man. That's what she does."*

Fuck, has Nadia been playing me this whole time? I've been falling in love with her, and she's been playing me?

"Take me back." I march toward the steps, my heart pounding. I need to get to Nadia. I need to look her in the eyes when I confront her about this. "Right now, Rocco."

"We're all going," Shane says, shutting down the equipment in a rush and then running after us. "Goddamn it, slow down. I have to lock up."

"This place is a fucking fortress. No one even knows it's here."

"I know," he mutters before we all jog out to the waiting helicopter.

"I'M GOING IN ALONE." Rocco doesn't even pull into the driveway, he just pulls up to the curb. "I'll come to the office after I'm done confronting her."

"Are you sure she's here?" Shane asks.

"The car's still in the drive," I say with a nod. "She's here. I'll see you in a bit. Go see if you can find out where Alex is."

Rocco drives away as I walk up to the house. Jesus, am I completely blind when it comes to Nadia? I didn't go into this with the intention of falling in love with her. My guard was up, I was careful. Watchful.

I reach for the handle, but movement through the window in the door catches my eye, and I stop.

"Fuck me," I whisper. Nadia is sitting on the couch, her back to me. And Alex, that son of a bitch, is pacing the living room, talking and gesturing with his hands.

Shane was right. The evidence is right here in front of me. Nadia didn't expect me back for hours, so Alex came over, and they're having a meeting in the house I'm paying for.

I pull my phone out of my pocket and call Shane.

"Yeah?"

"You need to come back here. Alex and Nadia are both here. I haven't gone in yet. I want backup. I know how badass she can be."

"On our way."

I shove my phone back into my pocket and decide to walk around the house to get a better view. We'll have to surprise them. Alex is weak and small, but Nadia is excellent at both hand-to-hand combat and with her weapon.

I ease my way around the opposite side of the room and peek my head around the window. Alex is standing in front of Nadia, his arms still flailing about.

And when he steps away, my blood turns to ice.

Nadia's hands are tied in front of her. Both eyes are blackened. Her shirt is ripped, probably from a struggle, and there's a gash in her shoulder with blood running down her chest.

The son of a bitch *hurt* her.

Nadia's eyes roam away from her brother and meet mine. They widen in surprise for a moment, and then she recovers. She watches Alex, who's still on a tirade, and then gives me a shake of the head.

It's barely noticeable, in case Alex sees her, but it's there.

She doesn't want me to come in.

Well, she's going to be very disappointed.

I hurry back around the house just in time to see my brothers hurrying up the driveway.

"He beat her up," I say quickly and bring them both up to speed. "She's not in on it, and he's going to kill her."

"No." Rocco takes out his sidearm and disengages the safety. "He isn't. How do you want to do this?"

"There are two entrances, aside from the garage." I point to the front door and then gesture to the side of the house. "Both are within his line of sight, so when we go in, we go in firing. But you have to be careful. Nadia's tied up on the couch."

"Rocco and I are going in on the side," Shane says, cool as a cucumber as he thinks it through. "Carmine, you go in through the front door as if you're just coming home and don't know what's going on. Play stupid with him for a bit. We need to catch him off guard."

"And if he just draws a weapon and shoots me?"

Shane smiles. "Duck."

"That's not helpful." I tap my piece at my ankle and the one at my back. "He's yelling. I'd say he's telling her everything he's done."

"Alex *would* brag," Rocco says. "He'll want to tell her everything before he kills her."

"I'm using that to my advantage," I say and walk to the door. "Get in position. I'm going in."

Without another word, I open the door.

"Hey, babe, I'm home! I hope there are still some donuts left. I'm starving. The gym was pretty empty today, so—"

I come up short when Alex points a gun in my face.

"Hey, hey, hey, what's going on? Nadia?"

"Hello, *darling*," Alex says with a sneer. "Go sit with her. This works out well. I can kill you both at the same time."

# CHAPTER 19

## ~NADIA~

*N*o. All I can think is *no*.

Alex is going to kill me.

And now, he's going to kill Carmine, too.

"Let Carmine go," I say through throbbing lips. "This is between you and me."

Instead of answering, Alex slaps me and then lowers his face to mine and sneers. "Papa didn't teach you to keep your cunt mouth shut, so I'm going to do it. Don't you fucking talk unless I tell you to."

"Why'd you do it?" Carmine asks calmly as he sits next to me. "Why'd you enlist Rich and go about this whole dramatic game?"

"Game?" Alex turns on Carmine but doesn't hit him. No, he's too much of a pussy to hit a man stronger than he is. "This isn't a game. This is brilliant. I was just telling little sis here all about it, but I'll explain it to you, too. She'll just have to hear it twice. But you don't mind, do you, sis?"

I shake my head no. From the corner of my eye, I see Carmine slip his phone out of his pocket. He taps on the screen, but I can't see what he's doing.

Hell, *he* can't see what he's doing.

"Papa is too set in his ways," Alex begins. "He's weak. He thinks we should respect the old ways of doing things. And because of that shortsightedness, he's missing out on a lot of money. I'm not willing to do that."

"You're not rich enough?" Carmine asks.

"Fuck, no. Who's *rich enough*? There's no such thing, you dumbass. Drugs. Drugs are where it's at. And when you have a new brew, all the better."

"That *new brew* you have kills people," Carmine says. "That doesn't make for repeat customers."

"That's not what we were selling." Alex laughs. "That was just to get people out of our way. The stuff we sell is the best high you can have. It's better than coke, better than meth or anything else. People will be *begging* me for it. They'll pay anything at all for it."

"What is it?" Carmine asks.

"It's a synthetic. You don't have to sniff it or shoot it. You pop the pill, and in twenty minutes, you're on the best ride of your life. I call it Hades."

"How original," Carmine says calmly. "So, you went to some of Sergi's people in New York, and they turned you down."

"Weak assholes," he says with the shake of his head. "They didn't want to do anything unless they ran it by Mick first. And I couldn't allow that."

"Why not?"

"Because this is *my* fucking operation," Alex yells and drives his finger into his chest. "Mine. Not theirs. And if they want to try to bring anyone higher up in, they get dead."

"So, what about Richard? Or should I say, *Dimitri?*"

*What? Who in the hell is Dimitri?*

Alex's smile falls, and he wipes his mouth with the back of his hand before smiling again, but I can tell he's nervous now.

"I figured you'd find out about that sooner or later," Alex says. "It was so pitifully easy. With his background, he was just itching to get into something on the down-low. Something big. It was his idea to marry into the family. I thought he should marry Nadia." He turns to me, and I want to throw up. "But he had a thing for Annika. He said Annika was weaker and would be easier to fool. And I hate to admit it, but he was right. She fell for the whole sappy I-love-you act—hook, line, and sinker. I mean, he actually got her to *marry* him! Women are so stupid. So easily manipulated. They're fucking worthless."

He turns to me and raises his hand, but Carmine stops him. He's up in a flash and has Alex's wrist in his fist.

"If you touch her one more time, I'll rip your goddamn arm off."

Alex shoves away like a pouty child. "Don't touch me. Don't fucking touch me."

He reaches for his gun, but it's gone.

"Looking for this?" Carmine holds it up, and Alex's face goes white.

Oh my God. We're going to live through this.

*We're going to live through this.*

Carmine throws the gun across the room and turns to me.

"Don't—" I begin, but it's too late. Alex hits Carmine over the head with the tray that was on the coffee table. Carmine turns and backhands Alex, but then, to both of our surprise, Alex retaliates.

Carmine takes as many hits as he dishes out. I rush across the room and retrieve the gun, my hands still tied with the twine Alex brought with him. Still, I'm able to point it down at my brother, who's now bleeding from the nose.

"Freeze."

Suddenly, Rafe and Shane run into the room, their weapons drawn, and Alex sags against the hardwood in defeat.

"Fuck," he says and then coughs and looks at me. "I will kill you. It may not be today, but it's going to happen. My men should have done it in France, but they were too weak. I knew I should have done it myself. And I will. Every minute of your life, you'd better sleep with one eye open and watch your back."

I look at Carmine. "Did you record everything he said earlier?"

He grabs his phone and nods. "It's on here. But I learned everything from Shane. That's where I was this morning."

I look over at Shane as Alex starts to moan and whine. "Do you have all of the evidence my father will need to prove that my brother was behind everything?"

"I do," Shane says with a solemn nod.

With the gun still in my hand, I look down at my brother, and I squeeze the trigger, killing him instantly.

"Call the cleanup team." I drop the gun and let Carmine fold me into his arms. I ache all over from the beating Alex gave me, and my heart hurts, too.

"Shh." Carmine rocks me back and forth. "I'm so sorry, baby."

"He was an ass. A complete ass. But he was also my brother. And there was a time that I loved him."

"I know." He kisses the top of my head. "Come on. Let's get you cleaned up."

"We've got this," Shane says, but before we can leave the room, he kisses my cheek. "You did the right thing."

"Sometimes, the right thing really sucks."

"I know."

"Don't worry about this," Rafe says kindly.

"I have to call my father. There's different protocol here."

"I know," Rafe says. "Don't worry."

Carmine leads me to the bathroom off the master, closes the door, and I fall into his arms, sobbing like I never have before.

"I'm a monster." I pull back, just out of his grasp. "Jesus, Carmine, I'm a monster. I killed my brother."

Without a word, he takes my shoulders and turns me to look into the mirror, pressed close behind me.

"Look at yourself."

My eyes are swollen and blackened. My lips are puffy and split. I have a cut on my shoulder from the kitchen knife.

"He knocked on the door about thirty minutes after you left," I begin and swallow hard. "Of course, I let him in. Turned my back. And he started in on me. He had a baseball bat. I couldn't react. Couldn't defend myself."

"He was a coward."

"He told me that he was behind all of the killings. Said that he was going to kill me, then Papa. That he'd be the boss. Said he'd turn our family into a drug lord empire—exactly what Papa doesn't want."

"And he was going to continue hunting you, would try to end your life, Nadia," he reminds me. "That wasn't an empty threat. If I hadn't arrived when I did, you'd probably be dead now. Can you look us both in the eyes and say that what you did was wrong?"

"No." I shake my head slowly. "I don't think it was wrong. Because he would have killed you, too, and I couldn't live—"

I turn back into his arms. "I couldn't live with myself if he hurt you, Carmine. I love you so much, I can't bear the thought. Oh my God, what would I do without you?"

He tips my chin up with his finger. "Do you mind saying that again?"

"What would I do without you?" I sniff, more tears falling at the thought of Carmine being gone.

"Not that part, baby."

"I love you, Carmine. I don't know how it happened or when. We went from being enemies to *this*. But I do. I love you so much it hurts. I really thought you'd come into this house and find me dead. That alone almost broke me. But then when I thought that he might kill *you*, as well, I just... You are the best part of my life."

"I think that's my line." His lips touch the side of mine, ever so gently so he doesn't hurt me. "I love you, too. With all of my heart and soul. You are meant to be with me. I feel that in my heart."

"I do, too." I snuggle into him for just a moment. "We'd better get me cleaned up so I can face my father. I don't know what he'll do."

"He'll love you," he says simply. "And he'll grieve."

"Yeah." I nod as Carmine reaches for a washrag. "We'll both do that."

SIX OF US sit in my father's living room in Atlanta. Carmine and his brothers flew me here this afternoon, and their father, Carlo, met us.

We didn't meet at an office.

We came to Igor Tarenkov's home.

"Your mother is lying down after taking a sedative," Papa says as he reaches for me. His eyes are shadowed and sad, but he touches me with tenderness. "How do you feel, little one?"

"A bit sore. It's not as bad as it was in Seattle when I got—" I stop talking at my father's furious look and swallow hard. "Oh, I guess I forgot to tell you about that."

"I suggest you tell me now."

I look over at Carmine, who's sitting next to his father. All four men are imposing. Carmine nods. "It's time, sweetheart."

So, I take a deep breath and tell them all about getting attacked in Seattle, and how Carmine and his people helped me get well.

"But that wasn't the first time."

I tell him everything, going back to when I was jumped in Atlanta, and my hair was cut.

"It seems your brother has been terrorizing you for a long time," Papa says quietly. "I'm sorry. I'm sorry that I never saw it. I should have known."

"He was good at covering his tracks," I remind him. "Papa, I understand if you don't want to see me again. If this is goodbye—"

"What kind of nonsense is this?"

"I killed your son." I bury my face in my hands and weep. "I murdered my brother in cold blood, and I would do it again. What kind of daughter does that make me? What kind of boss would I make?"

"No one asked for my opinion," Carlo says, catching my attention, "but I'm going to give it anyway. You would make an excellent leader, my dear. Because you did what you had to do to keep the rest of your family and those you care about safe. Your brother was the bad seed. And I hope I'm not speaking out of turn when I say we all saw that."

"You're not," Papa says. "I will grieve for the son I had and the man I needed him to be. But the punishment fit the crime here, Nadia. Don't torture yourself. You were defending yourself. And me."

Relief floods me. "Thank you."

"I'm sorry for the way this ended," Carlo says to my father. "If there is anything my family can do for you, we are always at your disposal."

"Thank you, old friend," Papa says. "And likewise."

"We still haven't figured out who killed Elena's parents," Rafe points out. "That goes back farther than Alex."

"That's something we'll have to keep digging into," Shane agrees. "We'll find them."

"I have something to say," Carmine says. "Mr. Tarenkov, I'd like to ask for your permission to marry your daughter."

My eyes fly to Carmine's in surprise.

Our fathers share a smile.

"Well, it's about damn time, my boy," Papa says. "Carlo and I have been throwing you at each other for years."

"I thought they'd never come to their senses," Carlo says with a laugh. "A couple of stubborn children we have here, Igor."

"Wait. You *wanted* us to marry?" Carmine asks.

"Of course. Why do you think we've allowed you to spend so much time together?" My father winks at me. *Winks!* I don't think I've ever seen him wink a day in his life.

"How do you like that?" Shane says with a laugh. "Pop's a matchmaker."

The brothers both laugh as Carmine crosses to me with humor in his chocolate brown eyes.

He lowers to one knee.

"Will you marry me, Nadia, and be the best part of my life until I'm no longer on this Earth?"

"Let me think about it." I grin as he digs into his pocket and comes out with a rock the size of a baby's fist. "Geez, Carmine. Did you have to get something so fancy?"

"Yes." He slips it onto my finger and then kisses my knuckles. "I'm going to give you everything you've ever dreamed of."

"I believe you." He kisses me carefully.

"Is that a yes?"

"That's a hell yes."

# EPILOGUE

## ĨVIE~

*I*t's been a long-ass day at the clinic. Annika took off for home about an hour ago, but I decided to stay and clean up a bit. Annika just hasn't been herself over the past month or so, not since her husband died.

I'm worried about her.

So, if I can stay late at work, make sure everything is perfect for her here and take some of the burdens off her, I'll gladly do it.

Annika is my best friend. She's the only person in the world who knows my deepest secrets. And I'll do whatever it takes to help her.

I hear the bell on the front door and hurry out to tell whoever it is that we're closed.

But when I get there, I stop cold.

"Hello, Ivie." He flips the lock on the door, and I dial Annika's number and leave my phone on the desk so she can hear everything. I hope with all my might that she answers. "Or should I say, *Laryssa?*"

I shake my head. "I'm sorry, I don't know a Laryssa. I'm Ivie. And we're closed for the day. But if you'd like to make an appointment, I can help you with that."

"You know, I thought for a long time that your father was an imbecile. Stupid. He didn't cover his tracks well."

I just raise my chin, determined not to let him see my fear.

"But you're different. You covered your tracks *very* well. And I know that you couldn't have done that alone. Which tells me that your father isn't as stupid as I thought."

"I don't know what you could possibly want from me. I'm just living my life."

"And a nice life it is," he says. "Good for you, Laryssa. I couldn't make your father pay for his sins when he was alive—and we both know that those sins were many. But now I've found you."

I shake my head as he walks around the counter.

"Now, don't do something silly like try to get away. You're coming with me. And you're going to pay for the sins of your father."

He jabs a syringe into my arm, and I immediately feel...heavy.

"There, now. Come along, Laryssa. We have plenty of work to do."

I HOPE YOU ENJOYED UNDERBOSS! If you'd like more from this mafia family, you can click here:

HTTPS://WWW.KRISTENPROBYAUTHOR.COM/MAFIA

# ABOUT THE AUTHOR

Kristen Proby has published more than sixty titles, many of which have hit the USA Today, New York Times and Wall Street Journal Bestsellers lists.

Kristen and her husband, John, make their home in her hometown of Whitefish, Montana with their two cats and dog.

facebook.com/booksbykristenproby

instagram.com/kristenproby

bookbub.com/profile/kristen-proby

goodreads.com/kristenproby

# NEWSLETTER SIGN UP

I hope you enjoyed reading this story as much as I enjoyed writing it! For upcoming book news, be sure to join my newsletter! I promise I will only send you news-filled mail, and none of the spam. You can sign up here:

https://mailchi.mp/kristenproby.com/newsletter-sign-up

# ALSO BY KRISTEN PROBY:

**Other Books by Kristen Proby**

**The With Me In Seattle Series**

Come Away With Me
Under The Mistletoe With Me
Fight With Me
Play With Me
Rock With Me
Safe With Me
Tied With Me
Breathe With Me
Forever With Me
Stay With Me
Indulge With Me
Love With Me
Dance With Me
Dream With Me
You Belong With Me
Imagine With Me
Shine With Me
Escape With Me
Flirt With Me
Change With Me

**Check out the full series here:** https://www.kristenprobyauthor.com/with-me-in-seattle

Easy Kisses
Easy Magic
Easy Fortune
Easy Nights

**Check out the full series here:** https://www.kristenprobyauthor.com/boudreaux

## The Fusion Series

Listen to Me
Close to You
Blush for Me
The Beauty of Us
Savor You

**Check out the full series here:** https://www.kristenprobyauthor.com/fusion

## From 1001 Dark Nights

Easy With You
Easy For Keeps
No Reservations
Tempting Brooke
Wonder With Me
Shine With Me

## Kristen Proby's Crossover Collection

Soaring with Fallon, A Big Sky Novel

Wicked Force: A Wicked Horse Vegas/Big Sky Novella
By Sawyer Bennett

All Stars Fall: A Seaside Pictures/Big Sky Novella
By Rachel Van Dyken

Hold On: A Play On/Big Sky Novella
By Samantha Young

Worth Fighting For: A Warrior Fight Club/Big Sky Novella
By Laura Kaye

Crazy Imperfect Love: A Dirty Dicks/Big Sky Novella
By K.L. Grayson

Nothing Without You: A Forever Yours/Big Sky Novella
By Monica Murphy

ALSO BY KRISTEN PROBY:

**Check out the entire Crossover Collection here:** https://www.kristenprobyauthor.com/kristen-proby-crossover-collection